**In the darkness outside the dome, silhouetted against it,
a great army had gathered.**

Goose bumps crept down her arms. A lean, angular man wearing spiked armour ran up a mound, raised his right fist and shook it at the city.

"Now!" he cried.

Crimson flames burst from the lower side of the dome and there came a cracking, a crashing and a shrieking whistle. A long ragged hole, the shape of a spiny caterpillar, had been blasted through the wall.

"Are . . . you . . . ready?" he roared.

"Yes," yelled his captains.

It was too dark for Karan to see any faces, but there was a troubling familiarity about the way the soldiers stood and moved and spoke. What was it?

"Avenge our ancestors' betrayal!" bellowed the man in the spiked armour. "Put every man, woman, child, dog and cat to the sword. Go!"

Karan's stomach churned. This seemed far too real to be a nightmare.

The troops stormed towards the hole in the dome, all except a cohort of eleven led by a round-faced woman whose yellow plaits were knotted into a loop above her head.

"Lord Gergrig?" she said timidly. "I thought this attack was a dress rehearsal."

"You need practice in killing," he said chillingly.

"But the people of Cinnabar have done nothing to us."

"Our betrayal was a stain on all humanity." Gergrig's voice vibrated with pain and torment. "All humanity must pay until the stain is gone."

By Ian Irvine

THE THREE WORLDS SERIES

The View from the Mirror quartet
A Shadow on the Glass
The Tower on the Rift
Dark Is the Moon
The Way Between the Worlds

THE WELL OF ECHOES QUARTET

Geomancer
Tetrarch
Alchymist
Chimaera

SONG OF THE TEARS TRILOGY

The Fate of the Fallen
The Curse on the Chosen
The Destiny of the Dead

THE GATE OF GOOD AND EVIL

The Summon Stone
The Fatal Gate

THE TAINTED REALM

Vengeance
Rebellion
Justice

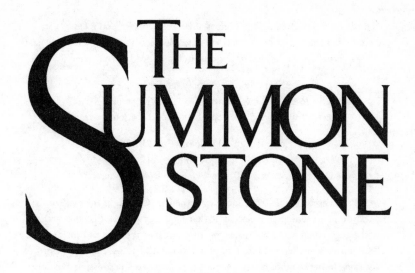

THE SUMMON STONE

BOOK ONE OF THE GATES OF GOOD AND EVIL

IAN IRVINE

www.orbitbooks.net

Copyright © 2016 by Ian Irvine
Excerpt from *Battlemage* copyright © 2015 by Stephen Aryan
Excerpt from *Hope & Red* copyright © 2016 by Jon Skovron

Cover design by Jack Smyth – LBBG
Cover images by Shutterstock
Cover copyright © 2016 by Hachette Book Group, Inc.

Orbit
Hachette Book Group
1290 Avenue of the Americas
New York, NY 10104
orbitbooks.net

Simultaneously published in Great Britain and in the U.S. by Orbit in 2016
First Edition: May 2016

Orbit is an imprint of Hachette Book Group.
The Orbit name and logo are trademarks of Little, Brown Book Group Limited.

The publisher is not responsible for websites (or their content)
that are not owned by the publisher.

The Hachette Speakers Bureau provides a wide range of authors for speaking events.
To find out more, go to www.hachettespeakersbureau.com or call (866) 376-6591.

Library of Congress Control Number: 2016933874

ISBNs: 978-0-316-38687-6 (trade paperback), 978-0-316-38686-9 (ebook)

Printed in the United States of America

RRD-C

10 9 8 7 6 5 4 3 2 1

CONTENTS

IAGADOR

SCALE

KM

0   25   50   75

0   5   10   15

LEAGUES

N

Salt Lake
Megaliths

R. Gannel

ELLUDORE
FOREST

DUNNET

Gance

Chanthed

FAIDON
FOREST

Thurkad

Feddil Rd.

Tullin

Muncyte

BANNADOR

Gothryme

Radomin

Tuldis

Casyme

SHAZMAK

Varp

Moyl

Plendur

IAGADOR

Dantoid

SEA OF
THURKAD

Narne

High Way

Furnisto

Sith

Vilikshathúr

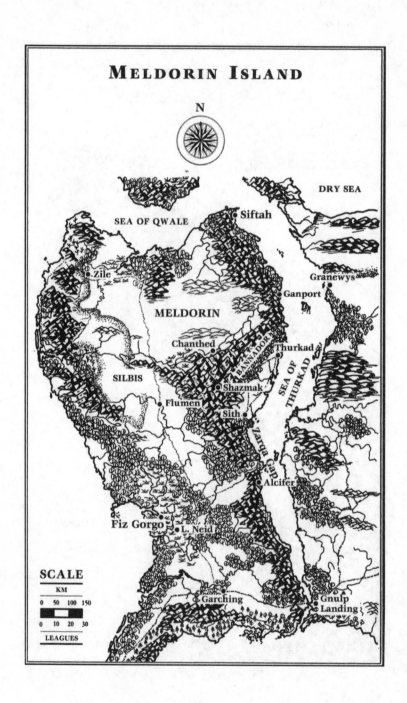

MELDORIN ISLAND

N

DRY SEA

SEA OF QWALE

Siftah

Zile

Granewys

Ganport

MELDORIN

Chanthed

Thurkad

SILBIS

Shazmak

SEA OF THURKAD

Flumen

Sith

Tarqa Gap

Alcifer

Fiz Gorgo

L. Neid

SCALE

KM

0   50   100 150

0   10   20   30

LEAGUES

Garching

Gnulp
Landing

PART OF THE SOUTHERN HEMISPHERE
OF SANTHENAR

LEGEND

Mountains
Hills
Desert
Salt Lake
Marsh, Swamp
Conifer Forest
Broadleaf Forest
Tropical Forest
Grassland
Reef
Main Road

Banthey
Fankster
Gendrigore
Nys
Huccadory
Bel Torance
Taranta
FARANDA
Strinklet
Tar Gaarn &
Havissard
Roros
Twissel
THE
DRY SEA
Mistmurk Mountain
Jepperand
Guffeons
Gosport
Katazza
Maksmord
Flude
Nithmak
Ashmode
CARENDOR
KALAR
STASSOR
Tifferfyte
Zile
MELDORIN
Morrelune
Fadd
Thurkad
Great Mountains
Nennifer
Burning
Mountain
Tirthrax
Fiz Gorgo
LAURALIN
MIRRILLADELL
Tiksi
KARAMA MALAMA
(Sea of Mists)
OOLO
HA-DROW
Ogur
LUUMA NARTA
SHAZABBA
Steppe
KARA AGEL
(Frozen Sea)
Noom
Grinding

N
W   E
S

SCALE
KILOMETRES
0 100 200 300 400 500 600 700 800 900 1000
0   40   80   120   160   200
LEAGUES

Maps by the author

20°
30°
40°
50°
60°
70°

THE SUMMON STONE

PART ONE

THE DRUMMING

1

THE EVIL MAN SAW ME

"No!" the little girl sobbed. "Look out! Run, *run*!"

Sulien!

Karan threw herself out of her bed, a high box of black-stained timber that occupied half the bedroom. She landed awkwardly and pain splintered through the left leg she had broken ten years ago. She clung to the side of the bed, trying not to cry out, then dragged a cloak around herself and careered through the dark to her daughter's room at the other end of the oval keep. Fear was an iron spike through her heart. What was the matter? Had someone broken in? What were they doing to her?

The wedge-shaped room, lit by a rectangle of moonlight coming through the narrow window, was empty apart from Sulien, who lay with her knees drawn up and her arms wrapped around them, rocking from side to side.

Her eyes were tightly closed as if she could not bear to look, and she was moaning, "No, no, *no*!"

Karan touched Sulien on the shoulder and her eyes sprang open. She threw her arms around Karan's waist, clinging desperately.

"Mummy, the evil man saw me. He *saw* me!"

Karan let out her breath. Just a nightmare, though a bad one. She put her hands around Sulien's head and, with a psychic wrench that she would pay for later, lifted the nightmare from her. But Sulien was safe; that was all that mattered. Karan's knees shook and she slumped on the bed. *It's all right!*

Sulien gave a little sigh and wriggled around under the covers. "Thanks, Mummy."

Karan kissed her on the forehead. "Go to sleep now."

"I can't; my mind's gone all squirmy. Can you tell me a story?"

"Why don't you tell me one, for a change?"

"All right." Sulien thought for a moment. "I'll tell you my favourite – the story of Karan and Llian, and the Mirror of Aachan."

"I hope it has a happy ending," said Karan, going along with her.

"You'll have to wait and see," Sulien said mock-sternly. "This is how it begins." She began reciting: "Once there were three worlds, Aachan, Tallallame and Santhenar, each with its own human species: Aachim, Faellem and us, old humans. Then, fleeing out of the terrible void between the worlds came a fourth people, the Charon, led by the mightiest hero in all the Histories, Rulke. The Charon were just a handful, desperate and on the edge of extinction, but Rulke saw a weakness in the Aachim and took Aachan from them . . . and forever changed the balance between the Three Worlds."

"I'm sure I've heard that before, somewhere," said Karan, smiling at the memories it raised.

"Of course you have, silly. All the Great Tales begin that way." Sulien continued: "In ancient times the genius goldsmith Shuthdar, a very wicked man, was paid by Rulke to make a gate-opening device in the form of a golden flute. Then Shuthdar stole the flute, opened a gate and fled to Santhenar . . . but he broke open the Way Between the Worlds, exposing the Three Worlds to the deadly void.

"This shocked Aachan, a strange world of sulphur-coloured snow, oily bogs and black, luminous flowers, to its core. Rulke raced after Shuthdar, taking with him a host of Aachim servants, including the mighty Tensor.

"The rain-drenched world of Tallallame was also threatened by the opening. The Faellem, a small forest-dwelling people who were masters of illusion, sent a troop led by Faelamor to close the way again. But they failed too.

"They all hunted Shuthdar across Santhenar as he fled through gate after gate, but finally he was driven into a trap. Unable to give the flute up, he destroyed it – and brought down the Forbidding that sealed the Three Worlds off from each other . . . and trapped all his hunters here on Santhenar."

"Until ten years ago," said Karan.

"When you and Daddy helped to reopen the Way Between the Worlds ... " Sulien frowned. "How come Rulke was still alive after all that time?"

"The Aachim, Faellem and Charon aren't like us. They can live for thousands of years."

Sulien gave another little shiver, her eyelids fluttered, and she slept.

Karan pulled the covers up and stroked her daughter's hair, which was as wild as her own, though a lighter shade of red. On the table next to the bed, moonbeams touched a vase of yellow and brown bumble-bee blossoms and the half-done wall hanging of Sulien's floppy-eared puppy, Piffle.

Karan stroked Sulien's cheek and shed a tear, and sat there for a minute or two, gazing at her nine-year-old daughter, her small miracle, the only child she could ever have and the most perfect thing in her life.

She was limping back to bed when the import of Sulien's words struck her. *Mummy, the evil man saw me!* What a disturbing thing to say. Should she wake Llian? No, he had enough to worry about.

Karan's leg was really painful now. She went down the steep stairs of the old keep in the dark, holding on to the rail and wincing, but the pain grew with every step and so did her need for the one thing that could take it away – hrux.

She fought it. Hrux was for emergencies, for those times when the pain was utterly unbearable. In the round chamber she called her thinking room, lit only by five winking embers in the fireplace, she sat in a worn-out armchair, pulled a cloak tightly around herself and closed her eyes.

What had Sulien meant by *the evil man saw me*? And what had she seen?

Karan's gift for mancery, the Secret Art, had been blocked when she was a girl but, being a sensitive, she still had some mind powers. She knew how to replay the nightmare, though she was reluctant to try; using her gift always came at a cost, the headaches and nausea of aftersickness. But she had to know what Sulien had seen. Very carefully she lifted the lid on the beginning of the nightmare ...

A pair of moons, one small and yellow spattered with black, the other huge and jade green, lit a barren landscape. The green moon stood above a remarkable city, unlike any place Karan had ever seen – a crisp white metropolis where the buildings were shaped like dishes, arches, globes and tall spikes, and enclosed within a silvery dome. Where could it be? None of the Three Worlds had a green moon; the city must be on some little planet in the void.

In the darkness outside the dome, silhouetted against it, a great army had gathered. Goose pimples crept down her arms. A lean, angular man wearing spiked armour ran up a mound, raised his right fist and shook it at the city.

"Now!" he cried.

Crimson flames burst from the lower side of the dome and there came a cracking, a crashing and a shrieking whistle. A long ragged hole, the shape of a spiny caterpillar, had been blasted through the wall.

"Are . . . you . . . ready?" he roared.

"Yes!" yelled his captains.

It was too dark for Karan to see any faces, but there was a troubling familiarity about the way the soldiers stood and moved and spoke. What was it?

"Avenge our ancestors' betrayal!" bellowed the man in the spiked armour. "Put every man, woman, child, dog and cat to the sword. Go!"

Karan's stomach churned. This seemed far too real to be a nightmare.

The troops stormed towards the hole in the dome, all except a cohort of eleven led by a round-faced woman whose yellow plaits were knotted into a loop above her head.

"Lord Gergrig?" she said timidly. "I thought this attack was a dress rehearsal."

"You need practice in killing," he said chillingly.

"But the people of Cinnabar have done nothing to us."

"Our betrayal was a stain on all humanity." Gergrig's voice vibrated with pain and torment. "All humanity must pay until the stain is gone."

"Even so—"

"Soon we will face the greatest battle of all time, against the greatest foe – that's why we've practised war for the past ten millennia."

"Then why do we—"

"To stay in practice, you fool! If fifteen thousand Merdrun can't clean out this small city, how can we hope to escape the awful void?" His voice ached with longing. "How can we capture the jewel of worlds that is Santhenar?"

Karan clutched at her chest. This was no nightmare; it had to be a true seeing, but why had it come to Sulien? She was a gifted child, though Karan had never understood what Sulien's gift was. And who were the Merdrun? She had never heard the name before.

Abruptly Gergrig swung round, staring. The left edge of his face, a series of hard angles, was outlined by light from a blazing tower. Like an echo, Karan heard Sulien's cry, "Mummy, the evil man saw me. He *saw* me!"

Momentarily, Gergrig seemed afraid. He picked up a small green glass box and lights began to flicker inside it. His jaw hardened. "Uzzey," he said to the blonde warrior, "we've been *seen*."

"Who by?"

He bent his shaven head for a few seconds, peering into the glass box, then made a swirling movement with his left hand. "A little red-haired girl. On Santhenar!"

Karan slid off the chair onto her knees, struggling to breathe. This was real; this bloodthirsty brute, whose troops *need practice in killing*, had seen her beautiful daughter. Ice crystallised all around her; there was no warmth left in the world. Her breath rushed in, in, in. She was going to scream. She fought to hold it back. Don't make a sound; don't do anything that could alert him.

"How can this be?" said Uzzey.

"I don't know," said Gergrig. "Where's the magiz?"

"Setting another blasting charge."

"Fetch her. She's got to locate this girl, *urgently*."

"What harm can a child do?"

"She can betray the invasion; she can reveal our plans and our numbers."

Pain speared up Karan's left leg and it was getting worse. Black fog swirled in her head. She rocked forwards and back, her teeth chattering.

"Who would listen to a kid?" said Uzzey.

"I can't take the risk," said Gergrig. "Run!"

Uzzey raced off, bounding high with each stride.

Karan's heart was thundering but her blood did not seem to be circulating; she felt faint, freezing and so breathless that she was suffocating. She wanted to scoop Sulien up in her arms and run, but where could she go? How could Sulien see people on barren little Cinnabar, somewhere in the void, anyway? And how could Gergrig have seen her? Karan would not have thought it possible.

Shortly the magiz, who was tall and thin, with sparse white hair and colourless eyes bulging out of soot-black sockets, loped up. "What's this about a girl *seeing* us?"

Gergrig explained, then said, "I'm bringing the invasion forward. I'll have to wake the summon stone right away."

Karan choked. What invasion? Her head spun and she began to tremble violently.

"So soon?" said the magiz. "The cost in power will be . . . extreme."

"We'll have to pay it. The stone must be ready by syzygy – the night the triple moons line up – or we'll never be able to open the gate."

The magiz licked her grey lips. "To get more power, I'll need more deaths."

"Then see to it!"

"Ah, to drink a life," sighed the magiz. "Especially the powerful lives of the gifted. This child's ending will be nectar."

Gergrig took a step backwards. He looked repulsed.

Karan doubled over, gasping. In an flash of foreboding she saw three bloody bodies – Sulien, Llian and herself – flung like rubbish into a corner of her burning manor.

"What do you want me to do first?" said the magiz.

"Find the red-haired brat and put her down. And everyone in her household."

A murderous fury overwhelmed Karan. No one threatened her daughter! Whatever it took, she would do it to protect her own.

The magiz, evidently untroubled by Gergrig's order, nodded. "I'll look for the kid."

Gergrig turned to Uzzey and her cohort, who were all staring at him. "What are you waiting for? Get to the killing field!"

Ah, to drink a life! It was the end of Sulien's nightmare, and the beginning of Karan's.

2

UNDER THE INFLUENCE

The darkness was a choking blanket, the hiding place of a killer.

Karan fought the shakes and the terror; she had to think things through, calmly and logically. She stirred the fire until it cast dancing shadows through the room, then held her cold feet and hands out to the blaze. It did not warm them.

How could she protect Sulien when she did not know who the Merdrun were, how they would attack, or where, or when? Could the magiz attack from the void, or would she have to come to Santhenar first? And how could Karan, whose gift for the Secret Art had been blocked as a child before it could fully develop, protect Sulien against an alien sorcerer?

Her right thigh throbbed, then the left. After being hurled against the metal side of Rulke's construct ten years ago, on the desperate day that had changed the Three Worlds for ever, Karan had broken so many bones that no one had thought she would ever walk again. Had it not been for the healing hands of Idlis the Whelm, once her enemy, she would be confined to a wheeled chair – or dead.

The pain kept intruding. She rose and paced, wincing with every step. The signs were clear now – it would get worse until it was unendurable; she would soon have to resort to hrux. But not yet; through force of will she suppressed the pain. She had to be stronger than she had ever been.

She had taught herself to put up with it a little longer each time. To do otherwise, to give in too easily, was to risk hrux claiming her. And hrux addiction was worse than any physical pain.

She took a small key from a drawer, grabbed a lamp and went out. Her hands were shaking so badly that she kept dropping the flint striker; it took twenty clicks to light the wick. In the larder she climbed the stepladder and, standing on tiptoe, reached for the little metal box at the back of the top shelf, out of sight. Karan unlocked it, the key rattling around the keyhole, then opened the lid – and threw her head backwards. Yuk!

The lump of hrux oozed yellow-green muck and the stench, like rotten prawn heads mixed with sour milk, was nauseating. She hesitated; there was barely enough left for two doses and she had no way of getting more. Panic stirred but she fought it down. Dare she try a half-dose? She cut off a pea-sized lump and impaled it on the point of her knife. The longing was desperate now, but not yet . . . not yet . . .

The pain howled, it shrieked, it battered at her like a mad thing. She could not bear it another second . . . and another . . . and anoth—

No! Hrux aided seeings and she was going to need it; she must not waste it on relieving pain. Karan rubbed the lump across her lips, licked them, shuddering at the stench, lied to herself that the pain would fade and dropped the hrux into her cloak pocket.

She returned to her thinking room and sat in the dimness. Pain sneaked up her thigh, though it was dull pain now; the placebo was working. She needed answers. Why did the Merdrun seem so familiar? What was the summon stone and why did it have to be woken right away, at such cost? How long was it until syzygy, the night of the triple moons – months, weeks or only days? And how, how was she to save her daughter?

There might be a way to answer the first question. Dare she peer through the ghostly webs and treacherous mazes of the void, using the nightmare to try to find Gergrig? Perhaps, under the influence of hrux, she could. It would be dangerous, though not as dangerous as doing nothing. But what if she unwittingly revealed where Sulien lived? The thought was paralysing; how could she take such a risk?

She could not sit here like a helpless victim, waiting for the bruise-eyed magiz to strike Sulien dead. *Ah, to drink a life!* Karan had to act.

She focused on the end of Sulien's nightmare, when Gergrig had been speaking to the magiz in the light of Cinnabar's jade-green moon, and slipped the lump of hrux into her mouth. It was covered in fluff from her pocket. She gagged, choked, swallowed. Her head swirled and tingles ran up and down her legs. She shut the door; she might shout or scream and that would wake the household.

Karan closed her eyes and saw fog, though it cleared suddenly to a true seeing of a place she had seen ten years ago and never wanted to see again – the limitless void between the worlds. It swarmed with savage creatures; she could sense them all around, and perhaps they could sense her too, even in her bodiless state.

She had to be careful, and she had to be quick. Existence in the void was desperate, brutal and fleeting. Even the fittest creatures survived only by remaking themselves constantly, and every being there was consumed by a single urge – to escape.

There were blurred shapes everywhere – some creeping, some scuttling, some waiting with the patience of twelve-legged spiders in steel webs. Karan's seeing shot past them, zoomed in through shadow into fierce light, focused, then she let out a yelp. All she could see was a pair of deep-set blazing eyes and a jagged black tattoo – a glyph she did not recognise – centred on a man's forehead.

She retreated until his whole face was in view. It was the first time she had seen Gergrig clearly. A completely bald, domed skull, a heavy beard cropped to a black shadow over an angular jaw, full lips set in a cruel curve, a thin nose and, ugh, a hook-shaped spray of blood on his right cheek. It had clotted in his beard.

Karan shrank back in her chair. Could he see her? What would he do if he did? But his eyes did not move; he was looking down at an object dangling from his neck, a red cube on a fine steel chain. He touched the cube and a faint drumming sounded in her head.

A burst of light from the cube illuminated his eyes, which were an alarming colour, indigo blue with flecks of carmine. Shivers ran across Karan's shoulders, for the eyes alone were enough to tell her what Gergrig, and presumably the other Merdrun, were.

They were Charon. And that was impossible.

Gergrig rose abruptly. He had to be a foot and a half taller than her, and hard and lean. He reached out as if testing an invisible barrier and momentarily the scene went out of focus, then he dropped his hand and looked over his shoulder.

His troops were gathered behind him. They were heavily armed, bandaged and battered and bruised, and many were red-handed as if they had come straight from the battlefield. All looked jubilant, and all had the jagged glyph on their foreheads. There were many thousands of them, a mighty force armed for war.

An army that could not possibly exist.

Karan cut off the seeing and scrambled to her feet, her heart thundering. How could this be? There were no Charon any more. After Rulke's death, Yalkara and the few dozen survivors, all age-old, had been the last of their kind. She had said they were returning to the void to face their extinction with dignity.

Had that been a lie?

3

THE DRUMMING

How long would it take the magiz to locate Sulien? And when she did, could she attack from Cinnabar?

Karan's fear exploded into panic. She belted up the stairs and into Sulien's room, gasping. It was dark now; the moon was on the other side of the manor and only the faintest glimmer of starlight came through the window. Her daughter lay still. Too still? Karan's heart missed several beats.

"Sulien?" she cried, clutching at her hand.

"What's the matter, Mummy?" Sulien said sleepily.

The panic eased. Karan felt foolish. "I . . . was just worried, that's all."

Sulien patted her hand. "It's all right. Go to sleep now."

How could she ever sleep again, knowing the magiz could attack at any time? Though if she did, what could Karan do about it?

"I want you to have this," she said, taking off her braided silver chain. "It'll help to keep you safe." She put it around Sulien's neck.

"Mmm," said Sulien.

Karan sat there for hours, too exhausted to think clearly, just listening to Sulien's steady breathing until, an hour before dawn, her own head began to throb and her belly churned and heaved. Aftersickness.

Holding her stomach, she stumbled down and out into the garden, where she threw up. She scooped water from a barrel by the door, washed her face and looked out across the shadowed yard of Gothryme Manor.

The ground was so dry she could smell it; dust, lifted by an autumn breeze, tickled the back of her nose. The coming harvest was going to be the smallest in her memory and she had no idea how she would feed her workers next year. One disaster after another had emptied Gothryme's coffers and only one thing of value remained.

But how could she ask that of Llian?

What choice did she have? They might have to flee at a moment's notice, and going on the run would take coin, lots of it. If only he hadn't been so foolish. But he had, and the ban on Llian working, which had been in place for nine and a half years now, was eating him alive.

He was not just a brilliant chronicler of the Histories of Santhenar. He was also the first tale-teller in hundreds of years to have written a new Great Tale, the twenty-third, the monumental *Tale of the Mirror*. The Great Tales were his life and his passion, and if he could not practise his art, what did he have left?

The ban should have been lifted years ago but Wistan, the aged and obnoxious Master of the College of the Histories, had refused, and there were ominous signs that he was going to make it permanent. A lifetime ban would destroy Llian.

Karan heard that faint drumming again. It felt like an alien heartbeat, freshly woken, and suddenly she could not bear the load any longer. She hauled herself up to her bedroom.

"Llian, wake up." She shook him by the shoulder.

He groaned. "Wassamatta?"

"There's a problem and we've got to talk."

He rolled over. "It's still dark."

"It's nearly dawn. Come downstairs."

She told him the story while she was cooking breakfast – egg-soaked bread fried with purple onions and small cubes of fatty bacon. He slumped at the table with his eyes closed, listening in silence.

Further down the north wing a door banged. Cook and his assistant, young Benie, would soon be here, and Karan did not want to talk to them. She and Llian carried their plates out to the table on the rear terrace, which faced the snow-tipped mountains.

"It was just a nightmare," he said when she finished. He forked up another piece of fried bread, loaded it with bacon and onions, and carried it towards his mouth. "It doesn't mean anything."

"My *seeing* proves it was real," said Karan.

An onion ring fell off his fork and slid down his shirt, unnoticed, until it caught on a button. It hung there, quivering with his every movement.

"You'd just taken hrux," he said.

"Only a half dose."

"Maybe it was a hallucination."

The dangling onion ring was profoundly irritating. "I know what a hrux hallucination is like," snapped Karan. "This was a true seeing. Thousands of armed troops, still bloody from battle, getting ready for war – on us. And they looked like Charon."

"The Charon are extinct," he said in the *I'm trying hard to be reasonable* manner that was so annoying. "Their elders went back to the void to die."

"The ones I saw last night were young."

"Then they can't have been Charon. Besides, they don't have tattoos."

"Who else could they be, with those eyes? Rulke must have lied."

"Telling truth from lies is part of my training."

"And I know when to trust my seeings."

"Even when you've taken hrux?"

Karan fought the urge to whack him. Stupid man! She picked

off the onion ring and flicked it away. A crow caught it before it hit the ground, then hopped across the terrace, eyeing her malevolently. Karan imagined it pecking at their bodies ... She shooed it away furiously.

"I hadn't taken anything when I lifted Sulien's nightmare," she hissed. "Or when I read it. Gergrig told the magiz to find Sulien, *and kill her*, and you'd better start taking it seriously, or ... or ..." She thumped her head down on her arms, on the table. "I'm terrified, Llian. I don't know what to do."

He drew her to him and put his arms around her. "Sorry. I'm never any good early in the morning."

She suppressed a sarcastic retort. "We've got to do something."

"We don't know how the magiz will attack, or when. What can we do except take Sulien and run?"

"How can we run? We're practically bankrupt."

He pulled away. "And that's my fault," he said bitterly. "I got myself banned."

"I know. I was there."

But Llian kept on, flogging himself, as if by doing so he could ease the burden of guilt. "I broke the chroniclers' first law. I interfered in the Histories, and a hundred prisoners were burned to death in the citadel cells." He looked around wildly. "I can still hear their screams."

"You didn't kill them. Mendark set fire to the citadel, trying to kill you!"

"But that wasn't enough for me – oh, no! I provoked Tensor."

This was too much. "You bloody idiot!" Karan cried, shaking him by the shoulders. "You were trying to save my life!"

"And because of my stupidity, Rulke was killed." Llian looked down at his hands as if expecting them to be clotted with blood. "That's why I was banned ... but being a chronicler and a teller is all I'm good for."

"I knew that when I chose you," she murmured.

"You couldn't have known how bad it was going to get."

"I can put up with anything as long as I have Sulien and you."

But a barrier had grown between them and she did not know how to overcome it. Karan looked across the swan pond, now dry save for a brown, reeking pool in the middle.

"Llian, we need money, fast. And the one valuable thing we have . . . *you* have—" The drumming was back, thundering in her head this time.

Llian cried out and made for the axe standing in the woodpile near the door.

"Ugh!" Karan yelped, clutching at her skull.

He froze, right hand outstretched. His fingers closed and opened, then with an effort he drew back from the axe. "Karan?" He turned jerkily, like an automaton, and his eyes had a feral glint.

The sound cut off. "I just heard the drumming again," she said.

The light faded from his eyes and he was the familiar Llian again. He lurched back to the table and took her hands. His fingers clenched around hers, and his breathing was ragged.

"Llian, what is it?"

"Just then I felt . . . I wanted to . . . "

It was as if he were afraid to say it. No, *ashamed* to say it. He jerked his head sideways. She followed the direction of his gaze to the axe.

He sat on his hands as if to keep them from misbehaving. "I felt a wild urge to . . . to run amok. Break windows, chop up the plates. Smash the wine bottles in the cellar."

"Given your prodigious appetite for red wine, that's really worrying."

The joke fell on its face. "I'm afraid, Karan. Afraid of what I might have done."

She swallowed. Llian had many flaws, but violence was not one of them. With him anger turned inwards, not out.

"How long have you been having these feelings?" she said delicately.

"Never – until just then. It took all my willpower to pull back from the axe."

And it had happened when the drumming started. An ugly possibility reared, but before Karan could think it through there came a hoarse cry from the back door.

"Karan, Llian! Come, quickly."

Rachis, their ancient steward, was hunched in the doorway, panting. Age had withered him; once tall and upright, now he was nothing but spindly, stooping bone and skin like wrinkled leather. In his eighty-two years Rachis had seen everything, and he was normally unflappable, but now his mouth was opening and closing, his watery eyes staring.

"Benie," he croaked. "Benie . . ."

"What about him?" said Karan. The cook's apprentice was a good-hearted lad of seventeen, though accident prone. "Has he cut himself again? Is it bad?"

"He's . . . he's murdered Cook."

4

STABBED HIM THROUGH THE HEART

"Benie . . . *killed* Cook?" cried Karan. It was preposterous.

"Stabbed him through the heart with the boning knife," said Rachis.

Karan ran into the kitchen. Fragments of a wide blue bowl and pieces of chopped cabbage, turnip and carrots were scattered across the flagstones. Cook lay on his back in front of the enormous cast-iron range, arms outstretched. Blood soaked the front of his apron and he was clearly dead.

Her cranky, wonderful Cook, the centre of her household for the past seven years, was gone — from some moment of madness. Why?

Benie, a stocky lad with untidy blonde hair and little scars all over his hands, was backed up against the door of the larder, a thin-bladed knife hanging from his left hand. A thick crimson drop of Cook's blood, not yet congealed, hung from its tip. His teeth were chattering.

Karan held out her hand. "Can I have the knife, Benie?"

He handed it to her at once, dazedly. His hands were trembling, his prominent larynx bobbing up and down.

"What happened?" said Karan. Her knees had gone wobbly. She clutched the edge of the kitchen table, looking from Cook to Benie, back to Cook. How could he be dead, just like that? She could not take it in.

"I . . . killed . . . Cook," said Benie, shaking his head as if he could not believe it.

"Did he attack you?"

"No . . . why would he?"

"Cook's got a sharp tongue," said Rachis. "But he's not . . . he *wasn't* a hard man."

"Why did you do it, Benie?" said Llian.

"I don't know."

"There's got to be a reason."

"No. None at all."

"Did you hear voices?" said Rachis. "Telling you to kill Cook?"

Benie shook his head. "I was boning out a leg of mutton and suddenly I felt furiously angry."

"Why?" said Karan.

"I don't know. It came from nowhere and I couldn't stop myself. I . . . just . . . stabbed him." Benie looked down at Cook's body, blanched, and Karan saw the little boy in him, bewildered and terrified. He began to shake. "Poor Cook," he sobbed, his nose running. "He taught me so much. I just wanted to be as good as him."

Benie let out a howl that pierced her to the heart. "Did anything odd happen before you did it?" said Karan.

"No," said Benie. "Except for that thumping sound."

"What thumping sound?"

He tapped it on the bench, the rhythm that Karan had heard. The drumming. "I heard it just before . . . "

Karan exchanged glances with Llian, who seemed to be thinking the same thing as her.

"What's going to happen to me?" Benie said plaintively. "They won't hang me, will they?"

Karan swallowed. He had been a mischievous little boy, always getting into scrapes and coming to her to say sorry afterwards, but there was nothing she could do about murder.

"I'll put him in the old cellar," Rachis said heavily. "And send for the bailiff. Come with me, lad." He led Benie away.

"I didn't want to hurt him," Benie wailed. "Cook was good to me. Karan, please help me!"

Karan stood there, fists clenched by her sides, utterly helpless. Why was everything falling apart?

"Sulien will be down soon," Llian said in a low voice. "We'd better do something about the body."

They carried Cook down to an empty coolroom, locked the door and cleaned up the mess and the blood – there wasn't much. Out in the stone-walled orangery, they sat on a granite bench spotted with circular grey patches of lichen, among the orange and kumquat trees. The small green oranges were sparse and the leaves hung down, badly wilted. Everything was wilted this year, Llian most of all.

"Is there anything we can do for him?" he said.

Benie had been part of Gothryme all his life and more than half of Karan's. His mother had died in childbirth and his father was unknown. He had simply been taken in; it was what people did around here.

"It's got to be the drumming," said Karan. "It affected you too."

"But not you."

She shrugged. "Nor Rachis."

"Why not?"

"Maybe only certain people are susceptible."

"Benie's a good lad," said Llian, getting up like a worn-out old man. "He's worked hard these past years . . . and we have a duty to him. Do you think we should . . . ?"

"Let him escape?" said Karan bleakly.

He pressed his forehead against a horizontal branch. "Yes."

"He killed an innocent man, for no reason. Will he kill again, the next time the drumming sounds? And the time after that? We can't take the risk, Llian."

"What if we hide him somewhere? Lock him up where he'll be safe."

"For ever? No, we can't. Cook's poor wife is now a widow, his three children are fatherless, and without his earnings they'll starve. I'll have to take them in, and they have to know what happened, and why. And know that justice has been done for their father." Karan shook her head. "How am I going to tell them?"

Llian paced in figure eights between the orange trees. "Benie will be convicted of murder."

"I'll plead for him," said Karan. "I'll do everything I can . . . "

"But he'll still be put to death."

She covered her face with her hands. There was no solution; the drumming had made sure of that. She could see the rest of Benie's brief life, all the way to the rope.

Llian came back and put his arms around her. She scrunched herself against the comforting solidity of his chest.

"Do you think they're connected?" he said after a long pause.

"What?"

"Sulien's nightmare and your seeing – and the drumming."

"I first heard it after Gergrig touched the red cube," said Karan. "Yes, I do."

"Is he trying to wake the summon stone with it?"

"He must be, though why does that come at such a cost in power? And what's the summon stone meant to do? What's the drumming for, anyway? And when do the Merdrun plan to invade us?"

"The Magister has to be told, urgently."

The Magister led the Council of Santhenar, which for many centuries had been an alliance of the most powerful mancers in the world. It had been formed for the protection of Santhenar fifteen centuries ago and for most of that time it had been headed by Mendark, a ruthless mancer who had renewed his life many times. On his death ten years ago Karan's friend Tallia had taken his place. Though the council was in decline now, its greatest members dead and its influence waning, she was Karan's best hope.

"I'll courier a letter to her this morning. And to Shand – he knows everyone." Couriers were expensive; another bite out of their almost empty coffers.

"What do you want me to do?" said Llian.

It warmed her; she felt as though they were working as a team at last. "What you're brilliant at – finding answers to the vital questions."

"Like what?"

"Who are these Merdrun, who look just like Charon?"

Llian thought for a long while, frowning. "I've never heard the name before. I don't think I can find the answer here."

"And, how could Gergrig see Sulien from the void? He looked into a little glass box and I saw lights flashing."

"At a guess, because of her seeing, though I didn't know she had the gift."

"Neither did I," said Karan. "But I'll stop her from ever doing it again."

"It came through a nightmare – how can you stop that?"

Karan's belly knotted painfully. What if Sulien saw Gergrig again, tonight, and the magiz used the nightmare to locate her?

"I'll have to find a way to hide her from the magiz. Next question – how do the Merdrun plan to invade Santhenar? Everyone knows how difficult it is to get out of the void."

"That's why Gergrig was going to wake the summon stone right away," said Llian.

"But what *is* the summon stone? Where is it and how is it woken? Why does that cost so much power, and what does the stone actually *do*? Can it be stopped or destroyed? And what's the drumming got to do with it?"

"If I had access to the secret archives of the college library, I might be able to answer those questions. But since I'm banned—"

"You've got to find out, urgently; do whatever it takes to get the ban overturned. And I . . ." Karan looked away.

The blood drained from Llian's face. "Please tell me you're not going to spy on them again?"

She avoided his eye. It had to be done.

"Karan?" he said desperately.

"The Merdrun want to kill Sulien. You and I have to protect her. It's as simple as that."

"Yes," he said hoarsely. "Well ... if you're quick." He frowned. "There's one question you haven't asked me to answer."

"How long until syzygy, when the three moons line up in the sky of Cinnabar?" said Karan. "That's my other job."

"But—"

"The only way I can know when syzygy is, is to do more seeings."

He choked. "They'd have to be really long ones."

"Yes."

"All right," said Llian. "But before anything, we've got to spread the word about the invasion."

"How will that help?"

"If everyone knows, the magiz has no reason to target Sulien."

Except malice – or hunger to drink her innocent life.

Karan went across to the nearest kumquat tree. Some of the little round fruit were ripe and she picked a handful and ate them whole, the pungent oils stinging the inside of her nose and clearing her head.

She had another, even more dangerous plan, one she dared not even whisper to Llian. If there was no other way she would try to attack the magiz, and Gergrig too. Though she did not know how.

"Don't tell Sulien about any of this," said Karan.

"Why not? She'll have to know before long."

"Until we know more, for her sake I'd like to pretend that everything is all right."

"But it's not all right!"

"No. And I've got a very bad feeling."

"What?" said Llian.

"That everything we care about, everything that matters, is about to be swept away. Until ... that happens, I just want Sulien to be a normal, happy little girl."

5

THE BIGGEST MISTAKE OF YOUR LIFE

Karan hurled her trowel into the vegetable garden. "How will the magiz attack?" she yelled at Llian. "How will I even know? I'm afraid to leave Sulien for a second."

Her family's survival depended on her and she did not have the faintest idea what to do. She could not protect Sulien twenty-four hours a day; sooner or later the magiz would find a way through and kill her, and the world would end.

It was mid-afternoon. She was picking leeks and onions; Llian was lifting little round potatoes out of the dry soil with a wooden garden fork. The leeks were thin and yellow, not much bigger than spring onions. Everything was withering away.

She had written to Tallia and Shand, the only powerful allies she had, asking them to spread the word about the Merdrun threat, but what could they do to help her?

Shand was like a wise old uncle, but he was also a dangerous mancer who, when one of his moods took him, could be downright unhelpful. And, she remembered bitterly, years ago his prejudice against the Zain had almost got Llian killed. Would he help now? *Could* he help?

"I'll look after her if you need to go to Tolryme," said Llian, scooping a double handful of potatoes into his basket.

"What can you do?"

Llian restrained himself with an effort. "I don't know. What can *you* do?"

"I've got to be here. I can't leave her."

"Gergrig saw Sulien through her nightmare. She's hardly likely to have another one in the middle of the day."

"You're happy to take the risk, are you?"

"Please stop attacking me. We're in this together."

But Karan was beyond being reasonable. "What if the drumming starts again, and you—" Fool, fool! If she could have taken the words back and swallowed them, she would have, but it was too late.

Llian went so white that she thought he was going to faint. He dropped the garden fork and said stiffly, "You don't trust me."

"Of course I do." How could a few thoughtless words make things so wrong? "I trust you absolutely . . ."

"Just not with Sulien. You think, when the drumming sounds again, that I'll help the magiz attack my own daughter."

"That's not what I meant at all," she cried.

"It's exactly what you meant," he said in a dead voice. He picked up his basket and stumbled away.

Karan's bones were aching again. She sank onto a garden bench and put her head in her hands. She had made things worse and did not know how to fix them.

"You must stop pushing Llian away," Rachis said quietly. "You've got to trust him."

She had not realised he was in the garden. "You heard?"

"More than I cared to."

"I'm afraid to trust anyone – except you, of course." She looked up at him. "You went to town this morning. Has the drumming caused any other attacks?"

"A few fights. No killings. Lots of people heard it, but most weren't affected by it."

"Is that good or bad?"

"It's bad for Benie. I argued that the drumming made him kill Cook, but the bailiff wouldn't listen. He insists it's murder, and everyone in Tolryme feels the same."

"And no one can prove otherwise." Karan had already written to the mayor of Tolryme and the judge who would come from Radomin to hear Benie's case, though she felt sure it was futile.

"No," said Rachis heavily. "Karan, about Sulien . . ."

"I don't know how the magiz will strike, or where. Or when." She looked up. "I've got to have a plan. Can you . . ."

He sat beside her, his knees clicking. "I'm just an estate manager, Karan. I know when to plant the crops and when to get them in, how to look after the animals and manage the farm workers. I don't know anything about your world, your special gift, or the kind of people you're dealing with."

"But you're wise and strong."

"I'm an old, old man and I'll soon be in my grave. Whatever you do, you must work it out with Llian first."

"But—"

"I can't believe you've forgotten everything he's done for you – and all he's sacrificed."

"Of course not," she said guiltily.

"He's brave and strong and clever, and he loves you – if you'll give him the chance."

"If I tell him what I'm up to, he'll only agonise, and that'll make it even harder."

"Sulien is his daughter too," Rachis said curtly. "It's his right to be involved – and to agonise! Don't cut him out, Karan."

"What happens when the drumming starts again? How can I trust—"

"You're making the biggest mistake of your life, and I'm not collaborating with it."

Rachis trudged up the dusty path towards the kitchen. He did not deserve the burdens she kept piling on him. Karan slumped back on the bench. She kept seeing the way Llian had gone for the axe before Benie had killed Cook. True, he had beaten the impulse, but could he resist the drumming next time, and the time after?

She was utterly alone. No one could help her now . . .

Except her Aachim kinswoman, Malien. The Aachim who dwelt on Santhenar were few, but they were clever and strong, and Malien was one of their leaders. But she was a thousand miles away in the great bastion of Tirthrax, carved deep into the highest mountain in the world. How best to contact her?

A mind-to-mind link could work, and Karan was skilled at using that rare talent, though it was risky. Links were related to seeings and it was possible the magiz might be able to eavesdrop on it. But there was no choice.

She slipped out the rear gate of the garden and headed through the
dusty fields to the River Ryme, where she sat on the end of her decrepit
jetty. It had fallen into disuse over the past twelve years of drought,
since the river was seldom high enough for boats to come this far
upstream. At the moment it was just a series of isolated pools separated
by meandering beds of cobbles.

Karan sat cross-legged on the weather-roughened planking and tried
to picture Malien as she had last seen her, a couple of years ago. The
Aachim were big people for the most part, with dark hair and dark eyes,
and remarkably long fingers. They were long-lived, brilliant designers,
and masterly workers in both metal and stone. But, bitter about their
long exile from their own world, Aachan, they now isolated themselves
in their mountain cities and lived in the past.

Malien was different. She was smaller, pale of skin, green of eye
and red-haired, like Karan herself. They were distantly related though
Karan, being only one quarter Aachim, was not considered one of
them. Malien was like a wise old aunt to her; she had tremendous
inner calm and a vast knowledge of the Secret Art, and Karan needed
both.

The link proved difficult and tiring, and when she finally made the
connection it was weak and wavering.

"What's wrong?" said Malien.

Mindful that the link might not last, Karan told her as briefly as
possible. Links also conveyed emotions and she felt the impact on
Malien as a series of sharp shocks, like a nail being hammered into a
tree.

"*Ah, to drink a life!* the magiz said. It was sickening."

"Go on," said Malien.

Karan told her about the drumming and Benie murdering Cook.
"Have you heard it too?"

"We have," said Malien, "though none of us has been affected by it."
Her tone hinted at superiority. After a long silence she went on. "This
is very bad."

The link was hard to hold, but Karan waited in silence.

"You know how much we feared the Charon," Malien said at last.

"They were the most powerful human species of all. A hundred of them took Aachan from you and turned your people into serfs."

"A fact we don't care to be reminded of, even after all this time," Malien said drily. "Yet I happen to know – I learned it by accident not long before their end – the Charon's deepest secret."

"Oh?" Karan said sharply.

"They were afraid of another human species in the void."

"Could that be the Merdrun?"

"I don't know."

"Except for the tattoos, they look just like Charon; at first I thought they were Charon."

"They aren't," said Malien. "The Charon fought their enemy for thousands of years and were beaten."

"Beaten?" It seemed impossible.

"They were being hunted to extinction, and they were desperate. That's why they fled the void and took Aachan."

"Gergrig said his people had been betrayed and exiled. They've practised the art of war for ten thousand years to get their revenge."

"I don't know anything about that, but anyone who could terrify the Charon and almost wipe them out must be formidable indeed."

Karan's entrails knotted painfully. How could Santhenar survive such an invasion? "Can the magiz attack Sulien from the void?"

"There's no way of telling."

"Then I'll have to spy on her again." Karan waited for Malien to talk her out of it.

"A mother must protect her child," said Malien, "whatever the cost."

"Do you think I can spy on the magiz via a seeing?"

"Spy on a mighty alien sorcerer and get away with it? Seriously?"

Karan swallowed. "Yes."

"No, I don't," said Malien. "You'll probably fail and be killed, very unpleasantly . . . but you have to try."

Karan's heart gave a single, leaden thud.

"Though not with hrux," Malien went on. "It's too dangerous and unpredictable."

"Then how?"

Again the hesitation. "We have a secret spell," Malien said reluctantly. "Forbidden to all but pure-blood Aachim. I could be exiled just for telling you about it."

"I can't work spells."

"You wouldn't need to."

"What is it?"

"An incantation of disembodiment."

"*Disembodiment?*" Karan squeaked.

"If I were to cast it on you, you'd be able to use all your senses to spy on the magiz on Cinnabar. You would be there in every way, except physically."

"I'll do it."

"It's a most unpleasant spell, quite unnatural. The body fights it all the way."

"As long as it does what I need, I don't care."

"You will care. You'll wish I'd never been born."

"I'll worry about that at the time."

"Impetuous as always," said Malien with a hint of amusement. "All right."

"When I'm disembodied, can I be seen or heard?"

"Not by ordinary people. But if you're sensed, a skilled mancer could make you visible. If that happens you must break the spell *instantly*."

"Can my spirit be attacked while I'm disembodied?"

"By a skilled mancer, yes. Also, over such a massive distance the spell could fade, or the connection between your spirit and your body could break. If that happened, your spirit would be lost and your witless body would wither and die. Be clear on this, Karan – using this spell is the most dangerous thing you've ever tried to do. And that's not the worst that could happen."

"What is the worst?"

"The magiz could force you to materialise on Cinnabar, then trap you."

"Is there any way that I can attack her, under the spell?"

Malien seemed to start, then said, "Don't even think about it."

"I was born with a gift for mancery," said Karan. "But—"

"Stop right there!"

"But when I was thirteen, Tensor saw my gift as a danger to the Aachim and blocked it so it would never develop. He robbed me of my birthright!" she said furiously. "Can you unblock it?"

"No!"

"I really need it, Malien."

"You're far too old. Your mancery can't be resurrected. And even if it could, it'd probably kill you."

"All right!" snapped Karan. "Can you cast the disembodiment spell on me via the link?"

"Are you sure you're ready?"

"Yes."

"I'll put a dormant spell on you – its effect will be ... mild. It's only when you trigger the spell that you'll really pay. Hold on to something."

Karan took hold of one of the splintery old planks. Malien cast the dormant spell and it wasn't mild at all; Karan felt a blistering pain from the back of her throat to the pit of her stomach as if a red-hot poker had been rammed down her throat, and the burning spread until the whole of her body was afire.

"You all right?" said Malien.

"Yes," Karan gasped, though she wasn't. She was burning up.

Malien told her how to set off the spell when she was ready. It was keyed to the single word *trigger.* The words *spell-stop* would undo the spell and bring her back to her body.

"Make sure Llian knows exactly what's going on," Malien added. "Under the disembodiment spell, your abandoned body will look ... frightening."

Karan did not have the strength to reply.

"I mean it," Malien said sharply. "You can't do this on your own."

Her voice went fuzzy. "Can't hold the link much longer," said Karan.

"Last thing!" cried Malien. "Your mad ancestor, Basunez, and your father, Galliad, both carried out reckless sorcery at Carcharon."

Carcharon, a remote part of Karan's estate, was a ruined tower high in the mountains west of Gothryme. Galliad, a half-Aachim, had been exiled by his own people for this crime.

"Sorcery that weakened the barrier between Santhenar and the void," said Karan. "I know."

"And their work could aid the Merdrun's invasion plans. If you have any of their papers, get rid of them."

"Why?" said Karan.

"If the Merdrun do invade, people will remember what Basunez and Galliad got up to, and their papers could be used to hang you for conspiring with the enemy."

The link vanished.

Karan remained on the jetty, picking splinters out of her fingers. Her insides still felt scalded; how could she endure the far greater pain of the triggered spell, then be competent to go spying? She felt hot and cold, and too unsteady to stand up.

What if the magiz caught her and killed her? Or the disembodiment spell went wrong and her spirit never returned to her body? Or the magiz attacked Sulien while Karan was separated from her body?

Was it hopeless? Was her little family doomed?

6

AND HE WAS DEAD!

Karan ran into her library and locked the door. In the secret passage she got out the rusty iron box that held Mad Basunez's documents, then flipped through the yellowed papers and stained parchments, the spell charts and coded incantations, shivering. His profane experiments at Carcharon almost six hundred years ago had allowed something alien in from the void, and it had slaughtered all but one of his seven grandchildren. It had nearly destroyed the family.

Karan often visited their graves, the saddest place on her estate. She imagined a seventh headstone, SULIEN, and it was more than she could bear. She hurled the contents of the box into the library fireplace and set everything alight. Good riddance!

Galliad's records were another matter. She had loved her big, handsome, half-Aachim father; he had been the mainstay of her life until he had been killed up at Carcharon, pursuing the same obsession. Karan went through his papers and picked out everything that was even remotely related to what he had done at Carcharon. At the library table, she watched another part of her childhood burn, then crushed the ashes so nothing could be read from them and went out.

She had to use the disembodiment spell and the sooner the better. Should she tell Llian? There was a strong probability that she would not make it back and she could not deceive him about that. He would be in agony and would try to stop her, but Sulien must come first.

At three in the morning she rose and prepared carefully in the empty guest room. She was crouched in the dark, bracing herself for the agony of Malien's disembodiment spell, when she heard a quavery moan coming from Sulien's room. Karan leaped up. Was the magiz attacking?

The bedroom door was wrenched open and Llian burst out, his face contorted in terror. He hurtled past without realising she was there and down to Sulien's room.

"Daddy!" she was howling as Karan ran in. "Daddy, Daddy!"

"It's all right," he said, holding her. "I'm here."

Sulien's green eyes took up half her face; she clung to him desperately. "Daddy, I *saw* you," she said, gasping. "And ... and ... "

A shiver made its way up Karan's spine. She sat beside them and took Sulien's hands. "What's the matter? Was it another nightmare?"

"I saw Daddy," said Sulien, her small chest heaving, *"and he was dead!"*

It knocked Karan sideways. Her eyes misted and her breath congealed in her lungs. She threw her arms around them both, crushing them to herself. It could not be true – *it could not!*

"I'm right here," said Llian to Sulien. "It was just a bad dream."

Karan put her hands around Sulien's head and lifted the nightmare from her. It was much harder than it had been the first time and when Karan finished her head was throbbing. Sulien's eyes returned to their normal size. She gave a trembling shudder.

Karan pulled the covers around her. "You'll be all right now. We're not going anywhere."

Sulien looked puzzled; the lifted nightmare was already fading.

"Go back to bed," Karan said to Llian. "I'll look after her."

He went still. Had she just reinforced her earlier rejection, and given him the impression that *his* life did not matter? She had not meant to. She reached out to him but Llian's face had already taken on the familiar closed look he used to protect himself. He nodded stiffly, kissed Sulien on the forehead and left.

Sulien's brow wrinkled. "What's the matter with Daddy?"

"He's all right. Go to sleep, it's late."

Sulien closed her eyes. Karan sat with her until she slept, then tiptoed out and back to the guest room. Her insides were burning again, but her hands were frigid and her bare feet were icy lumps. What had Sulien really seen? Was Llian going to die?

She restarted the nightmare and, in an image illuminated as if by a flash of lightning, saw him lying in the middle of an expanse of polished flagstones. He bore no visible signs of injury and she could not tell what had happened to him, but he looked dead.

Karan wrapped her arms around herself and rocked from side to side. She wanted to run to Llian and never let him go, but she had to know what was going on, and if it was real. She checked the image again, scarcely able to look at his lifeless body, but it told her nothing more. Could it be true? Or was it a threat?

She continued the nightmare, praying that it would reveal something hopeful. Another series of flashes showed the Merdrun army, led by Gergrig, charging up a mountain road towards a square fortress made of black iron and blue stone. The magiz's artificers blasted a fifty-foot-wide hole through the nearest wall, hurling dozens of sentries to their death, and the troops swarmed in as they had stormed the domed city in Sulien's first nightmare. But this time – flash, flash, flash – the blood-drenched nightmare followed them in.

During the Time of the Mirror Karan had seen more mayhem than she cared to remember, though it was nothing like this. On Santhenar warring armies normally did their best to spare civilians, but the Merdrun appeared to glory in bloodshed and destruction, as if the existence of ordinary people living everyday lives was offensive to them.

They butchered everyone they came across; only by doing so, it seemed, could they ease their own pain. The only people they spared were taken for torture, and they did not live long. And as the magiz stood by, gleefully drinking each life, she became stronger and the Merdrun more powerful.

It was awful, yet Karan had to watch the whole nightmare in case it gave her a clue to Llian's fate, or Sulien's – or indeed her own. But it did not.

Towards the end, when all the occupants of the fortress were dead, the Merdrun headed up through a rugged mountain pass towards a second fortress several miles away and half a mile higher. It was a breathtakingly beautiful castle carved from golden stone, with many slender towers and defensive platforms curving out over the walls. Another mile higher stood a third fortress, a vast curved structure hung with ice – or perhaps carved from ice. But what was it guarding?

She peered deep into the nightmare, up and up, and then she saw it. High above the curved fortress, on a flat-topped peak that stood above every other peak on barren Cinnabar, through drifting snow she made out a big blood-red trilithon – two tall standing stones with a third stone resting across their tops. Was it the gate that would let the Merdrun into Santhenar at the time of the triple moons?

"Mummy! Daddy!" screamed Sulien.

Karan raced into her room, dreading what she was going to find. Llian burst in after her.

"My head," Sulien gasped, clutching at it. "It's cracking open."

Karan's blood froze. The magiz was trying to kill her.

"What's happening to me?" Sulien whispered.

Blood gushed from her right nostril, then the left. Her eyes rolled up and she fell back on the bed.

7

I'M RESIGNING

"You're what?" cried Esea.

They were in the vulgar Pink Chamber of the citadel, a room so garishly overdecorated that Tallia bel Soon normally avoided it. The cornices were three feet deep and painted in a dozen colours, and each of the six glittering chandeliers would have filled a hay wain. Tallia had chosen it because no one would think to look for her here.

She turned away from the window and the streetscape of old Thurkad, the fabulously wealthy capital of Iagador and the most corrupt city in the world. For most of her time as Magister she had worked well with Yggur, the age-old warlord and mancer who had ruled Iagador for a dozen years.

But his mental breakdown and abrupt withdrawal six months ago had left Iagador leaderless and without an army, and the Magister had neither the authority nor the finances to fill the gap. Since then Tallia had spent all her time trying to hold back the warring barons who wanted to seize Thurkad for themselves, and the scum who just wanted to plunder it. Like the yellowcloaks she could see now on every corner. Who was their overlord? No one knew.

"I'm resigning as Magister and head of the Council of Santhenar," said Tallia. "Tonight."

For fifteen hundred years the council of mancers had been a powerful force in the west, but it was just a fractious rump now with little power and even less influence. It felt like her personal failure.

"Why?" said Esea, a small, striking blonde and a reshaper of rare skill, though neither attribute could prove her worth to the sternest critic of all, herself.

"Things are getting worse, not better. The council needs fresh blood and new ideas."

There was a long silence. Tallia looked from Esea to her seated twin,

Hingis, who had been kicked by a mule as a boy. His head and upper body were as ugly and misshapen as she was perfectly formed; the left side of his chest was caved in and his face was a tilt-boned monstrosity. It was not a mirror to the inside.

"The Magister can't resign," said Esea. "He or she can only be dismissed by the council or——"

"Die in office," said Tallia. "Too bad! I'm going. That's why I invited you two to this meeting."

"Why?" Esea repeated.

"I'm going home to Crandor."

"But you've lived in Thurkad for as long as I've known you. Longer."

"And I *hate* the place." A tremor crept into Tallia's voice and for once she did not try to conceal it. "My soul aches for my homeland: the tropic heat, the warm torrential rain, the wild and fecund jungle." She looked away and said softly, "And even more for my family. I can't bear it any longer."

"What will you do there?" said Esea.

"I don't have the faintest idea." Tallia stared through the grimy window as if she could pierce the distance to Crandor, four hundred leagues north. "Ryarin's murder tore the heart out of me. We were childhood sweethearts, did you know?"

"I didn't," said Esea. "I'm so sorry."

"We made promises to one another, and I kept putting him off – and he was killed because of what I am. I keep asking myself why I stayed here, and what it's all been for . . . and I have no answers."

"But we need you. In a corrupt world, a strong, decent Magister really matters."

"Thurkad would be better off if I'd been as ruthless as my predecessor. Anyway, I want children and I'm running out of time."

"You can have a family and still be Magister."

A faint drumming sounded in Tallia's head. She rubbed her tired eyes. She was always tired these days.

"The role of Magister is all-consuming. No one can do both." She kneaded her forearm. "My mind is made up."

"But who's going to replace you?" cried Esea.

Tallia glanced at Hingis, who used words as sparingly as gold tells, as if each syllable came at a cost and had to matter. Despite his ugliness, or perhaps because of it, he was a master illusionist so grounded in reality that he never succumbed to the lure of his art.

She had often heard Esea plead with him to fashion himself a more pleasing likeness. Perhaps she, afflicted by the rarest kind of beauty, truly believed such an illusion would help him, but Hingis always refused. Though hideous and in constant pain, he bore his affliction with a serenity his sister could not hope to echo.

Tallia, now uncertain, weighed their fitness. Hingis's illusions could make beauty from ugliness, something from nothing, order from disorder. But could a little, sickly man make peace between the warring factions who would rise as soon as she resigned?

Esea was his antithesis in the Secret Art as well. As a reshaper – a master of transforming matter from one form to another – she refashioned reality as well as he did illusion. Did she work so hard at her art because of the childhood dare that had led to Hingis's maiming and the guilt she could never escape?

Neither Hingis nor Esea could be Magister on their own. Their true worth lay in their ability to combine their separate arts – the shaping of both illusion and reality – into spells far greater than the sum of their parts. Mancers were rarely able to work together, and the twins' ability to do so made them invaluable. They were Tallia's worthy successors – as long as nothing ever came between them.

Hingis remained silent apart from the rasp of each indrawn breath into his good lung. He was hard to read.

"You don't have anything to say?" said Tallia, meeting his golden-brown eyes.

"You're impossible to replace." He spoke deliberately, in a hoarse and breathless voice, for the misshapen jaw and withered left lung made speaking an effort. "You've given your all to Santhenar, and we'll miss you. I wish you joy in your new life."

"But who will lead us?" Esea repeated.

"That's up to the council," said Tallia. "Though if you're willing to take the Magistership on I'll argue for you."

"I can't do it!" cried Esea. "I don't deserve it."

"I meant the two of you."

"It'd never work. We're not ready."

Tallia had not expected this. Esea was the reckless one, constantly trying to prove herself. Why was she being so timid? Had Tallia made a terrible mistake? She had no other candidate; the local councillors were utterly unworthy, and the others were far off and seldom made the long journey to Thurkad. "No one is ever ready to be Magister. I certainly wasn't when Mendark was slain."

"But you'd been his assistant for years."

"You and Hingis have been my assistants for four years," said Tallia. "May I put your names forward?"

Hingis exchanged glances with his sister and something unsaid passed between them, perhaps each agreeing because they felt the other wished it.

Esea nodded stiffly. "You'll stay to help us with the transition. A month? Two, even?"

"The new Magister needs a clean start," said Tallia. "Whether you two are confirmed as joint Magister or someone else is elected, my time is over. When I walk out of the council meeting, I'm leaving Thurkad."

"*Tonight?*"

"Yes."

"For good?" Finally Hingis showed some emotion.

"Crandor is two months away by ship. I don't expect to come back." She smoothed down her shoulder-length black hair, now threaded with silver, and took a deep breath. "We're late. Let's go in."

Hingis levered himself from his chair. His curved spine left him no taller than his sister. Tallia, lean and long-legged, towered over them both. She headed down the long hall to the iron-bound double doors of the council chamber, eased the left door open and stopped, looking into the vast room. Another Magister might have thrust the doors wide to crash back against the inner wall, but it was not her way to make entrances.

Seven councillors were seated at the table, a massive construction of ebony wood twenty feet long, six feet wide and weighing half a ton. They were bickering, as usual. Petty fools! There wasn't a man or woman here she would miss, not even her occasional allies, the triple-chinned glutton Lemmo Avury and squat, sour Cantha Pluvior. How could she have wasted a quarter of her life weaving paths through their small-minded opposition? She hoped she never saw them again.

The drumming sounded again, louder than before. Tallia surveyed the hall behind them, which was empty save for a pair of bent-backed clerks lugging armloads of journals on some pointless errand.

"What's that noise?" she said.

"Can't hear anything," said Esea.

"It's a thumping sound in my head," said Hingis, "and I don't like it."

Tallia put the niggle out of her mind. "Evening, Lestry," she said to the guard on the door. There were fresh bruises on his kindly face. "Long day?"

"Too long, Magister, but there's no help for it."

"We'll be quick tonight. You'll be home with your kids by eight." And your nigah-addicted shrew of a wife, poor man. Nigah, the narcotic bark of a tropical tree, stained the teeth black, and its addicts were violent and unpredictable.

"Thank you, Magister."

She passed her knife to him, and her staff. He put them in the Magister's compartment of the weapons cabinet. She went in and sat at the head of the table, nodding to the councillors. Hingis and Esea took their positions further along. Tallia looked down at her brown hands. Was she doing the right thing? Or selfishly putting her own interests above the welfare of Thurkad and the west?

Could Hingis, crippled as he was, and Esea, whose reckless streak seemed to grow worse each day, take her place? Or would one of the other councillors seize control and undo what little good she'd done in her decade as Magister? Tallia's resolve faltered. No, she had to stop finding excuses to cling to the past. No one was irreplaceable. It was long past time to go.

The drumming grew louder. Hingis clapped his hands over his ears; his broken face was twisted in pain. Esea stared at him, uncomprehending.

An argument broke out between Cantha and Rebnell, a red-faced little man with a big black mole on his chin. He slammed a fist down on the ebony table and cursed her, using the foulest oaths Tallia had ever heard. Cantha punched him in the face, squashing his tiny nose flat.

"Stop it!" yelled Tallia. "What's the matter with everyone today?"

A heavy thump on the locked door at the far end of the chamber. *Boom!* The door went skidding across the granite flagstones, its iron hinges squealing and leaving a trail of sparks in its wake. Splinters peppered the window drapes, the table and the councillors.

A band of armed men surged in, followed by a rail-thin mancer wearing a purple mask and one of those parchment-yellow cloaks she kept seeing on the street. Purple and yellow – what did that remind her of? Tallia leaped up, cursing her rule that weapons be left outside. She was a master of both armed and unarmed combat but there were far too many of them.

She kicked her chair aside, extended her right arm and cast a block on the running troops, who piled up as though they had run into a wall. The masked mancer directed his staff at her. *Zzztt!* Tallia's knees buckled and her block failed.

"Cut her down!" he roared. His voice was vaguely familiar.

Rebnell, who was at the far end of the table closest to the intruders, fell out of his chair, struggled to his feet, stumbled a few steps and was killed by so violent a blow that his little head struck the floor fifteen feet away, spinning like a top and spraying blood in all directions. Cantha was quicker but it did not avail her – a barrel-chested brute of a soldier thrust his sword through her chest and out her back. It made a ghastly crunching sound. He jerked the blade out, shouldered the falling body aside and ran at Hingis.

Esea let out a scream of fury and extended her hands towards the soldier. His bloody sword glowed red and smoked as the blood burned away, then went blue-white and turned to molten steel in his hand. He howled, clutched his charred hand, and began to scream and dance as the boiling metal ate through his boots. The reek of burning leather caught in Tallia's nostrils.

Though only half his size, Esea ran at him in a reckless fury. "No one touches my brother!"

She slammed a chair into his face and he went down, kicking and screaming, his boots and feet ablaze.

"Kill Tallia, the monstrosity and the blonde bitch first," bellowed the mancer. "Then all the others. Make damn sure they're dead. Then secure the library, the council's spell vault and the secret archives."

Three ruffians advanced on Tallia in a coordinated attack, one from the front and one from either side. She blasted the first man off his feet, kicked the second in the belly and the third in the throat. But as more troops stormed through the door she realised it was hopeless.

"Out!" she panted, shoving the surviving council members towards the main doors. "Run, you damned fools!"

As she turned back to face their attackers a muscle-bound fellow with protruding ears shot out from underneath the table. He propelled himself to his feet and thrust up at her with a yellow-clotted blade. Tallia twisted away but not in time. Icy pain speared through her shoulder as the point struck her right collarbone, slid through the flesh beneath and jammed against her shoulder blade.

She kicked him in the kneecap. He hopped back, grimacing, but did not fall. Blood poured from her wound, then a stinging numbness spread across her shoulder and her right arm flopped by her side, useless.

In the past Tallia had taken worse injuries, but numbness was spreading down her right side and up her neck. It did not feel like any spell she had encountered before. The yellow muck on the blade must have been poison.

Behind her she heard screams and the explosive gush of someone vomiting. Were the rest of the councillors being butchered? She did not have the strength to turn her head. She felt an immense sense of failure. How had her network of spies and informers, supposedly the best in the land, not warned her of this plot?

The muscle-bound thug swung his sword back and Tallia knew she was going to die.

8

CAN YOU STAY UPRIGHT?

Tallia slipped to her knees, watching the swinging blade that was going to end her life.

Behind her Hingis spoke three words in an arcane tongue: *"Rahgiz voluten shix."* Tallia's attacker let out a yelp as the blade appeared to reverse in his hand and spear at his own face. He swayed sideways and it sliced off his protruding left ear as it went past. On the floor, it looked like a bloody dried apricot.

He hurled the weapon from him, clutched at the side of his head, then stared at the blood all over his hand. Hingis's illusion was one of the finest Tallia had ever seen, though not enough to save her – the soldier was drawing a long knife.

Hingis and Esea faced each other. He nodded and spoke another two words. There was not a hint of panic in his voice.

At the same time Esea cried, "Chamber, crumble!"

The room began to shake, then wobble. The walls seemed to be vibrating in and out, the floor bucking up and down, the chairs clattering across the boards. White smoke billowed from a stack of paper scrolls. The muscle-bound soldier was thrown off his feet.

Esea pointed at the massive ebony table. It toppled onto its side, bounced as if the hard wood had turned to rubber, swung in a violent arc and slammed into the muscle-bound soldier, then the others. Bones snapped like dry wood. Two of the soldiers went flying backwards and the others disappeared behind the table, which pushed them across the chamber and crushed them against the side wall. Their screams proved that it was no illusion.

The chamber felt as though it was shaking to pieces. Statues of past Magisters toppled from their pedestals; framed portraits of councillors hit the floor and came apart. Hingis gestured at the ceiling, which cracked in many places. Chunks of lath and plaster pelted down, though oddly there was no dust. This *was* an illusion, though only a master could have seen through it.

Tallia tried to get up but her legs would not support her. Esea lifted her from behind and thrust a shoulder under her left arm, supporting her. Esea's face was bleached, her breath rasping. Attacking with such massive objects had drained her. Hingis was breathing in punctured gasps and his lips had a blue tinge.

The three surviving councillors were stampeding down the hall, Avury last, his prodigious buttocks wobbling like water-filled balloons. The seat of his trousers had burst.

Only two soldiers were uninjured and they hung well back, staring fearfully at the quivering ceiling. The masked mancer's lips were moving. Evidently he was trying to understand which aspects of the Secret Art were being used here, and how to counter them.

Esea turned Tallia and headed for the doors. Hingis lurched along beside them, grimly satisfied.

"Your best ever illusion," said Esea.

It was all Tallia could do to hold on. She glanced back. "They're coming again. Mean to kill us all. And I've got nothing left."

"Hold her up," said Esea.

Hingis gave Tallia his shoulder and she could feel his knees trembling. Esea raised both arms towards the far end of the chamber.

A quarter of the ceiling fell with a crash, burying the three soldiers. A chunk of plaster burst on the mancer's head, driving him to his knees and knocking the purple mask askew. Tallia saw a long lopsided face, a lantern jaw and pendulous ears like tree fungi – it was Scorbic Vyl, a dangerous mancer-for-hire. Who was he working for? He yanked the mask over his face and staggered out, calling for reinforcements.

"Come on," said Hingis.

Esea was on her knees. "Utterly . . . drained."

She forced herself to her feet and they hauled Tallia through the main doors. Hingis pulled them shut and locked them. Lestry, the door guard, had fled. Esea staggered to the nearest window and clung to its frame, looking out.

"Where . . . citadel guards?" gasped Tallia.

"Vyl must have dealt with them first."

Boom! Boom! The main doors were attacked from the other side. Tallia fell to her knees again.

"They can't hold more than a minute or two," said Esea.

They snatched their weapons from the cabinet. Esea hauled Tallia to the stone stairs on the left and, with Hingis's help, heaved her down five flights. He locked each set of doors behind them, though it could only gain them a few minutes. They were both gasping and Tallia still could not stand up by herself.

"What about . . . councillors?" she said.

"Running for their lives." Esea's voice dripped contempt.

"The council records—"

"Will fall into Vyl's hands," said Hingis. "This was well planned."

"Can't . . . end like this," said Tallia, slurring her words.

"If we don't get out of Thurkad before they take the gates," said Esea, "we're dead."

"Stables. My horses. Keep watch. Yellowcloaks."

They headed along a low, dripping passage to the citadel stables. Puddles of foul brown water on the floor smelled as if it had seeped from the cesspits. Esea wadded a rag against Tallia's oozing wound and bound it. There wasn't time to clean it. Tallia put a hand on the bandage and cast an antidote charm. The pain softened, though it did not ease the creeping lethargy that made the simplest thing an effort. Not knowing what the poison was, she could not counter it.

Her saddlebags were already packed. Hingis and Esea saddled the horses while Tallia clung to the side of a stall, feeling cold blood trickling down her side. It was taking all her strength to stay conscious.

They helped her onto her horse, a huge black beast, wild of eye and loyal only to her. Her head spun. With a supreme effort of will that she would pay for later, she forced the numbness back.

"Can you stay upright?" said Esea.

"Have to."

"Where are we going?"

"Was taking ship. Too risky now. Go . . . south-west gate. Split up."

"We're not leaving you."

"You must."

They rode for the gate, trying not to attract attention. It was very dark and the wind drove cold rain through the stinking yellow smog. There were few people on the streets and most were head down, trying to get out of the miserable weather.

They reached the south-western gate and were not challenged, though they were recognised and must soon be followed. Two miles south, at the junction of the Feddil Road and the High Way, Tallia reined in, shuddering with the cold.

"Got coin?" she said to the twins. Their stipend was small and Hingis's healers' bills must be enormous.

"We've got nothing but what we're wearing," said Hingis.

Esea pulled half a dozen small coins from her pocket, studied them ruefully and thrust them back.

"Magisters have . . . secret hoards," said Tallia. "One not far."

The rain grew heavier. She was shivering uncontrollably; cold was creeping out of the wound and all through her body. It took a desperate hour to find the place, between a cluster of boulders in a patch of scrub heavily grazed by goats. But as they passed behind the biggest boulder Tallia knew what she was going to find – she could sense the broken protection charm and smell the freshly turned earth.

The hoard, which had been hidden here for decades, had been freshly plundered. What if the other hoards were gone as well? She had savings but she was by no means wealthy. How was she to fund the fightback? Tallia slumped onto a grey boulder, shivering and shuddering, and cast her antidote charm again. It did nothing.

"What are we going to do?" said Esea.

Tallia lurched to her saddlebags, took out two coin pouches and handed one to each of them.

"We can't take your savings," said Esea.

"You can't go back. Lost everything."

"How will you get to Crandor?"

Tallia let out a bitter croak. "How can I go home now?"

"We can deal with Scorbic Vyl."

"But not . . . who's behind him." Vyl's colours had given that away.

"Who is behind him?"

"Yellow parchment on purple velvet – Cumulus Snoat."

"Who's he?" said Esea.

Tallia forced herself to focus, to speak clearly. "Greediest man in Meldorin. He's got a private army."

"But the City Watch—"

"Will have fallen. Snoat's yellowcloaks will control Thurkad by now ... and whoever controls Thurkad controls ... northern Iagador. But it's worse than that ..."

"What are you saying?"

"War!" she gasped. "And Iagador no longer has an army."

It was time for extreme measures. Tallia gripped her staff, focused on the wound and prepared the most powerful healing charm she could manage. Self-healing charms were rarely effective for long and the cost in aftersickness would be high, but she had no choice. She cast the spell. The wound burned as if a red-hot coal had been jammed into it, then her mind cleared a little.

"Thurkad is lost," said Tallia. "Race down the High Way to Sith. Don't stop, day or night. Send skeets."

Skeets were vicious hunting birds, bigger than eagles, and dangerous to handle, but they were the fastest way to send a message.

"Who to?" said Esea.

"Nadiril, the Librarian at the Great Library in Zile. And Wistan, at the college in Chanthed. And ... Yggur, too, I suppose." She pronounced his name as Igger.

"His abdication created this mess."

"You can't blame him for his illness. And he may be recovering by now – he may be able to help us."

"I wouldn't bet on it," said Esea.

"When you get to Sith, organise the resistance in the south: recruit allies and spies, raise money and form an army."

"That all?" Esea said sarcastically.

"Then await my skeet," said Tallia.

"Where are you going?"

"To Gothryme."

"A hundred miles is a hell of a ride in your condition."

"Must be done. Then I'll head to Casyme to see Shand."

"Who's he?" said Esea.

"Long ago he was known as the Recorder. Though he's an old man now – all my allies are old."

"Or damaged," said Esea, though she meant herself. She would never have said it about Hingis.

Tallia turned to go, then stopped. There was a high chance that she would be caught and killed, and the council's secrets must be protected. "Hingis, a word." She headed away between the boulders.

He followed, walking with a sideways rolling motion, his breath rasping. Esea came with him.

"A private word, please, Esea," Tallia added.

Hingis paused in mid-step, his eyes searching Tallia's. Gold flashed in Esea's eyes; she glared at Tallia, unblinking. Tallia met her gaze and they stood that way for a long moment, then Esea turned back.

Tallia went on until there was no chance of being overheard and waited for Hingis. He did nothing without effort but asked for no concessions.

"Esea and I work together," said Hingis.

"The more people who know the code to the council's spell vault, the greater the risk it'll be exposed. There are old spells and forgotten devices so deadly—"

His eyes widened fractionally. "I trust Esea with my life."

Tallia faltered. Was she doing the right thing, or making a terrible mistake? She could not think clearly. "While I'm Magister, I must protect our secrets."

"She won't take it well."

"If . . . if the need wasn't desperate, I wouldn't ask. Will you accept the code, use it if disaster strikes and there's no other way, and keep it secret no matter the cost?"

"If I do," said Hingis, "it will sunder us. And . . . that may turn out worse than if you never gave it to me."

There was no time to think that through. They had to leave *now*. "No one can see the future. For the sake of Iagador?"

His lopsided shoulders slumped, the left dropping lower than the right, then extended his right hand. She wrote the code on a scrap of paper and gave it to him. He read it, closed his eyes for a second, his lips moving, then nodded and handed the paper back. She tore it to pieces, put them in her mouth, chewed and swallowed.

"Fare well," said Hingis.

"And you."

He trudged back to Esea and they spoke briefly, after which she stalked to her horse and galloped away. Hingis hauled himself into the saddle like a crab trying to climb a wall and rode after her, as saggy as a bag of potatoes.

Pain stabbed through Tallia's shoulder. Had she made things worse? She mounted, turned onto the Feddil Road and urged her horse into a gallop. She could already feel her healing charm slipping, the aftersickness stirring. The hundred-mile ride was going to be brutal.

Yet her failure was more painful. Her decade as Magister had been wasted and she was never going home. The dream of tropical Crandor, a family and children at her knee, was over.

As soon as they were gone, a skinny bow-legged man whose arms and hands were thickly furred with black hair slipped down from his hiding place on top of the tallest rock, and raced back to Thurkad.

9

THE DISEMBODIMENT SPELL

Blood was smeared all over Sulien's face and she began to moan and kick. Was she dying? Karan could not breathe, could not think what to do.

"Is the magiz attacking?" Llian said wildly.

"I don't know!" Karan snapped. "Hold her still."

He held Sulien down by the shoulders. Karan extended her fingers across Sulien's forehead, desperately trying to sense how the magiz was getting to her. Her heartbeat thundered in her ears. Should she use Malien's spell and go after the magiz? With Sulien in this state, she dared not.

Precious minutes passed. Llian wiped the blood off her face but it kept pouring from her nose, and her legs were thrashing on the bed. *Ah!* When Karan had lifted the nightmare half an hour ago she had missed a small link implanted in Sulien's mind. That's how the magiz was attacking.

Karan reached down to the buried link, which was like a shiny black bead connected to a taut thread. She jerked the bead out and the thread whipped it away into the dimension from which it had come. Karan gasped; the pain was like an axe biting into the top of her own skull.

Sulien sighed and her eyelids fluttered. Llian tore off a pillowcase, wet it from the bedside water jug and wiped the blood off her face. The bleeding had stopped; she was asleep again, though it was interrupted by fits of trembling and whimpering.

"Watch her," Karan said weakly.

She sensed a distant pain, as bad as her own. She had hurt the magiz. Karan slumped onto the bed, holding her head. But the magiz would attack again and again; she would never give in. Karan got up and lurched out. This had to end *now*.

"What are you doing?" cried Llian.

She stopped in the doorway, swaying. "Don't come into the spare bedroom."

His eyes were despairing holes in his blanched face. "Karan?"

It hurt to see him in such torment, but nothing could be done right now. "I've got to stop the magiz while I still can. I'm going to use a disembodiment spell. Malien put it on me earlier."

"What for?" he said wildly.

"To find out how the magiz is attacking." There was no time to give him the details, no time for anything.

Not even to say, *I love you.*

In the spare room she prepared herself, knowing what a reckless thing she was doing. The magiz knew her link had been broken and she would expect Karan to strike back.

The disembodiment spell was a coiled spring inside her, which *trigger* would release. Every muscle was tense, resisting the agony to come. *Spell-stop* would return her to her body. She rehearsed the command; she might need to use it in a hurry. But what if she were confused or the magiz blocked her?

She filled a bucket with cold water and put it on top of the bookcase next to the bed, with a dangling rope attached to the handle. She had no idea if she would be able to use it in an emergency – during disembodiment her body might be comatose – but it was better than nothing.

Go, now!

She lay on the bed, closed her eyes and tried to picture the magiz as she had last seen her. It proved an unfortunate choice of image – she was torturing one of the prisoners taken in the attack on the square fortress, preparing to drink her life. Karan could not bear to watch. She triggered the disembodiment spell.

And knew what it must feel like to die by the most agonising death of all, anthracism, where the human body burned from the inside out. It felt as though molten lead had been poured down her throat. Her stomach was on fire and it was spreading to her lungs, her heart, her bowels and along her arteries to every part of her body.

Karan let out a desperate, croaking scream. Her head spun, the room whirled, bright sparks curved like meteor trails across her field of view, then, with the thud of a hammer striking human flesh, her spirit was ripped from her body.

She did not travel through the void, as she had done last time. There was no sense of movement at all, but she felt sharp gravel beneath her bare feet. It did not hurt; she had no body here, no weight.

Jagged rocks reared up all around and there was black ice in every cleft. She smelled blood and smoke and a sharp odour she did not recognise; it stung her eyes. It was bitterly cold and the air was thin; even her phantom lungs strained to draw enough. It had a metallic taste, like licking a piece of iron.

In the distance someone was screaming. Karan's bowels clenched. She was on Cinnabar, a quarter of a mile below the golden castle with the slender towers. It would be the next to fall.

The huge green moon stood at the vertical. Another moon, half its size and red, was sinking below the horizon to her left. The third moon, the little yellow one spattered with black, was not in evidence. She tried to pick up a shard of rock but her fingers passed through it. As Malien had said, the only thing she could do here was spy.

The Merdrun army was camped among the rocks in hundreds of orange tents. Sentries patrolled between them and around the perimeter. One was coming now – the round-faced warrior-woman Uzzey, whose blonde plaits formed a loop above her head.

She was marching towards Karan; it seemed impossible that she would not be seen. She backed away but Uzzey turned at the last moment and walked right through her. Karan felt a series of tiny impacts, like windblown feathers, and sensed Uzzey's exhaustion, then her hidden revulsion at the butchery she had been forced to carry out in the attacks.

Uzzey froze, then looked around wildly; she must have sensed Karan. Her eyes were startlingly blue and as clear as sapphires. She reached out with her left hand. She had slim, elegant fingers, though they were greatly scarred and bruised, and half her little finger had been hacked off; it ended in a brown scab. Her arm shook and she groped around her, then shivered and marched on.

Karan climbed an outcrop of red rock and studied the campsite. Apart from the sentries there were few people about and most of the tents were dark; the soldiers must be asleep. So where was her quarry?

Karan's gaze was drawn to the magiz and Gergrig, thirty yards away in a narrow space between two rock outcrops. A dead prisoner, a golden-skinned young man, lay on the bloody ground and the magiz was crouching over him. She stood up, a sick smile on her thin mouth. Her colourless eyes were glowing – she looked like a drunkard who had just opened the first bottle of the day. Karan's stomach heaved.

She drifted closer, her pulse pounding in her ears and every muscle taut. She had to kill the magiz, but how?

"You've drunk a hundred lives today," Gergrig said coldly. "You've got more power than you've ever had, but what have you *learned*? How can this child see us from so far away?"

The magiz took a step back. "I . . . I believe she's inherited talents that give her the gift of seeing."

"Who from?"

"Both parents are gifted, in very different ways. And I found . . ." She seemed reluctant to say it.

"What, damn you?"

She took another step back, hesitated, then said in a rush, "Both have been touched in the past by . . . by . . . *him*."

"By Rulke?" cried Gergrig, his dark features showing alarm, hatred, then a touch of fear. "Are you sure?"

"Yes."

"Is this another conspiracy against us?"

"Rulke is dead. He was killed on Santhenar ten years ago."

"Dead?" Gergrig repeated as if he could not believe it. "You're absolutely sure?"

"Yes."

For a moment he looked dazed, then he threw his head back and let out a chilling laugh. The jagged tattoo on his forehead shone green in the light of the vertical moon.

"Then we're free!" He glanced over his shoulder, then lowered his voice. "Rulke was the only man I ever feared. Nothing can stop us now. Soon Santhenar will be ours, our own world at last! And once we have it, we will plot our revenge."

To Karan's astonishment, this brutal man had tears in his eyes. He passionately, desperately wanted a world for his people. Well, he wasn't getting hers!

"There's still the child," said the magiz.

Gergrig's emotional moment faded. "Why is she still alive?" he snapped.

The magiz did not reply.

"No child could block your attack," he added.

"Someone lifted the nightmare from her, then tore out my link."

"Who?"

"I think . . . her mother."

Karan sank to her knees. The magiz knew too much.

"Can you attack her?"

"What's the point?" said the magiz. "She'll have told everyone about the invasion by now."

"It matters," said Gergrig, "because the red-haired brat has had other nightmares."

Karan stiffened. What other nightmares?

"What do you mean?" said the magiz.

"I've been searching my dreams," he said. "I . . . I think she's seen . . ." Gergrig seemed reluctant to say it aloud. He lowered his voice. "Something vital."

"What?"

"Our . . . one fatal weakness."

Karan gasped; she could not help it. Could this be the break they desperately needed? But as the dreadful implications sank in, her skin seemed to freeze all the way down her back. It made things worse, far worse.

The magiz started and stumbled back, her arms flailing. "Don't say any more!" She regained her balance. "Does the child know? Or is it buried in her subconscious?"

"Find out. Can you attack the mother?"

The magiz showed her teeth. "She was foolish enough to take the nightmare upon herself."

"Kill her, *now*! Then get rid of the child."

"It's not that easy. I'm burning power just to locate them from so far away. I can't keep it up, Gergrig. I'll need all that power later, to open the gate."

"Burn it now," he said harshly, "or we may not get to—" He broke off, then said more calmly, "The child is a danger and you've got to fix it. You will take no part in the battles for the golden castle, or the ice bastion. You will do nothing except find the girl, kill her, then eliminate the rest of the family. Erase the entire household, to be sure."

"It will be a pleasure," said the magiz, her colourless eyes glistening in those black, black sockets.

Karan slumped against the rocks. How could she hope to stop a sorcerer who was bursting with power after drinking so many lives? A sorcerer who was addicted to death.

"How are the preparations going?" added the magiz.

"The summon stone has woken," said Gergrig, "and the chaos has begun on Santhenar. Friend will turn on friend, sister on brother. Soon whole nations will tear themselves apart. By the night of the triple moons there will be no opposition." He grinned savagely. "What a month of war we will have then."

Karan reeled. Benie's murder of Cook wasn't an insignificant local tragedy. The drumming came from the summon stone and the Merdrun were using it to create chaos – and render Santhenar defenceless by the time of the invasion.

"Unless someone finds the stone," said the magiz.

"It can look after itself."

"Yet it also has a weakness. Will it be ready to bring us through by syzygy?"

"It must. Without the alignment of the triple moons we won't be able to open the Crimson Gate, and the next opportunity is years away. Have you done the final calculations?"

She hesitated. "To be sure, I need more lunar observations."

He glowered at her. "But you know approximately."

"Approximately," she said after a calculating pause, "eight weeks."

"Get your damned measurements. I need to know to the minute." Gergrig stalked away.

The magiz, now agitated, paced back and forth, the gravel grating underfoot, then loped towards the nearest tent. It was red with a green rope along its ridge, and was set apart from the others. Emerging with a small brass instrument like a navigator's sextant, she sighted on the red-brown moon, which was setting. She stood there, absolutely still, and as it passed below the horizon Karan heard a faint click.

The magiz made a note on a tablet and trudged back to her tent. Karan followed, digesting what she had learned. Only eight weeks until the invasion through the Crimson Gate – presumably the red trilithon she had seen in Sulien's second nightmare. She had to alert Tallia and Malien urgently.

And she had discovered vital information – both the Merdrun and the summon stone had weaknesses and were vulnerable. If the stone could be found and destroyed, the Merdrun wouldn't be able to come through. And if it could not, their fatal weakness had to be identified.

But that wasn't why she was here. She had to find a way to hide Sulien – no, her entire family – and that meant taking on the magiz. Karan stopped outside the tent and peered in.

Her enemy was standing at a table made from grey canvas stretched over yellow tent poles, entering numbers from her tablet into an almanack. It had four columns, the last three headed with coloured dots. Next to the red dot was the word Wolfrim. The green dot was labelled Stibnid and the yellow one Cromo. Karan assumed they were the moons.

The numbers in the columns must be the rising and setting times of each moon, which the magiz would use to calculate when the three of them would form a line in the night sky – syzygy – when the Crimson Gate could be opened into Santhenar and the Merdrun would invade.

Karan crept towards the entrance of the tent, but as she put her head through a horn blasted in her ear so loudly that she cried out. The magiz spun round, staring into Karan's eyes. Could she see her?

"Gergrig!" the magiz bellowed. "Spy in the camp!" She whirled, snatched a white rod off her blankets and thrust it out.

Karan hurled herself backwards, but a blast of red fire from the rod struck her in the chest, and a pale shimmering nimbus formed around her. Now the magiz could see exactly where she was.

The nimbus slowly faded but Karan could barely move; it was rapidly draining what little strength she had in the disembodied state. Malien had not warned her about that.

Gergrig came bounding down from outcrop to outcrop. He hit the ground outside the tent, skidded, scattering gravel in all directions, and roared, "Where?"

"She can't be far away," said the magiz.

"Guards, surround this place!" yelled Gergrig. "Who is it?"

"I think," said the magiz, who was red in the face and panting, "it's the mother."

"And she'll lead us straight to the child," said Gergrig savagely. "How did she get here?"

The magiz thought for a moment. "A spell of separation, or of disembodiment."

"How dare she think to oppose *me*!"

The arrogance, the assumption that nothing mattered save what he wanted, was staggering. "Spell-stop!" cried Karan.

"Materialise her!" Gergrig pounded a scarred right fist into his left palm. "I'll do the torturing; you'll stand by. The instant she reveals where the daughter is, put an end to the sorry business." He smiled grimly. "And I'll deal with the mother."

"Spell-stop!" Karan gasped. "Spell-stop, spell-stop!"

Pain seared through her innards again – terrible, blistering pain – but the command did not work. She said it again but knew it would fail – in her disembodied state she lacked the strength for it.

"Spell-stop, spell-stop!"

Nothing. The magiz pointed the rod at Karan. *Thud!* She was out-lined with orange fire this time. Now she was burning on the outside and on the inside. She tried to get away but Gergrig ran around behind her, his long arms outspread. The magiz advanced slowly, the rod pointed at Karan's forehead. Her teeth – yellow, crooked, pointed at the tips – were bared. She licked saliva off her fleshless lips; she ached to drink Karan's life.

"Materialise the little bitch!" snapped Gergrig.

"Spell-stop," Karan said feebly.

She tried to reach back to her empty body and rouse it; she imagined her right arm reaching up and flailing about for the rope attached to the bucket of ice water.

She sensed a distant splash but she was still here. Either the water had missed or it had not been enough to wake her spiritless body. Karan stood there helplessly as the magiz's knuckles whitened on the rod, bracing herself for the agony of rematerialisation and the torture that would follow.

Then black pain flared in her head—

"Karan?" cried Llian.

She was lying on the sodden bed and her head was throbbing. She opened her eyes. She had never been more glad to see him. "What did you do? How did I get back?"

"I didn't do anything. I heard you scream and ran in. There's a bruise on your forehead where the bucket hit you."

She felt the long, curving lump and winced. "Is Sulien . . . ?"

Karan tried to get up but did not have the strength. Llian helped her to a sitting position. Cold water ran down her back.

"She's asleep. What's going on?"

Karan clung to him like a lifeline. He was the only solid thing in her crumbling world and she had treated him very badly. She told him in broken sentences all she could manage, that Sulien had seen the Merdrun's fatal flaw, and it had condemned her.

"If we can find out what it is . . ." said Llian.

"I'll try."

"There's something else, isn't there?"

Karan looked at him blankly. She could not focus on anything except Sulien. "The magiz said the summon stone can look after itself, but it has a weakness. You've got to find out what it is."

"I will." He stared at the floor. "Do you think you can protect Sulien?"

"Maybe . . . if I can divert her nightmares – and the link – onto me. Then block the magiz."

"I don't see how that helps," said Llian. He looked as though he were about to throw up. "She can still attack you."

"It's all I've got. Help me up. Got to do it right away."

Karan could not walk. Llian, clearly suffering the deepest misgivings, carried her into Sulien's room and set her in a chair next to the bed. Sulien did not stir, though her sleep was racked by shivers and shudders and occasional little moans.

Karan took her daughter's warm hand in her own cold hand, rested her throbbing head on Sulien's forehead, then implanted a link that would recognise the magiz, block her from attacking Sulien and divert any attack onto herself.

"Mummy," said Sulien, half asleep, "what are you doing?"

"Looking after my lovely daughter. Have you had any other nightmares about the Merdrun? And their great weakness?"

"Don't think so. But I never remember my dreams afterwards."

When Sulien slept, Karan touched her on the forehead and tried to find that vital dream, but without success. The mind was an unmapped labyrinth and she did not know where to look. She fell back, gasping.

Llian carried her back to their bedroom, stripped her wet clothes off and put her to bed, and got in. "Karan, we've—"

"Can't talk," she whispered. "Exhausted."

He stared at the ceiling for a long time, his jaw knotted, then blew out the lamp and turned away.

Karan lay there, aching all over. She felt utterly boneless and longed for the release of sleep, but it would not come. She kept seeing Gergrig's savage smile and the colourless eyes of the magiz.

Little tapping pains began at the top of her skull. The magiz was trying to break through. Something oozed onto Karan's upper lip; her nose was bleeding.

She found a handkerchief in the dark and dabbed the blood away. By diverting the magiz's attack, all she had done was delay the inevitable. It was like a pygmy trying to fight a giant, and if she made a single mistake her family would be crushed underfoot.

But even if she could find the strength to block the attacks, sooner or later the diversion would fail and the magiz would attack Sulien directly. From this moment on Karan could never relax, day or night – she must constantly be watching for signs of an attack on her daughter.

There was only one solution, once she regained the strength for it. Return to Cinnabar and kill the magiz first.

10

OF COURSE SHE'LL FIND OUT

Llian watched Sulien playing a game with Piffle in the orchard. She was tossing the fallen leaves at him and laughing as he leaped in the air, trying to catch them in his mouth. There were yellow leaves in her red hair. In other circumstances it would have been a perfect day, for she had no memory of the nightmares Karan had lifted from her.

His eyes prickled. Time was hurtling towards the night of the triple moons and he had learned nothing about the enemy. How could he protect her when he couldn't fight to save his own life? Would he even know when the magiz found her, or would he just discover— Llian choked.

"What's the matter, Daddy? You look so sad." Sulien came up and took his hand. "Is there anything I can do?"

He rubbed his wet eyes. It wasn't right that she should be worrying about him. "Just thinking."

"What about?"

"Stuff. We'd better get these pears picked."

He plucked the last red pear on the tree, inspected it for grubs and put it in the orchard basket, then stood there, worrying about his reaction to the drumming. He'd felt a terrifying, almost uncontrollable urge to smash things, and what if it was worse next time? What if Karan was right about him? What might he do under its irresistible influence?

He had to be strong. He had to be prepared to fight the drumming when it next occurred.

How could Karan hope to beat the magiz, a powerful alien sorcerer, anyway? She was out of her depth, yet she would never give in. She would protect Sulien with her life – and lose it. Then the magiz would kill Sulien to protect the Merdrun's fatal weakness. But even if, by some miracle, Karan and Sulien survived the next eight weeks, the Merdrun would invade and the world would end.

Who were they, anyway, and why had they fought the Charon, whom they closely resembled, so relentlessly? What was the summon stone that would allow them to open the Crimson Gate and invade Santhenar on the night of the triple moons? Could he find it?

Karan had assumed that he could sort through his knowledge of the Histories like a librarian through a catalogue, but Llian knew he could not find the answers here. He needed access to the best libraries, though under Wistan's ban they were barred to him. The ban must be lifted urgently, but how?

"The old bastard should have died years ago," he muttered.

"You're not supposed to swear in front of children." Sulien gave him a stern look, though her furtive grin undermined it. She loved it when he broke the rules.

"Sorry. Though bast— *that* word, isn't really swearing. It's a true description of Wistan, the repulsive little swine."

She rolled her eyes, skipped off and climbed the next pear tree. Her big-eyed puppy trotted from one pile of cow dung to another, sniffing cheerfully.

"Hang on!" Llian lugged the basket across. "You know the rules. I climb the tree, you catch the pears."

"Piffle," said Sulien. It was her favourite word. "Mummy said—" She broke off, flushing charmingly.

Llian set the basket down and frowned at her, hands on hips. "Go on, what did Karan say?"

"She told me not to tell."

"Mummies and daddies shouldn't keep secrets from each other, should they?" Hypocrite! Llian could have written an encyclopedia on secrets.

Sulien brushed her red tangles back over her shoulder and took a deep breath. "If they love each other, they should tell each other everything."

"What else did Karan say, exactly?"

"She said . . . um, there were some rude words."

"About me?" He hid a smile. "You have my permission to repeat them."

"Really?" She beamed. "Mummy said, 'Don't on any account let that clumsy oaf climb the fruit trees . . . or next time he's liable to break his bloody bollocking neck.'"

"I've only fallen out of a tree once," he lied.

"Fibber! It's three times this year already. I've been counting."

"What a frightening little creature you are," he said fondly. "Do you spend your whole day spying on me?"

"I don't spy," Sulien cried. "I just . . . notice things."

"You'd make a great chronicler. What do you want to do when you're grown up?"

"Live here, of course. I love Gothryme. Though I wish it'd rain."

For years that had been their main preoccupation, yet now the drought was the least of their worries. "Me too."

She scrambled up and out onto a slender branch, which creaked alarmingly, then dropped pears to him. Llian caught them and put them in the basket.

"What happened to Cook?" said Sulien, reaching across to the next branch. "And why is poor Benie locked in the old cellar?"

Llian stumbled against the basket. Pears rolled across the dusty ground. "How did you know about that?"

"Daddy, *please*. Did Benie go mad, like Mummy's mother did when she was little?"

Llian leaned back against the fork of the tree, looking across the orchard to the dry riverbed.

"No," he said heavily. Sulien had to be told; she would find out soon enough. "Benie killed Cook. We don't know why. Did you hear anything strange yesterday morning?"

"No."

Not for the first time he wondered what other gifts Sulien had. "Do you see things in your mind's eye, the way Karan does?"

Sulien shrugged. "I don't know how Mummy sees things."

It was an impossible question. If she did have an unusual talent, it probably seemed normal to her.

"Why are you still banned from working, Daddy?"

"Because Wistan is a foul, malicious old warthog, and he hates me."

"Is that because you're a Zain?"

"Partly. Lots of people hate us." A treacherous alliance in ancient times had led to the Zain being despised outcasts for two thousand years.

Her bottom lip trembled. "Am I a Zain? Do people hate me?" She swayed on her branch.

He lifted her down and held her close, cursing his big mouth. "No one could possibly hate you." Except that callous brute Gergrig and his evil, life-drinking magiz.

"But am I Zain?"

"Not exactly. It comes through the mother's line, not the father's."

"Who are the Zain, anyway? Didn't they build the Great Library at Zile?"

"They did. They used to live in western Meldorin, and they loved books and writing. But long ago, during a terrible war, their leaders betrayed humanity to the Charon, and the Zain were exiled. They ended up in a hot desert land in the south. That's where I come from, a little town called Jepperand, next to the Dry Sea."

"Oh!" She scurried up the other trunk. "You didn't finish talking about the ban."

"Wistan was expected to die years ago, but he clings to life like a grub to a twig, and clings to the mastership too. And while he lives, he controls the vote, the ban and my life."

She dropped the pears, he caught them and they continued until the basket was full.

"What was Mummy doing in the library yesterday?" said Sulien.

"Writing to Tallia and Shand, I expect."

"No, she sneaked in and locked the door."

"How do you know?"

"I like to hide under the old desk in the corner and read. Mummy looked really pale. I thought she was going to faint."

It felt wrong not to be talking about the nightmares Karan had lifted from Sulien, but they had agreed to keep them from her for now. "What happened to Cook was a big shock," he said lamely.

"Mummy was reading papers in the secret passage."

He gaped at her. "What secret passage?"

Again that infuriating roll of the eyes, that pitying look: poor, silly Daddy. "It's ... um ... where she keeps the stuff she doesn't want anyone to see."

"What stuff?"

"Books and papers, hundreds of years old, I expect."

"Karan said Gothryme's old records were lost in the Great Flood eighty years ago," Llian muttered.

"She probably didn't want to worry you," Sulien said wisely. "I suppose that's why she burned them in the fireplace."

"Burned what?"

"I couldn't see," said Sulien, not meeting his eyes. "She had her back to me."

Llian knew she was lying but did not know how to get it out of her. She was as stubborn as her mother and better at keeping secrets than he was. He picked the heavy basket up and they headed back.

"What other secrets do you know?" he said idly.

"I know you've been writing to your old girlfriend in Chanthed. Even though you promised Mummy you wouldn't."

Llian walked into a low branch, setting his head ringing. His mouth had gone dry. How did Sulien know that? He put the basket down and rubbed his forehead. "That's my private business, and you're not to tell Karan."

"Why not?"

"Because if she finds out, I'll be in big trouble."

"Of course she'll find out. Mummy always does."

And when she did, Karan would crucify him.

"Are you going to leave us and live with your girlfriend?" Sulien said anxiously.

"Don't be ridiculous! Anyway, Thandiwe's not my girlfriend. That was ages ago, before I met Karan." He crouched down and took her hands. "Sulien, you've got to promise you won't say anything."

"If she's not your girlfriend, why are you writing to her?"

Her disapproval hurt, deserve it though he did. "Do you promise? This is really important."

"All right, I promise. But you've got to tell me why."

"Because Thandiwe was supposed to become Master of the College when Wistan died."

"But he never did."

"He will," Llian said savagely, "if I have to throttle him with my bare hands."

Sulien let out a squeak of alarm.

"I didn't mean it," he said hastily. "But Wistan's a very sick man; he can't even get out of his chair. When he dies, soon, there's a good chance Thandiwe will be elected Master. Then, if I'm nice to her, she'll overturn the ban and all our troubles will be over."

Llian wasn't sure that prospect was even relevant any more, but he had to keep up the pretence of normality for Sulien's sake.

She looked up at him with those deep green eyes that saw too much, and too deeply. "What does Thandiwe mean by being *nice to her*?"

11

I'LL DO IT – WHATEVER IT TAKES

Llian knew what Karan had been about to ask of him before Cook's murder. He had been dreading it, but it had to be done. They needed coin urgently and lots of it, though to get it he would have to sell the most beautiful thing he had ever created.

He sat at the battered library table, turning the illuminated pages of his *Tale of the Mirror* and remembering. His mother, Zophy, whom he had not seen since leaving home at the age of twelve to study at the college, had been a book illuminator. His late father, Llayis, had been a scribe. They had given him their love of stories and storytelling, and taught him their own crafts, ones he practised to this day.

His critical eye saw flaws on almost every page of the *Tale of the Mirror*, yet it was the most beautiful work he had ever done, and the most important. The story ranked highly among the twenty-three

Great Tales created in the four thousand years of the Histories. It was certainly the longest.

It told the tale of the deadly mystery Llian had uncovered twelve years ago, just before graduating from the college. After Shuthdar destroyed the stolen Golden Flute, three thousand years ago, a crippled girl with him had been murdered to conceal another crime.

While Llian had been trying to unravel that mystery he had been thrown together with Karan, who had been forced by Maigraith to steal a corrupt ancient artefact, the Mirror of Aachan, from Yggur. Karan was being hunted relentlessly by Yggur's servants, the terrifying Whelm, and she and Llian had gone on the run together.

Soon all the great powers on Santhenar – the Aachim led by Tensor, the Faellem under Faelamor, Mendark the age-old Magister, and Yggur – had been drawn into a titanic two-year struggle to get the mirror and crack the coded secret hidden within it – the way to make gates. Tensor had seized the mirror and recklessly freed his mortal enemy, Rulke, from the prison of the Nightland, planning to kill him.

But Rulke had escaped and then, in secret, had built his astounding construct – a flying machine powered by the Secret Art – which could also make gates. He had used it to bring the last of the Charon from Aachan in a desperate attempt to save them from extinction, but had been thwarted by his other enemy, Faelamor.

Llian had finally broken the code of the mirror and solved the mystery. Yalkara, another great Charon, had killed the crippled girl to conceal her theft of the enchanted gold from the destroyed flute, and soon everyone was hunting for it as well.

In the climactic battle, Rulke, Mendark and Tensor had been killed. Faelamor had died soon after and Yalkara had taken the last of the Charon back to the void to die. The Three Worlds had been changed for ever, and Karan and Llian had been at the heart of it.

Every word of the story raised memories of the desperate years he had spent pursuing the tale with Karan, until he finally stood on the stage of the College of the Histories and Master Wistan had grudgingly announced the result of the vote. The sixty-four masters had been unanimous; even Wistan had voted for Llian's tale.

"The *Tale of the Mirror* is a Great Tale, the twenty-third."

It had been the most overwhelming moment of his life, and it was followed by the most devastating – Wistan had banned Llian from practising his art, for corruption.

He turned another page, reading his book for the last time. He had seen the need coming a long time ago and had done everything possible to avoid it; he had even pleaded with Thandiwe for help after promising Karan he would have nothing to do with her. But there was no choice now. He had to sell his *Tale of the Mirror*.

It was difficult to price a manuscript that was utterly unique, though far lesser ones had sold for a hundred gold tells. His Great Tale had to be worth at least five hundred tells, enough for them to go on the run for a year or two.

Llian knew of three wealthy people who might be interested, but one was half a continent away in Crandor and another in the far east. However Cumulus Snoat lived in Iagador, and his library of rare books was unrivalled in the west, though Llian did not know anything else about him. He wrote to Snoat, describing the manuscript and asking what price he would pay, then gave the letter to Rachis, who was taking a horse and cart to Tolryme.

The manuscript, which no longer felt as though it belonged to him, lay open at the point of Rulke's death. Thinking about the tragedy and the unexpected discovery that Rulke had been a good man after all, Llian suddenly saw a clue to one of his questions – who the Merdrun were, where they came from and why they looked so like Charon.

As he lay dying, instead of cursing Llian for the fool he was, Rulke had given him a small silver key. *My spies told me that you lost a tale, chronicler*, he had said. *Here is a better! But you'll have to earn it.*

Llian, sick with guilt, had sworn to write the full story of the Charon one day, so their name would live on after they were gone. But researching that story and finding answers to his questions would take him to places only an unstained chronicler could enter. It always came back to the ban.

Taking a fresh sheet of paper, he wrote the date on top, then stopped, thinking about how disappointed Sulien had been in him, and how much it had mattered. Only nine, yet already she knew what a flawed man her father was.

But it had to be done.

Dear Thandiwe

You asked if I could help you gain the mastership. Yes I will, gladly, and in return you will overturn my ban, urgently. Just say what you want, and I'll do it – whatever it takes.

Llian

As he blotted the page, Sulien burst into the library. "Daddy, Daddy, they're taking Benie away."

He ran out. The bailiff from Tolryme was leading Benie down the track. His wrists were enclosed by heavy black manacles and he was escorted by guards twice his size. He did not call for help, nor look back at his lifelong home. Even from the rear he looked broken, uncomprehending and resigned to his doom.

Llian ran after him, then stopped. Benie was the property of the law now and there was nothing he could do. He watched until they disappeared over the rise, then turned back. Tears were running down Sulien's cheeks. He tried to pick her up and hug her but she threw herself down.

"Where's Karan?" said Llian, sitting beside her.

"I don't know." Sulien stroked Piffle's head. He licked her nose. "Benie was always nice to me," she said, her voice aching. "Why is this happening, Daddy?"

Because of the Merdrun and their damned summon stone! Sulien had to be told, soon. But not now, not today. "I don't know," he dissembled. "Sometimes bad things . . . just happen."

Remembering the letter he had left on the library table, he ran back, but it was gone. Fear closed like a thorny fist around his innards. Karan was bound to take his words the wrong way.

"What's the matter, Daddy?" said Sulien, who had followed him.

He shook his head. He was a dead man.

12

TAKE THE MONSTROSITY ALIVE

Hingis had been waiting for the moment for ages. Dreading it. And finally it came. His twin sat her horse in the middle of the road, watching him. He swallowed. Esea thrived on conflict, and he hated it. Was that why she had waited so long?

"What did Tallia give you?" she said in a deceptively mild voice. Deceptive because she was not one to hold back her emotions. Unlike him.

They were halfway up a stony hill, one of many on the rugged Coast Way south. The winding road, here gouged into brown and white layered rock, was as rutted as Hingis's face. It was a windy day, with scudding clouds and frequent chilly showers whistling in from the unseen sea to their left. He could smell salt and seaweed rotting on the shore. He glanced behind them. No sign of pursuit, yet.

"I can't tell you," said Hingis. Every jolting step his horse took hurt, and his ribs ached from the effort to breathe.

Wind whipped her blonde hair across her face. She raked it out of her eyes furiously. "We've always shared everything."

"It's a Magister's secret."

"Tallia was going to propose us to be Magister jointly. Why can't I be told?"

"She said this secret could not be shared."

"She's trying to drive a wedge between us," Esea said shrilly.

"She's just doing what the Magister must."

"After we risked our lives to save her!"

Hingis reined in, the agitation rising and sending his withered lung into spasms. It always started this way, and it was liable to finish with him on his back, feeling as though he was slowly suffocating. One of his recurring nightmares.

"Esea, please don't."

Raindrops peppered his face. He threw his shoulders back, trying to expand his chest, but the breath thickened in his throat, his sight blurred and his head spun. He swayed and clutched desperately at the saddle horn.

In a moment she was beside him, steadying him. "Sorry. I'm a mean-faced bitch. If it wasn't for me——"

Her reiterations of guilt and self-blame were almost unbearable. "Let's focus on getting to Sith."

"Of course," Esea said in an overly bright voice. She looked back the way they had come and swore. "They're after us!"

Hingis turned too quickly, vertigo overcame him and he would have fallen had she not caught his arm. He tried to focus and could not, though one thing was clear. They were in deep trouble, and in his condition they could not hope to outrun it.

"How many?"

"About ten."

Esea could not hold off ten by herself. Outdoors, her mancery was far less effective.

He clutched her wrist. "I'm sorry. I do care for you."

"I've never doubted it," she said harshly.

She pulled away and for a terrible second he thought she was going to leave. Reality intervened. Esea would give her life to protect him and he would do the same for her.

"We'll head up the hill," she said. "Can you ride by yourself?"

"Don't get too far ahead; I can't see far. What's at the top?"

"No idea."

The horses clattered up the corrugated track, Hingis lurching from side to side. It was all he could do to stay on. His ribs began to ache, then the bones of his ruined face. He forced the pain into the background; he had half a lifetime's experience in that discipline.

He began to prepare a defensive illusion. A mancer's power could either be drawn from himself, which was exhausting, or from a previously enchanted object, if he had one. Hingis's power came from his own meagre body, and the process of drawing it was long and painful.

He looked up and Esea was gone. He choked. Curse being so useless, so helpless!

"Esea!" he gasped. His vision was closing in; he could not see beyond his horse's head now.

"I'm right here," she said from a few yards away. "Come on, you can make it."

Make it to what?

The horses scrambled up a steep slope and then the ground was level beneath him; they were at the top. The gritty soil was littered with broken stone and the grass was scant, grey, tussocky. The hilltop had a mineral smell he could not place, a poisonous smell.

"What's it like, Esea? Any place we can defend?"

"Some broken walls a hundred yards ahead, barely high enough to hide behind, and what's left of a couple of chimney stacks."

"From a house?"

"Furnaces, I'd say. There are mining pits on the right – worked out long ago. And mullock heaps and piles of slag."

"What were they mining?"

"Lead ore, by the look of it, and smelting the lead out. Careful, there could be covered shafts."

He heard her dismount. She took the reins and led his horse forward.

"Between the chimneys and the wall is our best hope. It'll give the horses some protection."

The panic faded a little and Hingis's focus improved. The chimney stacks were about twenty feet high and eight feet across at the base. The closer one had a distinct lean to the right and a large crack half-way up, shaped like the profile of a hook-nosed man. There was little mortar between the stones – a crude job, only meant to last as long as the small ore deposits could be worked.

"Have we got a chance?" he said.

Her breast heaved and she said in a high voice, "There's a way down on the far side. If you go now—"

"No!"

"Tallia gave you a special job. If I delay them—"

"No."

"If we stay, we'll both die."

His eyes moistened. "You've always been beside me. If you're going to die, I'll die with you."

She stamped her foot. "Then you're a stupid bloody fool!"

"One of many personality defects," he said with a lopsided grin. "Help me down."

She reached up. He dismounted with the grace of a buffalo descending a ladder, almost bringing her down as well.

"How are we going to do this?"

"Start with your illusions. I'm at a disadvantage here."

Buildings were easily taken apart if you knew where to apply force, then gravity did the rest, but breaking or moving rocks was hard work for a reshaper.

The wind was stronger up here, and colder. Hingis's teeth chattered. He suffered from the cold at the best of times, there being little meat on his twisted bones, and it was worse in times of stress.

"I'll get your coat," she said, reaching up to his saddlebags.

"No, I need to be able to move freely."

That was a laugh, given that he had the dexterity of a warthog. He inspected the ruins and his spirits sank further. Two people could not hope to defend them against ten, for the enemy could attack from three directions at once, and there was enough cover on the hilltop for them to get within thirty yards unseen.

He studied the area more closely. The walls formed a series of small enclosures but, being only a few feet high, were little use for defence; a running man could leap them. They were higher on the north side, though not high enough. A series of low slag heaps, the poisonous soil bare of vegetation, occupied the northern and western edges of the hill. The enemy would be exposed if they came that way. Beyond, the land dropped sharply.

On the eastern and south-eastern sides he made out five irregularly shaped pits, some partly filled with water, surrounded by scrubby vegetation. There could be other pits or shafts, unseen. Further on the mullock heaps – piles of broken rock – ran in tongue-like landslides over the edge of the hill.

Esea led the horses in between the two chimneys, where they would be protected from arrows. "No point making it easy for them. I'll stay here. Go up there."

She pointed to the far end of the low walls, where an angle, higher than the rest, would cover him from two sides. She never stopped trying to look after him.

"I'll work on an illusion," said Hingis.

He lurched along between the broken walls. At the end he clambered up onto the highest section and teetered there, scanning the hilltop and planning his deception. Esea was watching him anxiously, afraid he would fall. He suppressed his irritation.

She cocked her head, listening. "They're coming up the hill."

The wind whined between the broken chimneys. Raindrops spattered his face and neck, and his feet were freezing. *Get on with it!* He had to form his illusion before they saw the reality.

First, blur the hilltop so they wouldn't see the dangers. The weather helped; it wasn't difficult for a master illusionist to turn the showers into patches of mist. It was harder to make it cling to the pits to hide them, though, and Hingis was breathing raggedly by the time he had done it.

He copied the pit outlines and moved them south so they lay across the enemy's most direct path, hoping to divert them towards the hidden pits. But large-scale illusions were difficult at the best of times; they would not fool the enemy long.

Esea was pacing back and forth next to the chimneys, moving her hands in the air. Hingis could not tell what she was trying to do; perhaps she did not know herself. She was as intuitive as he was logical, and often a reshaping only took form in the last desperate seconds.

He was creating wall illusions when their pursuers appeared at the top of the track. Nine soldiers, led by the gaunt mancer, Scorbic Vyl. He was unmasked and his head was bandaged.

Vyl's bony head turned this way and that, studying the hilltop, then he raised a snake-shaped staff. A thunder crack echoed back and forth, and when the echoes died Hingis's pit illusions were gone.

He felt that suffocating breathlessness again but fought it; he could not afford any weakness now. He crouched down and continued working on his wall illusions, afraid they would disappear too, but they remained. Perhaps Vyl's spell could only disperse what he could identify as illusion.

Vyl's cry rang out. "There they are! You two, take the monstrosity, alive. The rest of you, hold the blonde bitch for me!"

Hingis's heart missed three beats in a row and he lost his vision for a couple of seconds. When it returned the soldiers were racing towards the ruins, seven of them heading for Esea, the other two and Vyl coming his way. Pain seared through Hingis's jaw. What would Vyl do to his beautiful, tragic sister?

He lurched back towards her, vision blurred, breath ragged.

Esea raised her hands and pointed at the leading soldier. His pants fell down and he tripped and landed hard, the broadsword jarring out of his grasp. The next two men swerved round him.

She pointed at the first of them. He stumbled and landed prone – his boots had come to pieces. The man behind him yelped, dropped his sword, which had turned red-hot, and shook his smoking fingers. He snatched up the broadsword of the first man to have fallen and ran on.

The mancer let out a harsh cry and pointed his serpent staff at Esea. She screamed and doubled over.

"Take her!" bellowed Vyl.

Esea forced herself upright, her face twisted in agony. There was blood on her mouth and chin. She extended her hands towards the closest soldiers but nothing happened. Fear exploded in Hingis's chest as they ran at her, unhindered.

"Come out!" said Vyl.

Hingis had no choice. He limped out from behind his walls and the two soldiers took hold of him.

"Bring her here," said Vyl. "Hold tight to the monstrosity. He needs to see."

They dragged Esea across, then Vyl prodded Hingis in the chest with his staff. "You've got a secret, and I want it."

Hingis shook his head. He was too afraid to speak.

Vyl gestured to a bow-legged fellow with black fur coating his arms and the backs of his hands. "This man was hiding outside Thurkad when Tallia gave you the code to the council's spell vault."

"I don't know what you're talking about," said Hingis.

"Cut off his sister's littlest left toe," said Vyl.

13

THE SHADOW SNAKE

"No!" shrieked Hingis.

"Speak then," said Vyl.

But Hingis could not betray Tallia either. While the two soldiers held Esea, the hairy man removed her boots and socks. Her small feet were as perfectly formed as the rest of her. The drumming grew louder and Hingis felt a shocking pain in the middle of his chest.

"Well?" said Vyl.

"Keep your mouth shut, Hingis," said Esea.

Vyl gestured to the hairy man. "Do it."

He put the point of his sword on her little toe and glanced at Hingis. Hingis wanted to scream out the code. How could any secret, even the spell vault, matter as much as his sister? But he had sworn to protect the code; he did not speak.

The hairy man thrust. Esea screwed up her face but did not make a sound. He bent and held up her severed toe. Hingis wanted to tear the sky down on the man, and Vyl, and most of all himself.

"The code," said Vyl, "or it's another toe. I'll turn her into a monstrosity like you, if I have to."

"You wouldn't tell me," Esea hissed at Hingis. "Don't you dare tell him."

"I . . . can't . . . bear it," Hingis whispered.

"I'll gladly sacrifice a few toes to protect the secret — and your *honour*."

She meant it, and it proved that, despite her flaws, she was more honourable than he was. Her beauty was the only foil Hingis had to his own hideousness, and if she were mutilated protecting him, he would be doubly marred.

Vyl nodded to the hairy soldier, who removed her next toe and displayed it like a trophy. Esea tried to stifle a cry but could not. The drumming grew louder.

Hingis looked down at her bloody, maimed foot and knew Vyl would not stop with her toes. He would do exactly as he had threatened, and Hingis could not endure it.

"Well?" said Vyl.

"Shut up!" snapped Esea, her face twisted in pain.

Vyl gestured to the soldiers to move away from Hingis and approached. "The code," he said. "Whisper it to me."

The drumming pounded in Hingis's ears and the pain was more than he could bear. He whispered the words and numbers he had sworn to protect with his life. And he would have, but he could not protect it at the price of Esea's mutilation, or *her* life.

"You bastard!" she raged, raising her left foot. "Does my sacrifice mean nothing to you?"

"Kill her slowly," said Vyl, grounding his staff. "He can watch."

The soldiers were still yards away from Hingis and he saw a tiny chance. Acting on rarely used intuition, he drew more power than he had ever drawn before and cast a despairing illusion. But not at Vyl, at his serpent-shaped staff.

Vyl let out a shriek of terror as the staff became a gigantic snake, the most perfect and devastating illusion Hingis had ever created. The snake twisted in Vyl's hand, opened a bucket-sized mouth and went for his head. He knew it was illusion but, in that moment of terror, intellect could not override instinct.

Esea spoke a reshaping command and metal shattered to Hingis's left, embedding shards of one soldier's sword in the throat of another and the eye of a third. She bolted, hobbling on her left foot.

The snake's mouth closed around Vyl's skull, the finger-length fangs sinking through bone with an audible crunch. He screamed so loudly that the remaining soldiers froze, their weapons out.

Hingis rode the illusion with all he had, knowing it would not last; maintaining it was sucking the strength out of him. Then something rose like a misty sickness from the ground – no, from some source underground. A black miasma, born from poisons leaching from the slag piles and given life by the mancery used here.

It had a kind of power and he took it. Hingis gestured towards the screaming mancer and the snake shook him by the head. It levered its fangs out, widened its jaws and enveloped Vyl's head as if to swallow him whole. His scream was cut off; he thrashed on the ground and the snake's smaller sets of teeth moved back and forth, dragging him in until his neck and left arm were enveloped as well. His legs kicked uselessly and his free arm flailed.

The hairy soldier let out a war cry and ran to the mancer's aid. Vyl was grunting like a half-strangled pig, and brown muck, mixed with blood, was foaming out of the snake's mouth. The soldier stopped, gaping. The illusion faded a little. Hingis forced it back to reality. The soldier let out a roar, ran on and took a wild hack at the snake.

There was a sickening crunch and blood fountained from its mouth, then abruptly the illusion vanished. The snake staff fell to the ground and so did Vyl, blood pouring from his upper arm, which was almost completely severed.

The hairy soldier's mouth fell open and the tip of his sword thudded into the ground. Hingis lurched back behind the broken walls.

Vyl was moaning. "You – imbecile!" He groped for his staff with his good hand and sent a blast at the hairy soldier that hurled him backwards for twenty feet, as dead as the stones all around him.

"Kill the blonde and take the monstrosity," Vyl gasped. The staff fell from his hand. He clamped his fingers around his upper arm, vainly trying to staunch the bleeding. "Help . . . me."

Two soldiers ran to him. Another two went after Esea and the remaining two came for Hingis. The miasma coiled around his throat as if to choke him. He staggered and fell to his knees, his guts churning. Aftersickness had always been his bane, though this was unlike anything he had suffered before. There was something toxic about this place.

His hunters were approaching the outer walls. Hingis checked on his wall illusions. One was fading but the first one he'd created, when he was stronger, still held. He shifted the illusion fractionally and blurred the real wall.

Esea let out a shriek, but he could not see her and could do nothing for her. The leading soldier, a huge red-faced fellow, grinned and sprang over the illusion wall towards Hingis.

Crack! The soldier's groin came down on the broken top of the real wall with all his weight on it, jarring the sword out of his hand. The impact must have been agonising but he stifled a cry, rolled forward onto the rubble and crawled for the sword.

Hingis heaved a heavy piece of stone off the wall and dropped it on the flat of the blade, which snapped halfway along. But it was still a deadly weapon. The soldier rose, swinging the stub at Hingis's face. He swayed sideways. The soldier swivelled to attack; there came a second *crack* and he groaned and fell, his hip broken.

The other soldier, not trusting anything he saw, was probing ahead with the tip of his blade. He would soon discover what was real and what was not.

Hingis lurched down between the walls, looking for Esea, but there was no sign of her. Vyl lay on the stony ground twenty feet away, covered in blood and as white as an egg. Someone had removed his arm; it was a couple of yards off. A scar-faced soldier held the stump while a small wiry fellow tightened a bloody tourniquet with a piece of stick. The stump was still dripping blood; Hingis prayed that Vyl did not have much left in him.

The toxic aftersickness was getting worse; Hingis could not last much longer. The other soldier was clambering over the wall, five or six yards away. Hingis dug deep for the strength to cast another illusion but did not find it. He was spent.

"Esea!" he choked.

From behind the chimneys he heard gasping and the sound of metal striking stone. They'd trapped her too. His head spun and he fell against the broken wall. The rough stone drove into his ribs, driving the air out of his good lung. He slid sideways onto the rubble, breathless and unable to move. His pursuer, a swarthy fellow whose dark eyes were mere slits, loomed over him.

"By the powers, you're a hideous little bastard," he said disgustedly.

He struck Hingis across the head with the flat of his sword, then pressed the point of the blade against his throat until the skin broke. Hingis shrank away and the soldier grinned. Six of his top front teeth were broken off in a row.

"The little bitch is dead," said the soldier, prodding Hingis's mangled face.

He poked the tip of the blade between Hingis's lips and levered his mouth open. Hingis had no hope left and, having betrayed Tallia's secret and failed his sister, just wanted to die as quickly as possible.

"Look out!" a man shrieked.

The swarthy soldier raised his sword and whirled. A good distance away stone grated on stone, then a man cried out. The sound was cut off by a liquid thud, like a rock pulverising a melon.

"Is he . . . ?" called a different voice.

"As a maggot! Get out, get out!"

The north side of the first chimney came apart and fell with a thunderous series of crashes onto the chimney beside it, which began to collapse as well. A scream was cut off abruptly, then the narrow gap between the chimneys filled with rubble for a good ten feet. Dust swirled up and obscured the scene.

The swarthy man ran along beside the wall for a few yards, then stopped. His shoulders drooped as he stared at the place where the gap had been, then he turned back to Hingis, baring his broken teeth.

"Guess they won't need their shares. And maybe not Vyl either." He prodded Hingis with the sword. "On your feet!"

It was all Hingis could do to come to his knees. The swarthy man swatted him on the side of the head again, but the poisonous aftersickness was rising, and the air in Hingis's throat was as thick as glue. He could hear himself gasping like a stranded fish; little sparks were flashing in his eyes and his lips were tingling.

"Get up, you repulsive little swine!" The soldier kicked Hingis in the guts.

He folded over, unable to move.

"Get away from my brother!" said Esea.

Tears flooded his eyes. She was alive! She was on the wall twelve feet away, pointing a short stick at the swarthy man.

He put the blade to Hingis's throat again. "Drop it or he dies."

Esea tossed the reshaped stick down. But whatever it had been, it was no longer a stick. It landed at the swarthy man's feet and exploded with a little bang, scattering burning embers in all directions. Some of them landed on his trews and stuck. He tried to brush them off, but those he touched stuck to the side of his hand. Smoke trailed up from the embers, then a little patch of red grew around each one.

The swarthy man dropped his sword and tried to grind out the sparks on his hands. They stuck together. The right leg of his trousers burst into flame. He let out a pig-like squeal, vaulted the wall and raced towards the nearest pit, trailing flame and smoke.

Hingis dragged himself upright as the man dived over the edge of the pit and disappeared. Hingis heard no splash and the smoke continued to gush up.

"What was that?" he said dully.

Esea did not want to talk about it. Up close, he could see how much it had taken out of her; her normally beautiful features were slack, her skin pallid, her eyes dull and staring.

"Had to lure them right in," said Esea. "Didn't have the strength to do anything from a distance. Could barely pull the mortar out of the chimney from ten feet away." She reached out with both hands. "That snake illusion was brilliant."

"I don't know how I did it," he said numbly. "It just came to me."

"Well, it saved us. Where's Vyl? We've got to put him down."

To protect the secret code Hingis had given away. He staggered to the edge of the hill, but Vyl, escorted by the two surviving soldiers, was half a mile away, racing back to Thurkad. There was no hope of catching him.

As Hingis stood there, staring after them, guilt hit him like a land-slide. How was he to tell Tallia that he had betrayed the council's most important secret, and that Snoat would have the code to the spell vault within days? She had to be told urgently but he had no way to contact her. His stomach heaved and he threw up so violently that something tore in his belly.

Esea put an arm across his shoulders. "It's done, and we've got to make the best of it."

Hingis looked down at her three-toed foot. She was maimed now, like him, and he had allowed it. He shuddered and wrenched away.

"Hingis?" she said anxiously. Then she realised the source of his revulsion, and it crushed her. "I sacrificed my toes to keep the secret safe," she said very quietly. "And protect you. And now my foot *repulses* you?"

Hingis could not speak. Her perfect beauty had made his own hideousness bearable but there was no way to say it. Her lovely face crumbled and she went utterly cold. She dragged her sock and boot on over her bloody foot and rode away.

The pain in his belly grew worse. Hingis hauled himself onto his horse and rode past the pit. The swarthy man, desperate to put the fire out, had dived too soon and landed on the broken rock surrounding the greenish water. He had dragged himself to the water's edge, leaving a bloody trail behind him, and lay still, head and shoulders submerged, legs still burning.

The stink of burning meat was still in Hingis's nostrils an hour later. But the foulness of his twin betrayals would be there until the day he died.

14

THEY NEARLY KILLED ME

After the bailiff took Benie, Karan stalked into the kitchen and scrubbed the big table down violently. It did not help. She had done everything she could, yet it had made no difference. He was doomed and, if she could not find a way to stop the magiz, so was Sulien. Only Karan could save her but it was impossible to attack the magiz from the disembodied state.

She went looking for Llian. He was not in the library but the *Tale of the Mirror* lay open on the table. She sat down in front of it. It was the most beautiful book she had ever seen and it meant everything to him. But war was coming, they might have to flee at a moment's notice and they needed coin, lots of it. The book had to be sold.

A brief letter caught her eye on top of a stack of papers. It was addressed to Thandiwe. Karan turned away; it was none of her business. Then she turned back.

Karan had never liked Thandiwe. She was a man-hunter, and the man she wanted was Llian. She had visited once, years ago, and even talking to Karan at her own dinner table, Thandiwe had not been able to tear her gaze away from him, the greedy bitch! She could have any chronicler or teller in Chanthed, so why did she want him? Because he had a Great Tale to his name.

Karan looked sideways at the letter, headed for the door then, without conscious thought, turned back, snatched it up and read it.

Just say what you want, and I'll do it – whatever it takes.

Like hell! She thrust the letter into her pocket and went out. Her knees were shaky. She took deep breaths to steady herself, then went around the old keep to the entry track. It could not be called a road and was badly in need of maintenance, like everything at Gothryme. The bailiff, Benie and the two guards were out of sight.

In the distance a winding line of dust marked the course of the track. Someone was coming this way, riding fast. Not Rachis then. The rider topped the rise and pounded on, slumped sideways in the saddle.

Llian appeared with Sulien. He avoided Karan's eyes. She scowled at him.

"It's Tallia!" said Karan.

"And in bad shape."

Tallia's face was a greenish-grey and her shirt was dark with blood from the right shoulder to her waist. She tried to smile but could not.

"What's happened?" Llian reached up to support her.

"Council meeting attacked two nights ago," said Tallia. "Four councillors dead. Rest ran."

Karan shivered. *It was beginning.*

They helped Tallia inside and onto the settee in the sitting room, a long but narrow room whose pink granite walls were bare. Karan had taken the delicate old tapestries down to clean. Llian went back for the saddlebags.

She began to cut away Tallia's shirt, which was stuck to the wound with clotted blood. "How did this happen?"

"All it takes to tear down a system," said Tallia, "is one ruthless man prepared to kill everyone in his way."

"I can't believe they wounded *you.*"

"They nearly killed me."

Sulien came in with clean rags, a pair of scissors, a jar of ointment and a bowl. She went out and returned with a wooden pail of hot water. Karan cut the rest of Tallia's shirt away, tossed it into the fire and cleaned the caked blood off, revealing a deep, infected wound running below the right collarbone. She winced with every stroke.

It was a bad sign. If Tallia, one of the toughest people Karan had ever met, could be beaten so easily, what hope did they have?

Karan finished cleaning the wound, covered it with ointment and a pad of cloth, and bound it. Llian came to the door, put the saddlebags down and left, still avoiding her gaze.

"I remember the first time we met," said Karan. "You gave me some chocolate. I'd never tasted anything like it in my life."

"What's chocolate?" said Sulien, who was tossing the braided chain Karan had given her from hand to hand.

"Poor, deprived child," said Tallia fondly. "In Crandor, where I come from, my family has a big cocoa plantation." She gazed at Sulien and gave a sigh of longing. "I might give you some later . . . if you're good."

"I'm always good." Sulien blushed faintly.

"Off you go," said Karan. "We need to talk about grown-up things."

Sulien did not move. "Like Benie murdering Cook?"

"What?" said Tallia.

"I wrote to you about it yesterday." Karan told her about the drumming and the murder. "He lost all self-control when the drumming sounded. Is . . . is there anything you can do to save him?"

"What have you done so far?"

"I've pleaded with the bailiff, the sergeant and the mayor of Tolryme. Paid an advocate to defend Benie. Written a statement about his good character."

"Then there's nothing more anyone can do."

"But they'll hang him!" Karan cried. "I should have let him go."

"So he could kill again, the next time the drumming sounds?" said Tallia.

"It's not fair!" said Sulien.

"The chaos has begun," Karan quoted. *"Friend will turn on friend, sister on brother."*

"And Snoat is behind it," said Tallia.

The blood drained from Karan's cheeks. "Cumulus Snoat? What's he got to do with anything?"

"He instigated the attack on the council. He's taken Thurkad and his army won't stop there."

Karan stifled a gasp. "But Llian wrote to him yesterday, asking what he'd pay for the original manuscript of the *Tale of the Mirror.*"

Tallia sat up abruptly. "Has the letter gone?"

"Rachis took it," said Sulien.

"This is bad," said Tallia. "Why does Llian want to sell it anyway?"

"We're practically bankrupt," said Karan. "And with the other thing I haven't told you about . . . "

"I don't think I can take much more bad news. But I suppose I must."

"Sulien, go and help your father."

"He's just staring at the library wall," said Sulien.

"Go!" Karan cried.

Sulien went, furiously. Karan checked outside the door, then told Tallia about Sulien's nightmare and Gergrig ordering the magiz to kill her and the household. And how, using Malien's disembodiment spell, Karan had gone spying on the magiz and had nearly been caught.

"By the night of the triple moons there won't be any opposition," she ended.

Tallia slumped in her chair, breathing shallowly. "And we can't fight the Merdrun because we've got no idea where the summon stone is. Or *what* it is. Or what their fatal weakness is, that's buried in Sulien's unconscious mind."

"I looked for it, but I couldn't find anything."

Tallia looked at her sideways. "There are . . . other ways."

"Like hell!" Karan jumped up and stalked back and forth, trembling. "I thought you were our friend."

"You don't know what I was going to say."

"You want to prise the secret out of Sulien's head with *mancery*."

"It may be the only thing that can save us, Karan."

"Swear there's no risk to her and I'll think about it."

Tallia made as if to speak, stopped, then said, "I can't. But if we can discover the Merdrun's weakness and make sure they know we know, there's no reason for the magiz to kill Sulien."

"She's an evil, malicious woman. She'd do it for spite." Karan sat. "How risky is it?"

Tallia paused for a very long time. "The spell may have no effect at all, though it's dangerous and unpredictable."

"What's the worst that could happen to Sulien?"

"Catatonia. Incurable madness. Even death."

"Then the answer is no! Don't ask again."

Tallia sighed. "Well, at least Malien knows what's going on. She's the greatest power in Santhenar now."

"She doesn't know how my spying went," said Karan. "Or that the summon stone has a weakness and can be destroyed."

"Why not?"

"I haven't been able to get through to her."

Tallia frowned. "Maybe the magiz is blocking you. What are you going to do?"

"Protect Sulien. Llian is trying to find out about the Merdrun and the stone, then we'll go somewhere the magiz can't find us – if there is such a place."

"Promise me you won't attempt any more seeings."

"I'll do whatever it takes to save my daughter!" Karan said fiercely.

Tallia shook her head. "And I was about to resign."

"Why?" Karan said numbly.

"To go home and have a family while I still could, but that's impossible now."

"I thought it was never going to happen for me," said Karan. "What are we going to do?"

"Someone will have to find this summon stone and destroy it. Though I don't know who – or how."

"What about your old allies?"

"That's just it," said Tallia. "They're all old."

"Malien isn't old."

"But Tirthrax is a thousand miles away. I'm out of my depth, Karan."

Sulien came in bearing a bowl of beef soup, a chunk of brown bread and an apple, then tried to look inconspicuous. Karan pointed to the door. Sulien scowled and went out. Tallia ate a few mouthfuls of soup.

"Tell Llian not to sell his book to Snoat. Surely there's something else you can sell first?"

"Only this," said Karan, picking up the chain Sulien had been playing with.

"It doesn't look as though it would be worth anything. Can I see?"

Tallia put out a long brown hand and Karan dropped the chain into it. Tallia's hand jerked. She studied the chain.

"There's supposed to be a charm on it," said Karan. "Put there three thousand years ago by Shuthdar—"

"To protect a crippled young woman called Fiachra. But it failed." Tallia ran her long fingers along the chain. "He was the greatest craftsman who ever lived. And a great spell-binder. Karan, this is very valuable."

"Right now, it's only worth the time it can buy us."

"Well, here's a down payment." Tallia took a small bag from her saddlebags.

"I don't expect—"

"I know you don't."

Tallia finished her soup and bread, put the apple in her pocket and rose unsteadily. She swayed, steadied herself on the arm of the settee then turned to the door.

"Thank you," she said.

"That wound needs rest. At least two days."

"I've got to see Shand right away. After that I'll call our allies to an urgent meeting, probably in Chanthed. I'd like you there if you can manage it."

"Let me know the date and I'll see."

After Tallia had ridden away, and Karan was tidying up, she found the chain sitting beside Tallia's soup bowl along with a large slab of chocolate.

Karan picked up the chocolate, settled the bag of coin in her pocket and went out. Things might be bad and getting worse, but she still had friends.

15

THE CRY OF THE NIGHTJAR

Ooo-ooo-ooo-ooo.

The crippled girl trembled in her sleep and pulled the blankets up to her ears. Her herb pillow released the scent of lavender.

Ooo-ooo-ooo-ooo.

Aviel roused slowly, opened one eye and closed it again; it was still dark in her little perfumery workshop. She was drifting back into sleep when she heard it a third time. *Ooo-ooo-ooo-ooo* — the cry of a nightjar, a very bad omen. She felt a painful spasm below her heart, a sign that her luck was about to take a turn for the worse.

By which she meant worse than usual.

Aviel was a twist-foot, which signified bad luck, and a seventh sister, which was worse. But worst of all, she had been born a silver-hair, and the combination of all three meant prodigiously bad luck. It had dogged her from the moment she was born, except for the single lucky day that had landed her here.

There was an almighty thump on the door. She jumped.

"Aviel?"

It was Shand. "Yes?" she squeaked.

"Need your help. Quick!"

She rubbed her angled right foot and the twisted, lumpy ankle that never stopped hurting, dressed and limped up to Shand's big old house, a monstrosity of a place with undulating walls of intricately laid polychrome brickwork. The interior design was equally strange – rooms whose proportions changed from one end to the other as if they belonged in a house of mirrors, walls stepped from bottom to top and top to bottom, rooms with five, seven and even eleven sides.

Tallia, whom Aviel had not seen for a year, lay on the couch by the fire in the main living room, a very long room with a fireplace on each wall, though only one was lit. Shand had exposed an inflamed wound below her right shoulder. She looked half dead.

"This is days old," he said to himself. "Why isn't it healing?" He looked up at Aviel. "You've got the best nose I know. Tell me what you think."

As Aviel went to her knees beside Tallia, pain stabbed through her ankle. She sniffed, closed her eyes and sniffed again. "Blood, fresh and old. Infection. Ointment – comfrey and calendula, rosemary and other herbs."

"Anything else?"

"Should there be?"

"You're the scent master."

"I'm not even an apprentice." Aviel took another sniff. "There's a faint acrid smell."

"Some kind of balm?"

"No." She put her nose just above the wound. "It's griveline."

"What's that?"

"A herbal poison. Why is it there?"

"Poisoned blade, I'd say."

"I meant, why can I smell it after all this time? It doesn't last, save in a sealed bottle." Aviel's ankle throbbed. She rose painfully.

Shand dragged a chair across for her, and another for himself. They sat down, staring at Tallia. Her chest rose and fell fractionally. Her breathing was shallow and laboured.

"Is she dying?" Aviel whispered.

"Slowly. You're definite it's griveline?"

"Yes."

"Then there must be something in the wound. Bring me some hot water."

Aviel fetched a pot-full from the kitchen.

Shand probed the wound with a fine blade. "Nothing hard in there."

"What about something soft?" said Aviel.

She sterilised a little mustard spoon in the fire and allowed it to cool. Shand eased it into the ragged wound and scooped out some bloody muck.

"Your eyes are better than mine, girl."

Aviel stared at the spoon. The griveline smell was stronger. "I can see a tiny yellow dot . . . no, two."

She washed the muck through a piece of gauze. Half a dozen little beads lay there, no bigger than frog eggs. She probed one with the point of the knife. It burst and the smell bit into the lining of her nose.

"They're filled with griveline, slowly dissolving to release the poison."

Shand cleaned the wound out and Aviel washed each scoop of blood and pus through her piece of gauze until they had all the beads. Shand bandaged Tallia's shoulder. It was light outside now; the work had taken hours.

Aviel made tea and they sat by the fire. Tallia was sleeping peacefully now and her breathing was stronger.

"Who would attack the Magister?" said Aviel.

Shand did not answer.

"I keep hearing the cry of a nightjar," she added. "And it's a very bad omen."

Shand snorted.

Tallia let her breath out in a rush and her eyes shot open. Her left hand went to her right shoulder. She looked up at Aviel, then her gaze slipped to Shand. "Whatever you did, I feel much better for it."

"Thank Aviel. She identified the poison that was slowly killing you."

Tallia sat up and offered her hand. "Thank you, Aviel." She turned to Shand. "Why slowly?"

"Griveline." Aviel showed her the tiny beads trapped on the piece of gauze. "On the blade."

"He really wanted you dead," said Shand. "As uncomfortably as possible."

Tallia stood up, shakily. "I'm all hot and cold."

Shand hauled an armchair across, helped her into it and draped a blanket around her shoulders. Aviel went to the kitchen and prepared a tray with cold meats, cheese, boiled eggs, bread and butter and pickles.

"I assume you know about the fall of the council and Snoat's armies on the march?" Tallia was saying when Aviel returned.

"Nothing travels faster than bad news," said Shand. "You got out just in time."

"How do you mean?"

"His forces have taken Thurkad and all the land to the north as far as Elludore Forest. He'll soon move on central Iagador and then the south. If he can control that, he'll control everything west of Lauralin."

"And we've got to fight him, because there's a much bigger problem."

"Karan wrote to me about the Merdrun."

"There's more now."

She filled him in, including what Malien had said about the Charon being terrified of a remorseless enemy.

Ooo-ooo-ooo-ooo. The nightjar again. Spiders tap-danced across Aviel's shoulders.

"Only three Charon ever came to Santhenar," said Shand. "Rulke, Yalkara and Kandor. And look at the trouble they caused. I don't dare imagine what a whole army of *their* enemies would do."

"The summon stone must be found and destroyed," said Tallia.

"And we've got less than eight weeks to do it."

"Unfortunately, we have no clue as to what it is, or where."

No one spoke for several minutes, then Tallia said, "I'm worried about Karan. She's planning to go back to Cinnabar, but the Merdrun, and this mighty magiz, are way beyond her strength."

Shand just shook his head.

"We need a new leader, Shand."

"No!" he said explosively.

"I've seen you face down the greatest powers in the land."

"A man who doesn't want the job would make a poor leader."

"On the contrary, a man who doesn't want the job makes the best leader."

"We have to do something," Aviel said softly.

They looked up suddenly as if they had forgotten she was there, and she flushed to the roots of her silver hair. Who was she, a crippled girl who had never left the town she was born in, to tell the mighty what to do?

"The child is right," said Tallia.

"I'm not a child," Aviel muttered. "I'm sixteen – almost."

"I'll contact our allies, such as they are," said Shand.

"Call them to a meet in Chanthed in two weeks."

"Why Chanthed?"

"Wistan is dying, so we must go to him." Tallia stared into the fire. "Though he may not last a fortnight."

"What is it?" said Shand.

"He's got the greatest spy network in the land. Hundreds of his former students tell him everything that happens, and he keeps a 'dirt book' on everyone important. But when he dies it'll be unprotected, and if it falls into Snoat's hands it'll be ruinous."

Aviel could not sit still any longer. She took the plates out to the kitchen and washed them, and was returning for the platter when Tallia spoke again, "What about Aviel?"

She stopped outside the doorway.

"What about her?" Shand growled.

"We both know she's got a remarkable talent. And given that the old guard has utterly failed us, we must do everything we can to encourage the young."

Shand was silent.

"Have you shown her that grimoire of scent potions?" Tallia persisted.

"Shut up about it!" he hissed.

His chair squeaked. Aviel ducked across to the sink, sweat forming on her palms. Shand's footsteps approached the doorway, stopped, then went away. She heard him poking the fire, savagely, then the cork was wrenched out of a bottle and his chair creaked again. She crept back to the door.

"She can't go on working by trial and error," said Tallia.

"Nothing I can do about it."

"War is falling on us like a meteorite, Shand."

Aviel heard gulping, as if he was drinking from the bottle. Drinking *half* the bottle, by the sound of it.

"Grimoires are deadly," he said. "She might be ready for an apprenticeship in six months, but she'd need a good master."

"Then find her one! If we're to survive, we're going to need every talent we have."

Aviel slipped out and back to her workshop. She ached to be taught about scent potions, but masters in mancery were notoriously cranky, often abusive and frequently lecherous. And, it was said, reluctant to teach apprentices their greatest secrets. In the hands of such a master, what would happen to her? She might endure all manner of drudgery, abuse and misery yet still not learn what she needed.

Could she learn the Secret Art from a book? A master's grimoire? The very idea was absurd. Aviel stirred the ashy charcoal in her braziers, prepared her apparatus and began the day's work, extracting the scent from a bag of lemon verbena leaves.

But the thought would not go away.

16

I ALWAYS PAY FULL PRICE

Llian picked up the scattered books of the Histories, climbed the library ladder and replaced them on their shelves. He had learned nothing about either the Merdrun or the summon stone. Two days had passed since Tallia's departure, and two almost sleepless nights, alone, for Karan had taken to sleeping in Sulien's room.

He had never felt more useless. Karan, who was utterly focused on protecting Sulien, went about her work like an automaton, and she was so touchy that even Rachis tiptoed around her. She was trying to find a way to attack the magiz and Llian could do nothing about it. She was going to be killed, he knew it, and all he could do was stay calm and hold the family together, for Sulien's sake.

But he couldn't do it. He wasn't even sure he could hold himself together.

"The judge has come," Karan said from the doorway. "Benie is going to be sentenced this afternoon."

Llian started and almost fell off the ladder. "There's no trial then?"

"He admitted to killing Cook."

"He might have changed his story . . . "

"He hasn't. Benie just keeps telling the truth in that bewildered and desperate way. I'm going to plead for him one last time, but I don't think it'll do any good."

"Would it help if I came too?"

"I don't think the judge would see you."

"Why not?"

Karan's eyes slipped away from his. "The usual reason."

"Because I'm Zain," Llian said bitterly. "If I'd known the trouble I was going to bring you—"

"Please don't start that again," she said wearily.

"Karan?" he said, sensing an opening.

"What?"

"You said the old family papers were lost in the great flood, but I know you burned them in the fireplace."

She spun around. "Have you been *spying* on me?"

"Sulien saw you." He reached out to her. "Please don't shut me out. This is eating me alive."

She took his hands in hers, sighed and sat down. "I'm sorry. I can't think about anything except stopping the magiz." She looked up, flushing. "It's really hard to pass from the void into any of the real worlds, but the terrible sorcery Basunez and my father did made it a lot easier. I had to get rid of the evidence."

"All right, but we've got to work together."

Her mouth set in a hard line. She wrenched a crumpled sheet of paper out of her pocket and slammed it down on the table. "How is this working together?"

It was the letter he'd written to Thandiwe. "It . . . it's just asking for her help."

"That's not how it reads to me."

"How does it read to you?"

"As though you're planning to abandon your family for your mistress."

Why was she acting this way? He hadn't looked twice at Thandiwe in a dozen years. "You told me to find answers. *Do whatever it takes*, you said. I've got to have the ban lifted first."

"Thandiwe was your lover."

"More than twelve years ago!"

"She still wants you, Llian. I've seen it in her eyes, every time we've met."

Llian could not restrain himself. "So what?" he roared. "I don't want her."

"What if the drumming starts up the next time you're with her? Will you be able to resist her?"

"You don't trust me," he said bitterly. "With Thandiwe or Sulien."

Things were so tense afterwards that he was not displeased when Anjo Duril, a chronicler he knew from his student days, dropped in unexpectedly.

"Who is he?" Karan whispered after Llian had shown Anjo to a guest room in the southern wing that ran off the keep. "I've never heard you mention him before."

"He was a couple of years below me. Can't say I liked him much."

"Why not?"

"He never went to the taverns and got drunk. Never mucked around or went wenching." Llian flushed.

"Students!" she sniffed.

"Anjo wasn't clever but he was ambitious, and always sucking up to the masters. He just did his work and nothing else, a very tedious fellow all round."

"And now he's a chronicler and a master, earning good coin."

Again there was an edge to her voice, enough to sting, but Llian did not defend himself. He had let the family down.

After dinner, when they were sitting around the fire, he said to Anjo, "What's the latest news from Chanthed?"

Anjo sat back, a faint smile playing on his full lips. A well-fed, self-satisfied fellow rapidly going bald, he filled his clothes to bursting and his olive skin had an oily gleam. "About you?"

"No, about the college. How's old Wistan?"

"Fading. No, dying."

"He was dying when Llian was awarded his Great Tale," Karan said sourly. "At least, Wistan *said* he was dying."

"He spins a good story when he needs to," said Anjo, "though this time it's true. He can barely get out of his chair, and don't the other masters take advantage of it."

"How do you mean?" said Llian.

"Time was when nothing got past Wistan. If any student committed the slightest misdemeanour, he knew about it."

"I remember," Llian said ruefully.

"You would," said Anjo.

"Really?" said Karan waspishly. "Llian hardly ever talks about the old days at the college, even though he spent a third of his life there. I'd love to hear some of your stories, Anjo."

"What were you saying about the other masters?" Llian said hastily.

"They're taking the students for every grint they can get. Even the entrance scholarship has a fee these days. Seven silver tars."

"That's outrageous." Llian banged his goblet down, slopping wine everywhere. "The entrance test was always free, on principle."

"Not any more. The students pay until they bleed. Even to sit their exams. Even to get their marks." Anjo paused, then smiled wolfishly. "Even to pass."

"You mean if they don't pay, they don't pass?"

"Some of the masters — the corrupt ones — are doing very nicely," said Anjo, chuckling.

He was expensively dressed: thick rings on his plump fingers, a massive silver amulet on a heavy chain, and his coat was finest black lambswool. Anjo was so sure of himself that he was prepared to boast about the corruption. Or sure that no one would listen to anything a disgraced chronicler had to say?

Llian could feel his gorge rising but he forced himself to keep his temper. The man was a guest.

"How do you get on with Wistan?" Llian said carefully. He could suck up too, when he was desperate.

"I have his ear," said Anjo. "Good old reliable, boring Anjo. Asinine Anjo, I think they used to call me when I was a student. I don't suppose you'd remember that?"

"Can't say I ever heard it said," Llian lied. He had coined many such a phrase about the dull students, the unattractive ones and the physically afflicted, which went to prove what a shabby person he had been. Then, in desperation, he said, "I don't suppose you could have a quiet word with him?"

"What about?" Anjo's smile broadened.

"Me." It came out as a croak.

Anjo rubbed his glistening scalp with his fingers, studied the oil on them, then casually wiped them on the tablecloth. Llian felt an urge to throttle him. *If the drumming sounds now, you're a dead man.* He half hoped it would.

Anjo frowned. "What could I possibly say to Wistan about you?"

Llian flushed. Anjo wasn't going to make it easy.

"That I've served my time. Learned my lesson. The ban was originally for seven years, and that's well up."

"As I understand it," said Anjo, "Wistan's ban was unlimited."

Karan leaned forward. "But Thandiwe," the name sounded like spider venom, "commuted it to seven years."

"That's not strictly true," said Anjo. "Wistan said, 'A master who has been banned can't be considered for readmission in *less than seven years*. And that requires a two-thirds majority of all the master chroniclers.'"

"But Thandiwe, the Magister-Elect, said it would be reconsidered in seven years," said Llian.

"Unfortunately Wistan didn't die and her position lapsed years ago."

"That's ancient history," said Llian. "Will you—"

"But that's what we deal in, Llian. The Histories."

"Will you put in a good word for me with Wistan?"

"I'm not sure that would be wise – for me, I mean."

Llian suddenly felt that he was standing on a trapdoor and there was a snake pit beneath it. "Why not?"

"There are malicious rumours circulating about you."

"Rumours?" Again that desperate croak. Time was when Llian had had absolute control of his voice – it was part of the teller's art he had worked sixteen years to master.

"Apparently a cabal of the masters is determined to destroy what remains of your good name. Some of them – can you believe it? – even say that your *Tale of the Mirror* is a fraud."

"How dare you!" Llian cried, leaping to his feet and knocking his goblet over.

Anjo put his hands up, still smiling. "You asked what was going on at the college and I reported it . . . as an impartial chronicler should. I've no doubt that your tale deserves to be the twenty-third Great Tale . . . despite how it came about."

Always the sting in the tail. Llian sat down again.

"What are you talking about?" said Karan.

"What Llian was banned for," said Anjo. "There are those who say – and again, I'm not one of them – that he didn't meddle in the Histories just because he's a reckless fool, but . . . "

"What are they saying?" she said with quiet menace.

Anjo's head snapped back, as if he'd only now realised where the real threat lay, then the smug smile returned. "That Llian shaped the Histories to his will, to improve his tale."

Pain sheared through Llian's chest. A teller could be accused of no greater crime. It would destroy him so utterly that there could be no coming back. He reached out blindly for the wine bottle, which was empty save for a few teaspoons of purple, gritty dregs. He drank them anyway.

"Llian the Liar, they're starting to whisper in the halls," said Anjo.

"Why?" said Karan. The glint in her green eyes would have melted iron.

"Why what?"

"Why are the masters trying to destroy Llian's good name? How can he possibly be a threat to them when he's still under a ban?"

"I should have thought that was obvious," sneered Anjo. "The common people love the *Tale of the Mirror*. They ask for it to be told more than all the other Great Tales put together, and that amounts to a kind of power – a valuable currency in these troubled times."

"To lead an uprising?" Karan let out a hollow laugh. "Llian has many fine qualities, but he couldn't lead a hungry goat to a blackcurrant bush."

"Thanks," Llian muttered, trying to swallow the dregs stuck in his throat.

"In the past," said Anjo, "great tellers have twice become Master of the College through the weight of public acclamation. They're making sure it doesn't happen a third time – especially not a foul, treacherous and deceitful Zain, as they view you. So I can't possibly intercede with Wistan on your behalf. It wouldn't be wise."

Anjo rose, stretched, yawned. "Thank you for your hospitality, and I bid you goodnight. I've a long ride tomorrow and I must leave at dawn."

"I'll make breakfast and see you on your way," said Karan.

"No need to trouble yourself. I'll get a pie from the baker at Tolryme." Anjo bowed and left.

Llian looked up. Karan was gazing at him, the firelight shining on her red hair. She had never looked more beautiful, and he had never felt less worthy of her.

"That's it then," he said.

She launched herself at him and held him close, squeezing so hard that she was compressing his lungs.

"No, it's not. Come to bed. We'll talk about what to do after he's gone."

Llian rose late the following morning with a throbbing head and the feeling that things were going to get worse. Karan and Sulien were out somewhere. In the manager's office Rachis had his head bent over a ledger, his watering eyes just a few inches from the page.

Llian took his gruel to the library, put it down on the table and reached out to draw the *Tale of the Mirror* to him. It wasn't there. He looked across to the special place on the bookshelf where it was kept. It wasn't there either. Ice formed in his belly as he looked around frantically and saw, on the other side of the table, a small piece of notepaper with three battered copper grints resting on it.

I always pay full price.

Asinine Anjo

17

HE'S NEAR HIS END NOW

At a villa eleven miles east of Muncyte, Cumulus Snoat sat in his ermine-lined dressing gown on the marble terrace, sipping the day's first cup of *nim* tea, the finest in the world. It was shipped all the way from the rain-saturated forests of tropical Gendrigore for his delectation, and his alone. A brazier beside him burned laths of pink, subtly scented rosewood.

He reached for Goudry's *Blood Poems*, written twelve hundred years ago and forgotten by all save those of the most exquisite sensibilities. Only nine copies were in existence and his was by far the best, yet it irked him that rival collectors held the other eight books. He shrugged off the irritation and had just begun to read when a skeet came howling in.

"Can this be *it*?" he said. "No, expectation is the enemy of happiness."

Shortly a kimono-clad young woman hurried in, carrying a rectangular package. Her cheeks were overly pink, which marred her otherwise flawless beauty. Snoat sighed. His self-control was almost perfect and he expected no less from those around him. A mild rebuke was necessary, though he was determined not to allow it to spoil the day.

"Your face is flushed, Ifoli. Have I not told you, nothing is so urgent that it can be allowed to spoil your perfection?"

"I'm sorry, Cumulus," she said, for he preferred to be addressed by his first name. Even her voice was beautiful – high and lilting. "Knowing you were waiting for this, I became over-excited."

He had taught her such self-control that the pink tinge faded and she was perfect again. He extended his hand. The package had been wrapped in magenta silk and tied with sapphire-blue silken cords, precisely to his requirements. Ifoli knew what he wanted and took pains to deliver it, in every respect.

Snoat unwrapped the package deliberately, taking pleasure in every moment. If life wasn't for pleasure, what meaning could it possibly have?

"Is it necessary to crush and humiliate the people you rob?" Ifoli said softly.

Snoat set down the package while he considered the question. It was an emotive one, and it vexed him that she had asked it, but again he wasn't going to let it spoil this perfect day.

"I was the poorest of children, the son of a labourer and a maid-servant on a vast estate. Though I was polite and hard-working, I was constantly put down because of my humble origins. As a boy, I resolved to gain power over the greatest people in the land, then rob them of their treasures and show them what it felt like to be poor and power-less." He met Ifoli's eyes. "And so I do."

He drew the wrappings away and it stood revealed, one of the most precious books in the world and the only one of its kind that he, or indeed any collector, had been able to lay hands on. It was Llian's original illuminated manuscript of the twenty-third Great Tale, the *Tale of the Mirror*, and it was even more beautiful than his letter had said. Not just beautiful and infinitely precious, but a document of vast importance and significance to every living person on Santhenar.

And now it was his.

"And even more precious if the despicable Zain who created it should die," he said aloud.

"Pardon, Cumulus?"

"Never mind. Anjo Duril has done well. See that he is paid the market price."

"The *full* market price?"

"To pay less would be to diminish the book."

"Yes, Cumulus." She bowed, hesitated, then turned back to him. "When Anjo obtained the manuscript, he noticed an object that may be of interest."

"What kind of object?"

"The braided silver chain given by Shuthdar to the crippled girl Fiachra before he died. It was made by his own hands, and is said to contain an enchantment he put on it to protect her."

"Interesting," said Snoat.

"Only a handful of objects made by Shuthdar survive, though it may be the least of them. Not worthy of one of your collections, perhaps." She turned to go.

"Any object made by Shuthdar would be worth a place in my collections," said Snoat, "since I have nothing by him. Tell me about this protection."

"Anjo knows nothing about it, save that it exists."

"A charm put there by Shuthdar thousands of years ago," Snoat mused. "An enchantment so well crafted that it may linger to this day."

"You're thinking it might be possible to read the original spell," said Ifoli.

"The great folly of the Secret Art is that few adepts ever share their secrets. Rather, they do everything possible to conceal them with arcane codes, tricks and traps and deliberate deceptions."

"Mancery is a hazardous occupation. More of its secrets are lost than passed on."

"And thus the Secret Art dwindles. Few mancers of the modern age can equal the masters of ancient times, and no one has ever approached the spells that Shuthdar bound into his astonishing magical devices."

"Then this charm, if it could be read ..."

"I'll consider it another day. Send Ragred to me."

Ifoli bowed and went out.

Snoat dismissed further thoughts of the chain. He would allow nothing to distract him from the manuscript. He turned the pages, marvelling at the calligraphy, the illuminations and the quality of the writing.

Any collectable manuscript must have one of those three qualities, and sometimes two, but never had he seen one where the calligraphy, the illuminations and the writing were all of the highest order. Yes, he saw little flaws here and there, imperfections that would have marred any printed or hand-copied book. But original manuscripts were judged differently – flaws and imperfections were the author's signature, unique and endearing.

He realised that Ragred, a vast wart- and wen-covered monstrosity, was standing to one side, awaiting his attention. Snoat put the manuscript down and studied him, revelling in Ragred's hideousness. He was as ugly as Ifoli was beautiful, and Snoat appreciated the one as much as the other.

"What news of Tallia bel Soon?" he asked.

"Scouts lost her in Faidon Forest," said Ragred in a boar's grunt.

"How about Hingis and Esea?"

"Scorbic Vyl lost them, and most of his men. And his arm."

"Would you be so kind as to visit my displeasure on Vyl?"

"Er ... he has something for you."

Ragred would not have mentioned it unless it was vital. "Proceed," said Snoat.

"Tallia gave Hingis the code to the council's spell vault, and Scorbic extracted it from him."

Oh, perfect day!

"Do you wish to go there now?" said Ifoli, who had come in silently.

"Tomorrow!" said Snoat. "And then, depending what we find there, make ready to decamp to my villa near Chanthed."

He handed Ragred the copy of Goudry's *Blood Poems*. "Put this on the brazier."

Ragred hesitated in case he had misheard. Snoat appreciated that in a servant, for mistakes did happen. He also appreciated obedience.

"Onto the brazier," said Ragred and placed it carefully in the middle, where the fire was hottest.

Snoat watched the book burn with only a fleeting regret. It was marred in his eyes now. Everything was, before the prospect of the most perfect collection of all.

"Empty out my library," said Snoat. "Pile all the books up down there –" he indicated the manicured meadow below the terrace "– and burn them."

"Burn them," Ragred echoed, and this time he did not move until Snoat nodded. "Will that be all, Cumulus?"

Snoat laid a hand on Llian's manuscript. "This is the twenty-third Great Tale. Find out where the original manuscripts of the other twenty-two are – if they're still in existence."

"Library of the College of the Histories, Chanthed," said Ragred.

Excellent servant! Not just collectably gruesome, but vastly knowledgeable.

"However . . . " said Ragred.

"A problem?"

"May be difficult to . . . obtain."

"Why so?"

"Protected by a spell, bound to the Master of the College. While he lives, it's unbreakable."

"Master Wistan is in poor health, is he not?"

"Near his end."

"And when he dies, the protection will fade . . . until it's renewed by the new master."

"Yes, Cumulus."

"I have a tame master there, don't I?"

"Basible Norp," grunted Ragred. "Oily but effective."

"Contact him. We need to make plans. Then send for Gurgito Unick."

"Er . . . really?"

This time Snoat sighed. And yet he'd given three extraordinary orders in ten minutes. A good servant had to be sure.

"He's a vicious, untrustworthy drunk and lecher, very possibly the foulest man I've ever met. But he's also an intuitive genius and the best maker of magical devices in Meldorin . . . if not the world."

"Fetching Unick." Ragred bowed his wen-encrusted head and went out.

Cumulus Snoat turned back to the *Tale of the Mirror*. He was in such fine humour that not even the stench of burning leather from the brazier could mar his delicate sensibilities.

Could he put together the rarest, most beautiful and most important collection in all the world? If he could, his life would be as perfect as his collection.

One down, twenty-two to go.

18

NINEFINGERS

"There it is." Esea pointed down the crowded street.

The sign on the front of the tavern said NINEFINGERS. It was a three-storey building of soot-stained yellow brick, like all the other buildings in the street. The decorative arches around the front door and the windows were dark blue brickwork, save for the keystones, which were red-black haematite and carved with fiends' faces – pinched, sharp-nosed and pointy-chinned. Cunning-eyed, Hingis thought.

Esea had not mentioned his betrayal again, but it was not over. His reaction to her maimed foot had shattered her and he did not think anything would ever make up for it.

He despised himself. His disfigurement did not matter to her; indeed, it had brought them closer. So why did her small imperfection matter so much to him? He could not say; it just did. What a shabby person he was.

"You sure this is the place?" he said, clinging to the saddle horn with both hands. They had ridden non-stop for the past sixteen hours and every twisted bone ached, every muscle.

"Sith isn't so big a city that there are likely to be two Ninefingers."

She dismounted with a thump, staggered a couple of steps and turned to him.

"Go and make sure," he said, laying his head on his horse's neck. "Once I'm down, I'll never get up again."

She looped the horses' reins over the rail and limped up three slate-topped steps, across a wide porch whose well-scrubbed brown boards creaked, and inside. Hingis's horse dipped its head to drink from the mossy water trough. He clung on, capable of only three thoughts: hot bath, warm bed, endless sleep.

After some minutes Esea came out, followed by an immensely tall and strongly built woman in her early twenties whose skin was as black as anthracite. Without a word, she plucked Hingis out of the saddle.

"I can walk!" he cried, mortified.

Cradling him in one arm as though he weighed no more than a child, she unfastened his saddlebags and carried everything inside.

The bar was almost empty, it being mid-morning. A couple of old women sat in a corner, playing a game with dice and a circular board. A huge man stood behind the bar, stacking mugs on a shelf. He was middle-aged, his hair greying, a strong body thickening in the middle. It was clear that he was the young woman's father.

He jerked his head at her. "Put him down, girl. That's no way to treat a gentleman."

She flushed and set Hingis on his feet. He staggered. She steadied him. Hingis looked up into her eyes, expecting to see the usual revulsion, or at best pity. He saw only kindly concern.

"Thank you," he said, studying her more closely. She had a strong, handsome face and soft eyes – hazel, striking in her dark face – that seemed to be hiding something. She went out.

The huge man came out from behind the bar, wincing as he walked. "I'm Osseion." His voice was deep, rumbling, cheerful.

"Hingis," said Hingis. "And my twin, Esea."

"We've already introduced ourselves."

Osseion held out a four-fingered hand and Hingis shook it. Osseion's finger joints were swollen.

"Arthritis," he said. "I'll never wield a sword again. Could be awkward . . . considering."

"You were Mendark's personal bodyguard," said Hingis. "You're in the Histories."

"Doesn't bring customers through the door." Osseion surveyed the almost empty room. "Come out the back."

They followed him down a narrow hall, around a corner and into a small square room where coal smouldered in a tiny iron grate. The room was pleasantly warm, though stuffy, and had the tang of coal smoke and sulphur. The single window was curtained. A pine table by the window was surrounded by four chairs, their worn seat covers embroidered by a child's hand.

Osseion helped Hingis into a chair and went out. He sighed as the weight came off his feet and his warped bones shifted and settled. Esea stood with her back to the fire, rocking on her right foot. Her left foot rested lightly on the floor. It must be very painful. He shuddered, leaned back and closed his eyes. The daughter came in carrying a laden tray.

"I'm Hingis," he said, holding out his bony hand.

She smiled and shook his hand rather timidly. Her hand was much bigger than his, and callused across the palm and fingers.

"Ussarine," she said quietly, pronouncing it Oos-*sar*-een.

"And this is my twin sister, Esea."

Esea nodded stiffly but did not extend her hand. What was the matter?

Ussarine set the table, put bowls of soup in front of Hingis and Esea and a platter of bread, butter and cheese in the middle. Hingis salivated.

"You practise with a sword," he said to Ussarine.

"Every day since I was two," said Ussarine. "And other weapons too. How did you know?"

"From your calluses," said Osseion as he came through the door with four mugs of black beer. He put them on the table and sat down.

Ussarine stood there for a moment, awkwardly, then turned to go.

"Sit down, girl," said Osseion.

"I'm not sure . . . " said Esea warningly.

"We know why you're here," said Osseion. "Tallia sent word."

"Where is she?" said Hingis. "I need to contact her urgently." To advise her that he'd betrayed his word and given the enemy the code to the spell vault.

"No idea. She said to send any messages to Chanthed, but she may not get there for a couple of weeks."

"A couple of weeks!" cried Esea.

Snoat would surely have plundered the spell vault by then, and he would be unstoppable. Hingis wished he had died on that toxic hilltop.

"I can make your arrangements but I don't go out much – arthritis has me buggered. Ussarine will look after you and there's no better guard in all Meldorin." Osseion's voice rang with pride. "I've taught her all about weaponry, and when she was younger Tallia taught Ussarine everything she knows about unarmed combat – which is *everything*. Ussarine also holds the rank of captain in the Sith militia."

Ussarine sat at the far end of the table and took hold of her mug but did not drink. Esea did not look happy. She drew the bowl towards her and began to eat.

"What's happening up north?" said Hingis.

"Snoat's forces are moving slowly south and west from Thurkad," said Osseion. "There's no opposition worth a damn and the roads are full of refugees."

Hingis took a morsel of bread and butter. "You know about the Merdrun?"

"We're facing an invasion from the void, a martial race that even the Charon feared, and Snoat's chaos is preparing the way for them," said Osseion. "We have to get rid of him but first we need an army."

"Assuming we can fund it," said Esea.

"Sith's merchants are raising money. But what you need is fighting men –" he glanced at his daughter "– and women."

Ussarine caught Hingis's eyes on her and looked down at the table. Was her father's reputation too much to live up to, or did she think he would sooner have had a son?

"But that can wait," added Osseion. "When you've eaten, your baths will be ready, and your beds. We'll talk further in the morning."

He drained his mug and went out. Ussarine followed, carrying her untasted beer.

Esea closed the door, then said quietly, "I'm not happy with her being involved."

Hingis ate some soup. "Why not?"

"We don't know anything about her."

"If we can't trust people who come highly recommended, we'll never get anything done."

"You didn't trust the one person in the world who would never let you down, then blabbed Tallia's secret at my first squeak."

"Scorbic Vyl wasn't going to stop with your toes."

"You should have kept your mouth shut," said Esea.

"Would you, if he'd been cutting bits off me?"

She did not reply.

"Esea, I'm exhausted and every bone aches."

Hingis rose unsteadily. Esea's face was pale save for a red flush on each cheek. He went out and Ussarine showed him to his room, where a steaming bath was waiting. He undressed and slid into the blissfully hot water, scrubbed himself with thyme-scented soap, and for the first time in days he was not in pain. He lay back and closed his eyes, allowing the heat to ease his cares.

Now drowsy, he got into bed, but the pain grew and the further he reached towards blessed sleep the further it retreated. Shortly there was a knock on the door. Esea, he assumed. They had never been estranged this long before, and he relied on her as much as she did on him. He had to undo the damage.

"Come in," he said.

But it was Ussarine carrying a small jug of oil and a towel. She entered, leaving the door half open.

"Father sent me," she said, lowering her eyes. "He thought your back might need a rub."

"It's all right." Hingis did not like anyone seeing his sad, twisted body. He sat up, and such a spasm passed through him that a groan escaped.

"Father said to insist. If you would just turn over . . . "

The muscles in his back were like knotted tree roots. Hingis did not have the strength to resist.

She warmed some oil in her hands and set to work. Her fingers were immensely strong, yet she knew exactly where to press hard and where to be gentle. Within a minute he felt the tension leaving him and the pains in his distorted frame easing. He surrendered himself to the power of her hands.

"Hingis?" Esea said from outside the door. "Are you awake?"

She pushed the door open, came in and froze, looking from Hingis to Ussarine, then back to him. Her beautiful face warped. Ussarine, absorbed in her work, took a while to realise Esea was there. She started, her fingertips gouging into Hingis's back. They stared at one another, Esea in fury, Ussarine in puzzlement, which was slowly replaced by a mortified flush.

Esea turned and went out without a word, then slammed her own door so furiously that it shook the upper floor of Ninefingers.

"I'm so sorry," Ussarine said in a tiny voice. "I didn't mean to come between you and your twin."

"It's all right," said Hingis. "Thank you. My back feels better than it has in years."

She nodded distractedly, picked up the oil and the towel and went out, pulling the door closed behind her. Hingis sat up. His back was utterly pain-free and it wasn't the only thing to wonder about. Ussarine did not appear to see him as a monster. She had simply treated him like another human being, and this gave him the most inexpressible joy.

But it had made things even worse with Esea.

*

Hingis had made no progress with Esea, who rebuffed him every time he opened his mouth. He ached for the loss of her.

"Sorry it's taking so long," said Osseion after they had been in Sith for five days with little to show for it. They were at the back of the empty barroom by the fire. "With Snoat's forces heading our way, most of the people I need to talk to have gone into hiding."

"Sith's walls are strong," said Esea. "Surely it's not in immediate danger?"

"We're a city state on an island in a river and we rely on trade; we can't even feed ourselves. But if war comes to the south, there won't be any trade."

"What have you got for us?"

"Half a dozen experienced officers. Good leaders, all of them, and they'll know where to find the troops you need."

"Are they reliable?"

"Used to be."

"What's that supposed to mean?"

"I knew them well in the old days. Ussarine will take you to meet them tomorrow." He went out.

Esea was scowling. "That woman!"

"Why have you taken such a set against her? She's quiet, polite, reliable—"

"You know why!" she hissed.

He did but wanted to hear her say it. "Tell me."

"She wants to take you away from me."

"Rubbish. She's just a kind person."

"Who was rubbing your naked body when I came in the other day."

"She was massaging my aching back," he said coldly, "with the door open. Ussarine has no interest in me . . . that way."

"You want her though, don't you?"

"Don't be ridiculous. I'm a hideous little wreck that no woman would look twice at."

"You want a permanent bond, a soulmate. Where will that leave me?"

The door opened and Ussarine came in carrying a laden breakfast tray in one hand. She put down plates of steaming porridge laden with green mussels, crisp fried blackfish with yellow mushrooms and a large pot of red tea.

Hingis studied her surreptitiously. There was nothing meagre about Ussarine's figure: though she was huge, all was in proportion. Her face was not pretty, but neither was it plain, and it was kindly. Besides, compared to him she was an extraordinary beauty.

Esea wore a sour smile. *You see.*

Ussarine went out. She had a long vigorous stride; her hips oscillated as she walked and her trousers stretched across taut, splendid buttocks. Hingis swallowed and looked away.

Esea dug him in the ribs, smirking. He devoted himself to his mussel porridge, flushing. He wasn't naïve; Ussarine was simply being nice because that's the kind of person she was. And perhaps because Hingis, having no expectations, was not intimidated by her size and her mastery of the warrior's arts.

He had also noticed how lacking in confidence she was, despite being bigger and stronger than most men and a more accomplished fighter. Or did her lack of confidence come from precisely those things?

When she came back for the empty plates, to his own surprise he found himself asking if she would like to have dinner with him that evening. She looked down at him in surprise, and for a moment he thought she was going so refuse, or mock him as so many women had before he'd learned to avoid such humiliations. Then a shy little smile grew until it transformed her whole face.

"I'd love to," said Ussarine. "I'll be free at seven."

He was heading to his room when he saw the expression on Esea's face. She was furious. But what could she do?

"You're what?" he cried when Esea told him at breakfast the following morning.

"Going to the meeting in Chanthed. Right away."

"But we've got work to do here."

"It doesn't need both of us."

"Why so suddenly? The council isn't until the week after next."

"It's at least a ten-day trip from here."

"But I . . . " He almost said, *I need you*. Perhaps it would have turned out better if he had, but he was also thinking that the separation would do them both good. And, selfishly, that it would make it easier for him to spend time with Ussarine. They'd had a most pleasant dinner last night. He had quite forgotten that he was a hideous cripple.

"Yes?" she said eagerly.

"Nothing. If you feel you must go, that's all there is to it. Though I'll miss you."

"I'll miss you too."

A spasm struck him in the chest. "You know you're on Snoat's death list."

"So are you. Besides, I'll be going via the back ways."

"You don't know the back ways to Chanthed from here."

After a pause, she said, "My bodyguard does."

It fell into the silence like a hammer against a bell.

"What bodyguard?" A fist closed around his kidneys and squeezed until he was hard pressed not to scream.

Esea's smile was vengeful, malicious. "I talked Osseion into sending Ussarine with me."

19

A DINNER BEST FORGOTTEN

"What are we going to do for Daddy?" said Sulien to Karan.

They were walking back to the manor with a basket of mushrooms each. In the drought they were only to be found in damp places below the granite cliffs of the Gothryme escarpment, a mile and a half behind them.

The theft of his manuscript had shattered Llian, and not even Sulien could cheer him up. It was a devastating blow to Karan too. If war drove them out of Gothryme they had nowhere to go because their allies would be in the same boat. They would have to count every coin before they spent it, and what little coin she could scrape together would run out quickly if they had to pay for food and lodgings every night.

There was nothing to be done. Even if Llian accused Anjo Duril of stealing it, no one would take the word of a disgraced ex-chronicler over that of a respectable master.

"We'll cook Llian the best dinner he's ever—"

Karan looked around at the sound of hoof beats. "I wonder who that is?" They scrambled up a small hill and she squinted at the two riders. "Shit!" Was the whole world conspiring against her?

"You're not supposed to swear," said Sulien.

"It's Maigraith! What's she doing here?"

"Who's Maigraith?"

"Someone I knew years ago. She's . . . very powerful." And she always brought trouble.

"Powerful with what?"

"Mancery. She was trained by Faelamor, the greatest illusionist in all the Three Worlds. And Rulke taught her his own secret arts."

"Don't you like her?"

"She's . . . a difficult, manipulative woman. She almost got me killed half a dozen times."

"Who's that with her?"

"Looks like her son, Julken. He's the same age as you."

"I like it when we have visitors. Except for that rotten Anjo Duril."

"You didn't like him?"

"His mouth was always smiling but he's got snake eyes."

"I should have consulted you before I let him in."

"I can always tell if someone is good or bad," said Sulien.

"Really?" said Karan. "What about Benie?"

"There's not a bad thing in him."

"And yet he killed Cook," Karan said, to herself.

"The drumming *made* him do it."

That would not save him. The judge had made this clear when

Karan had pleaded for Benie's life a second time. The judge had warned her not to pester him again.

They barely had time to deposit the mushrooms in the kitchen and wash their hands before Maigraith arrived. Karan gave Sulien's hair a perfunctory brush, then her own, which made no difference to either, and headed to the front door.

Maigraith was just dismounting. She was slender, neither tall nor short, with silky chestnut-coloured hair cut across at shoulder length. Her eyes were indigo flecked with carmine and her oval face would have been striking save for a thin-lipped, unsmiling mouth. She had hardly aged since Karan had last seen her, but then, with both Charon and Faellem ancestors, why would she? Maigraith could be two hundred years old for all Karan knew, and might live as long again.

She did not greet Karan, but turned and reached up as if to lift Julken down from his horse. He smacked her hand aside with a meaty fist, half-fell off the black stallion, landed with a thump and turned, glowering at them. Karan took a step back – he was gigantic.

"I thought you said he was nine?" Sulien hissed.

Her face wore an expression Karan had never seen on it before – utter loathing. *I can always tell if someone is good or bad.*

Julken's father had been a big handsome man. Julken had the same black hair and dark complexion, but ordinary brown eyes. A broad, solid body was matched to a round head and a mean little mouth. He was already taller than Karan's five foot one, and fully grown he would be a giant.

"Julken," said Maigraith, "this is my old friend Karan. We were pregnant together. Shake hands."

Julken's lip curled in disgust at the word *pregnant*. He took Karan's extended hand and crushed it. She winced and he grinned, the evil toad.

"And Sulien," said Maigraith, looking down her nose at her. Sulien's clothes were grubby and there was dirt under her fingernails. "Little girls shouldn't be allowed to run wild."

And you should mind your own damned business.

Sulien reluctantly put out her hand, which wasn't half the size of Julken's. He enfolded it in his gigantic paw, squeezed as if he was trying to crush her bones, then yelped and jerked his hand back, shaking it furiously. There were swollen red stripes across his palm and fingers.

Karan had no idea what Sulien had done, or how she had done it, but she had never felt more proud of her.

Julken looked Gothryme up and down. "What a ruin! Do we have to stay here, Maig?"

Karan expected Maigraith to rebuke him, but she wore a smile that could only be described as doting.

"There's a fine inn in Tolryme," Karan said hastily. "Far better than the small comforts we can provide here. Better food too."

"Food is food," said Maigraith. "I don't care what I eat."

"I do," whined Julken. "They'll probably feed us on dog, or cockroach."

"We came all this way to see little Sulien," said Maigraith. She looked at Karan expectantly.

Cold feathers ticked the back of Karan's neck. What was going on?

"Yes, come in." She forced a smile.

Julken barged past Karan, knocking her sideways. "Bring my bags and be quick about it," he snapped.

Hospitality wasn't that sacred. Karan gestured Maigraith to the door and followed her through.

"Run and find Llian," she whispered to Sulien. "Ask him to make a *special* effort."

Julken continued in the same vein for the next half-hour while they took tea on the terrace. Gothryme was cold, cramped and ugly, and Rachis was a stupid old fool who should have been put down years ago. Karan was outraged for her old friend, who pretended that he had not heard, and even more outraged at Maigraith, who despite her criticisms of Sulien's wild upbringing, shabby clothes and general lack of grooming, failed to check her own son in any way.

Llian came around the corner, wearing his best clothes. Maigraith stood up abruptly. Her eyes had gone hard and she was quivering with suppressed fury.

What was the matter? There had been no tension between Maigraith and Llian the last time they had met, before the children were born.

She had been quite friendly towards him. Now it looked as though she hated Llian. Fear shivered through Karan. Maigraith was a very bad enemy and not one that Llian could deal with. What had changed?

"Julken," said Maigraith. "This is Llian, Sulien's father."

Llian put out his hand. Julken did not offer his own.

"*This man* killed my father?" Julken said incredulously. "I don't believe it. He couldn't even lift a real man's weapon."

"Tensor killed your father," said Karan. "He'd always hated Rulke."

"But Llian incited him," said Maigraith. "Words are the sharpest weapon of all, aren't they, Llian?"

Karan's fear sharpened. Clearly Maigraith blamed Llian for Rulke's death, but what was she really up to?

That night, after the worst meal Karan had ever prepared, Maigraith entertained them with a brilliant demonstration of the Secret Art – a mid-air recreation of the solar system, complete with six planets, their twenty-seven moons, a band of asteroids and half a dozen comets, all moving in their orbits. She expressed grudging surprise when Sulien named all the planets in the correct order.

Afterwards Sulien read a poignant little story she had written about Piffle.

"Well, that was crap," said Julken the moment she had finished.

"I'm sure she did her best," said Maigraith.

Karan only restrained herself with a superhuman effort. Hospitality was sacred at Gothryme . . . at least for the first night.

"Speaking as an impartial teller, I thought it was very well told," said Llian. He scowled at Julken. "I can't wait to see how *Sulken* is going to entertain us." He gulped from his goblet. Evidently he had decided that the only way to get through the evening was with as much wine as possible. Karan could hardly blame him.

"Don't want to." For the first time Julken seemed unsure of himself.

"Show them your art," Maigraith said to Julken. "He's been prac-tising for weeks."

"Yes, come on, Julken," said Llian thickly. "Your father was one of the greatest mancers of all time. You must have inherited *some* of his talent."

Karan jammed her elbow into his ribs so hard that wine went all down his front. Llian scowled and squeezed his shirt into his goblet. She felt like smacking him.

"Daddy!" Sulien hissed. "Manners!"

"You can do it, Julken," said Maigraith. "You'll surpass your father one day."

Julken's fleshy bottom lip quivered. Had he been told that over and again, but knew he would never measure up?

"I know a spell to boil water," he said reluctantly.

Llian passed him the decanter. "Try it on the wine. Boiling could only improve it."

Julken set the decanter in front of him, made several clumsy motions over it and cast his spell. Nothing happened. He flushed and tried again without success. His round head looked like an overripe tomato about to burst.

Maigraith, frowning, inscribed a sentence on a piece of paper and slid it across. Julken looked down at it, his lips moving, then sounded it out haltingly with wildly exaggerated motions of his meaty hands.

A wisp of vapour emerged from the mouth of the decanter, but that was all. Julken's face was on fire; he glowered at the table. Sulien let out a tinkling peal of laughter.

"Sulien!" cried Karan. "Apologise at once."

"I'm *sorry*," said Sulien, her eyes alive with glee. She poked the decanter with a fingertip and the wine boiled instantly, bubbling out of the top and onto the tablecloth.

Julken looked down at the petite girl, his fists opening and closing, and there was such rage in his eyes that Karan's heart missed a beat.

"You will be," he said in a grating voice. "When we grow up, we're going to be married . . . and you'll never laugh again."

Sulien let out a cry of terror, fled up to her room and bolted the door. Karan went after her, but neither threats nor promises could induce her to come down. When Karan returned to the dining room, Julken was stabbing the fire with the poker, showering coals everywhere. Llian, who'd already had more wine than was good for him, was destroying the cork in a new bottle.

Maigraith tried to laugh the incident off. "You know what boys are like. They say the first thing that comes into their heads."

"It sounded like a threat to me," said Llian. "And no one threatens my daughter. If you step out of line again, Julken—"

"This isn't your house, it's Karan's," snapped Maigraith. "You have no rights here, and if you ever lay a finger on my son . . ."

Karan linked her arm through Llian's. "Llian and I speak with one voice. Julken will apologise."

"Very well," Maigraith said coldly. "Where is Sulien?"

"She's gone to bed. I'll expect his apology in the morning."

Maigraith called Julken and they went to their room at the far end of the southern wing. Llian helped Karan carry the sorry remains of dinner into the kitchen and they cleaned up. "I'm sorry," he said. "I've made things worse, haven't I?"

Karan felt a great surge of affection for him. "You were defending our daughter, but please don't make an enemy of Maigraith."

"It's a bit late for that."

20

THE ARMS OF HIS MISTRESS

"Mummy, Daddy! Mummy, Daddy!"

Karan was shocked awake. Had Sulien had another nightmare? Had the magiz got to her? It was barely sunrise, yet she was sobbing and banging on the bedroom door.

Llian scrambled out of bed and pulled on a robe. Karan yanked the door open and Sulien fell in, hugging something fluffy in her arms. Something limp.

"It's Piffle!" She was howling, heartbroken. "He's dead!"

Karan took the sad little body, ashamed of her momentary relief. Piffle's tongue protruded and his neck was floppy. Llian folded Sulien in his arms.

"I'm really sorry," he said. "It must have been a wildcat from the mountains. With the drought, they're hunting further afield."

"There's no b-blood," sobbed Sulien. "No tooth or claw marks. And . . . and I heard the drumming."

Karan found no trace of injury, but under Piffle's fur its neck was bruised, as if huge hands had closed around it and snapped it.

"When?" she said.

"At dawn. He was barking furiously . . . and then everything went quiet. What could it be?"

A dreadful suspicion arose. Karan could see it in Llian's eyes too. She shook her head. *Not in front of her.*

"Take Piffle down to Rachis," said Karan. "We'll be down in a minute."

Sulien went out, the puppy hugged in her arms. Karan closed the door.

Llian yanked on his pants. "Julken's a monster and he's only going to get worse."

"What are we going to do?"

"Get rid of them, and make sure they never come back."

"We can't accuse him without proof," said Karan.

"We both know he did it. Make some excuse."

She went down the stairs, trembling, afraid of the confrontation. What would Maigraith do? She was in the kitchen with Rachis and Sulien, who was brushing Piffle's fur. A very surly Julken sat outside at the terrace table.

Karan took Maigraith aside and told her what Julken had done. "I want you to go, now! And *never* bring him here again."

Without a word, Maigraith hauled Julken off to his horse, saw him mounted, gave Llian a stare that shivered Karan's bones, and they rode away.

"If she ever comes back . . ." said Llian.

"There's nothing you can do. I'll take care of her." But how, how?

Half an hour later a courier appeared at the door, carrying an urgent letter and asking for an exorbitant sum, two silver tars, in payment.

"Who's it from?" said Llian dully.

"Doesn't say," said the courier, a plump grey-haired old woman on a gigantic bay mare. She turned the letter over in her hands. It was bent, battered and rather grubby.

"It isn't in very good condition," said Llian.

"Came by skeet, didn't it?"

Karan appeared beside him. "Here's your fee, and thank you, Lebla," she said, handing her the coins. "Take the damned letter, Llian."

He wiped off a skeet dropping. "I don't recognise the handwriting."

Karan took the letter from the envelope, sniffed it and handed it to him. "I'd know that perfume anywhere. It's from your *friend* in Chanthed."

Llian clawed his fingernails into his cheeks. "Just for one day let's think about Sulien first. I loved Piffle almost as much as she did."

"Sorry. What a bitch I've turned out to be." Karan gave him a quick kiss on the forehead. "I'll call you for the burial." She limped across to the kitchen.

Llian stared at the crumpled letter. Should he burn it, unread? But he could hardly do so after Karan had paid two precious tars for it.

He sat under a plum tree in the orchard. Thandiwe's perfume carried him off to those carefree student days before he had told the *Tale of the Forbidding* so sensationally at the Graduation Telling twelve years ago, and his life had changed for ever. He had first set eyes on Karan then, in the audience, and she on him, as though their meeting was fated to be. How could it have all gone so wrong?

Chanthed, 17 Mard, 3111

My dearest Llian

   Wistan is finally dying (yes, really dying, not pretending), and before he goes there must be an election for Master of the College. I think I've got the numbers, but I need all the support I can get and you have a surprising number of followers. Well, not surprising considering your Great Tale, but you know what I mean.

    I need your help urgently, and I know how unhappy you are, trapped in the backwoods of Bannador. Come to Chanthed in all haste, if not for the sake of our long friendship, then at least for what I can do for you. Once I'm Master of the College, your ban will be overturned and a junior post will be yours.

"A junior post!" Llian exclaimed.

    You deserve much more, but I've already promised the senior positions to my supporters. But there are other things I can offer you; just name it and it's yours. Anything at all!

    Please come with all possible haste. My rivals are well organised and none of them will do anything for you.

    Your oldest friend,

Thandiwe

Llian read the letter again. The offer of a junior post was an insult, but he had to get the ban overturned.

As to the barely concealed subtext, he did not even want to think about it.

After Piffle had been laid to rest along with his favourite bone, and Sulien's tears had subsided, she went up to her room and closed the door. Karan's heart ached for her but right now there was nothing she could do.

She turned round. Llian was standing awkwardly nearby, holding the letter in one hand. He was sweating.

"Come out to the orangery," said Karan.

He followed her and they sat at the cast-iron table. He handed her the letter.

"Just tell me what's in it," she said, making a supreme effort.

"No more secrets."

"All right." As she read the letter, the sick feeling in the pit of her stomach grew worse until she was on the verge of throwing up. *I know how unhappy you are* and *trapped in the backwoods* made it clear precisely what Thandiwe thought of Karan and Gothryme. She might as well have said *with that bitch of a wife.*

But there are other things I can offer you; just name it and it's yours. Anything at all! There was no doubt as to what she was offering.

"I know what you're thinking," said Llian. "She wants me—"

"In her bed," said Karan.

Llian looked despairing. "I won't go."

"But you need her help to find out about the summon stone. It's urgent, Llian."

"Wistan, Anjo, Snoat, Maigraith and now Thandiwe. It's as though someone is manipulating them to get at me."

Karan's fists were clenched so tightly in her lap that her knuckles ached. Thandiwe lived in Llian's world, and she could give him back the career without which he felt only half a man.

If Karan begged him to stay here, he would, but he was bound to confront Maigraith when she came back, and Karan knew she would. Maigraith would destroy him; she might even have come here with that intention.

It only left Karan one option. To save her family, she would have to push Llian into the arms of the woman who wanted to be his mistress.

21

THE WORST DAY OF MY LIFE

"I can't go," said Llian. "Not when Sulien—"

"You can't protect her from the magiz. But if you can find out where the summon stone is, and what it is, someone might be able to keep the Merdrun out."

"It would be expensive. Food. Inns. Stabling for my horse."

"There's coin enough . . . just."

"What if I get there . . . and Thandiwe tries to cozen me . . . and the drumming starts again."

"You'll resist it," she said as steadily as she could. The irony was sickening. "I trust you."

She *would* trust him, even if she had to force herself. But Thandiwe would stalk him and ply him with drinks and flattery, and flourish her ripe body in his face . . . and surely, sooner or later, under the influence of the drumming, Llian would crack. If he did, Karan would never get him back. How would she explain that to Sulien?

But then, how would she explain it if Maigraith decided to avenge Rulke? "I want you to go," she said softly. "Right now."

He looked stunned. Though not as stunned as she felt. Karan felt as though she'd been beaten with a club.

"There's no point getting there after Wistan is dead and the vote has been held," she added. "She'll owe you nothing."

"I can't leave with Sulien in such a state."

"It's only seven weeks until the invasion." Panic surged. Time was running out yet things were getting worse, not better. "I'll look after her. She'll understand."

"No, she'll feel that I've let her down when she most needed me, and she'll be right."

"You've got to go."

She peered between the orange trees towards the track to Tolryme. There was no sign of riders but the knot in her belly did not go away. Maigraith would be back.

"It's as though you're trying to get rid of me," Llian muttered. "What's going on?"

He was quick! "Nothing," Karan lied. "Go!"

"What, *now*?"

"Yes."

"All . . . all right."

Gloom settled over her. She stood up. "We'd better tell Sulien."

"I can't bear to leave her like this. Why don't you come too?"

Karan wanted to, but it was impossible. "The harvest has to be got in and we're short-handed as it is. Then there's all the preserving and drying and smoking and pickling to be done for the winter."

"We might not be here by then."

If the invasion succeeded, they might all be dead. "Our farm workers still have to eat."

His face sagged.

"But in six weeks or so," said Karan, "we could think about coming. Let's go up and tell Sulien."

"Tell me what?" said Sulien, coming in.

"I've got to go to Chanthed right away," Llian said dully.

Her green eyes flashed. "*Why?*"

"It's his best chance to get the ban lifted," said Karan.

"I don't want you to go," said Sulien.

"I don't want to go either," said Llian.

"You must!" said Karan.

Sulien swung around to Karan, fists on her hips. "You're sending Daddy away? Because of *Maigraith*?"

She was her father's daughter, no doubt about it. "It's nothing to do with her," Karan lied. "Llian, go and get ready."

An hour later, he rode off. Sulien was inconsolable. "Why did you send Daddy away?" she screamed.

"I didn't," said Karan, feeling sick.

"Yes, you did. I hate *everything*! This is the worst day of my life."

Sulien fled to her room and slammed the door. Karan stood by the track, all alone, tears flooding down her cheeks. She had never felt more alone, empty and burdened. At the crest of the rise Llian stood up in his stirrups, waving so furiously that he almost fell off. Clumsy oaf! She smiled sadly. Then he disappeared and she was wrenched in two. Would he even survive the trip?

She wiped her face and went to the kitchen, where she tried to distract herself by cleaning and blacking the vast iron stove. It did not help. Two hours later she heard the drumming again, very faintly, and ten minutes after that Maigraith was back, alone.

"What do you want?" Karan snarled.

"Where has Llian gone?"

Karan put down her brush and the jar of blacking in case she was tempted to decorate Maigraith's face. "To Chanthed. Something came up and he had to go at once."

"I suppose it makes it easier," said Maigraith.

Karan felt that she was not displeased. Perhaps she had manipulated things to this end. Maigraith had been taught by Faelamor, the greatest manipulator of all time.

"No!" said Karan. "Whatever the question is."

"I want Sulien to come and live with me for six months – even a year. She's a gifted child but she needs discipline."

Karan stared at her, open-mouthed. Only Maigraith could say such a thing.

"Julken murdered Piffle. He's a vicious brat and I wouldn't send Sulien to live with you and him for a day to save my own life."

Maigraith's lips compressed to a hard line. "Julken won't be there. I've sent him to Garching Nod."

"What's that?"

"The best mancery school in the west. It's a hundred and fifty leagues away. He needs discipline and he's too old to live with his mother; he's got to become a man. He won't be back for a year and a half."

The pain in Karan's chest was so bad that she could have been having a heart attack. "I don't understand why you want Sulien to live with you."

"You and I were the only two triunes in the world," said Maigraith. "You bear the blood of Aachim, Faellem and old humans, and I'm descended from Charon, Faellem and old humans. We're unique, Karan! No one can understand what we've been through and who we are."

"Sulien is the only child I'll ever have; I can't bear to be parted from her."

Then Karan hesitated. Maigraith had been a brilliant mancer even before Rulke gifted her with much of his own art. If anyone could protect Sulien against the magiz, she could. But could Maigraith protect her against Julken? Blind as she was to his flaws, would she even see the danger? Karan could not take the risk – there were worse things than death.

Maigraith reached into her saddlebags and pulled out a heavy leather bag. She weighed it in her hand, pursed her lips, then drew out another the same size.

"Things are desperate. You're close to losing Gothryme, and Llian will be in the arms of that curly-haired trollop within the week. I'm your only hope." She put the two bags on the kitchen table. "Five hundred gold tells in each. Enough to pay your debts, recapitalise the estate and still have a full bag left over."

Despite her penury, Karan wasn't tempted. It was a struggle to restrain herself from punching Maigraith in the face but she had to stay calm for Sulien's sake.

"How dare you try to buy my daughter?" she said with icy fury.

"What are you talking about?" Maigraith seemed genuinely bewildered. "I want us to be a triune family, and families look after one another."

"How would you know? You never had a proper family."

"All the more reason that I would want one now."

"You're not getting mine." Karan picked up the bags and threw them out the door. "Go, and take your bags of gold with you."

Maigraith picked them up and rode away without a word. Karan had not heard the drumming but she felt sure Maigraith was being affected by it. The summon stone was working on her too.

22

YOU WANT *ME* TO DESTROY THE STONE?

You'll never laugh again.

Why would a nine-year-old boy say such a thing? What irrational expectations had Maigraith given Julken? And what was Karan up to? Llian knew she was hiding something about Maigraith, and it frightened him.

The further he rode the more he became convinced that he was doing the wrong thing. The magiz had not shown her presence since Karan used the disembodiment spell, but she was still trying to get to Sulien. There was nothing he could do to protect either of them, but he should be there. Karan would take on anyone who threatened Sulien, no matter how powerful, and it was going to get her killed.

He could not bear to think about it.

It was ten in the evening when he finally reached Casyme, an untidy town of three thousand surrounded by forested ridges. Shand had moved here a few years ago and it took a while to find his house, which was set on a huge block of land that sloped down into the valley at the rear. The house had curved walls of bluish stone with pale inserts around small leaded windows, a tower on one corner with a conical steeple roof covered in silvery slate, and further back, rising above the clustered ornate chimneys, another tower topped with an onion-shaped dome.

Llian swung down, his knees wobbling as his feet hit the ground. It had been a long and unpleasant day and he wasn't sure what his reception would be, given Shand's prejudice against the Zain. Depending on his mood, Shand could be friendly and the best of company . . . or not.

He shrugged on his pack and headed up the path to the front door. Half a dozen black-faced sheep were asleep on the grass. He knocked on the door. No answer, and the windows were dark.

A long way down the rear yard he made out a small lighted building. He trudged down a path made of irregularly shaped paving stones. The door was closed but the place smelled as if flowers were drying inside. He went up three steps and pulled the door open.

"Shand?" he called cheerfully, looking into a many-sided room with benches running around the walls and a little bed at the rear.

A girl spun around, her mouth falling open in shock. She was slender with a hint of golden tan, silver hair so fine that it drifted with every movement, and wide blue-grey eyes. A glass flask in her left hand was a quarter full of a honey-coloured fluid, and the scent of lemon verbena was overpowering.

"Who are you?" she cried, backing away. She had a bad limp – no, a turned right foot.

"Llian. I'm looking for Shand. Is he away?"

"Llian?" she said, frowning.

A trifle piqued that she had not recognised his name, he added, "I'm a teller. Is Shand about?"

She did not reply. The benchtops were crowded with stills, retorts, crucibles and other equipment, all gleaming. Shand had been making his own wines and distilling spirits for decades. Llian remembered his gellon liqueur with particular favour.

"Are you his housekeeper?" said Llian.

"This is *my* place! And it's really late. Go away."

He retreated, caught his heel and fell backwards down the steps. His arms and legs waved as he struggled to get up with the heavy pack on his back. She stared at him, then, for a second, almost smiled.

"I didn't mean to offend you." He got up, wincing. "I've come a long way, and it's a cold night."

She softened. Evidently making a fool of himself had shown that he wasn't a threat.

"You can wait on the front porch. Shand will be back late."

"What's your name?" said Llian.

"Aviel. Goodnight!" She closed the door in his face.

He unsaddled his horse and led it to a water trough. The porch ran along the left side of the house and around the corner to the front. He sat in one of the cane chairs there, pulled his coat around himself and closed his eyes . . .

Someone was shaking him. "What the devil are you doing out here? Not that you aren't welcome."

Shand's iron-grey hair was greyer than the last time Llian had seen him, and thinner. His eyes were startlingly green in the lantern light.

"The house was locked up. And Aviel—"

"She's a prickly little thing. The key's under the fifth stone to the left of the back door. Come in."

Llian followed Shand through the front door, down a wide

undulating hall panelled to head height in dark wood, and into a large chilly room with a fireplace in each of the four walls. The fireplace to the left was set. Shand lifted the glass of his lantern, touched a scrap of papery bark to the flame and lit the kindling.

He indicated the chairs by the fire. Llian put his load down and sank into the nearest with a sigh. Shand went out, shortly returning with a tray, bread, slabs of cheese, a jar of pickled onions in dark brown vinegar and a jug of black beer. He filled two mugs, touched his to Llian's and said, "To old friendships."

"And happy times," said Llian ironically. "Did you see Tallia?"

Shand frowned. "Yes. What are you doing here?"

Llian filled him in.

Shand's keen eye fixed on him. "And Karan is happy about you helping Thandiwe?"

"Not really. She seems to think . . . "

"I dare say." Shand took a long pull at his beer.

Llian ate half a pickled onion, which was so spicy that sweat broke out on his forehead. "Then Maigraith turned up, with Julken . . . " Llian, remembering that Shand was Maigraith's grandfather, chose his words carefully. "And Karan told me to go at once."

"I haven't seen Maigraith in years," Shand said sadly.

"Why not?"

"Disagreement on the way she was bringing Julken up."

Llian told Shand about the disastrous visit, and Piffle. He just shook his head.

They sat in silence, Llian's worries weighing on him, then he burst out, "Shand, I'm terrified! Karan is planning to go back to Cinnabar."

"And do what?"

"Try to kill the magiz."

Shand choked on his beer. "Then why haven't you stopped her?"

Llian gaped at him. "It's impossible to talk Karan out of anything once she's set her mind to it, as you know very well. But she was lucky to escape last time; she can't do it twice."

"I can imagine how you must be feeling."

"Desperate. Helpless. Sick with dread."

Shand leaned forward. "The best way to help Karan is to find the summon stone, *then destroy it.* That will stop the invasion."

Llian sat back abruptly. "You want *me* to destroy the stone?"

"You've got the skills to discover what the stone is and where it is, and you have Rulke's key."

Which was hidden in a secret compartment in Llian's belt. "What's the key got to do with anything?"

"Do I have to do all your thinking for you?"

Llian tried to pull the fragments together. "The Merdrun hunted the Charon for thousands of years and almost wiped them out."

"Yet Rulke was the only man Gergrig ever feared," Shand prompted.

"So Rulke's secret papers – the Histories of the Charon – are bound to talk about the Merdrun's weaknesses. And perhaps the summon stone." Llian felt a vast weight leave his shoulders. "You're right: this is my job, and I'm going to do it or—"

"Don't say it! This calls for something special."

Shand cracked the wax on an old and dusty bottle, levered out the cork and filled two fresh goblets. He raised his own. "Cheers."

The wine was better than anything Llian had tasted in years. He sipped it in silence.

"I wonder if you might do me a small favour?" said Shand, refilling their goblets.

"Of course," said Llian.

"There's a young lad here in Casyme, seventeen. Fatherless, and his mother is desperately poor, but proud and wants the best for her boy. You know the situation."

"All too well."

"Wilm is a bright lad, and hard-working, but naïve and unworldly. His mother, by taking in washing and scrubbing floors, has scraped a handful of tars together, though not nearly enough to pay for an apprenticeship. Anyway, he thinks he wants to be a chronicler."

"And you'd like me to escort him to Chanthed, to sit the scholarship exam."

"Would you? Wilm never had any hope of rising from his lowly place in life until he did some work in my garden and I mentioned the college, and you." Shand seemed anxious, which was uncharacteristic. "He's desperate to make something of himself and feels that the test is his only chance. Realistically, it probably is."

"The test is brutal and the competition fierce. I'd hate him to spend all his mother's savings if he had no chance."

"So would I," said Shand, "but a man has to make his own way in the world – as you chose to do at the age of twelve, when Mendark came knocking."

It reminded Llian of Mendark the Magister, that great and terrible man, though not as he had been at that time. Rather the way he had looked near the end of his life – like a withered raptor. His nose had shrunk into a beak, his hands to claws and his skin had hung loosely, as if the flesh beneath had dried up. He had been greedy, manipulative and corrupt, yet he had given his all to protect the world he loved, and it had not been enough.

So how could Llian hope to succeed?

"You made quite an impression on Aviel," said Shand as they took breakfast on the front porch, "on your back, legs and arms waving like a stranded tortoise." He chuckled.

"She's not the friendliest person I've ever met. How did she end up here?"

"For a blow-in, you ask an awful lot of questions."

"I'm a chronicler," said Llian.

"I should report you for practising while under a ban."

Llian winced.

"Sorry," said Shand. "You know me – prone to saying what I think."

"I recall a unjust accusation years ago that nearly got me killed."

"And I've apologised. As to Aviel, I took her in."

"A man has to make his way in the world, but not a woman?" said Llian teasingly.

"She was only thirteen then," Shand said gruffly. "And crippled, and she had nowhere to go. She pays the rent on her workshop by making things for me."

"Stuff that needs to be distilled? Grog?"

"You've got a hide!" Shand thundered. "Grog is what the navvies swill in the crumbling wharf city of old Thurkad." Then he smiled. "As well as perfumes, Aviel makes the finest liqueurs and essences, and if you hadn't been in such a hurry you might have tasted some." He looked up. "Ah, here's Wilm now."

He was a hungry-looking lad, taller than average and broad in the shoulder but painfully thin. His brown hair was very short and he had big hands with prominent knuckles. He was dressed in the cheapest of homespun, a little threadbare but made with care, for his clothes fitted him perfectly. A canvas pack sagged off his back. Wilm caught Llian's eye on him as he approached. Wilm looked away, stumbled and almost fell.

"Seems a trifle shy," Llian said quietly. It wasn't a good start for a would-be chronicler.

"Perhaps it's you."

"Me?"

"Wilm loves the Great Tales. And since the day I told him that I happened to know you, he's been in awe." Shand shook his head in mock disbelief. "Clearly, I should have told him *all* about you."

Wilm shuffled up, glanced at Llian then looked down.

Llian stood up and held out his hand. "Hello, Wilm."

Wilm flushed and extended his hand, but so awkwardly that he missed Llian's by a foot. Shand sighed and dragged the lad's hand into Llian's. It lay there for a second or two, limply. Clearly Wilm had never shaken hands before and had no idea how to do it properly. He withdrew his hand as though it had been scalded and looked down at his large feet.

"So you want to be a chronicler?" said Llian.

"Mm," said Wilm. "Make something of myself."

"Would you like some tea?"

"No thanks."

Llian glanced across at Shand, who affected a blank expression, but Llian knew he was enjoying the situation. If the long trip to Chanthed was going to be like this, it would be excruciating.

Gravel crunched on the path and Aviel came round the corner, the sunlight catching in her drifting hair. Her limp was less pronounced this morning. She wore a contraption of wood and wire on her right boot, evidently in the hope of straightening her foot, though judging by her face it was excruciating to walk in.

She came up to Wilm, holding a small package. "You're so brave, going away to make your fortune. I don't suppose we'll ever see each other again, but I wanted you to have this. So you'll always remember where you came from and the people who wished you well."

She handed him the package. She was much smaller than he was, but entirely in command of herself, while Wilm was overcome.

"Thank you," he said at least fifteen times.

She stood up on tiptoe and kissed him on the cheek, then headed back down the path, hardly limping at all though it must have taken a supreme effort. Did she care for Wilm, or was she just being kind? Llian was good at reading people as a rule, but he could not tell.

23

HIS NAÏVETÉ WAS ASTOUNDING

The more Llian probed Wilm on the journey to Chanthed, the clearer it became that he was on a fool's errand.

Naïve as only a child brought up in rustic circumstances could be, he did not have a tenth – not even a hundredth – part of the knowledge required to succeed in the immensely difficult college scholarship test. As a final-year student twelve years ago, Llian had marked hundreds of test papers and listened to dozens of presentations. Only one of those students had gained a scholarship.

"Are you absolutely sure you want to do this?" he said as they crested the last ridge and headed down the long broken slope that would bring them to Chanthed tomorrow morning. "It's a tough test – and expensive."

"It's taken every grint my mother could scrape together," said Wilm. "How can I give up now?"

"There's no point attempting it unless you're confident you'll do well. And no shame in pulling out either."

"I can't pull out," Wilm said desperately. "I may never get another chance."

Because that would be admitting failure, and failure meant returning to Casyme and a life of drudgery? His determination to better himself was touching, and Llian saw echoes of his own life in the lad, though Wilm simply did not know enough.

"There could be a thousand ways of proving yourself. You've got to find the one that's right for you."

"You think I'm not up to it, don't you?"

"No," Llian lied. "But you have to be sure, otherwise you're wasting all your poor mother's savings for nothing."

Wilm jerked convulsively. Clearly, he was terrified that he was going to fail. "I'll work harder than all the other students put together. I've got to succeed!"

But it didn't work like that. Llian stifled his next objection and the one after. As Shand had said, *a man has to make his own way in the world.* And make his own mistakes, no matter how painful.

Wilm's mistakes were going to be very painful and there was not a thing Llian could do. He wondered what the lad would do when the inevitable disaster struck, and whether there would be any pieces left to pick up.

To while away the evenings Llian had been telling an abbreviated version of his *Tale of the Mirror*, and he finished it that night. Afterwards Wilm was silent for a long time. Then he said, "Is that why Shand took Aviel in?"

"How do you mean?" As always after a telling, Llian was in a state of exhilarated exhaustion.

"To cover up her theft of the enchanted gold from Shuthdar's destroyed flute, Yalkara the Charon murdered the only witness, a crippled girl. And much later, because Charon live practically for ever, Shand and Yalkara had a child together. He must have been terribly ashamed when you discovered that the woman he loved had committed such a terrible crime. Do you think he gave Aviel a place of her own as a way of making up for Yalkara's crime against that other crippled girl?"

As Llian lay awake afterwards, staring up at the stars, he began to see Wilm in a new light. Maybe he did have what it took to be a chronicler after all.

"The application fee was five silver tars, but it's gone up to seven," said Wilm, wringing his big-knuckled fingers. "I've got to pay it, but that won't leave anything for food . . . "

He was pacing back and forth in the tiny room Llian had rented in a decrepit three-storey rooming house. It had a dangerous tilt to the left, the roof leaked, everything including the bedding smelled of mould and rats, and the damp patch on the wall, the size and shape of a charging buffalo, was growing by the hour.

Some of the masters – the corrupt ones – are doing very nicely, Anjo Duril had said.

The college was much changed in the time Llian had been away, and not for the better. Unscrupulous masters had taken advantage of the bedridden Wistan's long decline to turn it into a palace of greed. Every student, and every applicant, had to pay until they bled, and every tale had a price now. It firmed Llian's resolution to support Thandiwe. The college urgently needed a vigorous new master.

He had also made several attempts to get an appointment with Wistan, hoping to gain access to the secret archives of the college library, but Wistan would not see him.

"Then there's an interview charge," Wilm went on, "one tar, and robe hire—"

"You don't need robes to do the scholarship test."

"The master in charge said a scholarship winner must look the part. He said I could do the test *dressed like a dung-shovelling hick* . . . but it would count against me by ten per cent. What am I going to do, Llian? These are my best clothes. My mother spent weeks sewing them."

With love and devotion and all the care in the world. As with Wilm's travelling clothes, they fitted him perfectly, but they were made in a rustic style that had gone out of fashion eighty years ago – if, indeed, it had ever been in fashion.

"Do you think I can beat all the other candidates by ten per cent? Please tell me you do, Llian. I've got to."

Wilm leaned towards Llian, his whole body quivering. It was unbearable how much he wanted to win.

"No, Wilm. You can't. Not even by five per cent."

Wilm crumbled but pulled himself together by an effort of will. "Then I'll have to hire the robes. That's another three tars."

"Three tars?" cried Llian. What were they doing to his beloved college? "You used to be able to hire robes for a term for that kind of money."

"That's the charge, and I'll have to pay it."

"Save your money. I'll borrow you a set of robes from one of my old friends."

"Thank you, thank you," cried Wilm. Turning his back on Llian, he took out his wallet and began a dismal count. "Application fee, seven tars; interview fee, one tar; test admission fee, one tar; rent for a week, one tar; food and drink, one tar and ten grints."

Wilm turned around. "That's eleven tars and ten grints! Everything is so expensive here. At home we can live for six weeks, food and rent and everything, for a single tar."

"How much do you have?" said Llian.

"Twelve tars and nine grints. I've got less than a tar left over, and there are bound to be other charges. I haven't got enough, Llian." His voice rose; he looked like a lost little boy. Then all the blood left his face. "I forgot the fee to use the college library – another tar! I've got to pay it too; I've got to study the Histories, but . . . even without paying for the robes, it won't be enough."

"Look, don't worry about the rent."

Wilm stiffened. "I'm a man now and I have to pay my own way. I'll tighten my belt; I can't possibly need one tar and ten grints for food. There must be cheaper places to eat."

"There are," said Llian, "though I wouldn't advise you to frequent them. You're liable to end up with food poisoning." He tried to make light of it. "It won't impress the examiners if you throw up all over them."

Wilm was beyond seeing the funny side of anything. "I've got a strong stomach. I'll be all right." He paced furiously, the sagging floor shaking underfoot. "I can manage it, but there won't be anything left for the trip home – if I fail."

"Forget about the rent. Plenty of people helped me when I was starting out, and when you're rich and famous I'm sure you'll do the same."

"If I start out in debt, I'll never get out of it." Wilm counted his coins again. "I'll get a job. I'm strong and used to hard work."

Llian kept his silence. In a town teeming with students all looking for work to pay the masters' outrageous imposts, work would be hard to find and poorly paid. But maybe Wilm was right. He'd had such a tough life, maybe he could work harder than anyone else.

"You've got to leave time for study, though," said Llian.

"Do you think I need to study that much?"

His naïveté was astounding. "How well do you know the Histories?"

"I went to school until I was twelve. And I've read some of Shand's books."

Llian sighed. Wilm had to be told. "The other candidates will be studying night and day, learning two thousand years of the Histories off by heart. Do you know them that well?"

Wilm's broad shoulders sagged. He lowered himself onto his bed, which groaned under him, and put his head in his hands.

"I'm a stupid yokel, aren't I? If I go for the scholarship it'll take every grint of my mother's savings and there'll be nothing to live on, even if I do win. But from what you say, I've been deluding myself. There's not a hope in the world, is there?"

"I would never say there's no hope," Llian said carefully. "It depends on the examiners. If I was one, I wouldn't be looking for kids who could parrot off a thousand pages of the Histories. I'd be looking for candidates with original ways of thinking."

"Should I take the risk and probably waste all the money? Or abandon my dreams and creep home, to become a miserable muck-shoveller for the rest of my life?"

"I don't know, Wilm."

Wilm's face contorted. Although he was only seventeen and had barely lived, his agony was as real as that of the characters in any tale Llian had ever told.

"You've travelled the world with some of the most important people in the Histories," said Wilm. "Mendark, Rulke, Tensor, Malien, Yggur! You've even *fought* some of them, and survived! You've succeeded at everything you've ever done, and you've written a Great Tale. You're brave and brilliant and generous and wise. Tell me what to do."

Llian's face grew hot. He had done some great things, but he'd also had a lot of disastrous failures. "Wilm, you have to make your own decisions, right or wrong, succeed or fail; that's what being an adult is all about. Besides, I've made a mess of my own life. I'm banned, remember?"

"It'll be overturned," said Wilm with utter confidence. "This time next week you'll be a master chronicler again."

"Maybe," said Llian, thinking about all his other failings. "But you're looking at your life in black and white – either you win the scholarship and become a chronicler, or you fail and go home to nothing. Life's not like that."

"If I fail, there'll be no money for me to train in any other trade."

"Life throws up opportunities all the time and most of them don't require payment – not in money, at any rate." Llian's belly throbbed. What would Thandiwe's real price be? And how far would he go to get the ban overturned? "You have to seize them when they appear, not knowing where they'll lead, but only that they'll take you to places you could never have dreamed of."

Wilm rose, a little unsteady on his feet. The light was back in his eyes. "You're right. I'm going to go for the scholarship – *and win it.*"

"Good for you. And now, if you're all organised, I've got to see Thandiwe."

24

BUT THAT WOULD RUIN
THE COLLEGE

"You've grown hard," said Llian.

He and Thandiwe were sitting on the grassy mound overlooking the main quadrangle of the college, enjoying the unseasonably warm weather.

"Betrayal will do that to you," she said darkly. "In the old days I did everything right; I got to the top by working harder than anyone else, only to have Wistan laugh in my face and cast me down again."

Thandiwe had a tendency to rewrite history. Hard-working she undoubtedly was, though after Llian's banning she had become master-elect because Wistan wanted to humiliate Llian even further. *I raised the least of us to the position of the greatest,* he had said, *to demonstrate that you could never be acceptable.* But the position had lapsed long ago.

"In the meantime," she went on, "the lazy but conniving masters, the corrupt ones and the well connected have all overtaken me. This is my last chance, Llian. I've invested everything in my campaign to become Master of the College, and I'm going to succeed, whatever the cost!"

"What if you fail?"

"I won't!" she said fiercely. "And my first act as master will be to crush and humiliate and utterly destroy that bastard Wistan. I'm sure you'll be delighted to see it."

Llian might have, once, but what would be the point?

She faltered. "When I said I'd invested everything, I meant *everything.* I've called on every friend, every favour, and everyone I know who has any influence." Thandiwe's beautiful face twisted. "It's hard to admit this, especially to you, but I've ... I've even assumed the horizontal position when there was no other way to get a vote. And I've laid out all my savings, and every copper grint I could beg or borrow, in bribes."

"How much have you borrowed?"

"Five hundred and fifty gold tells. So I *have* to win."

Llian rocked backwards; it was a fortune. "How are you going to repay it? A chronicler couldn't earn that much in five lifetimes."

"I can't repay it unless I become Master of the College."

"Have you got the numbers?"

She hesitated. "I've got more than enough promises, though I'd be a fool to count on all of them. Realistically, it's in the balance. If I fail, I'll be bankrupt."

"And a bankrupt can't work at the college."

"I'll end up in debtors' prison until my debts are paid. Which they will never be, obviously." She took his hand. "Llian, if I fail, I'm utterly and irrevocably ruined."

He pulled free. "What are you asking from me?"

"I want your support."

"You've got it."

"And your vote."

"I'm under a ban."

"After seven years, unless a ban is specifically renewed – which it hasn't been – a master chronicler is entitled to vote in all matters concerning the college. Including the election of a new master."

"Really? And in return you'll have my ban overturned?"

"Yes . . . "

"But?" said Llian. "Is there a problem?"

"Not in the least," said Thandiwe. "I'm trying to get you a senior post."

"I thought they were all spoken for."

"Students will flock here to be taught by the first teller in hundreds of years to have a Great Tale. I'm working on funding a new position especially for you – Master of the Tellers."

Llian choked. A senior mastership wasn't even a dream. But until the Merdrun were stopped, the only thing that mattered was finding out about the summon stone.

"And then there's us," she went on.

"Us?" Dread crept over him. Was this what she really wanted?

"Everyone knows you're not happy at Gothryme."

"My personal affairs are none of their business."

"Sorry, I could have put that better." She took his hand again, and Llian heard the sound he had been dreading – a distant drumming. "Llian, loyalty is one of your best features, but haven't you given enough? You're fading away at Gothryme. You've got to follow your calling . . . and I can make you happy too."

The drumming in his head grew louder. Thandiwe had never looked more beautiful, or more desirable. He leaned towards her. They had so much in common. She *could* make him happy, and he had not been happy in a long time.

Thandiwe moistened her lips. Her eyelids quivered.

A searing memory broke through the drumming, Sulien saying, *What does Thandiwe mean by being "nice to her"?*

He sprang up, gasping for breath, and backed away. Under the influence of the drumming he might even have betrayed Karan, but he could not betray his daughter.

"Llian?" she said anxiously.

The drumming was gone. He stumbled ten steps to the edge of the mound and stared across the dusty plains, despising himself. Was he really that weak?

And how dare she? In one breath Thandiwe was whining about her own betrayal, and the next she was asking him to betray Karan and Sulien. But she was offering more than his one vote and his tarnished reputation could possibly be worth. Why? All he saw in her eyes was the hard and desperate woman she had become.

"Llian, talk to me."

Her position must be precarious, and if she was going to fail, her offer was worthless. Indeed, since she had laid out a fortune in bribes already, being publicly associated with her could destroy his chances of getting the ban overturned. But if he turned her down he would make an enemy for life – and what if she became master after all?

"I'd better go," he said. "You've given me a lot to think about."

She looked dismayed. "What about your vote? I can count on it, can't I?"

"I'll let you know."

"I can sweeten the offer a bit more."

"I'm not out for everything I can get, Thandiwe."

He left her sitting there and headed down to the main street, shaken and chastened. He was far too susceptible to the drumming. He had to fight it *before* it sounded or he would never summon the willpower to resist it.

The streets were crowded. The next term was about to begin and Chanthed was full of students new and old. They did not recognise him, but many of the stallholders and innkeepers did, and most greeted him cheerfully.

But as he continued, his mood darkened. How had Thandiwe borrowed such a gargantuan sum? The stipend of a master chronicler was only five or six gold tells a year. Who would lend her a hundred years' salary on no collateral?

Only someone who expected to be repaid many times over. But how?

As far as Llian knew, Master of the College wasn't a highly paid position either, though there could be perks he did not know about. Who would know? He headed into the college and down to the purser's office. It was highly unlikely that Old Sal would still be there; she had been talking about retiring the last time he had popped in to see her, four years ago. But she had treated him well even when his so-called friends had fallen away, and she had been the purser's clerk as long as Wistan had been master.

He approached the counter. A plump, matronly woman frowned at him.

"I'm looking for Old Sal," said Llian. "I was a student here years ago, and I say hello whenever I'm in Chanthed. Though I suppose she's retired or . . . " He did not want to say "died'"

"Name?"

"Llian."

Her heavy eyebrows rose. "Not the Llian who told the *Tale of the Mirror* . . . "

"And was banned by Wistan. Yes, that's me."

"She retired two years ago."

"Oh!" said Llian. "Well, thank you anyway."

She smiled. "Sal still comes in to help out from time to time. She . . . um, knows where the bodies are buried." She held out her hand. "I'm Haience, her granddaughter. She often speaks of you. She's having lunch in the purser's courtyard."

Llian followed Haience down a series of narrow, high-ceilinged corridors, then out into a bright little courtyard paved with yellow sandstone flagstones. An ancient twisted jacaranda tree shaded the far corner and the table beneath it, where a tiny bird-like woman was bent over a yard-long journal.

"You have a visitor, Grandma."

Old Sal looked up, squinting at her. Her gaze shifted to Llian, then she smiled. "Master Llian, and as handsome as ever. What a sight for an old lady."

"I'll bring you some chard," said Haience and went inside.

Llian shook Sal's claw-like hand and sat. "How are you, Sal?"

"Shrinking and wrinkling a little more each year, but the figures still add up. How are things in . . . Gothryme, isn't it?"

"A terrible drought."

"But great blessings," said Sal. "The lovely Karan. Such beautiful red hair." Sal ruffled her feathery locks, a sparse white cap over her small head. "She hasn't cut it?"

"It goes halfway down her back. And Sulien—"

"We met last time you were here. A sweet child." She looked up at him over that beak of a nose. Her eyes were small and bird-like but intense. "Are you here for the election?"

"In a way."

Should he tell her? Thandiwe's candidacy was a matter of public knowledge, as were the enormous sums the candidates were spending on their campaigns. The townsfolk, Llian knew, strongly disapproved. He was prepared to bet that Sal did not like it either.

"I hadn't realised I was allowed to vote, but apparently I can, and Thandiwe Moorn has asked me to support her."

"Are you going to?"

"I haven't decided yet."

Haience returned with a tray, a pot of the yellow tea called chard, two cups and a plate of square biscuits filled with small green nuts.

When she had gone, Llian added, "I'm worried about what I'd be getting myself into."

"You should be." Sal turned her head, studying him. "Why don't you run for the mastership?"

He stared at her. "I'm banned."

"There's nothing in the rules that says you can't run."

"It's too late, the vote's in two days. And I don't have any money."

"You have a name." She poured the chard, the heavy pot shaking a little in her hand.

Llian nibbled on a biscuit. "How much does the Master of the College earn?"

She blew on her chard. "A lot more than a purser's clerk, but it's no fortune. Fifteen gold tells a year."

The interest on Thandiwe's debt had to be at least fifty tells a year, maybe a hundred, depending how desperate she had been. Even if she became master, the debt could never be repaid – not legally.

"Suppose an unscrupulous master is elected, or a corrupt one?" said Llian. "Would there be ways for them to make more money from the college?"

"Unfortunately."

"What kinds of ways?"

"It has a lot of property that could be sold cheaply to cronies. Not to mention priceless books and other treasures that collectors would pay a fortune for."

"Such as Cumulus Snoat."

Her beady eyes flickered. "An unscrupulous master could also double the fees or sell passes, honours and masterships to the highest bidder."

"But that would ruin the college!" he cried.

"Which you and I and old Wistan love. The master and *her* cronies would bleed it dry, and the college would not recover in a hundred years."

"The fees are already too high." Llian told Sal about Wilm's experience.

"I can't bear what those masters are doing to this place," said Sal.
He drank his chard in a single gulp and leaned back.

"Have I helped with your decision?" said Sal.

"Very much."

It was worse than he had thought. How could he support Thandiwe
now? But what if he did not, and she became master anyway? She did
not take rejection well.

"I'm damned either way," he said. "But thank you." He took her
small blue-veined hand and kissed it. "For everything."

On the way out a darker possibility occurred to him. If the new
master gained Wistan's dirt book, he or she could use it to extort for-
tunes from the people named in it. Or sell their secrets to criminals,
blackmailers or business rivals.

Maybe that was what Thandiwe's banker was really after.

25

HOW WILL YOU PAY IT BACK?

The scholarship examination was tomorrow and Llian could see that
Wilm was panicking. He was hunched in the corner, surrounded
by books on the Histories and dozens of pages of scrawled notes. He
snatched up a page, read it then closed his eyes and tried to repeat it
back.

"Aarrgh!" he cried, stumbling to a halt after a few sentences.

He flung the page down and grabbed another, with the same result.
He was sweating and his eyes were shiny, and he was breathing so
rapidly that Llian would not have been surprised had he passed out.

"I can't do it!" Wilm's voice cracked. "I've really tried, Llian, but the
words won't stay in my mind. A master chronicler has to be able to read
a thing twice, then remember it perfectly. You can do that, can't you?"

"Yes," said Llian. "But I had sixteen years of training."

"I'm going to fail. They'll laugh me off the stage."

"The examiners are professionals; they wouldn't think of doing such a thing. And you certainly won't be the worst they've seen. Why, I remember—"

It was the wrong thing to say. "I won't win though, will I? *I've got to win, Llian!*"

All Llian's coaching since they had left Casyme, and all his carefully reasoned arguments, had been forgotten. Wilm had reverted to the terrified rustic he'd been when they met. Llian felt for the lad, but he did not see what anyone could do about it.

He sat on his bed. "Have there been any messages for me?"

"What?" said Wilm. "Oh yes. Three. All from Thandiwe." He waved a hand at the grubby pillow on Llian's bed.

He lifted the pillow and found three envelopes. Llian broke the seals and read them one by one. They were increasingly urgent versions of the same message.

Where are you? The vote is TOMORROW! I've told everyone that you're supporting me but you've got to CONFIRM it to all my other supporters IN PERSON. Come and see me as soon as you get this. DON'T let me down, Llian. I'm a good friend but a BAD ENEMY.

The enemy part he understood. The friend he was still in two minds about, and the threat was as clear as a diamond. He showed Wilm the final note. They had already discussed Llian's dilemma. He saw it as a contribution to the lad's education.

"What am I going to do, Wilm?"

"You'll do the right thing. You would never do anything else."

If only he knew how many times Llian had done the wrong thing, and known he was doing it.

"But what is the right thing? Thandiwe is clever and hard-working and decisive; she's good with people, knows her own mind and isn't afraid to make hard decisions. She could make a fine Master."

"But is she honest?" said Wilm.

"I don't know that she's *dis*honest."

"Will she do her best for the college – or will she be out for what she can get?"

Llian shrugged. "But if I turn her down and she becomes master anyway, she could destroy me."

"If that's the kind of person she is, you shouldn't be voting for her."

"What if I turn her down and someone really bad becomes master?"

Wilm was breathing heavily again. Llian wasn't sure his own dilemma was helping. Or maybe it was – inner torment featured heavily in the Great Tales.

"And there's another thing, maybe the most important of all," he added.

"How could anything be more important than saving the college?" said Wilm.

"What if doing the right thing by the college means doing the wrong thing by my family?" said Llian. "With war coming—"

"Family always comes first," said Wilm.

"So you think I should support Thandiwe?"

Wilm leaped up, roaring, "I don't know and I don't care! I can't think. *I can't do this!*" He threw himself face down on his bed. "I'll have to creep home and work in that stinking tannery for the rest of my life. And Aviel, my only friend, won't want to know me because you can never wash the stink off."

It shocked Llian out of his self-obsession. What a thoughtless oaf he'd been, laying his burden on Wilm when he most needed calm and quiet.

"I'm sorry, Wilm. You asked me for advice the other day and I didn't give it to you, but now I will. You've come too far to turn back. Finish your studying and have an early night, then go to the scholarship test in the morning with a clear head and the knowledge that, whatever happens, you've done your best. That's all your mother can ask of you, and Aviel too, and if that's not good enough she's not a true friend."

"She *is* a true friend!" Wilm cried. "We've been friends since I was four and she was two."

"Then you've nothing to worry about, have you?"

Wilm sat up and rubbed furiously at his red eyes. "Thank you. I'll never forget how you've put yourself out to help someone you don't even know."

"Plenty of people have helped me." Llian turned away but swung back. "I'm off to see Thandiwe, and I still don't know what I'm going to say to her, but whatever happens it's going to be bad. I'll see you in the morning to wish you well."

As he went out, his racing heartbeat was an echo of the drumming that could ruin him. His stomach was cramping. He had never been good with confrontations, and if he refused to support Thandiwe it would be as bad as it could get. And what if she used her wiles on him again, and the drumming sounded? He had to keep her at a distance; he dared not allow himself to get too close. He rehearsed how to deal with her as he headed up the hill to her house but felt no better when he got there.

Had he not known about her prodigious debt he would have thought she had done very well for herself. Her home was a three-storey timber extravagance in the overly ornate old Chanthed style – a profusion of turrets and cupolas with carved demons, goblins and other mythical creatures leering from every alcove.

To support Thandiwe or let her down? Oh, to be able to work again, and know that his telling had held his audience enthralled from beginning to end. No small thing that.

His mind was made up. He would give Thandiwe his vote and his public support. The ban would be lifted and he would search out the secret of the summon stone. He had less than six weeks.

Llian knocked on her front door. While he waited, he worked out the numbers. There could never be any more than sixty-four masters, but three positions were currently vacant and the three candidates were not allowed to vote, though Wistan was. That left fifty-eight, counting Llian. To be elected, one master had to receive a majority of the votes, thirty or more. If no candidate received a majority, the one with the lowest number of votes was eliminated and a new round of voting began. In the event of a tie, Wistan had a casting vote.

Thandiwe opened the door and her face lit up when she saw him. "You came! I knew you would." She studied his face. "I do have your vote, don't I?"

Was he doing the right thing, or was this the most disastrous decision of his life?

"You look troubled," said Thandiwe.

He stepped into a long but narrow hall with dark panelling to shoulder height and pale lining boards above that. He could hear a crowd of people talking in a room at the back. There was a small cloakroom to his left. He drew Thandiwe into it. Mistaking his intention, she extended her arms.

"The debt," said Llian. "How can you pay it back when the master only earns fifteen tells a year?"

She lowered her arms. "There are other sources of income. Look, what does it matter? Your ban will be deemed unjust and you'll be compensated. Plus you'll have your career back, and a senior mastership."

"I've got to know, Thandiwe. In all conscience, I can't—"

"All right!" she hissed. "There are some ancient coins in the library, so old that no one knows where they came from. The eleventh master brought them back from a trip across the Western Ocean untold centuries ago. A private collector wants them, and they don't belong in the library anyway, so I told him he could have them in return for funding my campaign. But that's all. I've spent eighteen years of my life here, and I would never do anything to harm this place."

"Promise?"

"Yes, I promise. Do I have your vote?"

He nodded stiffly.

She beamed and threw her arms around him and kissed him on the mouth, and it was not the kiss of one old friend to another. Llian pulled away, scrubbing at his mouth with the back of his hand, but she was in such a state of euphoria she did not notice.

She led him back into the hall. "Come and meet everyone."

"Have you got the numbers?"

"Counting you, I've got thirty-four promises – four more than I need. So even if a couple turn their coats at the last minute I'll still be over the line."

Llian followed, wrestling with his conscience. The other candidates were Candela Twism, aggressively ambitious and probably honest, but lazy and of dubious intellect, and Basible Norp, a master Llian had never met. A fine chronicler, Llian had heard, but not good with people.

Should he or shouldn't he? Despite the loss of the old coins, Llian felt sure Thandiwe would be the best for the college. And unquestionably this was the best for Sulien, Karan and his quest to destroy the stone. So why was he still agonising?

She led him into a large double dining room. The tall doors across the middle had been folded back and the room was crowded with people.

"Press the flesh for a few minutes," said Thandiwe. "I've got to change."

"I thought you were in a hurry."

"But you're here now."

Llian moved into the room, greeting the masters by name. They were surprisingly friendly; he'd been led to believe that they disliked him and wanted the ban made permanent, but most of them complimented him on his Great Tale and a few said they looked forward to his joining them as a senior master.

Someone pressed a drink into his hand, a delicate etched-glass goblet filled with a pale fizzing wine. He took a sip and it was delicious. He looked up, into the cold eyes of Anjo Duril.

"You bastard," Llian said in a low voice. "Where's my book?"

"I sold it to Cumulus Snoat."

"I bet you made a handsome profit on the deal."

"I paid you what *I* thought it was worth."

"Three copper grints!" Llian called him every unprintable name he could think of, and threw in a few made-up ones for good measure.

Anjo's cold smile tightened. "And Snoat paid me what *he* thought it was worth. Five hundred and fifty gold tells."

Thandiwe wafted by in a gown that emphasised her voluptuous figure. "I see you've met my most valued supporter." She bestowed a winning smile on Anjo, who favoured her with a slightly warmer version of his glacial smile, and she continued.

Her *most valued supporter.* The coincidence of amounts, five hundred and fifty gold tells, was unlikely to be any such thing.

"So you're Thandiwe's banker," said Llian. "What are your intentions?"

"I merely serve."

"Serve who?"

"Snoat has been supporting my career for more than a decade. Now it's time to pay him back." Anjo's smile broadened. He was laughing at Llian.

Llian felt a sharp pain at the base of his thumb and looked down to see a shard of etched glass embedded there – he'd crushed the bowl of his goblet. Its contents was fizzing on the floor, his blood dripping onto the puddle and turning it pink. He pulled the shard out, put the broken glass on the nearest table and wrapped a napkin around his hand.

Duril was still grinning. Llian fought an urge to punch him in the throat. He went out. Snoat was behind Anjo Duril, and Llian knew precisely what Snoat wanted. To conquer Meldorin and plunder its treasures for his personal collection. But he was undermining the west when it most needed to be united against the Merdrun.

"What's the matter?" Thandiwe's hand was on his arm.

"Squeezed one of your goblets a bit hard. Sorry."

"I couldn't give a damn about the goblets. Come on."

She led him back in and up to the front, onto a low dais. She grimaced at sight of his bloody hand, tossed the napkin away and knotted a fresh one over the cut. She tapped a spoon against the bowl of a goblet until it rang out.

"Masters," she said in a voice equally ringing. "My last supporter, but not the least. Llian of the Great Tale, the *Tale of the Mirror*."

She put down the goblet and picked up two full ones, handing one to Llian. Thandiwe raised her goblet. "To Llian and the success of my campaign to become the seventy-fifth Master of the College of the Histories."

Everyone raised their goblets. Llian did not.

"Llian!" she hissed. "What's the matter?"

"Anjo Duril is your banker."

"So what?"

"And you know who's behind him."

"There's no one behind him."

But Thandiwe could not meet his eyes, and this confirmed his resolve. He could not be a part of it. The price was too high.

The assembled masters were waiting for him to say the words that would make her win certain. Anjo was at the front, smiling, and Llian wanted to smash his teeth in.

"See Anjo Duril there?" said Llian.

"What are you doing?" cried Thandiwe.

He shook her off. "He put up all the money for this campaign – five hundred and fifty gold tells! How can you repay such a sum?"

The masters were staring at him in consternation, muttering to one another and shaking their heads.

"It's not true," cried Thandiwe. "It's . . . not . . . true."

"There's only one way such a sum can be repaid," said Llian. "By plundering our beloved college – or debauching it."

"Anjo is a good man," said Thandiwe desperately.

"But Duril's master is Cumulus Snoat," said Llian. "Isn't he?"

He expected Duril to deny it, and Llian's first hint that things were going terribly wrong came when Duril did not.

"I owe Cumulus everything," said Anjo, "and I'm determined to repay him."

"You're saying that you'll control the new master, and Snoat will be telling you what to do."

"That's not precisely how I would describe our relationship. But the essence is correct."

"And we know what Snoat will do to the college," said Llian. "He'll plunder it, debauch it and, ultimately, destroy it." He raised his voice. "So I won't be giving Thandiwe my vote, and I urge you, all of you, not to give her yours either."

"You utter bastard!" shrieked Thandiwe. She hurled herself at Llian, slapping and punching and kicking and screaming. "I'm going to utterly destroy you." She took a deep breath, then turned to the masters, who were staring at her in shocked disbelief. "He's a liar and a cheat. I've heard rumours that he faked parts of his so-called Great Tale, and if I should be elected Master of the College I'll be doing my best to make his ban permanent."

She took a desperate, gasping breath, then forced a smile. "Get out!" she hissed.

Llian wavered his way towards the front door. He had blown all hope of getting the ban overturned, for nothing! What was Karan going to say?

The only person not upset was Anjo Duril. He was grinning like a fairground clown. The sick feeling in Llian's stomach churned into an all-consuming dread. Had he just made the worst blunder of his life?

Had he done exactly what Duril and Snoat wanted?

26

THANK YOU FOR CORRECTING ME

Llian had promised to wish Wilm well for the test but he had not come back, and Wilm was worried. Had things gone really bad with Thandiwe? She was desperate to get the mastership; was she desperate enough to harm Llian if he turned her down?

Wilm put on the clothes his mother had sat up late for many nights to make, working by the feeble glimmer of rush lights because they could not afford candles. He donned the dark green student's gown and cap Llian had borrowed for him and felt a momentary pride. He was a student at the College of the Histories, even if only for the day.

The gown was threadbare and none too clean, and had an unpleasant mouldy smell. He should have washed it. Too late now.

Seven o'clock and Llian still had not turned up. It was a bad omen. Wilm could not wait any longer because the doors of the Great Hall, where the test was held, would be locked at eight sharp, and any student not inside by then missed out.

He trudged down the street, going over all the facts he had tried to cram into his unwilling head over the past week. At whose behest had Shuthdar made the Golden Flute that had turned the Three Worlds upside down? Had he made it for Rulke, or Tensor the Aachim, or was it Pitlis? Why had Shuthdar stolen it, and what precisely was the Forbidding that he had brought down over the world when he destroyed it? Was the Clysm part of the Forbidding or a separate event? How many times had the great Magister Mendark renewed his own life – ten times, thirteen or twenty-two?

The list of questions the examiners might ask was endless. Wilm had known the answers yesterday but this morning his mind was as empty as a lost sock. What was the point of going on and throwing good coin after bad? If he pulled out now, at least he would save the admission fee. One tar would be more than enough to get him home. If he camped out most nights and only ate bread, he might get home with most of the tar intact. He might have failed but he would not be completely empty-handed. That mattered, now that he had given up hope of winning.

Each candidate was questioned on stage in front of all the other candidates, and he had never been good at performing before an audience. He became flustered and forgot things he knew perfectly. It would be worse with all those strangers judging him.

He almost turned back. He would have, save that he could not bear to see the disappointment on his mother's face when he confessed that all her savings had been wasted. Turning back would prove he didn't have the guts to stick to anything. What would she think of him then?

Wilm reached the entrance of the Great Hall half an hour early and was dismayed to see dozens of candidates there already. A few unfortunates were not wearing robes but the majority were, and they were all better than his. Still, he was used to that. Back home he had always been the poorest at any gathering, and his clothes the cheapest, the most worn and mended. He joined the line.

"Hello," he said to the girl ahead of him. "Where are you from?"

She was tall, and her gown was crisply ironed and edged with pure white lace. She looked him up and down, wrinkled her nose and turned away. A flush burned its way up his cheeks. She had judged him in a glance and dismissed him as unworthy of a single word. If, by some miracle, he did win the test, was the college full of rich snobs who would spurn him because he was poor and came from a tiny place no one had ever heard of?

Damn them all! What did it matter what anyone thought? He would show them.

The line inched forward. Two people were on the door – a handsome young man with swept-back wavy brown hair – a senior student, Wilm presumed – and a little old lady with a beaky nose, beady little eyes and feathery white hair. She was entering names and payments into a ledger half as long as she was tall.

"Name," said the student briskly.

"Wilm."

"Wilm who?"

"Tomyd. Wilm Tomyd. From Casyme. That's in Bannador."

"That'll be one tar."

The old lady looked up. "Wilm? You came here with Llian."

"Yes," said Wilm, wondering how could she possibly have heard his humble name.

"How do you come to know him?"

"I ... I've done some work for an old friend of his. A man called Shand."

"The legendary Recorder?" said the handsome student in astonishment.

"I just know him as Shand," said Wilm.

The student whistled. He looked Wilm up and down, taking in his gown and rustic clothes but evidently forming a different impression to the tall snooty girl.

"Isn't there provision to waive the admission fee in deserving circumstances?" he said to the old lady.

"Indeed." She smiled at Wilm and put a mark beside his name. "No charge."

The student put out his hand. "Good luck!"

"Thank you." Wilm shook it in a daze, then turned for the door.

"Wilm?" said the student. "If you don't win, don't think it's the end of the world. I took the test every year for five years and never even got close to winning. But then, as Old Sal here would tell you—"

"Stanzer is a scandalously lazy boy," said Old Sal, though affectionately.

"Wouldn't do a day's work to save my life." Stanzer waved Wilm through.

The unexpected kindness gave him a surge of confidence. He passed into an ancient hall with a high triple-vaulted timber ceiling supported on intricately carved beams. He gazed at it in wonder. Several hundred chairs had been set up, facing a stage at the far end. Half of the chairs were already occupied.

He counted the occupants. A hundred and sixty-one, and more boys and girls were streaming in all the time. Some were his age but many looked younger – some as young as eleven or twelve. Were they all competing for the one scholarship? If they were, it was hopeless.

The doors were closed. Three black-robed masters appeared on the stage, along with Stanzer, who carried Old Sal's huge ledger, and another student, a young blonde woman with curly hair and a broad, smiling mouth. The masters sat at the main table and the two students at a smaller side table, the volume open in front of them. Wilm stared at the master on the right, a lean, cold-eyed fellow with a pair of waxed moustaches that stuck out six inches to either side of his cheeks like black knitting needles.

"The examination begins," said the master in the middle, in a reedy voice that barely carried to Wilm. He was a tiny little chap with a bald, pointy head. "The names will be called in random order. Xix, Dajaes?"

A short girl stood up in the front row, stumbled over the hem of a robe that was too big for her and almost fell. She looked as though she was trapped in a tent. She climbed the five steps to the stage, bowed to the masters and stood with her hands folded in front of her, trembling visibly.

"What are the Forty-Nine Chrighms of Calliat?" said the master on the left, a statuesque woman with dark skin and iron-grey hair that stuck out in all directions.

"The Forty-Nine C-chrighms of Calliat," said the girl, "are a series of linked enigmas and p-p-paradoxes so complex that – that, more than th-thirteen hundred years after Calliat's death, only one has been solved." She bowed again and waited.

"Silly girl's learned it from an old textbook," said a boy to Wilm's left.

Wilm felt a surge of panic. The books he'd been able to get hold of had all been ancient.

"Wrong!" said the master who had asked the question. "The triune called Maigraith solved twenty-seven of them brilliantly, over a decade ago."

The girl's pale face crumpled. She bowed, said, "Thank you for correcting me," and headed back to her seat.

Was that it? They only got one question each? How could the examiners decide so quickly?

"Rebt, Norbing," called the master in the middle.

A large stocky boy hobbled onto the stage, supporting himself on a walking stick.

"What is the Gift of Rulke?"

"A stigmata on the Zain that—"

"Wrong! The Gift of Rulke, also called the Curse of Rulke, was knowledge given by Rulke to the Zain in ancient times, enhancing their resistance to the mind-breaking spells of the Aachim. The stigmata merely identified a Zain as having the Gift."

The boy hobbled away, fighting back tears. And so it continued for hour after hour as the morning passed, then the afternoon. The tall girl who had snubbed Wilm only managed half a sentence before she was judged wrong. She let out a cry of anguish, ran from the stage without thanking her examiner and slumped in her chair, weeping. Wilm took no pleasure in her downfall; he only prayed that he could do better.

Outside the light faded; within the hall more lamps were lit. In all that time almost every student had been judged wrong. The judges had said "Correct!" only five times.

Only five to beat, Wilm thought. So far! He had been keeping count of the candidates as they went up. Two hundred and sixty-six had been tested, and there were only three hundred and three in the room. It must be his turn soon. Please, let it be his turn. He was hungry and thirsty and exhausted, and it felt as though his brains were leaking out of his head. If he had to wait much longer he doubted if he would be able to remember his own name.

And please, let it not be the cold-eyed master with the waxed black moustaches. He had not said "Correct" once.

"Tomyd, Wilm!" said the master with the black moustaches.

Wilm started, let out an audible gasp, then scrambled to his feet. He could do this. He just had to clear his mind and answer the question. Wilm tried to visualise the judge saying that crisp, beautiful "Correct!"

It was a hundred miles up to the stage, and all the way he could feel the eyes of the other candidates on him, judging him for his threadbare and mouldy gown. Heat was rising to his face and he could not stop it; he felt so self-conscious he hardly knew what he was doing and, hurrying up the last step, he caught the toe of his boot and fell flat on his face in front of the judges.

Laughter rippled through the assembled students. Wilm got up. Could things get any worse? He had to say something.

He bowed to the judges and said, with a confidence that astonished him, "At least I fell into good company."

Only the statuesque master with the iron-grey hair smiled, and barely, but it was something.

The master with the black moustaches did not smile. His cold eyes smouldered and his thin lip was curled. "Recite the second paragraph of the *Tale of the Forbidding*."

And Wilm knew it! He could not believe his luck. Llian had told him his own version on the way from Casyme.

"Which version of the tale?" he said. "There are several."

His questioner looked startled. He turned to the other two examiners. The woman nodded. Was that a good sign, or a bad?

"The most recent one," said the master with the black moustaches.

It could be a trick question, but Wilm had to go with what he knew. He began, and as he did Llian's telling flowed into his mind. He looked out into the audience and fixed on one particular face, the girl in the front row who had been called first. He spoke as though he was a teller, telling her the tale as best he knew.

In ancient times Shuthdar, a smith of genius, was summoned from Santhenar by Rulke, a mighty Charon prince of Aachan. And why had Rulke undertaken such a perilous working? He would move freely among the worlds, and perhaps the genius of Shuthdar could open the way. So Shuthdar laboured and made that forbidden thing, an opening device, in the form of a golden flute. Its beauty and perfection surpassed even the dreams of its maker – the flute was more precious to him than anything he had ever made. He stole it, opened a gate and fled back to Santhenar. But Shuthdar made a fatal mistake. He broke open the Way Between the Worlds.

Wilm finished, and bowed, and knew that he had it word perfect, exactly as Llian had told it to him. He had done his very best, and surely it had to give him a chance. The master would say, "Correct!" He must!

"Wrong!" said the master with the black moustaches. "That is indeed the second paragraph of the tale, as told by Llian at the Graduation Telling on the seventeenth day of Thisto in the year 3098. However it is not the *most recent* version. It was told by Vizoria Di-lini at the Graduation Telling last year, where she changed 'broke open' to the more correct 'tore open'."

Wilm was crushed. How could anyone be expected to know that? He turned, tears starting in his eyes, then turned back and bowed. "Thank you for correcting me."

One of the students sniggered, and to his mortification Wilm realised that his nose was running. Having no handkerchief, he had to wipe it on the back of his hand, which provoked laughter in a dozen places. He fled the stage, trying to retain his dignity, but had to wipe his eyes, and then his streaming nose again, before he got back to his seat.

This humiliation wiped out the triumph he should have felt after having done the very best he could. But one thing was absolutely clear – Llian, his hero, had made it all possible, and Wilm did not see how he could ever thank him enough.

27

YOU PASSED A TEST

After "betraying" Thandiwe, Llian was too agitated to sleep, and reluctant to disturb Wilm on the night before his test. Going to a tavern was the most appealing option but he needed a clear head more than anything. Besides, he was going to need every grint now.

He paced the empty streets for hours in a chilly, misting rain. Had he ruined everything on a matter of principle? He had certainly destroyed any hope of having the ban overturned. If Thandiwe became master he was finished. And if she did not, what he had done would not endear him to the other two candidates. In their eyes he had betrayed a friend, so how could he be trusted?

Forget her, the mastership and everything else. It didn't matter now. Only his quest was important, and he could not waste any more time. He had to break into the secret archives of the library right now, search them for any mention of the Merdrun and the summon stone, then go after it.

The decision came as a great relief. He had been too focused on doing things the right way, but with his career in ruins, what did he have to lose?

It was long after midnight and he was striding down to the college when a hand caught his arm. Thinking he was being attacked, Llian tried to pull free, but the huge old fellow who had hold of him did not let go. He wore sandals and a scarlet-and-blue kilt, and the street lamp illuminated a bald head.

"Who are you?" cried Llian.

"I'm Bufo, captain of the college guard for as long as Wistan is around. The hour he goes, I go too."

He released Llian's bicep. Llian rubbed it; the captain's grip was as hard as a pipe wrench.

"Come, Wistan wants to see you without delay."

"But . . . it must be two in the morning."

"It's gone half past three," said Bufo. "You've tried to see him four times in the past week. Are you saying you don't want to see him?"

"Of course I do. Er, how is he?"

"He doesn't expect to live another week."

"I'm sorry to hear that."

"No, you're not. You always loathed him."

"It's true we were never the best of friends. But that was a long time ago."

Bufo did not reply to this absurd statement, but led him through the college gates and down to Wistan's rooms. Fires glowed in grates on either side of his small sitting room, which had teetering stacks of books and papers on every surface and was unpleasantly hot. Llian took off his wet coat and hung it on the stand.

"I've brought Master Llian," said the captain.

"Thank you," said a rasping voice from the darkness on the far side of the room. "Open a bottle of the Uncibular fifty-six, would you? Bring three glasses."

Bufo indicated a shapeless armchair, so old that the leather was criss-crossed with cracks. The colour might once have been purple, brown or even blue. Llian sat; the seat felt as though it was stuffed with cobblestones. Bufo disappeared into the darkness.

Something squeaked and creaked and he reappeared, pushing Wistan in a wheeled chair that dwarfed his puny body. He had been an ugly baby, an even uglier young man and a grotesque old man. As an ancient, he was undoubtedly the most hideous living creature Llian had ever set eyes upon.

Wistan had a small, oddly shaped head on a remarkably long and scrawny neck off which his loose skin hung in wrinkled folds. His face was dish-shaped, as if someone had put a hand across it and pushed the middle inwards, but the dish narrowed at the top and flared out to a lantern of a jaw at the bottom. His lips, the only fleshy part of him, were thick and grey, his eyes small and bulging, and his flat-topped head was as bald as a basalt boulder.

Wistan's body, which had always been spindly, had withered to skin and gristle. No wonder he could barely stand up, there was less muscle on him than on the lower leg of a chicken.

"Goodnight, Master Wistan," said Llian, rising from his chair.

Wistan grunted. "A better night for me than you."

Llian did not wonder about that. Wistan knew everything. He always had.

Wistan looked around. "It's damned cold. Where are my blankets?"

Bufo wrapped a pair of charcoal-coloured blankets around Wistan up to the neck, leaving his stick arms out. The captain laid a second blanket across his meagre lap.

"You want the ban lifted?" Wistan continued.

"Yes," said Llian.

From the corner of an eye Llian saw Bufo lever out a cork. He sniffed it, put it to one side, then slowly poured the red-brown wine into a decanter, swirled it several times and filled three glasses. He handed one to Wistan, gave Llian the second and took the third for himself.

"Thank you," said Llian, savouring the aroma of the fifty-five-year-old wine.

"To our beloved college," said Wistan, raising his glass. His arm shook.

Llian and Bufo echoed him. Llian took a small sip. The wine was sublime.

"To business," said Wistan.

Llian couldn't see what business they could have together, but he was prepared to eke out the moment as long as the bottle lasted.

"You passed a test tonight," said Wistan.

"I didn't know I was doing – Oh! At Thandiwe's place. How did you hear about that?"

"Two of the masters in the room are mine. I knew Thandiwe was ambitious but I hadn't realised her corruption had gone so far. Five hundred and fifty gold tells! That was a fine bit of sleuthing. How did Anjo get that kind of money?"

"From me," Llian said bitterly.

Wistan's dung-coloured eyebrows crawled up his pallid forehead. "I heard Gothryme was——"

"The bastard stole my manuscript of the *Tale of the Mirror* and sold it to Snoat."

"And this was the reason you decided to betray your old friend?"

"No! I'd planned to support Thandiwe, reluctantly, until I discovered that Anjo was Snoat's man. If she was elected, he would control the college, and when he finished there would be nothing left of it. I wasn't happy about her cronies' plan to blacken your name either."

"I would have thought you'd be delighted." Wistan took a thoughtful sip.

"Well, I'm not sure we'll ever be friends—"

Wistan's laughter was a crow choking on an over-large frog. "You hate my guts."

Llian considered the matter. "Time heals." He studied his glass, which was empty. "And the wine has a mellowing influence."

"Bufo, that's a hint to top his glass up."

It had not been, but Llian wasn't going to complain. Bufo filled it generously.

"The college made me what I am," said Llian. "I could not see it ruined."

"Even at the cost of ruining your career and failing your family?"

"If Thandiwe became master, I felt the college's ruin was certain."

"What about your quest to find the summon stone and destroy it?"

"How do you know that?"

"A skeet came from Shand, asking me to aid you."

"I need access to the secret archives."

"You'll have it in the morning." Wistan studied his glass. "I've often regretted banning you, you know. We've become too safe, too pedestrian, too rule-bound. No wonder yours is the only Great Tale in hundreds of years. We need to take risks and make allowances, don't we, Bufo?"

Bufo sipped his wine dreamily. "I just guard the gates, Master."

"You've had nine and a half years to reconsider," said Llian frostily. "I wrote to you many times after the seven years was up."

"The Master of the College can impose a ban," said Wistan, "but it takes a two-thirds majority of the staff to lift it. Over a third of the masters have always opposed it. Including Thandiwe."

"Thandiwe blocked me?" said Llian, stunned.

"Every time it came up."

This was a punch in the face. "For years she's promised to lift the ban if she ever took your place."

"She might have, once she had what she wanted so desperately. Until then the ban was a lever she could use to gain your support. But it lost her mine. I'd been going to make her master after me . . . until I realised she was betraying you."

"And she accuses *me* of betraying her." Llian gulped down half a glass. "The deceitful cow!"

"At least you know who your friends are," said Bufo, leaning back in his chair and crossing his long legs.

"As do I," said Wistan. "That's why I'm planning to put a new candidate into the ring at the election tomorrow. You, Llian."

Llian choked. Had Wistan been a joking man it would have been the best joke in the world, but Llian could not remember him ever cracking a smile. The other possibility was that he had gone insane, though there was no sign of that either.

"Having weighed the evidence," said Wistan after a long pause, "you've come to the reluctant conclusion that I'm in earnest."

"I . . . don't know what to say. Master of the College. Me?"

"Absurd, isn't it? And you'd still have to win the vote. But after the fracas earlier tonight, and with my support, you'll certainly be the leading candidate."

"But you hate me."

Wistan sighed. "I've never hated you, though you were exceedingly troublesome. The old forget that they were once young and bold – or if they weren't, that they would have liked to be. Both have their place: the old must ensure that the best of the past is preserved, while it's the job of the young to get rid of all that's useless and outdated. But when the balance goes too far one way or the other . . .

"You were the kind of student, and are the kind of chronicler, that we should be desperate to encourage. I've been master far too long; I allowed the college to become as fixed in its ways as I am in mine. It needs a new master who isn't afraid to prune the dead wood. Will you accept my nomination?"

Master! Llian was in a daze. He would have all the knowledge of the world at his disposal and plenty of coin – both would make his quest a hundred times easier, and much quicker. But what would Karan think? Well, she had told him to do whatever it took. For the first time since Sulien's initial nightmare, he felt hopeful.

"Yes," said Llian. "I will."

"Then I have something to show you. My dirt book – my notes on hundreds of the most powerful and important people in the west."

"What do you use it for?"

"Mainly to extort small sums for the maintenance and improvement of the college – I too am corrupt in my own small way. But this isn't the only weapon the master has. The college has many secrets . . . and a number of powers to protect our treasures."

"I don't know enough about the Secret Art to blow out a candle flame."

"Nor did the majority of the seventy-three masters before me. Those who can use the art do so; for those who can't, there are variety of devices that a non-adept can wield. There's another book about that. I'll show you another time. Bufo, my dirt book."

Bufo put a small brown-covered book in Wistan's shaking claw. He passed it to Llian.

"I thought it would be bigger," said Llian.

"The pages are rice paper," said Wistan, "and I write in a small hand. It suffices for the six hundred and seventy people I have information on. Don't look at it now; take it with you. Bufo will burn an identical book and dispose of the ashes in such a way that he'll be seen. Guard it with your life. When you're alone, you'll get a good deal of amusement from my pen portraits of our allies. I particularly refer you to the entry on yourself, though it's . . . a trifle out of date." Wistan almost smiled, but his facial muscles could not pull it off. "Go. I'll see you at the election, which is at two in the afternoon, sharp."

He extended his hand. Llian shook it. It was a collection of cold dry bones. "Thank you, Master."

"Thank *you*. The lack of a worthy successor is the only reason I've hung on so long." He hesitated. "What will you do first, as master?"

"Find the summon stone and destroy it. Until we're safe from the Merdrun, there's no point thinking about anything else."

Wistan nodded and closed his eyes.

Llian put on his coat, settled the dirt book deep in his pocket and went out. He was surprised to see that the sun was up. It was after seven, and he had promised to wish Wilm well in the test. He ran all the way to their rooming house but Wilm had gone half an hour ago.

Llian hid the dirt book under his mattress. No, too obvious. He pulled the mattress out, made a slit in the far corner and slipped the book an arm's length into the mouldy straw. Then he lay down fully dressed, but the long day and the sleepless night, the wine and all the dramas caught up with him.

He did not wake until the great clock in the market square tolled twelve, midday.

28

A DAMNED LIE

When Llian arrived at the chamber where the election was to be held, at half-past one, a third of the masters were already there. The door attendant, a small man greatly scarred about the face, checked his credentials, took his bag and put it in one of the storage compartments, and let him in.

Wistan was in his wheeled chair at the rear of the dais, enveloped in his charcoal-coloured blankets. Llian went across but he was sound asleep. Hardly surprising; he too had had a sleepless night. There was no sign of Thandiwe, Basible Norp or Candela Twism. Presumably they were doing last-minute campaigning.

He looked around, feeling more than a little uncomfortable, for most of the masters were watching him. Perhaps they were wondering how he dared show his face after the scene at Thandiwe's house last night. Llian knew many of them, including Master Laarni, a small dark fellow, rather loud and self-important though decent enough, and Master Cherith, plump and saggy but with an enchanting smile. They would probably support him.

"Changed your mind, have you?" said Limmy Tuul, a hard-faced master with a black wen on his right eyelid. He was one of Thandiwe's strongest supporters.

"We'll see," said Llian.

Candela Twism entered, walking ahead of a small coterie of masters. A solid woman, square in the body and short in the leg, with a broad face inclining to jowls and a mass of loose grey ringlets that quivered with every movement. If the effect was meant to be girlish, it was a failure. Llian thought she looked like an overweight merino.

She headed his way. "Heard about Thandiwe's party," she said without any acknowledgement that they had not seen each other in seven years. "Are you going to vote for me?"

"I don't know," Llian lied. As a candidate he would not have a vote, though no one would know he was standing until Wistan made the announcement, presumably after all the masters were here and the room was locked. "Tell me why I should."

"Stability, that's my platform. The college is running nicely and I wouldn't change a thing."

Because she was too damned lazy. Far easier to keep the systems Wistan had spent so long developing, whether they were suited to the college of today and the challenges of tomorrow or not. But she was reputed to be honest.

"In these troubled times we need all the stability we can get," he said obsequiously.

She moved on. Someone touched Llian on the shoulder. He looked around, then up, to a very tall master with sun-bleached hair and weathered skin covered in dark sun spots.

"You must be Llian," he said. "I know you by reputation – a truly magnificent Great Tale. Basible Norp, at your service."

"Thank you," said Llian. "I've heard you're a master chronicler of rare talent."

"I've had a few moments. Nowhere near your league, though. Can we have a chat?"

"It's nearly two. The election—"

"It'll be ages yet. These things always take a long time to get going."

"Tell me why I should vote for you."

"To be honest," said Norp, "I'm not sure you should."

"Pardon?" It was the oddest election pitch Llian had ever heard.

"Candela stands for business as usual, and that's no bad thing. The college has a few problems, but the students are good and its finances are in order. She wouldn't change anything."

"The college also has to be adaptable, especially in times like ours."

"True, true." His eyes widened; he was looking over Llian's shoulder.

Thandiwe had made her entrance, wearing a spectacular peach-coloured gown she must have been sewn into, for it revealed every luxuriant contour. When she saw Llian, her glare could have burned the heart out of an obsidian sphinx.

"Thandiwe's brilliant," said Norp. "Strong and a creative thinker. She would adapt the college to new challenges."

"There are one or two question marks over the direction she might take," said Llian.

"As you so sagely put it last night. I heard you created a sensation."

"All I want is what's best for the college."

"As do we all. Good talking to you."

Norp wrung Llian's hand and turned away without saying what he stood for or asking for his vote. Thandiwe stalked across. Llian braced himself, suddenly exhausted. He wasn't sure he was in a fit state to deal with her – or her fury when his own candidature was announced.

"How dare you come here, you bastard, after what you did to me last night."

"Maybe I've had a change of heart and want to vote for you after all."

She gave a small involuntary jerk, as if she was desperately hoping he would. "You haven't changed your mind. You're up to something. Who are you conspiring with? Certainly not Candela. So it's Norp.

Well, don't be fooled by his *Who, me?* manner. He's as cunning as they come and he can't be trusted any more than *you* can!"

"Or you," said Llian softly, so she had to strain forward to hear.

"What the hell are you talking about?"

"You've voted against overturning my ban every time it's been raised."

She paled. "That's a damned lie. I've always been your biggest supporter."

"It came from the most reliable source of all."

"Wistan?" she said incredulously.

He smiled thinly. "All this time you've been pretending to be my friend, yet supporting the ban so you could manipulate me when you needed my vote. I can't think what I ever saw in you."

"I know exactly what I saw in you," she hissed. "A treacherous snake. I'm going to destroy you, Llian. For the next thousand years, whenever anyone hears your name, it'll be Llian the Liar, the Cheat, the Perverter of the Great Tales."

He recoiled, shocked by her venom, but she was already stalking away. His heart leaped about in his chest. She would do it too.

A bell rang on the far side of the room. A uniformed aide went to the centre of the dais.

"The masters are all present and the doors have been locked. These are the candidates." He unrolled a sheet of paper and held it up in front of him. Llian's heart started to pound. What would Thandiwe do when Wistan nominated him? Her explosion would blow the roof off.

"Thandiwe Moorn. Basible Norp. Candela Twism." He frowned and turned towards Wistan, who was still swathed in his blankets but now awake. Llian could see the lamplight reflecting off his bulging eyes. "Are there any additional candidates?"

Wistan said nothing.

"Are there any additional candidates?" the aide repeated.

Why didn't Wistan speak? Had last night been a last twist of the knife by a malicious little man who never forgave or forgot? Llian struggled to believe it; he was good at reading people and everything Wistan had said rung true. Besides, Llian had the dirt book.

"Are there any additional candidates?" said the aide for the third time. "No? Then the voting will commence. Master Wistan has already indicated in writing that he does not intend to vote."

It had to be malice. Llian could see Wistan's eyes glittering. He was irrevocably ruined.

The three candidates took their places on the dais, Thandiwe on the left, Candela Twism in the middle and Basible Norp on the right. Now came the choice Llian had not expected to have to make. The masters were lining up before the candidates. Who to choose?

He could hardly vote for Thandiwe after the way he had denounced her last night and her years-long betrayal. He could not bring himself to vote for Candela, which only left Norp, the self-effacing but undoubtedly brilliant chronicler.

As Llian lined up in front of him, Thandiwe shook with rage.

The numbers were counted and the aide announced them. "There are fifty-seven voters. Twenty-nine votes are needed for a majority. Twism, eleven votes. Norp, twenty-two votes. Moorn, twenty-four votes. As there is no majority, Twism is eliminated."

Candela Twism looked around, smiled vaguely and ambled away.

"Second round," said the aide. "Vote for your candidates. There are fifty-eight voters this time, thirty votes needed for a majority."

The lines of masters ebbed and flowed. Some remained in front of Thandiwe, and some in front of Norp, but a surprising number changed position. Again Llian was put to the choice. It occurred to him that he knew remarkably little about Norp. Still, how bad could a man be who refused to blow his own trumpet?

The lines were almost complete and about the same length. He caught a pleading look in Thandiwe's eye. Was he wrong about her? She was one of the strongest people he knew; she might be able to resist Anjo. And since Wistan had betrayed Llian, maybe what he'd said about Thandiwe had been a lie.

Who was it to be, the known or the unknown? He had to rely on his judgement. He took a deep breath, turned away from Thandiwe and went to the back of Basible Norp's line.

The numbers were counted. "Thandiwe Moorn, twenty-eight votes,"

said the aide. "Basible Norp, thirty votes. Basible Norp will become
the seventy-fifth Master of the College of the Histories on the death,
retirement or incapacity of Master Wistan."

Wistan was still staring at them. He had not moved; what was the
matter with him? Had he had a stroke?

"You bastard!" Thandiwe shrieked. "You've utterly ruined me!"

She leaped off the dais, her peach-coloured sash trailing behind
her and her white teeth bared. When she hit the floor, the high heel
snapped off her left sandal. She kicked it off and launched herself at
Llian, who could not get out of the way in time. A small fist caught
him in the eye; he teetered and went down with her on top of him,
punching and clawing and using her knees and elbows. His eye was
starting to swell and he could hardly see. He tried to push her off but
her satin gown tore at the left shoulder.

Thandiwe drove her forehead at his face, striking his right cheekbone so hard that it dazed him. She was lunging at him again when
someone caught her from behind and dragged her off. The skin-tight
gown ripped down to her waist.

Basible Norp had her by the upper arms. She lunged again but he
was too big, his grip too strong. "Enough," he said quietly. "It's over."

"This betrayal rivals anything in the Histories," she said in a cracked
voice.

Llian was trembling violently and unable to speak. He had only one
hope left – that Norp would be grateful and lift the ban. He seemed
a reasonable man.

Thandiwe shook herself free and staggered away, trying to pull her
gown up onto one amber shoulder, then the other, but the satin was
shredded. She slumped onto a chair and wept.

With a mighty effort, Llian pushed himself upright. Either he was
swaying or the room was tilting back and forth. Blood flooded from
his nose, his chin burned where she had clawed strips down it, his right
cheek throbbed mercilessly and his eye was swelling. Everyone in the
room was staring at him, and clearly most did see it as a betrayal.

Everyone except the aide, who was running towards Wistan.
"Master?" he cried.

Wistan's head had slid sideways; he must be badly ill. The aide whispered to him. Llian pushed through the throng and heaved himself up onto the dais. It took a mighty effort; he felt like an old man.

"Attendant!" yelled the aide. "Call for a healer." He reached out towards Wistan but drew back as if afraid to touch the great man.

The scar-faced attendant came lurching across the room. Judging by his gait, there was something badly wrong with his legs. He stared at Wistan for a moment, then pulled the blankets away. They hit the floor with a sodden sound and a trail of red. The blankets were saturated with blood, and so were Wistan's clothes and the seat of his chair.

His throat had been cut.

Everyone gathered around, staring at the body. Thandiwe was gaping. Basible Norp looked dazed, as if he had never seen a corpse before.

"Murdered!" said Candela. "Attendant, call for the sergeant and lock the door. Let no one out, and no one in save the sergeant and his men. Everyone else, move back. Don't touch Wistan. And beware, the killer may still be here." She looked across at Norp. "Master Norp?"

He staggered to the far corner and vomited noisily.

"He did it!" said Thandiwe in a carrying voice.

"I beg your pardon," said Twism.

"I accuse Llian!" Thandiwe pointed a long bare arm at him. She was quivering violently. "He's always hated our master. Llian cut the throat of a helpless old man. Arrest him!"

Llian looked around wildly. This could not be happening. "I haven't been anywhere near him," he gasped.

"Arrest the murdering swine!"

"That's the sergeant's job," said Candela Twism, "after he's weighed all the evidence. Master Moorn, you're making an exhibition of yourself."

Thandiwe made another vain attempt to pull up her ruined gown.

"Master Rendi," said Candela. "Give Master Moorn your coat."

Rendi took off his grey jacket and handed it to Thandiwe, who wrapped it around herself and fastened the wooden toggles. The door attendant came lurching back, his hands still bloody.

"Master Candela?" His voice was prim and sounded vaguely familiar, though Llian did not recognise the time-ravaged face. "I know something that may bear upon this crime." He looked down at his bloody hands, then flinched.

She handed him a handkerchief and he wiped his hands.

"Yes?" she said.

He leaned towards her, lowering his voice. His thick lips were wet, his scarred cheeks oddly flushed.

"If you have something to say, tell everyone."

"I saw Llian slipping out of Wistan's rooms early this morning," said the attendant. "Not long before that, I overheard a furious argument."

"That's a lie," Llian cried.

"Do you deny you were in Wistan's rooms?" said Candela.

"No. We had private business to discuss. But there was no argument."

"He's lying," said the attendant. "Llian screamed, *I'm going to kill you for this* and stormed out."

Llian gaped at him. Why was he making up such an outrageous lie? Was he part of a conspiracy with Thandiwe? Then Llian realised who the attendant was.

"You're Turlew!" Llian turned to Candela. "He's always hated me."

"You seem to make an awful lot of enemies."

"He tried to rob and murder me in the mountains twelve years ago, when I was on a mission for Wistan. Wistan sacked him, then Turlew lost his legs in the war and blamed me for it, though I hadn't seen him in years. These were his last words to me, when I saw him in Chanthed a decade ago." Llian quoted them from memory, in a precise imitation of Turlew's screeching voice.

"*Curse you, Llian! Curse you until the earth bleeds and the black moon rots to pieces. Soon you will not have a friend in the whole of Santhenar. Your very name will be a curse, and before the coming Hythe you will wish you were as happy as Turlew the beggar man!*"

"Was Turlew sacked by Wistan?" said Candela to the aide.

"I don't know, Master Candela. That would have been well before my time."

"Find someone who would know. At once."

"Captain Bufo was with Wistan and I last night," said Llian. "Bufo will confirm everything I've said."

"Find Bufo as well," said Candela.

The aide ran out. Turlew stood there, shuddering and wiping his bloodstained hands over and over. Llian's stomach muscles were so tight that they throbbed. What if the aide could not find Sal? What if she did not remember? What if the sergeant just wanted an easy solution to the crime? He, Llian, had to make an emergency plan but his brain seemed to have frozen.

Shortly the aide returned with Old Sal. The masters were gathered in a bunch between her and the dais, concealing Wistan's body from view, and Candela did not explain why she had been summoned.

"You've kept the stipend book for fifty years," said Candela to Old Sal. "Do you remember the circumstances under which Turlew, here, left Wistan's employment?"

"He was dismissed without a reference," said Old Sal.

"For what reason?"

"Master Wistan sent Llian off on a vital mission to Thurkad and gave him a heavy purse for expenses. I understand that Turlew attempted to rob Llian, and kill him, but failed. That's all I know."

Llian let out the breath he had been holding. Maybe it would be all right after all.

"Thank you, Sal," said Candela.

Sal went out.

"It's true I hate Llian," said Turlew. "But everything I said is true."

"It's a lie, and Bufo will confirm everything I said," said Llian. "Wistan and I had an amicable discussion and made up our differences."

But the minutes passed, and Bufo did not appear. "Has anyone seen Bufo this morning?" said Candela.

"He brought Wistan here at midday," said Master Laarni. His hair had receded rapidly since Llian had last seen him a decade ago. "They spoke for a few minutes, shook hands and Bufo left."

"Was Wistan still alive?" Candela said sharply.

"Yes. I spoke to him half an hour later. That would have been at one o'clock. He seemed very cheerful. It was almost as if he had a joke he wasn't sharing with anyone."

"Wistan had a *joke?*"

"Yes. It was ... most unusual."

The aide reappeared. "Bufo left Chanthed an hour ago and said he wasn't coming back."

The hour he goes, I'll go too, Bufo had said early this morning. Had he known Wistan was going to be murdered? No, that was absurd. Perhaps Wistan, after ensuring that Llian had secured the mastership, had planned to end his pain-racked life. But someone had murdered him first.

"Until Llian's version of events can be corroborated, Turlew's accusation, enemy or not, must be given due weight," said Candela.

"I haven't been near Wistan since I entered the room," said Llian. "And I'm not carrying a knife. You can search me."

The aide searched Wistan's bloody corpse, the blankets and Llian, but no knife was found.

"He must have hidden the knife," said Turlew.

"I haven't left the room," said Llian. "I've been talking to people the whole time I've been here. The only person in this room with bloody hands is you."

"Check Llian's bag," said Candela. She studied Turlew, frowning. "No, stay where you are. Masters Laarni, Rendi and Tuul, bring in all the bags."

They did so. Llian's was opened first. Right on top was a long blood-stained knife.

"I told you he was the killer," gloated Turlew.

Llian kicked Turlew's wooden legs from under him, grabbed his bag and bolted.

PART TWO

PEM-Y-RUM

29

A STAGGERING CATALOGUE OF FLAWS

Nightfall, and Llian was huddled in the reeds beside a stinking drain. He had not eaten or drunk since leaving Wistan's rooms early that morning and he was desperately thirsty, but the water was too foul to drink. The stench was making his stomach churn, and his cheek throbbed where Thandiwe had headbutted him.

He had gambled everything, and lost. What on earth had possessed him? How had he so lost sight of his true goal, and how could he find and destroy the summon stone now?

A chilling thought struck him. As the accused murderer of a great man, the constables might have orders to shoot him down rather than allow him to get away. Only Bufo and the killer knew that he was innocent, but Bufo was long gone and no one knew where. There was no way to clear his name.

Who could the killer be? Llian's first thought was Turlew, though he was a sneak and a coward. It would have taken a far bolder man to cut Wistan's throat and stroll away in a room crowded with masters.

He lay back in the reeds, probing his cheek. Where could he go? He still had friends in Chanthed from his student days, though most had families now, and responsibilities. He could not ask any of them to risk everything by sheltering him.

The news of his crime would be a sensation; Karan would hear about it within days, and so would everyone else who knew him. Would they believe the story? Well, Karan already doubted him; she no longer trusted him to protect his own daughter.

How, after all their years together, could she have so little faith in him? Was it because she had invested everything in the only child she could ever have, or did she see a flaw in Llian that he had failed to recognise in himself? But Sulien, Sulien! It was unendurable.

He knew what Karan would think of his choice to support Norp over Thandiwe. She would be apoplectic with fury. *Why go all that way, at so much trouble and expense, only to betray the one person who could have helped us?* Would it be the last straw? Would he ever see her again? Or Sulien? Llian slumped on the smelly ground, overcome by despair.

Was there any way he could send a message to them? He dared not take the risk; he was too well known here. Besides, his quest was more urgent with every passing day. Only four and a half weeks remained.

He counted his money: twenty-two silver tars and half a dozen grints. It would not last long. He was putting the coins away when he realised that the scholarship test would have finished long ago. Given all the revelations about corruption at the college, the test would have been rigged; the scholarship would either go to a favourite of the judges or to the student who had paid the biggest bribe. Wilm, alone and penniless, must be in despair. And Llian had promised to look after the lad; he had to make sure Wilm had enough money to get home.

Which meant returning to their rented room. Would the rooming house be watched? Probably, though as a teller Llian was used to assuming a range of identities. He could use any of dozens of voices and accents, and change the way he walked and his physical mannerisms. If he kept to the night and no one saw him up close he might get away with it.

He turned up his collar, pulled his hat down so it concealed his face, assumed a slump-shouldered, defeated posture and a limp, and set off. The streets were crowded, for it was a mild evening, and in his mud-stained clothes he looked like a hundred other unfortunates. He kept a sharp lookout for constables and saw several, but by keeping well clear of them he attracted no attention.

At the rooming house the danger was immediate, for the old lady who ran it had eyes in all four sides of her plump little head. But she also had an appetite for chard and a weak bladder, judging by her frequent trips to the jakes out the back.

Llian concealed himself in the shadows in the rear yard and waited until she came out, her copper lantern casting beams of yellow light across the bare ground. The door of the jakes banged. He slipped up the stairs and opened the door to the top room, which was in darkness.

"Wilm?" he said, hand on the latch, ready to run.

No answer. Llian stood there, staring around him. He heard no movement or breathing, and as his eyes adjusted he saw from the light coming in through the grimy window that the small room was empty.

His pack was gone; the constables would have taken it when they searched the room. Wilm's canvas pack sat at the end of his bed. Llian retrieved Wistan's dirt book from the mattress and sat on the bed in the dark, planning his next move.

If the secret of the summon stone existed at all, it would be in the thousands of forgotten documents in the library archives. Breaking in would be dangerous but he had done it before. In his student days, in search of stories no other student had access to, he had taught himself a burglar's skills and cracked the locks. Such skills, once learned, were never forgotten.

There was still no sign of Wilm. Llian sat on the bed, opened the dirt book in a ray of light coming through the window and turned the pages until he came to his own entry, written while he was still a student and, evidently, never updated.

*Llian has so many flaws that, not knowing which to highlight,
I begin alphabetically – he is arrogant, audacious (bordering on
reckless), clumsy, conceited, cruelly accurate in his pen portraits
of the other students and masters (and even me, the disrespectful
villain!), drunk and disorderly, disorganised, egocentric, greedy for
knowledge, immature, impractical (except on nefarious forays such
as breaking into the forbidden section of the archives), insensitive, intolerant, irresponsible (especially when it comes to the
consumption of beer and wine), lazy, obdurate, rebellious, rude,*

self-satisfied, thoughtless of the feelings of those less fortunate than himself — which is almost everyone — unkempt, unrestrained (especially in relation to wine and women) and wasteful.

And he is Zain! Need I say more?

In spite of this staggering catalogue of flaws, Llian has passed his master chronicler's tests with the highest distinction. He also has a remarkable gift for telling, though time will tell if it comes to anything.

I don't like him and I don't trust him. But he has done brilliant things. And may do more, if he can only control his many vices and harness his few virtues.

Llian sat back. Wistan had been a trifle harsh but not entirely inaccurate. His words would have been hurtful had the glow not lingered from being offered the mastership.

An hour had passed and he dared not stay any longer. He took three silver tars from his wallet and wrote a note.

Wilm, I'm in diabolical trouble — you will have heard by now. This should be enough for you to get home and for a bit of a start in your new life. I know you have it in you to succeed, and the key to success is never giving up.

Llian

He wrapped the coins in the note and put it in Wilm's bag, then went to the window. As soon as the old lady's lantern approached the door of the jakes again he went down the steps and out into the cold night. He would find a room in the seediest tavern in Chanthed, a place where no one asked questions, fill his belly, then get started.

If he discovered anything about the stone, he would set out to destroy it. It would not be easy; Gergrig had said it could look after itself. But, unjustly banned from doing the work he loved, his life in peril because of a crime he had not committed, and cut off from his own family, the quest was all Llian had left.

30

YOU ALWAYS WANT MORE

Two weeks after Llian's departure for Chanthed, Karan and Sulien were feeding the swans on the rapidly drying pond when the harsh cry of a skeet sounded in the distance.

Karr! Karr!

Karan drew Sulien close, then ducked as the raptor shrieked overhead, so low that her hair was ruffled by its passage. It hurtled around the keep then raced down the track towards the old watchtower, two hundred yards away. Banking at the last second, it lifted and hovered over the ramparts, flapping its wings furiously.

Someone appeared there – a woman. Fear touched Karan's heart. "Is that . . . ?"

"Maigraith," said Sulien. "What's she doing in our watchtower?"

"I don't know. Stay here." Karan set off at a run for it.

Showing no fear of the vicious bird, Maigraith extended an arm. The skeet's claws enveloped her slim wrist. She opened the message pouch, withdrew a document and, with an effort, swung the heavy bird out over the edge. The skeet dropped like a rock until it gained airspeed and shot away. *Karr! Karr!*

Sulien had followed. "I told you to stay back," said Karan. "Maigraith is . . . dangerous."

"To Daddy?"

"How did you know that?" said Karan.

"You know that piece of sharkskin you use for rasping wood?"

"Mmm."

"Whenever Maigraith looked at Daddy, that's what it felt like."

Karan shivered. Maigraith came out of the watchtower, a folded piece of paper in her hand.

"What are you doing back here?" snapped Karan.

"Protecting you. This is urgent." Maigraith held up the paper.

"Go and do your next geography lesson, Sulien," said Karan. Sulien did not move. "Now!"

She went reluctantly. Maigraith handed Karan the piece of paper.

Master Wistan is dead in his wheelchair, his throat cut.
  Llian stands accused of his murder and is on the run.

Karan's knees buckled. This could not be happening – it had to be a lie. Maigraith caught her and held her up. Karan read the note again and again. There was no signature.

"Who sent this?" she croaked.

"A reliable source."

"It can't be true."

"Llian hated Wistan. Everyone knows that."

"He's not a violent man," said Karan. And yet when they'd first heard the drumming, he had gone for the axe. "If there was a fight, more likely Llian would have been killed."

"There was no fight. *Master Wistan is dead in his wheelchair, his throat cut.*"

"Llian would never attack a helpless man."

"Inexplicable things are happening all over the land – like your cook being murdered by his assistant."

"I don't believe it!" Karan trudged towards the manor.

"Even you, fanatically loyal as you are, must be thinking that Llian *could* have done it," said Maigraith.

"How dare you put words in my mouth!" Karan roared. "No one knows Llian as well as I do. He would *never* murder a helpless old man."

"There's no need to shout."

"Mummy?" said Sulien, appearing from behind a bush where she had been hiding. "What's the matter?"

"It's all right." Karan took several panting breaths. Sulien would have to be told, but not now.

"No, it's not."

"I'll tell you later. Off you go."

She went reluctantly, giving Karan anxious glances and Maigraith hostile ones. She knew there was a link between Maigraith and Llian's hasty departure.

"How do I know this note is true?" said Karan.

"Are you suggesting I made it up?"

"You've manipulated me before. You learned your trade from a master."

"I have many flaws, Karan," said Maigraith, her agitation showing in the way she precisely enunciated each word, the only sign that she was not speaking her native tongue. "But I am not a liar."

"Then whoever sent the message must be."

"It doesn't say Llian did it. It says he *stands accused* of the killing." Maigraith gained control of herself. "You must go to him. I will look after Sulien."

Karan stopped dead in the middle of the track and stared at her, dumbstruck. "You never give up, do you?"

"I know you love Llian . . ." Maigraith's thin upper lip curled, clearly thinking, *though I can't imagine what you see in him.* "You've got to race to Chanthed and you can hardly take a nine-year-old girl with you. For the sake of our fellowship as triunes, I'm prepared to put my own business aside to help you."

Had it been anyone else, Karan might have been tempted, but she knew Maigraith too well.

"No thanks." She walked off.

"Why not?"

Karan waited until she had reached the manor before answering. "As I learned after you forced me to steal the Mirror of Aachan, with you no obligation is ever discharged. You always want more, and more, and more."

"When you change your mind," said Maigraith, "I'll be here."

"Not on my land!"

Maigraith turned and headed up the track. Karan stood at the front door, fists clenched at her sides. This had to stop. Desperately needing someone to talk to, she headed down to Rachis's office, then remembered that she had asked him to go to Tolryme to make a final plea for

Benie's life. She had done everything she could to save him, but neither the mayor nor the judge would listen.

Sick at heart, she trudged back to the library. "Sulien?" She wasn't there. Karan's heart skipped a beat.

"Yes, Mummy?"

The panic eased as she saw Sulien's elfin face peering out from under the old desk in the corner. She was lying on the floor, her hair in a fan across her back, reading a book.

"I told you to do your geography lesson," said Karan.

"I did."

"Then you won't mind if I test you. Show me Gendrigore on the big map."

Without hesitation Sulien carried the library ladder to the huge wall map depicting the continent of Lauralin and the surrounding lands. She climbed to the top, stood on tiptoe and indicated a small peninsula in the tropical north.

"It's here."

"What's the chief product of Gendrigore?" said Karan. Sulien couldn't possibly know that.

"Mushrooms. It's the rainiest place in the world. The only things that grow there are grass and trees and mushrooms."

"Then why aren't its chief products meat or cheese, or timber?"

"It's surrounded by mountains and cliffs. The people can't get out anything that's heavy. But dried mushrooms are light. Porters carry great packs out over the Range of Ruin. Oh, and tea leaves too."

"That's enough work for today," said Karan, impressed. "Come for a walk."

As they went out the back door, Sulien called, "Piffle? Piff—" Her face crumbled. She reached up and took Karan's hand. Karan squeezed it, her heart aching for her.

"Where are we going?" said Sulien, sniffling.

"Is there anywhere you'd like to go?"

"Along the river. We might see some lizards."

They sat on a curving granite outcrop overlooking the largely dry bed of the Ryme. The sun darted in and out of high clouds moving across the mountains from the west. Karan looked up hopefully, but they did not promise rain.

"There's one!" said Sulien.

It was a couple of feet long. Sulien skidded down the outcrop and crept towards the gravel bank.

"Careful, they bite," said Karan.

"Everything bites, Mummy."

Karan's eyes misted as she watched her. How much longer could their time together last?

Apart from occasional pain spikes at the top of her skull, presumably the magiz trying to break through the block but failing, there had been no sign of her in over a week. But maintaining the block and being on alert day and night was taking its toll. Karan was exhausted, mentally and physically. There was no way she could keep it up until the invasion. Not with Llian to worry about as well.

This murder charge could not be a case of wrong time, wrong place. The evidence must have been fabricated to destroy him. Was this why Sulien's nightmare had shown him dead?

These were troubled times, and murdering an important, helpless old man was one of the worst of crimes. Llian's accusers could have him tried, convicted and executed very quickly. She had to go to him right away.

Sulien had crept to within a few yards of the lizard. The breeze ruffled her curls. Karan debated how much to tell her. The child was a worrier, and Llian's troubles were a huge burden to put on her, though Sulien was bound to find out. She always did.

"Sulien? Can you come here for a minute?"

She came back and perched beside Karan. "It was eating beetles. I could see halfway down its throat – disgusting bits of legs and wings and heads, all chewed up. Yuk!" She studied Karan's face. "Daddy's in trouble, isn't he?"

"I'm afraid so."

"Is it bad?"

"They're saying he murdered old Wistan."

"Who's saying that?" cried Sulien. "They're stinking liars!"

"Yes, they are," said Karan. "But I don't know what to do."

"We've got to save him. You've saved Daddy before, lots of times."

"Well, several times," Karan conceded. "But I was younger then."

"I'll help you." Sulien jumped up. "I'm going to pack." Karan did not move. Sulien looked down at her. "What's the matter?"

"Nothing."

Sulien shivered. "You're not leaving me behind. You're not!"

"I've got to travel fast."

"If you leave me here, Maigraith will get me. You can't leave me behind, you can't. *You can't!*"

It took half an hour to calm her down, by which time Karan was more rattled than before. Her healed bones throbbed, as they often did in times of stress. She wanted hrux.

She had a mental exercise to stave off the pangs. Karan imagined herself going to the larder and opening the little box, but closing it at once. There was only enough for one proper dose and, though it was nearly the time of year when Idlis brought more, his arrival time could vary by weeks.

But by the time she and Sulien had eaten lunch and the table had been cleared, the pain was worse.

"Is it really bad this time, Mummy?" said Sulien, watching her anxiously.

"It's not the worst—" A spasm struck her in the right thigh, where she had suffered the worst break. Karan lurched to a chair and fell into it, almost weeping. "It's pretty bad."

"Why is that rotten old magiz trying to hurt you?"

"I think she's trying to provoke *you* into a reaction, using your gift."

"*Me?* Why?"

"So you'll reveal yourself and she can attack you. Whatever happens to me, no matter how much pain I'm in, you must not use your gift to help me."

"But Mummy—"

"Promise me. No matter what."

"All right," Sulien said reluctantly. "Are you going to take more of that . . . nasty stuff?"

"There's hardly any left. And Idlis—"

Sulien shuddered. "He scares me."

"The Whelm are strange," said Karan. "But if not for Idlis and Yetchah, I would never have had you."

"I try to like him, but I just can't."

Rachis's cart rattled into the yard. Karan went out to help him unharness the horse. "How did it go?"

He shook his head. "Badly. The judge is hearing six more cases caused by the drumming: another murder, two assaults and three thefts, all by decent citizens who've never been in trouble before. The law sees it as an epidemic to be crushed without mercy."

"Should I plead with him again?"

"He isn't seeing anyone else. He only gave me a minute. It's hopeless, Karan. They're going to hang Benie at two-thirty." Rachis glanced at the angle of the sun, his old head nodding. In the bright sunlight he looked a hundred years old. "And it's two now. Even if you galloped all the way, it'd be . . . over before you got there."

Poor Benie – guilty yet innocent – and with only thirty minutes to live. Karan could not bear to think about it. Five minutes passed. Ten. Fifteen. The pain was very bad now. She tried her mental exercise again but this time the pain was too strong, the longing too desperate. She had to relieve it – she would never be able to think of a plan in this state.

She fetched the little case from the pantry and put it in her pocket – another small but necessary defiance. Twenty minutes. Twenty-five. The pain eased, as it sometimes did when release was close, but not enough.

Thirty minutes. Karan hooked her fingers around the edge of the table. It could not be happening, not to that kindly lad she had known all his life. She imagined him crying out for help and finding none. Then she felt a jarring pain in the back of her neck, a thud and nothing save emptiness.

She laid her head on her arms and wept.

Another half-hour went by. She had to come up with a rescue plan for Llian but could not focus on anything save an awful last image of Benie.

She found Rachis in his office, talking to Sulien. "I'm going for a walk," said Karan. "I need to think."

"Where?" said Rachis.

"Over to the escarpment. I might even go up to the forest, if I feel up to it, as far as the Black Lake."

"That's a tidy step," said Rachis, "in your—"

"*Condition*, you were going to say?" Karan said coolly. "I'm not an invalid."

Rachis and Sulien exchanged eye rolls, and they both laughed.

"If I don't get back till late, will you take care—"

"Yes, I'll look after Rachis," Sulien said, and giggled. Clearly, he had not told her about Benie.

Karan filled her water bottle and packed some bread and cheese, and headed off on the path to the broken cliff that separated the lower, productive part of her estate from the more extensive upland section, which, due to difficult access, was almost unused. The brisk walk helped; by the time she reached the base of the escarpment the pain had faded to a dull throb.

It quickly returned as she began to climb the steep natural stairs though, and by the time she reached the top, five or six hundred feet higher, she could barely walk. A grassy slope ramped up to her right, towards her Forest of Gothryme, which extended in a narrow strip for miles along the terrace above the cliff. The Black Lake lay just inside the upper edge of the forest. To her left the slope was broken by a series of rugged, thickly wooded gullies.

Karan took off her boots and socks and lay on her back on the cropped grass near the edge, the breeze cooling her hot feet. She closed her eyes and found herself drifting, the endlessly cycling terrors slipping from her mind . . .

She could not afford to sleep. She needed a peaceful place to escape her worries and plan how to save Llian, and the pavilion on Black Lake was the most peaceful place she knew, imbued with happy childhood memories. She headed up through the forest.

The pain returned as quickly as it had gone, and by the time she reached the lake she was fighting the urge for hrux with every step. The water looked black when in shadow, though now, with the sun angling through the trees onto the surface, it was a deep red-brown colour, like strong tea.

The granite pavilion beside the water was so old that no one knew who had built it; even the stone was crumbling. Its roof, a quintet of small metal peaks surrounding a tall central spire, was mostly intact, though stains on the paved floor showed that it leaked in half a dozen places.

A box with a stone lid held a few camping items – a battered old pan, a small cooking pot, some plates with the enamel chipped around the edges, and fishing lines with corroded brass hooks. Four blocks of stone arranged in a hollow square made a fireplace. Karan had often come up here with her father when she was little; they had caught fish and fried them in the pan, then sat by the water until late in the night, Karan swinging her little legs over the edge of the old jetty while Galliad had told her the *Tales of the Aachim*.

The drumming sounded, a triple thump followed by a double, two singles and another triple. It was stronger here. Her sensitive gift felt stronger too. She could visualise the ruin Snoat's army was spreading: families torn apart, livelihoods destroyed, long guarded treasures plundered.

Pain spiked through the girdling bones of her pelvis. Hrux, now! She fumbled in her pocket, trying to lift the lid of the case one-handed, then forced herself to stop. Hrux dulled the wits, and if ever she needed them about her it was today.

She sat where the balustrade had broken away save for a few crumbling stumps and waited for calm to come. The dark water teemed with fish, but their moving shadows echoed another shadow in her mind, one that was growing every minute – Maigraith had followed and was coming ever closer. How to deal with her? Karan had to, before she could go after Llian.

Driven by the drumming, Maigraith was bound to make another attempt to sway her, but what did she really want?

31

I WILL NOT ALLOW IT!

Karan had not eaten since breakfast; no wonder she could not think straight. She baited the hook of one of the fishing lines with a piece of bread and cheese squeezed into a lump and tossed it into the water. After tying the other end around one of the baluster stumps she gathered dry wood and kindling, and set a fire.

When she had been little, she and Galliad had often camped here for days, exploring the forest, catching fish and gathering wild herbs. She could see two varieties of bitter greens, creeping rogid and tall wild mustard with foot-long leaves mottled green, red and purple. At this time of year they would be as pungent as freshly mixed mustard, stinging the nose and taking the breath away. They would certainly clear her head.

The drumming repeated three times, then stopped. She lit the fire and gathered a pan full of shredded mustard greens and rogid leaves. Some of the mustard plants had gone to seed. She shook the seeds out of the papery pods for seasoning and collected some dandelion leaves as well. And lastly, three hard green limes from the tree she had planted here twenty years ago.

The line was taut. She drew the fish in, hand over hand. A small one. Karan killed and gutted it and tossed the line back, then scaled her fish and prepared it for cooking. It would soon be dark. Where was Maigraith?

She closed her eyes and tried to sense the shadow she had detected before, but it wasn't there. What if Maigraith decided to take Sulien? Rachis worked in the east wing, forty yards from the keep; he would not hear her cries. She would be gone, just like that. That fear was a physical pain, worse than the one in Karan's bones.

Now she was being silly; Maigraith was obsessive and single-minded but she wasn't a monster. Karan wiped sweat from her forehead and checked her line, which was jerking. A big fat fish this time, almost enough for two.

As she finished filleting it, Maigraith appeared on the forest path, moving silently in the gloom. She had learned such skills from the Faellem, who lived in harmony with nature – though not with the other human species.

"Has it helped?" said Maigraith.

"What?"

"The solitude."

"I haven't had enough of it," Karan said pointedly. She probed the fire with a stick, pushing the burning ends in so they would make a good bed for the pan. "Are you hungry?"

"Somewhat."

She filled the pot with water and put it in the corner of the fire, tore up a handful of dandelion leaves and tossed them in. They would make a slightly bitter but refreshing tea. The drumming started up again.

"What's that?" cried Maigraith, holding her hands over her ears.

Her indigo and carmine eyes flashed in the firelight, reminding Karan that she was very powerful . . . and very dangerous.

"That's the drumming."

"I thought people were making it up as an excuse for their own bad behaviour." The implication was, *Nothing like that could possibly affect me.*

"It's real. I've heard it many times."

"It doesn't affect you?"

She shrugged. "Nor Rachis."

"Why am I hearing it here?"

"It's getting stronger. Maybe it's even starting to affect people as insensitive as you."

Maigraith did not take it as the insult it was meant to be. She *was* insensitive, and knew it.

"About Sulien," said Maigraith.

"What?" Karan snapped.

"Since she's triune too, she may have a great destiny, but she needs to be nurtured and challenged. A change would broaden her outlook and give her new perspectives."

"Call me selfish, but I want my only child to live with me until she grows up." Karan banged the pan onto the fire, scattering embers across the stone.

"But this is bigger than both of us," said Maigraith. "Julken and Sulien are also triune."

Karan stiffened, for she had just remembered something Maigraith had said ten years ago, when they had been pregnant together. Now it struck her like a thunderbolt.

Who else can a triune's son mate with but a triune's daughter? From our loins spring a new people, a new species, perhaps with more of the strengths and fewer of the weaknesses than those that engendered us. Let us agree to pair them, now.

Karan had dismissed the idea out of hand and Maigraith had never mentioned it again, but clearly she had not forgotten it.

"Every single thing Rulke did in his long life was to save his people from extinction," said Maigraith, showing passion for the first time. She rotated a heavy gold ring on her finger – Rulke's own ring that he had shrunk to fit her.

"I'm aware of that," said Karan.

"But he failed, the Charon are gone, and Julken is all that's left of him. Karan, please listen. All their greatness and all their promise can't be lost. Julken and Sulien could found an entirely new line of people. Their children would be tetrarchs – four-bloods!"

It was outrageous. Karan trembled with fury but kept her silence. She had to know the worst.

"It could enhance our great gifts and best qualities," Maigraith went on, "and overcome the great flaws in triunes, like the constant threat of madness."

"It might also cancel out those gifts and amplify the risk of madness," Karan said coldly. "But even if every possibility was as you say, my answer would be the same. Sulien will make her own choice, when she comes of age."

"Karan, please . . ."

The drumming pounded in Karan's ears. "And *never* Julken. He strangled Sulien's puppy just because she laughed at him."

"That's a filthy lie!" screamed Maigraith. She leaped to her feet, her eyes flashing fire. "Take it back or . . . or . . ."

Karan sprang back, her heart racing. She had never seen Maigraith lose control so badly. If the drumming was behind it, there was no saying what she would do next.

The drumming roared; Maigraith's eyes flashed brighter. She stepped towards Karan, raising her hands. "I don't *want* to take her from you, but . . ."

This had to stop now. Karan stepped in a small hole and pain rippled down her right thigh. Hrux, hrux! She froze. What if she fed the last piece to Maigraith?

No, for all her pestering, Maigraith had done Sulien no harm. And hrux was a dangerous drug with unpredictable effects. There was no way of knowing what it would do to her ... though no permanent harm, surely. There wasn't nearly enough for a fatal dose.

"But if you leave me no choice, I will!" said Maigraith.

Dare Karan use it? Half mad with pain and terror as she was, she could not think straight, but how else could she stop Maigraith for long enough to get Sulien away?

"Calm down." Karan pointed to the fish to distract her. "I'm starving. We'll talk about it after dinner."

The flush retreated from Maigraith's face; she nodded and sat by the water. The pan was smoking. Karan greased it by rubbing it with a piece of oily cheese and slid the fillets in. When they were done she scooped them out onto two of the enamelled plates and squeezed the juice of one lime over the fish. The others she squeezed into the pan, tipped in a small amount of water and tossed in the greens. Their bitterness would disguise the taste of hrux, she thought in a curiously detached way – if she used it.

Pain shrieked up her leg as her body realised it was not going to get the hrux it craved. She wavered; whatever happened next she would soon be desperate for it. Then she thought about Sulien falling into Julken's brutish hands. It could not be endured, so her own pain must be.

She stirred the wilted greens around, then, when Maigraith was not watching, flicked in the piece of hrux and squashed it into the liquid on the far side of the pan. Karan poured the hrux-dosed sauce over one plate of fish and handed it to Maigraith, then dribbled the sauce from the near side of the pan onto her own meal.

"What's this?" said Maigraith, forking out a piece of red leaf.

"Mustard greens." Karan indicated the tall plants growing further up the slope.

"And this?"

"Rogid. It grows over there."

Maigraith studied Karan for a moment. Karan ate her dinner. Maigraith took a forkful of fish and greens, frowning at the taste, but ate it.

Karan tensed. Hrux only took a few minutes to act, but how would it affect her? Would she slide into euphoria? Pass out? Scream and shout? Become violent?

Maigraith's teeth began to chatter. She half rose to her feet, the enamel plate clattering to the stone.

She turned to Karan. "What have you . . . nnnnnhh? *Nnnnnhh. Guh! Guh!*"

Foam formed at the corners of her mouth; her eyes went a burning carmine and protruded from their sockets; her arms flailed; she reeled around in interlocking circles, knees bent, gagged, spat out a cupful of foam, reeled in the other direction . . . then stopped as if she had run into a post.

Blood ran down her chin from a bitten lip. Her eyes widened even further. "No!" She shrieked. "Rulke, it's Tensor! Look out!"

Her slim body twisted; she was wrenching at something immovable as if trying to get past. "No, *no!*"

Karan's flesh went cold as she realised what was happening. Maigraith was reliving the worst day of her life, the moment ten years ago when Tensor had attacked Rulke with that irresistible Aachim spell, blasting him backwards and impaling him on a long metal thorn torn out of the side of his ruined construct.

Maigraith went wheeling sideways, landed with a thump, rose to her hands and knees, then screamed so shrilly that it hurt Karan's ears. But then the iron self-control Maigraith had practised for decades asserted itself, even over the effects of hrux. She laboured across to the point where, in her addled mind, her dying lover must be, and stood like a marble statue, staring down at him.

"You gave your life for me," she said.

Then in Rulke's voice as if replaying the fatal moment, *"How we would have loved, you and I. But it was not to be."*

"I once loved, and was loved." She bent as if to kiss him. *"And the fruit*

of our love will shake the Three Worlds to their underpinnings. But this is the end of the Charon."

Maigraith's marble face twisted. "I will not allow it!" she screamed. "I will reach even beyond the grave to bring him back."

She thrust her hooked hands up as if to pull the sky down on their heads. "I . . . will . . . not . . . allow . . . it!"

She turned and stared at Karan, though she could not tell if Maigraith was seeing her or something else from that desperate day ten years ago. She ran at Karan, reaching out as if intending to choke her. Unable to get out of the way, Karan dropped to the stone with an impact that sent needles of pain up her bones.

Maigraith trampled over her, still screaming, and ran straight over the edge into the water. She sank out of sight, resurfaced, thrashed to the bank, slipped in the mud, clawed her way to her feet and pounded up through the black forest.

Her cries faded into the night. Silence fell, though for half an hour afterwards Karan could still hear Maigraith's psychic screams.

I will not allow it! I will not allow it!

Suddenly the pain struck like an avalanche. Hrux, *hrux*! Karan crawled to the frying pan and licked out the dregs of sauce, but her tongue did not even tingle. Every skerrick of hrux was gone.

Why had she come up here; and why had she done such a reckless thing? The drumming, so strong here, had turned Maigraith's foolish longing into obsession, and now the hrux had raised that obsession to a mania.

Sick with guilt and in such pain that she could not stand up, Karan began to crawl back down the dark path towards the cliff stair. She could not stop, even if she wore her hands and knees down to bare bone. She had to take Sulien away before the hrux wore off and Maigraith reverted to the quest she could never forsake, because she had just sworn it on the image of the love of her life.

Before she reached the cliff path Karan felt a small piercing pain in the top of her skull, as if a sharpened spike had been pressed against it. *Tap!* The pain increased. *Tap!* It increased again. It felt as though the spike was being tapped into her skull with a mallet. The magiz was attacking again, but far more strongly than before, and Karan could guess why.

The struggle had weakened her block, reducing her ability to keep the magiz at bay. And perhaps the drumming up here, so much stronger than at Gothryme, was also eating away her strength.

Tap, tap, tap. Crack!

The pain was agonising. The magiz was close to breaking through. And the moment she did, she would divert her attack from Karan to Sulien. Sulien could not resist the magiz; she would be killed in minutes and then the sorcerer would attack Rachis, everyone who worked at Gothryme, and go after Llian.

And all because of Karan's unbelievably stupid act.

32

AS BAD AS IT CAN GET

The shriek was so chilling that Aviel dropped her basket of bitter orange leaves – one of the ingredients for a phial of scent she was making to send to Wilm – in the mud. She gasped and stumbled, looking around frantically. It sounded like a skeet, but Shand's skeet cage was empty – he had sent his three carrier birds out before he'd left and none had come back.

Another shriek, louder and rising in pitch, approaching rapidly. It was above her! She let out a squawk of fear. The raptor was hurtling down in a vertical dive straight at her. And skeets were killers.

It was thirty yards to her workshop and the bitter orange trees were too small to shelter her. Aviel snatched up the basket, knowing it was a hopeless defence against such a creature.

Her heart was skipping all over the place, her breath coming in tearing gasps. Down, down the skeet hurtled, like a condor hunting a rabbit.

Hooked yellow beak almost as big as her hand, bloodstained claws that could tear her face off or her throat out, battering wings, evil eye.

It let out another shriek, folded its wings back and accelerated. Aviel's worn boots settled into the mud and pain throbbed through her bad ankle. She clutched the handle of the basket. Ready . . . now!

She swung the basket desperately, knowing how little chance she had. The skeet struck, tearing it apart, and shot past, leaving her holding the handle. She hurled it after the bird, missed, then hobbled through the onion patch towards the workshop, knowing she wouldn't make it. The skeet was already turning. She grabbed Shand's spade, which she had been using earlier, and raised it above her head.

Aviel was used to avoiding blows; she'd had plenty of them from her father and her six big sisters. But she had little experience in dealing blows out. The skeet swept in again, legs extended, wicked claws spread wide enough to enclose her head. She swiped at it with the shovel but it swerved and she only struck a wingtip. It slashed at her, one claw tearing through her sleeve, and she felt a stinging pain along her forearm.

She dropped the shovel, snatched it up again and flailed furiously around her, cursing the bird with the choicest of her father's swear words. It turned towards her and she caught a flash of red on its right leg.

"Get away from me, you horrible mongrel beast!" she yelled, sobbing in her terror. "Get away!"

It perched on the leafless branch of a small plum tree, eyeing her malevolently. Aviel gagged. It smelled like the rotting carrion that was its favourite diet.

"What do you want?"

It raised its right leg, then lowered it. A red case was strapped there, and they were only used for the most urgent messages. But Shand had left suddenly a couple of days ago, saying that his granddaughter was in trouble and racing to Gothryme, and she had no idea when he would be back. She had to get the message.

The skeet shot over Aviel's head, making her flinch, then wheeled around the wooden skeet house, folded its wings and squeezed through the one-way opening. It flapped up onto its perch and glared at her.

It wanted her to remove the message, but she didn't want to go anywhere near it. When only thirteen Aviel had seen a skeet tear a man's throat out, then feed on him while he was dying.

Yet Shand had been good to her; when no one else would think about helping an unlucky twist-foot, he had paid off her indenture to Magsie Murg's stinking tannery, asking nothing in return. He had given Aviel use of the workshop for a modest rent and kept her horrible father, Gybb, who wanted to profit from her good fortune, at bay.

Skeets were malicious creatures; it would attack her for the joy of it, and hungry skeets were doubly vicious. She let herself into Shand's house, went to the cold-room and cut off a hindquarter of rabbit, which she carried down to the skeet house. She took up a length of broom handle with a spike in the end, spiked the haunch and eased it in through the feeding hole towards the skeet.

It ripped the meat from the bone with its hooked beak and gobbled the pieces. Aviel watched the lumps move down its throat, shuddering. Get the snool over its head, quick!

She unlatched the door, but as she reached out with the snool, a narrow leather bag on a long handle, it shook wildly. If she whacked the skeet on the head it was bound to attack. She calmed herself and tried again. It took four goes before the snool slipped over the bird's head, and it went still.

Getting the message was the most dangerous part, and Shand usually asked someone to help him. Her heart was hammering and her stomach felt as though something was thrashing around down there, trying to chew its way out.

But delay was risky too. She crept in, small bones crunching under-foot and the stench of putrefying skeet droppings rising around her with every step. Holding the snool on with her left land, she reached out with her right. But the straps of the red case were tightly buckled; it would take both hands to undo them.

Aviel was not going to let go of the snool handle. If she did, the skeet would knock her down and eat her innards. Making sure the door was open behind her, she tied the handle of the snool to the side of the cage. The skeet moved sideways on its perch and the snool slipped up an inch. She froze, then slowly eased it down.

Taking a last step, she unfastened the lower buckle. As she began on the upper one the skeet stepped sideways and the snool slipped up again. Aviel's bowels turned liquid. She eased the snool down. The strap was very tight and slippery with bird poo. The skeet raised its head and cracked its wings. Aviel panicked and jerked at the strap. The message case came free, but the snool slipped off and the skeet let out a shriek of fury.

Aviel hurled herself at the doorway. The skeet cracked its wings again; it was after her! Agony shot through her bad ankle; she stumbled and fell to hands and knees in the manure, dropping the case. The stench burned the passages of her nose; she scrabbled forward, but as she reached the door the skeet landed, *thump*, on her back, its claws digging through her coat and shirt into the skin.

She hurled herself backwards, slamming the skeet against the side of the cage. It shrieked and struck at the top of her head with its beak, a tearing pain. Aviel slammed back again and again until its claws relaxed, then staggered out through the open door and around behind it, pulling it hard against her.

Through gaps in the boards she could see the skeet swaying from side to side. They were very expensive birds. What if she'd broken its neck? She crouched behind the door, guilty and afraid, her skull and back and arm throbbing. But after a minute or two it let out another shriek and flew out of the open doorway into the night.

Aviel retrieved the muck-covered message case. Blood was running down the side of her head — the skeet had torn her scalp open. She dipped a bucket into the water barrel outside Shand's back door and cleaned the muck off her boots, hands and knees, then returned to her workshop and scrubbed her hands with soap and warm water.

Skeet fed on carrion and an infected scalp wound could be deadly. She filled a bowl with hot water from the pot hanging over the fire and fetched a clean rag and a little green olivine jar of ointment.

Among the hundreds of items she had inherited in the workshop was a small cracked mirror. Aviel propped it up against the big mortar and pestle, pulled a stool up to the bench and perched on it, letting out a sigh as the weight came off her ankle.

The top of her head was red and blood had run down to her right ear, clotting her flyaway silver hair into scarlet strands. She dabbed at the wound until she could see it clearly, a hook-shaped tear an inch and a half long.

She smeared it with ointment, which burned like lemon juice in a cut, washed the blood out of her hair and attended to her other injuries. Her belly churned; she felt faint, in shock.

Aviel grated fresh ginger into a mug, added hot water and stirred it, pulled her stool up to the brazier, broke the seal on the message case, then stopped. It felt wrong to be touching Shand's mail. What would he want her to do? He was a private man; if the message was personal he might be furious, might even throw her out.

The thought of being homeless and penniless again, unable to pursue her dream and forced to take the meanest work of all because no one would give an unlucky twist-foot anything better, was unbearable.

Should she take one of Shand's horses and try to find him? She had never ridden a horse, and the thought of climbing onto such a great beast and trying to stay on was paralysing.

Surely doing the wrong thing was better than doing nothing. She took out the message and unrolled it. It was from Malien, whom Aviel knew to be one of the Aachim leaders.

As she scanned the letter, which was written in a sloping, elegant hand, a shiver began at the base of Aviel's spine and wove its way up until the hairs stood up on the back of her neck.

Malien
Tirthrax
27 Mard, 3111

The 27th of Mard was a week ago. Why had the letter taken so long?

Shand,
    Call our allies together, urgently. Then prepare for war.
    I don't know how Karan's spying mission to Cinnabar went — I can't contact her. But I've learned a little about the Merdrun and it's

all bad. They want an empty world for themselves and no species in the void is more versed in war. If they get through the gate they will take Santhenar in a very short time, and the only people spared will be as slaves. Before anything, you must find the summon stone and destroy it.

Snoat's activities are a deadly distraction that is aiding the Merdrun. Do whatever it takes to stop him. Assassinate him and his allies; take the reins of power yourself, if necessary.

I have sent word to my own people in the east, and the Faellem in Mirrilladell, but both are so far away I fear they can do little to aid us in time.

I will go to Chanthed by the fastest means possible but I can't get there in under a month. That may be too late.

Malien

The letter slipped from Aviel's hand. *They want an empty world . . .*

The brazier did not seem to be putting out any warmth. She shivered and hugged her arms around herself. *Call our allies together, urgently.* If it had been urgent a week ago it was far more urgent now. She had to find Shand, wherever he was, and give him the letter without delay.

She had to leave the only home she had ever known and go out into the dangerous world she knew nothing about, but feared with all her heart.

33

I'LL MANAGE

Karan thumped her bloody fists against the iron-reinforced front door of Gothryme over and over, gasping and sobbing and crying out desperately, "Rachis! Rachis!"

A minute or two later he hauled the door open. In the harsh lantern light he looked like a barely reanimated corpse. "It's three in the morning. You'll be the death of me, Karan."

"I'm sorry. I've—"

"Got to go. And you don't know when you'll be back. And can I please take care of Gothryme while you're away."

Karan allowed her head to fall forward until it struck the two-inch-thick planking. "I don't deserve you."

"I'll take that as a given. Maigraith?"

"How did you know?"

"Have her visits ever brought anything but misery?"

"Don't know where she is. Could be half an hour behind, for all I know. Got to fly."

"What do you want me to pack?"

"Enough for a week or two. I'm going to Chanthed and taking Sulien with me. You . . . heard about Llian?"

"Sulien often feels she has no one to talk to but some silly old fool out the back."

"She's told you everything?"

"Everything she knows, which is a lot." Tears formed in his rheumy old eyes. "I can't tell you how much I'll miss that child."

"I can't tell you how much I'll miss you." She reached out to him.

"Yes." He turned away hastily. "I'll get on with it then."

Karan cleaned herself up at the sink – things were bad enough without scaring Sulien witless – and went up the echoing stairs of the old keep on her hands and knees. At the top she pulled herself upright and leaned against the granite wall for a minute, panting and longing for hrux.

There was no hrux, and if something happened to Idlis on the long and dangerous journey north from Shazabba there would never be hrux again. Better get used to it. She opened Sulien's door, and the lamplight in her eyes was dazzling. Sulien was sitting on her bed dressed in green trousers and blouse, and her travelling pack was bulging.

"What . . . are you doing . . . awake?" Karan's thoughts were worms trying to swim through treacle.

"You had a fight with Maigraith," said Sulien. "Up at the Black Lake."

"How did you know that?"

Sulien shrugged. "I just know stuff."

"Not a fight, exactly," said Karan. "She went a little crazy. I stopped her, though I don't know for how long."

Sulien pulled on her socks, then her boots. She began to lace them up but could not seem to manage it. Karan knelt in front of her. "Sometimes you frighten me."

"I don't think you need to worry when I can't lace up my own boots."

Karan stood up unsteadily.

"Your hands are all bloody," said Sulien. "And your knees."

"Just scratches. From crawling. Come on."

"Where are we going?"

"To find Llian and get him out of trouble." She looked around the odd-shaped little room. "Got everything?"

"Yes," Sulien said in a whisper, as though realising that after this nothing would ever be the same again.

In Karan's room the great box bed was as she had left it, including the dimple in Llian's pillow that she had not wanted to smooth out. Stupid, sentimental fool! She changed her clothes and packed.

"Go down to Rachis," said Karan. "I need a few minutes to myself."

Sulien frowned but went out. Karan sat in the canvas chair by the window, braced herself, then made a link to Malien.

She expected it to fail, as it had every time she had tried to contact her in the past week and a half, but the link formed instantly and strongly. She could actually see Malien sitting on a stone platform cut into the side of Mount Tirthrax. The view, across the incomparable snow-capped wilderness of the Great Mountains, was one of the greatest on Santhenar, but Karan had no eyes for it.

It was windy there. Malien's hair had blown up into a corona around her head.

"About time," she said.

"You were expecting me?"

"I've used half my art to make sure you got through. I expected you to contact me after you spied on the magiz – assuming you survived."

"I tried over and over," said Karan. "Couldn't get through. But Shand and Tallia know what's going on."

"Tell me everything. Be quick."

Karan did so.

"I'm coming west," said Malien. "We're almost ready to leave."

Karan sagged; relief left her feeling peculiarly boneless. Malien led a powerful people and would know how to organise the defences. "You don't sound surprised at my news."

"I have other sources of information," said Malien. "It'll take us weeks to get to Bannador, of course."

"Months, surely?"

"Not the way we're travelling. So, what do you want?"

"Pardon?" said Karan, wondering how the Aachim, clever though they were, could get here so quickly.

"You linked because you wanted something from me. I think I can guess, but why don't you tell me?"

"I'm afraid that everything I've done – including my fight with Maigraith – is strengthening the magiz's link, and she'll soon be able to attack Sulien again. I can't guard her day and night, so there's only one solution."

"Go back and kill the magiz," said Malien.

"It sounds bad, said out loud."

"To protect our own, we do what we must."

"Last time, when I talked about attacking her while I was disembodied, you hesitated. Is there a way?"

"Yes and no."

"What does that mean?"

"Your father knew a way. He may even have used it."

"What are you talking about?"

"Mad Basunez's experiments let a savage creature in from the void and it almost wiped out your family, but that did not stop him. He simply invented a spell for killing such creatures. More than five centuries later, your father improved that spell."

"How do you know?" said Karan.

"It was contained in a forbidden object. That's the real reason we exiled him from Shazmak."

"How does the spell work?"

"It has the form of a death mask – in fact, the death mask of Basunez himself. It won't harm anyone who can't use mancery, but when used against a wizard or sorcerer it reverses the power they're drawing and directs it into the heart or some other vital organ. The more power they use, the more quickly it kills them. It's a horrible death."

"No more horrible than the magiz is planning for us."

"It's highly dangerous. A non-mancer taking on a powerful mancer is always fraught, and after your previous visit she'll be expecting an attack."

"You said, *Yes and no*. What's the *no?*"

"You can't attack her when you're in spirit form."

"You mean . . . ?"

"Before you can use the death-mask spell, you'll have to allow the magiz to materialise you." Malien paused.

Karan swallowed. "Can't I materialise myself?"

Malien hesitated. "I wouldn't recommend it."

"Why not?"

"Even for a skilled mancer, it's incredibly exhausting. Since you aren't a mancer, in the unlikely event you could materialise yourself at all, you'd be too weak to stand up."

"Can you put the spell on me to do it myself? So I'd only have to trigger it?"

Karan sensed her deep unease, and Malien did not speak for several minutes.

"I could . . . *All right*, but don't use it unless there's absolutely no alternative. Going back to what I was saying, if you can kill the magiz quickly it should dematerialise you again, and you can use *Spell-stop* to return. But if you fail, you will be taken . . . "

"It seems horribly risky," said Karan, reliving the screams of the prisoners the magiz and Gergrig had tortured to death before she drank their lives. Her fate, if she failed.

"Too risky, but you did ask."

"Is there any other way I can protect Sulien against her?"

"Not that I can think of."

"Where is the death mask?"

"Among your father's secret things, I expect."

"How do I use it?"

"Put it on, point at the magiz's heart and say *Transpose* as though you really mean it. The spell embedded in the mask should do the rest."

"What if it doesn't work?"

"You will die."

Karan thanked Malien and broke the link. Sulien did not know that the magiz was trying to kill her, but she would soon have to be told.

In the secret passage of the library Karan rifled through the dusty boxes of her father's possessions and found it at the very bottom – a grimy verdigris-covered copper mask of a hideous old man, clearly cast from a plaster mould of Basunez's dead, furious face. She shuddered and hid it in her pack.

Rachis was waiting in the kitchen with a bag containing travel necessities. She did not check it; there was no need. Her guilt deepened. How could she leave all Gothryme's troubles to him at such a time? The first time Maigraith turned up unexpectedly Karan had not returned for a year and a half. When she got back this time, if she did, would he still be alive?

"Will you be all right?" she said.

"I'll manage," said Rachis. "It'll probably rain tomorrow."

She embraced the old man. There seemed nothing to him. Tears pricked her eyes, something which was happening all the time lately. Was she cracking up? No, she had to be as strong as she ever had. For Sulien. And for Llian.

"Go!" Rachis shook hands with Sulien, gravely, like one adult to another. "Look after your mother for me, won't you?"

"I will," said Sulien, large-eyed and overcome by the moment. "Can you do me a favour, Rachis?"

"Of course."

"Can you water the flowers I planted on Piffle's grave?" Tears leaked from her eyes.

"Twice a day," said Rachis.

They went out into the darkness. Rachis and the stable boy had saddled the strongest horse, Jergoe, a compact bay. Karan boosted Sulien up, then climbed up behind her. Her worn-out muscles shrieked. The trip down from the Black Lake, a quarter of it on hands and knees, the rest at a desperate stagger, had drained her almost beyond endurance.

She looked back at her shabby manor, just grey shadows in the moonlight. Would she ever see it again? Sulien was sniffling. Karan put an arm around her and took the reins with her free hand. She nudged Jergoe with her heels, waved, and they headed away.

"Where are we going?" said Sulien.

"I'm so tired I can't think."

"I think we should go straight to Chanthed and find Daddy."

"That's what Maigraith would expect me to do."

"Then we've got to get there first. We'll be safe in Chanthed."

Karan wasn't sure they would be safe anywhere. "We'll ride until the sun comes up, then find a place to hide and get some sleep."

Sulien leaned back against her. Karan kept to the wheel ruts of the road, where the ground was hard and Jergoe's hooves would leave poor tracks. After half an hour she turned off the Tolryme road and headed right on a stony path that led up into the hills. Each jolting stride sent a spike of pain through her, and there was nothing she could do about it.

How long would the hrux affect Maigraith? If she was unable to travel for a day or two, there was a good chance Karan could stay ahead of her. But if she was only affected for hours, she might already be on their trail. And if she caught them, Karan had nothing left. Dare she open a spy link?

"No, Mummy," Sulien said softly.

"How do you know what I'm thinking?"

"When you start to make a link my head aches."

Another reminder that she did not know what Sulien's gifts were – or whether they were assets or liabilities. She pulled her close. "I'm sorry."

"Did Maigraith attack you up at the Black Lake?"

"Not exactly." Karan told her what had happened as briefly as possible.

"But *you* don't go mad when you take hrux."

"Maigraith and I could hardly be more different. She's a triune of Charon, Faellem and old human with the Charon side predominant. I'm a triune of Aachim, Faellem and old human with the old human side predominant."

"Am I a triune too?" said Sulien.

"Yes, though because Llian is old human, that side of you is even stronger."

"Old humans are the best, aren't we?"

"Of course," Karan said absently. "Maigraith was terribly damaged as a child. She learned early on that nothing she did would ever be good enough."

"Why not?"

"The Faellem and the Charon were deadly enemies, and Faelamor, who brought Maigraith up, hated and feared Maigraith's Charon side."

"Then why did Faelamor use her?"

"Because Maigraith could do something that no one else could. But, because she could never escape the pain inside her, she denied her feelings. Perhaps that's why, when she recognised her soulmate in Rulke, Maigraith fell so hard for him."

"Is Daddy your soulmate?" Sulien said sleepily.

"In . . . a very different way."

It reminded Karan how badly she had treated him. What was he doing now? Was he even alive? What if they had caught him, tried him and were knotting the noose? She choked. Sulien, who was dozing, whimpered.

They rode on until the eastern skyline showed the faintest blush of colour. Time to find a place to hide. Ahead a series of little stony gullies ran up to a lens-shaped patch of scrub. If she were careful the hard ground would show no tracks. She roused Sulien, then dismounted and led Jergoe up the gully and into the grey-leaved trees. Brown boulders marked with white scribbly quartz veins littered the slope. It would have to do, for she could go no further.

She found a relatively level spot near the top of the scrub in the lee of a small bluff. Karan settled Sulien there and lay on her bedroll, trying to think things through. Once she found Llian, then what?

What if, influenced by the drumming, he *had* killed Wistan? No, she had to believe in him. This irony was a particularly bitter one. She refused to believe he could have killed Wistan, yet could not bring herself to trust him – if under the influence of the drumming – to protect Sulien or resist Thandiwe.

34

NOT AFRAID ENOUGH

Malien's letter was urgent and Aviel had to get it to Shand at once. His mute stable boy, Demoy, saddled her a horse, an ugly cross-eyed beast called Thistle. The lad's expression said it all – you'll be lucky to get a hundred yards before you break your silly neck.

"How do I get on?" said Aviel.

Demoy rolled his baby-blue eyes, rubbed his coarse yellow hair, making it stick out in all directions, then led Thistle to the nearest stall. She climbed the rails, trembling. Animals could smell fear and she must stink of it. Demoy pointed to the reins. She took them in her left hand, extended her right leg across his back and landed in the saddle with a bone-jarring thump.

Thistle snapped his tail, leaped from the stall and bolted out the stable door.

"Help!" Aviel wailed.

She clung to the reins as he careered up Shand's drive and out onto the potholed road. She was bouncing and sliding from side to side. The stable boy had not shortened the stirrups and her legs weren't long enough to reach them. She was going to fall off and break all her bones.

Thump, thump. With every stride her bottom struck the hard saddle and the motion was chafing skin off the insides of her thighs. At the crossroads she needed to go left, towards the north. She hauled on the left rein and to her surprise Thistle went that way.

Her slight weight meant nothing to the big horse and an hour later he was still cantering, uphill and down, now through a scrubby forest. Her bottom was one massive bruise. He hurtled around a corner and ahead she saw half a dozen refugees, fleeing west from Snoat's war on Iagador. Their belongings were piled high in a cart and they were staring at their carthorse, which lay dead on the road.

A tall young man jumped out in front of Thistle, waving a knobbly stick. Aviel let out an involuntary cry. He wanted her horse and looked desperate enough to kill for it.

"Thistle, run!"

Thistle leaped straight at the young man, who swung the stick at her head. Aviel ducked and it struck Thistle on the back. He shrieked and kicked out. The young man dived out of the way, cursing her. Thistle raced on.

"Not that way!" cried Aviel as he headed right at an intersection. "Straight ahead!"

Thistle turned right. At the next crossroads she managed to turn him left, then left again, then right. She checked her sketch map, making sure she was back on the right road – the one Shand would take on the way home from Gothryme. She must not miss him.

Thistle was splashing along a muddy track snaking across a steep forested slope when she heard a drumming sound. He whinnied and reared up on his back legs. She slid backwards off the saddle, over his rump, landed on her bruised bottom on a wet slope and skidded down it.

"Thistle!" she screamed. "Wait!"

He kept going, carrying her food, water and sleeping pouch. Aviel tumbled over, twisting her right wrist, and cracked her head against a sapling.

She came round with a splitting headache. She had slid a good hundred feet down the grassy slope, and it was too steep and wet to stand up on. She began to crawl up, her wrist throbbing and twisted foot dragging, but halfway up she slipped on her skid marks, which had exposed greasy white clay, and slid down again.

Aviel tried again and slid down again. She looked right and left. The slope was wet with seeping water and looked just as slippery in both directions. She went left for about a hundred yards and tried again, but without the use of one wrist and one ankle it was hopeless. She considered going down, but the valley below was covered in forest and she had not seen any signs of habitation in the past hour. If she got lost she might never get out.

And she had lost Shand's valuable horse. He would be furious. She sank into despair.

A horse whinnied, though it did not sound like Thistle, then shod hooves clicked on the track above. Aviel was about to call out when a man's voice rose in a drunken song. Another man cursed him and they swore at one another for a minute or two. She hunched down, the backs of her hands prickling, until they were gone.

The sun was low now, her clothes were damp and it was very cold. Her belly was empty and her throat dry. She dug a fist-sized hole in the slope and lapped at the muddy water that collected there.

Then in the distance she made out a familiar male voice reciting an epic poem, the *Lay of the Silver Lake*. It was Shand, heading back to Casyme.

"Shand!" she screamed over and again until her voice went hoarse. "Help!"

Finally his head appeared above her. "Aviel?" He scrambled down the slope. "What are you doing here?"

"Urgent skeet message," she croaked. "Malien." Aviel reached into her coat for the message.

"It can wait," said Shand. "Let's get you up first."

"No!" she gasped, fending him off.

"What the blazes is the matter?"

She could not get the letter out. Her wrist was purple and very painful.

"Read the letter," she said limply. "Please."

Shand took it from her pocket, scanned it, then glanced at her, his eyes glinting.

"I d-didn't want to open it . . . b-but it said *urgent*."

"Idiot girl, be quiet!"

He lifted her and went up sideways, digging his heels into the clay and wheezing with every step. At the track he heaved her into his saddle.

"How did you get here?" said Shand.

It burst out of her. "I lost Thistle! I'm sorry. I shouldn't have taken him."

"Why did Demoy saddle Thistle for you, great cranky brute as he is?"

"I'll pay you back . . . somehow." But how? Horses were very expensive and she earned hardly anything.

He clambered up behind her. "Be quiet. I need to think."

Aviel clung to the sides of the saddle, aching with despair. He was bound to throw her out. The horse trod in a pothole, spearing pain through her. She cradled her wrist in her hand, choking down on a sob. Where could she go? Her beloved workshop belonged to Shand. All she owned was one little book on perfumery she had laboriously copied out. If she could not do her work she would fade away and die.

They passed out of the forest into grassy country littered with round grey rocks. Shand's weary horse plodded on. The light faded and frost began to settle; it was going to be a cold night. Aviel sank into a daze punctuated by spikes of pain. The horse stopped and Shand climbed down.

Startled back to wakefulness, she swayed in the saddle. A handful of stars glittered in the west.

"Where are we?"

"Lippity Crag, an hour and a half from home."

"But Malien's message is urgent."

"Nothing I can do about it tonight."

He led the horse up a winding track scattered with stones that rocked and slipped underfoot, towards the crest of a small hill. Dark rocks reared up out of the ground – spiky, threatening. A cold wind keened around them.

In between the black outcrops, which ran in lines the length of the hill, Shand lit a storm lantern. A trickle of water meandered through the rocks. He took off the saddle, rubbed his horse down and gathered firewood. Aviel set the fire, lit a piece of bark from the lantern and soon the dry wood blazed up. She sat near the warmth, watching him from the corner of her eye, afraid she had done the wrong thing.

"Hold out your wrist," he said.

She did so. He probed the swelling. His thick fingers were gentle. He bandaged her wrist.

"And your ankle."

"It'll be all right tomorrow," said Aviel, ducking her head. She tucked her twisted ankle under the other. She was lying; it was bound to trouble her for weeks. She closed her eyes. Cast out! Nowhere to go.

What would happen to her? A sob escaped her. She choked it off; she had to be strong.

"Nonsense," said Shand, going to his knees in front of her.

"No!" The thought of him studying her ugly ankle was unbearable. She stood up, wincing.

"What the blazes is the matter with you?"

"I don't like people looking at my ankle."

"Then I won't. But that's not the real problem, is it?"

"You're going to chuck me out," she whispered.

He frowned. "Why would I do that?"

"I read your private letter . . . and took Thistle without permission . . . and lost him."

"Useless nag," said Shand. "He's no loss – if he *is* lost, which I doubt. How did you get the letter anyway?"

"A skeet came in. With a red message case. I knew it was urgent, so I . . ."

His face set as hard as the rocks behind him. "You went into the skeet cage *by yourself?*"

"I was afraid something bad would happen if you didn't get the message."

"But you know what skeets are like – it could have torn your face off." Shand rubbed his leathery face. "I can't believe you're alive."

"You've been so good to me, I had to repay you. But it's all been for nothing."

"Nonsense. You might have saved the day."

"What do you mean?"

"I wasn't planning to stop in Casyme. If you hadn't come after me I might not have got Malien's message for weeks, and that would have been disastrous."

Aviel felt a small inner glow. She'd done the right thing after all.

He dragged a rock close to the fire. "Sit here. It'll do your ankle good." She made a convulsive movement. "Don't worry; I won't look."

He took blankets from his saddlebags, draped one around her shoulders and turned away.

"Where are you going?" squeaked Aviel.

"To relieve myself, if you must know."

"Oh! Sorry."

When he was out of sight she inspected her ankle. It was badly swollen and the bones were grating together. She tore a strip off the bottom of her shirt and hastily bandaged it.

Shand returned. They ate salted meat and toasted bread in silence. She sat with her head lowered, watching him sideways, fretting. He was worried about something other than Malien's letter.

"Is something the matter?" said Aviel. He seemed harder and grimmer than she had ever known him.

"My granddaughter's got herself into bad trouble."

He took Malien's letter from his pocket, reread it and tossed it into the fire.

She watched it burn. "Malien said *They want an empty world.* Does that mean . . . ?"

"If they get through the gate, they'll be aiming to wipe everyone out, except for those young and strong enough to keep as slaves."

The Merdrun would have no use for cripples. "What are you going to do?"

"Take you home at first light."

"And then?"

"What Malien asked. Call our allies together, then ride hell-for-leather for Chanthed. Take on Snoat. Find the summon stone and destroy it."

He lay by the fire. Aviel pulled her blanket around herself, trying to think things through. With no money and no skills to sell she was totally reliant on Shand, but he would soon be leaving. And with Snoat creating chaos on one side and the threat of annihilation on the other, he might never come back.

"I have to matter," she said aloud.

"You talking to me?" Shand said sleepily.

Her family were useless, but she *burned* to count for something. "But what can I do?"

He did not reply, and after a while she lay down and tried to sleep.

"Scent potions," Shand murmured.

"What?" said Aviel.

"Potion making is a neglected branch of the Secret Art, and *scent* potions – potions whose magical effect comes from the careful blending of aromatics, whether pleasant or foul – have scarcely been made in a thousand years."

"You talked to Tallia about them the other day," she said unguardedly.

"I *thought* you were eavesdropping," said Shand.

Aviel's pulse accelerated. Could she become a scent potion maker, an important, useful person?

"I probably don't have the gift," she said gloomily.

"You have an instinct for it, actually."

Her heart soared. "How do you know?"

"After I let you use the workshop, I watched over you for a couple of weeks to make sure you were working safely. And purely by instinct you were using techniques that alchemists and potion makers can take years to get right."

"Really?" Dare she allow herself to dream?

"One day, by accident, you made a simple scent potion."

"What was it?" she cried.

He grimaced. "A potent laxative. I won't go into the gruesome details."

Heat crept up her cheeks. "I'm sorry! How do you know about scent potions anyway?"

"I've made one or two in my time. I could help you with the basics – if you're interested."

Interested? She could have flown around the top of the hill. "What are they used for?"

"Anything that other forms of the Secret Art can be used for – healing, harming, protecting, bewitching, and even killing. Increasing strength or enfeebling, giving hope or courage, or creating despair . . . "

A shiver ran through Aviel at the possibilities. And the dangers. "Surely it can't be right for one person to have such power over others?"

"You might ask the same question of all kinds of people. For instance an archer, who can kill from a distance without being seen – though outside of war, archers rarely do."

"You would teach me?" Her face fell. "But you're going away."

"The Secret Art is mainly learned through practice. I'll lend you my primer on scent potion making. I copied it from the grimoire of my late master, Radizer. After my apprenticeship ended, um, precipitately."

Tallia had mentioned the grimoire, Aviel recalled.

Grimoires are deadly, Shand had replied. *She might be ready for an apprenticeship in six months, but she would need a good master.*

Then find her one! Tallia had replied. *If we're to survive, we're going to need every talent we have.*

"How did an apprentice end up with the grimoire of a master?" said Aviel. "Surely that's . . . unusual?"

"One of my master's experimental potions went badly wrong," said Shand. "It blew his workshop to bits, and him with it, but his grimoire, in its iron case, survived."

"You . . . um . . . filched it?"

"I couldn't leave such a dangerous book in the ruins for any passing fool or villain to find."

"But you never became a master."

"For a girl who's only fifteen, you ask a lot of impertinent questions."

"Sorry, sorry!"

"As a lad, I was easily distracted. I . . . um . . . pursued other career options and never went back to scent potions."

"What career options?"

"Mind your own business."

35

IT'S MY FATE

After the bitter ending to the scholarship test, Wilm needed to be by himself. His hopes of studying at the college had been dashed and he just wanted to get away, but he could not head home without thanking Llian.

Remembering the silver tar that Stanzer and Old Sal had saved him, Wilm stopped at a baker's shop and eyed a large plum pie. It was expensive, two copper grints, but after eating nothing all day he could afford it. It smelled glorious and tasted even better. As he walked along he ate it in small, delicate bites, savouring every sweet morsel.

It took him all the way to the western gate of Chanthed. He kept going, walking fast for an hour and more, until he came to a rivulet. He was miles out of town but it did not bother him; it was a pleasant night and he was used to walking. He had a long drink, washed his face and headed back.

Llian had promised to be there, yet there was still no sign of him when Wilm returned to their room after nine in the evening, and his pack and saddlebags were gone. Wilm was really worried now, for Llian was a man of his word. He must be in some trouble, no doubt to do with Thandiwe, who seemed a very poor friend.

Wilm took off his shirt, reached into his pack for a clean one and saw the folded piece of paper. As he unfolded it, three tars fell out. He read the note, then stared dazedly at the coins. Llian was in terrible trouble, yet he had taken the time to think of Wilm and give him money from his own small purse. Wilm's eyes moistened. He would not think of the money as a gift; it was a loan that he would pay back in full.

How could he find out what had happened to Llian? He was walking past an outdoor café when he saw a face he recognised, the short girl who had answered the first question in the scholarship test. The girl who, in the gown that had been far too big for her, had looked as though she was trapped in a tent.

What was her name? Dajaes Xix. Up close she was older than he'd thought, his own age or even a bit older. She was slowly sipping a lemon drink as if trying to make it last, and she looked desperately unhappy.

"Hello," said Wilm. "I saw you at the test. I'm Wilm. You're Dajaes, aren't you?"

She gave him a tentative smile. She had small white teeth and soft brown eyes, and Wilm thought she looked rather nice.

"You remembered my name?" Her voice was timid, almost inaudible. "You made a joke after you fell on your face. If that had happened to me, I would have died."

"I just opened my mouth and out the words came."

Dajaes shook her head. "And even after falling down, and people laughing at you, you gave a very good answer. You must be so clever."

She looked down at the table, her lower lip trembling. She looked as though she was about to burst into tears.

"Not really," said Wilm. "I'd heard the tale told only a few days ago. Do you mind if I . . . " He gestured to the empty chair.

"Please do. I . . . I don't know anyone in Chanthed. I'm so lonely." She paused then said in a rush, "I've spent all my free time for the last year studying for the test." Her lip trembled again and tears magnified her eyes. "Now I've got to go home and confess I failed because my books were too old, and Father will beat me black and blue."

She rubbed her arms and Wilm noticed several old bruises, faded to the palest yellow.

"That's terrible," he said. "I failed too. I don't know what I'm going to do now."

"I know what's going to happen to me. Father will marry me off to one of his disgusting old drinking mates, and he'll beat me too, and before you know it I'll have three or four screaming kids and then I'll die in childbirth like my mother and my aunt." She burst into tears.

Wilm squirmed. Not having sisters or close relatives, he had not encountered a crying girl at close range before and had no idea how to help her. Impulsively, he reached out and took her small hands in his own, holding them until the weeping fit passed.

"You're so kind," she said. "I'm sure I don't deserve it."

"I'm sure you do, since you've worked so hard. Anyway, you seem really nice. Did you really want to be a chronicler?"

"No, being a historian is a little . . . dry. I wanted to be a teller of the Great Tales. I've been writing stories since I was a little girl; it's all I've ever wanted to do. Father is a tin miner and he thinks telling is stupid, but I've got an uncle who loves the Great Tales and he talked Father into giving me this one chance. But hardly any of the questions were about the tales – they were nearly all chronicler stuff – and . . . and . . . What am I going to do, Wilm?"

She looked as though she was going to cry again. Wilm could hardly blame her; if his fate was to be married off to some foul old drunk who was going to beat him he would cry too. But there was nothing he could do; tomorrow they would leave Chanthed, go their separate ways, and never see each other again.

He squeezed her hands. "I'd better go. I'm looking for a friend. He's in trouble and I've got to help him."

Her face crumpled; she must have been hoping he would stay. "What's his name?"

"Llian. He's a teller."

Her eyes widened; she drew in a sharp breath. "I've read the *Tale of the Mirror* fifteen and a half times. I made my own copy from the one in the Ridsett library. I can't believe it's true."

"What are you talking about? The masters voted it a Great Tale."

Dajaes smiled, and for the first time her sad face came alive. "Not Llian's Great Tale, silly. What they're saying he did."

"What are they saying?" said Wilm.

"That he murdered Master Wistan before the election this afternoon, then ran for his life."

Wilm rocked back on his chair. "The master has been murdered?"

"His throat was cut." She shuddered. "That poor old man. He could barely get out of his chair."

"I don't believe it," said Wilm. "Llian is gentle and kind and generous. Look!"

He pulled out the note, which was still wrapped around the three silver tars. "Even though he was on the run and needed every grint he had, he came back and left this for me."

Awestruck, Dajaes reached out and touched a fingertip to the words written by the great teller. "He's been my hero ever since my uncle started reading me the tale. I was only nine, and I didn't know what a lot of the words meant, but it carried me away into another world."

"Do you believe me?"

"Of course I believe you. A man like Llian would *never* do such a thing."

"Then we've got to help," Wilm said impulsively. "We may be the only people in Chanthed who believe he's innocent."

Her brown eyes glowed for a few seconds, then she shook her head. "I've got to go home," she said dully.

"So your father can marry you to a drunken old brute?"

"It . . . it's my fate."

"No, we can change our lives." The blood was pounding through Wilm's veins; he felt inspired. "I've got no father and my mother is the poorest woman in Casyme, but she saved up her grints to give me this chance."

"But we failed, and now we have to go home."

"No, we don't. I'm going to make something of my life. When the opportunity comes I'm going to grab it with both hands and never look back. You can too."

"I only have eleven grints," said Dajaes. "Just enough to pay for my food on the river ferry home to Ridsett."

"How far is that?"

"Forty leagues. The ferry takes a week."

"I've got four silver tars," said Wilm impulsively. "You can stay with me and we can clear Llian's name. And then . . . something will come up." He knew it would; he felt transformed. He had a mission in life — he had to save his friend. *The key to success is never giving up.*

A flush appeared on her pale cheeks. Belatedly Wilm realised that she had taken his proposal in a different way. He expected her to smack him across the face and walk out, but she just sat there, staring at him.

"I . . . I didn't mean . . . " he said stiffly.

"I would be disgraced," said Dajaes.

"My mother brought me up to be a gentleman," said Wilm primly.

He had never been closer to a young woman than he was now, save for that friendly kiss from Aviel when he was leaving Casyme. In truth, Wilm was a late developer, and physical intimacy was too embarrassing to think about.

"My father would not see it that way."

"Would he come after you?"

She laughed hollowly. "He wouldn't waste the money. He would cast me out. I would never be able to go home."

Wilm did not think that would be much of a loss but was wise enough not to say it. "I'd hate it if I couldn't go home."

After a long pause, Dajaes said, "I'd miss my uncle."

Wilm stared at his hands. What could he, who was famous for getting things wrong, do to help Llian? He could not imagine where to begin.

"But Llian has been unjustly accused of murder," said Dajaes as if she were thinking things through as she spoke. "He's been framed by the real killer and we're the only people who believe in him. We have to try and save him." She stood up suddenly, and there was such solemn resolve on her young face that his own spirits lifted. "I will endure the disgrace. We're going to save Llian, together."

He extended his hand, but she moved in and gave him a quick hug, then stepped back as if to make clear that it was an entirely businesslike arrangement.

"How do we start?" she said.

Wilm was dazed. He had not imagined that she would agree. Now she had, the surge of energy that had carried him along faded, and the plum pie was a distant memory. "I'm so hungry I can't think straight. Have you had dinner?"

She shook her head. "Everything is so expensive – test entrance fee, library fee, robes fee . . ."

"I'd be broke if it wasn't for Llian," said Wilm, "and the woman on the door. She remitted the entrance fee because I knew him. It's a tar I never expected to have; let's spend it on the best dinner we can get."

"Let's not," she said sensibly. "It may take a long time to clear Llian's name and we only have your four tars and my eleven grints. Let's have the cheapest dinner that will fill us up, and get to work."

They had big bowls of vegetable soup and chunks of coarse freshly baked bread spread with rich brown dripping. It was delicious, though Wilm hardly tasted it; he had to keep grinding his knuckles into his thigh to remind himself that this was real. That he was sitting opposite a very nice girl who loved the tales even more than he did, and they were about to go on a rescue mission into the unknown with not the faintest idea where it would lead them.

"First we have to find out the facts," said Dajaes. "I've heard rumours but I'm sure most of them aren't true."

She had very good manners, always setting her knife and spoon down perpendicular to the table edge and never putting her elbows on the table. Wilm made sure he did not slurp his soup and worried about dribbling it down his front.

"I'd better go and see the sergeant," said Wilm. "He'll want to talk to me, since I came here with Llian."

"I'll come with you. He might not be so hard on you then. I'll . . . I'll pretend to be your girlfriend."

That warmed him. They finished their dinner and headed down to the watch house. Wilm felt self-conscious walking beside her, almost as self-conscious as he had going up onto the stage at the scholarship test.

But this time it was a good feeling.

36

I'LL HAVE TO BURN
ANOTHER LIBRARY

In his exquisite manse of Pem-Y-Rum, ten miles downriver from Chanthed, Cumulus Snoat frowned at Ifoli's news. He did not like to frown; it marred the perfection of his noble forehead, but in times of the greatest vexation he could not help himself.

"Are you saying Basible Norp has failed me?" said Snoat. Then, "Why do you cringe from me? It's not your lovely neck under threat."

Ifoli forced calmness upon herself, and the tension in her jaw muscles eased. "Apparently Wistan secured the college's treasures before he was killed, but neither the details of the protection spells nor the devices and talismans that maintain them can be located."

"Do you mean . . . ?"

"Basible can't break the protections."

"And therefore can't deliver me the manuscripts of the first twenty-two Great Tales."

Snoat touched the edge of Llian's manuscript with a fingertip. He was so enchanted by it that he had to have it with him wherever he went, and lived in terror that it would be stolen.

"Almost any spell can be broken if enough talent and effort is devoted to it."

"I can't bear to wait," said Snoat. "Nothing satisfies me any more; even my most priceless wines now seem tasteless. I'll have to burn another library – how else can I cope?" He felt another frown forming. "What about Wistan's dirt book?"

"Basible found the ashes of a small book, burned some hours before Wistan was killed. Nothing can be resurrected from it."

"Now I'm vexed!" cried Snoat. "Have you no good news?"

"Your army has swept all before it in the north. You now hold everything between Thurkad and Elludore Forest."

"Better than nothing," he said grudgingly, "but far greater prizes lie to the south."

"You'll need a bigger army for that."

"I'm raising one. What news of the despicable Zain?"

"He hasn't been found."

"I am most displeased. Go!"

Ifoli did not move. "Cumulus, you gave firm orders that you would see no one this week, but . . . "

This was almost an insurrection. And yet . . . "I value you for your ability to think and your appreciation that there may be times when you know my business better than I do. You may speak."

"The bankrupt chronicler, Thandiwe Moorn, wishes to put a proposition to you."

"She is utterly destitute?"

"And at the end of her rope. The bailiff will come for her within days, unless—"

"Send her in."

Shortly Thandiwe entered. Destitute she might be, but she put on a good show. Curvaceous bordering on voluptuous, a waterfall of black hair, a simple but elegant blue gown. She was nowhere near Ifoli's level of beauty, but for a woman who must have been thirty-six Thandiwe was rather fine. Nervous, though. Her left knee had a tremor. She bowed, a trifle too low.

"Speak," said Snoat.

"You have a passion for the Great Tales," said Thandiwe. "I think I can bring you a new one."

"You *think* you can bring me a new one."

"The only certainty in life is death."

"Especially when I deal it," he said pointedly. "Go on."

She squirmed. "A decade ago, in the months before Magister Mendark's death, he gave Llian almost unfettered access to his personal papers. Mendark wanted Llian to write the tale of his life – his often renewed lives, in fact."

"Mendark was a great man," said Snoat, "but fatally flawed."

"He was at the centre of the greatest events of the past thousand years, and shaped many of them. Yet the tale of his life has never been told."

"Why not?"

"Llian chose not to because of what he saw as Mendark's corruption. Llian put his notes into the college library and, as far as I know, I'm the only person who has had full access to them."

"What does this have to do with me?" said Snoat.

"I want to write the tale but . . ."

"Debtors' prison looms."

"If Basible Norp would give me access to Llian's notes, and you were to provide modest assistance . . ."

"You owe Anjo five hundred and fifty tells. Hardly modest."

"With your support I could make a Great Tale of Mendark's life and gift the manuscript to you."

To give away something so valuable she must be desperate. Yet to have the mastership in her grasp twice and lose it both times, lose everything, would make anyone desperate.

"I could not accept it as a gift," said Snoat.

Thandiwe's face fell.

"For such a treasure, *if* it should be voted a Great Tale, I would pay full price," he added. "After subtracting your debts. I will consider the matter. Ifoli will escort you out."

Thandiwe forced a smile. Clearly, she had hoped for a clearer indication. Or perhaps she feared he would give Llian's notes to someone else to write the tale. Perhaps he would.

When she was gone and Ifoli stood beside him again, Snoat said quietly, "Contact Basible. He will send Llian's notes for this tale with the utmost dispatch."

"With an armed escort?" said Ifoli. "To make sure they can't go astray."

"Quite."

"What do you think?" Snoat said to Ifoli the following evening.

He had read the key parts of Llian's notes. Ifoli, now desperately fighting off a beauty-marring weariness, had spent all night and half the day reading eight hundred pages in Llian's calligraphic hand.

"If certain questions about Mendark's work were answered, and it was supplemented by an account of his last days and his death, it could make a Great Tale."

"The twenty-fourth Great Tale. *My tale.*" He sighed.

"But is she the right person to tell it?"

"Thandiwe is more than competent but less than great. Yet she's ambitious, passionate . . . and desperate. No one would work harder to make it a glorious tale. I will commission her. But before I do, I've identified an intriguing possibility." Snoat was testing Ifoli. "I wonder if you saw it too?"

She did not answer for a good while and his congenital mistrust stirred. Was she merely gathering her thoughts, or was she choosing how much to tell him?

"I saw a number of possibilities," Ifoli said carefully. "To which do you refer?"

"One that might be connected to a certain incomplete device of Mendark's." Snoat wasn't going to give her any more than that. He wanted her unbiased thoughts.

"The one we saw the day we used the secret code to get into the council's spell vault?"

"Precisely."

"There could be a new kind of mancery. One that Llian, not having any talent for the Secret Art, did not recognise," said Ifoli.

"Put it into words for me."

"Mancery has always been limited because power can only be drawn from two places: within oneself, or from a painstakingly enchanted object ..."

"But there's a hypothesis, the *secret of mancery* ... " he prompted.

"That power – vast amounts of it – could be stored in certain natural objects, right under our noses."

"Until there's evidence of it, the secret of mancery remains mere speculation."

"Judging by Llian's notes, Mendark may have gained that evidence," said Ifoli. "He may have been close to mastering the secret, or at least the *theory* behind it."

"A theory can't give me my heart's desire. Besides, Mendark burned his library before he died and all his work was lost." Snoat looked at her expectantly. He did not think she was holding anything back, but he had to be sure.

After another long pause, Ifoli said, "Llian read all Mendark's papers, including his work on mancery. And whatever Llian reads twice, he can remember. What if his memory – what he doesn't know that he knows – could allow Mendark's work to be reconstructed?"

Snoat felt all choked up. "If I were capable of love, Ifoli," he sighed, "you would be the one."

"Thank you, Cumulus." He was not sure if she was being ironic.

"The device we saw in the spell vault may have been Mendark's failed attempt to tap this new source of power," said Snoat. "If the theory could be turned into a practical magical device, or devices I'd have the power to crack the protection on the twenty-two Great Tales."

"That could take years," said Ifoli.

"Unless a genius looked at the problem in an entirely new way."

"Will that be all, Cumulus?"

"When I was a young man," Snoat mused, "that doddering old fool, Nadiril the so-called Sage, chased me out of the Great Library with a broomstick. That very day I resolved to build a collection greater than his, then take his from him. With the secret of mancery I could do just that." Snoat realised that his megalomania was showing. "But I'm daydreaming. Can Llian be compelled to reveal what he knows?"

"With a murder charge hanging over his head he must be even more desperate than Thandiwe."

"Have her lure him here with a tempting offer. She will oversee his work and make sure he stays honest."

"And then?" said Ifoli.

"Llian will do a private telling of his *Tale of the Mirror*, just for me."

"And then?"

"Where is the pleasure if he can do a telling for anyone else? Where is the joy in owning the original manuscript of his tale if he can make a copy? Besides, if he can assist me to reconstruct the secret of mancery, he can assist someone else."

"So Llian has to die?" said Ifoli.

"I would apologise to him in advance," said Snoat. "He's a great man, even though he is a cursed Zain. I'd explain that I sincerely regretted having to put him down."

"You might have trouble getting him to appreciate your point of view," Ifoli said drily.

"One more thing. The chain made by Shuthdar?"

"Ragred has gone to get it from Karan."

37

IT'S BACK, MUMMY. *IT'S BACK!*

Karan's desperation grew with every hour of that interminable trip across the mountains. She felt sure they were being followed. Had her reckless use of hrux on Maigraith turned her into a deadly enemy? And if Karan did not get to Chanthed soon, Llian would surely be caught, tried for a murder he had not committed, then executed. She kept seeing the image from Sulien's nightmare – his body lying on that expanse of polished stone.

If she lost Sulien and Llian she would surely go mad, as her poor mother had. More than once Karan had felt the madness wrapping its tendrils around her, trying to drag her down into the pit she had visited once before. If it took her again, she would never escape.

Sulien sensed it too. She was normally an independent child, but Karan had never known her to be so solicitous, or so clingy.

That evening, after an hour-long search for a secure campsite, she chose a steep bare hill from which she would be able to see and hear anyone coming. The light was fading by the time they panted their way to the top, yet Karan was tempted to go straight down again. The crest was a grassy oval with a broken diamond of stand-ing stones and, at its centre, a partly collapsed tunnel tomb. Many of the stones of the diamond had fallen, but at the far end a single trilithon remained – like the gate from Sulien's dream, only smaller. The stones were grey, not red; nonetheless, it was an unfortunate coincidence.

Karan reminded herself that tunnel tombs and stone arrays were common in Meldorin – she had seen them in dozens of places. Besides, they could go no further; she was exhausted and Sulien was asleep on her feet.

After a scrappy dinner, the same as all their previous ones, Sulien crawled into her sleeping pouch and went to sleep. Karan sat up, knife in hand, watching and listening. If Maigraith was following, what could be done to stop her?

Restless now, she walked around the rim of the hill, which fell away steeply on all sides save the east, the way they had come up. A light mist heightened the similarity between this place and the flat peak with the Crimson Gate, the gate that on the night of the triple moons would bring the Merdrun to Santhenar.

The hairs rose on the back of her neck; she should not have come here. She was running back to Sulien when she let out a shriek: "Mummy! *Mummeeeee!*"

Karan fell to her knees beside her daughter. Sulien was sitting up, eyes tightly closed. Her hands were clutched to her head again and she was shaking it from side to side as if trying to dislodge something clinging there.

"It hurts," she whimpered. Her voice faded. "Hurts really bad." Her eyes shot open. "An evil old woman. Pointing at me! She's got horrible eyes. Mummy, she's trying to kill me! Help, help!" Blood trickled from her nose. "Help," she said more faintly.

Then Sulien began to scream, a shrill, awful sound, but each scream was softer than the one before, as if the life was being drained out of her.

Putting her hands around Sulien's head, Karan tried to lift the attack from her, as she had lifted the nightmares. She heard a great sigh, *Aaahhh!* Had she done just what the magiz wanted?

"Get away from her, you murdering bitch!" Karan snarled. "You're . . . not . . . touching . . . my . . . daughter."

She looked deeper, found the new link the magiz was using and tried to break it. But it was far stronger this time; she could not touch it.

Her only option was to take the attack on herself, as she had done before. Karan wrenched the link out bodily and Sulien shot to her feet as if she had been jerked up on a rope. She teetered on the tips of her toes for a few seconds, then slumped to the ground, gasping. Her mouth and chin were covered in blood. She wiped it away with her sleeve, smearing it across her left cheek.

"Mummy?" whispered Sulien.

Karan could not move; she was on her knees on the frosty grass, and the spike in the top of her head was back, though it no longer felt as though it was being gently tapped into her skull. Now each thud was a hammer blow, bruising and brutal. She could not think for the pain.

"What's the matter, Mummy?"

"Mglpf!" Karan could not get any words out.

Sulien threw her arms around Karan, and at her touch the pain eased. Karan could still hear the thudding, but it seemed more distant, and each impact was duller and more remote, until the pain faded away.

Sulien's eyes widened and she gave a low moan. She was staring over Karan's shoulder. Karan looked round but the hillside was empty.

"What is it?" she gasped.

"I had a nightmare ... weeks ago," said Sulien. "But you took it away."

"Yes," said Karan, her skin crawling.

"It's back, Mummy. *It's back!*"

"What's back?" Karan said carefully, not wanting to alarm her more than necessary.

"The big bald man who saw me. He's got a jagged black tattoo on his forehead." Her eyes widened; Karan could see the rest of the first nightmare coming back, bit by bit. "His name is Gergrig and his army was attacking a beautiful city and killing everyone. He wants to invade Santhenar on the night of the triple moons."

"It was just a nightmare."

"That's a fib!" cried Sulien. "Gergrig knows I saw him. He ordered his evil magiz to kill me. And you and Daddy ..."

She broke off, staring into space again. Her pupils widened and contracted over and over, as if she was staring at a series of bright flashes.

"There was another nightmare," Sulien said slowly. Her brow furrowed; she peered into Karan's eyes, and there was nothing she could do to stop this one coming back either. "Daddy was dead! I saw him lying on the cold, cold stone."

"That was just the magiz, trying to frighten us," said Karan.

"But Daddy's been framed for murder. He's running for his life, and if they catch him they'll hang him just like they hanged poor Benie! You've got to save him, Mummy."

Clearly Sulien had to be told everything. "The magiz just attacked you," said Karan. "And I can't do anything for Llian until I . . . deal with her."

Sulien said nothing.

"Do you remember any other nightmares about the enemy?" said Karan. Her heartbeat was a series of slow heavy thumps.

"No. Should I?"

"Gergrig once said that you'd seen their greatest weakness. If we knew that, we'd know how to beat them. It's really, really important."

Sulien pressed her spread fingers against the sides of her head, closed her eyes and sat still for a minute or two. Then her eyes sprang open. "Is that why the magiz wants to kill me?"

"Yes."

"I'm sorry. I don't remember it at all."

"Maybe it'll come back later." Karan got up and put more wood on the fire.

"What are you going to do?" said Sulien. Her voice had a tremor, as if she felt she had let everyone down.

"I have to go back to Cinnabar, the little world the Merdrun are attacking," Karan said slowly. "Your Aunty Malien put a spell on me – a disembodiment spell – so I can get there in spirit."

Sulien wrapped her arms around Karan. "Are you going to attack the magiz?"

"If I don't kill her, she'll kill us all. And I've got to do it soon, before she attacks again. But . . . "

Sulien looked up at Karan, breathing shallowly and fast. "You're scared to leave me here, all alone."

No parent should ever have to tell their child such things. Karan took Sulien's hands. "I . . . I might not come back. And that would leave you all alone, with . . . with . . . "

Sulien took a very deep breath. "Of course you'll come back. That rotten old magiz couldn't possibly beat you."

"She's a powerful mancer, and I'm just a sensitive who can do a few things with links and seeings. She might beat me, and before I take her on I've got to know you'll be safe."

Sulien's lower lip wobbled. She wiped her eyes. "If – if you don't come back, I'll ride straight to Chanthed. It's only a day from here. I'll be safe there."

Until the magiz was dead Sulien would not be safe anywhere, but there was no point saying so. Karan told Sulien exactly what she was going to do, and how, then got out the hideous copper mask.

"Aah!" cried Sulien, burying her face in Karan's chest. "What's that?"

"Mad Basunez's death mask."

Sulien took another peek. "How can anyone be that ugly?"

"He was a very evil old man."

"Don't use it!"

"The mask was made by your grandfather Galliad. It's safe."

It was clear from the expression on Sulien's face that she thought using it was a very bad idea. "How will I know?"

"Know what?" said Karan.

"If the magiz has . . . got you. And you're not coming back," Sulien ended in a rush.

Malien had explained that. "My body will stop breathing."

"But before you can attack the magiz, you've got to let her materialise you. Your body won't be here."

Sulien's wits were in better shape than Karan's own. Not a good sign. "If I disappear, wait a quarter of an hour. If I don't come back by then it means she's got me, and you must leave at once. Ride to Chanthed, without stopping, and find . . . Thandiwe. She'll look after you until Shand or Tallia or Malien gets there." Karan crossed her fingers behind her back.

Sulien looked astounded, as well she might. *"Thandiwe?"*

"She likes Llian. Of course she'll like you."

This irony was even more sickening than sending Llian to Thandiwe. Could she protect Sulien? It hardly seemed likely but Karan did not know anyone else in Chanthed.

"All right," said Sulien, very quietly. She gave Karan a tremulous hug. "You'd better . . . "

"Yes," said Karan.

She took the death mask in her right hand, made sure her knife was in its sheath on her hip and focused on the golden castle the Merdrun had been planning to attack next.

"Trigger!" she said.

Karan's insides burned like an oil-fed fire, then her spirit was inside the castle, though it no longer resembled the beautiful place she had seen weeks ago, when the magiz and Gergrig had so very nearly caught her. Under the light of the little yellow moon and the middle-sized red one, the castle was a ruin.

Weeks of bombardment with siege engines had brought down the tops of the towers and battered away most of the tens of thousands of wall carvings; only smashed fragments remained. The streets were a mess of golden rubble, twisted green copper roofing and broken black slates, and there were corpses everywhere. The defenders were little better than corpses themselves; they were battered, staring-eyed zombies who looked as though they had not slept in a week. They knew what would happen when the Merdrun broke in, as soon they must, but they were determined to fight for what was theirs.

In other circumstances Karan might have fought beside them, for she could see a desperate nobility in the defenders that was entirely lacking in their attackers. She rose into the air to see how long they had left.

Not long at all. The top of the wall was almost empty of living guards, and knee-deep in dead ones. She imagined Sulien kneeling beside her body back on the hilltop, desperately watching to make sure she kept breathing. Karan had to close off the image – it was too painful.

She was looking over the edge when the great wall began to collapse up from the base. There had not been one of the magiz's explosions this time; some dark mancery, long in preparation, had eaten away the rock below a hundred-yard section of the wall, leaving it unsupported.

Within minutes, broken stone filled the hole where the rock had been removed, and the attackers were scrambling in intent on slaughter. Karan could not bear to witness it. She was roaming back and forth, looking for the magiz, when she remembered that Gergrig had ordered her to take no part in the attack until she had eliminated Sulien and her household.

Karan drifted lower, searching for the red tent with the green rope along its ridge, and found it where it had been last time, but it was empty. Where was the magiz? She floated higher, scanning around the ruined castle and then above it, and her eye caught a faint flash as off a glass surface – the magiz's sextant.

The upper edge of the huge green moon was just cresting the horizon to Karan's right. Her heart lurched painfully – all three moons would be in the sky at once – though a swift glance told her that they would not line up. The middle-sized moon, the fastest-moving of the three, was diving towards the left horizon and would set within minutes.

Karan took a firm grip on the death mask and headed up towards the magiz. It was bitterly cold at this altitude: the ground was sheathed in thick ice, every vertical surface was hung with blue icicles, and even in her bodiless state it was numbing her fingers. The magiz, her stringy form made shapeless by heavy furs, was entering another measurement in her almanack.

Karan instinctively looked up towards the ice fortress high above. It was a series of igloo-shaped masses, lit dimly from within by haloes of orange light like strings of glowing beads. There was no sign of guards. A long way above the fortress she saw the flat-topped peak with the red trilithon – the gate the Merdrun were fighting towards – but the mist up there was too thick to make it out.

She landed fifty yards from the magiz and stood there, watching warily; the magiz might have set out any number of detectors and traps. Karan headed slowly towards her, psyching herself up to do something utterly foreign to her nature – kill in cold blood. It was not an easy thing to think about, but if the magiz lived, Sulien would die.

Forty yards. Thirty-five. Thirty.

Crack! A dazzling white nimbus sprang up around her. Karan let out an involuntary cry of fear and saw the magiz turn slowly, smiling that blank-eyed smile. Her trap had been sprung and again Karan's strength drained away.

Five slender green beams fixed on her from all sides. Were they part of her enemy's materialisation spell or did they have another purpose? As she continued towards the magiz, the green beams dragged on her; she felt as though she was hauling an increasingly heavy weight. Twenty yards. Fifteen. Ten.

The magiz waved her white rod in the air, rather as a conductor would, then snapped it down and pointed the tip at Karan. The green rays thickened and began to sting.

"Materialise!" hissed the magiz. "How I'm going to drink *your* life."

Karan's skin burned and the heat sank into her like a reversal of the blistering internal heat of the disembodiment spell. Then, in an explosive and painful instant, her spirit outline filled with real flesh and bone as her body dematerialised on the hill next to Sulien and materialised here.

Instantly Karan knew she had made a terrible mistake – she had failed to dress for the cold, which was so bitter up here that each breath burned all the way down her nose and throat and into her lungs. It was a killing cold and she could not survive it for more than a few minutes. Already her fingers were stiffening; soon frostbite would set in.

What must Sulien be thinking? That Karan was already dead and the magiz would soon attack her directly? Don't wait fifteen minutes – run *now*! Get away from the trilithon.

Karan fitted the copper mask to her face, but the moment she took her hand away the mask went with it – it had frozen to her fingers. She pressed it against her forehead until it stuck and slowly worked her fingers free. If she ever got out of here she might be scarred for life, though that was the least of her worries.

She thrust out her right arm, her fingers throbbing, and pointed at the magiz's heart – but could not speak a word. Her fingers and toes, her ears and lips and nose, and even her eyes were burning with the cold. It hurt so much that she could not remember the word to release the killing spell in the death mask, the spell that would turn the magiz's power back on her.

Then she had it. "Transpose!"

No sound came out; her vocal cords must be too cold. Karan rubbed her throat furiously with her free hand.

The magiz thrust the white rod high in the air and fired a blast of red. Horns went off in the distance and heavily armed Merdrun came from everywhere, charging towards Karan.

"Tranzbose!" she slurred. "Tran*spose*! *Transpose!*"

Only on the third attempt did she manage to say the word clearly. The death mask grew hot and fell off her face, and her hand wobbled; instead of pointing at the magiz's heart the spell was directed at her left leg. Karan saw no beam or flash or any other evidence that it had worked, but suddenly the magiz was screaming and rolling around on the icy ground with white smoke billowing up from her left leg, then flame and black smoke. A small popping explosion spread thousands of little fragments of char across the ice and ...

The magiz's left leg was gone.

It was horrible, and Karan's spell had done it. But the troops were closing in and coming fastest of all was Gergrig. Was there time to finish off the magiz? Karan had to try. She snatched up the frigid death mask, held it to her face and pointed again.

"Transpose!"

Her arm shook and the reversal spell missed. There was no time for another attempt; she had to flee now or die.

"Spell-stop!" she cried. "Spell-stop!"

It did not work, though the death mask grew hot again. Could it be interfering? Gergrig was charging in, only twenty yards away, swinging his serrated sword back for a blow that would hack her in two. At the same moment the magiz managed to sit up and point her rod at Karan.

"Spell-stop!" Karan yelled.

Of course it wasn't working; she had been materialised. Before she could dematerialise, the magiz's spell had to be broken.

"Transpose!" screamed Karan, pointing at the magiz.

The rod blasted at the same instant that the transpose spell struck it, and blew the rod to pieces, embedding hundreds of little white splinters in the magiz's hand and releasing a torrent of power that created a fireball and a mushroom cloud of yellow smoke. The magiz fell back screaming and, as Gergrig swung, Karan dematerialised.

"Materialise!" shrieked the magiz, pointing with her splintery fingers.

"Spell-stop!" yelled Karan. "Spell-stop!"

She materialised in a black nowhere, then burst out of it into moonlight and fell a couple of yards onto the hilltop directly under the grey trilithon, thirty yards from Sulien, with a bone-jarring thud. Karan rolled over, groaning.

"So hot here," she whispered. Her fingers and toes and the tip of her nose were throbbing.

"Mummy!" cried Sulien, running to her. She stopped suddenly, staring. "Mummy?"

"I'm all right," gasped Karan. "I didn't kill her, but the transpose spell destroyed her rod; that's how I got back. I've stopped her for a while, and I'm all right!"

"No," said Sulien, holding both hands out in front of her as if to block a bright light. "No, no!"

"What's the matter?"

"She's put her mark on you."

"Where?" said Karan, checking herself over. "I can't see anything."

"In here," said Sulien, tapping Karan's forehead. "It's like . . . a mental lighthouse, flashing out of you."

Karan's blood ran cold. The magiz must have marked her with a psychic stigma, and it was the perfect defence. Karan would not dare attack again because the magiz would always know where she was, and what she was doing, before she could act.

But it was worse than that. The magiz would always know where Sulien was too. She would never be safe while she remained with Karan.

There was only one solution. She had to send her away, though who could she possibly entrust her daughter to?

38

A LIFE THRICE OWED

"What's that funny smell?" said Sulien late the following afternoon. They were winding down the last pass towards the foothills and would reach Chanthed tomorrow.

Karan sniffed, and her healed bones gave an anticipatory throb. Whelm! She had been hoping to meet them, knowing Idlis would come this way on his annual trip to bring her hrux. And they were close.

"The Whelm feed those strange horses of theirs some stinking herb. I never learned why."

She looked over the brink, down to the road far below. There, moving in a steady line, were half a dozen cadaverous Whelm horses and their equally gaunt riders. They were all bony, with grey skin and big ugly feet and hands. It was Idlis and Yetchah – she recognised them – plus another four Whelm escorts. Or spies. An insecure people who lived in a cold and inhospitable southern land, they saw threats everywhere.

The Whelm lived to serve a master. First Rulke; then, after he was imprisoned in the Nightland, they had served Yggur instead, though they had never respected him. They had spent a thousand years aching for the time when Rulke would finally free himself. *Oh, perfect master!* they had called him when the great day came. His death not long afterwards had left them masterless and bereft, and masterless and bereft they remained to this day.

"They frighten me," said Sulien.

"Me too, yet Idlis and Yetchah have been good to me," said Karan.

"I know," Sulien muttered. She had heard it too many times. "Idlis hunted you halfway across Meldorin once. But you spared his life, three times, and that means he owes you for ever."

Karan started. Could they be the answer to her prayers? Maigraith certainly feared the Whelm, who had tortured her many years ago. If anyone could protect Sulien from Maigraith, they could. And perhaps they could hide her from the magiz too.

No! She could not even *think* about doing that to Sulien.

As they went down, the reek grew stronger until it tore at the passages of her nose and stung her eyes. Sulien's eyes were watering so badly she could barely see. They turned the last hairpin bend and found the six Whelm arrayed across the track in front of them, enveloped in robes and hoods to protect their sensitive grey skin from the autumn sun, weak though it was. Their black eyes blinked behind slitted-bone eye covers.

"Karan," said the bone-and-skin man second from the left, Idlis. "To have come all this way, you must be desperate for hrux."

His face was terribly scarred, the skin like thick paper torn to pieces then crudely glued together in overlapping layers. His voice was as gloopy as boiling porridge. He attempted a smile but it failed and died – any form of levity was anathema to the Whelm. Nonetheless, Karan could tell he was pleased to see her. A bond had grown between them over the years, the strangest imaginable.

"I am," said Karan. "But that's not why I'm here."

"You're hunted," said the woman to his left, whose name was Yetchah.

She had approached prettiness when she was young, in a gaunt black-eyed way, though she had lost weight and looks since Karan had seen her a year ago. All the Whelm seemed more meagre than she remembered them. How they must be suffering in their masterless exile.

"How do you know?"

"Echoes from a sending," said Yetchah, which meant nothing to Karan. She looked down at Sulien with a strange, almost yearning expression. "The little one has grown."

"Sulien," she said. "My name is Sulien!"

"We will camp," said Idlis.

They rode into the trees and down a gentle slope until they were out of sight of the track, and dismounted. Two Whelm began to clear the ground in two places – one circle for themselves and another, forty yards away, for Karan and Sulien. Another two gathered firewood. Idlis and Yetchah stood by while Karan removed Jergoe's saddle, rubbed him down and carried her gear across to the smaller campsite. Yetchah headed down to a rivulet for water, stopped, then turned and cast a longing look at Sulien.

"Sulien, could you help Yetchah fetch the water?" said Karan.

Sulien's eyes widened. She began to say no.

"No one would take better care of you," said Karan. "Except me."

"And Daddy!" Sulien snapped.

Yetchah had been there for Karan's dreadful labour, which had nearly been fatal to mother and baby. In the end, under Idlis's direction, Yetchah had drawn Sulien safely out.

Sulien raised her chin, untied the water pot and went with Yetchah, though she maintained a good distance between them. Karan watched her out of sight then turned to Idlis.

"Our business first," he said, throwing back his hood and taking off the eye covers. Neither were needed in the cool shade under the trees in the hour before sunset.

Karan took the little box out of her pocket. He opened it and pressed in a lump of hrux with thick-knuckled spatulate fingers. It only half filled the box.

"The harvest was bad this year," he said. "I fear you must endure more pain than usual."

"Whatever you bring, I accept with gratitude."

He bowed. "It is poor recompense for a life thrice owed." The black eyes searched hers. "You are in trouble."

"So much trouble that I can scarcely bear to talk about it."

"Yet a trouble shared is a trouble cut in half."

In some respects she found it easier to unburden herself to Idlis than she had to Rachis or even Tallia. Karan had no idea what Idlis was thinking, though, since he felt contempt for everyone she knew save her and Sulien, he was bound to be on her side. But where to start?

"Llian is on the run," she said, "accused of murdering Wistan, the Master of the College of the Histories."

"Llian is a fool," said Idlis. "No one could understand what you see in him."

She wasn't going to try and explain. "It's love."

"Ah!" Idlis seemed to be trying to comprehend the notion. Yetchah had once appeared to love him, though Karan was not sure to what degree Idlis had been capable of returning her affection. "Llian would kill, if forced to it." He worked his grey eyelids up and down with his fingers. "But he is not a murderer," he added.

"Will you stand up in court and testify to that effect?"

Idlis's grey lips stretched halfway across his flat face and he made a peculiar squawking noise that she could only assume, never having heard it before, was laughter. She laughed too. The notion of a Whelm testifying on behalf of a Zain was absurd enough, but the idea that any old human court would admit a character reference given by a Whelm was beyond preposterous.

"I have to get to Chanthed and save him," said Karan.

"I understand the need. But you have another problem."

"Maigraith. You know her."

"A desperate woman."

Karan told him the whole story.

"This Julken should have been strangled at birth," said Idlis.

"No!" she cried.

"Some pairings are wrong. Rulke, our perfect master, believed he had found his match and his soulmate in Maigraith. We all believed it at the time, and we were wrong. There is a flaw in her, as is often the case with triunes."

"Like me."

"Yetchah and I drew forth the girl-child Sulien from your body, alert for any such flaw."

"And?" cried Karan.

"In choosing to mate with that buffoon Llian, somehow your womanly instinct led you to select the complement that was right for you. Sulien is not flawed."

Karan wasn't sure whether she had been complimented or insulted.

"But Maigraith's choice was a disastrous one. By mating with Rulke, the flaw was magnified. No child of hers by our perfect master could ever be anything but a monster."

"Then her quest is doomed," said Karan.

"Yes, though she will pursue it, with increasing bitterness, until the very stars wink out. But there is a third problem."

"We're being hunted," said Karan. She was about to tell Idlis about the Merdrun and the magiz when an instinct warned her to keep silent. She could not have said why.

"And they're close," said Idlis.

"Maigraith!"

"No."

"How can you tell?"

"We are far from home, and the people of Meldorin do not love us.

We search our surroundings for danger using a kind of . . . sending. It creates echoes, and one is coming down the way you came."

It had to be someone sent by or under the control of the magiz. "I'll be careful," said Karan, "but what am I to do about Maigraith?"

"There's only way to put an end to it. Kill her."

"I'm not a murderer!"

"If she tried to kill Sulien, would you not defend her to the death?"

"That's different."

"It's only a matter of degree," said Idlis. "The sooner it's done, the less trouble you'll be put to."

"Maigraith is Shand's granddaughter, and he's my friend."

"You would put friendship before the life of your own flesh and blood?"

"It's not that simple."

"It is very simple. If you kill Maigraith, you solve the problem and save your daughter, and all it costs you is one friend. Allow Maigraith to live and you will eventually lose your daughter, she will suffer a terrible fate at the hands of a monster, and you'll blame your friend and lose him too."

He had a point, though it was like being struck in the midriff with a battering ram.

"Then help me," she said, reaching out to him, the words tumbling out spontaneously. "I've got to get to Llian and I can't risk having Sulien with me. Take her! Take her with you to the frozen south. Hide her and look after her until . . . "

Idlis's ruined face heaved. He liked the idea even less than she did.

"If you ask it," he said, "I will do it because of the lifelong obligation I owe you. But such an exile does not please your daughter."

There came a clang and a cry of "Mummy, no!"

Sulien had dropped the pot of water she had carried all the way from the rivulet. Her trousers were wet up to the knees and she was staring at Karan in betrayed desperation. Then she turned and bolted up the slope into the trees.

Karan ran after her, but her bones must have shifted in the week-long ride from Gothryme. Every step sent shivers of pain up to her hips and Sulien was leaving her behind. The forest was scrubby at the top of the hill, then Karan descended into a series of parallel grooves, miniature ridges and valleys no more than thirty feet from crest to trough, with bands of dark shale angling out of their sides.

Sulien passed over the crest of the third ridge and out of sight. Karan stumbled after her, topped the ridge and stopped. Sulien had only been thirty yards ahead but there was no sign of her.

"Sulien?"

No answer.

A band of olive-green bushes meandered along the base of the valley, not tall enough to conceal a standing adult, though enough to hide Sulien. The ground showed no tracks. At the bottom Karan saw a small boot print in the moist earth, then a strand of red hair caught on a twig. Sulien had gone up the little valley, under cover.

She had a rebellious streak that Karan, recognising much of herself in the child, had not tried hard to curb. She followed the intermittent tracks up. If Sulien broke out of the bushes to either side, she was bound to see her.

The tracks led up the base of the little valley to a dripping hump where the bushes were sparse and the finely banded shale outcropped like the pages of a book. Karan lost Sulien there. She climbed the wet hump, stood on top and looked around. Ahead, a dip in the rock had created a shallow pool ten feet long and three wide at its widest point, though only six inches deep. The water was clear, the dead leaves lying on the bottom undisturbed. Sulien had not gone through it and there were no tracks to either side.

Hairs lifted on the back of Karan's neck. Something was wrong. She looked to either side and back, trying to gauge how far she had come. A quarter of a mile at most, but too far to call Idlis; he would never hear her through the trees.

"Sulien? Come out at once!"

It would soon be dark. A line of pregnant clouds was moving up from the south and the air had a heavy, moist odour she had not smelled at Gothryme in ages. It was going to rain.

She trudged up the valley. The bushes were sparser here, the ground rockier, and a hundred yards ahead it rose steeply to a fist-shaped knob that thrust outwards, providing an outlook over the surrounding woodland.

Karan headed to the left around the knob, the front face being too steep. Low-growing ferns brushed her calves. The rock here was a yellow, gritty sandstone that rasped at her fingertips as she climbed. The top of the outcrop was oval-shaped and almost flat, like a beret. She was scrambling up when a warty hand slapped across her mouth and nose, and she was dragged backwards then shoved to the ground.

She looked up into the face of the ugliest man she had ever seen, a huge lumpy fellow with scarred and mottled skin covered in warts and wens and grotesque pustules.

"Where is it?" he said in a thick grunting voice, as if his insides were as nodular as his exterior.

Idlis had been right. Maigraith wasn't her closest pursuer.

"Who are you?" said Karan.

"Name is Ragred."

39

YOUR ADMIRER WANTS YOUR HELP

No matter how much Llian scratched, he could not stop the itching. He was filthy and covered in red lines of bedbug bites. The innkeeper had snorted into his ale when Llian asked about a bath; the place did not have one.

He was lurking in the darkest corner of the barroom of the seediest tavern in Chanthed, waiting for the hue and cry to die down so he could sneak across town and break into the college archives. He had spent long days here while the invasion clock ticked ever more loudly. More than three weeks had passed since Sulien's nightmare and he had made no progress. Less than five until their world ended. The thought was paralysing.

As was the knowledge that the magiz could be attacking Karan and Sulien right now. He was desperate for news but had no way of getting any.

"You *have* come down in the world," said Thandiwe, slipping into the seat opposite him. She was also dressed cheaply but, being Thandiwe, her clothes enhanced her figure. She would look magnificent wrapped in a tent fly.

"How did you find me?"

"You're predictable."

"What do you want?" he hissed.

"I may be able to do something for you," said Thandiwe.

"What happened to *I'm going to utterly destroy you?*"

"I happened on a secret admirer of your work."

"Bully for you."

"I'm trying to help you, Llian."

"For the next thousand years, whenever anyone hears your name, it'll be Llian the Liar, the Cheat, the Perverter of the Great Tales. Remember?"

"There's gold in it for me," she said grudgingly. "For arranging things."

And she needed it desperately. "Go on."

"Your admirer can get you out of Chanthed and give you a hiding place . . . "

Llian's eyes narrowed. It seemed too good to be true and probably was. "What would I have to do in exchange?"

Thandiwe's mouth turned down. "Write a brief tale and dedicate it to him."

She envied Llian. She wanted a Great Tale desperately, and private commissions were the icing on a very rich cake. For the privilege of dining with such a teller and having a tale dedicated to himself, a wealthy connoisseur would pay more than a master at the college would earn in a decade.

"What's his name?"

"I can't say."

"Sorry," said Llian. "Not interested."

She had not expected that. "Why the hell not?"

Llian hesitated. The fewer people who knew about his quest the better, but if he thwarted Thandiwe she would have the constables here in minutes.

"You know about the Merdrun?" said Llian.

"Of course; all the chroniclers are talking about them."

"I've got to get into the secret archives." He sketched out his plan.

Thandiwe sat back, weighing it up. Since she always had an ulterior motive, she was bound to think he had one as well. "Your admirer can easily get you in."

"You're sure?" said Llian.

"Absolutely. But he'll want to meet you first."

What choice did he have? If he refused she could — no, would — betray him. "All right."

She stood up. "Let's go."

"Right now?"

"He doesn't live far away. Have you got any reason to delay?"

Thandiwe led him out the back door. A large coach was waiting around the corner. He climbed inside, she joined him, and they were rolling down the street when it occurred to him that this was a little too convenient.

"I've got to know who—"

She pulled the window blinds down. "You'll soon be safely out of Chanthed, in a place where no one would think of looking for you."

"Assuming we can pass the city gates." Llian had not been game to try.

"We'll pass."

The knot in his belly tightened. How could she be so sure? Where were they going? Who was the patron? He was tempted to kick the door open and leap out into the night, but then he would be hunted again, and public feeling against Wistan's cowardly killer was running high. If they caught him they might hang him without a trial.

"There's another thing," said Thandiwe after they had been waved through the town gates and the coach was rolling along the north-eastern road not far from the meandering River Gannel. "Your admirer wants your help."

"What for?"

"A secret project."

He sat up, his interest piqued. "Oh?"

"Something Mendark worked on for ages, before his death."

"What about?"

"Mancery."

"I hardly think *I* can help anyone with mancery. What about it?"

"I wasn't told."

An hour passed. They might have gone as much as ten miles. The coach stopped and Llian heard the coachman's deep voice, then another man's laughter. A gate was opened and the coach passed through onto a driveway. Gravel crunched under the iron-shod wheels. Llian reached for the nearest window blind.

Thandiwe caught his hand. "Leave it."

Rich men could be obsessive about their privacy. The coach took a sharp turn to the left, throwing her against Llian, and she clung to him far longer than was necessary. Considering her previous threats, it was disturbing. What was she up to?

The coach stopped and the door was opened. The coachman was holding up a lantern; they were in a coach house that smelled of fresh paint. The floor, which was pale pink marble, was almost impossibly clean. Llian climbed out. A liveried servant was waiting, and also a tired young woman with black hair, wearing a green kimono of watered silk. She was extraordinarily beautiful. She studied Llian and he caught the faintest hint of disgust.

"You will bathe and dress. This way."

He followed her down a tiled path, her lantern casting moving fans of light to either side. The grass was so neatly clipped it might have been done with scissors. He looked back and Thandiwe was still standing by the coach. She looked anxious, lost and not a little afraid. Llian felt not a trace of pity.

The young woman led him in through the back door of a villa, a large rectangular building of three storeys with two-storey wings running off either end. Inside, all was in darkness save for her lantern beams, which did not reveal anything above waist height. She went up two flights of stairs, along a corridor, opened a door and ushered him into a large bathing room, beautifully tiled in green, banded serpentinite. She lit the lamps and turned on taps in a large tub. Hot and cold water gushed out.

"Put your clothes in the basket for burning," she said. "Your boots as well." She studied him in a measuring way. "I will fetch clean garments directly, and ointment for your bites." She went out.

What kind of a man was Llian's patron? Well, for the luxury of a hot bath, clean clothes and easy access to the archives, he could be any kind of a man he damn well pleased. Llian dumped his ruined clothes and battered boots but kept his belt, for Rulke's little key was hidden in it.

After Llian had bathed she led him into a room the size of a ball-room, though its only occupant was an elegantly dressed, bronze-haired man sitting at a leopardwood desk at the far end. His forehead was high, his nose regal, his chin cleft and his Cupid's bow lips full and sensual. A large armchair near the window had its back to him.

She escorted Llian over to the desk, which was bare save for a bound book the man was reading. After several minutes he looked up into Llian's eyes.

"Thank you for agreeing to come," he said in a rich, slow voice in which each word was perfectly enunciated. He rose, came around the desk and extended his hand. Llian shook it. "You know my subordinate, I believe."

The armchair rotated to reveal Basible Norp. Cold crept over Llian. *Subordinate?*

"Yes," said Llian, "though I don't know *your* name."

"A scandalous oversight on Ifoli's part," said the bronze-haired man. "I am Cumulus Snoat."

The scales fell from Llian's eyes. Snoat, who had tried to kill Tallia and nearly succeeded, who was now making ruthless war on Iagador and trying to take control of the college. Llian had been manipulated – no, conned.

He stared at the book on the table. It was inside a protective cover, which was why he had not recognised it before. It was his *Tale of the Mirror*, and there was nothing he could do to get it back. He felt a mad urge to drive his head into Snoat's belly, grab the book and dive through the window.

How disastrously he had blundered by writing to Snoat in the first place. And how catastrophically he had compounded that error by voting for Norp instead of Thandiwe.

Wistan must be turning in his grave, and one of Snoat's cutthroats had probably sent him to it. But Llian's final blunder was by far the worst. Why, after all Thandiwe's threats, had he come here with her? Because he'd had absolutely no choice.

With heart-stopping horror, something even worse occurred to him. If Snoat got Wistan's dirt book he could identify and attack the allies, and it would undermine any defence they tried to make against the Merdrun. Why hadn't he hidden it when he'd had the chance – or failing that, burned it as soon as he'd been framed for murder?

"I've been thinking about your proposal," said Llian. "I'm afraid it's not for me, but thank you for the offer."

Snoat raised a hand and a squat, muscle-bound man appeared in the doorway to the left, wearing only a groin strap. His head was as round as a melon and his entire body had been shaved about a week ago. All over his body stubs of hair stood out like bristles on an old, coarse boar.

"Yorgee," said Snoat. "Would you be so kind as to convince the Zain to stay?"

By the time Llian appreciated what Snoat was saying, Yorgee was only a yard away. He was half a head shorter than Llian but must have been twice his weight. Yorgee caught Llian by the shoulder in a grip that ground the bones together, then punched him in the belly so hard that it drove the wind out of him.

"Cumulus wishes you to stay until the job is done," said Yorgee.

"I'll stay," gasped Llian.

"Cumulus thanks you," said Yorgee.

He thumped Llian again to reinforce the point. Llian flew backwards and his impact with the floor jarred a small book from his pocket. The beautiful woman picked it up and, after a small hesitation, handed it to Snoat.

"Ahh!" he said.

Wistan's dirt book, and all its secrets, was now in the hands of the enemy. Llian's quest was in tatters; there was no hope of finding out about the summon stone now. He would be lucky to get out of here with his life.

40

YOU EXCEED YOUR LICENCE

"You will tell me everything Mendark ever told you about the Secret Art," said Snoat, "and everything you read about mancery in his personal papers."

"Why?" said Llian.

"Yorgee, answer Llian's question."

"Never mind," Llian said hastily.

The loincloth-clad brute thumped Llian in the belly, lifting him off his feet. He got up, breathless and aching, staggered to the podium prepared for him, searched his perfect memory and began to recite. He could recall hundreds of conversations on the topic and many pages of documents, though, having no talent for mancery, they meant nothing to him. What was Snoat looking for?

Everything Llian said was written down by a pair of secretaries, then compiled into a master copy by Snoat's beautiful assistant Ifoli. Snoat sat quietly in the background, eyes closed and one silk-slippered foot tapping. Occasionally he raised a hand. Ifoli stopped Llian, checked with the secretaries and, without notes, gave Snoat a perfect summary of what Llian had remembered.

On the second morning, before he began, Snoat said, "Is Unick here yet?"

Ifoli looked uneasy. "He arrived an hour ago."

"Call him in."

Gurgito Unick was a red-faced bull of a man, well over six feet tall and powerfully built. He had the scarred face and knuckles of a barroom brawler and bloodshot eyes that seemed too small for their sockets. The smell of stale drink preceded him into the salon.

He caught Llian's eye and sneered. "Stinking teller!" He spat on the floor and dropped into a chair.

A servant ran across and cleaned the spittle up.

"Continue, Llian," said Snoat.

Llian wondered why Unick was there, since he did nothing save slump in his chair, breathing noisily through a badly broken nose. His clothes were shabby and none too clean, his nails were chewed to the quick and the sole was coming off his left boot.

Llian's recital continued until he had told Snoat everything he knew about Mendark's use of the Secret Art. Unick disappeared.

The following day Llian was allowed to read, or write in the journal he carried everywhere with him, but nothing more was asked of him. Snoat spent hours conferring with Ifoli regarding one detail or another and making pencil sketches.

Her duties were assigned to another young woman of almost equally perfect beauty, a tall grey-eyed redhead. Ifoli began to turn Snoat's sketches into working drawings done with a draughtsman's precision and lettered in an elegant hand. Llian had no idea what they were about.

Later that day Unick was brought back. He was sober this time and his raw eyes darted around the room as if he suspected everyone of conspiring against him. As he lumbered to Ifoli's table she rose abruptly, leaning away from him as if her skin was crawling.

Snoat shot Ifoli a sharp glance. She calmed herself and began to describe the first of her drawings in a low voice. Unick snatched it out of her hand, studied it for a few seconds and tossed it down. He did the same with all her other drawings.

"Well?" said Snoat.

"Worthless rubbish," said Unick.

"What about this?" said Snoat, opening a black ironwood box and showing Unick the contents, which Llian assumed to be a device of some kind.

Unick reached for it greedily. Snoat moved it out of reach.

"Where did it come from?" said Unick in a thick voice.

"The Council's secret spell vault."

"It looks like Mendark's work."

"Yes."

Unick took another look, then grinned. "I know how to do it."

"*Really?*" cried Snoat.

"Yes."

"How many devices will be required to use the secret of mancery?"

"Three."

"Only three?"

"Origin. Identity. Command."

"What do they do?"

"Origin allows one to find and study sources, previously unknown, of great natural power, and it can also find enchanted objects. Identity identifies people who are using mancery, allowing one to spy on them. Command allows one to control and use the sources of power, and also control other mancers. A mancer who has all three devices will be more powerful than all other mancers put together – assuming he has the strength to wield such mighty and ruinous artefacts."

Llian was staggered. Such power, vastly greater than anything the world had ever known, would change Santhenar for ever.

"And if he doesn't?" said Snoat.

"The Command device will splatter his remains across a hundred acres." Unick grinned at the thought.

Snoat's breath hissed between his perfect teeth. "All right. Show me your drawings when they're done."

"No drawings. All I need is head and hand and eye."

Unick slumped in Ifoli's chair and stared hungrily at a glass-fronted case. It held ten cut crystal bottles, all different. Snoat had said that they contained the rarest liqueurs in the world. Unick licked his scarred lips.

Snoat looked out the paired windows for a minute or two, then called Ifoli. "What do you think?" he said quietly.

"Mendark may not have known what he was doing. He may have been mistaken, or—"

"Unlikely – he was both brilliant and careful. And over his many lifetimes he analysed the work of dozens of other great masters."

"Yet he sought –" Ifoli lowered her voice but Llian could read lips "– that which no other master ever found."

"Continue."

"Alternatively, Mendark may have been led astray to protect the secret."

"Who would do such a thing?"

"Mancers are notoriously jealous of their art. Some would sooner it died with them than hand it on, even to a valued protégé."

"I feel the same way about my collection," said Snoat. "Why should some unworthy person benefit from my hard work after I die? It would diminish everything I've done. I'd sooner burn this place to the ground, and everything in my collection, than allow anyone else to possess the least part of it."

Ifoli stiffened. She was part of Snoat's collection, and so was Llian. He shivered. Their lives were in the hands of a perfect narcissist.

It was warm in the salon but Ifoli's arms had goose pimples. After a minute of silence she said, "There's another possibility, Cumulus. A disturbing one."

"Go on."

"Mendark may have been used. His work on this secret project may even have been *directed*."

"He worked on it for hundreds of years, and outlived dozens of great mancers. How could any of them have used him?"

"It could have been these Merdrun we keep hearing about."

"They're a fantasy designed to rally support against me." Snoat walked back to Ifoli's table.

"Cumulus?" she said urgently.

"Yes?" he said without turning around.

"I must warn you that this is a very dangerous project."

"You exceed your licence." He gestured to Unick. "Begin on the Origin device."

Unick was still staring at the bottles, his throat moving as if he were swilling grog. He left without a word. Snoat left as well. Ifoli gathered her sketches and locked them in a drawer, then removed the chair Unick had used and washed her hands. A servant carried the chair out and brought her another one. Ifoli sat at her desk, staring into space. Every so often a shudder racked her.

Llian wondered how Mendark's meteoric rise to power had come about. The Histories were silent on the matter, though he was aware of the rumours, all unsubstantiated, that as a young man he had "done a deal with a demon".

There were no such things as demons, but could the rumours be true in another way? He knew from personal experience how ruthless Mendark had been.

And, remembering the corruption only revealed at the very end of his life, could Ifoli's stab in the dark be true? Could Mendark have been used all that time by the Merdrun?

Three devices to find, take and master. Origin. Identity. Command.

They were the real reason Snoat had brought him here. And if he got them, how could he ever be defeated?

41

OR YOUR MOTHER DIES

The name Ragred meant nothing to Karan. She struggled furiously but he was strong enough to hold her down with one hand, so she went still. She had been in a lot of fights in her time and had won more than she should have, given her small size. She pretended to be beaten and waited for her chance.

"Where's Sulien? What have you done with her?"

Ragred's smile revealed a mouthful of white, well shaped teeth. In so hideous a man this little quality made him seem even more frightening. He shifted his weight and Karan drove a knee into his groin. His grip relaxed for an instant; she headbutted him in the nose and rolled aside while he was still dazed.

Pain rang up and down her thigh. She hopped away to a safe distance. "Where's my daughter?"

His squashed nose gushed blood down his face and all over his perfect little teeth. "If you come here, I'll tell you."

Karan should have run but she didn't. Had he found Sulien? She had not been out of sight for long, but one blow from his fist or foot or elbow or knee would be enough to take her from this world.

Ragred took a step towards her. "Where is it?"

She checked behind her; there were no obstacles to fall over. She took a step backwards, and another step. "Where's what?"

"The chain."

"What chain?" said Karan, though he could only mean the one that had belonged to Fiachra. It was the only valuable thing she possessed. She had given it to Sulien.

The bloody teeth snapped together. He extended his warty right hand.

She retreated another step. "What do you want it for?"

Ragred stepped forwards gingerly, evidently still in some pain. Karan backed towards a patch of rough ground where the angled shale broke the surface.

As she turned, he sprang further than she would have thought possible. She tried to get out of his way but he flung out an arm, caught her by the hair and jerked her towards him so hard that she thought her scalp was going to tear off. Her feet left the ground, she landed on her back and before she could recover he was on her.

He shoved a hand down her shirt and groped around. She struck at him furiously but she might as well have been whacking a piece of teak. He caught both her wrists in one hand and thrust his repulsive visage at hers.

"Where ... is ... the ... chain?"

Ragred wrenched at her right pocket, tearing it. Then Sulien appeared behind him, creeping up with a fist-sized piece of rock, and Karan had never seen such fury on a child's face.

She tried to signal Sulien with her eyes – *Run away* – but she took no notice. Karan dared not call out to her; one bound and Ragred could have them both.

He was groping with his free hand when Sulien brought the rock down on his skull with all her strength. He sprayed bloody saliva all over Karan, then slumped on top of her.

But he was not quite unconscious, and his hand held her wrists in a grip she could not break. She tried to push him off but he was too heavy. Sulien was to Karan's left, bouncing from one foot to the other.

"Stay – back," gasped Karan, unable to draw a full breath.

Sulien bit her lip, then bent for the rock again. Ragred's long arm swung out and back.

"Look out!" cried Karan.

Sulien sprang aside. His fingers grazed her left shin but could not grip.

"Run!" yelled Karan.

Ragred sat up and put a knee on her chest. "Come here, girl, or your mother dies."

Sulien stood frozen, looking from Karan to Ragred.

"If he gets you too, he'll kill us both," said Karan. "Run!"

Sulien ran.

Ragred hauled Karan to her feet, held her by the shirt and back-handed her twice across the face, a pair of heavy blows that rocked her head from side to side. She could feel her cheeks swelling.

"She'll be back," said Ragred. "Nowhere to go, has she?"

He licked his little white teeth clean. Karan watched in fascinated repulsion.

"I'm not by nature a violent man," he said softly, "but I can't go back without the chain. The quicker you give it to me the less damage I'll do to you."

Karan felt sure he was going to kill her and nothing she could say would make any difference. He headed after Sulien, dragging Karan by the wrists. Several minutes later she saw something dart through the trees behind them. Something strong but awkward, with arms and legs moving in jerky arcs. She lost it but saw another, thirty yards away. Should she tell him? He might react badly. She must.

"They're after you," said Karan.

His head jerked round. He must have sensed something wrong, for his eyes were wide and darting.

"Who?"

"Whelm."

He stiffened; he was afraid of them. He stopped for a second, searching for tracks, but the ground was hard here and there were none. He went on, then stopped again, looking around wildly.

They were stalking him, appearing and disappearing between the trees, and for the first time she saw real fear on Ragred's face. Whelm were slow and awkward but tireless, and they never gave in.

Suddenly they were all around. He lurched in a circle, trying to keep them all in sight and holding Karan in front of him as a shield. As they moved in, he closed his hands around her throat.

"Back," he gasped. "Or I choke her to death."

But the Whelm were immune to such threats. Idlis would do everything he could to save her, but if she died during the rescue he would be released from his obligation.

Ragred kept rotating, kept squeezing. Karan was gasping, kicking her legs and trying to tear his hands away, but could not break his grip. Spots floated before her eyes; she could feel the darkness rising and the Whelm were still twenty yards away. By the time they reached Ragred she would be dead. The light faded . . .

"Mummy!" Sulien was shrieking in her ear. "Mummy! Wake up."

Karan was on the ground and Ragred was half across her, his fingers closing and opening around her neck.

"Get off, you bollocky bastard!" screamed Sulien, whacking the back of Ragred's head with a stick.

What had happened to him? His breath was gurgling in his throat. Sulien caught one of his nodule-studded wrists and heaved with all her weight, but it barely moved. His fingers clenched and again Karan began to choke.

Idlis lurched up, put his narrow boot on Ragred's face, took hold of his wrist and heaved. He could not budge it either. He drew a wavy-bladed knife, put it against Ragred's wrist and forced it outwards, cutting his hand off. Blood pumped all over Karan's front.

Ragred let out a howl and convulsed backwards, but only the upper part of his body moved. The severed hand clung to her throat for a moment then the fingers slowly relaxed. Idlis flicked it away with his knife. Sulien caught Karan under the arms and tried to drag her away.

Ragred shrieked, "What have you done to me?" His stump flailed, spurting blood in all directions.

He tried to get up but his lower body remained where it was. He clawed at his back and Karan saw a double-bladed throwing axe embedded there. It must have severed the spinal cord. She shuddered and came to her knees. Idlis had just missed her with a similar axe twelve years ago, during his month-long pursuit after her escape from Fiz Gorgo with the stolen Mirror of Aachan.

Ragred's fingers touched the axe handle.

Idlis put the blade to his throat. "Why?" he said thickly.

Ragred did not answer. Idlis pressed the point into his neck. Blood flowed. The other Whelm closed in and Ragred looked at them in naked terror.

With Sulien's help, Karan came to her feet. "Let me," she croaked. The words stung her bruised throat.

She approached Ragred warily. He had gone a muddy grey; he must be bleeding internally. But he was a strong man; he might heave the axe from his back and hurl it at her.

"Ragred, in ten minutes you'll be dead. You said you weren't a violent man. You can prove your quality before you die."

He did not answer.

"Your master's hold on you is about to break. Who is he?"

She thought he was going to defy her, then he said, in a wisp of a voice, "Snoat."

"Why does he want the chain?"

"Hopes . . . recover . . . Shuthdar's spell."

"I didn't know Snoat was interested in mancery."

"It's why . . . framed Llian. And took him."

"Snoat has Llian?" Karan hissed. Sulien let out a cry. "Why?" said Karan. "He couldn't cast a spell to save his life."

Was this better than him being on the run from the law? In the short term, perhaps. Snoat would keep Llian safe until he got what he wanted. But after that . . . Karan knew that he hated Zain.

"Don't know . . . " Ragred was fading rapidly now.

"Is Llian all right?"

"For . . . now."

"Where is he?"

"Pem-Y-Rum."

"Where's that?" Karan said frantically.

"Estate near Chanthed. Snoat soon . . . put him down."

His severed wrist was hardly bleeding now. He toppled onto his face, bubbles popping thickly in his throat. His arms thrashed. Idlis walked across, put his iron-shod boot on the uppermost blade of the double-bladed axe and shoved. The thrashing stopped. Ragred was dead.

And the clock was ticking for Llian. If Karan could not free him, Snoat would put him to death. Soon.

42

YOU WILL SAVE DADDY, WON'T YOU?

Idlis must have sensed Karan's need to be alone with Sulien, for he moved the Whelm's camp over the ridge, out of sight. Karan limped back and forth, gathering firewood and collecting water, then setting up their little tent, for it was already sprinkling.

She cut up strips of fatty bacon, sizzled them in the pan with an eye-stinging yellow onion and the shrivelled remains of the carrots and beans she had brought from Gothryme, added water and stirred in cracked wheat to thicken it. They had eaten the same meal every day but she was too hungry to care.

Sulien sat under a tree twenty feet away. She had not spoken since Ragred's death, which was worrying. She was normally such a chatterer. Karan could not imagine what Sulien must be thinking. It was a wonder she had not shut down completely.

Karan was close to it herself. She kept reliving Ragred's attack and the axe in his back, the magiz's agony as her leg had been destroyed and, most chilling of all, Sulien clutching at her head as that slow trickle of blood ran from her nose.

And then there was Llian, held prisoner by Snoat and soon to die. He must be desperate.

Karan filled two bowls with soup and took them to the tent, one at a time. She was shaking so badly that she had to use both hands. "Come here."

A wary look crossed Sulien's face, then she ran and snuggled under Karan's left arm. They sat in the entrance and ate their soup in silence. The fire crackled. Raindrops pattered on the roof of the tent.

"How is your throat, Mummy?" said Sulien very formally.

"The hot soup stings, going down."

"It'll be better in the morning."

"Yes."

The stilted exchange died. Karan ran through her options again but saw no solution. The magiz would take time to recover, though when she did she would pursue them even more relentlessly – it was personal now. She would trace Karan through the psychic stigma and attack Sulien, so what choice was there but to send her away with the Whelm?

Though if she did, Sulien could only take it as a betrayal by the one person she had always relied on. Besides, Idlis's actions had reminded Karan that the Whelm could be inhumanly ruthless.

The rain grew heavier and they retreated to their sleeping pouches. Sulien laid her head on Karan's breast, sighed and wriggled around, then settled. Karan did not. Trying to rescue Llian with a child in tow was out of the question. If she was caught or killed, Sulien would be alone and defenceless in a land where she knew no one.

"Are you worrying about Llian?" Sulien said softly.

She hardly ever called her father by his name. It was a troubling sign. Karan did not want to burden her any more than she was already, but if they were to part she had to know everything.

"You didn't hear Ragred's last words," said Karan. "Once Snoat gets what he wants from Llian he's going to ... "

"Kill him." Sulien clung to Karan. "We've got to save Daddy."

"But the stigma the magiz put on me means I can't be with you. It's too dangerous."

Sulien said nothing for such a long time that Karan felt sure she had fallen asleep. She stared at the fire through the triangular opening. There was no solution.

"Thank you," said Sulien.

Karan started. "What for?"

"For talking to me like a grown-up."

Karan hugged her.

"The Whelm are very strange, aren't they?" Sulien added.

She crawled out of her sleeping pouch into Karan's, and soon she slept.

Hours passed and Karan was still turning possibilities over, desperately seeking a solution where there was none. There had to be a way to protect her. Malien had to unblock Karan's gift for mancery, whatever the risk. Karan reached out to her but could not make a link; she could not sense Malien at all.

The logs crumbled to winking coals, the coals to ash. A breeze drifted smoke into the tent. Sulien coughed once without waking. The pattering rain died away to occasional spatters of heavy drops as the breeze shook the branches above the tent. Finally, Karan slept.

She woke with a start, more tired than when she had lain down to sleep, to find Sulien up and dressed, cooking bacon and toasting stale bread. Her hair was freshly brushed and tied back in a curly pony tail, her pack stood outside the tent and the water pot was boiling.

Karan staggered out, rubbing her bruised throat and swollen cheeks. The Whelm were coming down from their camp, lugging their gear towards the track and saddling their emaciated mounts. Sulien heaved out Karan's pack and the saddlebags. Karan choked down her bread and bacon, washed it down with bitter herb tea and wiped her mouth with the back of her hand. Tears kept forming in her eyes; she scoured them away.

Sulien, who was down on the track talking to Yetchah, came solemnly up the hill, lifting the silver chain over her head. Yetchah was close behind.

"I want you to have this back, Mummy," Sulien said, holding out her hand. Fiachra's chain formed a small silver pool there.

She was normally a grubby child, but her hands were clean and pink as if they had been freshly scrubbed, her fingernails were clean, and she was wearing her best clothes. A chill settled over Karan. It was as if Sulien was preparing for a funeral.

"You need it more than I do," Sulien added. "For protection."

Karan took the chain but did not put it on.

"What protection?" said Yetchah, frowning.

Reluctantly, Karan gave it to her. Yetchah stroked it, both ways.

"The protection is blocked and I can't unblock it," she said, handing the chain back. "It's useless."

"War is coming," said Karan, shivering and clutching Sulien tightly, "and Snoat has weakened us when we most need to be united."

"War *is* coming," said Yetchah. "I can almost touch it." The Whelm exchanged glances.

"You've got to save Daddy," said Sulien.

Karan felt hot and flushed; she was drenched in sweat. She swallowed. "I don't see how I can."

Sulien looked up at her, then at Idlis and Yetchah and the other grim-faced Whelm, then back at Karan. She squared her small shoulders. Her lower lip trembled but she managed to still it.

"I'd only be in the way. I'll go with Idlis and Yetchah." She turned to Idlis. "You will take me, won't you?"

Suddenly his ugly face was lit by an astounding inner glow, unlike any expression Karan had ever seen on the face of a Whelm.

"We will take you home with us, little one," he said, almost as overwhelmed by the moment as Karan was. "And treat you just like our own children until Karan comes for you."

It was far worse than if she had sent Sulien unwillingly. No child should have to make such an act of self-sacrifice.

"You *will* save Daddy," said Sulien, staring at her with a mixture of hope and desperation. "Won't you?"

Karan lifted Sulien and squeezed her tightly, her tears raining down on the child's upturned face.

"Whatever it takes," said Karan, "I'll do it. And after we've finished the magiz and broken the summon stone, we'll come and take you home."

Karan could not tell if Sulien believed her preposterous statement. Nevertheless she swallowed audibly, wiped her eyes and went to Idlis and Yetchah.

The dreadful parting had come. The Whelm were heading south-west across the rugged hills, and Karan was going west to Chanthed. Her sole consolation was that Sulien would soon be beyond the reach of the magiz.

They said their goodbyes, then, frozen in despair, Karan watched Sulien's small white-faced figure ride away. No moment in Karan's life had ever been as bad. Would she be safe? What if the magiz found her anyway? Could the Whelm do anything to save her? Would they even know she was being attacked, or would they just find her small, cold body after the magiz had gleefully drunk Sulien's life to feed her own sick addiction?

When they were out of earshot, Karan screamed until she tasted blood in the back of her throat and every bird in every tree for a hundred yards around had taken flight.

She looked after the Whelm but even their small dust cloud had dispersed. It was done, and she had to be just as strong.

"Let's get moving," she said to Jergoe. He felt like the only bit of home she had left.

Jergoe flicked his ears. She wheeled and galloped for Chanthed.

Whatever Yetchah had done to the silver chain, it had also heightened Karan's sensitive's gift. She could sense the ruin inflicted by Snoat's armies; if she closed her eyes and imagined a map of Iagador, a stain was creeping down from Thurkad and the conquered lands to its north.

It was inching west towards Bannador and south towards central Iagador. Once they fell, only one great force would remain, the Free City of Sith. Sith was strong, but it had fallen to Yggur twelve years ago and it could fall again. When that happened, there would be no effective resistance left. And then the Merdrun would invade.

It was a distraction she could do without. She slipped the chain into a pocket and buttoned the flap.

"Faster, Jergoe."

43

IT COULD BE AWKWARD

In Chanthed, Karan checked Jergoe into a stable and trudged up the street to the markets, where she bought a sweet bun and picked pieces off it as she walked. Her burning drive to get here had been replaced by panicky despair. How could she hope to rescue Llian from the most powerful man in the land?

Her head was aching. She took off her broad-brimmed hat, unbound her hair and shook it out. Someone tugged on it and she whirled, thinking it was a mischievous child, and was confronted by a beaming young woman her own height. She was thin with a long plain face and short platinum-coloured hair. Karan blinked at her for a few seconds before recognising the child she had been the last time they had met, a dozen years ago. Lilis, a street urchin then, had helped Llian escape from Thurkad and Karan would always think kindly of her for it.

"Lilis! What a coincidence meeting you here."

"Hardly. We're here for the meeting. Aren't you?"

"What meeting?"

"Of our allies – Nadiril, Shand, Tallia, Yggur . . ."

"Oh yes, Tallia did mention a meeting, weeks ago. I'm glad Nadiril's here. If anyone knows where the summon stone is—"

"He hasn't heard of it," said Lilis. "Tallia already asked."

"Oh!" said Karan, deflated. "But it's so good to see you. You look . . ."

"Like a future librarian, I hope." Lilis studied her anxiously. "I'm so sorry about Llian."

Something burst inside Karan. "He's not *dead*?"

"I meant the murder charge," said Lilis. "Obviously he's been framed."

"By Snoat. He's got Llian in Pem-Y-Rum," said Karan, low-voiced. "And Snoat hates Zain."

"Shh!" Lilis drew Karan into a side street. "He's got spies everywhere. And I have to tell you, Shand isn't happy with Llian."

"You just said he was framed!"

"It's what Shand says he did beforehand that's the problem."

"What?" said Karan.

Lilis did not reply, but took her to a large but ramshackle timber house in a tree-lined street. Karan spent the time fretting. Yggur was a difficult man, and even when they had been allies years ago they had not got on. She was not looking forward to seeing him again.

They went through a series of connecting chambers of varying sizes and shapes. There was no hall, and rooms appeared to have been added randomly as the need arose. The owners must have grown wealthier over time though, for the rooms towards the back were larger and grander.

In a square high-ceilinged chamber that looked out on a stable and an overgrown rear yard, Tallia sat wrapped in blankets, her chair pulled close to a rusty iron firebox in the centre of the room. She was thinner than Karan had ever seen her, and shivering though the room was warm.

"I thought you were better," said Karan.

Tallia tried to smile but could only manage a spasm. "Infection keeps coming back. I've never been so weak."

"I'd hoped you could . . . " Karan stopped herself.

"What?" said Tallia.

"I don't want to add to your burdens."

"A Magister has to carry the burden, whatever it is."

"I'd hoped you might help me . . . rescue Llian."

Tallia mouth spasmed again. "If I can."

The back door opened and a very tall man entered, limping on his right leg. His hair was long and black as crow feathers; frosty eyes were set in deep sockets under jutting black eyebrows, and his face was all hard planes and sharp angles. He saw Karan, missed a step, gave her a jerky nod and continued across to the far side of the room, where he sat in a corner, his head lowered.

Karan stared after him. Knowing about Yggur's breakdown, she had not expected much from him, though surely some recognition that they were in this together was in order.

Another man entered. He was almost as tall, but ancient and with-ered to strips of muscle and sinew stretched over a collection of clicking bones. His bald head was a dome and his eyes were clouded, though a spark lit in them when he saw Karan standing there. He smiled and took her hands in his.

"Very pleased to see you, my dear," said Nadiril, the Librarian of the Great Library at Zile. "Ah, but Llian. Not good at all."

Nadiril always looked as though he was clinging to the underside of death's trapdoor, but he was a kindly man who had been good to her and Llian in the past. She felt better for knowing he was here.

Shand followed, grim of face, and glowered when he saw her. What was the matter? What had Llian done?

"So," said Tallia, looking around the room. "Is this – my apologies – *all* we have to lead the fightback?"

Karan studied them. Nadiril, an old man who spent his time study-ing books. Shand, who had renounced most of his powers after suffering a terrible loss and a great rejection. Yggur, a great but mentally unstable mancer who wanted to hide from the world. Tallia, ill and desperate to go home to Crandor. Lilis, who might become a worthy successor to Nadiril, but was young and inexperienced and no fighter. And herself, unable to focus on anything but saving her family.

"Malien is coming with some of her people," said Shand, "though she'll be weeks yet. And we may get some help from the Faellem."

"The world will be lost long before they get here from Mirrilladell," rumbled Yggur.

"After what Llian's done, it's probably lost already," said Shand.

"What has he done?" said Karan.

"Wistan was going to make Llian Master of the College. Next thing we know, Wistan is dead, apparently by Llian's hand."

"That's a stinking lie! And if you believe it, you're an even bigger fool than you look."

"Karan, please," said Nadiril. "No one's made any accusations."

"I'm making one," said Shand. "Llian came here to support Thandiwe, and she would have made a fine, strong master." His voice rose. "Instead, he voted for Basible Norp, Snoat's lackey! Now Snoat controls the college, its wealth and its secrets – and that's not the worst."

Karan was shocked speechless. Why would Llian come all this way, at such cost, then vote for Snoat's man against Thandiwe?

"What is the worst?" she croaked.

"Wistan gave Llian his dirt book and told him to protect it with his life. But it's clear from the number of our supporters who've been blackmailed, killed or have disappeared in the past few days, that Snoat has it. Wistan protected it for forty years, and within three days – *three days* – of Llian taking it, it was in Snoat's hands."

Ever so faintly, Karan heard the drumming. Shand winced.

"Llian loathes Snoat," Karan said furiously. "He stole Llian's manuscript."

"Maybe Llian has done a deal with him to get it back."

"Snoat hates the Zain," Karan said coldly, "almost as much as you do, you bigoted old bastard!"

"It wouldn't stop Snoat doing a deal. And where is Llian now, Karan?"

"He . . . he's in Pem-Y-Rum," Karan whispered. "He's Snoat's prisoner."

"My information is he went willingly, with Thandiwe, in Snoat's own coach. Llian is probably blabbing our secrets right now."

"That's a lie! Snoat's going to have Llian killed." Her voice cracked. "Ragred said so."

"Who the hell is Ragred?"

Karan bared her bruised throat. "He was Snoat's man. He did this to me yesterday – before the Whelm killed him."

There was a long silence. "You'd better tell us about it," said Nadiril.

Karan told the story. At the end, when everyone started to speak at once, Nadiril held up a withered hand.

"Let's not do the enemy's work for him. And Shand, please refrain from making unsubstantiated accusations."

"What Karan did to Maigraith isn't unsubstantiated," snapped Shand. "Nor is what her ancestors did up at Carcharon, is it, Karan?"

"I have no idea what you're talking about," Karan lied. This was getting dangerous.

"I think you do," said Nadiril. "We must know what's going on, Karan."

Karan told them about Maigraith's visit with Julken, her obsession revealed by the drumming at the Black Lake, and how, when there was no other option, Karan had dosed her with hrux.

"I heard her psychic cries and went looking for her," said Shand. "And I found blood further up the range towards Carcharon. If she's dead," he said harshly, "Karan killed her!"

This hurt, coming from someone she had thought of as a friend. "I will do whatever it takes to protect my daughter. Anyway, Maigraith isn't dead."

"How do you know?" said Tallia.

Karan, afraid they would ask her to prove it, said nothing.

Tallia clutched at her injured shoulder. "If we're going to be at each others' throats from the beginning, we might as well stop this right now and wait for the Merdrun to kill us all." She looked pointedly at Karan. "Please set Shand's mind at rest."

"The very first time Maigraith *used* me," Karan said icily, "she forced me to create a link between us so she could get into Fiz Gorgo and steal the Mirror of Aachan from Yggur."

Yggur scowled. "Which is where it all began."

"It began with Shuthdar's Golden Flute, thousands of years before that," said Nadiril, "and will go on for thousands of years after we're gone."

"A trace of my link still exists," said Karan. "If Maigraith were dead, it would be gone."

"Then open the link," said Tallia. "Show Shand."

"What if it reveals me to her? She's out of her mind."

"If you want our help . . . " Shand said remorselessly.

Why was he so changed, so cold? Could the drumming be affecting him? Surely not Shand. But if she did not cooperate they would never help her.

Karan closed her eyes, settled her hands in her lap and rifled through her memories for the long-buried link to Maigraith. She teased it up to the surface and opened it gingerly. The drumming roared through her mind.

Shand clutched his temples. "Ah, my head!"

Karan swayed, opened her eyes, and the pain faded a little. "She's in a cave. Or underground."

"Where?"

"Can't tell."

She felt a psychic pressure, like trying to hold a door closed while someone far stronger was determined to force it open. Pain rippled through her skull as though the bone was being prised apart, then the drumming went *boom-boom*, *boom-boom-boom*.

There was a burst of brilliant light, like a lantern being thrust into her face. A pair of indigo and carmine eyes were blazing into her own, then Maigraith forced the door open.

The link set like a solid white beam between them and she shrieked, "I'll get you for this, Karan! Llian is a dead man. And you'll never see your daughter again."

With all the strength she had left, Karan forced the rage back. Maigraith cried out. Karan snapped the link, tore it out by the roots, then aftersickness overcame her and she toppled and struck her head on the iron firebox.

She roused, her head throbbing worse than before. Lilis was dabbing at her forehead with a handkerchief spotted with blood. The others were all around her: Nadiril, Tallia and Shand, his face now a mixture of anxiety and guilt. Yggur had not moved.

"I'm sorry," said Shand, whose tanned face had a grey tinge. "Maigraith's . . . not herself."

There had been such rage in her eyes. Had Karan created her own nemesis?

"Where's Sulien?" Shand said suddenly.

"I sent her away with Idlis and Yetchah. They went south to Shazabba and I don't know which way."

Shand's anger flared again. "To stop us from searching her mind!"

"I sent her away to protect her from the magiz."

"Whose side are you on, Karan?"

"She doesn't know the Merdrun's weakness."

"How the hell would you know?"

"Because I asked her . . . and looked into her mind."

"Karan, I'm disappointed," said Nadiril. "We have to identify their only weakness."

"No one is using deadly mind spells on my daughter," she said flatly.

"But you've just put her in danger," Yggur said quietly. "The Whelm are unreliable – as servants or as friends."

Karan shivered. They had served him for a very long time, only to betray him when a better master had come along. Had she made a terrible mistake?

"We've got to deal with Snoat before we can defend against the Merdrun," said Nadiril.

"What's the plan?" said Tallia.

"Do what Malien asked in her letter to Shand. Kill Snoat, and find and destroy the summon stone. And in case that fails, raise an army to hold the Merdrun back."

"How?" said Karan.

"*You* don't need to know. Walls have ears, Karan."

"What does Snoat want, anyway?" said Lilis.

"He's a power-hungry narcissist. He sees the world as his personal toy box, to use, plunder or destroy at whim."

"How do you know?"

"I have sourc— I just do," Nadiril amended hastily.

44

WE COULD BE KILLED

The top of the ten-foot wall around Pem-Y-Rum was lit by lanterns and Snoat's sentries paced it night and day. Wilm and Dajaes had spent days watching from the forest, trying to find a way in, but the sentries did twelve-hour shifts and never slackened off . . . save the one time.

Wilm and Dajaes were forty feet up, squashed together in the fork of a big tree; from it they had a line of sight through the forest to the main gates and part of the wall. A warm breeze rustled the leaves all around. It was exciting; they were on a great and important adventure together. And he found it very pleasant to be pressed up against a charming and attractive girl who admired him.

A exhausted guard, a hollow-eyed youth with huge ears and sandy hair that stuck out in all directions like a badly made broom, stopped by the guardhouse, leaned back against the wall for a moment and fell asleep standing up.

The next guard to pass by discovered him and shouted for the sergeant, who came running. Half a dozen sentries assembled. A captain appeared and conferred with the sergeant.

"What are they going to do?" whispered Dajaes.

She smelled like roses. Wilm found it distracting. "I don't know," he said slowly. "Though sleeping on duty isn't good. In wartime—"

"It's not wartime, and this is just a country estate."

"Sometimes my imagination runs away with me."

The captain and the sergeant broke apart. The broom-headed youth pulled free of the man who was holding him and reached out with both arms towards the captain as if begging. Wilm could not make out what he said, though it was clear the captain wasn't receptive. He spun on one foot and snapped an order to the sergeant, who gestured to the sentries.

The broom-headed guard ran as if intending to leap off the wall. Another sentry tripped him. He was lifted to his feet, his wrists were bound behind his back and then, as he was held from behind, one of the guards thrust a sword into him.

Dajaes gasped and caught Wilm's right hand in her two hands, squeezing it tightly.

The youth doubled over. The sergeant hauled him upright. Blood began to puddle on the walkway. The other five sentries put their swords into him, one after another. The sentry holding the guard let him go. He folded up and fell, and did not move. The blood spread until it was the size of a kitchen table. The sergeant snapped an order and the guards went back to patrolling, stepping carefully around the dead man as they paced.

Dajaes was shivering violently. Wilm put his arms around her and she pressed her face against his chest. When she pulled away, her face was wet with tears and her nose was running.

He found a rag in his pocket and wiped her tears away and then, self-consciously, dabbed at her nose.

Dajaes looked up at him. "What have we got ourselves into?"

"I thought it would be an exciting game," said Wilm, "but if we're caught breaking into Pem-Y-Rum, we'll be killed too."

He imagined someone taking the news to his mother. If she could see him now, she would be out of her mind with worry. *Work hard, do the right thing and never attract attention to yourself.*

Dajaes was holding his hand again.

"This changes everything," said Wilm.

She shook her head. "It doesn't change anything. Llian is in even more danger than we thought, and if we don't rescue him, he'll be killed as well."

"But we're just kids!"

"You're seventeen and I'm eighteen. If I'd gone home, father would be marrying me off any day now. That makes me an adult."

"What if we told the sergeant in Chanthed what Snoat's up to?"

"We don't have any proof. Besides, how can a town sergeant take Snoat on? Llian's only got us, Wilm."

Her logic was unarguable. "But what are we going to do?"

"Find him inside Pem-Y-Rum. Get him out. Help him to clear his name."

Wilm felt utterly overwhelmed. He lowered his head onto his bony knees. "I don't even know where to start."

"I do," said Dajaes. "We're going back to Chanthed. Come on."

"Pem-Y-Rum was originally built by Odio Lossily," said Dajaes.

"Who's he?" said Wilm.

They were in the sub-basement of the college library, in a section that, judging by the dust, had not seen much use in decades. Shelves full of boxes, books, scrolls and paper folders stretched for thirty yards in every direction.

Dajaes shook her head in disbelief. "You must have read about him when you were studying for the scholarship test."

"I can't remember anything. I crammed so many facts in that they all got mixed up."

"Odio Lossily was a legendary teller of eleven centuries ago." She was reading a page attached to the plans. "He crafted the eighteenth Great Tale, the *Tale of Rula*."

"Rula was a Magister during the Clysm, wasn't she?" said Wilm.

"In the Annals of the Magisters, she's regarded as the greatest of all."

"Greater than Mendark, who lived more than a thousand years and renewed his life thirteen times?"

Dajaes smiled. "It's good to see one of those facts has stuck."

"What did Rula do that was so great?"

"If you read the Great Tale you'll find out. Getting back to the point, Odio Lossily became fabulously wealthy and built himself a magnificent country manor, Pem-Y-Rum."

"Yes?" said Wilm.

"He was one of the first of the great collectors. Maybe that's another reason why Snoat bought the place."

"Um . . . ?" Wilm did not have the faintest idea where she was going with this.

"Lossily was also a master at this college, and all his papers are here. I read that when I was studying for the test too."

"Go on."

"Before the builder started work he would have needed drawings and detailed plans of everything. And if we can find them—"

"We might be able to get Llian out. Let's get to work."

It took long and weary hours of searching before they found the plans, but they turned out to be less use than they had hoped.

"Pem-Y-Rum looks nothing like that," said Wilm, riffling through the drawings again. They showed a large but simple one-storey villa with a courtyard in the centre, completely different to the current house.

Dajaes lowered her head onto the papers. "So tired. Even my eyes ache."

She closed them for a minute or two, then sat up. A smudge of dust on her left cheek was shaped like the letter P. "Eleven centuries is an awfully long time. It might have burned down."

"Or been torn down and rebuilt several times. Few houses would have survived unchanged all that time."

She gave a weary sigh. "Would you mind awfully if I had a little nap?"

"Odio Lossily was also a master of wine," said Wilm. "He wrote books about the wines of Iagador and established the first vineyard in the area."

"I've never tasted wine," she said drowsily.

"Llian drinks it; I tasted some a couple of times." He made a face. "It wasn't very nice."

"Perhaps he couldn't afford anything good."

"A vineyard would need a big wine cellar," said Wilm. "And even if the place was torn down and rebuilt, why would they rebuild a perfectly good cellar?"

He went through the plans again. "Here we go."

Dajaes did not answer. She was asleep. He studied the plan of the cellars, which ran under the manor and back into the hill in two wings for fifty yards, then tossed the plan on the pile and leaned back in his chair, rubbing his eyes.

"It's no damn use!" he muttered.

"What were you looking for?" said Dajaes, sitting up with a jerk.

"I was hoping the old cellars came out past the boundary wall."

"If they did, the entrance would be guarded." She checked that there was no one within earshot and picked up the plan. "Wilm, this tunnel goes close to the wall."

"How does that help?"

"What if we tunnelled under the wall from the forest?"

"It'd take years to tunnel that far through rock," said Wilm.

"It isn't rock. The soil is ten feet deep there. We saw it in the road cutting near Pem-Y-Rum, remember?"

Why would he remember that? "It would still take ages to tunnel that far – if the tunnel didn't collapse on us."

Wilm shuddered at the thought of being trapped underground,

nose and mouth and ears filled with dirt, unable to breathe, choking, gasping, dying.

"I used to go underground with Father all the time," said Dajaes. "Before he took to the grog and they sacked him." Her small fists clenched. "He taught me everything he knew about tunnelling in hard rock – and soft earth."

"We'd have to start a long way back from the wall, otherwise the guards would see us."

Dajaes measured distances with her fingers. "Eight yards from the end of the cellar to the wall. Plus three yards for the wall. And another forty to here," she tapped a point in the forest, "where we could start a tunnel out of sight. Fifty-one yards. Fifty-five, to be safe."

"Fifty-five yards!" He did a quick calculation. "But if the tunnel was a yard square, say, the soil would fill about . . . dozens of four-wheeled wagons."

"Twenty-eight, actually, if a wagon holds two cubic yards."

"It'd take weeks. And where would we put it?"

"If the tunnel was *half* a yard square it would only be seven wagon loads," said Dajaes. "We can dump it in that old quarry we saw in the forest. No one goes there."

"Half a yard! That's not much wider than my shoulders."

"A smaller tunnel is safer than a large one."

"But still not *very* safe. It gives me the horrors just thinking about going down one."

"Can you think of any other way to save Llian?"

"No."

"Then we'd better get on with it." She stood up, studying him with her head tilted to the side. "It'll be the hardest work you've ever done."

"Everything I've done in my life has been hard work."

It took every grint they had left to equip themselves with a rusty iron pick, a wooden shovel, food for a week, a lantern and fuel, some rope and a couple of buckets so Wilm could carry the soil to the quarry.

Using discarded boards, they made a little wooden cart with rounded corners and skids instead of wheels. Dajaes tied a length of rope to either end so Wilm could heave the full cart out and she could haul the empty one back to the tunnel face, where she would work alone. There would not be room for two, and Wilm did not have the experience to know which soil was safe and which was not.

The following morning she began the tunnel in the side of a mound-like hill, out of sight of the wall and surrounded by shrubs. It was easy work at first, and Wilm, returning from dumping his buckets of earth over the side of the quarry a hundred yards away, watched anxiously as she crawled out. The tunnel was four feet long already.

Dajaes was filthy and her eyes were streaming, the tears carving runnels through the dirt on her cheeks.

"What's the matter?" said Wilm.

"Lantern fumes. And they'll get worse as the tunnel gets longer. Can you check on the guards?"

He crept through the forest to the nearest vantage point, a rounded hillock. The wall guards were pacing, following their normal routine, though this did not ease his anxiety. He had never seen anyone go into the forest, but if a guard should choose to, for any reason, they would be discovered. And killed.

He went back, hauled the cart out, filled his buckets, lifted the wooden carrying bar onto his shoulders and trudged off to the quarry. So the morning went. He called a halt for lunch and Dajaes backed out, then flopped on her face on the dirt.

Wilm helped her up. "The fumes?"

"Got a shocking headache."

He handed her a water skin. She gulped at it, washed her face and hands and gave him a feeble smile.

"I ... I'll take a turn after lunch," said Wilm, cringing at the thought of working underground.

"The hell you will! I'll do it in the dark, by feel."

"That doesn't sound very safe."

"Safer than breathing lantern fumes all day."

They ate bread and cheese and an apple each; it wasn't enough for either of them but they had to ration the food, since there was no money to buy more.

"How far have you got?" said Wilm.

"Four yards."

"Great progress!"

"But the further I go, the slower it'll get."

She continued, working in the dark, every so often coming out for air, and occasionally lighting the lantern and crawling in to check the face of the tunnel. By sunset they had done nine yards and were feeling very pleased with themselves.

"That's enough," said Dajaes. "We can't use the lantern after it gets dark; it'd be spotted from the wall."

They put their gear inside, covered the entrance with dead bushes, scattered leaves over the bare earth outside and headed through the forest for half a mile to a secluded place Wilm had found earlier, a copse not far from a rivulet.

"Can we have a fire?" said Wilm. It was already getting cold. "I'd love a cup of hot chard."

"Too risky," said Dajaes. "After we've been here a day or two, and we know if there's anyone around, it might be all right."

They sat shoulder to shoulder, eating their meagre dinner and talking quietly about the day's work and their plans for tomorrow. They were going to start at first light.

Soon it was too cold to sit out in the open. They had no tent, though fortunately it did not rain often at this time of year. As the light faded, Wilm got out his sleeping pouch, then realised that Dajaes did not have one. Travelling by ferry, she hadn't needed one.

"You should get to sleep," he said, offering the sleeping pouch to her. "You must be exhausted."

She looked up at him. Even in this light he could see that her cheeks were flushed.

"You worked just as hard, carrying all that dirt."

"It's all right," he said. "I like sleeping out."

"At this time of year? You'll freeze."

She picked up the sleeping pouch, put it down again and took a deep breath.

"I can't possibly sleep in these filthy clothes," she said, undressing. "And I don't think you should either."

45

A NASTY, GREEDY MAN

In Karan's dream, Sulien was hunched on a rock at the edge of the camp-site, gagging as she tried to force down a mouthful of the Whelm's chunky black and grey gruel. It had grub-like things in it and looked revolting.

I can't get it down, she kept saying, *I just can't.*

A bony grey hand, a Whelm that Karan could not see clearly, took the stone dish from her. *No dinner then. And for breakfast this again. You will finish it.*

It's disgusting. How can you eat such horrid things?

You asked us to take you. You're a Whelm now.

Karan saw no more, but when she woke in darkness she sensed far too much. Sulien was hungry, exhausted and utterly miserable, and her heart went out to her. As the Whelm had said, they were treating Sulien just like one of their own children – harshly.

Karan started to make a link to her, but broke it off. The magiz might locate Sulien and *drink her sweet little life.*

How could she have allowed her gentle daughter to make such an awful and dangerous choice? Since Idlis had saved Karan's life ten years ago, he had been utterly reliable, but what if Yggur was right? What if the Whelm betrayed her as they had betrayed him?

Was there anything she could do? No, because they might have taken any of half a dozen routes south to their homeland, and even if she started searching now, she would never catch them.

Fury overwhelmed her, at the magiz and the Merdrun, at Snoat and Shand and Thandiwe, and Llian too. Karan punched her pillow, hurled it across the room, groaned then burst into tears. Things were getting worse, not better, and the Merdrun would soon invade.

"Karan," said a scratchy voice, "what is it?"

Lilis was kneeling beside her in the gloom. Karan had forgotten that they were sharing a room.

"How could I do it to my daughter?" she wailed. "I can't eat, can't sleep. Can't even focus on rescuing Llian."

She jumped out of bed. It was just past dawn and the sun had not yet risen. "Sorry," she said. "Go back to sleep." She dressed.

"Where are you going?" said Lilis.

"For a ride. I need to think."

"Do you mind if I come? Llian was kind to me when I was a street kid; I can't bear to think of him in Snoat's hands."

"I'd love you to come," said Karan.

They were riding down the drive when two horses turned in at the front gate. The first was a gigantic red stallion, eighteen hands high, on which sat the biggest woman Karan had ever seen. Her skin was coal-black and her hair was coiled on top of her head. Behind her, on a piebald mare, was a small blonde woman.

"Is Tallia here?" said the big woman. "Or Shand?"

"Who are you?" said Karan. She had never seen her before, yet there was something familiar about the shape of her face.

"Ussarine?" said Lilis, doing the clumsiest dismount Karan had ever seen. She caught her left boot in the stirrup and almost fell on her head. "What are you doing here?"

"Bodyguarding." Ussarine sprang down and they embraced. It was like a bear hugging a child. Karan got down too.

"You must be Karan," said Ussarine, looking at her hair. "You know my father, Osseion."

"I do!" said Karan. "I didn't know he had a daughter. How is he?"

"Very well, apart from the arthritis. It troubles him to walk."

"I'm sorry to hear it." She went across to the blonde woman, who had her arms folded across her chest and was scowling at Ussarine. "I'm Karan."

The blonde touched hands. "Esea. Where's Tallia?"

"Still abed. She hasn't recovered as well as she should have. Is something the matter?"

"I bear very bad news." Esea hesitated. "You'll soon hear, anyway. The enemy, Snoat, has the code to the council's spell vault."

"How did he get it?"

Esea's mouth set in a hard line. She rode on without answering and, at the stables, dismounted and yelled for the stable boy, then limped into the house.

"How did this happen?" said Karan.

"I wasn't aware it had," said Ussarine. "But I'm just a bodyguard. Where are you off to so early?"

Karan did not answer.

"Ussarine came to the Great Library with Osseion," said Lilis. "Eight years ago. We're the same age, can you believe it?" She looked up at Ussarine, beaming. "It's so good to see you. Won't you come with us?"

"Ussarine must be exhausted after riding all the way from Sith," Karan said pointedly.

"You can trust her with your life. And Llian's," said Lilis. Then, as if the matter needed settling, "I showed Ussarine all around Zile when we were girls. We spent a month together."

"One of the happiest months of my life," said Ussarine. "Is there something I can assist you with, Karan? Any friend of my father, and of Lilis, as the saying goes."

They rode out of town together, Karan in the middle, Lilis hunched in the saddle on her left, her hair shining in the sun, and Ussarine towering to her right. Karan explained the situation.

"And Pem-Y-Rum is where Llian is held?" said Ussarine.

"I'm not sure it's wise to show your face outside Pem-Y-Rum, Karan," said Lilis. "Since he's after you too."

"I'm sick of doing what's wise," Karan said irritably. "No sensible approach is going to get Llian out, so I have to consider reckless ones."

"Talk to Esea," said Ussarine. "She makes an art form of recklessness."

"Maybe I will. What's she doing here by herself, anyway?"

"What do you mean?"

"Tallia said she and her twin brother were inseparable."

Ussarine's face turned into a mask. "You'd have to ask Esea about that," she said in a dead voice.

Karan glanced at Lilis, who looked as puzzled as she was. Oh well, none of her business. Karan stopped in the middle of the road.

"You're right, Lilis. It's not a good idea for the three of us to go sauntering past Snoat's estate in broad daylight. Together we're quite . . . "

"Unforgettable," Ussarine said wryly.

"Why don't you two go back? I'm going to make a quiet sortie past the place and see what I can find out. I'll be back tonight."

They headed back to Chanthed. Karan urged her horse on. A mile from Pem-Y-Rum, according to her map, she took a side track into the forest. When she judged that she was opposite the gates, she cast around for a suitable tree to climb.

She had been a brilliant climber once, but her bones were aching before she found a suitable perch, thirty feet up, from which she could see the gates, the villa and outbuildings. Guards patrolled the walls and there were more at the gate. Beyond, hundreds of people toiled in the gardens, orchards, vineyards and fish ponds. The place was the size of a small town.

She spent an hour watching and making notes in a little book, then lingered, hoping to spot Llian, but in vain. She was grimly contemplating the climb down when a furtive movement in the forest caught her eye.

It was a sandy-haired young fellow with a big frame, though with not enough muscle to fill it out, dressed in grubby homespun. A girl appeared, small but well fleshed. She stood up on tiptoe to kiss him and he put his arms around her. Young lovers with nowhere to be alone but outdoors. Karan smiled and wished them well.

She climbed down and limped back to her horse. Pem-Y-Rum could not be entered by normal stealthy means. She would have talk Tallia into a rescue mission.

46

FIND THE SOURCE

Every passing refugee – and there were more every day – heightened Aviel's fears for her own future. They staggered into Casyme with nothing more than they could carry on their backs, and she had never seen such beaten people. Their eyes were hollow, their clothes dirty, and none looked as though they had eaten a decent meal in a week. Snoat's armies were stripping the land of everything that had value.

Yet he was a minor problem compared to the Merdrun. What would happen when they invaded? Mass hysteria? A complete breakdown of civilisation, in which people like herself would be the first victims?

She tightened the clamps on her smallest still. She was distilling lavender oil now and it was a laborious process – a bucket of lavender, after hours of distillation, produced less than half a teaspoon of oil. But what use was lavender oil in a world at war?

After bringing her home yesterday Shand had sent out all his message skeets then raced off to Chanthed, saying he would not be back for at least six weeks. He had taken the little phial of perfume Aviel had blended for Wilm to remind him of home, but had forgotten his promise to teach her the first lessons in scent potion making.

She knew no more than he had told her on the ride home: *Mancery works by mentally locating a source of power, finding a way to draw some of that power safely, focusing it to the purpose in hand, then releasing it.*

Power either came from within or was drawn from an enchanted device. And using mancery came at a cost: aftersickness. But if a mancer was reckless like Shand's late master, Radizer, or unskilled or just unlucky – both of which applied to her in spades – the cost was liable to be a painful or gruesome death.

She could not imagine what an inner source of power was, though surely it had to do with willpower, determination and focus, all things she had in abundance. And Shand had said she had a gift for scent potions. Dare she try by herself?

How had she made that accidental potion that had so disabled him three years ago? Aviel lit a candle and sat up in bed with her journal, reading what she had done that day. Where had she found power to turn a cleansing blend of perfumes into a laxative scent potion?

She had been standing at her bench when the room around her faded into darkness and an image had slowly come into focus. Aviel relived the moment. She was looking into a well, narrow but deep, and the water was so far down that she could only make out the faintest reflection. Though it did not look like water; it had an oily appearance. She mentally reached down to it, stretching as far as she could reach, then further, further. Her arm seemed to elongate; it really hurt. She scooped up some of the liquid in a cupped hand and brought it back up, the liquid dripping through her fingers.

Her hand was empty, the liquid gone save for an oily, glistening wetness. She rubbed her forehead with her damp fingers, smelled the scent blend she had made that day – jasmine, cedar, hints of woodsmoke, citrus, sage and other things – and light exploded behind her eyes.

Aviel roused herself. She was in her bed and her head was throbbing, as it had after she'd made the laxative scent potion, though she still did not know what she had done. Was the well some inner source of power? She could not guess; she needed Shand's primer.

She lit a lantern and splashed up the track to the house. Perhaps he'd left her a note. He sometimes did when he went away in a hurry. It was raining heavily now, cold and depressing. She unlocked the back door and went inside. The air was stale and the house felt abandoned. The scrubbed kitchen table was empty, and so was the bench. He hadn't left her anything.

The cold heightened the ever-present pain in her ankle. She sat down at the table. What to do? She heard a faint drumming, the summon stone working its evil on the land, and shuddered.

Shand would be furious if she searched his house for the primer, but the invasion could occur before he returned and she had to protect herself. Her only hope was to start learning about scent potions right away.

She started at the back of the house and worked forward. The bookcase by the main fireplace held dozens of handwritten books, mostly volumes of the Histories and copies of several of the Great Tales, but also a book of epic poems, a bestiary that had been read so many times the pages were coming out, and an atlas with a series of blank pages at the end entitled *The Unknown Lands*.

She went up the long staircase, which made a right-angle bend halfway up. There were four rooms upstairs, plus the observatory under its little dome. It was furnished with a stool, a squat mirror telescope and an almanack in which he had entered astronomical readings over a period of years. Aviel sat on the stool, idly turning the pages. She had not seen any mention of the Secret Art, though he would hardly leave such valuable and dangerous books out in the open.

Shand had lived for hundreds of years, his life extended by a gift from his lover, Yalkara, who had subsequently rejected him. Therefore the primer, which he had used as an apprentice, must also be ancient, and ancient books had a particular smell.

The rain grew heavier; it was pounding down now. She limped down the stairs. He must have a secret hiding place, probably protected by a spell or charm so it could not be seen. But would he have thought to protect his hiding place against a book's smell?

Aviel went back and forth, sniffing. Nothing downstairs and nothing upstairs. What about the cellar? A musty smell led her to a trapdoor in the far corner of the living room under the little round rug, and a ladder ran down for fifteen rungs. She winced her way down it into a cavern hewn out of layered yellow and brown rock. There were puddles of seepage on the floor and a mouldy smell. Beads of moisture on the far wall glistened red and orange in the lantern light.

Behind her a series of iron racks contained dusty bottles and stop-pered glass flasks, a dozen ten-gallon barrels of wine, and six small barrels of the raw spirit Shand used for making brandies and liqueurs. But there was no smell of old books.

Until she sniffed along the wine barrels, and the one in the far corner had the faintest aroma of aged parchment. She hesitated. This was wrong; Shand would be apoplectic.

She found a hidden catch at the back and opened the barrel. Inside, wrapped in canvas and then in layers of waxed paper, was a book, eleven inches square, with covers of pink polished rosewood inlaid with camphor laurel, sandalwood, incense cedar and other scented timbers. It contained several hundred pages of fine cream-coloured parchment, though many of the pages were stained, some smelled bad, and the combination of odours made her nose prickle. But it wasn't Shand's primer – the name on the cover was Radizer and the title was *Scent Potions*.

Shivers crept up the outsides of Aviel's thighs. This was the grimoire of Shand's reckless master, who had blown himself to bits while trying to make one of the potions. It was a deadly book, one no apprentice would be allowed to open save under the supervision of her master. Yet she, who had never done anything really reckless in her life, was thinking about using it by herself.

If she began there would be no going back. No regaining Shand's trust either, and after all he had done for her she could not so betray him. She replaced the grimoire in the barrel and was splashing down through the puddles to her workshop when she heard the crack of huge wings and a furious shriek from the direction of the skeet house.

Not again! She got a fist-sized piece of rabbit, headed to the skeet house and, with some difficulty, removed the red-cased message. Aviel opened it in the workshop, hunched up against her brazier.

West of Tirthrax
2 Pulin, 3111

Shand,
Our very existence is in peril and every second counts now.
Find the summon stone, the source of the drumming, with the utmost haste. Destroy it by smashing it to pieces, burning every fragment in the hottest fire you can make — but NOT mage fire — then pounding the fragments to dust and scattering it far and wide. Do not use mancery near it. Under no circumstances attempt to draw upon the power of the source — this could be catastrophic.
I am hurrying to Chanthed by aerial means and should arrive in three weeks, though at best that will only be a fortnight before the night of the triple moons. If you're not there I will take charge of our defences — though I fear it may already be too late.
Desperate times, old friend.

Malien

The brazier gave out no heat. Aviel's feet and hands felt as though they had turned to ice.

Our very existence is in peril . . . every second counts. Destroy the stone . . . not *mage fire.*

Why not?

Even if she could find someone who knew how to direct a skeet to Chanthed, Shand would not get there for the best part of a week. But the summon stone had to be found urgently and if seconds counted, a week was out of the question.

Aviel was forced to a terrible conclusion. It was up to her to locate the summon stone right away so, when Shand got the message, he could destroy it.

But to do that, she would need his grimoire.

47

WAS THAT THE DEATH CRY?

When Aviel finished the first half of the grimoire it was five in the morning and her eyes were starting out of her head in horror. She blew the lantern out and collapsed on her bed, shaking as if she had a fever. The book was dreadful, dark and deadly.

And she had to use it.

The mancery of scent potions was nothing like she had imagined. She only ever used her scents for positive purposes: healing, enhancing moods, disguising bad smells and generally making people feel better in one way or another. She knew there were darker potions, though she'd had no idea just how depraved and terrible they could be.

Now she did.

The dark scent potions in the grimoire greatly outnumbered the good ones: potions to enfeeble, confuse or control a person; potions to make an enemy ill and potions to prevent a wound from healing; potions that would drive whoever smelled them insane; potions to utterly corrupt. Potions to poison an enemy in a dozen sickening ways.

And potions to kill.

Some were dangerous to make, as Radizer had discovered when he was blown to bits. All the dark potions were dangerous to test, and some were so perilous that they could only be tested on the intended victim.

Dark potion-making began with the collection and purification of a variety of scents, fumes, stenches, miasmas and reeks. Some were foul, acrid, corrosive or poisonous, and some had to be sourced from grave-yards, charnel houses, cesspits and other terrible places.

She wondered how the summon stone had ended up where it was. Was it lost, or had it been deliberately hidden? The answer mattered – a scent potion for finding something lost could not be used to locate a deliberately hidden object, or one concealed by spell or illusion.

Every second counts now.

Such a powerful enchanted object was unlikely to have been lost. It had probably been carefully hidden long ago. A guess, but it gave Aviel something to work with.

The grimoire contained three scent potions for finding hidden objects, though the Wild Goose Exhalation, the easiest of them, hardly seemed appropriate, and the Revelatory Reek could not see through spells of hiding, illusion or misdirection. That only left the Eureka Graveolence, which began on page 421. Aviel had no idea what gra-veolence meant, though it suggested both grave and violence. It was one of the scent potions in the final and most difficult section of the grimoire – the "Great Potions".

The section began with three pages of warnings about making the potions and a further two pages of warnings about their use. Their effects were liable to be stronger, less predictable and more dangerous each succeeding time they were used.

She turned the pages, reluctantly. Even the names were unpleasant – the Revelatory Reek, Murderer's Mephitis, An Essence of Ague, the Putrid Potion – and she wondered why Shand had been apprenticed to a mancer who was clearly attracted to the dark side. There was a dark side to Shand too, though it had never been turned on her.

It would be once he discovered what she was up to.

Aviel reached page 420 and went to turn to the next page, but it was stuck to the one after and she had to ease them apart with a knife blade. As soon as she opened the pages, her nostrils were attacked by a repulsive stench. She dropped the book and hurled herself back.

The grimoire appeared to be smoking. No, a red-brown fume was oozing from the pages of the Eureka Graveolence, though it hung above the surface as if trying to get back into the parchment. She tried to waft it away with her fingers but the fume spun into a trio of whorls, spinning sluggishly, that coiled away from one another. The pages, Aviel now saw, were spattered with thick greenish-brown muck, long congealed.

The whorls rotated around the edges of the pages, approached one another, combined and were drawn back into the largest of the spatters with a faint squelching sound, like muck gurgling down a plughole.

But the smell was even worse, and it was coming from the three middle fingers of her right hand, where they had passed through the fume. Her fingertips had gone the greenish-brown colour, and it was spreading. She scrambled across to the washbasin, poured some water in and scrubbed her fingers with the strong yellow soap she had made last week. It had no effect; the stain was creeping down past the first joint of her three fingers, staining the skin and turning it thick and lumpy, like – she imagined – the skin of a troll. Aviel tried sandsoap, scrubbing until her fingers throbbed, but that did not stop the stain either.

What if it kept spreading until it turned her into a fifteen-year-old monstrosity? How her sisters would gloat. The thought stopped her heart for several beats.

She tossed the water out the door, took a flask of aqua vitae distilled from fermented fruit, which she had planned to use for tincture making, and poured a cupful into the basin. Aviel jammed her fingers into it and yelped as the pure spirit stung and burned. The liquid went the same foul brown as the fume, but when she withdrew her hand the stain was still spreading slowly down her fingers. What if it got into a cut and started to grow inside her?

Apart from cutting the affected fingers off, Aviel could only think of one remedy. Last year she had extracted a flask of fruit acid from a case of bitter oranges. It had lifted the skin off her hands and left them red and flaking for weeks afterwards. She had labelled it with a warning, put it on a high shelf and forgotten about it.

She tossed out the reeking spirits, wiped the basin with a rag and measured a small quantity of the fruit acid into the basin. After taking a deep breath she plunged her fingers in. Her eyes wandered to the cleaver hanging on the wall behind her chopping bench. She used it for cutting up woody herbs. If the fruit acid did not work she would have to take desperate measures.

Her skin stung, burned, throbbed. She stared at the wall as she rubbed her fingers together, working the liquid into every pore. Aviel did not look down; she did not want to get her hopes up prematurely. Only when she could bear the pain no longer did she lift her fingers from the fruit acid.

The stain had stopped moving at the second joints of her fingers. But would the acid kill the stain? She might not know for hours so she put a glove on her wet fingers and tried to put it out of mind.

The grimoire lay open on her bedcovers. It was a malevolent book, dangerous even to a careful master and deadly to an apprentice. Since she was the greenest novice, the sensible thing was to put it back where she had found it and never think of it again. After all, it wasn't up to her to carry out Malien's orders.

How could she have read the grimoire *in bed*? The thought of it lying on the covers where she slept sent tingles of horror through her. She took it to the little scrubbed table where she ate her meals, but reading it there felt just as bad. Aviel put it on the scarred, zinc-covered workbench that old Quintius the alchemist, whose workshop this had been, had used for his unsuccessful experiments, and felt the tension ease.

She went to close the book, then stopped. Would the fume rise again if she reopened it at the Eureka Graveolence? Was the book safer closed or open? She pulled up a stool and scanned the instructions for making the scent potion.

It was the most complicated recipe she had ever seen — it used twenty-eight ingredients and had fifteen steps, some involving processes she had never used before. Some of the ingredients she already had or could find without too much trouble, such as the pong extracted from a rotten crow's egg and the distilled essence captured from a pile of aged horse manure, but others would be difficult. And at least two would be dangerous, both to obtain and to use.

Thrice-warmed sludge from the base of the de-hairing pits of a leather tannery.

The de-hairing pits had the foulest and most disgusting stench Aviel had ever smelled, and getting some of the sludge would be tricky because there was only one tannery in Casyme and it belonged to Magsie Murg, a rich and nasty old lady who would have owned Aviel's indenture for seven years had Shand not intervened. Magsie was a law unto herself and she had most been unhappy about losing Aviel to Shand. If she was caught in the tannery while he was away, she could end up enslaved there.

The stench from the burning skull bone from a hundred-year-old grave.

Grave robbing was an offence against the dead, not to mention a serious crime, and it brought shockingly bad luck.

Aviel sniffed the glove. The reek was gone; she could only smell bitter orange now. She peeled off the glove and the lumpy skin came off her fingers, leaving them red, wrinkled and very tender.

She went back to the recipe. Some of the weights and measurements were indecipherable because of the noxious muck spattered across the pages, and two of the ingredients were illegible. She took a fine-bladed silver knife and worked it under the largest of the spatters, hoping to lift it off.

Aaarrghhhh!

A dying shriek echoed back and forth in her inner ear. Aviel whipped the knife away as more stinking fumes oozed out. She threw herself backwards, her hair streaming all around her head and crackling with sparks. Her heart was thundering and sweat prickled on the backs of her hands.

Was that the death cry of Master Radizer? Had he been making the Eureka Graveolence before he died? Could the stains be the residue of his failed scent potion? Or his own decayed remains? Or both?

And if she were so extraordinarily foolish as to attempt the potion untutored, would her exploded innards end up beside his?

48

A PERFECT BRUTE

Llian was slumped in a chair, his head still echoing from the drumming, which had gone on half the night, when Ifoli burst into Snoat's salon. Her breathing was ragged, her ivory cheeks tinged with pink, and she stumbled as she entered. Her left hand was pressed to her stomach as if she were in pain.

"Ifoli!" snapped Snoat, clearly irritated that she had strayed so far from the perfection he demanded.

"Gurg—" Her voice was higher than usual, almost shrill.

Snoat scowled.

With a visible effort of will she calmed herself, regularised her breathing and pressed her left hand down by her side. Llian could not remember seeing anyone so young – she could not have been twenty-five – having such extraordinary self-control.

"Gurgito said he'll come when he's damn well ready." She bowed and stood back, trembling a little.

"Did he now?" A muscle jumped in Snoat's jaw, then he laughed. "What a fellow he is."

"I'm not sure what you mean, Cumulus."

"In his way, Gurgito Unick is as perfect as you are. You are perfectly lovely, perfectly competent and, *almost always*, perfectly composed. Unick is a perfect brute who lacks all impulse control. He's as vicious a mongrel as you will ever see, and one of the prizes in my collection."

"He's worse now! The Origin device has corrupted him."

"Come now. He only finished it at midnight."

"And it's utterly transformed him. He's a danger to you, Cumulus."

Llian sat up. The drumming had began suddenly at midnight, louder than he had ever heard it. He had lain in bed for an hour, fighting an almost overwhelming urge to sneak down the hall to Thandiwe's room. He had tried everything to defeat it, though in the end only one thing could hold him back – the thought of Sulien's crushing disappointment in him.

"He hates men like me," said Snoat. "But he hates clever women even more."

Ifoli's hand slipped to her stomach again. "He hates all women."

Snoat frowned. "He *struck* you?"

Ifoli unfastened the central buttons of her gown. Her midriff bore a fist-sized red mark. She fastened the buttons. The flush reappeared on her cheeks but faded at once.

"Have him brought here. By the tetrad."

"Sir!" cried Ifoli. "I implore you—"

"At once! And *never* call me sir again, or the tetrad may pay a visit on you."

She bowed and went out.

Snoat, now agitated, dismissed the secretaries and Thandiwe. He turned to Llian, who had no idea what was going on or what the tetrad was.

"Unick is the most brilliant maker of enchanted devices in the world," said Snoat. "There's no one else like him. But I can't allow him to damage my possessions, can I?"

"Am I your possession?" Llian had begun to think he was.

"You're a unique and precious part of my collection, the teller of the first new Great Tale in hundreds of years. Though I'm not sure you're going to be a permanent part . . ."

Chills formed on the back of Llian's neck. Snoat's words could be interpreted in a number of ways but he could only focus on the obvious meaning. Snoat planned to have him killed, and, trapped in this walled and heavily guarded estate, how could he hope to escape?

The drumming sounded, very faintly this time. Some distance away a man roared like a mad beast, then let out a stream of obscenities fouler than anything Llian had heard since his reckless student days. Then came an almighty crash, as if one of the exquisite vases that lined the corridors had been smashed to pieces, followed by another series of berserk roars, obscenities and crashes.

Ifoli burst through the doorway, skidded on the polished floor, recovered and said redundantly, "They're bringing him now, Cumulus. He's . . . reluctant."

"The Oolian vases?" said Snoat.

"Three of the four."

"Bring the last."

She went out. The roars grew louder until they rattled the windows, then Gurgito Unick was dragged in. He was a very big man, but the tetrad who had tamed him were bigger. They were giants, as muscular as weightlifters, yet it took three of them to hold him, and his wild lurches and furious lunges were dragging them several feet one way and then the other.

It was hard to comprehend how anyone could have changed so radically, so quickly. Unick's face was as bloated as that of a five-day corpse, his tiny eyes were so red they seemed to be dripping blood, and he stank as if he had slept in the same clothes for a month. Had his Origin device focused the drumming on him?

His ruddy eyes touched on Ifoli, who had returned with the last of the Oolian vases, a lovely piece almost three feet tall. He leered at her. Then Unick noticed Llian staring at him and rage overwhelmed him.

"Stinking teller!" he roared.

In an explosion of violence he tore free of the tetrad and ran at Llian, who was in a corner and had nowhere to go. The tetrad lumbered after Unick but he was too quick. Llian was sure he was going to die – one blow from those mighty fists would drive his nose out the back of his head.

He put up his own fists, though he had never won a fight in his life. Unick sprang ten feet, landed in front of Llian and swung at him with terrible force. Llian ducked late and the blow clipped him on the side of the head, knocking him to the ground. He lay there, stunned, seeing the threat but unable to move.

"Ifoli!" said Snoat.

Unick leapt, intending to land with all his weight on Llian's head. This would have killed him had Ifoli not leapt into Unick's path like a ballet dancer, swinging the Oolian vase by its rim. She slammed it into Unick's face and it shattered, driving him backwards. Llian crawled the other way, then the tetrad had hold of Unick again.

For a moment he was silent, dazed by the blow, which had broken his nose and cut his face in a dozen places. Ifoli stood there, her breast heaving, staring at the fragments.

Snoat scowled. "For pity's sake, Ifoli, close your mouth. You look like a yokel." She did so, and he smiled. "You saved the life of one of my most precious possessions and I won't forget it."

"But . . . the vase was the last in existence," said Ifoli.

"It was one of a set. Better none at all than an incomplete set."

Another insight into the character of the man. Llian liked Snoat less every second, and feared him more.

Snoat addressed the tetrad. "You will beat Unick to a pulp and lock him in his workshop. Then you will beat each other to a pulp for so failing me."

The tetrad battered Unick with ruthless efficiency, sickening to watch. Such a beating would have killed Llian, but Unick, an experienced brawler, had an astonishing ability to absorb punishment. He did not look at his attackers or try to resist them. His bloody eyes stayed fixed on Llian the whole time.

Finally he slumped into unconsciousness and the tetrad dragged him out. Servants came in, barefoot so they would make no noise, to clean up the blood and the shattered porcelain.

"It doesn't do to let me down," Snoat observed.

Llian squirmed.

A messenger appeared at the door. Ifoli spoke to him for half a minute. "Ill news, Cumulus. Will you hear it now?" She looked meaningfully at Llian.

"I will," said Snoat.

"Ragred caught up with Karan some miles east of Chanthed but failed to get her chain, and now he's dead. A Whelm killed him."

"A *Whelm?*" cried Snoat, vexed. "What name?"

"We don't know. Karan gave her daughter into the Whelm's safe custody."

"Why would she give Sulien to *them?*" cried Llian. He appreciated all Idlis and Yetchah had done for Karan but did not share her faith in them. "Where are they taking her? Is she all right? Where is Karan now?"

Snoat raised an eyebrow at Ifoli.

"The messenger did not know where they were taking Sulien, chronicler," she said to Llian, "but Karan was heading to Chanthed."

Snoat looked Llian up and down. "Escort Llian to his room. He's got a lot to think about."

The night that followed was one of the worst of Llian's life. Possibly, *the* worst. What a fool he had been, voting against Thandiwe. Karan must have heard that he had been accused of murder and had come after him, and then she had been attacked. He could only imagine what she and Sulien had gone through before Ragred was killed.

But why had she sent Sulien away with the Whelm? She had been afraid of them since Idlis lurched up the path to Gothryme when she was a toddler. She had screamed herself hoarse.

It did not make sense, for she came first, always. Llian could only think of one reason why Karan would send her away. The magiz must have got to her, and she believed that Sulien was safer with the Whelm than with herself.

It must be Karan's worst nightmare. It was certainly Llian's.

49

CONTROLLING THE SOURCE

Llian was at the window of the salon when a six-horse carriage drew up outside, just on dark. Snoat got in, accompanied by Ifoli, and the coach drew away. It was followed by his mounted escort, the tetrad, their muscles straining their purple and yellow uniforms to bursting point.

Llian knew where Snoat was going because he had gloated about it — to the same place he had gone last night and the night before. He kept returning to the private library of the College of the Histories, to sigh and drool over the manuscripts of the other twenty-two Great Tales.

Snoat could not touch them, for they were protected by an

enchantment of such potency that not even the demolition of the library would have released them. But he was determined to have the tales, and Unick was working on a means to break the enchantment. Llian had no idea if it was a task for a week or a decade, though, judging by Snoat's demeanour, it was going well.

Unick, however, looked worse every time Llian saw him. The drumming was corrupting him by the hour, which suggested that the summon stone was the source of the power he had found, and that his newly completed Origin device was linked to it. Dare Llian sneak into the workshop to find out? The best part of a month had passed since Sulien's nightmare about the Merdrun, and his thwarted quest to find the stone grew more urgent by the hour.

Unick would be drunk by now – he always was by dinnertime – though drunk could mean more dangerous, not less. But Llian had to try. If he could locate the stone and get a message to Shand or Tallia, they could go after it. It would begin to make up for all the damage he had done since arriving in Chanthed.

Unick's workshop was at the back of the South Wing, below ground, in a part of the villa that was little used as it was close to the river and had a problem with damp. The door was not locked, and the smell of him was muted, as if he had not been there in hours. Even so, Llian hesitated. If he was caught snooping, Unick might well kill him.

It had to be done. He entered a large pentagonal room containing a labyrinth of tables and benches, haphazardly arranged. Half of the benches were covered in clockwork mechanisms and other mechanical devices in various stages of disassembly.

The others held a variety of alchemical equipment, all as filthy as Unick himself. The contents of one distillation flask had congealed to a festering brown sludge covered with blue and red mould. A zinc-covered bench was corroded through to the timber, while pits in the metal were coated with fantastic growths of white and yellow crystals.

The stench became gaggingly strong, then the door slammed. Llian whirled. Unick stood there, holding a flask in each hand and rocking like a dinghy in a heavy sea. He was clad in the same stained trousers he'd been wearing during his attack on Llian the other day. His bare chest and belly were covered in a thicket of wiry hair, the hair of his armpits was six inches long and clotted into rat-tails, and his feet were filthy.

"Looking for another Great Tale, chronicler?" sneered Unick. "Stick around and I'll write it with your broken bones."

The bruises from his beating had faded, though his bloated face was as purple as ever, as if he was only seconds away from apoplexy. Llian prayed it would take the brute sooner rather than later.

He edged along the benches, always keeping one between him and Unick.

"If you want to know what I'm up to," Unick said conversationally, "all you have to do is ask."

He seemed in a rare good humour tonight and Llian wondered why. "Why would you tell me?"

"Snoat doesn't want anyone to know, and I hate him even more than I hate you."

Unick upended one flask into his mouth, drained it and tossed it into a pile of rubbish in the corner. He wrenched the bung out of the other one.

"All right," said Llian, suspecting a trick. "I'm asking. Have you found the source?"

If the source was the summon stone, which was corrupting people to gain enough power to let the Merdrun through, how could it ever be used safely? Was that why Unick was decaying so rapidly?

"Snoat wants the Command device to break the college's protection and steal the twenty-two Great Tales," Llian added. "How far have you got?"

"I built the Origin device in less than a day," Unick boasted, "then tapped the source for the very first time."

And it had corrupted him. Ifoli was right – this secret was too dangerous to use.

"Snoat has ordered his artisans to copy each device as soon as I finish it," Unick added, "but they'll fail. It's not that simple."

"Have you made the other two devices?"

"Very soon."

"Can I see the Origin device?"

Unick shrugged. "I might even test it on you."

He waded through the mess to a bench next to the mould-streaked south wall and picked up a long brass tube. It resembled a telescope but had a cluster of blue needle-shaped crystals on one end and a pair of glass lenses in the other. Silver and gold wires were wound tightly around the middle, and more crystals, red rubies and green emeralds, could be seen through the windings.

Unick gave the tubes a half-twist and the blue needles began to glow. He touched the jewels in a complicated sequence, raised the device and put his eye to the lenses, and swung the tube from left to right.

The drumming swelled and Llian felt a mad urge to attack Unick. Though it would have been suicidal, it took all his strength to beat the compulsion.

Unick's tiny eyes were darting now, his fists balling up. Then, in an instant, he went into a berserk rage and hurled himself at Llian, who leaped back, crashed into a bench and dodged behind it, trying to get to the door.

The Origin device jerked so wildly that Unick lost his grip on it. It went flying through the air; he dived after it but it bounced off a bench and the cluster of blue crystals fell out. The drumming stopped instantly.

Unick pulled himself to his feet, rubbing a bruise on his forehead. He turned slowly and for a second Llian heard the drumming again, though this time it seemed to be thumping inside Unick's head. His eyes bulging, he sprang onto a bench, then to the next one and launched himself at Llian.

He gave in to the call of the drumming, using it to defend himself. The closest object was a two-foot-high glass still. Its cooling jacket was full of water and it was very heavy. He grabbed it and smashed it down on Unick's head, scattering glass and water everywhere and knocking him to the floor. Unick should have been unconscious but he was tearing his fingernails on the floorboards as he clawed his way towards Llian.

He bolted.

*

"What the hell have you done now?"

Thandiwe was shaking Llian by the shoulder. As he sat up she gave him a last furious shake, banging his head on the head of the bed.

"What do you want?" he muttered. It was just getting light outside.

"Why has Snoat stopped questioning you? I haven't got nearly enough for *Mendark's Tale*."

Llian took a malicious pleasure in enlightening her. "He doesn't give a damn about it. The tale was just bait to get me here."

"What an ego you've got! Why on earth would he want a failed chronicler and murderer, anyway?"

"He framed me! And you know it."

"Answer the bloody question!"

Llian told her about Snoat's plan to make the three devices, and what Unick had done so far.

"So it's all been for nothing," she said bitterly. "No! I've got to have the tale, or I'm ruined."

"Right now we've got more important things to worry about."

"Like what?"

"Once Unick completes the Identity and Command devices, Snoat will get rid of us. We know too much."

Thandiwe's full lips moved but no sound emerged. She scrubbed her mouth with the back of her hand. "But—"

"Surely you thought about that before you approached him?"

"Why would he hurt me? I'm—"

"Beautiful?" said Llian without sarcasm. "Clever? A great chronicler?"

"I don't believe he would just . . . *kill* me. For nothing."

"Believe it!"

"What am I supposed to do?"

"Make yourself useful to him."

"You mean sleep with him?" said Thandiwe.

"I'm not sure you're his type."

"You mean I'm too old! You're a cruel bastard, Llian."

"I didn't mean that at all. Besides, aren't you forgetting something?"

"What?"

"I said he'd get rid of *us*. We're in this together, and *you* put us here, but your only thought has been about how I can help you."

"I didn't have my college fees and stipend paid for by one of the most powerful people of all. Everything I've gained in life, I've had to work for."

"And there was nothing you wouldn't do to get it."

She slapped him, a stinging blow that knocked his head sideways. "You slimy hypocrite! How dare you?"

"What are you talking about?"

"*A great chronicler you may be, Llian, but you are not a worthy master,*" she quoted in a passable imitation of Wistan's voice from the never-to-be-forgotten night when he had banned Llian. "*Your tale proves your dishonour.*"

"I'm sorry," he said after a mortifying minute of self-analysis. "I've no right to point the finger at anyone."

She sat beside him, a trifle mollified. "What are we going to do?"

"Sell him on *Mendark's Tale*."

"I tried that already."

"No, *really* sell it. He's a rapacious collector, remember? The moment he got my manuscript and realised how rare and important it was, nothing would satisfy him except owning all the Great Tales. But what then?"

"I don't understand."

"Collectors have to keep collecting, but once Snoat steals the other twenty-two Great Tales he'll have the perfect collection – the originals of all the greatest tales ever written, the very core of the Histories. Nothing can ever be more valuable, except . . . "

"A twenty-fourth Great Tale," Thandiwe said slowly.

"And if it also featured Snoat – as one of the great people in the Histories – his ego would drive him to have it."

"Doesn't necessarily mean he'd want me to write it."

"You underestimate yourself. If anyone can sell you as the best person to tell the story, you can."

Thandiwe stood up, her breast heaving, and walked around the room. Llian's news had shaken her, but she was as resourceful as anyone he had ever known.

"I think I can do it," she said.

"Unless you *know* you can do it, you'll never convince him."

"I know I can do it." She sat beside him again. "Thank you, Llian. We . . . we could have been good together." She looked at him expectantly, almost coquettishly.

He wasn't going down that road. "I don't know what I'm going to do, though. He could come for me at any time."

"You've got a ready-made means of making yourself useful."

"What's that?"

"A private telling of your Great Tale."

"What a good idea. If I drag it out I could increase my life span *by days.*"

50

I, A MERE COLLECTABLE

Llian was staring at a blank page of his journal when Ifoli entered his room. She wore a simple gown of emerald silk and silk slippers of the same colour. Her black hair, freshly cut, was a feathery cap around her head. In all his life he had never seen anyone so beautiful.

He rose, conscious of his own awkwardness. She bowed, then presented, on a lozenge-shaped platinum tray, a white card with silvery writing on it in a calligraphic hand even better than his own.

Llian took the card.

Lord Cumulus Snoat
and Ifoli Saquarin

request the pleasure of your company at dinner tonight,
9 p.m., in the gallery of the private library.

Llian read it again. Why would Snoat invite when he could command? Had Unick completed the three devices? Was Llian no longer
needed? Was he going to be killed tonight? Nine o'clock was only three
hours away.

"Do you accept or decline?" said Ifoli.

"What would you advise?"

"How could I, a mere collectable, presume to advise the greatest
living teller?"

It was the first hint that she was unhappy with her status here, and
again he wondered where she came from and how she had come to
serve Snoat.

"Currently I'm a disgraced ex-chronicler, accused of murdering the
man who rightly banned me from practising my art."

"Your achievements stand. You beat the incomparable Rulke in a telling competition. And your tale was voted a Great Tale, unanimously."

Previously, Llian had rarely sensed any emotion in her speech, yet
now he detected a hint of admiration. Why would Ifoli, the perfect
servant, admire him? Because she loved books, or the Great Tales? If
so, why was she helping Snoat? He studied her face, searching for a
hint of what was to come. Could she remain impassive if he were to
be killed tonight?

She was too good; she reflected his gaze like a mirror.

"Please tell Lord Snoat that I would be . . . delighted to accept."

Ifoli bowed, then looked him up and down.

"Something the matter?" said Llian. The clothes he had been given
when first brought here were respectable enough.

She seemed to be measuring him. Height a little above average, leg
length average, shoulder width broad, feet large.

"Go to the bathing chamber." She frowned, considered. "No, you
will use mine. Go to the top floor and down the hall to the very end,
on the right." She handed him a small brass key. "A cutter will attend
to your hair at eight. Your outfit will be ready at eight thirty-five. Lord
Snoat would prefer that you be punctual."

"Translating that," Llian said sarcastically, "I'll be punished for
being late."

"This dinner is exceedingly important to him. Do nothing to spoil it."

Or else?

She went out. Llian returned to his journal but could not concentrate. Where had Snoat found such a perfect servant anyway? Her features, and the name Saquarin, hinted at the far east, the lands between Fadd and Tiksi, though it was a part of Lauralin that Llian had never visited.

Why dinner? Why now? What was going on?

The servants' bathing chamber, which he normally used, was plain but clean. Why was it unacceptable? He went up to the top level. The hall was wide and the ceiling high, with extravagant cornices made from carved pale-yellow soapstone. Ifoli's bathing chamber, small but elegantly finished, was clad in venous golden travertine. It smelled faintly of her musky perfume.

Llian felt a trifle abashed at bathing in her personal tub, but as she had said, she was as much part of Snoat's collection as Llian was.

For how long?

And how long for her? Would Snoat replace her the moment her looks began to fade, or when he found someone whose beauty and self-control were more perfect? Of course he would, but what would he do with her?

I'd sooner burn this place to the ground, and everything in my collection, than allow anyone else to have the least part of it.

Was her fate to be disposed of the moment her perfection faded? It had to be, and Ifoli must know it. So what held her here? Or was she as much a prisoner as he was?

The water was beginning to cool. He ran more hot in – a luxury he had not enjoyed in ages. The complicated hot-water plumbing at Gothryme had failed last year, and Karan could not afford to repair it, since that would have involved demolishing and rebuilding several walls.

How did Ifoli cope? Did she cling to the illusion that her master would take her for his partner? If she did, she was gravely mistaken, for Snoat was a narcissist to the core and cared about nothing except himself. Status and appearance being everything to him, any consort who fell short of perfection would diminish him, and must be replaced.

Finally, when his fingers and toes were prune-like, he drained the
tub, scrubbed it clean, wrapped a towel around himself and returned
to his room. It was after eight, and a young man, almost as handsome
as Ifoli was beautiful, was anxiously waiting to cut his hair.

Llian did not ask his name and the young man did not volunteer it.
He trimmed Llian's hair, shaved his stubble, cleaned up and went out
without a word. Immediately a short man and a tall woman entered,
each carrying a leather bag.

The woman provided Llian with underwear, a cream linen shirt,
black knee britches and a red silk coat, and inspected each garment
after he put it on. The shirt proved slightly too small across the shoulders. She took the seams apart and restitched them, her needle moving
faster than Llian's eye could follow.

The old-fashioned buckled shoes, made from olive-grey chacalot
hide, weren't quite wide enough for Llian's feet. The short man, with
the skilful use of a stretcher, had them fitting perfectly within minutes. They went out. Llian sat on the bed but got up again. There were
knots in his stomach. Was this going to be his last meal? Did Snoat
require everything to be perfect because he intended to dispose of Llian
afterwards?

Someone knocked on his door five minutes before the hour of nine. It
was the tall redhead who had taken Ifoli's place while she was working
on the drawings.

"It is time," she said. She inspected Llian, straightened his collar and
removed a thread from his left sleeve.

"What's this dinner all about?" said Llian.

"It's about Cumulus."

"Everything is about him," Llian muttered.

The redhead, whose name he did not know, looked him in the eye,
and for a second Llian thought she was going to reveal something. Then
she said, "Yes, everything is. Come."

He followed her out. Thandiwe was waiting outside her own door.
She wore silver-grey silk satin, a calf-length gown that clung to her
figure but did not shout about it.

"You too?" said Llian.

She nodded stiffly. Her fears surely ran on the same track as Llian's. The redhead went ahead.

"Take my arm," whispered Thandiwe. "We're in this together."

Llian did so reluctantly; he could only imagine Karan's reaction to this scene. Where was she now? Was Snoat still hunting her? And Sulien? Had she come to terms with the Whelm, or did she live in terror of them every hour of the day? They were hard, cold slave-drivers who were incapable of kindness. He could not bear to imagine her suffering.

A longcase clock struck nine as the redhead reached the double doors of the gallery. She pushed them open and announced, "Llian, teller of the *Tale of the Mirror*, with Thandiwe Moorn."

Thandiwe stiffened; the announcement had made her no more than Llian's partner. It was not a good start.

They went through and the redhead pulled the doors closed behind them.

The gallery might have been eighty feet by forty, though the ends lay in shadow and all he could make out were a number of widely separated display cases. Directly ahead stood a rosewood table lit by lamplight. It was not a long table, only eight feet by four. Presumably Snoat wanted the dinner to be intimate.

The gallery was above the library, which could be seen through an oval opening in the floor. A broad staircase curved down to the reading room, though it too was unlit.

Above them a square skylight had been opened, for it was a mild evening. There was no moon, but the stars were diamonds scattered on black velvet and a scented breeze wafted in from the perfumed roof garden.

Snoat appeared out of the darkness with Ifoli on his arm. He bowed, then went to one end of the table and Ifoli to the other. He was immaculate in blue and not a hair was out of place; Ifoli was dressed in pale yellow satin, a simple sheath. The table was set with silver and glassware that looked brand new. It might have been designed and made solely for this dinner.

Snoat greeted Thandiwe and Llian as if he were the perfect host and they were honoured guests. He ushered them to their chairs, drew them out and pushed them back in as they sat down. He bowed to Ifoli, who sat, then took his own chair. He looked as if he had gained his heart's desire. Was that good — or very bad?

A servant came, a bald old fellow with an upright military bearing. He poured green wine into four tall glasses and withdrew. Snoat took up a black baton, pointed it at the lamps, and their light faded until only the glowing wicks could be seen. He raised his glass.

"To the most perfect and vital books ever created on Santhenar," he said. "To the Great Tales."

Llian almost choked. So that's what this was about. But, mindful that he was utterly in Snoat's power, he put on a teller's smile and echoed, "To the Great Tales."

"To the Great Tales," said Thandiwe, her voice hoarse with longing.

The lust for a Great Tale burned more strongly in her than in anyone Llian had ever known, save himself. What would she not do to get one?

Snoat gave a little flick of the baton, over his shoulder. In the ceiling four long narrow cylinders emitted a golden radiance from their downward-pointing ends. Some kind of lightglass, Llian assumed. The light grew until it illuminated a second table, on which, artlessly arranged, was a series of old, battered books, and one new one which Llian knew instantly, for it was his own.

"The original manuscripts of all twenty-three Great Tales," said Snoat. "And now they are mine."

"The perfect collection," said Ifoli without a trace of irony.

Llian's fists clenched so tightly that his knuckles throbbed. The stinking mongrel bastard! How dare he flaunt his stolen goods as if he had earned them, deserved them? For all Snoat's airs, for all his pretence to be a man of culture and discernment, he was nothing but a thief and a murderer. Llian felt an urge to leap onto the table, trample the silverware and smash the glasses, then kick Snoat's perfect teeth down his throat. He wished the drumming would sound, to give him the excuse.

Thandiwe gave a tiny shake of her head. *Pull yourself together. He has the power of life or death over us.*

Snoat's lips twitched. He knew what Llian was thinking, and he was loving it. Llian's impotent fury was part of the joy of the occasion, another proof of Snoat's own supreme power and importance.

Llian drained his glass, not tasting the surpassingly good wine until the last drop. He felt another overpowering urge – to get drunk, make a boor of himself and spoil Snoat's perfect dinner. Though that might also be part of the plan – to contrast his own calm and measured character with the behaviour of the people who surrounded him.

Llian wasn't going to give Snoat the satisfaction.

The aged servant removed the glasses and brought others, and a different wine. It was lemon-yellow, full of tiny rising bubbles and refreshing in a tongue-tingling way. Small courses came one after another, each matched with the perfect wine. It was one of the most memorable meals of Llian's life, possibly even shading the time old Nadiril had interrogated him at a dinner in Thurkad that had taken all night and until lunchtime of the following day.

Snoat began as the perfect host – charming, considerate, attentive to his guests' every need – but as the evening wore on he became increasingly distracted by the table containing the twenty-three Great Tales. His glances at it became longer, more frequent and more longing.

Then, when Llian at Snoat's request was telling a brief tale about the long-disappeared race who had constructed the levels below the Aachim city of Shazmak, he rose abruptly and went to the other table.

Turning one's back on a teller in mid-tale was so rude that it was beyond Llian's experience, but he was nothing if not a professional and carried on with barely a pause. Thandiwe did not react apart from a narrowing of the eyes and a thinning of the lips. However, Ifoli, who was listening raptly, let out an audible gasp. She was shocked. No, she was furious!

Llian allowed the tale to reel off in his mind, and continued to tell it, but his thoughts were elsewhere. Why, when she knew everything about Snoat's life of villainy, had this small discourtesy so shocked Ifoli? Compared to stealing the twenty-three Great Tales, it did not rate.

He puzzled away at the question. Where had Snoat found her? She was highly educated and clearly had an appreciation of tales great and minor. But why this reaction to Snoat insulting a teller?

Telling must mean a great deal to her.

Snoat returned to the table. Llian finished his tale, and the next course was carried in. But soon Snoat was up again, drawing on gloves and opening one manuscript, then another, caressing the cracked leather, and once, Llian was astonished to see, wiping a tear from his eye. He sat down again and had just taken up his fork when Thandiwe tossed her bombshell.

"What are you going to do now, Cumulus?"

The fork halted, halfway to his mouth. "I don't follow you."

"The Great Tales are the perfect collection. Only twenty-three have ever been written, they're the most important creative and historical works on Santhenar, and you have the original manuscripts of all of them. It's a collection that can never be topped."

"Yes?" said Snoat, frowning.

"Surely it must make everything else you've collected a bit . . . second-rate?"

"There can be perfect collections of all kinds of things," he said with a hint of brusqueness.

"I don't see how. Take emeralds for instance. You have the best known collection but it can never be perfect."

"Why the hell not?" Snoat's manicured accent was slipping, revealing . . . what? A man of low birth who had painstakingly erased his old self?

"A new and better emerald could be found at any time," said Thandiwe, "or even a new mine full of them, and a better source of emeralds could render your collection *ordinary* overnight. The same applies to everything else you collect. Whether it's from nature or from the work of some great artisan, it can always be surpassed. Rendered second-rate. Even made valueless. Only the Great Tales endure, though . . . "

She trailed off and attacked the delicacies on her plate with gusto. Ifoli was staring at her in astonishment tinged with fear. Llian smiled; he knew what Thandiwe was up to.

"But?" said Snoat when she did not go on. He was showing definite signs of agitation now. "Get on with it!"

"Ah," said Thandiwe. "I had a second point, didn't I?" She pretended to consider it while she chewed.

Snoat seethed. Llian tucked in, finally enjoying the beautiful food and the magnificent wine. This might go badly wrong but he was going to enjoy it while it lasted.

"Twenty-three," Thandiwe said ruminatively. "It's an ugly number."

"I don't see why," said Snoat.

"Twenty-four, on the other hand, is a remarkable number with many attractive properties. If you had twenty-four Great Tales it'd really be something to boast about."

"There aren't twenty-four."

"There could be, if you allowed me to complete *Mendark's Tale*. His was a great life; it would certainly make a Great Tale."

"It *could* make a Great Tale," said Snoat, "but that requires the acclamation of the masters of the College of the Histories."

"If you sponsored the tale . . . "

"Any Great Tale acclaimed by corruption would be valueless to me," he said coldly. "Besides, a Great Tale has to have a great ending. The end to Mendark's life was unsatisfactory."

"Who's to say the tale has ended?" said Thandiwe. "You're continuing the greatest work of his life, and if it can be completed you'll change the world. That would be a most satisfactory ending." She paused, then added softly, "And you would be one of the towering figures in the Histories."

Though Llian had given Thandiwe the idea in the first place, he had to admire how she had spun it. It was the dream of everyone on Santhenar to be in the Histories, and even more so to be in a Great Tale. A narcissist like Snoat could not be immune to this desire; on the contrary, it could become his most profound motivation.

"You're a collector to your bones," she said. "You can't stop now – you have to make your perfect collection *more perfect*."

"Do you think I don't know what you're up to?" Snoat grated. The ugly accent was stronger now.

"It benefits us both," said Thandiwe.

"Yes, it does," he mused. "There's more to you than I thought. What do you say, Ifoli? Has Thandiwe saved herself?"

"She has a rare gift," Ifoli said ambiguously.

"I believe she'll do after all."

"Cumulus?" said Ifoli.

He chuckled. "I don't need *two* tellers, do I?"

Ifoli's gaze flicked from Snoat to Llian, and again he saw that she was shocked.

"But Llian wrote, *and illuminated*, the twenty-third Great Tale," said Ifoli. "Of all the manuscripts, it's the most beautiful and the most perfect."

"And all the more valuable if he's not around to make another copy," said Snoat. He poured himself a small goblet of brandy without offering any to anyone else and sniffed it appreciatively.

"Or ever tell the exquisite tale again . . . after he does my private telling."

51

WHO *WAS* MENDARK, ANYWAY?

Two agonising days had passed for Llian, and two sleepless nights, and he had never seen Snoat more cheerful. Only one thing could bring him more pleasure than obtaining an exquisite new piece for his collection, and that was planning the destruction of a treasure he no longer found good enough – to make sure no one else could have it.

Thandiwe was now the Chosen One, the teller with an almost certain Great Tale. Despite what Snoat had said, Llian knew it would be voted a Great Tale. The current masters knew which side their loaf was buttered on, and who did the buttering.

And Llian was the Doomed One. The man whose life would be measured in minutes after he completed Snoat's private telling. Whenever that would be.

His only distraction was his quest, fruitless though it seemed. Where had the summon stone come from, and where was it now? Had Mendark known? Llian could not recall him ever mentioning it.

Where had Mendark come from, for that matter? He had risen to power towards the end of the ruinous era known as the Clysm, when Santhenar had been devastated by a series of wars between Charon and Aachim lasting for almost five hundred years. Mendark had been elected Magister of the Council of Santhenar at the unheard-of age of twenty-three, thirty years younger than any Magister before him, and there had been rumours that he'd had unholy aid.

Though Llian had known Mendark since the age of twelve, had travelled halfway across the world with him, owed his career to Mendark and at times had thought of him as a friend, he knew nothing about his early life. He had been a secretive man. A mercurial man too, and his cold rages were legendary. After Mendark set fire to his own library while Llian was trapped in it, he had spent most of the past decade hating the Magister. But had he unwittingly been led astray by the Merdrun? And if he had, did it change anything? Llian would reserve judgement on that.

He was trudging back to his room after another fruitless day when Snoat turned the corner, and he was cock-a-hoop.

"Llian!" he said cheerily. "Come and see what I've added to my collection."

"Another stolen treasure?" Llian said sourly.

"This one walked in through the front door. Well, to be precise, the side window."

"A book walked?"

"Who said anything about a book? Come!"

Llian followed him into the other wing of the villa. Snoat entered a guarded room that smelled of ointment, passed between a series of screens and there, lying in a bed with her dark skin covered in bandages and bruises, was Tallia. Llian reeled. It was a catastrophe.

Snoat chuckled. "What a prize!"

"How . . . ?" said Llian.

"I dare say she'll tell you all about it."

"You're leaving us to talk?"

"I've made sure she can work no mancery. And I know you to be singularly inept." Snoat went out.

Llian carried a chair across to the bed and sat beside it. Tallia had two black eyes, so swollen that she could barely open them.

"Tallia," he said softly. "It's me, Llian."

One eye opened to a slit. The other quivered but remained closed. She raised her left hand, winced and let it flop down again. Her wrist was encircled by a metal band mounted with a pink amethyst and fine silver wires wound around it in five places. Llian recognised Unick's work: ugly, but presumably effective at preventing her using the Secret Art.

"Is there news of Karan?" he burst out. "Snoat's been hunting her. I can't bear to think—"

"She's safe. She's with us."

"Who's *us*?"

"Me, Shand, Yggur, Nadiril and Lilis."

Relief drained the strength from him and he slumped on the bed. "What – what's your plan?"

Tallia lowered her voice. "Bring down Snoat any way we can. And destroy the summon stone."

"Why did Karan send Sulien away with the Whelm? Or did they *steal* her?"

"You're being silly. She volunteered to go with them."

He could not hold back a cry. "Why?"

"Partly because of a stigma the magiz put on Karan when she went back to Cinnabar."

The blood drained from Llian's face. His head was spinning, his vision breaking up to whirling streaks. "What?" he said shrilly. "She went back *again*? When?"

Tallia told him what she knew.

His breath came in great shuddering gasps. "Are you saying the magiz is in Karan's mind . . . and knows everything she does?" He felt so faint he had to lower his head onto the bed. She was doomed.

"Pull yourself together," said Tallia. "The stigma is more like the lantern on the outside of a coach – it only reveals where Karan is, and only some of the time."

Llian managed to sit up. "What was the other reason she sent Sulien away?"

"Isn't it obvious? Karan couldn't attempt a rescue while she had Sulien with her."

Guilt fell on him like a collapsing wall. Karan had put herself in even more danger because of his stupidity, and Sulien had sacrificed herself to the hideous Whelm to give her mother the chance to save him.

He rose and staggered around the room. "This is a nightmare, and I'm to blame. I don't deserve Karan's love, much less Sulien's."

Tallia sighed. "Since you have it, deservedly or not, you'd be advised to draw comfort from it. Anyway, Sulien has linked to Karan a couple of times, and she's safe. The Whelm are treating her like one of their own children."

Llian let out a despairing cry.

"What is it now?" said Tallia.

"The Whelm are harsh, cold and emotionally dead. Their children get hard labour and daily punishment whether they've done anything wrong or not. Tallia, I've got to get out of here."

"There's no way out of Pem-Y-Rum. And you've got a job to do." She opened one black eye and studied Llian. "You look well enough."

"He's fattening the pig," Llian said bitterly.

"Beg your pardon?"

He explained his situation, then told her about Unick's work and the devices he was making. "And it's all connected to the summon stone," he concluded. "Somehow."

She did not speak for several minutes. "It's no wonder he caught me so easily. The Identity device would have detected me the moment I tried to break in."

"Did you come alone?"

"Yes. Karan kept on at us to rescue you. And I had to make up for . . . my utter failure as Magister."

"You've been a great Magister."

Tallia laughed hollowly. "I neglected to foster talented young leaders to replace old and tired ones. I failed to build strong alliances, and I couldn't fill the power vacuum Yggur left when he had his mental breakdown. Because of my failures, Snoat had an easy road to power, and when the Merdrun come . . ."

In four weeks. Panic flared; Llian wrested it to the ground. "What happened to you?"

"The moment I sneaked into Pem-Y-Rum, a red-faced brute laid into me as though he wanted to batter me to death."

"Gurgito Unick. You're lucky he didn't kill you."

"You forget who I am, Llian. *He's* lucky I didn't kill *him*."

"I hope you hurt the bastard."

"I broke his jaw with a kick that would have snapped any other man's neck."

"Good!" said Llian.

"Then the guards held me while Unick, broken jaw and all, attacked me." She shivered. "I've never seen such hate in a man. He locked the mancery-blocking bracelet on me and that was that."

"What do you know about Mendark's extraordinary rise to power?" Llian asked, after a pause.

"Why do you ask?"

"There were rumours that he'd done an unsavoury deal to get there. Or incurred a debt that had to be repaid."

She frowned. "Why does it matter now?"

"Unick's Origin device is connected to the summon stone. And we know Mendark started working on the secret of mancery hundreds of years ago. Plus, Snoat mentioned finding an incomplete device in the Council's secret archives, that—"

Tallia groaned.

"What is it?" said Llian.

"A few weeks ago I made a disastrous mistake, and already it's come back to haunt me."

She told him about entrusting the code to the spell vault to Hingis, despite his and Esea's protests, and how he had been forced to reveal it within days.

"That's how Snoat and Unick have made such brilliant progress," she said bitterly. "They had Mendark's prototype for inspiration."

Llian said nothing. Given that he had lost the precious dirt book within days, he could hardly blame her.

They sat in silence for several minutes, then she added: "No one knows anything about how he came to power. It was a very long time ago, and he was a secretive man."

"I've got to find out, but all his papers burned with the citadel library."

"Maybe not all," said Tallia, leaning towards him and lowering her voice. "He had a number of secret caches, where he kept copies of secrets that must never be lost. One was at the salt lake megaliths north of Chanthed."

"Whereabouts?"

"Inner base of the tall squared-off stone in the outer line of stones."

Llian heard the door open and leaped up as Snoat appeared with Ifoli.

"Go with Ifoli, Llian," said Snoat. "You've got to prepare for my private telling – tonight."

"And then?" said Llian.

Snoat smiled. "Your death will make the Great Tale even more exquisite, because you will never tell it again."

It was like a hammer blow to the heart. It seemed to stop beating. "Damn you!'" Llian cried, gasping for air. "I'll spoil the tale! I'll ruin it!"

"Your pride wouldn't let you, teller. If you are to die tonight, and you are, you would have to make your last telling your very best."

52

I'M THE SENIOR MEMBER

Karan's heart was beating so rapidly that it was painful. She leaned forward, staring at the little leather model of a mouse's snout on the table. It was linked to a tiny mouse ear hidden behind Tallia's right ear. Nadiril made the silly little devices for spying. He took a wry amusement from their absurdity.

The leather snout opened.

"Go with Ifoli, Llian," it said in a cool drawl that had to be Snoat's voice. "You've got to prepare for my private telling – tonight."

"*And then?*" said Llian.

Karan could hear the fear in his voice, and she could tell that Snoat was smiling. "*Your death will make the Great Tale even more exquisite, because you will never tell it again.*"

"*Damn you! I'll spoil the tale! I'll ruin it!*"

"*Your pride wouldn't let you, Teller. If you are to die tonight, and you are, you would have to make your last telling your very best.*"

The connection broke and there was silence. Everyone was avoiding Karan's eye. Damn them! Shand had made it clear that rescuing Llian was low priority. She leapt up, shoved her chair under the table with a crash and stalked out.

"Karan!" said Shand.

"Go to hell!"

She stood there for a few seconds, vainly trying to hold in her tears, then ran to the stables and raced out of town, taking the road to Pem-Y-Rum. There was no plan; she just had to get as close to Llian as possible.

In the forest she made her way to a point opposite Pem-Y-Rum and climbed the same tree as before. It was mid-afternoon and he was to tell his tale tonight. And Snoat would kill him when it was done.

How long did he have?

That would depend on how Llian told the tale. The original draft, written in his notebooks, took ninety-three hours to read aloud, though to the best of Karan's knowledge he had only done this once and it had utterly exhausted him. The final version, the Great Tale, took thirteen hours, and at the college he had told it over four nights. Llian had told it many times since, though usually a condensed version four to five hours long that made a far better story. It had to be the one – Snoat had said Llian was to die tonight.

Assuming he began the tale after dinner, say at nine, and it took five hours, since Llian was hardly likely to accelerate his demise, she had until two in the morning, at the very latest, to save him.

She had no idea how. But what if her assumption was wrong? If Snoat made Llian begin at six and only took a short break for dinner, the tale could be done by midnight.

Panic exploded and she almost fell out of the tree. As she steadied herself she saw the gangly youth from the other day, trudging between the trees. A pair of leather buckets was suspended from a pole across his shoulders, though clearly they were empty. He disappeared into a clump of bushes.

What was he doing? The sun was low, the light in the forest starting to fade. He reappeared, heading back the way he had come. The ends of the pole were bent now, which meant the buckets were full, but what was he carrying?

Several minutes later he returned and went into the bushes. A minute after that he came out with the girl and they walked off together. Karan waited a few minutes in case they came back, though she did not think they would.

The sun went down; it would soon be dark. She headed across to where she had seen the youth and discovered a path that had been trodden hundreds of times recently. It ended at a quarry with a mound of fresh earth at the bottom, partly covered by dead branches. It could only have come from a tunnel.

She hurried back. The entrance was concealed, but she knew it was there. She eased the dry scrub aside and found a small black opening, half a yard across, heading towards Pem-Y-Rum. The youth and girl must be thieves, probably working for a master thief. It made any rescue attempt doubly dangerous; if the tunnel was finished the thieves could come back tonight, and no doubt they would be armed.

There were few things more unstable than an unsupported tunnel through soil, and it was highly unlikely that it went far enough, but the time for hesitation was past. Karan crawled in, cracking her knee on a little handcart. She pushed it to one side and went on into the impenetrable darkness.

Though she had inches of space all around, the earth seemed to close in on her. If the roof fell in it would be a most unpleasant way to die. But not as unpleasant as Llian's death would be! This thought drove her on, and she counted her arm movements as she went, trying to make each one a foot long so she could estimate the distance.

At one hundred and sixty feet – as near as she could judge – she reached the end. Karan thought back to the view of the estate she'd had from the tree. She had to be at least five yards inside the wall.

And well below ground level. After several hours of unpleasant vertical tunnelling she could be inside the grounds. She sat there for a moment, thinking things through, then scurried out and raced back to Chanthed. She had to convince her allies to mount an extremely risky attack. It would not be easy and there was no time to waste.

"How do you know Snoat's guards haven't discovered the tunnel already?" said Shand when she finished. "You could be walking into a trap."

"Not to mention the risk of the thieves coming back," said Nadiril.

"I know the risks!" snarled Karan. "But Llian will be killed once he finishes his telling, and probably Tallia. I know you couldn't give a damn about Llian, but surely Tallia means something to you."

"We can do without the emotional blackmail, Karan."

"It's seven-thirty," she said hoarsely, stalking back and forth in front of them. "By two in the morning – at the very latest – Llian will be dead." Her voice became shrill. "If we're going to save him we've got to be in the grounds of Pem-Y-Rum by one. It'll take an hour to ride to the tunnel and three more to dig up into the grounds. We've got to be mounted with all our gear by nine o'clock, so if you're going to do anything it's time to pull your damned fingers out!"

They were staring at her, mouths open. Tears formed in her eyes. She dashed them away.

"Damn the lot of you!" she cried. "I'll go by myself."

"You won't!" said Shand, climbing to his feet. "You're not jeopardising—"

"Jeopardising *what*? You haven't done anything but whine since you got here."

"I'm with Karan," said Esea, standing up. "We've spent a week debating things and what have we got to show for it? Sod all!"

Ussarine rose, towering over them all, even Nadiril, who was the height of a bean stake and not much wider. "Since I'm Esea's bodyguard I have to go with her. But if I wasn't I'd go anyway. It's time to stand up and be counted."

Lilis was moving forward when Nadiril stretched out his withered arm and took her by the shoulder. "We all have our work to do and this is not yours. You're a librarian now."

"Snoat's already plundered the college library. How long before he moves on ours?"

"You're not a fighter, Lilis."

"I lived on the streets for seven years after Father was taken by a press gang. I'm a good spy."

"What if I said, disobey me in this matter and I won't take you back?" said Nadiril.

Lilis's thin face twisted in the most terrible anguish. She stood there for a few seconds, staring at the ancient Librarian, then said, "Llian was very kind to me. I have to stand by my friends, no matter what."

"I thought as much," said Nadiril with a ghostly smile. "Then go and save *our* friend, with my blessing." He looked around the stunned group. "Karan's right. It's time we stopped jawboning and actually did something." He tottered forward. "Karan, Esea, Ussarine and Lilis. Where are the men?"

"We don't need men to do the job for us," snapped Karan.

"I'm sending one with you anyway. Off you trot, Shand."

Such a look of outrage passed across Shand's weathered face that Karan burst out laughing.

"Who the hell do you think you are," he cried, "telling me what to do?"

"In Tallia's absence I'm the senior member of this council," said Nadiril. "And when other leaders fail, as is manifestly the case, it's my job to take command."

"You've no experience," sneered Yggur. "You couldn't lead a chicken to a bowl of wheat."

"And you're still in your pyjamas at dinnertime. Rescue team, it's eight o'clock and here are your orders," Nadiril said crisply. "Dress in dark clothing, arm yourselves, fill your water bottles and grab something to eat. We'll provide you with trowels, a hand pick, a small shovel, a handful of lightglasses and bootblack for your faces."

"Except mine," grinned Ussarine.

"Lilis, put your hair up and wear a cap. Shand, you'll need something to make a diversion with – a smoke-maker or two. You know how to make such things, I assume?"

"Before you were born," Shand said sourly.

"You've got twenty minutes."

"Lucky I made some the other day, then."

"Get going!"

To Karan's astonishment, Shand went. The rest of the team followed him.

"Been wanting to do that for a good fifty years." Nadiril chuckled. "Are you ready?"

"Yes," said Karan. "Thank you, Nadiril."

"Giving orders is the easy part," he said gruffly. "I'll be sweating every minute you and Lilis are gone."

"And Shand too," she said cheekily.

"He's a good man, but he has the most ridiculous ideas."

"Do you think we can do it?"

"I think you can."

She considered that. "But do you think we will?"

53

CAN YOU PICK THE LOCK?

"Karan?" yelled Lilis. "Wait!"

Karan reined in, swearing under her breath, then rode back. What with one delay and another it had been nine-twenty by the time they'd left Chanthed, and her nerves were as taut as fiddle strings. "What now?"

"Horse has gone lame," said Ussarine, who had dismounted and was holding its front right hoof up in one hand while shining a lightglass on it with the other. "It's picked up a spike."

"Can you get it out?"

"I expect so, but it won't be galloping on it for the next week or two."

Shand swung down, inspected the injury and nodded. "It's in deep. You'll have to go without Ussarine."

Karan swore. "No, I'll ride back and get another horse. The stable boy can take hers back."

She scrambled into the saddle and raced back through the darkness, calculating times and distances. She had planned on reaching the tunnel by ten, but at this rate they would be lucky to be there by eleven. Then they had to tunnel up and be in the grounds by one in the morning. Any later and they ran the risk of only finding Llian – assuming they could – in time to see him executed.

She galloped up the drive and roused the sleepy stable boy. "Sumey," she yelled. "Ussarine's stallion's gone lame. We need another horse right away."

He rolled out of his straw bed, rubbing his eyes. They heaved a saddle onto a strong, stocky grey mare and Karan tightened the straps.

"Come with us, lad. You'll have to bring the stallion home."

He mounted the mare, barefoot, and they galloped back, Karan compulsively checking the stars every minute or two. When they arrived, somewhat after ten, Ussarine had worked the spike out and Shand was rubbing horse liniment into the wound.

"Will you be all right with him?" said Ussarine to Sumey, who could not have been more than eleven.

"Course!" he said brightly. Clearly he would not have missed this for anything.

She shook his small hand, pulled a coin out of her pocket and handed it to him. "Thank you."

"Wow!" said Sumey. "That's – wow!"

They rode away. "How are we doing?" said Ussarine.

"An hour and a quarter behind," Karan said grimly.

They raced through the darkness, slowing before they approached Pem-Y-Rum so they would not attract attention, and headed through the forest. At the tunnel Karan closed her fingers around her lightglass and shone a glimmer into the entrance.

"You expect me to go in *there?*" said Ussarine. "I'm not sure I'll fit."

Esea muttered something scurrilous. Ussarine merely grinned.

Karan felt as though she was choking. What if her calculations were wrong? What if Snoat had made Llian tell the tale *before* dinner? Or Llian only told a three-hour tale? Three hours was exhausting, even for an experienced teller, and he was out of practice. He might be finished by now. They might be taking him away for execution this minute.

She banged her forehead with her fists. Her back was aching, and her thigh bones, and she no longer had the strength she had once been able to rely on to do the impossible – like the time she had climbed the outside of the Great Tower of Katazza to save Llian from Tensor. That had been a climb to rival any in the Histories, but she could no more do it now than she could swim to the moon. She wanted to scream.

"There's time, Karan," said Lilis in her scratchy little voice. "We'll do it."

Karan, Shand, Esea and Lilis blacked their faces. Ussarine watched them, smirking. Lilis twisted her shining hair into a bun under her cap.

Karan crawled into the dark. Behind her came Lilis, making little squeaky sounds like a terrified mouse, then Shand, grimly silent, then Esea and finally Ussarine, muttering to herself. Karan left them well behind. She needed to be alone to settle her nerves.

The tunnel had a gentle down-slope for the first hundred feet, then rose slightly for another forty. She stopped at the highest point.

"What's after this?" said Shand, his eyes reflecting the lightglass.

"Runs down a bit for another twenty feet, then stops. No way of telling how much further they planned to go. But we're well inside the grounds here, and the land above should be in shadow, so if we tunnel up . . . "

"How far?"

"Maybe six feet. Maybe ten."

"It's going to take a long time."

Karan probed the hard-packed roof with her pick and brought down a few clods onto her head and shoulders. She picked grit out of her eyes and attacked the soil furiously, but it was tiring work in such a cramped position, and after ten minutes she could barely hold her arms above her head.

Lilis wriggled past and began to toss the dirt down the tunnel with her trowel. Shand took over from Karan, then Esea, but after half an hour they were all exhausted and they had only dug up two feet.

"We can't do it!" Karan wept. "It's nearly midnight. It's going to take another four hours at least."

"Give me a go," said Ussarine, who was lying further up the tunnel. All Karan could see were the whites of her eyes.

"You'll never fit; it's barely four feet high."

"Better than lying here waiting for the tunnel to fall in. Move up."

They got out of her way. Ussarine took the pick in her big hands and, with a mighty upthrust, jammed it a foot into the earth at the side of the hole. She levered and a bucket-sized piece of earth fell out. She pushed it aside with her knee.

"Get rid of that." She attacked the roof, bringing down huge clods.

"You're going up at an angle," Karan said after a few minutes, when the shaft was twice its former diameter. The air was stale and she had a headache.

"Yes."

"It'll take even longer."

"Actually it'll be quicker. The dirt won't be falling on my face."

So it proved. In twenty minutes the shaft was four feet above the roof of the tunnel and Ussarine was bringing the clayey earth down as fast as they could clear it away. Karan watched in awe; she was a magnificent machine.

"I'll take a turn," said Shand. "You must be exhausted."

Ussarine shook her head. "On my days off I practise with a heavy sword for six hours straight. Sometimes eight hours."

"Why?" said Lilis.

"Soldiers don't live long unless they're the best and the strongest." Ussarine rested the pick against the side of the hole, smiling ruefully. "And often, not even then."

"What made you want to be a soldier, anyway?"

"When you're a girl . . . and gigantic, people taunt you all the time. If you're a good fighter they don't do it to your face."

"They taunt you if you're little and skinny too," said Lilis.

"Or if you're Zain," said Karan. "Llian . . . " She choked. "Llian suffered dreadfully simply because he was born a Zain."

She glared at Shand, who looked away. Ussarine renewed her work, seemingly no more tired than she had been at the beginning.

The shaft was eight feet high now. No one else could have dug it; no one else had the reach.

"Must be close to one o'clock," said Shand. "How far to go?"

"Won't know till I reach the surface," said Ussarine.

Karan's headache was piercing. The air was really bad now; they should have waited outside. Her legs were twitchy but there was nothing she could do about it; they had tossed so much dirt along the tunnel that there was barely room to move. She felt a terrifying bout of claustrophobia, but fought it.

The minutes dragged like hours. Finally, when she was almost vomiting with despair, Ussarine gave an almighty thrust, jammed the pick in as far as it would go, levered, then threw herself back against the side of the shaft as a section of earth fell in. *Thud*. Beautiful cold air swirled around them and starlight filtered down.

"Someone take a look," said Ussarine.

Karan crawled forward and Ussarine boosted her up the shaft. The hole was in shadow but they were only five yards from the wall. Judging by the stars it was around one-fifteen in the morning.

"We'll have to go carefully," Karan whispered. "Keep your faces turned away from the wall or the guards might see your eyes."

Ussarine lowered her to the floor. Karan gathered her gear and they extinguished the lightglasses. "Our next problem is where to go," she whispered.

"Ussarine and I will attack Snoat's library," said Shand, "making as much noise and chaos as possible so as to draw the guards, and Snoat, to us . . . "

"And then?" said Karan.

"We'll kill the swine and run for it."

"While I, Esea and Lilis look for Llian and Tallia."

"How will you find the library?" said Esea.

"I know where it is," said Shand. "In the old days I often dined here with the previous owner, Lanciver Gleag."

"We're wasting time. What do you want me to do?"

"You can't use mancery until we find Llian," said Karan. "But after that, do whatever it takes to get us out. You can bring Pem-Y-Rum down around Snoat's ears for all I care."

Esea's eyes lit up at the thought of chaos and destruction.

"Any idea where Llian might be?" said Karan to Shand.

"For so great a tale, Snoat will want a beautiful setting. Either the gallery above the library, in the North Wing, or the Little Theatre on the top floor of the main building. Lanciver used to have his private concerts there; it's a lovely chamber."

Ussarine boosted them up the hole, took Shand's down-stretched hand and scrambled up. For a few seconds Karan thought her weight was going to pull him in, then she was out and on the grass. Karan checked on the wall; no sign of guards. Silently, Shand indicated which way to go.

They made their way through the landscaped grounds, taking advantage of trees and shrubs to keep out of sight of the guards and, when they got close to the villa, anyone who might look out the windows. There was no moon yet but the starlight was bright enough to reveal them to a keen-eyed observer.

"The library and museum are there," said Shand, pointing, "in the North Wing. It runs off the main house, there." He indicated a taller building to the right. "We can't see the South Wing from here."

"How many people work here?" said Esea.

"Hundreds," said Shand, "though mostly in the vineyards and gardens, a long way from here. Snoat's got about twenty wall and gate guards, and there may be others patrolling the grounds."

"What about house servants?

"They have their own quarters half a mile away. He likes his privacy. The only other people here at this time of night will be Tallia, Llian, Thandiwe, Ifoli and Unick. And perhaps one or two night staff."

And Snoat's executioner, thought Karan. Was he preparing to do the job . . . or had he already done it?

They reached the North Wing and Shand tried the first door he came to. Karan peered in through a window made of many lozenge-shaped panes, but the room beyond was in darkness. The door was locked, and so was every other door they encountered.

"I can soon have it open," said Esea, flexing her fingers.

"If we use the tiniest peep of mancery," said Shand sharply, "the Identity device will detect it."

"Can you pick the lock?" said Karan.

"I don't have the tools. We can't force the door either; it'd make too much noise."

"What about a window?" said Karan. "Those little panes are set in lead. If we cut it out we could remove enough panes to climb in."

They went back and Karan attacked the lead with her knife, though after five minutes she had made little progress. It was old and brittle, and harder than she had expected.

"It's taking too long," she said.

"Shh!" said Lilis, who was on watch. "Someone's coming."

They slipped into cover behind a shrub whose leaves smelled like peppermint. Shortly a sentry appeared, pacing along the winding path from the greenhouses to the East Wing, then stopped twenty yards away. He yawned, scratched his backside, sat on a bench and got out a wrapped package.

"What's he doing?" whispered Karan.

"Eating his dinner," said Lilis.

After several minutes Karan said, "This is taking too long. What if we go for him?"

"It's too risky," said Shand. "We wait."

Karan's nerves felt like spiny wires. Even if Llian had done a five-hour telling, it must be ending by now.

Finally, after an agonising half hour, the guard moved on.

"We're clear," said Lilis.

Karan set to work again, but her hands were shaking and she made little progress.

"Give me a go," said Shand.

He forced the point of his knife into a gap and levered. The pane cracked in two. He prised it out, then the panes around it, leaving the framework behind.

"It's nearly two," Shand said. "We can't waste another minute. Ussarine, do you think ... ?"

She took hold of the lead, gave an almighty heave and, with a squeal of metal on metal and the crunch of cracking glass, the window came out. She propped it against the wall.

"The next time the guard comes past, he'll see that," said Lilis.

They climbed in. Shand took a number of egg-shaped objects from his pack and checked them one by one.

"What are they?" said Karan.

"A little bit of fire and a lot of smoke."

"Make it good."

"The Little Theatre is your best bet. It's that way." Shand pointed to the right, towards the main building.

"What if Llian's telling his tale in the gallery above the library?" said Karan.

"We'll see him. After making the diversion, we'll head for the South Wing and Unick's mancery workshop, trying to cause as much chaos as we can so we can get Tallia out. But don't wait for us. Get out any way you can."

Shand and Ussarine headed to the left. Karan, Esea and Lilis went right along a hall, then up a staircase.

Esea was limping badly. "Any idea where we're going?" she said after they had been walking along empty corridors for several minutes.

"The Little Theatre is on this level," said Karan. "Somewhere."

She choked. Everything was taking too long, and Llian's telling must have finished ages ago. Snoat might have killed him already.

They searched half the top floor without locating the Little Theatre. Then, from outside, someone yelled, "Fire!"

A bell began to ring. *Clang! Clang!* A deeper bell joined it. Karan ran to the nearest window. A ruddy glow was visible where she knew the library and museum to be, and smoke was gushing out through a broken window.

"There's too much fire," said Lilis. "They're in trouble."

"And there go the guards," said Esea.

54

THIS IS TOO EASY

"It's got to be down this way," said Esea.

Karan raced after her down a high, wide hall, then skidded to a stop outside a set of double doors carved with bunches of grapes and vine leaves. "This must be the theatre." She tried the doors. They were locked.

Esea pressed her open palms against the doors, whispered words of command and they tore off their hinges. Karan ran in. The stage of the Little Theatre was lit by two small side lamps and a spotlight focused on the centre. Before the front row of seats a small goblet, one third full of a green lime-scented liqueur, sat on a little round table. The seat of the chair was cold.

Karan moaned. "We're too late. Snoat's put Llian—"

"Don't say it!" said Lilis.

"Strong smell of brandy here," said Esea, who was at the top of a set of curving stairs.

Karan ran down to a well-proportioned mahogany-panelled room which contained sixteen flasks and decanters, each in its own display case. Each decanter was a masterpiece of the glassblower's art. There was also a stack of small barrels, four by three by two, a flood of brandy on the floor and a loose bung. Near the base of the stairs a cut crystal decanter lay on its side.

"What happened here?" she cried, the panic rising again. "Where's Llian?"

Lilis caught Karan's hand and squeezed. "We'll find him."

They went back up and searched the rest of the top floor but it was empty. There was a great commotion going on in the North Wing, however – flashes, booms and gushing smoke – and through the window she saw guards running back and forth outside the library.

Karan clattered down the first stairs she came to, turned the corner, and a guard yelled, "Stop!"

He must have dressed hastily, for he was barefoot, but the sword in his hand was longer than she was tall. She skidded to a stop, then backpedalled.

Esea came running up and thrust out her right arm. *Zzzt!*

The flash struck the guard in the chest, knocking him off his feet, and the sword went flying. Karan grabbed it, but it was far too heavy to use; she sent it skidding down the corridor into the darkness and ran on.

"Llian? Tallia?" she yelled. "Llian? Tallia?"

"Here," a voice said weakly.

Esea shattered the door and Karan burst in, elbowing screens out of the way. Tallia was sitting up in bed and looked wan.

"Where's Llian?" said Karan.

There was nothing Tallia could tell them. She had not left this room since her capture and had no idea where Snoat might have taken Llian.

"What do you want to do?" said Esea, now wincing with every step. "We're running out of time."

"Escort Tallia back to the tunnel," said Karan. "I'm not giving up yet." But in her heart she almost had. Was Llian lying dead on the stones Sulien had seen in her nightmare?

Lilis, who was at the door, hissed, "Library's on fire and there are people everywhere. We'll never get to the tunnel."

"Do you know where the mancery workshop is?" said Karan to Tallia. "Shand and Ussarine were heading that way."

"South Wing, the level below the ground floor. You'll smell Unick."

"We'll go down, keeping a lookout for Llian on the way. If Shand and Ussarine aren't there we might have to fight our way out."

They hurried down. Karan ran ahead, but as she reached the ground floor a big purple-faced man burst up the stairs from the basement. He was looking back over his shoulder and slammed into her, knocking her off her feet.

Karan skidded backwards across the polished floor, his stench thick in her nostrils. His jaw was misshapen as if it had been broken. He reached over his shoulder into his pack; the ends of several brass cylinders protruded from it. His whole body was trembling.

"Karan Fyrn," he said thickly, stepping towards her. "You're going to ice my cake."

She scrambled to her feet, whipped out her knife and raised it, ready to throw. "I can put this in through your windpipe and out your backbone faster than you can blink."

He froze; even the trembling stopped. Rage suffused his face and for a second she thought he was going to attack, but he must have read certain death in her eyes. Unick shuddered and ground his teeth.

"You won't always have the advantage."

He spun on one filthy foot and ran.

Shand and Ussarine reached the reading room of the library without incident. Every part of it, walls and ceiling, was of hand-carved timbers, the wood and the grain seamlessly matched. She gazed around herself in wonder. "It's the most beautiful room I've ever seen."

"The museum next door is its twin," said Shand. He took two of the grey egg-shaped objects from his bag. "Smash that window." He indicated the tall one at the far end on the right. "And another one on the other side, then run for that door. It leads into the museum, and that's where we're going next."

"What are you doing?"

"Making a diversion. When I break these, they burn with a small fire and vast amounts of smoke. Most of Snoat's treasures are here so it's bound to bring him and his guards, thinking the place is on fire. We'll sneak out the other side and look for Unick's workshop."

Ussarine picked up a chair and hurled it through the first window. As she ran for the second, Shand lobbed a smoke egg at the wall. It burst with a small *boom*, a lick of crimson fire, then thunderheads of white smoke exploded out of it. She joined him at the door. He hurled his second egg. She kicked in the door leading into the museum.

"The same here," said Shand.

She smashed the windows and he hurled the eggs. The room filled with choking smoke clouds within which small crimson flames glowed. They ran out into the darkness and headed for the other wing.

"This is too easy," said Ussarine.

A door along the long side of the South Wing was wide open; they went in and down.

"What's that horrible smell?" said Ussarine.

Shand sniffed. It was like a mixture of sulphur, grog and vomit and stale sweat, and oil of vitriol which would normally only be found in an alchemist's workshop.

"The place we're looking for."

As he took the last two smoke eggs from his pack a little glass phial fell out. He snatched at it but missed and the top broke off as it struck the floor, releasing an enchanting fragrance that reminded him of Aviel. He swore.

"What was that?" said Ussarine.

"Aviel asked me to give it to Wilm, a young lad Llian escorted to the college. But after Llian was accused of murder, Wilm disappeared. Oh well."

They searched the workshop, gagging at the stench, but there were no papers or journals, and no sign of the devices Unick had made.

"It was a long shot," said Shand.

As they turned to go, a colossal *boom* rocked the South Wing. Several benches overturned, the equipment piled on others was hurled onto the floor, and Shand heard the crackle of fire.

They ran out into the hall and through the open outside door. One end of the main house was enveloped in flames, roaring forty feet high.

"All things considered," said Shand, "I'd say it's time to go."

55

WE RUN LIKE BLAZES

Wilm lay in Dajaes's arms, staring up through the branches at the starry sky. After their lovemaking she had drifted into asleep, but he could not. Whatever happened tonight, their world would change and he did not want it to. The past five days, toiling with her to dig the rescue tunnel, and the past five nights, clinging together in his sleeping pouch, had been the happiest he had ever known. He wished this time could continue for ever.

But in a few hours they might be dead, or captured and tortured. Or they might fail and have to run, knowing they could not try again. Dajaes might come to her senses and realise that she could have no future with a feckless youth without money or skills.

He squeezed her tightly. She murmured in her sleep and hugged him back. His eyes prickled.

The wheeling stars told him that it was after midnight, almost time. This last quarter-hour might be all they would have together. A great sadness crept over him, a feeling that it was almost over. He let out an involuntary whimper. Dajaes rolled over and stroked his brow.

"Thank you," she said softly.

"What for?"

"For showing me that life doesn't have to be about drunks who beat you, and endless, useless, loveless toil. And thank you for helping me find a purpose. Every aching hour underground I knew we were doing something right and good."

"Me too."

"I suppose we'd better get up."

He checked the stars again. "We've got five minutes. Do you think—"

"There isn't time." He sensed her sad little smile.

"I was going to say, do you think we should rehearse our attack?"

"We go to the end of the tunnel, clear away the dirt I packed against the cellar wall, push the loose block out and crawl through. After that we'll have to make it up. We haven't got a clue where Llian will be."

"What if we're discovered? And attacked?"

"I light the fuse on my blasting charge and we run like blazes."

A fist clamped around his entrails. He almost choked.

"Wilm?" she said anxiously. Her small hand clenched on his upper arm.

"It's . . . not much of a plan."

"It's almost hopeless," said Dajaes. "What were we thinking?" Her fingers unclenched, clenched again. "We don't have to go in."

No one could blame them if they did not.

"Say something, Wilm."

"You first."

"No, you first."

"I'm really, really afraid . . . "

"But?" said Dajaes.

"Nothing has changed, has it? Llian's life is in more danger with every passing hour, and we're the only ones who can save him."

"If we thought it was suicidal, though, we'd be mad to go."

"We could leave with honour."

"But?"

"You first," said Wilm.

Her fingers went clench-clench, clench-clench on his upper arm, like a beating heart.

"I say we go in," said Dajaes.

Ten minutes later she crawled into the tunnel. Wilm stopped outside for a moment, sweating. It felt like an earthen tomb and could well become one. His pulse accelerated and his breath thickened in his throat.

"Could you light the lantern, please?" he said hoarsely.

Dajaes did not reply.

"Is something wrong?" said Wilm.

"Someone's been here," she whispered.

His heart buried itself in his intestines. "How can you tell?"

"The handcart is on its side. That's not how I left it."

"I'll bet Snoat's guards are waiting at the other end."

Dajaes sniffed. "The air's fresh. No one's lit a lantern in here in hours."

"They could have used mage light. I think we should get out."

Dajaes did not argue. They crawled out.

"What now?" she said quietly.

"We walk away, making a little bit of noise. If the guards are in the forest, watching the tunnel, they'll come after us. Then we run for our lives."

They walked away for a hundred yards. The forest was silent.

"I don't know what to do," said Dajaes. "They could still be waiting at the other end."

Wilm knew what he wanted to do. Run with her and never look back.

"Let's go in," he said. "Very carefully. If anyone is ahead, we bring the tunnel down between them and us and back out."

"All right," she said doubtfully.

Dajaes slung the miner's blasting charge over her shoulder and crawled in. She had made it with charcoal, sulphur and an unspecified ingredient she'd obtained from an alchemist in Chanthed, carefully mixed and packed into a hollowed-out piece of wood the size of a small tankard.

Wilm followed, his shoulders brushing the sides and his head the roof. Dirt fell in his hair and down his neck. The darkness was absolute and so was the silence. The earth felt as if it was closing around him. This was madness. If the guards knew they were here they could cave the tunnel in. Or wait until they emerged and spear them.

Snoat had a terrible reputation; he would certainly torture them to find out what they knew and who had sent them. He would never believe that two kids had done all this of their own accord.

It felt as though Wilm had been crawling for hours, as if he had gone miles. Where was Dajaes? Had she been taken? What was he supposed to do?

Ahead he heard a series of miners' oaths.

"What's the matter?" he said, crawling towards her.

Shortly a faint light appeared. Grey light – starlight! A shaft had been dug nine feet up to the surface, and whoever had done it had thrown the dirt further up the tunnel, almost blocking it.

"It's got to be robbers," said Dajaes.

"Why didn't they go through into the cellar?"

"Maybe they didn't discover it. What do we do now? It'll be a lot more dangerous with robbers in the grounds. If they're seen, the place will be swarming with guards."

"We'd better check." Wilm stood up in the shaft. "Climb onto my shoulders."

She squeezed up past him, knelt on his shoulders and eased her head up. "All quiet." She clambered down and wriggled through to the end.

"Let's go in."

Dajaes lit the lantern and scraped away the packed earth to reveal a block-work wall. She had previously sawn the soft mortar out around one block. They pushed it inwards. It made a loud scraping sound, then thudded to the floor.

"If there's anyone in the cellar . . . " Wilm fretted.

"It's after one in the morning!" She carefully put the blasting charge inside, then the lantern, and wriggled in. "Come on!"

Wilm had to hunch his shoulders to get through, and scraped a lot of skin off his outer arms. He flopped into the cellar. The lantern revealed a flagstone floor, hundreds of large barrels along the far wall and bare stone on this side. The place was remarkably clean, though the flagstones were stained where barrels had leaked, and it smelled of red wine.

Dajaes looked left, looked right, closed her eyes for a moment as if casting her mind back to the old cellar plan, and turned to the right.

"This way. Hurry, Wilm!"

He did not need to be told. With the robbers somewhere in the villa, the risk of being discovered grew with every passing second. They reached the end of the cellar and a large, solid door, which was locked.

"Blast it!" said Dajaes.

"Snoat's a greedy man," said Wilm. "We should have expected he'd lock his wine up. What are we going to do?"

"Blast it!" she repeated. "Run back to the hole and get a big handful of clay."

He did so. When he returned she was sitting cross-legged on the floor, scooping powder out of the blasting charge and wadding it into a square of rag torn from her shirt to form a small cartridge. She inserted a short length of her home-made fuse and tied it tightly.

After taking the bung out of the nearest barrel, Dajaes moistened the clay with a few drops of wine, then shoved it as far into the large keyhole as it would go. She inserted the cloth cartridge and held it in place with more packed clay, careful to keep the fuse dry, then put the top back on the blasting charge and replaced the shortened fuse.

"Don't stand in front of the keyhole," she said. "I've seen my father do this, but I've never tried it before."

Dajaes lit the fuse from the lantern and retreated. The little spark sputtered its way along then winked out at the clay. Wilm stirred.

"Stay back!" she snapped.

BANG! Clay blasted across the cellar, the hinges groaned and the door sagged. It had split from top to bottom at the lock. She yanked it open; they went up a flight of steps and looked out into a long corridor that was in darkness save for starlight coming through tall windows. Again Dajaes seemed to be consulting her mental map.

"We go right."

She shuttered the lantern. They hurried down the corridor.

"What if we run into the robbers?" said Wilm.

"Shh!"

Dajaes turned at the end and went up one hall, then another. Wilm had no idea how she knew to find her way. Perhaps she was just searching randomly in the hope of finding a clue to Llian's whereabouts. Having no better idea, he kept silent.

They were passing another set of windows when he saw a light flash, some distance away. "What was that?"

She looked out. The light flashed again. "The robbers?"

"Careless robbers! They're bound to be seen."

They continued, Dajaes now opening each door they passed, looking in and closing it again. The third door emitted a sweaty, unwashed stench and a reek of stale grog, and Wilm felt such a premonition of danger that he yanked her back by the shoulder.

"Don't go in there!" he said and closed the door again.

She rubbed her shoulder, looked up at his face and shivered. "Thanks."

They headed away as fast as possible, climbed a set of stairs and turned into a wide hall. There was no one about but they trod carefully and checked around each corner before they turned it. Dajaes was opening doors again, and at the next one Wilm caught the faintest whiff of brandy. He had never tasted brandy, or any strong drink, but he'd smelled it once or twice when helping out at Shand's place.

He looked into a panelled room. At the far end a series of display cases contained brandy bottles and decanters, each different in shape and design, plus a number of small wooden barrels. The room was faintly lit by light coming down a curved satinwood staircase. Then Wilm heard a man's voice, rich and melodious, up above.

"That's Llian!" he whispered in Dajaes's ear. "And he's *telling.*"

They slipped into the brandy room and closed the door. Dajaes set the shuttered lantern down.

"It's the *Tale of the Mirror,*" she said, eyes wide with awe. "Almost the end. Wilm!" She clutched his hand. "I'm actually hearing Llian *tell* it!"

There were tears in her eyes, tears of joy, and more than anything Wilm would have loved for her to hear the end of the tale, but it could not be risked. How to get Llian out? Surely he could only be telling to Snoat himself.

"Hide behind the stairs," he said in Dajaes's ear. "Get ready to whack Snoat when he comes down."

She did so, putting the blasting charge down beside her. "What are you doing?"

He darted to the nearest barrel and prised out the bung. *Glug, glug, glug* went the contents. The aged brandy was a deep, golden red-brown, and the smell was intoxicating, almost overpowering. Wilm's head spun. He lifted down a cut crystal decanter, an exquisite object with a solid silver stopper and a base of silver basketwork. He tapped it against the panelled wall, hard, then ducked behind the stairs beside Dajaes.

Above them Llian broke off in mid-sentence.

"What the hell was that?" said another voice. Wilm heard footsteps on the stairs. "Why can I smell brandy?" Then the man cried out in outrage. "It's . . . it's the Beacons barrel!"

A slim middle-aged man came storming down the steps, resplendent in a dress uniform and wearing a ceremonial sabre in a jewelled sheath. It had to be Snoat. He reached the bottom of the steps and stood there, staring at the flood pouring from the barrel and the bung lying on the floor.

"The tale is *ruined*!" he cried.

His right hand groped for the hilt of his sabre. Wilm rose and swung the heavy decanter at the back of Snoat's head, connecting with a soggy *thud*. The decanter did not break but he toppled into the pool of brandy and lay still.

Dajaes gasped. Wilm stood there, looking down the body in horror. Suddenly his hands and feet were freezing and he began to shake.

"Is he . . . *dead*?" said Dajaes, pressing up against him.

"I think so."

"What are we going to do?"

"Wilm!" Llian said in evident astonishment. He was looking down over the rail. "Did you do that? Well bloody done! But . . . what are you doing here?"

"We broke in to rescue you." Wilm paused, his head whirling, then remembered his manners. "This is my friend, Dajaes. She dug the tunnel."

"Did she?" said Llian. "Dajaes, I'm deep in your debt."

She was too overcome to speak.

"She's a big fan of yours," Wilm added. "She's read your tale fifteen and a half times."

Llian smiled and extended his hand. "When we get out of here I'll dedicate a tale in your honour."

She flushed, looked down, then up again. "Thank you," she whispered.

"We'd better go," said Wilm.

"One second." Llian ran up the stairs. "I'm ruining the bastard's perfect collection."

Snoat lay unmoving. In the slanting lantern light the brandy surrounding him looked like blood. Wilm's stomach churned and he ducked behind the stairs and threw up.

Llian reappeared, carrying his journal and his *Tale of the Mirror* in one hand and a sheathed knife and Snoat's leather manuscript bag in the other. He slipped his journal and the manuscript into the inner case, which was made of waxed cloth to protect the contents against the elements, closed the waterproof seals and hung the bag over his shoulder by its strap.

Dajaes opened the door and looked out. "No one in sight. Let's go."

"You armed?" Llian said to Wilm.

Wilm shook his head.

"Take his sabre. We may have to fight our way out and I'm hopeless."

Wilm unbuckled the belt of the magnificent, gleaming weapon rather gingerly, and strapped it on. He had never held anything more dangerous than his mother's carving knife.

"I suspect he planned to have me beheaded with it once my tale was finished," said Llian.

Dajaes stifled a cry.

"What about you?" Llian said to Dajaes. "Got a weapon?"

"Um, no."

Llian gave her the knife, then picked up the cut crystal decanter Wilm had used to strike Snoat down. Dajaes belted on the sheath and led them out, so overcome by all that had happened that she forgot the lantern and the blasting charge.

Before Llian's telling began, Thandiwe had secreted herself in the darkness at the back of the Little Theatre. She wanted to hear the telling for herself, partly as an act of defiance because Snoat believed it was only for him, and partly to learn from Llian, who was the best teller she had ever met. But the telling was a long one and she had been working eighteen hours a day, and halfway through the tale she drifted into sleep.

Snoat's cry, *"What the hell was that?"* shocked her awake. Had she been discovered? She was creeping along behind the seats, keeping low, when she heard footsteps on the stair down to Snoat's brandy room, then a thud.

Then Llian spoke. "I'm ruining the bastard's perfect collection!"

She peered over the seats as he grabbed his manuscript and ran down the steps.

Thandiwe scurried down the centre aisle of the Little Theatre, peered down the stairs and saw Snoat lying on the floor, as still as death, in a huge pool of what looked like blood. Llian had murdered him! Yet again he had ruined everything for her.

The dream was over – Snoat would not be sponsoring her Great Tale now. Every time she glimpsed the top of the mountain, someone sent her tumbling down again. It reinforced the message beaten into her at an early age – the only person she could rely on was herself.

She was going to get a Great Tale, no matter what it took. And revenge herself on Llian too. Thandiwe hurtled back to her room, grabbed her pack with her precious notes and her other meagre possessions, rifled Snoat's pockets and followed silently.

Behind her, brandy spread across the flagstones towards Dajaes's shuttered lantern and the blasting charge she had left behind the stair.

56

YOU'RE JUST A BOY

Wilm, Dajaes and Llian went looking for Tallia, but the room she had been in was empty. They crept along the dark halls, trying to find her, without success.

"We have to go," said Dajaes, who was becoming increasingly anxious. "If anyone comes . . . "

"Yes," said Llian. "There's nothing we can do for her now."

From outside, someone roared, "Fire!"

Through the window Wilm saw smoke belch out from the other wing of the villa, near where they had seen the flashes of light previously.

"What the hell was that?" said Llian.

Wilm told him about the shaft up from their tunnel.

"I'm not sure we can get to it now," said Dajaes.

She tried another way, but again they saw guards ahead. Dajaes stopped suddenly, standing on tiptoe to look out a high window.

"The library's burning and there are guards and servants everywhere. Wilm, I don't see how we can get back to the cellars."

"It wouldn't do any good if we could," said Wilm. "See those guards?" He pointed to a trio standing near the outer wall. "They're watching the shaft; they'll see us if we go near the tunnel."

"What are we going to do?"

"Steal some horses," said Llian. "Get to the front gate and hope the guards have run to the fire. It's our only chance."

Wilm thought it a poor hope but could not think of anything better. Then, as they approached a corner, Dajaes in the lead, he caught an unpleasant, sweaty stench.

"Wait, Dajaes!" hissed Llian. "Where's your knife?"

She indicated the sheath.

"No bloody use there, is it?" said Llian. "Wilm, draw your sabre."

He did so gingerly, holding it in both hands.

"Back away," said Llian. "Dajaes, you too!"

She drew the knife and took a couple of steps back, only to freeze as a huge red-faced man reeled around the corner. He carried a canvas satchel with an arcane device sticking out of it. Wilm saw a stubby brass tube, a dark, glowing crystal and some wound copper wires.

"Dajaes, get back!" snapped Llian.

She was staring at the drunken brute, frozen to the spot in horror.

"Don't try anything, Unick," said Llian, advancing.

Unick grinned, revealing a mouth full of broken teeth. "Just how I like 'em," he said thickly. "Small and helpless."

Wilm raised the sabre, then hesitated. Unick roared, "You haven't got the guts," and pulled the brass device out of the satchel.

Llian swore, dropped the manuscript bag, snatched Wilm's sabre and hurled it at Unick.

Unick sprang sideways and the sabre missed by inches. He pointed the device at Dajaes. A pitch-black flash burst from the crystal on the end and struck her in the chest, lifting her off her feet and hurling her back several yards. She landed on her back, her arms spread wide and her mouth gaping. Silent. Still.

Wilm screamed; he could not help himself.

"A real man could have saved her," sneered Unick. "But you're just a boy, a terrified little pup."

He turned and lurched back around the corner. Wilm's paralysis lifted; he ran after Unick and grabbed the sabre. Unick whirled, blasted it out of his hand, then skidded on something spilled on the floor. He bent, picked up the broken top of a phial and sniffed it.

His eyes widened. His head shot around; he seemed to be staring through the stone wall into the far distance.

"I'll have her too," he said mockingly and slipped the piece of glass into his pocket.

He took a second brass tube from his pack; this one had two red crystals on the end. He swung it back and forth horizontally as if seeking something, and the red crystals lit momentarily.

"Ah!" He smashed his way out through the nearest door and disappeared into the darkness.

Wilm staggered back to Dajaes, praying that she was only stunned. Llian was kneeling beside her small body, cradling her head. There was bright blood on her lip but no life in her eyes.

"I'm sorry." Llian wiped his eyes. "I'm really sorry, Wilm. I should have . . . " He shook his head. "There's nothing you could have done, not against Unick."

Wilm picked Dajaes up, then just stood there. He couldn't think. He could only feel, and everything was agony. Why, *why*? This was all his fault. He had talked her into trying to save Llian; it had seemed like a wonderful, unreal adventure. And now she was dead, because of him. She had done everything he had asked of her, done it perfectly, and he had failed her the very first time she needed him.

He barely noticed when Llian, who had retrieved the sabre, thrust it back into the sheath. Llian picked up the broken phial, sniffed it, frowned, retrieved the bung and jammed it into the phial, and pocketed it.

There came a tremendous *boom* from the other end of the villa and within seconds that part of the building was enveloped in flame.

"That was the brandy room," said Llian. "Why did it explode?"

"Dajaes's blasting charge," Wilm said in a dead voice, then howled in anguish.

"No stopping it now," said Llian. "The whole villa will be lost. And maybe the twenty-two Great Tales too." He stood there for a moment, staring out the window towards the library. "They're not worth another precious life. This way, Wilm."

Wilm followed him numbly. Though small, Dajaes had been a sturdy girl, but he did not notice her weight in his arms. He followed Llian out the side door and, keeping to the shadows, across to the stables. In the distance the servants and guards, under the direction of a kimono-clad young woman, were trying to save precious items from the library.

When Wilm entered the stables Thandiwe was inside, saddling several of the best horses.

"You utter bastard!" she hissed. "You've ruined everything for me, again!"

"If you're talking about Snoat," said Llian, "I didn't touch the swine."

"I did it," Wilm said dully. "I did it, I did it, I did it."

"I blame you anyway, Llian." Thandiwe was beside herself with rage.

"He was going to kill me as soon as I finished my Great Tale."

"I wish he had. One day you'll wish you'd never been born."

"I dare say," said Llian, "but it might be an idea to sheath our daggers until we get well away from Pem-Y-Rum."

She nodded stiffly. Llian saddled another horse and, knowing they would have to ride long and hard, looped three spare horses together. He stuffed several horse blankets into the saddlebags, tied on a water pot, grabbed a pair of cloaks hanging behind the stable door then cut the stirrups off all the other saddles. "It'll gain us a bit of time."

Wilm got himself into the saddle without knowing how, still holding Dajaes.

The gates of Pem-Y-Rum were unguarded; everyone was at the fire. Llian and Thandiwe rode out, leading the three spare horses on a rope. Wilm followed, cradling Dajaes's body and wishing he could have given his life to save her.

Karan was sick with failure. There was no way of knowing if Llian was alive or had already been put to death, and no way of finding out. The North Wing was surrounded by hundreds of guards, servants and field workers, all trying to save what they could – Shand and Ussarine had done their work too well. There was no sign of them either; no way of knowing if they were dead, alive, escaped or captured.

After an explosion in the main building it was ablaze from one end to the other. If Llian was trapped inside there was no way to get him out. Karan stood behind a screening row of bushes with Esea and Lilis, staring hopelessly at the flames. It felt as though they were consuming her life. Tallia lay on the ground with a coat around her, shivering.

"We'd better try for the gates," said Lilis. "The guards are bound to come this way."

"Yes," Karan said dully.

She helped Tallia up, supporting the much taller woman on her shoulder. Lilis led them on a meandering course towards the gates, taking advantage of every scrap of cover. They rounded the greenhouses and there, to their joy, they stumbled into Shand and Ussarine, who were covered in soot and ash but unharmed.

Lilis embraced them both. Karan stood there, unable to speak.

"Llian?" said Shand.

"No sign of him," said Karan.

"Guards," said Ussarine. "Coming this way."

"Do you want me to make a diversion?" said Esea. She looked as though she was dying to.

"Yes, quick," said Shand.

Esea thrust both hands towards the vast baroque cast-iron greenhouses, each of which was thirty feet high and a hundred feet long.

"All to ruin!" she screamed as if she wanted to tear the place apart.

The glass exploded out of the greenhouses towards the advancing guards, and they were no longer there. Karan took a hasty step back, shocked by the rage in Esea's eyes.

"Lead the way, Lilis," said Shand.

Lilis led them, under cover, towards the gates. It was darker there, the area being shielded by an avenue of trees. They were sneaking along, fifty or sixty yards from the unguarded gates, when three riders burst out of the stables, leading another three horses.

They passed under the lamps illuminating the gate and the watch house. Karan had not seen Thandiwe in years but recognised her instantly. The second rider was hidden from view behind her, but Karan also recognised the third, who carried someone small in his arms.

"That's the lad I saw in the forest with the girl," said Karan. "The lad who was carrying the dirt from the tunnel."

"It's Wilm!" said Shand. "What the hell is he doing here?"

"And who's he carrying?"

"I don't know, but she looks in bad shape."

They turned at the gate and Karan saw the second rider clearly.

"Llian!" she cried.

He did not turn; he would not have heard her over the roar of the fire and the clamour from behind them.

"Llian!" Karan shrieked.

He rode through the gate beside Thandiwe as if he did not have a care in the world, and they disappeared into the darkness.

"You bloody bollocking bastard!" she wailed. "Come back."

Shand gestured to Ussarine, who swept Karan up in her arms. They ran for the gates, but by the time they passed through the riders were gone.

57

BLOOD MOON

Thrice-warmed sludge from the base of the de-hairing pits of a leather tannery.

Dare she? Aviel had no choice. Unless she followed the instructions in the grimoire exactly, there was no hope that the scent potion would work – and a high likelihood that it would go wrong and splatter her all over the inside of the workshop.

Magsie Murg's tannery was at the end of Tannery Row, half a mile away, and when the wind blew from the east the whole town gagged. Aviel went out at three in the morning, dressed in her darkest clothes and carrying a scoop on a long handle plus a jar for the sludge. She had no lantern – evil old Magsie trusted no one and if there was any light the watchman would see it.

Aviel knew how the tannery worked; her father had taken her there

once while he negotiated some unsavoury deal with Magsie. The fresh
hides were washed in the stream down the hill to remove dirt, dung and
blood, then suspended in pits full of urine for weeks to loosen the hair.

The miserable workers then scraped it off the outside of the hide,
plus every last scrap of rotted flesh off the inside, and it was the most
disgusting job in the world. The hides were then immersed in dog
manure or bird droppings, then drenched in stale beer, washed and
finally hung in the tanning pits for a year and a day.

It was a dark night and getting darker, for the waxing moon was
almost completely hidden by clouds. A little too dark, Aviel realised
when she arrived at the tannery. There were pits all over the place, large
and small, and if she fell in one she would never get out.

She opened the gate and crept into the yard, and the smell was
almost unbearable. Had Shand not bought her indenture, this disgusting place would have been her life and her death. Taking the grimoire
was a poor way to repay his kindness.

Ahead to her left stood a huge barn-like building. The far end, used
for storing the finished leather, would be locked up. The nearer end was
open and had a series of tanning pits, but she did not need to go there.
Where were the de-hairing pits? She could not remember, nor could she
separate the reek of urine and rotting flesh from all the other stenches.

Aviel glanced up at the moon, hoping it would peep through the
clouds long enough to give her a glimpse of the layout, but no such
luck. Ah, now she remembered. There were a number of open-walled
sheds further down the yard; the de-hairing pits were in them.

Using the long handle of her scoop like a blind girl's cane, Aviel felt
her way down the yard. There was stuff everywhere between the open
pits: stacks of timber and roof tiles, piles of firewood, a set of wagon
wheels and, all over the place, oozing heaps of reeking sludge scraped
out of one pit or another.

The end of the handle sank six inches into a putrid muck heap before
she realised it was there. Aviel wished she could have collected what
she needed from it, but she could not be sure which pit it was from. If
she used the wrong sludge there was no chance of getting the Eureka
Graveolence to work. And every chance that it would kill her.

She went on, her stomach heaving, struggling to keep her dinner down. As she skirted a foul trench, suddenly there was nothing under her stick – a second pit had been dug only a foot from the first. Her left foot slipped; she threw herself back and landed hard on her bottom.

Aviel sat there for a minute, gasping. It had been so close. She was about to get up when she heard a tap-tapping sound from further up the yard, like a pebble skidding across a hard surface. The watchman! Had she closed the gate properly after she came through? Aviel could not remember the latch clicking. If it had swung open he would know someone was here.

A lantern flared and was raised high. It barely revealed the watch-man, a tall old fellow with only one arm, but it showed his companion all too clearly. Aviel shuddered. Magsie Murg was small and thin and well past her prime; she had a hooked nose, a sour mouth and fluffy white hair so sparse that the outline of her skull could be seen through it. And she was as nasty a piece of work as Aviel had ever met.

"If you ever leave the gate unlatched again I'll have you ducked in the tanning pits," Magsie said coldly.

"I never did!" cried the watchman. "There must be someone here."

"Search the yard. I'll check the leather store. If there's a square inch of leather missing, it comes out of your hide."

She let out a high-pitched giggle, presumably at her feeble wit, then unshuttered her lantern and hurried towards the barn-like shed.

If Aviel stayed, she risked being caught and, since Shand was away, Magsie would be able to do whatever she wanted to her – no one in Casyme would even know she was missing. Aviel fought the impulse to sneak out and run, for if she did she would not be able to come back for days – Magsie was bound to put on extra guards. No, she had to get the sludge now. The blood moon was in a few days and the next one might not be for months.

The clouds had thinned enough to reveal the yard, though dimly, and Aviel recognised the shed over the de-hairing pits. She went towards it, moving as silently as she could. The watchman was heading towards the other end of the yard but it was only a couple of hundred yards long and would not take long to search.

She slipped into the de-hairing shed, which smelled even more disgusting than the rest of the tannery. There were a number of pits but it was pitch dark inside; she couldn't even tell where they were. She probed about with the scoop handle. Ah, there was a pit in front of her. She reversed the handle and reached in with the scoop but there was no splash. The pit was empty.

She checked on the yard. The watchman was closer, and Magsie's light was moving around in the tanning shed. Aviel probed the next pit; it was empty too. She was starting to panic. What if they all were? She swung the scoop back and forth, feeling her way. The stench grew stronger.

There was a tiny *plash* as her scoop went below the surface of the urine the hides were soaking in. At last! She reached down as far as she could, having to stretch a little, then the scoop slipped into the sludge at the bottom of the pit. It would be made of hair and manure, earth and scraps of rotting flesh and who knew what else. Why would anyone invent a scent potion that used such revolting ingredients?

But it was the only way she could locate the summon stone. She dragged the scoop through the sludge and brought it slowly up to the surface. She was uncapping her jar when she noticed that the watchman's lantern was closer, and Magsie's too.

Aviel's hands were shaking and the wooden cap clicked loudly on the side of the jar. She hastily filled it with the putrid muck, capped it and slipped it in the pocket of her apron. It was all over her hands now.

"What was that?" said Magsie. She raised her lantern. "Watchman, *here!*"

He ran to her, panting. "What is it?"

"There's someone in the de-hairing shed."

"Why would a robber go in there?"

"How would I know? Get after him, you imbecile!"

The watchman ran down, swinging his lantern. Aviel backed away carefully; she must not fall in and be trapped here. Magsie was coming too, but she must have shuttered her lantern because Aviel lost sight of her. She probed ahead with the scoop. She would have to go around the far side of the pits and sneak along the wall to get out.

She pulled her hood down over her hair. If she was spotted, she must not be recognised, though Magsie would only have to see Aviel's limp to identify her.

The watchman entered, holding up his lantern. Aviel ducked behind a pile of fresh hides; she could smell the blood and dung on them. He went down the other side of the shed. There were several pits between her and him. She was creeping towards the door when a shadow appeared there. Magsie! Trapped! She was going to be caught and it would be the end of her life.

"Where is he?" Magsie said in an eager screech.

"No sign," said the watchman.

"I'll guard the door. Find him or you've got no job."

"Yes, Magsie."

His life must be utterly miserable if this job mattered to him, poor man. Magsie was moving back and forth just inside the doorway, blocking Aviel's escape. Her only hope was a diversion. She heaved the top hide off the pile. It was very heavy and made a wet, slapping sound as it hit the floor.

"What's that?" cried Magsie, unshuttering her lantern and shining it on the stack of hides, then the hide on the floor.

Her head darted this way and that; she made a gobbling sound in her throat, then moved towards Aviel's hiding place. She was going to be discovered. Acting on instinct, Aviel swung the half-full scoop at Magsie. She tried to get out of the way but it struck her on her hooked nose and the stinking muck splattered across her face.

She shrieked, choked, spat out muck, then, her arms flailing, fell backwards into the de-hairing pit with an almighty splash. Aviel stood there, frozen. She could not let the evil old lady drown, but to save her meant certain discovery. And Magsie would not be grateful.

Aviel had just stepped towards the edge when the old woman surfaced, spluttering and gasping and spitting out sludge, and shrieked, "Get ... me ... out!"

She was standing up and the urine level was only up to her shoulders.

The terrified watchman came running. Aviel slipped out the door and limped, as fast as she could, up to the gate and out.

That had been too close. She was never going near the tannery again, not even for a hundred summon stones.

Was the Eureka Graveolence the most dangerous and terrifying scent potion in the grimoire? It was unquestionably the most sickening and Aviel was uncomfortably aware that she was trying to create a scent potion many years above the level of her experience.

Extracting all the required scents, odours, reeks and stenches took five days of perilous toil, and most of those nights, plus more furtive trips to places she had no right to be, in terror the whole time that she would be caught. Her last trip was to the Casyme graveyard to collect ancient bones – the final ingredient for the graveolence was *the stench from the burning skull bone from a hundred-year-old grave.*

The graveyard was a haunted place, and in the misty moonlight it seemed to be full of angry ghosts. After digging up a long-dead body, shuddering all the while, she ran all the way home with her pilfered skull bone, imagining the ghosts' threats echoing in her ears. It was the wickedest thing she had ever done, and there was worse to come. Would using the bone to make a dark potion forever stain her young soul? Had she taken the first step on the road to ruin?

But she had to keep going. The invasion had to be stopped, for her own survival.

Aviel had also planned to create a Paralysis Stench for self-defence on her journey, but it required *the sour earth from beneath a long-gone body.* She wasn't going back to the graveyard either; no way was she going any further down the black path.

Finally the disgusting work on the Eureka Graveolence was done. She had completed the fifteen-step process and produced the last of the nine odorous oils. They had to be blended in just the right proportions, in exactly the right sequence, on the night of the eclipse of a blood moon – four days from now. If she had done everything properly, it would create the graveolence.

But would it show her where to find the source of the drumming, the summon stone? And if it did, what was she to do? There had been no word from Shand. Was it up to her to destroy it? She was alone in uncharted waters, carrying a burden far too big for her.

That night something woke Aviel from a deep sleep. The stars told her it was after two. She rolled onto her back and piled her herb-stuffed pillows up under her head. The fragrance reminded her of the scent she had made for Wilm. She hoped Shand had given it to him, and Wilm had liked it, and things were going well for him in Chanthed.

She was lying there, smiling, when she felt the pain in her midriff that always signified really bad luck. Then a sickening reek filled her nostrils, almost as bad as the sludge she'd taken from the de-hairing pit. But this was worse because she could tell it came from someone depraved and malevolent.

Someone far away had just detected her.

PART THREE

THE MEGALITHS

58

IT'S RUINED!

The pain in Snoat's head was exquisite, but not in a good way.

He lay on the floor, exploring the sensations. True physical pain was something that he, in his carefully managed life, rarely experienced. He must explore it further, but not now. There was something he had to do urgently. Something had gone terribly wrong.

His specially tailored dress uniform was sodden; he was lying in a puddle. He raised his head and it spun as if he were intoxicated. He had got drunk once, for the experience. It had not been pleasant and he never wanted to do it again. How could anyone bear to lose all self-control? How could they stand to numb their senses so? He did everything possible to sharpen his.

His head throbbed. He took a deep breath and the smell of spirits was so strong that it burned his nasal passages. Brandy, the Beacons barrel! He was lying in one of his finest; some swine had deliberately run it out onto the floor.

Then memory came flooding back, and the horror of the interruption that had utterly ruined his private telling. He had stormed down the satinwood stairs and . . .

The next memory was gone, though the evidence was clear; the back of his head bore the imprint of the cut-crystal decanter that had been used to knock him out. Snoat pushed himself up to a sitting position and his eyes went instinctively to the empty place on the shelf. The decanter of Driftmere, the finest brandy ever made, aged for one hundred and seventy-eight years, was gone.

Had Llian attacked him? No, some villain had discharged the barrel of brandy to ruin the tale and bring him down here. But Llian had to be in on it.

Then Snoat was struck by a thought so hideous that he groaned out loud. He came to his feet, swaying and staggering, drunk on the brandy fumes. He hauled himself up the stairs, clinging to the rail, and into the Little Theatre.

It looked just as it had before. The lights were low save for the spotlight illuminating the centre of the stage. But Llian was gone and so was the manuscript Snoat had been fondling as he had listened, awestruck and overcome, to the greatest telling of the greatest tale he had ever heard.

Both the telling and his perfect collection had been ruined, and the pain was so excruciating that it overwhelmed the agony in his skull. His famed self-control was no good to him now. He screamed.

Then, from outside, someone bellowed. "Fire! Fire!"

The screams, the yells and the clanging of warning bells took a long time to penetrate. Snoat looked around him, unable to work out where the racket was coming from; there were no windows in the Little Theatre. He stumbled down through his brandy room, out the door and into the hall. There, through a window, he saw something so awful that his knees gave under him.

He clung to the window frame, staring at his library and making a keening sound in his raw throat. Brown smoke was boiling out through the tall windows and the skylight above the gallery, where his formerly perfect collection had been on display.

He could lose everything in his library and museum and still smile. Even if every other precious thing in his life's collections was to be destroyed he could bear it as long as he still had the core, imperfect though it now was. As long as the first twenty-two Great Tales remained his, he could dream and scheme to get the twenty-third back.

He staggered across to the library, gasping like a sprinter at the end of a race. Foamy slobber was oozing down his chin but he did not have the strength to wipe it off. Half his staff and many of his guards were outside, and faithful, perfect Ifoli was directing them to save all the most precious things they could get to.

Some of his staff were helping her. Others, people he had trusted, were secreting precious items in pockets and behind bushes. Time was when he would have had them executed, after appropriately exquisite excruciations, but only one thing mattered now.

"Ifoli?" he said in a cracked voice. "The Great Tales. Are they safe?"

"We can't get up to the gallery, Cumulus."

"We must! Find a way."

Fear fleeted across her perfect features – she was afraid of fire. But then, and he had never admired her more, she overcame it. She nodded, took a square of cotton from her sleeve and wiped the slobber off his chin. Momentarily, Snoat was overcome by a feeling he had never felt before: tenderness. After this he should give her what she clearly wanted – his name.

She gave orders crisply, and his people raced to obey. Wet blankets were brought. She wrapped him in one. The foreman of his fish ponds ran up with two pairs of goggles. Ifoli fitted Snoat's, then her own, and tied a wet pad across his nose and mouth. She fixed her own in place and pulled a dripping blanket over her hair. Her eyes searched his as if weighing his resolve.

"If I can't save my Great Tales," said Snoat, "I might as well be dead."

Another servant appeared, carrying two dripping satchels and several large pieces of oilcloth. Ifoli folded the oilcloth inside the satchels to protect the precious books from fire and water.

She enveloped herself in her wet blanket and they went into the burning library. The smoke whirled and tumbled, boiled up around him and plunged down again like a waterfall. He turned round and round but could not see a foot in front of him. Despite the wet pad he was drawing smoke in with every breath; it was searing his nasal passages and burning his throat.

Panic swelled and he felt an awful urge to scream, tear off the confining rags and run, but he no longer knew which direction he was facing. Ifoli's warm hand caught his cold one and her face emerged from the smoke.

"This way. Don't let go of my hand."

Snoat did not plan to – she was the only solid thing left in his crumbling

life. He allowed her to draw him across the library, bumping into shelves
that were invisible until he was a few inches away, knocking over stools
and crashing against tables. Precious books rained down behind him. He
had no idea how she was finding her way; he could not have done it.

There was less fire than he had expected, though it was growing at
either end of the great room. And the smoke would be worse up on
the gallery level.

"The stairs!" said Ifoli.

She doubled over, coughing so hard he expected her to bring up
blood. Despite the goggles, her eyes were streaming. They went up.
His battered head was throbbing again; the smoke was much worse up
here. Every breath scorched tracks up his nose and down his throat, and
his lungs felt as though they were filled with mud. It hurt to breathe,
and no breath gave him enough air.

As they reached the top the air cleared a little, but then flames licked
up the stairs, bony fingers of fire that might have been directed at him
by a malevolent enemy. They played across his face and he smelled
burning hair; the folds of blanket over his head were smoking.

Snoat threw up his hands to protect himself but the fire, as if
enchanted to attack him, curved around and over his fingers – the
pain! – then shot at his face. The rag across his mouth and nose caught
fire. He wrenched it off. His nose was blistering and his hands were
burning but he could not move.

Ifoli jerked him out of the path of the flames. "The Great Tales, quick!"

Her perfect control of body and mind was fading. Her face was
white, her eyes blood-red, and every breath was a gasp. But her loyalty
to him was absolute. Almost too absolute?

Snoat wondered where that thought had come from as she dragged
him across the gallery where he'd had that wonderful dinner with Llian
and Thandiwe the other night. An *almost* perfect dinner.

He crashed into a table, so hard that it bruised his hip. He was
doubled over, rubbing it, when Ifoli screamed, "Get the books!"

She had done it; this was the display table for the twenty-two Great
Tales. He reached out, his hands shaking. His fingers were blistered and
blackened and terribly burned, but he felt no pain. He began to gather

the books, holding each one up to his face to be sure before sliding it into the oilcloth wrapper inside his satchel. His fingers left black smears and weeping fluid on the covers.

He could not see Ifoli; he assumed she was doing the same at the other end of the table. The air thinned again. Flames roared up the stairs and he felt that panic again – there was no going down them now.

"I have fourteen," yelled Ifoli. "How many have you got?"

He counted them. Suddenly his fingers were excruciatingly painful, and so was the tip of his dripping nose, and his chin. "Seven. There's one missing."

She scrambled onto the table, sweeping her arms from side to side. He felt around as well.

"Here!" she said. "The *Tale of Rula*."

He packed the slender volume into his satchel, folded the oilcloth down and closed it. The satchel was dry now and his wet blanket was rapidly drying in the fierce heat. Fear stroked his backbone. Dry wool would provide only a little protection from fire. Could it be enough?

"Come on!" said Ifoli.

He looked around what he could see of the beautiful gallery for the last time. It contained many of his finest treasures, collected over a lifetime, and in a few minutes they would be gone. Agony racked him. But all was not lost; he might yet get the Great Tales out. If he could not, burning to death would be the lesser torment.

Ifoli took his hand again and dragged him towards the secret stairs, but doubled over in a coughing fit. There was blood on her lips when she finished. Useless woman! Don't fail me now!

It was desperately hot and getting hotter; Snoat's head was spinning and his mouth was so dry that when he moved his tongue it crackled. They reached the location of the secret stairs. He pushed the hidden catch that opened the way in, but it did not budge. It was locked and he did not have the key with him. He could not have used it anyway; his fingers had locked into blackened claws.

"We're dead!" said Snoat. To his chagrin, his voice, which he had worked so hard to make refined, had a self-pitying whine. "It's all been for nothing."

He saw the whites of Ifoli's eyes, and in them something he had never seen before. Fury? Contempt? She reached down to her hip and unfastened a hatchet. Was she going to cut him down?

She attacked the wood around the catch, hacking at the polished cedar. Splinters flew. She exposed the catch and slammed the back of the hatchet into it over and over, until the lock broke.

Ifoli put her small foot against the door, kicked, and it opened. Inside, it was blessedly free of smoke. They went through and she shoved the door closed, but it swung open again. She put her shoulder to it, jamming it shut.

"Go down, Cumulus!" she said softly. *Her* voice, though it had a slightly smoky rasp, was still beautiful. How dare she be more controlled than he?

He stumbled down into the dark. It was incredibly hot in the stairwell, sandwiched between the fire in the museum and the blaze in the library. Stiflingly hot. Down and down. Something in the museum collapsed with an almighty crash. Above them a fiery gust blasted the door open and a rain of red cinders came whirling down, making beautiful spiralling patterns against the blackness. He was unable to appreciate their beauty as fully as he once would have.

They reached the lower door, which was also locked. This was a far more solid door and it took a long time for Ifoli to break it open. She was so exhausted now that she could barely raise the hatchet.

"Hurry up!" said Snoat, his voice like sandpaper rubbing on steel.

She gave a last, desperate hack, slammed her shoulder against the door, and it opened. Ifoli stood aside.

"You first, *master*," she said with a bow that might have been ironic — or even contemptuous.

He was too dehydrated to think about it. He shoved past and staggered away to a safe distance. The library and museum were burning fiercely now, and so was the gallery upstairs.

His servants and soldiers retreated, leaving an empty semicircle around him. Snoat tore off his blanket, laid it on the lawn, smoky side down, and tipped the manuscripts out of the satchel. He could not open his charred fingers to pick any of them up. The pain was awful.

"Ifoli! Bring my books."

She lugged her satchel across. It was far heavier than his. She swayed, coughed up more blood and wrenched off her goggles, mouth cloth and blanket. She looked haggard; her eyes were red-raw and surrounded by goggle-shaped soot rings, and blood from her lip was smeared across her right cheek. He felt a surge of irritation. She looked far from perfect now, almost *ordinary*.

Her eyes were expressionless. She had regained her self-possession. Perhaps he had imagined it earlier.

She called for a healer, and an extremely short man toddled up with his bag. Snoat could not recall his name. He bathed Snoat's ruined fingers in a sequence of coloured lotions – a stinging orange one, a burning mustard lotion and a soothing green balm, and bandaged them. He did the same for Snoat's nose and chin, picking away pieces of carbonised skin and flesh with stubby little fingers. Snoat cringed at his touch.

"The scarring will be . . . bad," said the healer. He leaned away as if expecting Snoat to strike him.

"And my fingers?"

The healer shook his head. "Only powerful mancery will be able to restore them."

Snoat squirmed at the thought of having mancery done on himself, but appearance was everything. Until then he would be a monstrosity and he would have to hide himself away.

Ifoli unpacked her manuscripts and laid them out in order. Snoat studied the covers one by one. They were all there and, apart from minor smoke stains and smears of blood and charred skin, were undamaged. He did not care about the stains; they were part of the Histories of the Great Tales now.

But when he looked at the empty space at the end, where the *Tale of the Mirror* belonged, a knife twisted in his guts and he let out a howl of grief.

"Cumulus?" croaked Ifoli. Her voice had also lost its beauty. She sounded like a desiccated frog. "What is it?"

She didn't know! Ifoli, who normally had his world at her fingertips, was ignorant of his loss. She would have been woken in the night by the fire and had run straight to the library to try and save his treasures.

"There's . . . been . . . a break-in," he choked. "It's gone!"

"What's gone?" She looked at the empty space on the blanket. "You don't have Llian's manuscript?"

"It's gone, and so is he!"

"Who broke in?"

"You tell me! My perfect collection is ruined!" he wailed.

That expression was back in her eyes again.

"My private telling has been *desecrated*," said Snoat self-pityingly. "Someone emptied the Beacons barrel onto the floor and struck me down with the decanter of Driftmere."

"They might not be gone yet."

Ifoli ran to the guard captain and gave swift orders. He bellowed at his men, who pounded towards the villa, but before they reached it the far end went up in a tremendous blast that blew out every window and scattered the silvery roof slates like brittle confetti.

"My brandy room, *gone*," Snoat said limply.

Brandy-fuelled flames leaped above the rooftop. They would soon consume the Little Theatre and everything else. Snoat watched his life burn. He felt empty, lost, ruined.

Ifoli came back. She had washed her face and brushed her hair, and changed into a red kimono. She looked almost beautiful again, but he could not erase two memories: how haggard and ordinary she had allowed herself to become during the rescue, and the look of contempt on her face when he had been at his worst. She had let him down and, as soon as he could find a suitable replacement, he would have to get rid of her.

"Llian is gone," said Ifoli, her voice still a little hoarse. "Also Thandiwe and Tallia, and the intruders." She hesitated. "And . . . Unick."

Another bitter blow. "Unick has bolted?"

"Ten minutes ago. He took three of your best horses."

Curse him! "And, presumably, the Origin, Identity and Command devices."

"He was carrying a large bag."

"Why didn't you stop him?"

She did not reply at once. She was staring at the flames. Finally she said, "I did not know, Cumulus. I was saving your perfect collection."

Fury surged through him. He would have struck her but his hands were too painful. "Who's my most reliable assassin – the fellow who cut Wistan's throat for me?" He could not remember the man's name; he could hardly remember his own name.

"Jundelix Rasper. But he's a day away, south-west."

"Find him! He will get my manuscript back and the devices Unick stole, and bring me the heads of Llian and Thandiwe, preserved in salt – or lose his own."

"What about Unick?"

"He's a danger to my plans. Tell Rasper I don't need Unick's head – *just his face.*"

Ifoli shivered but went to give the orders. Snoat called for a chair and someone brought him one. Ifoli returned, and suddenly he could not bear for anyone to see him brought so low.

"Clear everyone away!" he screamed. "Then get out of my sight! You've failed me. *Everyone* has failed me tonight."

She gazed at him for a moment, almost in pity, then gave the orders. He choked. How dare she pity him! He turned his chair to face the library fire and sat down, alternately looking down at his manuscripts and up at the fire.

Why had his guards not prevented this attack? And how had they allowed the attackers to get away? Ifoli should have known it was coming; she should have stopped it.

Pem-Y-Rum was valueless to him now. After tonight he would be a laughing stock. He would head east to his coastal estate, Morgendur, and take command of his army.

He had made a mistake by overthrowing the Magister and simply plundering Iagador. Predators like Thyllan the Impotent, a former warlord and perennial troublemaker who had been banished from Iagador long ago, were already taking advantage of the chaos Snoat had created over the past month to carve out little empires for themselves. He should have conquered Iagador and ruled it with a steel fist. Well, it was not too late.

But how was he to protect the manuscripts? He could not bear to let them out of his sight ever again. Distrust raised its head like a maggot through the skin of a peach. The twenty-two Great Tales had the worth of a nation, and anyone could take them from him with a knife thrust in the back, or a poisoned morsel at his dinner table.

He could only trust himself. He would protect the manuscripts the only way he could, with a spell tailored for the purpose. But for that he needed Unick's Command device, since his artisans had signally failed to copy any of Unick's mechanisms.

He stared at the empty place on the blanket. The loss of the twenty-third Great Tale was a cancer eating him from the inside. He had to have his perfect collection back.

And then he was going to burn Iagador from one end to the other.

If his enemies no longer envied him, let them fear him.

59

IT'S ALMOST BEYOND CONTROL

"The mongrel!" screamed Karan. "The slimy, treacherous bastard."

Her head felt as though it was about to explode. How could Llian do this to her after all she had gone through to save him? How could he do it to Sulien after she had sacrificed herself to the Whelm for him? When Karan caught him she was going to drag him off his horse, beat him until he wept for mercy, then start on that bitch Thandiwe. How she was going to pay!

They hurried through the forest to their hidden horses. The starlight was barely enough to see. She scrambled into the saddle and whirled Jergoe to ride after Llian.

Shand grabbed the reins. "You're jumping to conclusions."

"Let go!" Karan said icily.

"Damned if I will."

She knew she was behaving badly but was too overwhelmed to care. "I'll ride you down."

Ussarine shoved Shand out of the way and took Jergoe's head in both hands. "You won't ride *me* down."

Karan considered it. Her heart was pounding, there were bright flashes inside her head and she was shaking so badly that she could barely stay in the saddle. Tears welled. She fought them and failed.

Inside Pem-Y-Rum, part of the main building collapsed with a crash that sent sparks whirling a hundred feet into the air.

"Until his dying day Snoat won't forget what we've done to him tonight," said Shand. "Come on!"

"One of the finest libraries in Meldorin is burning to the ground," said Lilis, distraught. "How am I going to tell Nadiril? My life is all about saving books, not destroying them."

"Later." Shand went across to Tallia. She was propped up against a tree and did not look well.

"I'll be all . . . " She groaned and slid sideways to the ground.

Karan dismounted and ran to her guiltily. She had nagged Tallia ceaselessly about rescuing Llian. Was that why she had gone to Pem-Y-Rum while she was still unwell?

"Back to Chanthed," said Shand. "We'll tell Nadiril what's happened and decide what to do." His eyes flicked sideways towards Karan, then away.

About Llian! She felt sick.

Ussarine lifted Tallia onto Lilis's horse and boosted her up behind. Lilis put her arms around Tallia's waist.

"How are you feeling?" said Lilis.

"None too good," said Tallia. "If I collapse, let me go."

"I'm not letting you go," Lilis said stoutly.

They reached the house at five in the morning. It was dark at the front though a lamp glowed in the back room. The stable boy took their horses, then Ussarine plucked Tallia off, carried her inside, laid her on a settee and wrapped her in blankets.

Nadiril, who had been dozing in his chair, heaved a couple of billets into the iron firebox and put the kettle on top.

"Something stronger is called for," said Shand.

"Celebration or sorrows-drowning?" said Nadiril.

"The former," said Shand. Then, with a glance at Karan, "Mostly. Where's Yggur?"

"Snoring."

"Are you going to wake him?"

"He hasn't felt the need to make a contribution so far."

Shand took a large flask out of his pack and fetched glasses.

"What's that?" said Nadiril, a gleam in his eye.

"Spoils of war."

Shand decanted a generous tot into each of the glasses, handed them around and held his up to the firelight. It glowed golden red.

"You forgot me," said Tallia, sitting up. She looked a little better.

"I should not have presumed," said Nadiril, handing her his own glass. He fetched another.

Esea quaffed her drink in a single swallow, curled up in her armchair and closed her eyes.

Karan waved her glass away. She felt like a whirlpool in a raging river and did not want to replay the events of a night that, for all its successes, she could only think of as a catastrophe. If she did not ride after Llian right away she might never find him, but since she was practically bankrupt and reliant on her allies for everything, she had to wait on their dubious pleasure.

Shand told his part of the story baldly, including the destruction of the library and museum.

"That was one of the most important libraries in Meldorin!" cried Nadiril, taking an angry gulp. "Thousands of books and manuscripts that existed nowhere else."

"Do you think I don't know it?" snapped Shand.

Lilis described their rescue of Tallia, the fruitless search for Llian, the explosion that had turned the villa into an inferno, and the escape. She stopped, casting anxious glances at Karan.

"Out with it," said Nadiril.

"Your bastardly friend Llian has run off with that evil slut Thandiwe," Karan cried, and to her chagrin the tears she had been holding back for the past two hours flooded out of her.

"Tallia has been badly beaten," Shand snapped, "and you're whining about Llian. You're the very limit!"

Karan was mortified. "I'm so sorry," she said to Tallia. "I didn't think."

Tallia gave Shand a cold stare. "Given all that Karan has been through over the past month, and all it's cost her, she has every right to shout and scream."

Shand gritted his teeth — he was building up to another of his rages — but Tallia held a hand up.

"We heard about the Merdrun threat a month ago, and in that time Karan is the only one who has done anything worthwhile about it. She's risked her life repeatedly, her family has been torn apart, and we all owe her. As far as I'm concerned, she can say what she damn well pleases." Tallia drained her drink, closed her eyes, then added, "Besides, she's a *sensitive*! She feels things more deeply than we do. I imagine that's why the Merdrun see her and Sulien as such a threat."

There was a long silence. Everyone was staring at Karan, and her cheeks were burning. "Thank you," she whispered. The fury was gone.

"We don't know the circumstances of Llian's going," said Shand. "Save that, first, Wilm and his friend dug the tunnel that allowed us in, and they rescued Llian before we could get to him."

"And second?" said Nadiril.

"Llian didn't know we were there."

"How could he not know after you'd set half the estate ablaze?"

"It was chaos," said Shand. "We thought Wilm and his friend were robbers, and when they discovered our shaft they probably thought *we* were robbers."

"If you *had* been robbers," said Nadiril sourly, "some of Snoat's treasures might still exist."

"Moving on," said Shand.

"How could Llian ride away without making sure Sulien was safe?" said Karan, incapable of thinking about anything else. "And . . . me."

"He knew you and Sulien were safe," said Tallia, "because I told him."

"When?"

"When we talked in Pem-Y-Rum. He was beside himself when he

heard what had happened to you, until I told him that you were here, safe. But when he heard that Idlis and Yetchah had Sulien, I thought he was going to drop dead at my feet."

"Oh!" said Karan.

"You've been through a lot," Tallia added, "but so has he, and what he needs now is your trust and help."

"But he's done such stupid things."

"As have I, though I don't see you attacking me. And . . . surely you noticed how beleaguered Llian has been since the drumming began?"

"What are you talking about?"

"Anjo, Maigraith, Snoat, Unick, Turlew and Thandiwe have all attacked him, one after another."

"And Shand!" Karan muttered.

"It's strange how he attracts enemies. Uncanny, actually . . . " Tallia mused.

"To work," said Nadiril. "Snoat is an obsessive narcissist and Pem-Y-Rum now represents his biggest failure. He'll abandon the place and go back to Iagador, and we should head east."

"I'm going after Llian," said Karan. "And if I don't leave now—"

He held up a blue-veined hand with no more meat on it than a chicken's foot. "I was about to say you can't go alone."

"I know where Llian's going," said Tallia. "The salt lake megaliths."

"Why?"

"He thinks there's a connection between Mendark's work and the summon stone. Mendark's secret cache there might help Llian find it. And then he plans to destroy it."

"How can Llian destroy a dangerous enchanted object?" said Karan.

"He feels that he's let everyone down; that he hasn't contributed anything."

"What utter rot!"

"He can't destroy it," said Nadiril. "That's up to us."

"Us?" said Shand, an edge to his voice.

"Well, *you*. And you'd better be quick because I have other ill news. Two pieces of it."

"Go on."

"The first is from Hingis in Sith."

Ussarine sat up, watching Nadiril eagerly. Esea's head swivelled towards her and Karan was shocked at the fury in Esea's eyes.

"He's put a small army together, five thousand," said Nadiril. "Not nearly big enough, but a start. But the storm is gathering. That perennial troublemaker Thyllan the Impotent came across the Sea of Thurkad a few days ago with a raiding party. He's taken Dantoid, in the middle of Iagador, and declared it his. And with Snoat suffering such a humiliating defeat last night, other wolves will be emboldened to carve Iagador up between them. It's going to get bloody."

"Did Hingis send any message for me?" said Esea. "Or ask after me?"

She looked haggard and in pain, and had visibly lost weight in the few days Karan had known her.

"No," said Nadiril.

Esea ground her fists into her belly.

"What was the other piece of bad news?" said Karan.

Nadiril took a folded piece of paper from his pocket. "This came in by skeet at midnight." He read it aloud.

The mountains east of Booreah Ngurle
9 Pulin, 3111

Nadiril,
The drumming is getting worse; some new kind of mancery must be feeding the summon stone, strengthening it. Find the stone with the utmost urgency and destroy it. Do NOT use mancery near it. NEVER attempt to draw on its power.
I'm at least ten days away. Send word of progress, and where I should meet you, by the usual means.

Malien

"'Some new kind of mancery' surely means Unick's devices," said Shand.

"That would be my assumption," said Nadiril.

"Then it's all the more urgent that we find Llian," said Karan.

"Yes it is. Get a few hours sleep, then ride for the salt lake megaliths

with all possible speed. Shand, go with Karan. You'll need a guard."
He turned to Esea.

"Not me," she said.

"Why not?"

"My brother needs me; I'm going back to Sith." She gave Ussarine
a very cold look. "Take Ussarine. If you get to the source, you'll need
someone who hasn't got a skerrick of mancery."

"That's a bit rude," said Lilis hotly.

Ussarine laughed. "I'm glad I don't have a skerrick of mancery; I can't
think of anything worse. When do we start?"

Karan was happy to have Ussarine, though she was uneasy about
why Esea hated her so much, and what would come of it.

In Sith the following afternoon, Osseion came to Hingis's room bearing
a message that had just come in by skeet. "Tallia and the others are
coming east," he said. "Your sister will soon be back."

"And Ussarine?"

"It doesn't say."

He handed Hingis the message and went out. He read the note,
which summarised what had happened at Pem-Y-Rum. Esea was
coming home! They had never been separated this long before and he
missed her desperately, but he missed Ussarine even more. What would
Esea do when she realised?

She would force him to choose, and either way it would be a disaster.

60

THE BROKEN SABRE

"You're holding out on me!" said Thandiwe as the sun rose. "You know
something about Mendark that you're not saying, and I'm going to find
out what it is."

Llian clenched his fist in his pocket. She had been at him from the moment they rode out the gates, trying to wear him down. The technique was infuriatingly familiar by now and he was not going to give her the pleasure.

Despite their situation he could hardly keep his eyes open. Last night's telling had lasted for five hours and he had put his soul into it. Snoat had been right about him: even believing he was going to die when it was done, Llian could do no less than the best telling his enemy had ever heard. It had been utterly draining, especially the abrupt truncation of the tale only minutes before its completion, which had left the ending recycling through his mind. Normally after such a performance he would have slept for sixteen hours. Now, with the lack of sleep and the traumas of the night, he was practically climbing the wall.

Thandiwe started in on him again, and Llian snapped.

"This is why you'll never be a great teller," he said venomously. "You go on and on and on until everyone is bored out of their wits."

Her mouth closed with a snap and she gave him a look that would have melted brass.

"And you're utterly and offensively insensitive," he added, jerking his head towards Wilm.

He sat bolt upright in the saddle, so rigid that he might have frozen solid, holding Dajaes's body in his arms. Wilm had wept until his tear ducts ran dry and his bloodshot eyes squeaked when he blinked. His thin face was swollen and his knuckles were chewed almost to the bone.

Llian could not bear to witness his grief. How much worse must it be for Wilm, a lad of just seventeen? To have found such a girl; to have worked with her for a week on an utterly impossible project, and pulled it off magnificently; to have loved her, then lost her to the casual malice of a vicious brute. Llian could not have endured it; he would have tried to claw down the heavens.

They were leagues north of Chanthed, travelling across a dry, sparsely grassed plain in the direction he knew the salt lake megaliths to be. Thandiwe, her face like stone, galloped off. Llian nudged his horse up alongside Wilm.

"I never thanked you or Dajaes."

Wilm stifled a howl.

"I wish I'd known her," said Llian. "She must have been a wonderful girl."

"She was the nicest, smartest, sweetest woman who ever drew breath," said Wilm, almost choking, "and she loved your Great Tale. Dajaes thought it was the greatest story ever written, and the moment she heard about your troubles she had to save you. It was her idea to dig the tunnel, and she had to do all the work. I'm useless underground; I panic."

"Yet you overcame it."

"I just carried the dirt. She did the hard work and the clever stuff."

"If you hadn't whacked Snoat over the head with the decanter I'd be dead."

Wilm's face went blank. He wasn't interested in talking about himself, only about her, and who could blame him?

"How did you meet?" said Llian.

"She was the first student at the scholarship test. She gave the right answer, and they failed her because she'd used an old book!" he cried, outraged all over again. "I saw her at a café that night and we . . . became friends."

Wilm looked down at her still face and his own crumpled. It was awful to watch. Llian looked away, giving Wilm a few minutes to compose himself.

Llian could not bear to cause him any more pain, but it had to be said. "Wilm," he said gently, "we'll have to find a place – *you'll* have to find a place – to bury Dajaes."

Wilm's mouth became a gash twisted by a silent scream. Llian could not tell whether the lad wanted him there or a thousand miles away, though on balance he thought he should stay close. It was the least he could do for someone who had done so much for him.

"I know," said Wilm after several more minutes. "It's just . . . laying her in the ground makes it final. I don't . . . I can't . . . "

He could not find the words. Llian, who had the vocabulary of four thousand years of the Histories at his disposal, wasn't sure that he could express what Wilm was feeling either. Perhaps his grief was best left unarticulated.

They rode on, and after another mile or two crossed a small rivulet running in a series of meanders like green brush strokes through the undulating brown landscape. The trees were taller along the river, the air cooler. It was a pretty place.

"Here," said Wilm at the foot of a gentle green rise with a view of the sandy river. He stopped, went to dismount then realised he could not do it with Dajaes in his arms. "Llian?" he croaked. "Would you take her for me?"

Llian swallowed. In Wilm's eyes it must have been the greatest honour he could bestow. Llian steadied himself, then reached up. Tenderly, reluctantly, Wilm lowered her and Llian took her in his arms.

Wilm scrambled down, hit the ground with jarring force and almost collapsed. His muscles had locked from holding her, unmoving, these past four hours. He steadied himself, took her back and walked around for a minute.

"Here," he said, marking a spot with his heel.

He laid Dajaes down several yards away, where he could see her, then set to work on the soft turf with Snoat's sabre, cutting a rectangle and lifting the turf out. He attacked the exposed dirt furiously with the magnificent weapon, as if he wanted to ruin it because of his fatal inability to use it when Unick had taunted him.

Digging a grave with a sabre was hard work, and when the hole was only a foot deep the predictable happened – the blade snapped halfway down. Wilm continued with the hilt and Llian joined him at the other end, cutting the gritty soil with his knife and ruining the edge in the process.

So it went until the hole was four feet deep, where they hit a layer of hard clay.

"We won't get through that," said Llian.

They scooped the last of the earth out. Wilm glanced at the body, at Llian and at the hole.

"Would you like to be alone?" said Llian.

"No!" Wilm cried. "She did it for you. She'd want you here."

He strewed the yellow clay with green grass and wildflowers, gulped, knelt beside Dajaes and kissed her eyelids, then arranged her earth-stained clothes as best he could and lowered her into the hole. He remained there for some time, head and shoulders over the edge, weeping silently, then stood up and looked uncertainly at the earth pile.

Thandiwe rode up and took in the scene in a glance. She withdrew a square of blue silk from her pack, bent and gently placed it over Dajaes's face.

"To keep the earth off."

Wilm thanked her, nodded to himself, then took a double handful of soil and allowed it to stream down on Dajaes. After she was covered with a thin layer Llian and Thandiwe joined in until the grave was full and the turf replaced. They weighed it down with cobbles from the river, then retreated. Wilm stood over the grave, his lips moving.

He rearranged some of the cobbles and turned away. "Thank you," he said. "If you would ride ahead now."

They did so. When they were a hundred yards off, Wilm let out a howl of anguish. Shortly he joined them and did not look back.

But Llian did. Cutting off the stirrups would not delay Snoat's guards for long, and his fear of pursuit was growing by the minute. Wilm and Dajaes had believed Snoat to be dead, but Llian had not checked to make sure. Why hadn't he choked the swine where he lay?

The euphoria of the telling. Every teller was familiar with the phenomenon, especially after telling one of the Great Tales. After such a towering performance it could take hours, even days to return to normality, and if the telling was abruptly cut short, as Llian's had been, the return could take even longer. With everything that had happened afterwards, he wasn't yet back to his normal, analytical frame of mind.

There was another reason why Llian hadn't killed Snoat on the spot. It wasn't in him to murder an unconscious man, even one who had been planning to have him killed. It was a serious defect in his own character, Llian knew, one that he would probably rue.

If Snoat was alive, they had humiliated him in a way that no narcissist could endure. He would make it his life's work to destroy them.

It occurred to Llian that he had not checked on Rulke's key for some time. He turned away from Thandiwe and surreptitiously inspected the stitching of the secret compartment in his belt. It was still sound.

They bought food at a goat herders camp – a hindquarter of goat, a grubby round of crumbly white cheese and a bag of sprouting onions. Thandiwe respected Wilm's grief and they rode north across the arid plains in blessed silence.

Llian was wrestling with his unruly memories, trying to discover how Mendark's rise to power had come about at such an early age. The Histories were so silent on the matter that he suspected they had been rewritten at Mendark's behest.

History is as it is written. Or rewritten – the true historian's bane.

But Llian's memories would not yield up this secret. He was too exhausted.

"Where are you going, anyway?" said Thandiwe.

Llian jerked out of his daze. "The salt lake megaliths."

"What do you hope to find *there*? Something you can't find at that dreary old estate with your wife and daughter?"

He ignored the barb. He wasn't going to give her anything she could take advantage of. He lapsed into the daze again, only to jerk awake as he began to slide sideways out of the saddle. Ahead, occasional twisted trees marked the course of a dry riverbed. He rode to the nearest tree and dismounted. Wilm did too. Thandiwe stayed on her horse.

"I've got to sleep for half an hour. Wilm, can you keep watch?"

Wilm roused himself from his dark place. He looked haggard. "Of course, Llian."

"No, you need sleep more than I do."

"Nothing could bring me sleep," Wilm said in a cracked voice. "It's bad enough being awake. I keep seeing it, over and over and over. Why did he do it? Dajaes had done nothing to him."

"He's an evil man. And the device called Origin is linking him to the summon stone, corrupting him even more."

Llian sat on the dry ground, wrapped his coat around himself and focused on sleep.

"Llian?" Wilm said tentatively.

"Yes?"

"Can you teach me how to use a sword?"

Llian snorted. "You do realise who you're talking to."

"In the *Tale of the Mirror* it says you saved Karan's life with a sword. You fought and killed a lorrsk – a huge, savage beast that had clawed its way in from the void."

"So I did," said Llian, momentarily taken back to that desperate time, "but entirely by accident. As Karan describes it, I chucked the sword at the lorrsk the way a labourer shovels manure into a cart. The blade just happened to slice into its neck and sever an artery."

Wilm shook his head. Clearly he thought Llian was being far too modest. "Can you teach me?"

"Why do you want to learn?"

"I've got to be able to defend the people I care about."

"We all should be able to do that."

Llian searched his memory, then got out his journal and began to write and sketch at the back. "I once read a pamphlet on the seven basic strokes of sword fighting. It's just the elements but I suppose it'll be better than nothing."

He wrote down the descriptions of the seven basic strokes and knew they were word perfect, for that was the first of a chronicler's arts. Under each description there had been a diagram showing the movements of the stroke. Llian reproduced them as well, tore the pages out and handed them to Wilm.

He studied them for a few minutes, nodded to himself, then began to practise strokes, thrusts and parries with the broken sabre.

"You should wait until you have a decent sword," said Llian. "The weight and balance will be all wrong."

"I've got to learn now," Wilm said between his teeth. "Tomorrow could be too late."

61

BAGS OF GOLD

Wilm woke Llian after an hour. They changed horses and continued north at a fast pace, leading the spares.

"Where's Thandiwe?" said Llian.

"She rode ahead." Wilm glanced sideways at Llian. "Why is she so angry? I thought she was your friend."

"I thought so too, until I found out that she's been blocking me for years, refusing to agree to my ban being overturned."

Wilm was outraged. "Why would she do that?"

"Perhaps she got sick of doing the right thing and getting nowhere."

"What kind of a person would betray a friend!"

"I suppose she saw me as a threat. But that's not why she's angry."

He told Wilm about the election for Wistan's replacement, and how he, Llian, had made the disastrous decision to give his vote to Norp instead of Thandiwe.

"How could you have done otherwise?" said Wilm. "You could never vote for someone you knew to be corrupt."

He saw things in black and white, but it wasn't that simple. If only Llian had voted for Thandiwe ... But it was no use following that train of thought.

They rode on.

"What's at these megaliths?" Wilm asked after they had gone several more miles. Then, hastily, "Sorry, you don't have to tell me."

"You saved my life," said Llian. "I'm happy to tell you. Though I'd prefer you didn't say anything to Thandiwe."

"Not even if she tortures me."

"I think Mendark might have known about the summon stone."

"Known what?"

"Where it is. Where it came from. How the drumming works."

"I'd like to learn mancery," said Wilm.

Llian looked at him in surprise. "I thought you wanted to study at the college?"

"I haven't got the heart for it any more. Dajaes so wanted to be a teller, and she would have been a good one." He rubbed his eyes. "But if I became a mancer . . . "

Wilm was flailing around, trying to find his place in the world, but mancery wasn't it. "You've got to have the gift," Llian said kindly, "and a gift for mancery isn't common. Have you ever done anything strange or inexplicable?"

"No. My life was very boring until I met you."

"Does your mother have a gift?"

"I wouldn't think so. She's had a very hard life, and surely if she had—"

"What about your father?"

"I don't know anything about him," Wilm snapped. "And I don't want to. He never gave us so much as a holey grint!"

"Does he know he has a son?" Llian said mildly.

Wilm didn't answer. Llian did not pursue the topic.

"Do you think there could be a magical talisman in Mendark's cache?" Wilm said later.

"I don't know what he kept in his caches, apart from bags of gold."

"*Bags* of gold!" Wilm sighed. "In my entire life I've never seen a gold tell."

"Don't expect too much. Not all caches are full of treasure."

They rode on across a tussocky brown plain. A chilly wind came up, blowing from the south. Llian pulled his collar up over the back of his neck. Wilm was practising moves with the broken sabre again. Llian did not see the point.

Yet the lad had to make his way in the world, and it would help with his grief if he were actively doing something to protect the people he cared about. A lesson he, Llian, would do well to emulate. He had to find the summon stone, fast.

"Wow!" said Wilm.

The diamond-shaped standing stones, three times the height of a tall man, had been cut from red and black ironstone, presumably from the low range of hills called the Ironstones further on. They were arranged in the shape of a figure eight about three hundred yards long and half as wide, with the tallest stones being where the lines crossed. Each loop of the eight contained two smaller concentric loops. Some of the stones had fallen and a number of the others were tilted.

At the centre of the figure eight the ground dipped down into a stone-lined reservoir sixty feet across and shaped like a saucer, presumably so stock could water at it safely even when the level was low, as now. The stones ran down through the water. They led the horses down to drink and filled their water bottles.

The country was dry, the vegetation restricted to scattered tussocks of grey grass and the occasional stunted multi-trunked tree with small blue-grey leaves. Between the stones and the hills the westering sun struck dazzles off a thumb-shaped salt lake a couple of miles long.

"Do you want me to unsaddle the horses?" said Wilm.

Llian looked back, wondering why there was no sign of pursuit. And where had Thandiwe gone? She had been remarkably quiet since Dajaes's burial. She was up to something.

"No, we might need to leave in a hurry."

"Who built the megaliths?"

"Nobody knows."

"Why not?"

"We know they're more than eight thousand years old because they're mentioned in the oldest written records from Meldorin. But how old, no one can tell."

"There's an awful lot of them. How are you going to find the cache?"

"Tallia said it's at the inner base of the tall squared-off stone in the outer line of stones."

They walked around the figure eight. There were dozens of squared-off standing stones among hundreds that were unfinished. However only two stones in the outer line had been squared off, and one was stumpy, the top having broken off long ago.

Llian headed for the other, which was shaped like an obelisk. The stone was two yards across at the base. Using his knife, he gouged at the grey earth, which was littered with flat pieces of ironstone. He worked his knife a foot into the ground, almost to the hilt, and struck something hard. Llian thumped the hilt with the heel of his hand. The knife went no further.

"Looks like the place."

He began to dig. Wilm attacked the ground with his broken sabre and within a few minutes they uncovered a long rusty iron box. They had just heaved it out of the ground when Thandiwe rode up, her hair streaming out behind her in the wind. A greedy gleam came and went in her brown eyes.

"I don't think you'll find anything in this to help you with *Mendark's Tale*," said Llian.

"He might have secreted anything in so ancient a hoard."

"How do you know it's ancient?"

She swung down. "The box is practically falling apart. It'd take decades to rust in this dry country."

"Why are you here, anyway?"

Her eyes slid to the box.

"You're broke," said Llian, "and you need a lot of gold to stave off your creditors for the year it'll take to write your tale."

The box was locked with a padlock but a blow from Llian's boot heel tore the hasp out. Wilm reached for the lid.

"No!" Llian said sharply.

"Sorry," said Wilm, ducking his head.

"Mancers *always* protect their treasures."

A little dead tree stood a hundred yards away. Llian snapped off a branch, worked it under the lid and heaved it up. *Bang!* The rusted base of the box slammed into the standing stone and crumbled, scattering its contents across the ground. The top howled through the gap between Llian and Thandiwe and struck the ground forty feet away.

Wilm had gone very pale. "You saved my life!"

"Turn and turn about."

The contents included half a dozen little bags, one of which had burst releasing a double handful of gold tells, two knives in cracked leather sheaths and a sword in an embossed copper sheath, the like of which

Llian had never seen before. The copper was mottled with verdigris and both the sword and sheath were marked with the letter M. There was also a small book written on what appeared to be papyrus reed.

Thandiwe dived for the book. Llian reached it first, shoved it into an inner pocket and buttoned the flap down. "You've got all you're going to get from me."

"One betrayal after another," she said bitterly.

"You're such a hypocrite. If you'd helped overturn my ban instead of blocking it, you'd have been master years ago."

"I don't bel— Why do you say that?"

"Wistan was going to make you master until your betrayal of me, your *friend*, convinced him that you weren't of good character. A lovely irony, isn't it?"

Thandiwe did not storm off, as he had expected. There was gold to be divided up, after all. Llian withdrew the sword from its sheath and a shiver crept up his arm — it had a definite presence. It was lighter than he would have expected, and the blade, of some black metal, was uncorroded. He tested the edge, which was still sharp, and sheathed it. Wilm was staring at it, his eyes wide with hopeless longing.

Llian handed it to him. "This is a fine sword. Take it and practise your strokes."

Wilm shook his head. "I was brought up to not touch what isn't mine."

"Mendark is ten years dead," said Llian, "and since he had no heir, this cache is treasure trove. Legally, it belongs to whoever finds it."

"Are you sure?" said Wilm.

"Absolutely."

Wilm had not even looked at the gold, but his thin hand was trembling as he took the sword. He stared at it for a moment as if he had felt something too, then removed the sabre scabbard from his belt and attached the copper sheath. He worked the sword up and down several times, walked away, checked Llian's notes and began to practise the seven basic strokes again.

Llian counted the gold and divided it into three piles each containing two hundred and ten gold tells. "Yours," he said to Thandiwe.

She put it in her pack. Llian was bagging his and Wilm's shares when he noticed Thandiwe watching Wilm with a curiously yearning look. Despite all he had suffered recently he remained an innocent, and perhaps she longed for the days of her own innocence, long lost.

"He blames himself for not saving Dajaes from Unick," said Llian.

She rubbed her face with her hands. "It'll take more than a fancy sword to bring down that mongrel!"

"Did he have a go at you too?" said Llian.

She shuddered and closed her eyes, but not before he saw what she wanted never to reveal.

"It might be an idea to warn Wilm about that sword," said Thandiwe.

"What about it?"

"A mancer's weapon could be enchanted."

"Why are you telling me this? You hate me."

"Wilm has suffered enough. And life won't be easy for him . . . with you as a friend."

"Why don't you take your gold and go?" said Llian.

"Because you want me to."

Damn. She'd worked out why he'd given it to her. Thandiwe sat in the shade, took bread and cheese from her bag and ate, watching Wilm all the while. He worked on the first of the basic strokes for several minutes, repeatedly checking Llian's notes and diagrams, before moving to the second, then the third.

"He looks like a ploughman trying to chop wood," said Thandiwe.

"But he's utterly determined to succeed," said Llian.

She wandered down the slope towards the pool, a hundred yards away. Wilm made a particularly agricultural stroke and swore a miner's oath he must have learned from Dajaes. He studied the instructions then rehearsed the stroke over and again in a rather more professional manner. Llian smiled. Not so hopeless after all.

He yawned, climbed a sloping stone and checked for signs of pursuit. On finding none he had a drink from his water bag and sat in the shade of the stone. He felt desperately tired. He thrust a hand in his pocket to make sure Mendark's little book was safe, then closed his eyes . . .

Llian jerked awake, thinking that something was badly wrong. He scrambled to his feet and saw Wilm fifty yards away, still practising. The angle of the sun indicated that less than an hour had passed. Llian breathed a sigh, rubbed his eyes, checked for pursuit and saw a small dust cloud to the south.

"Wilm! Someone's coming."

Wilm sheathed his sword and came running.

"Bring the horses," said Llian. "I'll pack up."

Wilm ran down towards the pool, then stopped. "Where are the other four horses?" he yelled.

It struck Llian like a punch in the mouth. The dust cloud wasn't someone coming, it was Thandiwe going. He raced back to where he had left the bags, already knowing what he would find.

The gold was gone. Every last tell.

62

A SOURCE OF DARK POWER

Karan, Shand and Ussarine tracked the three riders north-east, then north. It wasn't as hard as Karan had expected; the six horses had left clear hoofmarks on the dry plains north of Chanthed. They were heading directly for the salt lake megaliths.

She hardly spoke all day. She no longer knew what to think. Was Llian a much put-upon hero or a fornicating scoundrel? And why, why had he gone with Thandiwe?

After much agonising she put the question out of mind. Only time would tell, and her other problem grew more pressing with every mile they headed north, away from the Whelm and Sulien, who would be going further south, and further out of reach, every day.

In the desperate moments that had led to Sulien going with Idlis and Yetchah, Karan had been in no state of mind to consider what it would actually be like for her. But in every sending, every fleeting link and unguarded emotion Karan had picked up since, Sulien's anguish was more apparent. She should have known better that to entrust her to them.

The Whelm were hard, cold and repressed; they had no sense of fun or joy and took no pleasure in any of the good things in life – the scent of a flower, a lovely sunset, a simple meal or the company of friends. Their lives were entirely given over to hard labour, duty, sacrifice – and punishment.

"She's having a dreadful time," Karan said to Ussarine. "And I don't know what to do."

"If she were my daughter," said Ussarine, "I'd be riding after her right now."

"I would if I knew where to look for her . . . though that would mean abandoning Llian."

"Children must come first."

"But if I went anywhere near her, the magiz's stigma would reveal Sulien to her."

"Then . . . I feel for you."

Ussarine never judged – she simply was there when needed, as solid as a small mountain. It was something rare in Karan's experience, but wonderful.

"Have you known Hingis long?" she asked.

It was as if the sun had risen, full in Ussarine's face. "We were only together five days before I had to leave with Esea."

"You and Hingis must have made quite an impression on each other?"

She smiled dreamily. "He treated me like a normal woman."

"And perhaps the converse . . . "

"He's in great pain – in all kinds of ways."

"But Esea came between—"

"They're very close, and they've both suffered," Ussarine said quickly. "I won't say a word against her." Her jaw tightened and she stared into the distance.

I will, Karan thought. Esea was utterly selfish. She would do whatever it took to keep them apart. "I wish you and Hingis all the joy in the world," she said and rode ahead.

"We've done twelve leagues, I'd say," said Ussarine at sunset. "We must be close."

"We're close," said Shand.

A keen southerly was blowing, and it was getting colder as the day waned. They were walking their horses now, keeping in cover as best they could, though Karan felt sure the precaution was wasted. Llian, Thandiwe and Wilm had changed mounts several times that day and their original five-hour lead must be far greater now. How could she ever catch them?

"Been here before?" said Ussarine to Shand.

He let out a dry chuckle. "I've been everywhere before."

"Lilis said you're twice as old as Nadiril."

"Lilis is an impertinent little—"

"Who is also Nadiril's nominated successor and wise beyond her years. If we're going to travel and fight together, and very probably die together, we should know each other's warts."

Another chuckle. Karan could not remember when Shand had last laughed twice in the same day. Though years ago, before Llian discovered that the love of Shand's life had murdered crippled Fiachra, he had been the best of company. Perhaps he resented Llian for that reason.

"I'm sure you don't have any warts, my dear," he said to Ussarine. "While I – I'm practically all wart."

"Lilis said you used to be called the Recorder. And also Gyllias."

"Gyllias is my real name. I was an important man for a hundred years or so."

"How did you come to live so long? If you don't mind me asking."

"I do mind. But those who are about to die should know they can rely on each other. I was given an extended life by my lover, Yalkara."

"Yalkara the Charon? The greatest of them all?"

"Most people would say that Rulke was the greatest, but yes, it was that Yalkara."

"Oh!" said Ussarine.

She seemed to be seeing Shand in a new and greater light. Or perhaps she was wondering how and why he had fallen so low. Karan certainly was.

"Since we're talking about personal matters, can I ask you a question?" said Karan.

"I suppose so," Ussarine said warily.

"Why does Esea hate you?"

"Because I like Hingis, and he likes me. Though I don't see why it should upset her so . . . " Ussarine looked bewildered and, for the first time, a little teary.

"She fears you'll come first and she'll be pushed away. So that's why she engineered it for you to come with us," said Karan. "To keep you as far away from Hingis as—"

"I smell smoke," said Shand.

They followed it upwind and shortly a vast set of standing stones loomed ahead of them.

"A good enough place for a camp," said Shand.

"Let me check all around first," said Ussarine.

"You go that way," said Karan, pointing left. "I'll check this way. Where was Mendark's hoard, anyway?"

"How would I know?" said Shand.

Karan walked around the outside of the figure eight. Here and there the stones had toppled and lay like fallen sentinels on the barren ground. On coming to one that was tilted at an angle of fifty degrees, she scrambled up the dark ironstone to the top, twelve feet above the ground, and balanced there, looking around her. She saw no movement in any direction. Llian was long gone.

"Hello up there," called Ussarine. "Anything to see?"

Karan did another rotation. "We might be the only people left alive in the world."

"Don't say things like that."

Only a month until the night of the triple moons, when the world would end. Suddenly exhausted, she climbed down and they headed back. Shand had collected a pile of dead scrub, all that could be found in this largely treeless land, and was striking sparks into tinder.

"All clear," said Ussarine. "They found Mendark's cache." She pointed. "Back that way a hundred yards."

"Anything left in it?" said Shand, feeding the fire.

"A rusted-out iron box, a couple of knives, bits of burned paper."

"Recently burned?"

"Yes. By Llian, I expect. I'm going to look for tracks while the light holds." Ussarine rode off, holding up a lightglass Shand had given her.

Karan followed him to a hole in the ground at the base of a tall smooth-sided stone. He touched a little yellow lightglass until it glowed, and held it up, revealing a torn canvas money bag, two knives and three charred flakes of paper.

"You need a knife?" said Shand.

Karan shook her head.

He dug a battered notebook out of his back pocket, lifted the flakes onto it, enclosed the notebook with his hands and headed back to the campfire. There he picked off the first of the flakes with the knife and held it over the coals. Two words, *dark power*, glowed briefly and faded. The second flake yielded one word, *bleeding*, which he thought was from the same sentence, and the third, *betrayed*.

"Disturbing," said Shand.

"But unhelpful," said Karan.

Llian felt in his pocket. The little book was still there. He had gone to sleep holding it and presumably Thandiwe had not dared to try for it.

"What are we going to do?" said Wilm very quietly.

Get drunk on Snoat's brandy, Llian thought, assuming she hadn't taken that as well. Yet he felt more relieved than angry. Thandiwe had been draining him for years, and it was worth Mendark's gold and the spare horses to be rid of her.

"Don't suppose you've got any money left?" said Llian. Snoat's guards had taken his.

"We spent every grint buying stuff for the tunnel."

"Ah, but I do have *this*." Llian rummaged in his bag and held up the purloined crystal decanter.

Wilm blanched. "Is that the one I . . . killed Snoat with?"

"It's the one you whacked him with. I wouldn't bet on him being dead."

"He looked dead to me."

"How many dead bodies have you seen?" Llian could have bitten his tongue out.

"N-none."

Evidently Wilm wasn't counting Dajaes. "I've seen hundreds," said Llian softly, and the worst of them flashed into his inner eye. They would haunt his dreams tonight. "It'd be safer to assume Snoat is alive and bent on revenge."

Wilm swallowed. His eyes returned to the decanter. "What good is that?"

"It's the finest brandy in existence. A collector would pay at least a thousand gold tells for it . . . assuming there's any left by the time we find a collector rich enough."

"You mean . . . every teaspoon is worth a *gold tell?*" whispered Wilm.

"At least."

"You wouldn't drink that!"

"Bloody oath I would. I might be dead tomorrow."

"Mother would have a fit. She doesn't earn a gold tell in a year of scrubbing floors."

"We don't have to tell her," said Llian.

"That's all very well," said Wilm primly, "but wherever we go we'll have to buy food."

"We'll drink the brandy and sell the decanter. The silver stopper must be the weight of thirty tars." Llian twisted it to crack the wax that held it in place.

"Aren't you worried that we're being followed?"

Llian paused. "You're right. We should get going."

He put the decanter away and opened Mendark's book. There were some scrawls on the first few pages, though the rest of the book was empty. He turned to the first page, which held six lines written with a fine nib in purple ink. It was dated ninety-four years ago, presumably when the box had first been hidden here.

Though Llian had plenty of experience in deciphering Mendark's writing, this scrawl was more impenetrable than usual. The lines were short, some of the words were underlined and others in capitals; it might have been written in terror or drunkenness. Or both. He looked up. Wilm was practising again, and his strokes had a hint of desperation now.

Llian scanned the page and closed his eyes to recreate a mental image of it. Mendark's impenetrable scrawl became his voice as Llian remembered it.

The drumming, the drumming!
  You bloody fool, the enemy has used you.
  It's a source of dark power bleeding into the world.
  And you've been manipulated **all your adult life**.
  To find it for them – AND WAKE IT.
  If you had, you would have betrayed Santhenar and
everything you believe in.

Llian tore out a blank page and copied the lines. Sometimes the act of copying helped in deciphering the meaning. *The enemy* must mean the Merdrun and *it* was surely the summon stone. And *all your adult life* suggested they had got to Mendark as a young man. Had they given him the power to wake the summon stone because they, from the void, could not? Was that Mendark's 'deal with a demon' that explained his astonishing rise to power?

The next page had been written thirteen years later, using a thicker nib and green ink.

Can the secret of mancery be used to block them?
  Or would that be playing into their hands?
  Might the summon stone feed on mancery?

Llian knew that Mendark loved Santhenar and would never knowingly betray his world. That must be why he had tried to crack the secret of mancery, hoping to block the enemy permanently.

The third and last page was dated only eleven years ago, not long before his death, and was written in what appeared to be silverpoint. Mendark had pressed so hard that the page was torn through in places.

*I was also sure nyphalle would work – it eats through wood,
metal, glass, porcelain and stone – but no one could create any. I
can't destroy it, but maybe the future can. I've got to SLEEP it –
and there's only one way to do that.*

*   The fatal way.*

"What does *the fatal way* mean?" said Wilm, who had approached
silently and was clutching his sword as if it were the only safe thing
in the world.

"It means that the Histories have to be rewritten," said Llian. He
burned the copy he had made of the first page, then laughed aloud.

"What's so funny?"

"It's ironic, really. Thandiwe did whatever it took to get herself a
Great Tale, and corrupted herself in the process, but this book proves
she's got the ending wrong. Mendark wasn't corrupt at the end, nor had
he gone mad. He was fighting to save the world."

"How did he die?"

Llian looked back through the years. "He was gutted by a thranx, a
savage winged humanoid that got in from the void when the Way Between
the Worlds was opened. Mendark gave his life to save the rest of us."

Wilm shivered. "Are you going to tell Thandiwe?"

"Should bad behaviour be rewarded?"

"What are we going to do?"

"After burning his library," Llian mused, "Mendark raced up
to Carcharon, then made a gate to Shazmak, where he was subsequently killed. But as to what he was *really* trying to do, no one
knows."

"Is Shazmak where the summon stone is?"

"I don't know. But Carcharon is a very dark place."

What had Basunez and Karan's father really got up to there? If only
Karan hadn't burned their papers.

"I think," Llian added, "we'd better head for Carcharon."

"What if it's there?" said Wilm.

"I've got to destroy it . . . "

"But?" Wilm said perceptively.

"It's a magical device of great power that can defend itself. It corrupted Unick in a twinkling, and he's a greater mancer. So how can *I* hope to harm it?"

Mummy, Mummy?

Karan, who had been dozing behind a megalith, shot upright.

Mummy, they're going to initiate me! Idlis keeps saying, "You're one of us now, my little Whelm." What if . . . what if they won't give me back?

Then Karan sensed a greedy alertness and felt a tiny spike of pain at the top of her head. The magiz again, picking away at her like a sore, trying to wear her down. She tried to send feelings of warmth and comfort to Sulien, but they felt pathetic and useless.

Mummy, where are you? You've got to come and get me.

Karan could hardly breathe. Could Sulien be right? Were the Whelm planning to keep her? Tears poured down her cheeks but with the magiz so close she dared not reply.

If they did plan to keep Sulien, how would she ever find her? The frozen wilderness of Shazabba was vast and the Whelm must have a thousand hiding places. In trying to save Sulien, had she delivered her to a fate that was almost as bad?

Mummeeeee?

Sulien's link faded away. Karan could sense nothing now. Would it be like this for the rest of her life – just emptiness? She screwed herself up into a ball, wrapped her arms around herself and rocked back and forth, but it could not ease her torment. Nothing could. She had given Sulien away and was never going to get her back.

Ussarine rode in, carrying something rectangular under her arm, and jumped down. Karan looked up listlessly, unable to care.

"What's that?" said Shand.

"The lid of the box. It must have been booby-trapped, and the lid was blasted off when it was opened."

Karan stood up. "Was anyone hurt?"

"There's no sign of blood," said Shand.

Ussarine turned the lid over. A small canvas money bag was caught in a snag in the metal.

Shand opened the bag. "Silver tars. I dare say Llian would have taken the gold."

"How do you know there was gold?" said Karan.

"It's worth twenty times as much as silver, and a Magister on the run would have great need of it for bribes, the hire of horses, coaches, ships and guards. And to encourage reluctant allies."

He tossed the bag to Karan. "Share it with Ussarine."

Karan let it fall. "I'd sooner starve than touch Mendark's silver."

"You're broke, Karan. You may need it to save your daughter."

Karan's eyes burned. *What if . . . what if they won't give me back?* She stumbled away, choking.

"Karan, what is it?" said Ussarine, running after her.

"Sulien is calling out for me, calling and calling, and I'm terrified to answer in case the magiz gets to her through me. She's addicted to death and she aches to drink Sulien's life. And I . . . don't know . . . what to do."

Shand shook his grey head. "I'm sorry."

"I just want to reach out to Sulien and comfort her. If I'm quick . . . it'll be all right, won't it?" Karan turned her tear-stained face up to Ussarine.

"You have to do whatever keeps Sulien safe," said Ussarine.

"But is she safe with the Whelm?" Karan cried.

"I don't know," Shand said heavily.

"I also found tracks," said Ussarine after a minute's silence. "Going two ways."

"They split up?" said Shand.

"Not deliberately."

"Sorry?"

"Judging by the tracks, one person left with their own horse and the three remounts. The other two people headed east with the remaining two horses."

"Who was the one and who were the two?" said Karan dully.

"We'd better take a look," said Shand.

Ussarine led them to the spot, and he studied the tracks of the person who had taken the four horses. "Definitely not Wilm. He's got big feet and a long stride."

"Not Llian either," said Ussarine. "These footmarks are slender; it's got to be Thandiwe."

Karan felt a vague stirring of relief but suppressed it. Not yet!

"Funny-looking tracks," said Shand.

"How do you mean?" said Karan.

"There are hardly any heel impressions. It's as though she was walking on tiptoe. Yet the toe impressions are really deep and dug in at the front." Then he laughed. "What a gall she's got!"

Karan looked at him blankly.

"Thandiwe's sneaking away carrying a lot of weight."

"She's tall," said Karan, "but she's not a heavy woman."

"She was when she made these footprints. She must have nicked all Mendark's gold, then stolen the spare horses and run for it."

"South-west towards the Hirthway," said Ussarine. "Doesn't sound like Llian's dearest friend to me, Karan."

"The treacherous bitch!" said Karan, but she felt an exhausting sense of relief. And a degree of guilt that she had so misjudged and mistrusted Llian.

When they arrived back at the campfire she counted out the bag of silver and gave Ussarine half. Karan put some in her pocket and the rest in her pack, and retired to her sleeping pouch. Once the camp was silent she looked up at the stars and imagined that one of them was Llian. If only she knew where he was.

If only she could link to Sulien.

63

THE BROKEN PHIAL

Wilm and Llian rode due east from the megaliths to the River Gannel, which they reached late in the afternoon. Wilm took no notice of their surroundings. He could think of nothing but Dajaes, her short life and terrible death, of throwing the dirt onto her cold body, filling the grave and riding away. Would he ever return? Would he even be able to find her grave again in this arid wilderness?

How could he have failed her so? Why hadn't he attacked Unick with the sabre? If he had she might still be alive. It was all his fault. The thoughts went round and round; he could not escape them.

"Come on, Wilm," said Llian, who had ridden into the sandy river-bed until the water came up to his horse's belly.

The Gannel was low at this time of year, broad but shallow. Wilm realised that he was staring blindly at the pebbles beneath the water. The round stones were just like the ones he had scattered on Dajaes's grave.

"We'll ride up the river for a while," Llian added, "to hide our tracks."

"How do we get to Carcharon?" said Wilm.

"We can't risk the track via Tullin . . ."

Llian trailed off. He had been preoccupied ever since reading those pages in Mendark's notebook. Wilm knew the look by now; Llian was sorting through his prodigious chronicler's memories, trying to find links between the past and the present.

"And?" Wilm prompted after another silent minute.

"There's another way across the mountains. It's shorter than the route through Tullin, but higher, and often closed by avalanches in winter."

"How do you know it'll be open now?"

"You don't get many avalanches in autumn."

Wilm looked ahead to an expanse of woodland that appeared to stretch all the way to the mountains. It was close to sunset.

"Shouldn't we find a campsite?"

"Not on the plains," said Llian. "Campfire could be seen for miles."

They rode through the woodland for half an hour, by which time it was almost dark. The land was undulating here and, as it rose towards the foothills, the open woodland became forest. They reached a freshet chuckling over a series of rocky rills between two knobbly hills, like an old man's knees. Llian headed upstream to a place where the trees were tall and there was plenty of cover.

"This'll do. The only way we can be seen is if someone stumbles right on us." He yawned. "Hardly keep my eyes open."

Wilm gathered wood and fetched water. Llian charred chunks cut from the goat hindquarter in the fire. Wilm didn't taste a single mouthful; he just sat there, staring at the flames and picturing Dajaes's lovely face, her soft brown eyes. How could he have failed her so?

Llian was writing in his journal. Wilm rose abruptly, turned away so Llian would not see the tears in his eyes and practised the seven basic strokes with desperate fury. He kept it up for an hour, by which time his arm was aching all the way to the shoulder and his knees were rubbery. He stopped for a minute, panting. Llian did not look up.

Sword fighting was one of the most exhausting activities of all, and few people could keep it up for long, but Wilm continued, fighting against the pain. He had to master the seven basic strokes and both strength and endurance mattered. He had not said anything to Llian, but Wilm planned to take Unick on and kill him. He could not be allowed to do to anyone else what he had done to Dajaes.

Wilm could not hope to match Unick after a few days' practice, for he was a cunning, experienced brawler. But he also looked like a sick man. Wilm had to stay alive long enough to wear him down, exhaust him. And then . . .

"I can't think," Llian said. "I'm too bloody tired." He got out the brandy decanter. "Want some?"

"No," Wilm said miserably.

"I guess it's not the time." Llian slipped the notebook into his pocket. "Ow, what's that?"

The tip of his middle finger had a spot of blood on it. He felt in his pocket and brought out a little stoppered phial.

"Where did this come from, anyway?" Llian sniffed it.

A troubling memory surfaced in Wilm's mind but sank again before he could identify it.

"There's a label on it," said Llian. He carried it across to the fire and studied the tiny writing. "It says, WILM. Did you drop it on the way into Pem-Y-Rum?"

"I've never seen it before," said Wilm. "But Aviel uses those perfume phials. She must have made it for me."

"Then how did it get there?"

"I don't know."

The phial set off a flood of memories – Dajaes and himself going every step of the way, rescuing Llian, trying to find the way back to the cellar but discovering they could no longer get to it, then deciding to head for the gates of Pem-Y-Rum. He saw the three of them walking down that fatal corridor . . .

Llian passed the phial to Wilm. "Unick picked up a bit of glass. He sniffed it and put it in his pocket."

Unick's final words exploded in Wilm's mind and he let out a cry of anguish.

Llian must have realised what it meant at the same second, because he said the words aloud: *"I'll have her too.* Why would Unick say that?"

"Aviel!" cried Wilm.

"Why would Unick care about someone he's never heard of, a hundred miles away on the other side of the mountains? It was just a meaningless taunt, because that's the kind of swine he is."

"Yes," said Wilm, so relieved that he felt dizzy and had to put his hands on the ground. "He wouldn't have the faintest idea where she lives."

"Is she a special friend?" said Llian.

"I remember the first time I saw her." Wilm stared into the fire. "I was four; she must have been two. All the little kids used to play in the paddock across from the butcher's shop, and Aviel was on the other side, trying to walk like everyone else. She was trying so hard, but her ankle was never going to go straight and the other kids made fun of her – *Twist-foot, twist-foot!* You know how cruel kids can be."

"I know."

"Mum rounded on them and asked me to take Aviel home. She was trying not to cry, and her ankle was red and swollen. I offered to carry her but she refused. She took my hand, though, and I walked with her all the way, and we talked about . . . stuff. We were both different. Me because I had no father, and Aviel with her terrible family. And being a twist-foot. Plus the silver hair and the seventh-sister business . . . "

"What about it?"

"They all mean bad luck, and Aviel has the worst luck of anyone I've ever met."

Llian smiled indulgently.

"It's true!" said Wilm. "She once tossed a coin fifty times, and forty-eight times it came up the opposite of what she called."

"I could use a skill like that at the gaming tables," Llian said dreamily.

"If she calls heads but secretly hopes for tails, heads nearly always comes up. She's tried to beat her bad luck but she can't."

"It doesn't explain what the phial was doing in Pem-Y-Rum."

Wilm held it up to the firelight. There was still a trace of liquid in the bottom. He worked the stopper out and took a careful sniff.

"It smells like the herbs and flowers in her garden."

"I wish I had a scent to remind me of home," said Llian gloomily. "I'm going to turn in."

He wrapped himself in his cloak and one of Snoat's horse blankets, and was asleep within a minute. Wilm put the phial away. He was desperate for sleep but it did not feel right to put Dajaes out of his mind on the day she had died.

It seemed impossible that it could have happened this morning. It felt like a hundred years since he had been young and innocent, going on the great adventure with her through the tunnel to rescue Llian. He had to stay with her as long as he could.

He sat there for hours, grieving and remembering the good times, and only when he knew from the wheeling stars that it was past midnight and the awful day was done at last did he finally let go.

But later on he jerked awake, hearing Unick's voice, over and over. *I'll have her too. I'll have her too. I'll have her too.*

Wilm felt for the phial in his bag and eased the stopper out. Pressing the broken end to his nose, he took a deep sniff, then stoppered it and put it away again. He sensed Aviel, far away in Casyme, smelling the same scent and smiling. It was all right; Unick's words didn't mean anything.

But then she gasped, doubled up and slapped a hand over her nose, though not before Wilm smelled it too – a disgusting reek that he would never forget if he lived a hundred lives. Unick!

I'll have her too.

It wasn't a dream and it wasn't some vision of madness. Somehow Aviel's perfume had connected her to himself, *and to Unick*. Wilm remembered him swinging another device back and forth. What had Llian called it? Identity! Then the two red crystals on the end had lit up, and Unick had said, "*Ah!*"

He was after Aviel, and he had to be stopped. Wilm kicked the sleeping pouch away, drew the black sword and ran this way and that, staring into the darkness. But there was nothing to see – Unick would be east of Chanthed by now, and Aviel was a hundred miles away in Casyme.

Though with the Identity device he could find her.

With quiet desperation Wilm began to practise the seven basic strokes, and did not stop even when bloody blisters formed on his palm and fingers, or even after the blisters burst. Every so often he paused to check his instructions by the firelight, correct his stroke and go at it again.

He was still practising three hours later when Llian woke with the dawn.

"You're up early," he said, smiling.

Wilm kept going mechanically for another half-dozen strokes before grinding to a stop. He turned towards Llian, bleakly, knowing he must look like a madman.

"Wilm, what is it?"

Wilm explained what had happened in the night, expecting Llian to dismiss it as a nightmare. Hoping he would.

"Why would Unick want to harm her?" said Llian.

"He's a monster!"

"No, there's got to be more to it. He must see some kind of a threat in her."

"How could Aviel be a threat?"

"I don't know. But Unick left Pem-Y-Rum the same time we did," said Llian, walking around the fire and thinking aloud, "and he took spare horses. It's a week's ride from there to Casyme, via the Tullin path. Less if he rides his horses into the ground, though parts of the path are so steep that riding is no quicker than walking."

"He could get to Casyme in another four days."

"He might."

"And we're further away than he was when he left," Wilm said dismally. "We'll never catch him."

"The mountains narrow rapidly as you go north," said Llian. "It's only a four-day crossing from here by the old path. Then we can race south to Casyme in another day."

"That's still a day too late."

"If we ride a couple of hours longer each day, we might make up the difference. Come on."

They stuffed their gear into the saddlebags, mounted and ate breakfast as they went.

"But what are we going to do if . . . when we get there?" said Wilm. "He's a great brute of a man."

"He's also a middle-aged drunk with the trembles. You're young and fast, and you've got one of Mendark's lucky swords. At the rate you've been practising, you'll be a master swordsman by then."

Wilm laughed hollowly. "What if he goes for you?"

"I'll talk him to death! Take heart, Wilm; we'll beat him, I know we will."

But Wilm knew they would not.

64

A WHIFF OF BURNED BONES

According to Shand's almanack, the eclipse of the blood moon would begin around half past eight tonight, and it would be over by a quarter to ten. The Eureka Graveolence had to be mixed at the full of the moon, though the almanack was silent on how long that would last. Aviel thought it might only be a few minutes. She would have to work fast, and accurately, for there would be no chance to try again.

She made everything ready, packed her bag with food, clothing and other necessities, plus a hammer to smash the summon stone as Malien's letter had instructed, and a metal flask containing a pint of oil so she could burn the fragments to ash.

She put her entire wealth, four silver tars and five copper grints, in her wallet and asked Demoy to make Thistle ready – the horse had found his way back to the stables a week previously. She was not looking forward to riding him again, though at least his quirks were familiar.

What else? To deal with unknown dangers she might need to blend a scent potion on the way. Aviel had once made a belt with many small loops, each sized to hold a phial. She filled phials with all the common scents, plus several uncommon ones and a couple that were rare or dangerous, and made sure they were all stoppered tightly and secure in their loops.

Darkness had fallen hours ago and the moon was rising. Not long to go. She checked in case her horrible sisters were creeping up to throw stones at the workshop or fill her water barrel with manure, but all was clear. The moon was just beginning to turn ruddy. A snail seemed to glide down her spine.

She went back inside, slipped the bolt and extinguished all the lamps but one, which she turned down so there was just enough light to see what she was doing. The potion making must not be interrupted. She drew the curtains, save the one on the upper part of the eastern window. She needed to check the moon constantly as the time approached.

Ooo-ooo-ooo-ooo.

The nightjar – not a good beginning. Aviel stood the nine phials on the bench in the order that she had to use them and checked the labels. She could do nothing about ill omens or her intrinsic bad luck, but she could eliminate simple mistakes.

She yawned, rubbed her eyes and laid her head on her arms. So tired. Her eyes closed for a second. She snapped them open and stood up.

She stared at the phials, her eyes unfocused, her mind on the coming journey. Assuming the Eureka Graveolence didn't go terribly wrong and splatter her all over the workshop, it would point her to the source of the drumming – the summon stone. Then, unless a miracle happened and Shand turned up, it was up to her to go there and try to destroy it.

Aviel shuddered. She hated leaving her workshop, and her previous dash on Thistle had taught her how dangerous the open road was for someone who could not run away. This would be a far longer trip – how long she did not know – with great danger at the end of it and no one to help her.

Ooo-ooo-ooo-ooo.

Why was the oil in the fourth phial a pale yellow? It should be colourless. She checked the label. It was correct but the oil wasn't. She took a careful sniff – mustard oil. It had nothing to do with the Eureka Graveolence; it was one of the phials that should have been in her belt. Despite all the care she had taken, she had mislabelled it.

She went through her belt, found the scent that should have been the fourth of her nine – the foul gas from a rotten death adder's egg – relabelled it and checked the nine again, twice, to be sure. Using mustard oil would have been a disastrous mistake.

Aviel glanced up through the window. The moon was full and ruddy all over. She'd already wasted a minute. Go!

She panicked, reached for the first phial and her trembling hand knocked it over. Aviel forced herself to stop and recite a list of herbs backwards to calm herself – yucca, wormwood, vervain, valerian . . . She picked the phial up and clamped an empty phial – the one in which the Eureka Graveolence would be blended – to a stand so she could not knock it over.

After selecting an eye dropper from a tray of them, she twisted out the bung of the first phial, drew some up in the eye dropper and dripped exactly seven drops into the tenth phial. She returned the rest to the first phial, capped it, then with a fresh eye dropper took one single drop of the second scent, the putrescent one she had extracted from the de-hairing sludge. All that effort and danger for one drop!

She focused on working to a careful rhythm and shaking the potion phial in the correct way and the correct number of times each time, and continued until only the ninth scent remained.

The nightjar called again. *Ooo-ooo-ooo-ooo.*

The moon was starting to eclipse; she could see the faintest shadow on the upper right. Aviel drew up the ninth oil in a clean eye dropper and caught an unpleasant whiff of the skull bone she had stolen and burned after violating an unknown person's grave. Her first step on the path to darkness.

Her arm trembled. She steadied it and carefully released ten drops onto a dry part of the inside wall of the phial, then watched the thick oil ooze down.

Not ten, you fool! Nine drops!

Aviel squirted the rest of the oil back into the phial it came from, then put the tip of the eye dropper into the oozing oil on the wall of the Eureka Graveolence phial, and drew up a quantity. But how to make sure there were nine drops in the phial? She released all she had drawn up save for the last, hanging drop, removed the dropper and shook the phial.

The Eureka Graveolence was made. But would it work?

Never sniff a scent potion directly.

Scent potions could never be perfectly duplicated since the strength of each scent could vary according to its source ingredients. One time a scent potion might be ineffective, yet the next time it was made the same amount could be an overdose. With her free hand she wafted some of the potion towards her, then stoppered the phial and took a careful sniff.

Bang!

Her limbs convulsed so violently that she shot backwards off her stool, cracking her head on the bench behind her. Pain shrieked through her skull. Choking sounds were coming from her throat and her heels were drumming on the floorboards. The lamp went out. Through the window the moon grew huge, as if it were toppling out of the sky right at her. It burst into shards and everything went black.

Aviel could see again, though her field of vision was spinning like a compass needle: mountains with tips of snow; a ruined mill of black stone in a mountain forest; an undulating landscape, brown and withered; a neglected manor with a green slate roof and walls of pink granite; an orchard with hardly any fruit; an escarpment. Then a series of barren hills rising steeply to a rocky horn on which stood a bizarre half-ruined tower built of violet-coloured rock.

The drumming sounded so loudly that it deafened her, and the tower wobbled as if it were made of rubber. Something slid off the bench behind her and landed on her forehead. A glass stopper.

Aviel groaned. Lights flashed before her eyes and she saw the ruined tower again. Was that where the summon stone lay? She could not tell, though she was sure of the direction, north-north-east. But how far? Five miles or fifty? Or five hundred?

She got up, rubbing her bruised forehead and the back of her head, picked up the stool and relit the lantern. The moon was still red, though just a thin crescent now, almost completely eclipsed. She had been out for some time.

Aviel checked the scent potion, which was safely stoppered. She tied a piece of thread around it so she could identify it in the dark if she needed to, wrapped it in a scrap of cloth for extra protection and jammed it into the last belt loop.

She tidied up the workshop, carefully washed out the eye droppers and left them to drain. Everything was ready. Time for bed. She would leave at dawn.

Aviel woke to a disgusting smell in her nostrils, the same reek she had detected several nights ago when she had realised that someone evil had become aware of her existence. But this was different, worse.

He was after her.

Was he in the workshop? She hurled herself out of bed and lit a lamp. The door was still bolted; she was alone. She tried to tell herself that it was just a waking nightmare but knew it wasn't. How had he discovered her? Was it because she had used the scent potion to locate the summon stone? Was it fighting back?

How close was he? She could not tell, and there was nowhere she could hide, no one to protect her. Her only hope was to get to the stone and destroy it before he caught her. Aviel dressed in the warmest clothes she had, checked her list three times, carried her gear to the stables and packed it into Thistle's saddlebags.

She collected the grimoire, locked the workshop and let herself into Shand's house. She thought the run-down manor with the green slate roof and the pink granite walls was probably Gothryme, where Llian lived. It made sense; she knew from the Histories, and bits she had read of his Great Tale recently, that strange and uncanny things had happened in the mountains behind Gothryme.

Aviel checked Shand's wall map and made a sketch map of the back way from Casyme to Gothryme. Remembering how easily she had become lost last time, she marked the distances to important intersections and landmarks on her map.

She left Malien's second letter in the middle of the kitchen table and scribbled, "Gone after it, Aviel," on the letter. She also did a sketch of the broken tower she had seen in the night, though she could not imagine it would tell Shand anything.

She had planned to put the grimoire back where she had found it, but instead Aviel returned to the stables, wrapped it carefully and tucked it into her saddlebag. It might be the only defence she had. She mounted, waved to the silent stable boy and rode out.

She would head for Gothryme. Perhaps she could get food and shelter there, since she was a traveller and had news, old though it was, of Llian. Then she would use the Eureka Graveolence again. If the source was close it should be easier to locate.

It was good to have a plan. She turned Thistle onto the back road and nudged him into a steady pace.

Then the waking nightmare came back.

65

IT'S HIM! IT'S HIM!

Aviel was hopelessly lost and there was only one way to get back on track, though she was reluctant to try the scent potion again just yet. Her stomach muscles still ached, and when she stretched she felt a sharp pain to the left of her belly button, as if she had torn something there.

Her map said that it was forty miles from Casyme to Gothryme, a couple of days' ride at her slow pace, but even in daylight she struggled to reconcile the lines on the paper with the landscape she was passing through.

There were no towns or villages here, no farmers to ask for directions, and somehow she had taken a wrong turning. It was late afternoon and the track was taking her up a ridge through tall, dripping forest.

How could this be right? The track did not appear to have been used in weeks. She stopped at a little cascade, where Thistle drank noisily, deposited an enormous amount of manure on the bank and cropped the grass. She urged him up to the top of the ridge and dismounted, wincing.

Her bottom was bruised all over and the insides of her thighs were chafed again. She looked left and right and up, though she could only see ridges, rising ever higher, and hints of snow on the tops of the highest.

Aviel consulted her map again but it was hard to focus on the lines; having had so little sleep last night, she was exhausted. Was there any point going on? She made mistakes when she was tired and her bad luck was always worse. It was after four in the afternoon now, and the sun had passed behind the mountains ages ago. Better find a safe campsite and get a fire going. She still felt shivery whenever she thought about what had happened in the night, and that stinking brute coming after her.

Through the trees she glimpsed the ruins of a mill, its rotting water-wheel still in place. It would be good to have walls around her again, even broken ones. She limped across to Thistle, took hold of the saddle and tried to lift her good foot into the stirrup. Pain speared through her ankle and her thigh muscles gave way; she could not raise her foot high enough. She tried again but was too low by a foot.

Tears of frustration sprang into her eyes. She wiped them on her sleeve, cursing her turned ankle and the miserable luck that had plagued her all her life.

"We'll just have to walk, Thistle. That'll be nice, won't it?"

Thistle turned his long head, looked her in the eye and snorted.

Aviel looped the reins around her fist. They crossed a cascade. The light was fading; it was getting cold and a ground mist was rising. She glanced to her left and saw the wheel again and the broken black walls behind it. And she recognised it – she had seen it after sniffing the graveolence. Had it led her here? If so, why?

"Home, sweet home, Thistle!"

Thistle whinnied; his eye was huge and the white was showing all around.

"It's all right," she said, stroking his neck. "We're safe here."

The ground mist rose in a series of wraith shapes. A chilly breeze twisted and coiled, then drifted the shapes towards her. She passed through one and it chilled her to her aching bones.

The mill loomed up. It had been built over the stream on the wall that dammed it, and the dam still stood. The stone walls were covered in moss as high as her head, and the mill was dank and unwelcoming, but it was the best shelter she was going to get. Aviel tied Thistle on a long lead so he could crop the grass and reach the water, and went in through a broken archway.

The mill had once been two storeys, but its roof had fallen in and the wood of the upper floor had rotted away except for a couple of beams festooned with wraith-like fungal growths. The ground was littered with decayed timbers and broken roof slates. Parts of the far wall had collapsed, leaving a series of ragged stone stumps like scattered teeth in a black jawbone.

Home sweet home indeed! She found some dry boards in the lee of the left-hand wall and used a little bag of tinder she had brought with her to light a fire.

It sputtered and shot sparks at her, and the smoke hung low between the walls. It had an unpleasant smell; the boards had been painted with wood tar to preserve them, and Aviel started to feel nauseous. She sniffed some oil of orange blossom, which helped, then took a blazing board outside to look for more dry wood. She found none; everything was sodden, and now it began to rain.

Thoroughly dispirited, she ate a lump of hard cheese, found a dry corner, put out the reeking fire and lay down in her sleeping pouch with her cloak wrapped around her. But though she was utterly exhausted, Aviel could not get to sleep.

With her hammer and her pint of oil, smashing the summon stone and burning the fragments should be easy enough. But she had to think of all the ways it could go wrong. The stone might be in a place that was dangerous to get to, or it might be protected in some way.

She was too tired. She closed her eyes and tried to put everything out of mind, and finally slipped into a troubled sleep.

The purple-faced man made his drunken way east across the mountains. He rode the last of his horses to death, abandoned it in the middle of the road and continued in a grunting lurch, swilling from a flask until it was empty then smashing it to pieces on the road, wrenching another from his saddlebags and continuing. Once, when his agony broke through the numbing effects of the drink, he screamed until blood ran from his nose.

He met an old man driving a cart and singing an offensively merry tune. He leaped onto the cart and threw the old man off on his head, cursing him for being happy in so wretched a world. The drunk turned the cart around and ran over the old man, then flogged the old horse into a gallop until it collapsed. He ate nothing and did not stop, day or night.

The rampage went on, one mindless brutality after another until the drunk crested the range of mountains separating the dry lands to the west from wealthy Iagador. There he stopped, took a fragment of dusty glass out of his pocket and sniffed it. He pointed a brass tube with two red crystals on its end to the left, then the right, his eyes blazing, then settled on a direction and staggered on. He had to stop her before she ruined everything.

Aviel screamed and threw herself out of the sleeping pouch. The stench had congealed in her nostrils, a reek so offensive that it made the Eureka Graveolence seem like a cleansing aroma.

"It's him!" she gasped. "It's him."

66

OUR VERY EXISTENCE IS IN PERIL

Karan was sitting on her horse, staring into nowhere, when Shand and Ussarine rode up.

"I've lost Llian and Wilm's tracks," Shand said. "I suspect they've gone east but we've got to be sure. Come on."

"Can't think about anything but Sulien," said Karan. "I'll catch you up."

He gave her a cold stare, then rode off. Good riddance! She was fed up with his suspicions and accusations.

"Don't do anything rash," Ussarine said softly, and followed.

Karan made a mug of herb tea, using the aromatic leaves of a twisted little mint bush, sat with her back to the trunk of a small tree and focused on her breathing, in and out, trying to eliminate everything from her mind. In and out.

But she kept seeing Sulien's tormented face as she'd offered to go with the Whelm. Why had she allowed her to do it? The thought of gentle Sulien being punished, starved and made into a little Whelm was unbearable.

Karan had to know she was safe but a link was out of the question. This left only one possibility, one she prayed the magiz would not be able to detect. She unlocked the little box and studied the lump of hrux inside. The smell did not seem as bad as the last batch. She cut off a small piece, then decided she needed more, to be sure.

No, that was the hrux talking. A smaller piece, not a larger one. Her hand had a tremor and her pulse was racing. She *really* wanted it, and the urge had to be resisted every time. She fought it until it faded, cut off a tiny piece, locked the box and put the piece in her mouth. Karan went to lick the knife – no, resist it *always*.

Her surroundings vanished as if she had been thrown through a hole into another land. She tried to focus on a mental image of Sulien but saw Unick instead.

He was staggering down a winding mountain track, gasping and grunting, brandishing his bloody fists at the sky and crying out for the source that was now lost to him. Its loss was eating him alive.

You bloody bastard, Llian! he cried. *I'll smash you to bits, you bloody, bloody bastard.*

Unick took a little circle of glass from his pocket and sniffed it. He turned left and right, his shrunken eyes jerking around in sockets too big for them. *You too, you little bitch. I'm not letting you ruin it.* Karan shrank back, only to realise that he was not talking about her.

It was all she saw of him, thankfully, and she must have slept, for she suddenly realised that she was sagging forward, her hair sweeping the ground. She sat up, surprised that she was not suffering the after-effects of hrux.

What news from our new world? said a familiar voice, Gergrig's.

Mist cleared and she saw a steep slope sheathed in crevassed blue ice. It was more than half a mile higher than the place where she had destroyed the magiz's leg; the wall of the bulbous ice fortress that guarded the flat mountaintop and the great Crimson Gate was only a few hundred yards above her.

Gergrig and a big man with a flattened nose and a rounded metal plate where the top left side of his head should have been were standing around a roaring fire fuelled with chunks of black oily rock. The mountainside was dotted with such fires, and the smoke curling up from them had collected in every hollow, making brown pools in the blue-white.

Between the two men, the magiz, swathed in grey furs, was perched on a rock ledge while an attendant strapped a mechanical leg, made of black iron and shiny brass, onto her stump.

The magiz looked up at Gergrig. Her thin face was gashed by pain lines but she seemed happy. *The fools don't even know I've a spy in their midst,* she said. *Not even the spy knows.* She laughed mirthlessly.

What do they know? said the man with the plate in his head.

They think the drumming is causing all their troubles, sneered the magiz. *They don't realise I'm pulling their strings.*

Even the man called Snoat?

Especially him. He's my greatest work of art. I've even convinced him that the summon stone, and ourselves, are a fantasy. She let out a revolting, snorting giggle.

There are two strings you're not pulling, Gergrig said, looking pointedly at her mechanical leg. *The mother's and the daughter's.*

They're both at breaking point. And the moment either cracks, I'll drink both their lives!

Karan snapped the connection and sat there, mouth dry and heart pounding. *The moment either cracks* meant that Sulien was also vulnerable, and there was not a thing Karan could do about it.

"Karan?" Shand was shaking her.

Her head was throbbing, one of the after-effects of hrux. Another was weakness in her limbs. Her legs and arms were trembling and her mouth was so dry she could not speak.

"Don't tell me!" Shand said sharply. "Not again!"

"What's the matter?" said Ussarine.

"The damn fool has taken hrux. Karan. *Karan!*"

"Water," she croaked.

Ussarine pressed the spout of a water skin through her lips and squeezed it. Warm water spurted in. Karan rinsed it around her mouth and swallowed. "I'm all right. Help me up."

Shand and Ussarine came into focus. "Did you find Llian's tracks?" said Karan.

"Heading east. Why hrux, Karan? You know how dangerous—"

"There was no other way."

"What did you see?"

Her memories were jumbled up and it was a struggle to put them in order. "Unick! East of Tullin. He sniffed a little circle of glass and said, 'You too, you little bitch. I'm not letting you ruin it.'"

"A little circle of glass?"

"Like the neck of a tiny bottle."

"Or a perfume phial," Shand said grimly. "Aviel asked me to give it to Wilm but I broke it outside Unick's workshop. And like a damn fool, I left it there."

"I don't see—" said Karan.

"She accidentally made another scent potion; I smelled it and it linked me to her. It must have affected Unick the same way."

Karan's skin crawled. "And he's terrified Aviel will find the source."

"The summon stone," said Shand. "We've got to go."

"There's more," said Karan. She told them what the magiz had said.

"An *unwitting spy.*" He studied her calculatingly. "Who?"

"The magiz didn't say." Could Karan herself be the spy, betraying the allies through the magiz's stigma? No, the idea was absurd. Then who? She had no way of finding out without going back to Cinnabar, and she wasn't going to do that.

"Can we get to Casyme before Unick does?" said Ussarine.

"It'll be touch and go," said Shand.

They raced after Llian and Wilm, riding all the hours of daylight and whenever there was enough moonlight to see, only sleeping three or four hours a night. But Llian and Wilm must have been going just as hard and they did not catch them.

Karan's terror grew with every step, for she kept picking up flashes of incoherent fury that could only be coming from Unick. Llian would not last a minute in a fight with him.

After four of the hardest days' riding in her experience they reached Casyme in the evening, but they were too late. The lock on Aviel's workshop was broken and she was gone.

"No sign of a body, at least," Ussarine said bleakly.

"Maybe he took her with him," said Shand.

"Hello," said Karan, smiling at a grubby, yellow-haired boy who had appeared out of the darkness.

He made wild movements with his hands. He was clearly terrified.

"My stable boy, Demoy," said Shand. "He's mute."

He squatted down in front of the lad and they exchanged signs for a minute or two. Shand shook Demoy's hand and gave him a silver coin. Demoy took their horses into the stables.

"Unick came through around midday," said Shand, "hunting Aviel. When he found she was gone he broke into my house, then stole my best horse and went after her."

"Where did she go?" said Karan.

"Demoy doesn't know. But she left in the night, in a tearing hurry."

"What about Llian and Wilm?"

"The lad's been hiding ever since Unick left. Doesn't know anything about them."

"So we don't know if they're ahead or behind us."

"No. Come into the house."

Karan was so tired that she was starting to hallucinate and she dared not risk that; visions could link her to Sulien or even take her back to Cinnabar. The house was undisturbed apart from the cellar, from which Unick had stolen several flasks and two little barrels of raw spirit.

"The bastard must be able to smell liquor," said Shand.

"Lucky he didn't tear the place apart."

"He's in too much of a hurry. Come into the kitchen when you're ready." He indicated the washroom. "There won't be any bread but the larder is full."

Karan washed her face and hands and went into the kitchen. The old table was piled with sausages, cheeses, dried fruit and jars of pickled vegetables. Shand was studying a sheet of paper, a letter from Malien.

"It's weeks old," he said. "Must have come after I left for Chanthed. It doesn't tell me anything new."

But below it was written in a hasty scrawl, "Gone after it, Aviel." She had sketched a tower which, though crudely drawn, drove thorns into Karan's backbone. The drumming sounded in her inner ear, long and low.

"Carcharon," said Shand. "I might have known." He gave Karan a very cold glance. "We're coming to the point where you have to make up for what your ancestors did up there."

"What . . . do you mean?" whispered Karan.

"You've got to go back to Cinnabar and do the job properly."

"It's like the South Pole up that mountain. In what I'm wearing I wouldn't survive five minutes."

He stalked out, shortly returning with a down-filled coat, hood and trousers, and a pair of fur-lined boots. "Take these."

"Shand," said Ussarine, "I don't think—"

"Who asked you?" Shand snapped. "Karan's ancestors corrupted Carcharon, weakened the barrier between the world and the void, let savage creatures through . . . and may even have allowed the summon stone through in the first place."

His words were a series of hammer blows. Could her father's work have allowed the summon stone into Santhenar? She could not bear to think about it – it tainted every memory she had of him.

Shand was packing the food when an awful thought occurred to him; Karan saw it in his leathery face. "Aviel has never been anywhere near Carcharon. How could she know what it looks like?"

He ran into the main room; a trapdoor crashed open and Karan heard him thumping down a ladder.

"What's going on?" said Ussarine.

"I don't know." Karan was numb, incapable of thought. She stuffed the cold-weather gear into her pack. Not Cinnabar again; it was a death sentence.

Shand reappeared, panting. "The little cow!" he said, part furious and part impressed, and raced down to the workshop. Karan and Ussarine followed. He sniffed various jars and flasks, then said, "She's taken my grimoire – and used it."

"Wouldn't that be dangerous?" said Karan.

He shivered and rubbed his forearms. "There's only one scent potion Aviel could have used to locate the summon stone, and it's one of the most deadly in the grimoire. I wouldn't even be game to make the Eureka Graveolence."

"She must be a remarkable woman," said Ussarine.

"Aviel is undoubtedly remarkable but she's not a woman. She's a girl, not yet sixteen, who's afflicted with very bad luck."

"She's already used the scent potion successfully," said Karan.

"To locate the stone she'll have to keep using it, and the more she does the worse its effects will get. And the greater the risk that it will be fatal."

67

DRINK THIS!

As the delays mounted and it became clear that Unick must beat them to Casyme, Llian could see Wilm shrivelling before his eyes and shrinking into despair.

"I failed Dajaes," Wilm cried, "and I can't help Aviel either. I'm useless!"

"We'll make it," said Llian without conviction.

Wilm was incapable of taking comfort from anything. He was a desperate wild-eyed automaton who slept three hours a night and practised the seven basic strokes every hour he was not on horseback. But it was all in vain.

In Casyme they surveyed the abandoned workshop, then discovered Aviel's note on Shand's kitchen table.

"See," said Llian, putting his arm around Wilm's shoulders. "She left before he got here. Maybe days before."

Wilm perked up a little. "But where did she go?"

Llian had known before he saw the sketch. He had been expecting it ever since he'd read Mendark's notebook at the megaliths.

"Carcharon! I'll raid Shand's larder; we'll need food for a week. Then I'll give the horses a good feed of oats and a rub down. Anything you need to do?"

Wilm started. "See my mother."

"You'll have a lot to talk about. What say we leave in an hour and a half?"

"An hour will do. She'll be working."

Wilm slipped his bag of silver into his pocket and ran off. Llian got on with his work, but before the hour was over Wilm was back, his shoulders sagging.

"Something the matter?" said Llian.

"I couldn't find her; she cleans houses all over town and no one knew where she was today. I left her a note and most of the silver . . . "

"But it's not the same as seeing her."

"There's too much to explain. She'll worry."

"Yes, she will."

"How far ahead is Aviel?" said Wilm.

He was desperate for comfort but Llian could give him none. "No way of telling. We'd better go."

"All right," said Wilm, "but I'm not stopping for sleep."

"You may be able to do without it – though you look like a walking corpse – but I can't and neither can our horses. There's no point arriving in such a state that we can't do a thing for her."

They rode for what remained of the afternoon and half the night, only stopping at midnight. Wilm could not sleep. He practised and paced, paced and practised until Llian could take it no longer. The lad's despair was infecting him too, and at this rate they would both collapse before they reached Carcharon. At one in the morning Llian wrenched the stopper out of the decanter of Driftmere, poured three fingers' worth into a mug and got up.

"Drink this!" He used a commanding tone.

"What is it?" said Wilm.

"Drink the bloody stuff! One gulp."

Wilm, inured to obedience all his life, drained the brandy, choked and spluttered.

"Gahh! That's horrible."

Llian winced. The finest brandy in the world was utterly wasted on him. Llian wanted some too, but he liked good drink too much and everything had to be sacrificed to their quest. He stoppered the decanter and returned to his horse blanket.

Wilm restarted his sword practice but after a couple of minutes said, "Head's spinning. Just have a little lie-down."

Without taking his boots off he lay down and crashed over a cliff into the first proper sleep he'd had in seven nights.

Llian lay awake. What would they find at Carcharon? If Aviel was there, how could they rescue her? He had lost far more fights than he had won, and his wins had mostly been due to luck. Wilm was strong and hard-working, but he was also an untutored youth with one week of training using instructions that, for all Llian knew, could be badly flawed.

Unick was one of the most vicious street brawlers Llian had ever known, and if he got within range of those scarred fists, he would die.

Wilm was still somewhat intoxicated when Llian woke him four hours later, though the sleep had done him good: he had regained hope. They ate a hasty breakfast – one of Shand's blisteringly spicy sausages, a handful of stinky blue cheese each and a few carrots. Llian made sure

Wilm drank plenty of water and they rode on, Wilm dozing in his saddle, Llian trying to formulate a plan.

He had still come up with nothing when they reached the Forest of Gothryme in the afternoon. They camped by the Black Lake, dined on ham and eggs and apples, and bathed in the dark icy water. Afterwards Llian's skin tingled for an hour.

"We'll sleep for a few hours, though we can't ride much further."

"How far is Carcharon now?" said Wilm.

"A good few hours. The last part is quite a climb, but there'll be a bright moon for it. I want to get there before dawn."

"What about the horses?"

"Plenty of water on the plateau, and plenty of grass. They'll still be here when . . . "

They stared at one another. The sentence didn't need to be finished.

"I don't suppose I could have another drop of Driftmere?" said Wilm. "For courage."

"I could do with a bit myself." Llian poured a generous slug into each of their mugs. "We who are about to die," he said, raising the mug and inhaling the glorious bouquet, savouring it.

Wilm clinked mugs, sipped, set it down and closed his eyes for a moment. "Actually," he said, "it's not all that bad."

"Not bad!" cried Llian. "If I were Magister I'd have you put down for that."

Wilm smiled, though it quickly faded. "We probably will die up there, won't we?"

"Our hopes aren't brilliant."

"I've always been a bit of a duffer," said Wilm. "Never could get anything right."

"Oh, I don't know."

"It's true. I've never known what I wanted to do with myself."

"Knowing your path in life makes a huge difference," said Llian. "From the moment Mendark came to our door in Jepperand, when I was twelve, I knew I wanted to be a chronicler and a teller of the Great Tales. I *burned* for it."

"And now?"

"I still ache for it, particularly telling."

"But if you wanted it more than anything, you wouldn't be here now," Wilm said perceptively.

Llian did not feel the need to talk about it. Clearly, Wilm did. Llian felt that the lad was on the verge of discovering who he really was.

"And you?" Llian prompted.

"I want to stand up for what I believe in," said Wilm. "And fight for what is right."

Llian took an exploratory sip. The Driftmere exceeded his lofty expectations. He almost purred. "Will you continue with your sword practice?"

"The moment I can afford it I'm going to have lessons. I've got to do it properly." He flushed in the firelight. "Sorry! I didn't mean . . . "

Chroniclers weren't easily offended. "I just wrote down the basic strokes as I remembered them. I've no idea if they're any good." Llian took another sip and sighed. "We'd better turn in."

He was settling down by the fire when Thandiwe's words resurfaced. "About your sword . . . " said Llian.

"I still can't think of it as mine," Wilm said dreamily. "What about it?"

"Mendark was a truly great mancer, and a mancer's weapon could well be enchanted. I thought you should know."

"It might give me an edge," said Wilm, and laughed.

"You're quite the witty young blade," said Llian, and went to sleep.

68

STRONGER, FOULER, CLOSER

"Light, I need light!" gasped Aviel.

He was coming for her; he was desperate to stop her from reaching the summon stone, the source of his power.

She pounded half a dozen of the tarred boards until they split, bound the pieces into a bundle and set the end alight. The black wood blazed three feet high, making wraith shapes dance and whirl on the stone walls of the mill.

She had to get out, now. She jerked her boots on so violently that she wrenched her ankle and the pain brought tears to her eyes; today was going to be a very bad day. Aviel hobbled out to Thistle. He must have been woken by her scream, for his eyes were wide and fearful. He whinnied and tossed his head and kicked out.

"Good boy," she said, stroking his muzzle. "Practise that kick; we're going to need it."

She led him to a block of stone and used it to mount, holding her blazing bundle high. Thistle kept moving; he didn't like the flames. She directed him back to the track and turned his head downhill.

"Down," she said.

The brand burned down to a stub. She tossed it into a stream and black night enveloped her. She laid a hand on Thistle's warm neck.

"You'll smell him a mile off. You'll warn me, won't you?"

The night was overcast and she could not see a single star. Aviel had no way of telling what time it was, though she still felt dull-headed; perhaps she had not slept long at all.

How far away was he? She thought he had been in a high place, looking down, though every ridge around here was a high place. He could have been five minutes away, or five hours.

The forest was full of small noises – the steady *thump, thump* of a bounding animal, a swooping flap that might have been an owl or even a bat, the rustle of small branches rubbing in the treetops. A tiny cry cut short, perhaps the owl taking a rat.

Those sounds had nothing to do with him. He would not come quietly through the black night; he would rampage through the forest, smashing down everything in his path.

She would have plenty of warning, though Aviel did not see how it would help her. Since she had to sleep, and evidently he did not, sooner or later he must catch her, and she had no way of defending herself against such a man. Her only hope was to outrun him, but first she had to know where to run to.

She had to use the Eureka Graveolence again.

Aviel did not want to. Her first experience had been most unpleasant, and the grimoire said the effects of the Great Potions were liable to be more dangerous each time they were used. But she had no choice.

She removed the cloth-wrapped phial from the last of her belt loops and checked it with her fingers. A thread was tied around it; it was the right potion. She took the stopper out, dampened the cloth with the potion and put the phial away. She could not risk losing it if something went wrong.

Very gingerly, she sniffed the cloth.

Thud-thud. It was as if Thistle had kicked her in the belly. The pain was so agonising that she doubled over, howling and gasping. The dark forest lit up, the tree trunks glowing a luminous white and bending down to trap her in a cage of live branches.

They toppled as if a thousand trees had been mown down by a single blow from a scythe. Lightning split the sky in two, the halves opened, and she saw that ugly ruined tower again, a long way off to her left. It had to be the place.

Minutes passed before Aviel was capable of sitting upright. Her belly was aching, and the muscle she had torn the previous night caused shards of pain with every movement. The darkness closed in, though she saw that the overcast was clearing away from the west, the stars coming out. She fixed on the direction where she had seen the tower and looked for a star she could use as a pointer.

If she took the angle between the red Scorpion Nebula and the yellow Triplets it would always point north, and the broken tower had been almost due north from here. It was enough to go on. When she came close the tower should be easy to spot – it was on the peak of a horn of bare rock.

She rode through the night, using the nebula and the Triplets to maintain her heading, and after a while Thistle got the message. Aviel dozed in the saddle, and whenever she roused he was heading in the right direction.

The sun rose. She emerged from forest onto a grassy plateau, a narrow strip of sloping land bounded on her left by rugged hills rising

to high mountains, and on the right by a cliff hundreds of feet high.
The plateau ran north, sometimes widening to five or six miles, sometimes pinching down to a rind only a few hundred yards across. It made
it easy to navigate. As long as she kept to the plateau she would be
heading roughly in the right direction.

It also made it easy for her hunter to follow.

In the mid-morning Aviel had to stop for a toilet break and a brief
sleep. There was no sign of anyone behind her so she dismounted in
the most open area she could find. She lay down in her sleeping pouch,
closed her eyes and was drifting into a desperately needed sleep when
she caught her hunter's putrid odour: stronger, fouler, *closer.*

Get away while you can!

She scrabbled out of the sleeping pouch, blind with panic.
Abandoning her pot and pan, her knife and spoon and even the sleeping
pouch, she half ran, half hopped towards Thistle, hauled herself into
the saddle and snatched at the reins.

"Go, Thistle!" she screamed. "Run as though the greatest demon of
the underworld is after us."

Thistle took her at her word and bolted north along the plateau, far
faster than Aviel had ever gone before. She hunched down, hooked her
cold fingers under the saddle and tried to stay on as he leaped rivulets and
cascades, swerved around boulders that had rolled down from the rearing
mountains on her left, and tore through patches of scented shrubbery.

Finally he slowed to a canter, trotting through a forest and past a still
black lake with a half-ruined pavilion, then up to the foot of a steep,
bare ridge that no horse could have climbed.

Thistle stopped. His great chest was heaving and his flanks were
covered in overlapping trails of foam. He looked her in the eye as if to
say, *I dare go no further.*

She stroked his muzzle. "Thank you, Thistle."

Aviel dismounted stiffly, took her pack out of one saddlebag and put
it on. It contained food and water, the hammer and flask of oil and the
deadly grimoire. It was a cold day and would be a colder night. Why
had she abandoned her sleeping pouch? Even if her enemy was riding,
he must be hours behind.

She hugged Thistle around the neck. "You deserve a rest and the sweetest grass on the plateau. But keep a sharp lookout."

She limped onto the ridge and began the climb. It was very steep and at first she had to go up on her hands and knees because she wasn't able to stand up. But she knew where to go now, for she had fleetingly glimpsed the broken tower on the headlong ride.

She could not see it from here but knew she had a climb of many hours. If she could locate the stone, smash it to bits and burn it, she might stop the invasion. With any luck that would hurt her hunter too . . . No, what was she thinking? The only luck she ever had was bad.

Up she went, ever up. The path turned into a sinuous track along the top of the ridge. It was only a few feet wide and there was a deadly fall of hundreds of feet to either side into gorges choked with boulders.

The way steepened again. Steps had been cut into the top of the ridge here, though they were broken, icy and littered with frost-shattered rock. Aviel's bad ankle was so swollen that she could not stand upright and she had gone back to hands and knees. She dragged herself up the abrasive rock with bleeding fingers, but she was not going fast enough.

She kept detecting him — ever stronger, ever fouler, ever closer. He was far stronger than her and utterly obsessed. She had to rest every hundred yards now but knew he did not stop at all.

Suddenly, after a climb of about eight hours, she smelled him again and almost fell off the ridge. How could he be here already? She had to be imagining it. But she looked down and there he was, huge, red-faced, driving up at a reckless speed. He was where she had been an hour ago, though at the pace he was going he would be here in twenty minutes. Could she reach the tower in that time? At her current rate it would take her another hour.

Aviel tried to climb faster, but her strength was fading and the heart had gone out of her. What was the point in enduring all this agony when she had no hope left?

69

IT NEEDS FEEDING

He was less than four hundred yards behind her and closing fast. Aviel looked for a rock to attack him with, but the ridge was so steep that every loose rock had fallen away.

She struggled up, leaving bloody fingermarks on the stone. Now he was only a hundred yards below her, gulping noisily from a flagon. He drained it and hurled it back over his head to smash on the steps far below.

He carried a pair of little barrels in a frame on his back, and he was now close enough for Aviel to recognise them as Shand's. They contained the raw spirit he used to fortify his sweet wines, and make his fruit liqueurs.

Had she been an apprentice mancer with command of a basic fire spell she might have turned her hunter and his barrels into a living torch that would have been visible in Tolryme town, ten miles away. How she would have watched him burn! The thought shocked her. How had her life been reduced to a single urge – kill or be killed?

Twenty yards behind now. Time for desperate measures. She took the Eureka Graveolence from her belt and removed the stopper, praying that it would hurt him as much as it hurt her. She would throw it in his face, hoping the concentrated potion would make him convulse and fall to his death. She could not be sure of hitting him from a distance; she would have to wait until the last second and pray that the potion worked quickly. If it did not, he would kill her.

He looked up and for the first time she saw his face clearly. His head was enormous, bloated and purple, his face covered in dozens of scars, some infected and oozing. His nose was a scarlet segment of cauliflower, his teeth were broken and his jaw was lopsided. But his eyes were the most horrible sight she had ever seen. The eye sockets were raw red holes, as if his eyeballs had shrunk. His eyes flicked back and forth as he tried to focus, and mucus oozed down his cheeks.

Aviel gasped and her elbow struck the rock so hard that a drop of the potion splashed across her hand. She tried to wipe it off with her other sleeve but spilled another drop on her trousers. She jammed the phial back into her belt, caught a whiff of the scent potion and threw up so violently that she sprayed the rock for yards ahead.

Pain speared through the torn muscle in her belly. Her stomach churned violently, sickeningly; her head felt hot, then icy cold. The muscles in her hand began to twitch uncontrollably, then in the leg where she had spilled the potion, and the twitching spread up and down until the only parts of her body not trembling were her head and her left arm.

Now he was ten yards below. He bared his broken teeth.

"W-w-who are y-you?" she whispered. Even her tongue was twitching now.

"Gurgito Unick, at your service."

Now he was five yards down. Those awful eyes darted back and forth.

"W-w-w-w-why?" Aviel could not get anything else out.

Two yards down. He smelled as if he were rotting inside, and rolling shivers and shudders were passing through him from one end to the other. Why was he so determined to kill her? Was it to protect the summon stone, the precious bane whose drumming had made him what he was, yet was eating him alive?

Aviel had to try again or die. With her left hand, which had now begun to twitch, she slipped out the bung of the Eureka Graveolence phial. As he bent over her his eyes slipped out of focus and she flicked the phial, spattering drops of the scent potion across his upper lip.

The drumming sounded thunderously, shaking the ground and flaking off chips of rock, which went skidding down the sides of the ridge. Unick's eyes opened so wide that his shrunken eyeballs protruded, then he reeled back, throwing up his arms. The weight of the barrels on his back overbalanced him and he crashed down the broken steps, landing so hard that Aviel felt sure he would have caved the back of his head in.

But she could not take advantage of his fall. Her twitching muscles were totally uncoordinated. After a minute he rolled over, almost toppling over the edge, but his luck was as good as hers was bad and another thrash took him back to the centre of a step. He sat up, staring at her blearily. Blood was streaming down the side of his head.

"What ... did ... you ... do?" He had to force each word out.

"S-s-scent potion. I used it to f-find the summon stone."

"Why?"

She told him about the Merdrun and their plans. Unick rubbed his head, then stared at the bloody smears on his hand. He was trembling worse than before. He wiped his hand on the seat of his pants and stood up, staring towards where the ruined tower stood. The drumming was fading.

"They'll never get past me," said Unick. "All the power of the summon stone will be mine."

"Malien said never use near mancery near it. It's got to be destroyed." She should not have told him; he would kill her for certain now.

"And *you* think you can do that?" he sneered.

She did not reply. She could not speak.

"The source," he whispered. "Oh, let it be up there."

"W-w-what's the matter?"

"Lost the source ... after I used my devices. It's tearing me apart."

"What d-devices?"

He partly withdrew one from his pack – a long thin brass tube with a cluster of needle-like blue crystals in one end – then shoved it back. "Origin."

The next, a thicker, shorter brass tube with paired red crystals at the end, was Identity. She had visualised it the first time she had been connected to him; he had used it to locate her. The final device, a stubby brass tube the size of a large beer tankard, with a single dark crystal on the end, was Command.

"What are they for?" Her tongue wasn't twitching so badly now.

"Greater mancery than has ever been imagined. Get up!"

"C-can't move."

The tiny eyes flicked back and forth, focused on her again. "Why not?"

"Spilled the scent potion on myself."

"Pathetic little fool! No one can teach themself mancery."

If he thought she was no threat at all, it might give her a chance.

He rose, picked her up, swayed towards the edge on the left and recovered only to sway even more dangerously towards the right. The hairs stood up on the back of her neck.

"Where are you taking me?"

He rubbed his eyes and worked his thick neck back and forth, struggling to focus. He was half blind close up.

"The stone needs feeding."

The twitching faded and she felt a splintery pain in her ankle. She cried out.

Holding her with one arm, he yanked up the leg of her trousers and stared at her swollen ankle. "Disgusting twist-foot! Should have been put down at birth."

Aviel felt the heat moving up her throat to her face. "I didn't ask to be born like this. But you're a monster – and you've created yourself."

He thumped her in the ribs. "You know nothing about me."

"What did you mean, *it needs feeding?*"

"The drumming is also a call. The stone wants power, but first it has to feed."

He staggered up the broken steps, lurching from side to side. Most people would have climbed on hands and knees but he seemed to have no fear. She had enough for both of them.

Finally she saw their destination ahead. The ruined, nine-sided tower, perched on the highest, steepest, most windswept and barren ridge in all Bannador. It loomed above them, unreal, deformed, the product of one man's insane obsession.

The ridge and tower wavered before her eyes and grew solid again. She knew where she was now. This was Carcharon, a terrible place where in ages past profane experiments had been carried out by reckless men, with tragic consequences.

Was that why the summon stone was hidden here? Had it been attracted to this evil place? Or was Carcharon evil *because* the stone was here?

She could sense something else now. A strangeness in the air and a warping of the ground, as if the great mancery done here in ages past had corrupted even the rock from which the ridge was made. Her stomach roiled and churned.

Unick stopped suddenly, gasping for breath. His breath reeked of spirits; she was half-drunk on his foul second-hand air. Feeling was coming back to her lower limbs, though. Was there anything she could do to save herself?

Do not use mancery near it, Malien had written. *Under no circumstances attempt to draw upon the power of the source – this could be catastrophic.*

Unick was a deluded fool and he was going to cause a disaster. She had to stop him. This must be why she had been given her special gift. And why, after she ran away from her family, she had been taken in by Shand, the only person in Bannador who could have helped her to learn the use of her gift. And why Malien's letters had come to her. It was meant to be.

It would be a fight to the death. A fight she had to win to keep the Merdrun out of Santhenar.

But first she had to save herself from being sacrificed.

70

A POISONED PLACE

Unick carried Aviel into Carcharon after dark. The drumming was now so loud that it shook the stone beneath their feet, and it appeared to be beating inside his head as well, each thump wobbling his bloodshot eyes in their wet sockets.

"It's here!" he said thickly.

The place was littered with splintered timbers and fragments of copper roofing, some melted. There was a large ice-filled depression in the floor, as if the stone had softened long ago, then had been moulded like jelly. A warped stone stair ran down into darkness.

The walls were deformed as though parts had flowed and set again, and there was a strangeness about the whole tower that she could not fathom. It was different each time she looked at it, and from the corner of her eye things seemed to shift, as if Carcharon wasn't quite of this world. It was the most unsettling place Aviel had ever been.

Now desperate for drink, Unick broached the first of the kegs by driving his fist into the top. He tilted the little barrel and gulped a cupful of raw spirit, gasping.

"Aaahh!" he gasped. "Good grog."

He left her to search the nine-sided tower, but soon returned. "Where . . . is . . . it?" he bellowed.

For the next few hours he huddled in the icy depression, drinking until he was almost mindless, his filthy pack beside him. The ends of his three devices protruded from its open top. Every so often black flares radiated from the dark crystal in the tip of Command.

"Power is flowing from the stone," he said to himself, "but where is it going?"

The Merdrun are taking it, thought Aviel. They're getting ready to invade. She could not work out exactly how many weeks had passed of the original eight, but it must be close to six.

An owl flew in and circled under the broken roof. Unick fired two ragged blasts at it with Command, though he was shaking so wildly that there was little chance of hitting it. A single pinfeather spiralled down, as if the owl had dropped it to taunt him, then it flew out.

"Death bird," he croaked. "Lives in haunted places. Comes to remind me I've got to pay."

She felt sure he was right; she kept seeing wispy figures slipping in and out of the walls. Ghosts, watching Unick. They paid no attention to her.

"Where . . . is. . . the . . . summon stone?" he roared.

He took another pull at his barrel, hefted it onto his shoulder and staggered down into the lower levels. She heard him blundering about, cursing and gasping and crashing into walls, then there was silence.

He thought that finding the source would ease his torment, but Aviel suspected his troubles would double the moment he located it. And hers too. The stone had drawn him here from a hundred miles away, and not for his benefit.

She sat down to think things through. She had been shying away from the obvious for ages because thinking about such things was foreign to her nature, but it was time to face it. Unick would never allow her to destroy the summon stone, yet that was the point of everything she had done since reading Malien's letter. He was planning to feed her to it.

So she had to kill him first.

The quickest way would be to steal his knife when he was dead drunk and cut his throat, though Aviel felt sick at the thought. It would live with her for the rest of her life.

But at least it would be quick. If she did it right it would disable him within seconds. But what if her nerve failed and he caught her? What if she made a mess of it and failed to kill him?

The drumming in Unick's head was so loud that Aviel could hear it all the time now. He was out of his mind from it.

"Where is it?" he screamed.

He staggered up the steps, hefted the second barrel onto his shoulder, turned to go down again but slipped on a broken piece of stone and the barrel flew out of his hands. It crashed down the steps, slammed into the wall and broke open.

Unick howled and hurled himself after it. He lay on the landing, lapping at the dusty stone until his tongue bled, but less than a cup of muddy spirits remained. The rest had soaked into the cracks between the stones and disappeared.

"Where is the summon stone?" he shrieked.

Nothing else could ease his torment, which was worse than ever now that he had no way of staying drunk. Unick was trembling so violently that he could barely walk; he kept throwing up blood and seeing nightmare visions. He stalked up and down, pointing his Origin device in every direction, fruitlessly trying to locate the summon stone in the maze under Carcharon.

He came crawling up the stairs, gasping and holding his belly. "Aftersickness. Worse than . . . ever felt. This . . . a poisoned place."

Aviel said nothing.

"Potion!" he snapped. "Give it here."

She handed him the phial with the thread tied around it.

Unick studied it suspiciously, then shook the last of the Eureka Graveolence, two drops, onto his filth-encrusted palm.

"That's way too much," said Aviel. "It only takes a sniff."

She caught a whiff of burned bones and felt a throbbing pain behind her temples. Unick snorted a drop up each nostril. The drumming roared; his feet pounded up and down, then he convulsed so violently that he turned an involuntary backwards somersault and hit the floor.

He got up, clutched at his belly and heaved, but he had eaten nothing in a week and all he brought up was blood streaked with green bile. He wiped his mouth on his sleeve and laughed maniacally.

Taking Aviel by the wrist, he jerked her so violently that it felt as though her arm had come out of its socket, then dragged her down the steps. She went thumping down on her bottom, her bad ankle twisting under her. He descended four levels, struck the wall with the side of his fist and a section swung open. He went through into darkness.

He released her; she heard a sizzling sound and blue light throbbed from the Origin device. He shone it around in all directions, the flaring light picking his features out from below. He looked demonic.

Unick caught her wrist again and continued down, following a tortuous path through a myriad of passages. Aviel, fearing that she would never find her way out, surreptitiously dripped scent from one of her belt phials, then another.

"Shh!" he said.

Now his movements became exaggerated, caricature-like. Aviel could no longer hear the drumming, though she could hear a repetitive rasping, as if one stone was sliding over another. A circle of dark red light appeared, outlining a deep shaft or well. She could not see anything at the bottom.

Suddenly Unick caught her about the waist and leaped into the shaft. Aviel screamed. His free hand slapped across her mouth and nose. He landed on a projecting block a yard down with a thump that rattled her teeth, sprang to another block around and down from the first, then another and another.

The shaft was like a spiral staircase with most of the treads missing – any misstep and they would plunge fifty feet to the bottom. He hit the floor hard, staggered through a stone slot, hauled her around a U-shaped bend and into a long gloomy chamber lit by a dull red glow. The nearer end of the chamber was lobed, like an arm ending in stubby fingers.

Unick thrust Aviel away from him and she fell to a stone floor, though it was not paving, as the upper levels of Carcharon had been. Here the stone appeared to have been eaten away.

"It's here," he whispered. *"It's here!"*

The glow brightened to a crimson radiance, outlining something near the far end of the chamber. And the summon stone was nothing like she had expected.

Malien had said to smash it to bits and burn the pieces, so Aviel had expected a small rock, a crystal or a stone artefact.

But it consisted of three tall slabs of stone, each seven feet high and two feet across. Two of the stones were upright and touching, while the third lay across their tops to form a closed trilithon, one with no space between the uprights. A deep red light ebbed out from the core of the stones, washing everything in the chamber blood red.

"The source!" sighed Unick.

He picked Aviel up, crushing her face into his reeking armpit, carried her to the three-lobed cavity at the other end of the chamber and tossed her into the middle lobe. Turning back towards the trilithon, he drew the Command device from his rucksack.

"Don't use mancery near it!" cried Aviel.

He pointed it at the trilithon. "I command—"

The crimson light flared and he was hurled back against the wall. He rose shakily, made an adjustment to the device and tried again. Again it flung him back. He made another adjustment and tried a third time. This time the trilithon flared so brightly that Aviel was dazzled. When she could see again Unick lay on the floor, unconscious, and the Command device was in a dozen pieces, though she felt sure he could put it back together.

She had to act quickly; he no longer needed her.

Smash it and burn the fragments. But Aviel was afraid to go near the trilithon, and her hammer was useless. Even if she'd had a sledgehammer, she would not be able to break such massive stones. How could it ever be destroyed?

Feed it!

It was a harsh, alien voice – female, she thought. Aviel shuddered. Was it the magiz Karan had seen?

Unick got up and dragged her towards the trilithon, smiling dreamily. Had the summon stone taken control of him? She struggled but he was far too strong. This was it, she thought with a dreadful calm – she was going to die.

The trilithon flared and the drumming began again, so deep that the three stones vibrated against one another and the walls of the cavern shook.

He stopped six feet away, tremors racking him and sweat forming puddles around each filthy foot. She sensed that he was afraid, that the summon stone was nothing like he had expected either. He raised her above his head. She tried to kick him in the face but could not reach.

"It has to be fed," he said, and hurled Aviel at the trilithon.

She was trying to cover her face with her arms when she struck an invisible membrane that depressed under her weight and sprang back, catapulting her at Unick. Her shoulder struck him in the throat and he went down, choking.

She crawled away. What had just happened?

Feed it!

"What with?" gasped Unick.

Start with a finger.

He drew his knife and headed after Aviel.

Not ... corrupt ... enough. Your finger!

Now, for the first time since she had met him, Unick showed fear. "But I've helped it to wake. And look what it's cost me."

First a finger, best given in terror.

He retreated, slipped in his oily sweat and fell to one knee, then pushed himself up to a kneeling position and raised his hands. The palm of his left hand was bloody. He looked down at it, then up at the trilithon. His face was distorted, his little eyes starting out of their red sockets. He slowly put his left hand on the floor and extended his little finger.

"Don't do it," said Aviel.

Unick slammed the knife down on his finger, severing it. He bared his teeth, picked the bloody finger up and in a swift movement tossed it at the trilithon. It burned to smoke before it reached the surface, and the smoke was drawn to the point where the three stones met.

The drumming, which had been sounding all this time, cut off. Unick toppled over and lay on his side, his knees drawn up. Blood dribbled from the stump of his finger. His eyes were open and staring, though he did not seem able to move.

But Carcharon now seemed disturbingly alive and only tenuously connected to the rest of the world. What was it connected to?

71

NOT SUCH BASIC STROKES

Llian had not been to Carcharon since the Time of the Mirror and it had been bad enough then. Now it was so polluted by waste mancery that even he could sense it. They were still hundreds of yards below the tower, on the steep path, but the air felt thicker here and had a visible shimmer.

"Careful now," he said over his shoulder to Wilm. "Unick might be watching."

"What about Aviel?" Wilm said desperately. "Do you think she could still—"

"I don't know, Wilm. But we can't stop hoping."

It was a miserable day — overcast, windy and exceedingly cold. Patches of black ice glazed the rudely cut steps.

Llian studied the sky. "Looks like snow."

"Bit early in the year, isn't it?"

"Not up here. We're three thousand feet higher than Casyme, and it's been known to snow here on Midsummer Day. I hate this place!"

Some of the worst moments of his life had occurred here. Ten years ago Rulke had held Karan prisoner in the tower and Tensor had ordered an archer to shoot her dead. Llian had been alone, isolated and in shackles, accused of betraying her to Rulke, and back then none of the allies, except for thirteen-year-old Lilis, had believed in him.

What were they getting into? Why had Karan burned those old family papers? Whatever her ancestors had done here, it must have been really bad. Had Basunez helped wake the stone the first time, more than five hundred years ago?

They reached the top. The wind was strong here, whirling powdery snow from drifts into their faces. They crept up to the tower and through the broken doors. The upper level, where Llian had once challenged Rulke to a telling competition and beaten him, was empty. The only sign Unick had been here was an empty spirit barrel with the top smashed in.

Wilm started to speak. Llian put a finger across his lips and led him down, then out into the walled yard that extended from the rear of the tower up the ridge for hundreds of yards. It looked like a rowing boat with its bow in the air and its stern weighed down by the hideous tower.

The floor of the yard was the native rock here, an intensely hard, violet-coloured gabbro. There was moss in shady places and lichen on parts of the wall, but no other plant had taken root in the accumulated dust. Carcharon was too cold and hostile to support any higher form of life. Including us, Llian thought.

He drew Wilm behind a broken wall where they could not be overlooked from the tower.

"What are we doing out here?" fretted Wilm. "We've got to go after Aviel."

"This is a strange and dangerous place."

"But you know it well. Where would Unick be holding her?"

"I don't know. It all seems different now."

"How can an empty tower be different?"

"That's what bothers me."

Llian stepped in a scatter of gravel and something went clinking across the ground. "What's that?"

"It's a ring," said Wilm, handing it to him.

A thick, unusually heavy ring – a man's ring, surely, though sized for a slender finger. "I've seen it before." The outside of the ring was unmarked but on the inside Llian made out a number of glyphs in what he knew to be the Charon syllabary. "This is Maigraith's! Rulke gave it to her, and it's a powerful talisman. How did it come to be here?"

He slipped it on his little finger, where it fitted snugly.

"The wind is really howling," said Wilm.

"It never stops. Only a madman would want to come here."

Llian knew that Carcharon had been a strange, ghost-ridden place long before Basunez had bankrupted his family by building this tower. Who had been here before, and what had they done in the unexplored levels far below Basunez's lowest basement? And did they have anything to do with the summon stone?

Suddenly everything he looked at was surrounded by a faint rainbow. Was Unick working mancery? Or was it the ring? Llian slipped it off and the coloured outlines vanished.

He put it on and was gazing around him when he noticed scratches on a tilted slab of stone, a section broken off a longer block. Scratches in a hand that was very familiar to him, for he had read hundreds of pages of it, written on paper, parchment, beaten copper and even polished stone. It was Mendark's hand, though it was hard to read on the raw stone. Llian closed his eyes and felt the marks with his fingertips, trying to work out the meaning.

A shape under his fingers made his heart race – the jagged Merdrun glyph. "These marks on the stone," said Llian. "Mendark made them."

The scratches weren't fresh but neither did they look ancient; they weren't overgrown by lichen.

"The last time Mendark was here was just before he died," he added. "Could it be a warning?"

He turned over the longer section of the slab and found more writing.

Can the secret of mancery protect humanity from the Merdrun?
  Or is it designed to raise the summon stone to the final stage and open the way for them?
  Was I duped in this too?
  Be warned. Be afraid!

It started to rain, the wind driving it at Wilm's face in stinging drops that were rapidly turning to sleet. Mist formed, whirled about and disappeared. He stamped his feet. Why was Llian taking so long? And where were Unick and Aviel?

He drew the black sword and practised the basic strokes, but now they were clumsy and ugly; his arm had forgotten the lessons. How could he have thought to learn sword fighting from a few scribbled notes?

"Every minute we waste—" said Wilm.

"I know," said Llian. "But this place is a labyrinth, and I need to sort it out in my mind before we go down." He huddled in the most sheltered corner of the yard, his lips moving.

Wilm prowled about, the black sword thrust out, ready to avenge Dajaes and spit Unick the moment he appeared. Ahead of him a doorway loomed; he had not noticed it earlier. It was stone, on heavy iron hinges, and open just enough for him to put his head through. He peered in and saw an empty room, though a foul smell lingered. Unick had been here.

Wilm slipped inside and across to the further door, which stood open, and saw stairs running up and down. He crept down, the darkness thickening with every step.

One step, two, three, four. He caught the faintest hint of citrus oil and his heart leaped. Even in this cold, the scent would not last long. Aviel could still be alive. He edged down into the gloom, reached a landing and went down another couple of steps. It was almost dark here. Now he caught a different scent – black pine, and a few steps below that, cedar oil. She must have laid a scent trail in the hope that someone would come after her.

The drumming sounded and the steps quivered underfoot, a deep, slow reverberation. He went a few more steps and his foot slipped in something thick, almost jelly-like. He sniffed it.

Blood!

Had Unick discovered the trail and killed her as coldly as he had killed Dajaes? Despair overwhelmed Wilm but he had to fight it. One little patch of blood meant nothing. She was down here and he wasn't going to fail her.

He went down another flight, then another. It was utterly dark, dank and oppressive; he felt almost as confined as he had in the cramped tunnel into Pem-Y-Rum. The drumming was all around him now. Everything was vibrating, even the bones of his skull, and he had an unscratchable itch in his left inner ear.

A scraping sound, like a boot dragging across rough stone, was followed by a hissing breath and a stench he would never forget. The reek he had smelled when Unick had—

Wilm could not afford to go there; not now. He thrust the black sword into the dark. The dragging sound grew louder, the stench fouler and so thick that he could barely breathe. The vibration was stronger here; it felt as though the walls were moving in and out.

He was panting. Something brushed his arm and panic swelled; he was trapped, slowly suffocating. He turned round and round but could not tell which way was up and which was down. Then, in an instant, claustrophobia overwhelmed him. The walls felt as though they were moving in, the ceiling dropping on him, the air being sucked from the passage. He had to get out!

He tripped on steps that ran upwards and bolted up them, despising himself for a coward, a loser and a failure but unable to stop. After several flights he burst up into the empty room near the stone door. He stood there for a second, gasping.

"Hand over the manuscript," said a man's voice from outside.

"Be damned," said Llian.

Clang – a sword glancing off stone. And Llian didn't have a sword. He was under attack!

Llian was so preoccupied with mentally trying to recreate the labyrinthine lower levels of Carcharon that he did not realise Wilm had disappeared. The wind was rising, the sleet turning to snow and, hunched in the most sheltered corner he could find, neither did he notice the lean, cloaked figure of Jundelix Rasper, Snoat's most reliable assassin, enter the yard.

Rasper's short hair was thick but white; his lean face was tanned to the colour of tea. He must have been fifty though he moved like a younger man. He drew a slender knife, so sharp that it could slit a throat without its owner noticing, and crept towards Llian.

A concealed door opened on the far side of the yard and Unick slipped out, pack on his back. Llian did not notice him either; Unick was upwind. Rasper gagged, though it was inaudible over the wind.

Unick drew the stubby brass Command device and pointed it at Llian. Rasper sprang, slashing at Unick, who blasted at him. Rasper swayed aside and kicked the Command device out of Unick's hand, then whirled and ran at Llian, trapping him in the corner.

"Hand over the manuscript."

"Be damned," said Llian, feeling for his blunt knife.

Unick came after him, moving in on the left as Rasper approached from the right. Llian waved his feeble weapon in front of him, cursing his own inattention. Where was Wilm? Had they already finished him?

Wilm burst out through the narrow opening of the stone door and went for Rasper, who was closest. He whirled and in a fluid movement hurled his slitting knife at Wilm's throat. Llian let out an involuntary cry.

The black sword flashed up into the fourth basic stroke, and the ten thousand times Wilm had practised it in the past week must have ingrained the movement, for he executed it flawlessly. The flat of the blade covered his throat; the hurtling knife struck it full on and the thin blade snapped.

Wilm moved instantly into the second basic stroke. Rasper drew his sword and lunged to gut him. Wilm sidestepped, swung the black sword with all his might, and Rasper barely ducked in time as the blade cut a tonsure through his white hair. He turned and ran into the sleety snow, vanishing from sight.

Llian didn't have time to admire Wilm's swordplay. Unick had put the Command device back together and was pointing it at him. It was the weapon with which he had killed Dajaes.

"Die, you bastard!" he said thickly.

But before he could fire, Wilm thrust his sword out in the sixth basic stroke and it pierced through the back of Unick's thigh to the bone. He howled and flailed around, dislodging the dark crystal at the front of the Command device. His pack fell off, landed on a block of stone, and the Identity device broke apart. The Origin device skidded across the stone-surfaced yard, caught on a projection and the tubes separated, exposing the device's innards.

Unick, blood pouring down the back of his thigh, hopped after the Origin device. Wilm stood over it and swung the sword back.

"This blade can cut rock," he said softly. "It'll chop you in half like a lump of suet."

He leaped at Unick, clearly intending to avenge Dajaes. The drumming became a shuddering roar, though for once it did not affect Llian.

Unick's fists balled like small melons. He had recently lost the little finger of his left hand, for the stump was scabbed and oozing blood. He let out a screech; he was going into one of his berserker furies and Llian did not see how Wilm could deal with it.

Llian ran three steps and swung the heavy manuscript bag by its strap at Unick's head. It slammed into his right ear, knocking him off his feet, and when he tried to get up his right leg refused to cooperate. He looked down at the blood, shook his head as if he could not believe this was happening to him, then ran in a scuttling limp up the yard and in through the stone door.

"Well done!" said Llian. "Yet again you've saved my life."

Wilm was shaking but managed a wobbly smile. "I can't believe I did that."

He lifted the Origin device, which looked remarkably heavy. Its brass tubes had separated, revealing a glass cylinder almost full of quicksilver. Wilm thrust it into his pack.

"Believe it," said Llian. "Keep watch while I take a look at this."

He picked up the Command device and put the dark crystal back in its socket. The drumming sounded, soft but compelling. Could he destroy the summon stone with the device? Yes, he could. He must! Now!

"Come on," cried Llian. "We're going down to the stone. I know the way now."

"Are . . . you sure?"

Fury flared. "How dare you question me!" Llian swung the device towards Wilm. "Are you with me or . . . ?"

Wilm froze, his eyes searching Llian's face. Llian felt a momentary unease but the drumming sounded again, overwhelming all restraint. With the Command device he could blast the wretched summon stone to dust and keep the Merdrun out for ever. He ran for the door.

No, Daddy!

Llian stopped dead. The drumming was gone and so was the compulsion. "Sulien?" She had never spoken to him mind to mind before. "Sulien, where are you? Are you all right?"

No answer, of course. He lacked the gift.

He looked around. Wilm was gaping at him and Llian realised that he was still holding the Command device, that he had threatened Wilm with it, that under the influence of the drumming he had actually imagined *he* could use it. He shuddered and dropped it in the snow. A burning flush made its way up his face.

"Sorry, Wilm. The drumming . . . "

"Yes," said Wilm, watching him warily. "I saw."

"I heard Sulien's voice." Shame crushed him; his nine-year-old daughter had far more sense than he did.

"Is she all right?"

"I couldn't tell." Her contacting him was troubling. Llian desperately wanted to reach her, speak to her and make sure she was all right, but he had no way of returning her call. "We'd better go after Aviel."

"Yes," Wilm said hoarsely.

Then Rasper reappeared out of the whirling snow, and this time he had four subordinates, all armed with swords longer than Wilm's.

72

HIS LEGS ARE GOING

"I can't believe how changed Carcharon is," said Shand, peering at the ruined tower through eyes slitted against the icy wind. "It . . . feels as though it's part of another world."

Karan was profoundly shocked. She had been thinking the same thing. "It feels like the sickest part of the void I ever saw."

"What have we got ourselves into?" said Ussarine.

"What have Karan's corrupt ancestors got us into?" said Shand, though mildly this time.

"Is there anything you can do?" said Ussarine.

Only in dire circumstances did Shand practise mancery, and then with the greatest reluctance. But Karan had seen him do remarkable things, and despite his protestations of being "past it", she felt sure that he still could do them.

"The power at work here is way beyond my ken," he said.

They were half an hour's climb below the tower and the weather was closing in rapidly. Scudding snow showers were starting to blur Carcharon into grey.

"We'd better get a move on," said Ussarine, studying the weather.

"If we ever get out of here," said Karan, "I'm going to tear Carcharon down, stone by stone." She considered the monumental labour that would be. "No, I'll bring a hundred barrels of blasting powder up and blow the wretched place to bits."

"I'll help you carry them," said Shand. "Stay here. I'm going to take a look."

He laboured up and out of sight.

"He's afraid I'll betray him," said Karan.

"Via the stigma?" said Ussarine.

"Yes."

"I don't believe it for a second."

"Thank you. But ... I'm starting to think that I'll have to go to Cinnabar again."

"How?"

"I don't know. The second time I used Malien's spell, the magiz was waiting with traps set. It'd be suicidal to use it a third time."

"And yet?" said Ussarine.

"If I don't go back and kill the magiz, will Sulien ever be safe? Will I?"

"There's no point going back to Cinnabar unless you have a new way to attack." Ussarine looked up. "Shand's waving; he wants us to go up." She strode up the track.

Mummy, where are you? Mummy, you've got to answer.

Sulien's link was full of child-like bewilderment. Why wasn't her mother answering? Then, desperately, *Mummy, are you all right?*

Karan doubled over, digging her fists into her belly, trying to distract herself from one pain with another. It did not work; she could not take any more. Surely it could not hurt to reassure Sulien ... just one sentence? One word.

She began to make the link, then forced herself to stop. Before she could go back to Cinnabar she had to convince Malien to unblock her gift for mancery. Malien's dire warnings surfaced but Karan forced them down again. It simply had to work.

She slogged after Ussarine and reached the tower, now an outline through whirling snow.

"I think we should go in a rush," said Ussarine, "just in case."

Shand was grey-faced and breathing hard. "If I drop dead, don't try to revive me."

Karan clapped him on the shoulder. "I dare say you'll live to a greater age than I will."

"Given that you've got both Aachim and Faellem blood, that's debatable."

"Well, I've got neither," said Ussarine, "so I win!"

Shand chuckled. Karan managed a smile. "Let's go."

The wind dropped momentarily and she heard the clashing of swords, followed by a familiar, desperate cry.

"That's Llian!"

She ran, drawing her knife. The doors were open and she burst through them, sliding on the icy floor almost to the stair. She looked around wildly. Where was he? The wind had resumed with greater ferocity, howling around the battered tower and through the window holes.

Ussarine came flying in and went skidding across the room towards the steep stair. If she fell down it she was liable to break her neck. Karan grabbed her outstretched left arm and heaved, and went spinning around Ussarine like a small red moon orbiting a giant dark planet.

"Thanks," said Ussarine.

Shand entered less precipitously. Close by, swords clashed. "They're out in the yard!"

Karan raced through the partly open door. The wind blasted snow into her eyes and for a few seconds she could not see. She rubbed it away.

Llian was on his back, desperately trying to hold off a snarling Unick, who was trying to strangle him. Wilm, a few yards away, was attempting to keep five armed men at bay. They were led by a wiry white-haired fellow, and all wore shoulder badges indicating that they were Snoat's men.

Karan left the five to Shand and Ussarine, and ran at Unick. Llian's face was purple. She leaped into the air and drove both feet at the back of Unick's head.

His face slammed into the rock with a crunching sound. Karan hoped it was his neck; if ever a man deserved to die, he did, though she suspected it was only his cauliflower nose. And his huge hands were still around Llian's neck.

She took hold of one shoulder and heaved, trying to drag him off. Unick rolled over and let Llian go, and she saw his ghastly face close up. His nose was gushing blood, his face was scarred and bloated, and his flip-flopping red eyes were one of the most sickening sights she had ever seen. She froze, staring at him. Beside him, Llian choked and gasped.

Unick's hands closed around Karan's shins, then he wrenched her legs apart so hard that she went over backwards. He came to his knees, still holding her shins. She kicked furiously but could not break his grip. The stump of his missing finger made bloody smears on her calf. Karan groped for her knife but it wasn't there; it had fallen out of its sheath in the struggle.

"Shand?" she cried.

He did not hear; he was fighting one of Snoat's five. Ussarine was defending against three more, and Wilm was trying to hold off their white-haired leader.

Unick came to his feet, changed his grip and she realised what he planned to do – swing her around by the shins and smash her head into the wall. She tried to double up and punch him in the face. He laughed and fended her off. He began to swing her, and there was nothing she could do to save herself; he was far too strong.

Llian scrabbled across, caught Unick's left leg with both hands and sank his teeth into the back of his calf. Unick howled and let go of Karan, who went flying over a pile of tumbled stones into a snowdrift. Unick flailed at Llian, who bit him again then reached up and punched the bloody wound on the back of his thigh.

Unick shrieked, toppled, recovered and hopped away into the snow, blood pouring from his nose, his calf and the back of his thigh.

Karan stared at Llian, who was gagging and spitting and scrubbing his mouth with the back of his hand. There was no time for a reunion. Shand had just gone down and his attacker was looming over him, sword raised for the death stroke.

Karan snatched up a fist-sized piece of rubble and hurled it at the man's head. It went wide and struck him on the right elbow. The sword fell from his hand and hit the ground point first between Shand's ribs and his arm. The man threw back his head in silent agony – the rock had struck him on the funny bone. Shand caught the hilt of the sword as it toppled towards his face, thrust it up into the man's middle and rolled out of the way as he fell.

"You all right?" said Karan.

"Bastard stabbed me in the arse," said Shand. "Left cheek."

"Want me to take a look at it?"

"No, thank you."

She looked around, dizzy from all that had happened. Ussarine had efficiently dispatched two of her opponents and now took on the third man, but he turned, snatched up the Command device and ran.

"Send word to Snoat!" said the white-haired leader, who was still fighting Wilm.

Wilm had a small patch of blood on his right shoulder and a cut on his chin. The white-haired man was wounded in the left ribs, and there was a smear of blood across his hair.

He lunged at Wilm, who barely evaded the blow. His own sword strokes were starting to look clumsy and he was panicking. Karan could not imagine how he had lasted this long against a man who was clearly a professional killer.

But the white-haired man was also middle-aged. He'd had a week-long pursuit and an exhausting climb at the end of it, and perhaps he was more used to slitting throats in the dark than fighting a long duel face to face. Karan, who had seen more fighting than she cared to remember, saw what Wilm could not.

"His legs are going, Wilm! He's tired; he can't take much more. Wear the bastard down!"

Wilm's legs did not seem tired. He was just a youth and used to hard labour. He flashed her a strained smile, parried the next blow, then lunged and pinked the white-haired man on the breastbone.

It wasn't a serious injury, but it could have been, and the white-haired man knew it. He checked and Karan saw the moment that he started to panic. He tried to fight it and went at Wilm with a series of furious blows, but his knees were wobbling, the heavy sword had exhausted him and none of his blows went quite where he wanted.

Wilm had his confidence back. He wielded the black sword as though it was an extension of his arm – he parried three blows then struck between the white-haired killer's ribs and into his heart. He fell back, dead.

Wilm stood there for a moment, panting, his face covered in sweat. Then, in a moment that showed his quality, he bent, closed the dead man's eyes and stood before him for a minute, head bowed, acknowledging his victim.

Karan's knees were wobbly; she was too old for this. She staggered across and shook his hand. "Thank you for rescuing Llian. And for all you've done for him."

"No more than he did for me," Wilm said simply.

Karan wondered at that but did not ask. "Did you find Aviel?"

"I think Unick has her trapped below. At the . . . summon stone."

"We'd better do something about it."

She surveyed the yard with its litter of bodies. Ussarine was uninjured. Shand was pressing a rag against his backside and grimacing.

Finally she turned to Llian, who had put on his pack and was watching her anxiously. There was blood on his face and purpling bruises where Unick had encircled his throat with those great hands, almost finishing him. He looked exhausted, and a little afraid.

Karan noticed a familiar ring on his little finger. "That's Maigraith's ring! Where did you get it?"

"It was in the dirt, just over there." He pointed. "Come here."

Karan hesitated for a second. But against all expectations he was alive, and safe, and she knew he had done his best. And he had done what he'd set out to do – found the summon stone for them. She took a flying leap into his arms. He caught her, staggering backwards, and held her tightly.

Then Llian's left hand went around her neck and Maigraith's enchanted ring, which had once belonged to Rulke, touched Fiachra's chain, which had been made by Rulke's enemy Shuthdar. The ring lit with an eerie yellow radiance, and Karan felt something wake in it.

The whole of Carcharon answered, echoing the same yellow radiance. It waved up from every stone, every twisted metal fragment of the ruined roof, and every one of those weird projections in the outside walls.

The drumming returned, louder yet deeper than ever.

There came a cry of agony from the depths.

Then a gate opened in front of Karan and Llian – an oval, shimmering tunnel – and humid air gushed out of it, instantly condensing to fog. The tunnel contracted then expanded again, sucking the air in. It lifted Llian off his feet and tumbled him backwards, his arms still wrapped around Karan, into the gate. She felt a blow to the belly, like being struck with a fast-moving ball, and clung to him more tightly.

Llian went "Oof!"

Then they hurtled into darkness.

73

IT WAS WORTH THE SACRIFICE

As Wilm stared into the whirling gate, every hair on his head and body stood up. It was awe-inspiring yet terrifying. He could feel the power all around him; the hilt of the black sword was crackling and sparks kept jumping from it to the copper sheath.

His unease was mirrored on Ussarine's face. Shand was looking into the gate too, his jaw knotted. Wilm, who had read every part of the *Tale of the Mirror* that featured Shand, knew that he had not only passed through gates, he had actually created at least one. So why was he looking so anxious?

"My ring!" a woman screamed, and staggered out of the ruins.

Thin almost to gauntness, she looked as though she had lost a lot of weight in a short time. Wilm saw shoulder-length brown hair, matted and tangled, and a long face that might have been attractive once. Tears streaked her cheeks – tears of desperation, swiftly turning to fury. She stumbled towards the gate, reaching out with one thin arm.

"Maigraith?" cried Shand. He limped towards her, his arms out-stretched. "Maigraith, stop!"

She ran past him as if he wasn't there and leaped into the gate. It flared bright, cleared inside, and Wilm saw a dark alien city – tall towers, gigantic, barely supported domes, sweeping arches and sinu-ous aerial stairways – at the end of a long tunnel. Maigraith turned, her gaze passing over Wilm, Ussarine and even Shand with seeming indifference, then shook her fist over her head and the gate winked out of existence.

The yellow radiance streaming up from every part of Carcharon vanished, and the drumming cut off.

"This is bad," said Shand. "This is very bad."

"What was that place?" whispered Wilm.

"Alcifer! Rulke's abandoned city."

"Will Karan and Llian be all right there?"

"Not with Maigraith hunting them."

"What are you going to do?"

Shand let out a bray of mirthless laughter. "Alcifer is two hundred and fifty miles south of here – a fortnight's ride."

"Are you going to reopen the gate? I've read that you've made gates before."

"You read too damn much for my liking. Go away and let me think."

"What about?" Wilm persisted.

"Destroying the stone. And saving Aviel – *if* she's still alive." Shand walked away.

It was a brutal reminder of why he was here. Wilm had to sit down before his knees gave under him. "Aviel," he said softly. "Aviel!"

Ussarine laid a hand on his shoulder. "You did well, Wilm. Who taught you how to use a sword?"

"I taught myself. From some notes Llian gave me." He looked at the four bodies. Snow was already an inch deep on them.

"Must've been good notes. Come inside."

He was following her to the door when Shand said, "Wilm?"

Shand was bent over something lying on the floor of the yard. Wilm went across. It was the separated brass tubes and crystals of Unick's Identity device.

"What's this doing here?"

Wilm explained about the earlier fight, when they had been attacked by Rasper and Unick. "It came out of Unick's pack and fell apart."

"I wonder if it can be put together again?" Shand gathered the pieces and stowed them in his pack.

"Shand, there was a message! From Mendark!"

"What?" said Shand in astonishment.

Wilm showed him what Llian had found. Shand studied the scratches on the stone, frowning.

"There was another device," Wilm said.

"What?" Shand said sharply.

"The one he murdered . . . murdered Dajaes with. Llian called it the Command device, but the assassin who got away took it."

Shand cursed. "He'll be taking it to Snoat."

Wilm was uncomfortably aware of the Origin device in his own pack. He should give it to Shand. He might be able to do something with it, while Wilm almost certainly could not. Yet something made him hold back – a tiny hope that he might be able to find Aviel with it.

They went inside. "First, find a place we can defend," said Shand. "Then a fire and food."

"What about Aviel?" said Wilm.

"If Unick's found the stone, he doesn't need her any more. It's hard to imagine she's still alive."

"I'm sure she was when I started to go down earlier." Wilm explained about the scent trail.

"What did you see?"

"Nothing. I didn't go all the way down. I . . . I panicked and ran."

"What you did outside proves your courage," said Ussarine.

"But I came here to save Aviel," said Wilm.

"We've got to destroy the stone," said Shand. "But how can we, if it's dangerous to use mancery near it?"

Shand could be a hard man, and if it came to a choice he would probably put destroying the stone ahead of saving Aviel. Wilm was glad he'd kept the Origin device secret. She came before everything else.

"What about blasting powder?" said Wilm.

"It'd take barrels of the stuff to do the job, and I'd have to go to Radomin to get it, then hire porters to carry it up. That'd take at least a week and we can't afford the time – or to leave Unick to his devices all that time."

"We've got to deal with him first," said Ussarine.

They went down the way Wilm had before, and though Shand and

Ussarine were with him he did not feel much better. The air seemed thicker and fouler, the darkness darker; it felt as though it was congealing around him. The only positive was the occasional waft of one of Aviel's scents. She had to be alive, she just had to.

They reached a shaft with a downward-spiralling step-stair. Shand peered down and blanched.

Ussarine, beside him, said, "Not without a rope."

"I didn't bring one," said Shand. "A blunder, in the circumstances."

It took a long time to find another way down, into deep caverns where the rock had been eaten away in smooth curves. The air was warm down here and getting warmer the further they went.

"We're below the part that Basunez built," said Shand. "This could be a thousand years old . . . or ten thousand."

"Perhaps it's why he came here in the first place," said Ussarine.

They continued along downward-winding passages like gigantic grub holes. Wilm's feeling of being stifled and his claustrophobia grew until he was close to panic. A scream was building up in him, and the only thing stopping him from bolting was that he was utterly lost.

"Getting close," said Shand.

"How can you tell?" gasped Wilm.

"I can feel the power. Stay behind me. You too, Ussarine. This is mancer's work."

"Didn't Malien warn you to not use mancery near the stone?" said Wilm.

"I don't see that I have any choice," said Shand. "If I don't, Unick will."

"What's the plan?" said Ussarine.

"Kill Unick. Find Aviel, in the unlikely event that she's still alive, and get her out. Destroy the stone and run for our miserable lives."

They turned a corner and an elongated cavern opened up in front of them.

"And there it is," said Shand, exhaling in a rush. "How the hell am I supposed to destroy *that*?"

The trilithon was an ominous glowing red. Everything in the cavern was red, even the shadows.

Unick stepped out from behind the trilithon. His hands were empty and he was smiling.

"What's happened to your fancy devices?" sneered Shand.

"While I'm here, all the power in the world is at my command," said Unick.

"Didn't save your little finger."

Unick's marble-sized eyes flicked towards the summon stone. "It was worth the sacrifice."

Wilm couldn't take it any longer. "You bastard, *where's Aviel?*"

Unick grinned, a truly horrible sight. "She had nothing left to give save her sad little life. The stone didn't think much of it; it doesn't like cripples. Or gutless boys like you."

"You're lying!" Wilm drew the black sword.

Ussarine's hand clamped onto his shoulder, holding him back. "He's taunting you, Wilm. His only joy comes from destroying anything good."

Without a hint of what he was planning, Shand pointed a little green crystal at Unick. White light shot towards his eyes, but Unick threw up his four-fingered hand and red light coiled from the summon stone, reflecting Shand's blast back at him and shattering the green crystal.

Shand cursed and wrung his scorched hand. Unick lazily pointed at Wilm, who knew he was going to die. But Ussarine knocked him aside with one hand and hurled a throwing dart with the other. It buried itself inch-deep in Unick's breastbone.

As Wilm hit the floor, the flap of his pack came open and the Origin device went skidding across the floor. Unick extended his hand, drawing the device across the chamber to him.

"Why did you keep that from me, you imbecile?" roared Shand.

Unick scrambled backwards, the dart still in his chest. He took cover behind the stone and reached up to it as if drawing power. Ussarine dragged Wilm around the corner with one hand and Shand with the other. Unick fired blast after blast, melting the wall where they had been standing. The cavern lit up like the inside of a furnace and the sound echoed back and forth, deafeningly loud.

They ran up for fifty yards to a place where they would see him coming, and stopped.

Shand clouted Wilm over the side of the head. "Explain yourself!"

Wilm knew he'd been an utter fool. "I . . . I thought it might help me find Aviel."

"You're . . . not . . . a . . . mancer," Shand ground out. "You don't have the gift."

"No." Wilm could not look Shand in the eye.

"And even if you were, Malien said not to use mancery near the summon stone."

"You used it."

"Only after weighing the risks," Shand said with menacing softness. "And I do have several hundred years of experience in the art. Aarrgh! Get out of my sight!"

Wilm crept away to where it was darkest and hunched down.

"It's hopeless," said Shand to Ussarine. "The stone is greatly enhancing Unick's mancery, giving him the power to defend it. With the Origin device I might have drawn enough power to do something about him. But now . . . " He gave Wilm a look that would have frozen molten lava.

"Is it feeding off Unick?" said Ussarine.

"I think so, but he's bonded with it too. It's corrupted him, the way the drumming corrupts susceptible folk, but it's also *made* him."

"I don't understand."

"Before Unick used his Origin device he was just a brilliant but unpleasant mancer, going nowhere," said Shand. "But the moment he drew on the power of the stone with the Origin device, back in Pem-Y-Rum, the drumming released all the inner restraints holding him back. Unick was willing to do whatever it took to reach the stone, and now he has."

"Is it a thinking device?"

"I doubt it," said Shand. "From what Karan said, it's being directed by Gergrig or the magiz. Or both. A pity Karan's gone, or I'd get her to go to Cinnabar again."

"Wouldn't that be dangerous?"

"Not as dangerous as the Merdrun invading," Shand said carelessly. "Let's go up."

Wilm's eyes narrowed. This was a harder Shand than the man he had come to know over the past few years. Was the stone working on him too, warping him so he took no account of all the little people who would be hurt on the way?

"What about Aviel?" said Wilm.

"You heard Unick," snapped Shand. "She's dead!"

"I don't believe him."

"He glories in killing. He sacrificed her to the stone."

"If you believe that, you're a bigger fool than I took you for," Wilm said furiously.

"Who the hell do you think you are?" snarled Shand.

"Someone who cares about people, not power! If you're going to abandon Aviel on the word of that madman, why did you come all this way?"

"Shand, Wilm," said Ussarine placatingly. "Can't you see it's the stone working on you?"

"I came here because Malien told me to destroy the summon stone," Shand said coldly to Wilm. "But if we're to beat Snoat we need all the power we can get."

"You've got it arse about," said Wilm. "If we destroy it, the Merdrun won't be able to get through. That's a far better outcome than letting them through and going to war against them."

"How the hell would you know?" Shand cried, apoplectic with fury. "You're a seventeen-year-old kid whose life experience consists of labouring jobs in the back end of nowhere."

"And you're a bloody old fool who can't see that he's being corrupted by the very thing that he thinks he can control."

The temperature in the passage dropped twenty degrees. Wilm knew he had gone way too far but it was too late to take the words back.

"Is that so?" Shand said nastily. "Then you can clear out because you're not welcome in my camp. Come on, Ussarine. The little shit can find his own way out."

Shand headed back the way they had come. Ussarine made hand signals to Wilm. They weren't hard to interpret. *Follow us but not too closely. I'll see what I can do to change his mind. In the meantime, keep your bloody gob shut.*

Despite his pounding heart and overwhelming feelings of claustrophobia, Wilm did not follow, for he had caught another whiff of scent – freesia – which could only have been left here by Aviel, and recently. To leave now would be to abandon her.

He loosened the black blade in its sheath and, in what was undoubtedly the bravest yet most reckless moment of his life, forced his claustrophobia beneath the surface and headed down to the summon stone cavern. He was almost there when he recalled Llian saying that his sword could be enchanted. *Do not use mancery near it*, Malien had said. Did that include taking enchanted objects near it?

Wilm dared not take the risk. He took off his sword and sheath, laid them beside the wall in the thickest darkness, then went the rest of the way on hands and knees, and peered in. The cavern was empty and the stench of Unick was so faint that he must have been gone for some time.

Dare he search the cavern? If the stone could sense his presence, it would call Unick and, unarmed, Wilm would be doomed. But if he left, he did not think he would ever find the courage to return.

There was no sound save a breathy whisper of circulating air. He supposed the warm air from the cavern would follow the rising passages and icy air would flow in from outside to replace it. He crept around the cavern and behind the stone. It looked the same from behind. He went up the other end and checked the lobes one by one. The first one smelled only of warm rock. Wilm was losing hope. He looked over into the second, which bulged down for about twelve feet. The light was poorer down there and he had to wait for his eyes to adjust. It was empty too.

Then he caught it – the faint but unmistakeable tang of citrus and daphne. It wasn't one of the blends he associated with Aviel's workshop, but rather the scent she wore herself. And it would not last long in such a warm place. She had been here recently. She could still be alive. No, she *must* be alive!

Why hadn't Unick killed her? Wilm could only think of one reason. He was saving her for some terrible purpose to do with the summon stone.

Perhaps to feed it.

74

IT BEGGARS BELIEF

At the bottom of her deep prison hole, over the rise and fall of the drumming, Aviel heard people shouting some distance away: Unick, followed by a deep female voice she did not know, then a broad voice she knew very well. Shand! Hope surged; she might survive after all. But how could old Shand hope to deal with Unick, a huge brute of a man with all the power of the summon stone behind him?

"Shand!" she yelled. "Down here."

The drumming swelled and drowned her out. The crimson light flared, bathing everything, even this far below the chamber of the stone, but shortly the light reverted to normal. Had Unick fed them to the stone? Was that why it had flared so brightly?

No, for she heard the voices again, arguing, though she could not make out what they were saying until one voice soared above the others.

"You've got it arse about," cried Wilm. "If we destroy the stone the Merdrun won't be able to get through. That's a far better outcome than going to war against them."

Aviel's heart lurched. What was he doing here?

"How the hell would you know?" bellowed Shand. "You're a seventeen-year-old kid whose life experience consists of labouring jobs in the back end of nowhere."

"And you're a bloody old fool who can't see that he's being corrupted by the very thing that he thinks he can control."

"Shand!" Aviel screamed into the silence. "Wilm!"

She shouted until she was hoarse, but when there was no reply Aviel plunged into an abyss of despair. Wilm was her oldest friend but she had no illusions about his abilities. Unick would kill him for the joy of it.

And why had he said Shand was *being corrupted by the very thing that he thinks he can control*?

Shand had taken Malien's first warning very seriously, so why was he now thinking about using the deadly power of the stone? Was it corrupting him, trying to make him do the worst thing he could possibly do? And Wilm, who was normally so quiet and polite?

How was she to get free and destroy it? Scent potions only worked on people. Could she force Unick to destroy the stone with a potion of command or control? Could she even make such a potion with what she had?

She dredged the grimoire up from the bottom of her pack, eased her bad foot into the least uncomfortable position and turned the pages. The darkest scent potions were in the last section, and there were several that might be used to control another mancer, though all required scents and stenches she did not have.

It was the same in the middle section of the grimoire, which described the Lesser Potions, and even in the first section, "Introductory Scent Potions". Only in the "Preface, Practice Potions" was there a scent potion she could make with what she had – the Electuary of Compulsion. The trouble was, it simply wasn't strong enough to use on Unick.

She was stymied.

Then she saw the answer. She had to escape and convince Shand that the stone had to be destroyed, not used – by using the potion on him!

Aviel was surprised at her own ruthlessness. Maybe the summon stone was working on her too, but she planned to use it. Shand must have doubts about going against Malien's warning, and Aviel had to heighten his self-doubt at the same time as she reinforced Malien's authority. The scent potion might just do that.

She was halfway through her blending when Unick popped his grotesque head over the wall of her prison and leered down at her. "If you think they're going to rescue you, think again."

She stared at him, wondering what he was on about.

Unick held up a slender black sword. "This is a famous enchanted blade once owned by Mendark the Magister. Your feckless friend Wilm found it, and when he comes back for you I'm going to lure him into a trap with it."

"What did he ever do to you?"

"He wounded me with this sword, and for that he has to die."

*

Wilm never knew how he found his way out of the labyrinth. Within minutes of leaving the cavern he was lost in a claustrophobic nightmare, and it took hours, and dozens of false turns, before he encountered a narrow conduit where he felt a current of icy air on his face. Outside air.

He followed it up, but it steadily narrowed until he had to hunch his shoulders to squeeze through. Should he go on? What if he got stuck here? What if he could not get out? The claustrophobia was rising again. He wanted to shout and thrash his arms but did not have the room to move them.

Just another yard. He could manage that, surely. And then, just another yard, until he dragged himself around a gentle curve and saw gridded daylight ahead, coming through a cast-iron grating over the end of the conduit.

The pins that secured it to the rock had rusted, and after three desperate heaves he snapped them off and forced it out. It was still snowing though the wind had eased. The quality of the light suggested that it was late afternoon.

He wriggled out onto a foot-wide ledge, then let out a squawk of fear. He was on the edge of a precipice. The yard wall loomed above him and the ledge ran along the base of the wall in either direction, out of sight. What was he to do? If he went back down the conduit he might not find another way out. He dared not spend the night down there.

He could not climb the wall either. His only option was to shuffle along the ledge until he got to the end and hope a way out would present itself. But which way? The outer wall of Carcharon was shaped like a tilted boat, with the tower at the lower end and the bow a couple of hundred yards further up the ridge and at least a hundred feet higher. He was halfway along the left side and he knew there was no ledge around the tower itself; it must end where the wall joined the tower. He would have to head up towards the bow.

Wilm stood up, swayed, his heart gave a terrified lurch and he slammed his back against the wall. A foot-wide ledge was plenty to stand on, so why was inching along it so terrifying? He took a step, and another, sweating so much that he could smell himself.

The light was fading quickly now; he had to move faster. On he went, step after step after step. The ledge sloped up steeply here and was icy; he had to dig the sides of his boots in to prevent himself from slipping.

Finally, however, the ridge curved away to his left and the curving wall – the bow of the boat – went right. With no danger of falling he made faster progress and soon reached the end, though the wall was as high above him here as everywhere else. He had to find a way over it and into the yard – without shelter, he would not survive the night.

Wilm continued until he found a place where the mortar had crumbled out of the joints between the blocks, leaving spaces where he could insert fingers and toes. He went up the first ten feet easily enough, though after that the cracks were shallower and it was an increasing strain to support himself. Fifteen feet to go. Could he do it? He had to, though after another five feet the tips of his fingers were bleeding and his grip was slipping. It was so cold he had no feeling in his fingertips.

Ten feet to go. The wind was stronger up here, catching his coat and pack, and trying to tug him off the wall. His fingers felt as though they were being pulled off at the knuckles, and the strain of supporting his weight on his toes ran from his heels up to the base of his skull. But he had to keep going. If he failed, Aviel would be fed to the stone.

Five feet and he could go no further. He tried a new mantra, *Just one more block, just one more block*, but it didn't work. The willpower was there but his muscles had nothing left.

"What the hell are you doing down there?" Ussarine was leaning out over the wall.

"Falling off!" Wilm gasped.

She lay on the wall on her belly and extended her long arm, but could not reach him by a foot. "Push yourself up."

"Can't do it."

"Yes, you can."

He tried and failed, tried and failed again. She slid sideways off the wall, evidently holding onto the inside with her other arm, and gained another six inches of reach.

"Go back!" he said. "We'll both die."

"Nonsense." Ussarine's voice projected calm confidence, though her teeth were bared under the strain. "Take my hand but don't put all your weight on it."

He strained up and managed to touch her fingers. She stretched down and caught his hand, then closed her fingers around it in a crushing grip and lifted him. But she pulled his toes out of the crack and suddenly he was swinging across the face of the wall, and the only thing holding them up was her other arm locked over the inside of the wall . . . and she seemed to be slipping.

His toes scrabbled at the wall, bumped across a crack but slipped out again. He jammed the fingers of his free hand into a higher crack, drew his knees up, then slid his toes down the wall until they found a deeper crack and took some of his weight. Ussarine rolled back the other way, lifting him. He went up another block, then she came to her knees and swung him up onto the wall.

"Thanks," he gasped. His calf muscles hurt so much that he had to sit down.

She rubbed her right arm, which was grazed from elbow to wrist, even through her coat and shirt. "Pleasure." She squatted down, frowning at him. "Though all things considered, I don't think I'll mention it to Shand."

"He might get a bad impression about me," said Wilm, and they both laughed.

But it was miserably exposed here and, now he was safe, the cold crept into his bones. Cold and fear.

"This way," said Ussarine.

He followed her down steps into the upper end of the yard. "What were you doing up there anyway?"

"Keeping watch. And staying away from Shand – he's poor company right now. Why did you keep the device?"

"I just thought—"

"Have you ever displayed the slightest aptitude for mancery?"

"No . . . but . . . "

She made an exasperated sound. "Anyone can learn sword fighting if they work hard at it, but without the gift for mancery you could study it all your life and still not be able to scratch your bum with it."

"I'm sorry. I've been stupid."

"Unbelievably!"

"Do you think I should apologise?"

"I'd give Shand a while to cool down."

"How long?"

"A couple of decades *might* do it."

Ussarine did not seem to be joking. She opened a door and, holding up her lightglass, passed into an old workshop. It was empty except for a few broken, rusting tools and some crumbling wooden benches. "You can sleep here."

She turned to go out again and stopped. "Where's that fine sword of yours?"

Wilm slapped his thigh, then sweat burst from his forehead. "After you and Shand went, I . . . I left it in the shadows by the wall, before I went back into the cavern."

"*You went back?*"

"Dajaes was killed because I failed her."

"How?"

How could she not know? How could *anyone* not know? But then, why would Ussarine know the story? Only he, Llian and Unick had been there. And Dajaes. He told Ussarine what had happened back in Pem-Y-Rum, and how he should have attacked Unick but had choked.

"How can you blame yourself?" said Ussarine after a long silence. "Before you got within striking distance he would have blasted you down as well."

"I didn't have the courage to try," Wilm said miserably. "That's why I had to go back down. I can't fail Aviel as well, I just can't."

"You're taking too much on yourself."

"And now I've lost my only weapon. I'm the biggest fool that ever drew breath."

Ussarine shook her head. "It beggars belief how you've survived to be as old as you are. Old Mendark would be turning in his grave."

"Why?"

"It was his favourite sword."

"How do you know?"

"My father used to talk about it."

"Who's your father?"

"Osseion. He was Mendark's personal guard for many years."

"Thandiwe said the sword could be enchanted. Is it?"

She hesitated fractionally. "Father never said, and neither did Mendark. He was close-mouthed about such things."

"You knew Mendark?"

"I often went to see my father at the citadel in Thurkad, where Mendark lived. I was thirteen when he was killed." She handed Wilm the lightglass and headed for the door.

"What's happening?" said Wilm. "With you and Shand?"

"He's trying to contact Malien and Nadiril. After that he'll decide what to do and where to go." She went out, came back and said, "Did you find anything in the cavern?"

"No." He told her what he'd seen and done.

"You may be a bloody idiot," she said, thumping him on the shoulder, "but your heart is where it should be."

75

TO LURE, ENSNARE AND CORRUPT

"Malien?" Shand was calling wearily. "Malien?"

Wilm looked down from his vantage point up in the smoke-stained rafters. Shand, who had taken refuge with Ussarine in the ruined stone bakery at the end of the yard, was sitting in the front half of the partly collapsed baking oven. The brickwork arched over his head and ran back like a cave for six feet.

He had been repeating the call for the last hour, without success. Whatever mancery he was using, it was exhausting; his voice was slower and wearier with each call.

Wilm could only see one side of Ussarine's face from here. She had glanced across as he settled into his hiding place, and though she had not looked his way again he felt sure she knew he was there.

Shand suddenly leaned forward. "Where are you, Malien?"

"Almadin." Her voice sounded impossibly distant. "Thirty miles west of Morgadis. What news?"

"Bad! I'm at Carcharon. We've seen the summon stone."

Succinctly Shand described what had happened and what they knew, including how Unick's Origin device had been gained and lost. Wilm squirmed.

"Is Karan with you?"

"She was." Shand explained about Karan and Llian being taken by the gate to Alcifer, and Maigraith going after them.

"I don't like this at all," said Malien. "Alcifer is a construct built to a purpose that only Rulke ever knew . . . "

Her voice faded, then returned strongly.

"You must destroy the stone at once."

"Can't get near it," said Shand. "And if I could, each piece weighs tons."

"Tons?" Malien sounded alarmed. "I thought it would be small enough to hold in the hand."

"It's a trilithon and each stone is seven feet high. Besides," he added in a low voice, "we're going to need its power."

"No, no, *no*! Don't even think that way."

"I've spoken to Nadiril. Snoat's moving south with an army of sixty thousand men. Hingis has only been able to raise five thousand, and we're struggling to equip them because Snoat's armies have robbed our allies of most of their wealth. Only Sith and the far south remain free, but if he lands an army there he could roll over our little force in a day."

"And a few days later the Merdrun will invade," said Malien, "and there'll be no resistance."

"Because they planned it this way," Shand said bitterly. "What about your people? They're strong."

"The bulk of them are four hundred leagues away in Stassor, and they can't get here for at least eight weeks. If the stone can't be stopped, we're finished."

"This fight has to be fought now, Malien, but there's only one way to get the power we need – the summon stone!"

"It's designed to lure, ensnare and corrupt. *Never* think that you can use it safely."

"How do you know?" Shand said with a return of the simmering anger Wilm had seen in him earlier.

"Because Karan saw it all. Meet me in Vilikshathûr in a week."

There was a snapping noise like a dry stick breaking underfoot, and the connection was gone.

After a long pause Shand turned to Ussarine. "I don't know what to do."

"Nadiril wants you to use the power of the stone," said Ussarine.

"And Malien says I must not. But indecision was ever the Aachim's greatest flaw."

"What if she's right?"

He rose and paced, hands clasped behind his back. "Malien won't arrive for a week, and it'll take us longer than that to ride to Vilikshathûr – assuming we can get through at all. I've got to act now. Do I use the stone? Or try to destroy it though I don't know how? Or ride away and hope we can find a way to beat Snoat, whose army is twelve times bigger than ours? Then, with only a few days to prepare, face the most brutal fighters Santhenar has ever seen."

"Rasper told the fellow who escaped with the Command device to send word to Snoat. If he had a caged skeet below, it will have reached him by now."

"It's got to be a gate then," said Shand. "Assuming I can find the strength for it."

"How long will it take to make one?"

"I don't know. I'm ... out of practice. A day or two, I expect. I'll make a trial gate first, and if it looks safe I'll go down to the stone. That way, if things go wrong we'll have an escape route."

"Using the summon stone should be a last resort."

"Oh, it will be," Shand said darkly. He looked directly at Wilm's hiding place, scowled and said to Ussarine, "Another thing."

"Yes?"

"Do you think I don't know you've been helping Wilm behind my back?"

"He means well."

"Some of the biggest disasters in the Histories have been created by people who meant well. Keep the wretch out of my way. This is going to take everything I've got." He rubbed his old eyes. "Maybe more than I've got."

Wilm slipped away but did not return to the workshop. Whether Shand succeeded or failed it would be bad for Aviel. Wilm had to try and rescue her now and he wasn't going to think about what could go wrong; he was just going to do it.

He went down, following the path he had taken with Shand and Ussarine. Could his sword still be there? He allowed himself to hope.

He had thought it would be easier this time, since he knew what he was facing, but going down turned out to be harder. The darkness was blacker than before, the air hotter and thicker and more stifling, and his claustrophobia was more overwhelming. If Unick chose to, he could kill Wilm as easily as he had Dajaes.

Finally he saw the ruddy glow ahead and knew he was close. He located the spot along the deeply shadowed wall where he had left his sword. It was not there.

The drumming started again, though softly now, a heartbeat slowly fading towards death. Aviel! Wilm checked along the wall in case he had the place wrong, though he knew he did not. The floor began to judder beneath his feet and for a few seconds it felt as though the walls were squeezing in around him.

He pressed his hands against the wall and took deep breaths until the panic passed. It was swelteringly hot here. He took off his coat, left it by the wall and continued down, around the corner and, after a heart-pounding hesitation, into the cavern. It was empty. He headed across to the summon stone, slowly, warily.

"Lost something?" said Unick.

Wilm jumped and looked around frantically. The trilithon brightened until the scalding red light hurt his eyes. He shielded them and made out Unick standing to the left of the stone. He was barefoot and missing two middle toes. The stone had fed again.

"You won't find her," said Unick.

"What do you want Aviel for?" Wilm's voice was a squeaky croak.

"I don't want her. The summon stone does – when it's ready."

"So she *is* alive!" cried Wilm. He almost choked.

Unick bestowed a sour smile on him.

"When ... when will it be ready?" said Wilm.

Unick shrugged. "Soon."

"Does it want me too?"

"Not particularly." Unick stretched up on the tips of his remaining toes to the top of the capstone and grasped something lying there – the black sword. He raised it to the vertical and scarlet light reflected off the blade. "But it's going to have you."

Unick swung at Wilm's right arm with all his strength. Wilm barely got it out of the way; the blade shaved hairs off the back of his hand. But the fury of the blow threw Unick off balance; he slipped in the curdled blood on the floor and Wilm attacked. He swung his right foot at the leg supporting Unick's weight, hooking it out from under him. Unick went down hard and the sword jarred out of his hand.

Unick scrambled after it on hands and knees, but his toe stubs scraped across the floor and he threw back his head in a silent scream. Wilm got to the sword first and swung at Unick's face. Unick threw himself backwards, came up against the stone, and his whole being seemed to fill with crimson light.

The pain lines faded from his ghastly face; he slowly stood up and smiled. It was the ugliest smile Wilm had ever seen: malicious, venomous and utterly corrupt. The stench of him in the hot room was so overpowering that Wilm was hard pressed not to vomit.

Unick extended his right hand. His remaining fingers were twisted as if they had been broken many times, and the nails were black. There was no time to think, only to react by instinct. Wilm swung the black sword round and flung it up at Unick's throat.

Unick jerked sideways and the sword speared through his right shoulder into the crack where the two vertical stones touched, impaling him. Blood sizzled and smoked on the stone; it flared more brightly than it had ever done before and red lightning radiated out from the sword's hilt. The drumming grew louder, the juddering of the cavern floor more frantic.

Unick was not smiling now. He wrenched the blade out with his shaking left hand. The sword was so hot that the blood on it was steaming. Awkwardly he swung it at Wilm, who dived, propelled himself up and drove the top of his head up under Unick's chin. Unick's head cracked against the wall. Wilm snatched back the hot sword and a shock zipped up his arm. His vision blurred.

"She's dead now, you little swine!" snarled Unick.

When Wilm's vision cleared a few seconds later, he was gone. Gone to kill Aviel.

Where? His reek was everywhere in the chamber but drops of blood on the floor showed the way. Unick had gone behind the stone, then down through a low archway into a tunnel that plunged down at a steep angle. The stumps of his recently lost toes left twin blood spots every yard. Larger, less frequent spots were from the wound in his shoulder.

Despite the injuries he was moving faster than Wilm, who dared not risk falling and injuring himself. He went down for fifty or sixty yards. This tunnel, like the summon stone chamber, looked very old and not man-made, but appeared to have been eaten out of the rock.

He turned a corner and caught a fleeting glimpse of Unick looking back – he knew Wilm was following and probably wanted him to. Wilm turned another corner and stopped. Ahead the tunnel branched like a three-fingered hand. Where had he gone?

Aviel's voice rang out: "Wilm, it's a trap. Go back!"

Her voice came like a physical blow. Wilm struggled for breath and tears formed in his eyes when he most needed to see. He looked around frantically. Where was she? Where was the trap?

He was struck over the head, then a blow in the back sent him skidding down and down.

76

HE'S COMING. HE'S CLOSE!

Wilm slid on his back, head first down a smooth, steep slope, then slowed as it shallowed out, and the top of his head thumped into something warm and sweet-smelling. No, *someone*. She let out a yelp as the impact pushed her a foot across the floor and he heard the tinkle of small objects being knocked over.

"Sorry," he said.

Wilm opened his eyes. He was at the bottom of a steep-sided pit, perhaps twenty feet deep and the same in width. He looked up at Aviel, who was sitting on the floor, cross-legged. It was hot; her feet were bare and her sleeves rolled up, and many little phials were set up in a line in front of her. The impact had knocked some over and she was picking them up and putting them back in their places, looking at him from the corners of her eyes.

He sat up and embraced her a trifle awkwardly. She clung to him for a couple of seconds, then gave a little twitch; he let go and moved away. She tucked her twisted foot out of sight under the other.

"Why didn't you go back?" said Aviel.

"I came to find you. To help you."

"But—"

"I had a friend," he said haltingly. "A student I met at the scholarship test." How meaningless the test seemed now, how silly the whole idea of becoming a chronicler. "Dajaes was her name. We rescued Llian from Snout, who was about to kill him, then Unick murdered her right in front of me, for no reason at all."

She laid a hand on his hand. "I can't imagine what that must be like. What you've been through."

"I've lived a lifetime in six weeks." A shudder racked him. "And when I realised that he was after you too . . ."

"How did you know?"

"After he killed Dajaes he picked up your broken scent phial – Shand dropped it – and sniffed it and said, 'I'll have her too.' Though I didn't realise it was yours until days later."

"I made it for you – to remind you of . . . home. But I'd accidentally made a scent potion and when Unick smelled it, it linked him to me."

"That was bad luck!"

"It's the only kind I have. Unick must have realised I was a threat to the stone."

"Why would he think that?" said Wilm.

She lowered her voice. "Because I'd read Malien's second letter. I couldn't contact Shand, so I had to destroy the stone."

"That was taking a lot on yourself."

"Malien said the world was in danger," she said simply. "And when Unick was linked to me for those few moments, I was already working on an . . . um, dangerous scent potion to find the stone."

"How did you know how to make it?"

"I'd rather not say."

He looked around. "Where's Unick gone?"

She gave him a sad little smile. "He planned all this, Wilm. He told me you'd left your sword behind and he was going to use it to trap you, so he could feed us both to the stone."

"I've made it worse," groaned Wilm. "I always get things wrong."

"I . . . I wish you hadn't come." She gave him another of those enigmatic sideways looks. "But I'm so glad to see you. I've been so alone. Just me and him."

"What are we going to do?"

"Escape, of course. Then I'm going to use the scent potion I'm blending to make Shand destroy the stone." She gestured at her array of phials.

How she had changed! Her self-confidence was astonishing. "Are scent potions a kind of mancery?"

"Yes."

"How did you know you had a gift for it?"

"Shand told me. I made one by accident years ago, and it gave him a terrible case of the runs." She laughed.

Wilm felt a small unworthy joy at the thought, but suppressed it. Shand might be a cranky old sod, but he had treated Wilm well enough. Better than Wilm had repaid him.

"But in a way I've always known," Aviel went on, thoughtfully. "Being a twist-foot, a silver-hair and a seventh sister, it's only right that I should have a gift to balance my bad luck."

"Is it a good idea to use mancery so close to the summon stone?"

"No. I'm planning to use it up in the tower, after we escape."

"How?"

"The stone feeds every few hours. It forces Unick to ... cut off a finger or a toe. After each time he collapses for a few minutes. That's our chance to get out."

"How will we know?"

"The drumming gets louder and the crimson light is really bright, and it flares in time to the drumming."

"I wonder why it takes his fingers and toes," said Wilm, "and not yours?"

She looked down at her foot. "Apparently I'm not corrupt enough, though the way I'm going ... "

"You'll never be like him!"

"I can feel the stone working on me. Maybe that's where I got the idea of using a scent potion on Shand." She went pink. "I'm so ashamed; he's been so good to me."

"The stone is working on me too. Only it's got more to work on."

Wilm felt the need to confess his folly in keeping, then losing, Unick's Origin device.

She did not judge or criticise him. But then she never had. Aviel nodded. "We have to look out for each other, Wilm. If you see signs that the summon stone is taking me over or making me do something I shouldn't, you've got to tell me."

"All right." It was impossible to imagine Aviel ever doing anything really bad.

"I've got to finish this potion now. Don't talk to me. See if you can find a way out. We may not have long."

Her face took on the familiar closed-off look she wore when she was working. Wilm felt pushed away, but told himself that it was just her being focused.

He studied the pit, which was smooth-walled in some places, such as where he had slid down, and slightly corrugated in others, like the back of a caterpillar. The rock consisted of alternate light and dark layers, sometimes in gentle undulations, sometimes twisted and contorted. It was very hard and there were no cracks in it, but the pale layers stood higher than the dark ones, providing small handholds.

Could he climb it? The shallowest angle was about sixty degrees. After his experience on the wall earlier, Wilm thought he might be able to manage it, and if he fell it would not be fatal. But how to get Aviel out? She could not climb such a steep slope, and neither could he carry her up it. Unick had chosen their prison well. The possibility of escape was enough to give them hope, but it surely could not be done.

Nevertheless he began. The first ten feet proved easy enough, though after that it was steeper and the handholds were shallower. It took five attempts before he made it up. He sat at the top, looking down. Aviel was carefully adding tiny amounts of one scent, then another, to a phial, shaking it then setting it down while she uncapped the next.

The drumming started. The light went from a dull brick-red to a lurid crimson and began to pulse.

"It's feeding on him!" said Aviel, with a little shudder.

"Is the potion ready?"

"It's way off. Can you get me out?"

She packed the phials in her belt loops. Wilm felt a momentary panic. With a length of rope or strong cord it would have been easy, but he hadn't thought to bring any from Shand's house.

"Have you got any spare clothes in your pack?"

"Yes . . . ?" she said hesitantly. "Trousers and shirt and . . . underwear."

"Chuck your pack up. I'll tie the clothes together."

She did not move.

"It's the only way," said Wilm. "Hurry."

She threw the pack up. It didn't go high enough. She tried again with a similar result.

"Sorry," said Aviel.

Wilm checked the passage behind him. There was no sign of Unick. He was turning back as Aviel swung her pack by the straps and gave it a mighty heave. The edge of something hard and heavy struck him across the forehead and knocked him off his feet.

"Wilm?" she cried.

He sat up, his head spinning, then crawled to the edge and looked down. Blood dripped off his forehead down the slide.

"I'm really sorry," she said. "I didn't mean . . ."

"It's all right."

He opened her pack and took out a pair of trousers and a shirt, and some underwear. He hastily shoved the underwear back in, tied her shirt to the legs of the trousers and tested it. It would not take his weight but it might hold hers. She had climbed as high as she could go but could still not reach his makeshift rope.

"Can I have your coat?"

She tossed it up and he tied it on. Still not long enough. He took off his sweaty blood-spotted shirt and tied it to her coat. After checking each knot, he lowered it down to her.

"Can you grip tightly enough?" he said.

"I'm not sure."

"Make a loop in the sleeve."

She did so, took hold of it with both hands and he began to raise her. Though she was slender and small-boned, it proved surprisingly hard work and his head was throbbing by the time she stood beside him. She flicked a glance at his bare chest and looked away hastily.

"How are we doing for time?" said Wilm, untying his shirt and putting it back on. "The drumming doesn't sound as loud as it was."

She stuffed her clothes into her pack. "The light isn't as bright either. That usually means he's rousing."

They hurried up the passage and came to a fork. "Which way?" said Wilm.

Aviel gnawed at her lower lip. "This way . . . I think." She indicated the left.

They continued. Wilm's pulse was racing, and he felt a troubling prickling on the backs of his hands. He wanted to run but the best

Aviel could manage was a fast hobble. They turned a corner and she said, "Ugh!"

"What's the matter?"

"I can smell him. He's coming. He's close!"

Wilm could see the fear in her blue-grey eyes. He felt a fierce surge of protectiveness, followed by black rage. She reached out to him without realising it. He took her hand. They turned another corner and Unick stood in their path. He was dripping with rancid sweat, swaying from side to side, and a filthy flagon dangled from his right hand. Two more of his toes were gone.

"I was hoping you'd get her out," said Unick. "Saves me the trouble."

Whatever he had in mind, it was bound to be bad. Wilm's fury surged. He pulled free of Aviel and, without thinking, ran at Unick.

Unick blinked at him, then smiled and began to raise the flagon. He was by far the heavier man but his reactions were dull, his movements slow. Wilm lowered his head and, running full bore, drove it into Unick's midriff and kept going, forcing with all the strength in his legs. The impact lifted Unick off his feet and hurled him backwards several yards. His head struck the floor and he lay still.

Wilm stared at him, breathing hard. His head was throbbing again. "Is he . . . ?"

"It would be too much to hope for," said Aviel. "That was reckless, Wilm, but well done."

It was his chance to avenge Dajaes. He was standing there, trying to convince himself to strangle Unick, and that it was the right and only thing to do, when the brute leaped up and bolted into the darkness.

"I should have done it," Wilm said bitterly. "Why did I hesitate?"

"Because you're a good man, not a cold-blooded murderer."

"What if he kills someone else? Or lets the Merdrun in?"

"What if, by sparing his life, you've done the right thing?"

"Ha!"

"We can't see the future, Wilm."

They hurried on and shortly emerged outside the summon stone cavern. Wilm headed in.

Aviel grabbed his arm. "Every time you go near it, it's more likely—"

"I've got to be armed."

He darted in and knew that Aviel was right. The drumming was not as loud as before yet he could feel the stone trying to get at him. The black sword lay on the top, though it was in its copper scabbard this time. He lifted it off. It was blood warm. He raced back to Aviel, took her hand, and they headed up through the thick, confining darkness. He retrieved his coat.

"How long was your sword on top of the stone?" said Aviel.

"Hours."

"What if it's picked up something from it?"

"I have to be armed."

"Where did you get it? I've never seen black metal before."

"Neither have I." Wilm explained where it had come from, and that it could be enchanted.

"Mendark wasn't a very nice man," said Aviel, her eyes searching Wilm's.

As he hurried on, she stifled a cry. He realised that he was walking faster than she could manage.

"Would you like me to carry you?" he said without thinking.

"No!" she said sharply. She had always been fiercely independent. Her hand went round his wrist. "But thank you. You've done more for me than I can ever repay. Is it much further?"

"No." He hesitated. "I should warn you that Shand isn't happy with me at the moment." He explained. "Ussarine is nice, though."

He told her how everyone had ended up here and what was going on in the outside world. They went the rest of the way at a slower pace and emerged in the tower at the level of the yard. It was dark outside and still snowing gently. There must have been well over a foot of snow in the yard, for the bodies had been reduced to elongated mounds.

"What time is it?" said Aviel. "I lost track down there."

No stars were visible; there was no way to be sure. "Maybe four in the morning."

As they squeezed out through the door into the yard, Wilm saw a bright flare of white light up the far end, not far from the workshop.

"What was that?" said Aviel.

The light grew brighter and he made out two figures to one side, Shand and Ussarine. The light appeared to be coming from a hoop-shaped woven structure propped between blocks of stone.

"Looks like he's trying to make the trial gate," said Wilm.

They crept up the sloping yard, keeping to the shadows. Ussarine was on the left side of the hoop, holding it vertical.

"What do you think?" she said to Shand.

"Done as much as I can right now," he said wearily. "We'll get a fresh start in the morning. With luck we'll have a working gate by dark."

He walked across in front of the hoop, staring at it.

Suddenly the ground shook, then crimson light fountained up through the stone directly under the hoop. Ussarine yelled and leaped aside. The white light outlining the hoop went pink, then a brilliant red. Shand brandished a fist and it turned white again, but the whiteness only lasted a second before it became red once more. Then, in an instant the hoop became a gate, a whirling tunnel like the one that had taken Karan and Llian to Alcifer.

"Look out!" roared Shand.

He turned to run but the gate lifted him off his feet and sucked him through. Ussarine cried out but she could not resist its pull either. They vanished.

"Did the summon stone do that?" said Wilm.

"I'd say it opened the gate before Shand was ready, to get rid of him."

"What do we do now?"

"We can't break the stone by ourselves. We should go to the gate."

"Are you sure it's safe?"

"It can hardly be less safe than here."

They ran hand in hand for the gate, but it turned white again, bounced them off their feet and faded away, leaving them all alone in one of the most dangerous places in the world.

"Ah!" gasped Aviel.

"What's the matter?"

"Twisted my ankle."

Wilm picked her up and this time she made no complaint. "We've got to go."

He carried her down the yard and through the tower to the front doors of Carcharon. There he stopped, contemplating the steep and icy path. It would be incredibly dangerous in the dark; they would literally have to feel their way. But it was not as dangerous as remaining here.

"Ready?" said Wilm.

"No," said Aviel.

"Why not?"

"Wherever Shand's gone, I don't think he'll come back. He's got Snoat's army to deal with. It's up to us now."

"But you just said we can't affect the summon stone."

"If the Merdrun come through, it'll be the end of the world, Wilm."

"You're right. It was Llian's job to smash the stone but he's gone. It's up to us now."

"We've got to find a way. No one else can."

PART FOUR

SYZYGY

77

NOT YOUR FINEST HOUR

If there was one thing Karan knew about gates, they seldom took you where you wanted to go and usually made things worse.

Torn away from Llian in the transit, she tumbled through the air, flashed through light and darkness and more light, then plunged into warm deep water. It went up her nose. She gasped, ended up with a mouthful that tasted of sulphur, thrashed and saw the surface a couple of yards above her. The panic eased and she swam up.

"Llian, Llian?"

She was in a pool with curving sides, forty yards by twenty, tiled in blue and surrounded by a large expanse of orange and black tessellated tiles. A scalloped roof, unsupported by beams or columns, curved high above.

Splash!

"Llian?"

"Glmpf!"

His head surfaced ten yards away. Was he in trouble? He kept plunging his head under the water and coming up again, spitting and heaving.

"Blurrggh!" he gasped. "Gaaah! Yuk!"

Karan swam to him. "Something the matter?" she said coolly. He had just saved her life but they had a lot of issues to deal with.

He rubbed the inside of his mouth with his fingers, spat out a mouthful, trod water and eyed her warily.

"Can't get the taste of Unick's leg out of my mouth."

"Why did you bite the filthy brute anyway?"

"Only to stop him killing you."

"You're a bloody idiot," said Karan.

"I've always thought so," said Llian.

"What the hell were you thinking?"

"About what?" he said warily.

Karan wanted to fling herself at him and never let go; she also wanted to whack him. To avoid both temptations she swam away, putting a few yards between them.

"Let's see. Voting down the friend you went to Chanthed to help in favour of Snoat's lackey. Getting yourself framed for murder, then scampering off to live in Snoat's villa. The processes that go on in your mind beggar belief! Telling Snoat all about the secret of mancery! Then escaping with your *girlfriend* at the very second we tore Pem-Y-Rum apart to rescue you ... " She faltered.

Llian stared at her. "The burning library, was that *you?*"

"With Shand and Lilis, and two others."

"Lilis! But—"

"She's a grown woman now – and fiercely loyal to you for some odd reason."

He managed a smile. "Little Lilis. Is she well?"

"Very. And we got Tallia out."

"Thank you – we looked everywhere for her." Llian began twisting his fingers back and forth. "Thandiwe hates me, Karan. She's sworn to do everything in her power to destroy me."

Karan sniffed. Six weeks of torment could not be laid aside that easily. Then she noticed Maigraith's ring again – the ring that, on touching Fiachra's chain, had formed the gate that had brought them here. It reminded her of her own bad decisions: using hrux on Maigraith, and sending Sulien away with the Whelm. Who was she to judge him when he had always done his best? It was time to mend fences, not pull them down.

"I've missed you so much," she said softly.

He came closer. "It's been the worst time of my life, and that's ... "

"Saying something!" she said fervently.

"Ever since Sulien's first nightmare, I've felt as though people were queuing up to attack me."

He had said a similar thing a long time ago, and suddenly it hit her.

"They *were* queuing up. The magiz couldn't get to you directly because you don't have a gift for the Secret Art, so she's been manipulating people like Unick and Snoat, and maybe even Thandiwe, to get at you."

"How do you know?"

"I ... um ... saw the magiz boasting about pulling our strings."

And all this time Karan had doubted Llian and made light of his problems, thinking only about her own. It was a wonder he had survived at all. "I'm really, really sorry."

Llian's eyes narrowed. "You *saw* the magiz? When."

Oops! "I took some more hrux a week ago. I had to know."

He shivered and caught her hand, pulling her through the water towards him.

"But we're together again," said Karan. "That's what matters."

"It's not *all* that matters."

Karan almost cracked; she only held back the tears by plunging her face under the water. Llian took her into his arms and they trod water together.

"It's been an absolute nightmare," said Karan.

"Is Sulien ... ?"

He seemed on the verge of saying something important, but stopped as if afraid.

"I'm afraid to contact her in any way in case ... "

"The magiz attacks her through you?"

"Or discovers where she is. But I get little moments from time to time. Sendings. Links."

"Is she ... all right?" said Llian. "Tallia said—"

"Sulien's safe, but utterly miserable. The Whelm treat her just like one of their own children – foul food, long hours of hard labour, no kindness."

"And daily punishments."

"How did you know that?"

"I know what they're like. But that's not all, is it?"

Her arms tightened around his neck, then it exploded out of her.

"Idlis keeps saying, 'You're one of us now, my little Whelm.' Sulien is terrified that they're not going to give her back, and so am I. And I dare not answer her. She must think I don't care, must think I've abandoned her. *I can't bear it!*"

Llian crushed her to him so hard that she lost her breath. Her iron self-control shattered; she howled and heaved and wept a bucket of tears, and did not stop until she realised that her nose was dripping down his back.

"Sorry!" she said, splashing it off.

They swam to the side, climbed out onto the warm tiles and lay there. Karan was too emotionally exhausted to sit up.

"There's . . . more," said Llian.

"What?"

"Just before you got to Carcharon, after Wilm and I drove Unick off the first time, I . . . um . . . gave in to the drumming."

Chills rippled down her back but she tried to make light of it. "You're still alive, and so is Wilm, so you can't have done any harm."

"I felt a mad delusion that I could destroy the stone with Unick's Command device. I was about to storm down when . . . something brought me to my senses. *Someone.*"

Her unease deepened. "What? Who?"

"*No, Daddy!*" he said in Sulien's voice.

Karan lurched to her feet, then dragged him up to face her. "*Sulien spoke into your mind?*" Her knees shook. "This is bad, Llian. Really bad."

"I don't understand."

"The Merdrun are close to achieving the dream they've been working towards for ten thousand years. It's only weeks away, yet one little thing can stop them. Their secret, fatal weakness, hidden somewhere in Sulien's subconscious. They're desperate to find her before we get the secret and ruin their plan." She gasped for breath. "And when she warned you . . ."

Llian had gone white. "You think it may have told them where she is."

"I don't know. But I'm scared. Really scared."

"You were right about me and the drumming," he said bitterly. "I can't—"

"Stop that! You're no more to blame than poor Benie was. The drumming is doing exactly what the enemy intended. Anyway . . . "

"What?"

She had to tell him. "I . . . I made a terrible mistake, Llian."

"Sending Sulien away with the Whelm?"

"Thus putting the secret beyond our reach. I can't imagine what I was thinking."

"You were trying to protect her," he said softly. "And Idlis will defend her with his life."

"He's just one man, and I don't think the other Whelm liked the idea. What if they—?"

He broke in. "Karan, don't! We've got to focus on what we *can* do."

She swallowed, looked around. "I suppose so. Where are we, anyway?"

"At a guess, Alcifer. Do you think, if we touched the ring and your chain again, it would take us back?"

"So you could have a go at destroying the stone?" said Karan.

"Yes."

"No, I don't. The ring was meant to protect Maigraith, and I think it brought us here because this was the safest place Rulke knew." She shuddered. "The summon stone is Shand's job now. If anyone can do it, he can. Who lives here, anyway?"

"I don't think anyone does. People have tried to occupy the city from time to time but none lasted long – it's held to be an unlucky place. And I suspect it was designed to keep people out."

"Meaning we could be ejected at any moment."

"Not us." He held up the ring. "I reckon it's a key to every door in Alcifer."

"But you've already got a key. 'Begin in Alcifer,' Rulke said before he died, and gave you that little silver key."

"It's a different kind of key."

"Well, that's your job now – to find what Rulke knew about the Merdrun and their one fatal weakness."

And her job was to protect their daughter. All this time, Karan realised, the magiz had been hurting her to provoke Sulien into revealing where she was. It had failed, but could the magiz locate her through the fleeting link she had made to Llian? It was a troubling thought.

They wandered the halls and the curving pathways, not talking. Alcifer was unlike any place Karan had ever been. In the first half mile they passed many clusters of slender red or black towers, in groups of three and seven and nine, some only a few levels high but others soaring straight up, without ornamentation, for hundreds of feet.

And there were domes, some hundreds of yards across and roofed with glass, covering gardens that must have looked after themselves, since they were perfectly ordered. There were sweeping aerial walkways, some in red metal and others in black, running from one cluster of towers to another. There were bowl-shaped lakes set on the tops of towers, and tall, narrow spikes, without windows or stairs, that seemed to have no purpose. Alcifer was beautiful, incomparable, and Karan could not take it in.

Llian was looking around in wonder and awe, clearly delighted to be here, but the place disturbed her; it felt like yet another threat.

She remembered a night in the mountains twelve years ago when Llian, dangerously ill with mountain sickness, had told her the great and terrible *Tale of Tar Gaarn*: the tragedy of Pitlis, the greatest designer and builder of all the Aachim. He had designed Alcifer, a unique and perfect city, on Rulke's instructions, and Rulke had used it to betray him.

Alcifer was magnificent, Llian had said that night. *A city vain and proud, cruel and predatory, majestic, perfect. So Rulke had made it. But it was also a construct, built for a purpose only he knew.*

She stopped suddenly. "Llian, we've got to—"

"I didn't have much sleep last night, or the week before that, and I'm so tired I can't think straight. Let's start afresh in the morning."

Karan looked up. "Isn't that the pool?"

All the pathways of Alcifer, local and city-wide, were curved, and they had returned to their starting point. They laid out their food on a little stone table: half a smoked sausage, a slab of dried deer meat, a packet of spicy dried prawns, rather soggy from the pool, two small pieces of cheese, one hard and red, the other yellow and oozing in the warmth. Some pieces of dried gellon, the queen of all fruit, now wet and sticky.

Llian took his manuscript and journal out of Snoat's waterproof leather bag, wiped drops of water off the journal cover and wrapped them up again. He ate some sausage, chewing slowly as if he lacked the strength to swallow.

Karan picked at the cheese. "I'm too tired to eat. Let's find a place to sleep."

They packed the food up and walked around the pool. There were rooms off two sides, though all unfurnished. Further on they came to a small pavilion with a dark green roof held up by six slender columns of silky smooth red jasper.

Karan hung her damp clothing over a rail and lay on the floor. Llian got down beside her. "This is nice," she said, snuggling up, and was asleep within a minute.

She woke to a soft dawn glow. Llian was writing in his journal by the light of a stub of candle. She rolled onto her back, watching him. It felt like old times, before Sulien's first nightmare had changed everything.

"How long do we have until the invasion?" she asked. She had lost track of time.

"Two and a half weeks."

He told her his story and what he had learned about Mendark's work, including the scratched writing on the broken slab at Carcharon.

"We can't do anything about the stone," he concluded. "That's up to Shand now. But we might be able to discover a weakness that can help us fight the Merdrun."

"How?" she asked.

"The Charon fought them for thousands of years; they must know everything about them."

"Where are Rulke's papers?"

Llian shrugged. "He just told me to begin in Alcifer."

"You'd better get started then," said Karan.

He slid his belt out of its loops and ran it through his fingers. And froze, staring at the belt's lower edge.

"It's gone!" It was a cry of agony.

An inch of the stitching had been cut to remove the little key from the secret slit.

"When did you last check?" said Karan.

"After Wilm and I buried Dajaes. I remember walking away from the grave and making sure the stitching hadn't worn through. The hag! The utter cow."

"I assume you're referring to Thandiwe?"

"Who else could it be? She must have taken it the day she pinched the gold and the horses. I wondered why she wanted three spare horses."

"Why did she?"

"It's a hell of a ride from the megaliths to here. A hundred and fifty leagues, at least."

"Why would she want to come here?"

"She lost everything when—"

"You voted Basible Norp Master of the College, instead of her," said Karan. "Not your finest hour."

"You picked a fool, Karan."

"I knew that within a minute of meeting you. 'My name's Llian. I've come to save you,' you said so very pompously, then fell down the steps and knocked yourself out at my feet." She giggled.

"Thandiwe *burns* for her own Great Tale. She's been pursuing Mendark's story, but she must have realised I had secret information about him that could invalidate parts of her tale, so she switched to an even better one – Rulke's."

"How did she know you had the key?"

"It's mentioned in the *Tale of the Mirror*. She swore she was going to destroy me, and this is her revenge."

"How long before she arrives?"

He mentally traced the route. "Even a council courier, changing horses several times a day, couldn't do it in less than eight days. So for Thandiwe at least ten."

"And she left the megaliths, what, eight days ago? She could get here soon. You'd better find Rulke's papers first."

"I'll get started."

"And I'll keep watch and take the key back the moment she enters."

"Be careful! She's a dangerous woman."

Karan's green eyes glittered. "Not as dangerous as I am, when someone of mine has been wronged."

"You speak as though I'm your possession," said Llian.

"And don't you forget it!"

He smiled ruefully. "Am I also your plaything?"

"There's every possibility – if you behave yourself."

78

I MUST WARN YOU

When Ifoli entered Snoat's oval reading room carrying a note, he gained the impression that she was afraid of him. Her fear did not bother him, though he was irked that she showed it.

Despite her exemplary service he would have got rid of her had there been anyone to replace her, but he no longer found it easy to recruit the best. It could not be because of his wealth and power, which had grown considerably since the catastrophe at the place whose name he had erased from the map. It must be because he was maimed, repulsive and an object of derision.

"Is that message from Rasper?" he said. Even his voice had lost its former honeyed perfection. These days it was grating and monotonous; he lacked the strength of will to speak properly.

"A subordinate," said Ifoli. "Rasper is dead and all but one of his men."

"How?" cried Snoat, shocked. "And where?"

"He tracked Llian and the youth, Wilm, to Carcharon, a ruin in the mountains west of Tolryme."

"I know where Carcharon is. Why did they go there?"

"The message does not say," said Ifoli. "Though Shand, Karan and Ussarine arrived only hours later, following Unick."

"Why did Unick go to Carcharon?" said Snoat.

Realising that he was rubbing his scarred chin through the silken mask that covered his nose and the lower half of his face, he dropped his hand to his side.

"Rasper's man did not know," said Ifoli.

"Take a guess."

"Unick went there because his devices—"

"My devices!" snapped Snoat.

"Your devices told him the summon stone was there."

"There is no summon stone! It, and the Merdrun *invasion*, are a fantasy concocted by my enemies to try and unite the west against me."

Ifoli went perfectly still. "I believe it, Cumulus."

He made a dismissive gesture, both crude and clumsy. His decline was humiliating and someone had to pay.

"Rasper's man has recovered the Command device," said Ifoli. "He's sending it by skeet the moment the bird returns to him. You'll have it by dinnertime."

"Without the Origin and Identity devices, it'll be severely limited. Have my artisans made copies yet?"

"Yes, but they can't get them to work."

Snoat cursed. Using profanity was another illustration of his decline, but he no longer cared. "Tell me about Unick."

"He's utterly debased now; he left a trail of ruin all the way across the mountains."

"He'll soon drink himself to death," said Snoat carelessly.

"I must warn you, Cumulus—"

"You already have," he snapped. "Don't mention it again."

"I have a duty of care."

"Enough!" he roared.

She nodded stiffly and stepped back to her place, her salmon-pink kimono rustling. Snoat flushed. He, who had always prided himself on his mastery of self, had so lost control as to shout at her. What was happening to him?

"What about Thandiwe?" he said in a deliberately flat voice.

"After splitting with Llian she headed south in the direction of Flumen, with four of your horses. She has not been seen since and you have few spies in those lands. It will take time to find her."

"Put more spies to work."

"Yes, Cumulus."

"But never lose sight of my first objective – my collection of the Great Tales must be complete. Find Llian and get his manuscript back."

"And then?"

"I want his mummified head spiked on my bedpost." He turned away to adjust the mask. "What progress on . . . the other matter?"

He meant restoration mancery to give him back his perfect nose and chin, and the three fingers so burned that they'd had to be amputated.

"Slow," said Ifoli. "Such mancery has been done before, though the results have rarely been ideal. However there are illusionists who—"

"I don't want the *illusion* of perfection. It's not for the world, it's for me."

He dissembled. It mattered a great deal that the world saw him as a perfect specimen, but it mattered more that he *be* one in his own eyes. Presently he was maimed and it could not be endured.

"It may take a greater power than old human mancers have ever used before, even such mancers as have taken renewal."

"The Command device will give me power; all I need are the restoration spells. Find them!"

She shivered, and again he felt she was afraid. Not of him, but of it.

"To the war," said Snoat.

"Sith won't be easy to take."

"The allies only have five thousand men, and they're led by a geriatric librarian." He snorted, then had to wipe his eroded nose, another humiliation. "I have three armies and my fleet is big enough to carry any one of them. Send one army south to besiege Sith. Embark another to take Vilikshathûr from the sea, then sail upriver to attack Sith from the east."

"It . . . will be done," said Ifoli.

79

A WAR OF HONOUR

"What the blazes is that doing here?" Llian said to himself. He had been searching Alcifer for Rulke's papers for days, without success, or indeed any sign that he had ever been here. Until now.

It was an eighteen-foot-high statue of Rulke – a nude carved from a single block of granite – on a broad stepped platform in the middle of a vast but otherwise empty chamber. His stone eyes were fixed on the opposite wall, which was covered in intricately embossed silver. Llian studied the embossing, realising that it was writing in the secret Charon script, a few paragraphs repeated over and over. It called to him but without the key it was unreadable.

He turned back to the statue. It was a good likeness and brilliantly finished, not an easy thing to do in such a hard and crystalline stone. As he was walking around it, wondering who had put it there, Llian saw that it showed the huge gash in Rulke's side that had killed him ten years ago. Or was it some older injury from his immensely long life? No, the wound matched Llian's memory of the fatal moment.

Given that the statue would have taken years to carve and polish, it could not have been here more than seven years. But who had commissioned it and brought it all this way? It would have been a major undertaking, for there was no granite near Alcifer. Only a wealthy patron could have done so, yet Rulke had been a much-reviled figure, still widely known as the Great Betrayer.

Surely only another Charon would erect a statue to him, but Yalkara and the other handful who had survived had gone back to the void to die. Then who, and how, and why?

Llian was still circling the platform when Maigraith's ring tingled and a rainbow of colours outlined a foot-wide oval at the base. The colours faded and so did the oval. Llian poked its middle with the toe of his boot and a concealed hatch, well matched to the rest of the stone platform, swung out.

Inside was a sheaf of copper leaves, each the size of a sheet of paper and held together with a broad ribbon made from beaten platinum. And they were written in the common script, in wine-red ink.

Every hair stood up on Llian's head. Was this this the breakthrough he had been looking for ever since leaving Gothryme?

Karan was hidden in the shadows above the north gate of Alcifer, waiting for Thandiwe, and she was looking forward to the confrontation. How dare Thandiwe try to seduce Llian? How dare she rob him? Karan indulged in little fantasies of revenge.

Llian slipped in beside her, holding some copper sheets. His face was flushed and his eyes were shining. "Look what I found. And I can read them."

"Are they the lost Histories of the Charon?" said Karan.

"No, they'd fill volumes. And they're in the secret Charon script that no one can read without Rulke's key."

Karan glanced out the window at the track winding down from the mountains behind Alcifer. Thandiwe could not be far away. "I'm going to enjoy taking it from that curly-haired strumpet."

"She fights dirty," said Llian. "Don't go near her on your own."

That was exactly what Karan planned to do. This was between her and Thandiwe, woman to woman. Besides, she did not want Llian to see her fighting over him – it was undignified and was bound to go to his head, which was already overly swollen.

Nonetheless, she was anxious. Thandiwe was big and fit, and Karan was small. She would be at a disadvantage in any fair fight, not that she was planning one. She knew how to fight dirty too. She flicked through the copper sheets.

"Where did you find them?"

He told her. "It wasn't difficult. Clearly, they were meant to be found. And they're in Rulke's handwriting."

"Who put the statue there?"

"I don't know. I'm not sure it matters."

"I'm sure it does," said Karan. "Does he mention the summon stone?"

"Not a word, but lots about the Merdrun and where they came from."

"Anything that'll help us to beat them?"

"Possibly."

"I wonder why they're written in the common script?" said Karan.

"I suppose, since the Charon were heading for extinction, the secret didn't matter any more."

"What secret?"

"For thousands of years the Charon and the Merdrun fought a civil war right across the void."

"A *civil war*?"

"The most savage creatures they faced in the void weren't the myriads of ever-changing beasts, as we've always been told, but their mirror-selves, created at the dawn of their exile."

"The Charon were originally called Mariem," said Karan, recalling a story she had not thought about in years, "and they came from Tallallame."

"They shared Tallallame with the Faellem," said Llian, slipping into his teller's voice, "who came to fear the Mariem's rapidly advancing civilisation. The Faellem used mass illusions to lead them through a portal, making them think they were going to another beautiful world, but the Faellem's real intention was genocide.

"The Mariem were trapped in the void with no hope of escape, because the Faellem had sealed the portal behind them. Within a month, their millions were reduced a hundredfold. It's the most monstrous crime in the history of the Three Worlds."

"And still shaping the worlds to this day."

"Then the Mariem took a new name, Charon, and a new leader, Stermin."

"Never heard of him," said Karan, turning away to scan the track again.

"But here's the vital part." Llian looked down at the copper sheets. "'Stermin was a flawed man, and after their betrayal he became obsessed with the nature and the power of evil. He saw it everywhere, even in the most innocent of acts, and set out to test his people's moral fitness.'"

"This isn't going to end well," Karan murmured.

"'On an uninhabited little world called Cinnabar,'" Llian read, "'Stermin forged sky-fallen metal and cut naturally empowered stone to make the Gates of Good and Evil that split the Mariem into Charon and Merdrun, and began the civil war that raged the length and breadth of the limitless void for more than 10,000 years.

"'He created two huge linked doorways, side by side – the Azure and Crimson Gates – to sort the Charon into those who were worthy and those who were not. But secretly! He told them nothing, save to choose a gate.

"'The Crimson Gate was enchanted to offer a person's greatest desire, yet weaken their self-control, while the Azure Gate was the opposite – it was ennobling. Many people resisted the lure of the Crimson Gate, perhaps sensing something wrong. But those could not resist it emerged with the stigmata of evil burned into their forehead, stigmata that even their children were born with—'"

"The tattoo the Merdrun wear," said Karan.

"'—and Stermin cast them out. The stigmatised ones so were outraged at being called evil when they had done nothing to deserve it that Merdrax, their leader, named them Merdrun and swore eternal revenge.'"

Llian turned another leaf, the thin copper making a small crinkling sound, and read on.

"'He cut a cube from the keystone of the Crimson Gate, hung it around his neck as the sign of his authority and led his people deep into the void, where he and his successors reshaped them to fit the stigmata. They slew every child born without it, and all who failed to live up to it, thus embedding the darkness in their bloodlines and proving Stermin right after all. By naming them evil, he had created a greater evil than he could ever have imagined – the Merdrun were a dark mirror to we Charon, and henceforth dedicated their lives to wiping us out. It was the only way Stermin's insult could be erased.

"'He died in the first battle, using the Merdrun as proof of his thesis and quite unable to see his own part in it. Far from the Gates of Good and Evil saving his people, they were the means of our destruction.'"

"I'd have thought they'd be evenly matched," said Karan.

Llian continued: "'No outrage or depravity was forbidden to the Merdrun, while we Charon still fought according to the old rules. War raged across the void and down the aeons, and the Merdrun ground us down until we were almost extinct. Our only hope was to disappear to a place where we would never be found – a real world separate from the void.'"

"Why was it kept secret all this time?"

He put down the copper sheets. "We know that the handful of surviving Charon, led by Rulke, vanished from the void and took Aachan, and afterwards parts of Santhenar, but they were surrounded by enemies who were far more numerous – the Aachim, Faellem and us old humans. Had the Charon's enemies known about the Merdrun, Rulke feared they would seek them out and tell them where his people were hiding."

"Is that what Alcifer was really for?" said Karan. "To defend the last of Rulke's people?"

"I don't know," said Llian.

"But the Merdrun found them anyway."

"Yes, but they couldn't get through the Forbidding that, back then, sealed off the Three Worlds from the void. That's where Rulke's note ends," said Llian, "but this is what I think happened. About twelve hundred years ago, the Merdrun managed to send the summon stone through a flaw in the Forbidding to Santhenar."

"Twelve hundred years ago! Then it couldn't have anything to do with my ancestors." Her father hadn't been an evil man after all; perhaps he had just been warped by the stone, as Benie had been.

"No. The summon stone was meant to create chaos, via the drumming, and the Merdrun planned to take Santhenar and wipe the Charon out."

"What went wrong?"

"They couldn't wake the stone, and eventually they took the

desperate step of remotely gifting power to a young adept on Santhenar, so he could do it for them."

"And that adept was Mendark," said Karan.

"They chose him because he was both brilliant and ruthless, and assumed he was infinitely corruptible. But after he had renewed his life a number of times, Mendark realised he was being used. He set out to find out who was doing it and stop them."

"But he failed."

"The summon stone was waking by itself by then, but he didn't know how to destroy it. He had come close to the secret of mancery but hadn't solved it either. In the end, I think he realised that there was only thing to do – sacrifice himself."

"How would that help?"

"When a great mancer dies, immense power is released. Mendark used it to freeze the summon stone until a way could be found to destroy it."

"Why did it unfreeze and the drumming start?"

"I don't know."

"Did you find the answer to the most important question?"

"The Merdrun's single weakness? No."

"Then no one knows it except Sulien," said Karan. "And I sent her out of reach."

80

I CAN KILL YOU IN ONE SECOND

Eleven o'clock and Maigraith was keeping watch on the north gate, as she had for days. She was not yet ready to take Karan and Llian on; there were too many unanswered questions. Who had created the great statue of Rulke? Why was Karan watching the gate? Who was she expecting?

She wasn't here now; she had left an hour ago with Llian. Maigraith turned back to the track. Her Charon heritage meant that she had little need of sleep and she planned to watch all night. Whoever was coming, she was going to get to them first.

And half an hour later a tall woman appeared, riding a weary grey mare and leading another. Maigraith recognised her at once – Thandiwe Moorn. What was she doing here? Causing trouble, no doubt.

Maigraith went down to the north gate and peered through a spy hole. Even covered in dust and exhausted, Thandiwe was a striking woman. She dismounted wearily and led the horses to a watering trough.

Maigraith threw the double gates open. Thandiwe spun round, staring at her.

"Are you . . . Maigraith?"

"What's your business here?"

After some hesitation, Thandiwe said, "Rulke's papers. May I come in?"

Since she was Karan's enemy, Maigraith might make use of her. She gestured Thandiwe in.

The moment she passed through the doors Maigraith heard a distant *tchunnk* and felt a small vibration pass through the tiled entrance hall. Then a humming sound began, at the lower edge of hearing, as if something in Alcifer had woken – but why would it wake to Thandiwe? Unless . . .

Maigraith caught Thandiwe's right arm, spun her and twisted it up behind her back. "You're carrying something. What is it?"

"I'm not," Thandiwe blustered.

"You know how powerful I used to be."

"Yes," Thandiwe said, tensing.

Maigraith jerked her arm up, hard. "I'm far more powerful now. I can kill you in one second . . . or draw it out for a week."

The resistance drained out of Thandiwe. "I've got Rulke's key."

Maigraith hissed between her teeth. "The one he gave to Llian so he could tell the true story of the Charon?"

"Yes," Thandiwe whispered.

"Llian would never have cast away so great an obligation. You stole the key."

"He betrayed me!"

Maigraith released Thandiwe's arm. "Come with me."

Thandiwe eyed her warily. "What do you want?"

"I'm sorely in need of news about Karan and Llian, and everything else that's happened in the past month."

"What's in it for me?"

"Your life," Maigraith said coldly. "Anything else depends on the quality of your information. And its veracity! But if all is well, I may be of some benefit to you."

"If you're so powerful, why do you need me?"

"The job needs two."

Maigraith led Thandiwe to the bulbous upper floor of a pencil-thin tower where she often sat to look over the sea or the mountains. Maigraith had a store of preserved Charon food there, found in one of the pantries. Rulke must have stocked them on his last visit ten years ago, and the meats, cheeses, smoked fish and pickles were now fully mature. She brought out a bottle of yellow wine. Maigraith rarely drank but she assumed Thandiwe, being a former friend of Llian's, would share his greed for it.

"Eat and talk," said Maigraith.

Thandiwe ate for an hour and talked for three, by which time Maigraith had as thorough an account of the doings of the past month as any chronicler could have given her. She poured Thandiwe another goblet of wine and sat back. Thandiwe was regarding her anxiously, perhaps wondering if she would get out of here alive. Maigraith was wondering the same thing.

"I judge that you have spoken the truth," said Maigraith. "Though the accounts of your dealings with Llian are slanted in your favour." Thandiwe stirred. "But what do I care?" Maigraith went on. "I hate him!"

Thandiwe sipped her wine. Maigraith poured herself a half-goblet. Rulke had brought it here for his own use, so it must be the best.

"The secret of mancery," she said thoughtfully. "A great opportunity, but also a great danger."

"How do you know it's a great danger?" said Thandiwe.

"I spent a month in the mountains, my mind in a . . . *numinous* state after Karan dosed me with hrux. I know about the summon stone and how it came to be there."

"How did it?" Thandiwe said eagerly.

"Show me the key."

Thandiwe reluctantly opened an enamelled locket and tipped the silver key onto the table. It was only the length of a finger joint and the shaft was no thicker than a needle. Maigraith shivered. It had been Rulke's; he had worn it on his body, and as he lay dying he had given it to Llian to ensure that the story of his people survived. Could it be right to thwart his will and take it?

Thandiwe was watching her anxiously. Maigraith touched the key with a fingertip and felt an unpleasant stinging prickle. A warning. She put her hands in her lap, below the level of the table so Thandiwe could not see, and studied her fingertip. It was red and covered in small blisters. Clearly she was not meant to use this key, and yet it had not affected Thandiwe. Maigraith took that as a sign that Thandiwe should tell the story instead of Llian. He did not deserve it!

And the key was linked to Alcifer, since something in the city had roused the instant it passed through the north gate. It was something to investigate at a later date.

"I know you to be a fine chronicler and a gifted teller," said Maigraith. "Therefore, after you've done me a small favour, I will show you where the Histories of the Charon are and allow you to keep the translation key. Then you will leave Alcifer with the records and never return." She raised an eyebrow.

"Yes," said Thandiwe. "What is the favour?"

"Had you been less desperate you would have asked before agreeing. But what I say, I do. First you will help me to trap Llian – via Karan."

"With the greatest pleasure. She doesn't deserve him."

"Yes, she does," Maigraith said ominously.

"Where will I find her?"

"She watches the north gate from dawn until dusk – for you,

presumably. When you ride up after dawn, she will be waiting. Lead her to me and I'll do the rest."

Maigraith mapped a small part of Alcifer on a piece of paper, then marked the route Thandiwe was to take from the north gate.

Thandiwe traced the route with her finger, her lips moving, then rose. "I'll see to my horses and move them out of sight. After that I'm at your disposal."

"Yes, you are," said Maigraith.

81

I'M GOING TO DRINK HER PRETTY LITTLE LIFE

"I don't want you to go back to Cinnabar," said Llian.

"I don't want to go either, but time is running out," said Karan.

Only a couple of weeks left. He felt a panicky nausea at the thought.

They were on the roof of a ragged spike of carved greenstone that Karan called The Spine, the highest point of Alcifer. The sun was shining, but with a keen southerly whistling across the rough stone it was chilly even in the middle of the day, and she was wearing the down-filled clothing and fur-lined boots Shand had given her. The top of The Spine swayed in the wind and sometimes shook alarmingly.

"There's got to be another way to stop the Merdrun."

"I can only think of three ways," said Karan. "Destroy the summon stone, though we don't know how and we're too far away; prevent the Crimson Gate from being opened from Cinnabar; or kill the magiz, who's gathering power from her victims to open the gate."

"How do you know the gate—"

She rubbed her watering eyes. "Gergrig said, 'Without the alignment of the triple moons we won't be able to open the Crimson Gate, and the next opportunity is years away.' But the gate was made by Stermin, a mighty mancer, so how can I stop it opening? That only leaves the magiz."

"*Another* mighty mancer," said Llian, shivering. "But Karan, the Merdrun kill everyone in their path for a reason. How can you take her on?"

"If I don't, she'll kill Sulien. Then you and me."

"All right! What's your plan?"

"Return to Cinnabar and use the dematerialisation spell to spy on the Merdrun from on high, then attack."

"The same as last time then," he said despairingly.

The pain in his chest, that had developed when she'd said she was going back, was like pincers wrenching his flesh until it tore. The magiz would kill her and laugh about it.

After a long pause Karan said, "It's all I can come up with."

"At least talk to the defenders in the ice fortress first."

"What for?"

"They had three massive old fortresses, all guarding the path up to the Crimson Gate, but why? What can they tell us about the gate? And about their enemy?"

"All right, but I'll have to be quick. Malien's spell is exhausting; I'll be lucky to last an hour."

He slumped against the roof wall. "Poor choice of words."

Karan looked into his eyes and he saw his own fear reflected there – that it was unlikely she would return.

"Can you sense what the magiz is doing now?" said Llian.

"Yes," she said quietly. "She's drunk so many lives she's high as a kite and much stronger than before. She's . . . looking for Sulien."

Then it happened – a wail of desperation so loud that it rang in his ears. *Mummy, Daddy, the Whelm have initiated me. They say I'm theirs now. All theirs!*

Llian reeled.

"You *heard*?" said Karan, clutching him with both hands.

A sudden gust hammered the spine, swinging it in a sickening oval. His stomach heaved; the pincers tore his flesh again.

Mummy, I know you can hear me. Why won't you answer? Don't you . . . want me?

Ahhh! It was a glutton's sigh. *I'm going to drink her pretty little life, very soon. The bliss!*

"This ... stops ... *now!*" Karan said savagely. "Trigger!" Her eyes rolled up, her knees buckled and she crumbled to the floor.

Llian fell to his knees beside her. Her eyes were empty and her pulse very slow. Her body was an empty shell – her spirit had gone to Cinnabar and she did not expect to come back.

He sat beside her, holding her hand. Never had he felt more useless. There was nothing he could do for her or for Sulien. He waited ... and waited, his throat so tight that he could scarcely breathe, his heart thumping leadenly. He felt so very cold, yet Karan's hand was colder.

An hour later she vanished. She had used the materialisation spell on Cinnabar. Or else the magiz had used the spell on her and was drinking her life right now.

The tearing pain in his chest grew worse. What was he supposed to do? He lurched around the oval top of the spine, only to realise that if Karan did return, it could be anywhere in Alcifer.

Llian ran all the way down, more than a thousand steps, reaching the ground so exhausted that his throat was burning and his knees would not hold him up. But it did not take away the fear or the pain. He checked the pavilion, the pool, the watch post high above the north gate and the other places Karan went to frequently. There was no sign of her. She was not coming back.

Sulien's fate rested on him now, yet he had never felt more out of his depth. What could he do to help her, or Karan, or anyone?

All three moons were in the sky now, and they weren't far off alignment. Syzygy should have been a week and a half away but Karan could tell it was only a few days off. Had the magiz lied when she had said eight weeks, to make herself look good now? She must have.

It was too soon! Even if the allies, by some miracle, killed Snoat today, they couldn't possibly be ready to fight the Merdrun in a few days.

Floating high in the bitterly cold air, in spirit form, Karan saw that the ice fortress, which she had thought to be a stronghold guarding the steep track up the mountain, was actually a gigantic ring-fortress a couple of miles in circumference, surrounding the entire flat-topped peak and the Crimson Gate at its centre. There must be many thousands of defenders; surely they could beat the enemy, who had to be exhausted from months besieging the domed city and the two lower fortresses.

The Merdrun army was dug into the crevassed ice below the ring-fortress. Karan could not tell their numbers, though they seemed greater than she had previously thought. And with every life the magiz drank, her power grew.

Her big red tent with the green rope along its top was surrounded by three rings of guards and another ring of cloaked figures that Karan assumed to be her acolytes or assistants. There was no way she could get through them all.

She swooped down towards one of the watchtowers of the ring-fortress, straight through the ice wall and into a long, narrow room, rectangular on three sides and curving gently on the fourth. It was constructed of sawn blocks of bluish ice with little streaks and flecks of red through them. There were woven rush mats on the floor and hundreds of weapons hanging on the curving wall. More were stored in little round compartments cut into the ice. A long workbench, also made from ice, ran along the centre of the room.

"Who are you?" cried a stocky black-haired boy, nine or ten years old, who was polishing a double-edged sword at the bench. He reached for the hilt.

"A friend," Karan said quickly. "You can see me?"

"We're protected against magic here."

Karan threw back her hood and shook out her red hair, which fell halfway down her back. The boy stared at her, then at her hair, as if he had never seen such a colour. "You're not . . . one of *them*."

"The Merdrun are our enemies too. My name is Karan."

He put down the sword but did not give his name. He was a very serious little boy. "You must see my father."

She followed him along halls of rough-sawn ice. Old tapestries, so faded that they were just blurs of green and blue and grey, covered most of each wall; the floor was strewn with brown rush mats. The air smelled of onion soup and oiled armour.

They entered a low, dome-shaped room where half a dozen men and women, all compact, stocky and short-haired like the boy, stood around a low table spread with battered old maps drawn on fawn leather.

"Father," the boy said to a weary man wearing green leather armour. His grey eyes were bloodshot. "A friend has come. Her name is Karan."

The people around the table stared at her.

"You're *here*," said the boy's father, reaching out to touch Karan's arm but not meeting any resistance. "Yet not!" He took a step back, watching her warily.

Karan explained where she came from, how she had reached Cinnabar via Malien's spell, and that she was trying to protect her daughter from the magiz.

"The Merdrun invaded Cinnabar eighty-eight weeks ago," said a plump black-eyed woman with ink-stained fingers. She laid down her pen on a blue plate, careful of the map. "They immediately attacked our cities in the lowlands, one after another. They've been fighting their way to us ever since. We don't know why."

"Thousands of years we've lived here, in peace," said the boy's father. "We—"

"Then why the massive fortresses?" said Karan.

"When we were given Cinnabar in ancient times, we promised the givers that we would guard the Crimson Gate against all comers. And so we guard!"

"I know why they're here," said Karan. "At the time of syzygy the Crimson Gate can be made into a portal to another world. Our world. It's called Santhenar."

"We haven't heard of it," said the woman with the ink-stained fingers. She had the air of a leader.

"Santhenar is what the Merdrun really want, and if they get through, we can no more resist them ..."

Karan broke off.

"Than *you* can, you were going to say," said the woman coolly. "You need have no fear. I swear by the Fallen Gate that we *will* resist them.

We'll crush the Merdrun and hurl them into the bottomless crevasses to feed the flesh-sucking ice worms."

But Karan saw from the faces of the other adults, and even the boy, that they did not believe it. They would fight to the death, and they would be defeated. The Merdrun had never been beaten.

"I hope you do," said Karan, bowing to them in turn.

She pulled her hood up and floated up through the ice roof. It was sickening to think that the depraved magiz and her assistants would drink the lives of these noble defenders like drunkards; that they would get high on their lives like the miserable nigah addicts of Thurkad.

She drifted towards the Crimson Gate, which consisted of two oval lens-shaped uprights with a similarly curved capstone on top. It was even bigger than she had thought – a good thirty feet tall. She settled between the uprights, looking up.

The Gates of Good and Evil, she thought with a shudder. And this was the evil gate, so what had happened to the good one, the Azure Gate? Had the Merdrun destroyed it after finding out what Stermin had done to them?

Karan reached out to touch it, expecting to get a shock or sense a surge of power, but felt only a cold more bitter than anything in her experience.

She must not give up hope. Even with the summon stone woken, Gergrig had said it would take an enormous amount of power to open the gate, and first the Merdrun had to break through the massive defences of the ring-fortress. She eyed the three moons. It was not long at all until syzygy. How could the enemy do it in the time left?

The ground shook violently, grinding the capstone back and forth on the uprights. She hurled herself backwards, but it stilled. Away to her left, in the direction of the green moon, clouds of snow boiled up. She floated up, trying to see what had happened.

There was a breach in the ring-fortress. The Merdrun had under-mined part of the lower wall, collapsing a thirty-yard-wide section of the fortress, and they were swarming up the ice to the attack. The defenders tumbled ice rubble down at them, driving them back, but they attacked again and again. They were relentless.

Karan took advantage of the chaos to slip lower, scanning the attackers for any sign of the magiz. Many of the defenders lay dead and dying below the broken section; she was bound to be there, drinking their lives.

Karan found her several hundred yards below, where a section of the ring-fortress had slid down in one piece before breaking apart and strewing nine crushed and bloody defenders across the ice. The magiz, accompanied by three acolytes in grey fur-lined cloaks, was hobbling from one body to the next, doing the gruesome business. Karan glided down, keeping low.

"We've lost thousands attacking this fortress," said one of the acolytes. It was a woman's voice, though Karan, being behind, could not see her face. She was as round as a dumpling in her heavy clothing. "We're really hurting, magiz."

"Not as much as they are," said the magiz.

She bent over another body, a young soldier whose chest had been crushed, though he was still kicking. Karan heard a revolting slurping sound and the magiz said, "Aaahh! that was a good one." The young man went still.

Karan clenched her fists helplessly. The evil old slukk had to die.

"Won't be long now," said the magiz, panting.

"How can you tell?" said the acolyte.

"A while ago I jerked Snoat's string again. I warned him of an assassination attempt by his enemies. He'll strike back very soon, and it will be the end of all resistance in western Santhenar."

"How did you know about the assassination plan?"

"I embedded a link in one of the enemy leaders a month ago. What he sees, I see, the fool!"

Karan, who had forgotten about the spy in their midst, froze. *He* and *one of their leaders* could mean Nadiril, Shand, Yggur or even Hingis at a pinch, but who? Yggur was the most likely traitor, given his previous mental breakdown and fragile emotional state.

She remembered the odd look he had given her in Chanthed, when she'd revealed that she had sent Sulien away with the Whelm. Could the magiz manipulate Yggur into hunting her down? Well, no one alive knew the Whelm better than he did. But would he hurt or kill an innocent child – even under the magiz's compulsion?

Yggur had been a ruthless warlord once, but there was also a soft side to him, a kindness in him. And he was tough – he had survived ordeals, mental and physical, that would have broken most other men. Karan did not want to think him capable of killing a child . . . yet she had not thought Benie capable of killing either.

The magiz hobbled to another dying defender, twenty yards away, while the three acolytes remained where they were, staring at the corpse of the young man whose life she had just drunk with such sickening ecstasy. Was this Karan's chance? There were no other Merdrun within a hundred yards; they were much further up the slope, occupied with the attack.

She would have to be quick, though. Malien had said that materialising oneself was incredibly exhausting. Karan drew her knife. One quick thrust was all it would take, then she would dematerialise and return to Alcifer.

She zoomed down and, just before landing a few yards behind the magiz, triggered the materialisation spell. Her boots struck the ice, but the moment her weight came onto her knees, they buckled. She had no strength at all; she could not even hold the knife! It went *click-click* as it hit the ice, then skidded past the magiz.

She whirled, colourless eyes shining out of those horrible soot-black sockets, grinning savagely. "I've pulled your string too, you little fool."

The magiz lunged, surprisingly quickly for someone who had an artificial leg, and caught Karan by the left shin. Her hands were as cold as the ice beneath her; so cold that they burned. Karan tried to dematerialise but could not speak the words. She could barely move.

"Make a link to your daughter," said the magiz.

Karan managed to shake her head.

The magiz laughed. "You can't save her. When I have direct contact, you can't stop me."

The magiz let go then, with the bony forefinger of her other hand, tapped Karan on the top of the head three times, and each tap was like a metal spike being driven deeper. "Link to your daughter!"

Karan managed a grunt of defiance, but it wasn't enough – the magiz was forcing a link to form. It was already complete in Karan's mind; it was questing out, searching for the emotional connection to Sulien, and she could not stop it.

No! she thought desperately, as if she could stop the link through will alone. No, no, *no*!

But the magiz's will was stronger, and her mancery was overwhelming. "Yes," she said. "And the moment it's complete, I'll drink her little life."

She forced so hard that the spike seemed to spear right through Karan's head. She could not make a sound, but every fibre of her mind was screaming.

Mummy, what's she doing to you?

The magiz had succeeded, and Karan was crushed by a terror so complete that for a moment she could not think. Then it burst out of her: *Sulien, break the link!*

"Ahhhh," sighed the magiz, then tensed. She was preparing to send a killing blow across the link, and Karan could do nothing about it; the pain had utterly disabled her.

But she's hurting you, Mummy, said Sulien. *She's trying to kill you. Break the link! NOW!*

The pain grew; the magiz was about to strike Sulien dead. Karan had to do something. Her tongue unfroze and she screamed.

Leave . . . my . . . mother . . . alone! cried Sulien.

Karan sensed her desperate rage. *Don't, Sulien!*

"I've found the brat, Gergrig!" yelled the magiz. "I know where she is."

Sulien's fury exploded and a searing, blue-white flash burst in front of the magiz's eyes. She shrieked and tried to shield her eyes but little blisters formed all over her face, then her eyes turned blood-red.

"I can't see!" she howled. "Gergrig, I can't see."

"I'm coming!" he roared.

And then it happened. Across the link, through Sulien's eyes, Karan saw the Whelm stand up, a dozen of them, and they were staring up at the sky as if in awe.

Gergrig? said a squat bony man. *Master?*

Every hair on Karan's head stood up. No, *no*!

We have no master, Idlis said coldly.

But we could have, said the squat Whelm yearningly.

The pain in Karan's head was gone and she could move again. *Sulien, get out of there now!*

There was no reply. *Sulien, did you hear me?*

The magiz flailed around blindly and caught Karan by the shin again. Karan kicked but could not break free; the magiz's hand had frozen to her skin. But Gergrig was only yards away. She had to break the link and go.

"Dematerialise!" she gasped. "Spell-stop, spell-stop!"

Rip! She felt an agonising pain in her lower left leg — the skin had torn off in a bloody inches-wide strip all the way around.

"Amplify the drumming, magiz!" bellowed Gergrig. "Corrupt every-one on Santhenar."

Karan tumbled into blackness, the drumming loud in her ears, then went skidding across the polished stone floor of Alcifer, dribbling blood from the ragged skinless ring around her shin. Everything, including Sulien's earlier cry, had been part of a lure to bring her back to Cinnabar — and into the trap.

She forced herself to her hands and knees, realising that she had been gone a long time and Llian must be in torment. She had to find him. But before she could stand up, something hard pressed into the middle of her back.

"Welcome back," said Maigraith.

82

THEY'RE AS GOOD AS DEAD

"Ussarine?" bellowed Shand.

"What's happening?" Ussarine cried as they tumbled through the gate. "Where are we going?"

"I don't know." The wind was howling in his ears and he could barely hear her. "I was trying for Alcifer, but—"

They were jerked one way then another, as if two people were fighting over them. Ussarine's flailing fist struck Shand in the nose so hard that his eyes watered. He grabbed her wrist with both hands and held on. They were spinning in a flat circle now. Ussarine pulled him against her.

"I'm afraid—" he said.

"Of where we're going?"

"And who's sending us there."

"Did the summon stone open your gate?"

"Yes, to get rid of us," he said grimly. "But I'm not sure it's controlling it now."

"Who is?"

"Either Snoat or the magiz." Could the Command device really give Snoat the power to seize control of a gate? It was a troubling thought.

"Wherever they're sending us, we don't want to go there," she said.

"Hang on! I'll try to find Tallia."

Ussarine clamped her arms around him. Shand closed his eyes and attempted to visualise her, but all he could see was old Nadiril, sitting at a table with another of those ridiculous ear-shaped listening devices in front of him. He would do.

The gate ejected them and they landed with a thump that tore them apart. Shand skidded across a tiled floor on his knees, *bump-bump-bump*, and crashed into a row of chairs, knocking them over one by one. Some distance away a table was turned upside down. Crockery smashed and cutlery went ringing and tinkling across the floor.

"What the blazes is going on!" A door was thrown open and Yggur stood there swaying. "You!"

"Displeased to see you too," said Shand.

Both knees had been torn out of his trousers and his knees were bleeding. He rubbed them furiously, then went looking for Ussarine. She was lying under the ruins of the table, which had lost three of its legs in the impact. A long bruise ran from one side of her forehead to the other.

"Shand?" said another man. "Is Ussarine . . . ?"

"Here," said Shand, heaving the top of the table aside and helping her up.

Ussarine probed the bruise with her fingertips, winced, then stood up, beaming. "Hingis!"

The ugly little man was staring at her, his eyes shining. She ran four steps and threw her arms wide. "It's so good to see you."

Shand scratched the back of his neck. They made an odd couple. Though, he supposed, not much odder than he and Yalkara had been. Esea appeared in the doorway, frowning at the commotion, and when she saw Ussarine with her arms around Hingis, Esea's breath hissed between her teeth and she stalked out.

"About time you got back from holidays," said Yggur to Shand.

Yggur looked stronger now, almost like his old commanding self. Shand felt a surge of hope; he could be a powerful ally, and he had gifts that no one understood.

"I might say the same to you," said Shand.

He went into the adjoining room, where Nadiril sat in a chair by a fire, toying with the enchanted leather ear and talking to Tallia. They shook hands. The others trooped in. Hingis was sweating, and Esea very pale.

"I gather things aren't going so well here," said Shand. "Wherever here is."

"Vilikshathûr," said Tallia. "I wonder how you got here if you didn't know where you were heading."

"I was originally aiming for Alcifer."

"Why there?" said Nadiril.

Shand summarised what had happened in Carcharon. "How goes the war?"

"Bad," said Tallia. "Snoat's armies are rampaging down the length of Iagador and there's nothing we can do to stop him." She summed up the situation. "Since he lost Pem-Y-Rum, he's been making war like a man obsessed."

"It undermined his very identity," said Shand, "and to a narcissist that's unbearable. He's got to prove himself all over again. Any news from Malien?"

"No."

"Are you riding back to Carcharon?" said Hingis.

"Only if there's no other way. It's more than a week's journey, through lands occupied by Snoat's army. We don't have the time, and if we're caught our last hope will be lost."

"What are you going to do about the summon stone, then?"

"I'll *try* to reopen the gate," Shand said wearily. "That won't be easy or quick, and given that the stone just expelled us, I can't imagine it'll let us return."

"Someone has to kill Snoat," said Tallia.

"Where is he now?"

"On the flagship of his fleet, offshore, blockading Vilikshathûr."

"It's not easy to protect a ship, even in the middle of a fleet. On a dark night, one man can sink a ship if he knows where to place the charge."

"How would we do it?"

"Not with mancery. We'll send in a dozen saboteurs in black canoes, carrying incendiaries and barrels of blasting powder."

Tallia nodded. "It could work. Nadiril?"

"Do it!"

She rose. "I'll get it organised for tonight." She went out.

Shand sat with Nadiril and Yggur, telling them the grim details of the past week and a half. It felt good to be working as a team again.

Before he finished, Tallia ran in. "Snoat's flagship separated from the fleet an hour ago and is racing south."

"Why south?" said Yggur.

"He must have traced Llian's gate to Alcifer," said Shand. "Snoat wants Llian's manuscript back desperately."

"Can we get there first?" said Nadiril.

"We might, if we had a fast enough ship."

"I've made an arrangement with a fat lout of a fellow called Pender," said Hingis. "Can't say I like him much, but he does have a lot of ships."

"I used to know him well," said Shand. "Tell him we want the fastest one he's got and we need to leave in —" he consulted the chalcedony clock on the mantelpiece "— three hours. Have your saboteurs ready to embark, Tallia. If we can catch him, we'll send him down with his ship and put an end to the bloody business."

Hingis was sweating as he lurched into the little room at the back where Esea was waiting. Since her return from Chanthed three days ago they had maintained an uneasy peace based on never mentioning the betrayal that had torn them apart, but he had known it could not last if Ussarine came back.

Esea looked haggard. Their schism was eating her up as much as it had him.

She forced a smile. "Hingis—"

Breath rasped into his good lung. "Please don't force me to choose."

"I wasn't going to. I want you to be happy, and if that means you have to be with *her* . . . "

"It does."

"Then as long as we're reconciled, I'm happy too."

She did not look it, but he said, "Thank you."

"I'll even give you my blessing . . . if you can do one little thing for me."

"Anything!" he said hoarsely.

"Would you change my bandages? It's hard to do by myself."

He froze. It was a test, one he must not fail. "Yes," he croaked. "Of course."

He could do this. He went down on his knees, took off her left shoe and sock, then slowly unwrapped the bandages. He told himself that the loss of two toes was insignificant; Esea was still a hundred times more perfect than he.

The ragged wounds where her toes had been were almost healed now. Their loss hardly changed her at all. His twin was still beautiful, and Hingis needed her to be, to balance his own hideousness – inside and out. He looked up. There was a sheen of sweat on her lovely forehead; she was desperately hoping he could do this.

He smiled. It was all right after all. Esea let out her breath.

The drumming sounded, very soft, very low, but not low enough. Hingis looked down at her maimed foot, gave an involuntary shudder and ruined everything.

83

IT CAN'T BE FAKED

Maigraith always appeared at the worst possible time.

Karan could not deal with her now. The magiz knew where Sulien was and might attack her at any time. And the Whelm had seen Gergrig — what would they do? She could think about nothing else.

Her bloody shin throbbed, dragging her into the here and now, and she forced herself to focus. Maigraith had lost so much weight that her arms were like jointed sticks, and her face was a skull dominated by the eyes that betrayed her Charon heritage.

They were locked on Karan, unblinking. "Your hrux nearly killed me," said Maigraith. "Perhaps you hoped it would."

"I had to protect my daughter," Karan whispered.

"You knew there would be a reckoning, and now it's come. Who are you going to give up? Sulien or Llian? You can't have both. Refuse me Sulien, and Llian dies. It's that simple."

Karan's only hope was to act instantly, exhausted though she was. She caught Maigraith by the ankles and heaved. Maigraith teetered, but before Karan could topple her a cord flashed over her own head and tightened around her throat.

"Lead us to Llian," said Thandiwe. "Now!"

Llian had been searching for hours in deepening despair. There was no sign of Karan in any of her usual haunts. He was pacing around the great chamber containing the granite statue of Rulke, when Maigraith's ring on his finger clicked against the embossed silver wall. A section slowly dissolved to reveal a cubic vault of lustrous black obsidian, twenty feet on a side. It was empty but for a table, two chairs and a plain rectangular chest made of the immensely hard black metal, titane.

The chest had no lock. He opened it, looked down at the neat stack of journals, codexes, scrolls and loose parchments, and choked.

This was it! After ten years of dreaming about them, and days of searching, he had found Rulke's records right where he should have expected them to be – at the point where the statue's gaze was focused.

He took the documents out one by one, handling them lovingly, and sorted them into those he could read, one small pile, and those written in the secret Charon script – three larger piles. The unreadable documents, written in indigo ink on pages made of beaten silver, would be Rulke's true Histories of the Charon from the time they were exiled into the void.

Llian doubled over, scarcely able to breathe. Rulke had devoted his long life to protecting his people from the Merdrun, and he would have had a plan in case they found a way into Santhenar. But to find that plan, Llian needed the key Thandiwe had stolen.

He was flipping through the silver pages of a slim codex, aching to read it, when he heard a gentle thump behind him. His heart soared. "Karan?"

"Perfect timing," said Thandiwe. "Put the book down and raise your hands, or she dies."

The codex hit the floor. Karan was on her knees and Thandiwe held a cord tightly around her throat. His heart stopped. A gaunt, feral Maigraith stood to one side, and from the look on her face she wished him dead. Join the queue!

With aching slowness Llian picked up the book and laid it on the table. Dust wafted up in little clouds, one from either side. The leather cover had a small patch of mould on its centre shaped like a bee in flight. He raised his hands.

"Let her go," he whispered. "She hasn't done anything wrong."

"She dosed me with hrux," grated Maigraith.

Karan tried to speak but the cord was too tight; she could only make choking sounds. His mind raced. There was no point arguing or laying out the litany of Maigraith's crimes against Karan, and Julken's against Sulien. Maigraith held an unshakeable belief in the rightness of her own actions.

"Loosen the cord," he said quietly.

Thandiwe pulled it tighter. Would she really kill Karan, who had done nothing to harm her, to take revenge on Llian? How could he save her? Ah!

"You're a chronicler, not a killer," said Llian, using all the power of his teller's voice to enthral and convince.

Thandiwe did not move. Neither did Maigraith. What had happened to her? She looked like a flesh-coloured skeleton animated by an all-consuming rage, and there had to be more to it than hrux. Something had utterly transformed her in the five weeks she had spent at Carcharon, and surely it had to be the summon stone.

"If you take revenge this way," he said to Thandiwe, though he was also speaking to Maigraith, "it will undermine everything you do from this moment forward."

Thandiwe loosed the cord fractionally. Karan sucked at the air.

"Even if you get your Great Tale," he added, raising his teller's voice to a higher plane, "and gain the highest honour, even if the world acclaims you as the greatest teller of all, it will avail you nothing because in your heart you'll know you didn't earn it."

"I've earned it," she grated. "No one has ever worked harder."

"You used to have a beautiful teller's voice, the best natural one I've ever heard, but listen to it now. It started to fade the moment the drumming took you over."

"The drumming has nothing to do with it." There was a tremor in Thandiwe's voice now.

"Are you saying that all the bribes you paid, the lies you told, the betrayals you did, starting with denying me my career, were the *real* you?"

"I deserve a Great Tale and I'm going to have one."

Karan was staring at him, trying to work out what he was up to. Llian wished he knew. He was making it up as he went along, though he did not see how it could work.

"Thandiwe," he said softly, "tellers aren't like normal people. You don't get a Great Tale simply by writing well; you also have to tell it aloud to the assembled masters. Every tale is also a performance, and a Great Tale has to be a towering performance, but you must believe, in your heart, that before everything else you *are* that great teller. If you don't believe it, your teller's voice will show it. It can't be faked."

"I *am* a great teller," cried Thandiwe, "and I *will* have my Great Tale!" But her voice cracked.

"I hope you get it," said Llian. "I really do. But if you steal the tale or kill for it, in your own mind that's what your real identity will be when you tell your tale to the masters: not a teller, but a thief or a murderer. You can't be both. In reaching for the prize, you will have put it forever beyond your reach."

Thandiwe stared at him, then at the top of Karan's head, then at Maigraith. A shudder racked her.

"I've done plenty of bad things but I'm not a killer!" she cried. "I'm not!"

The cord fell from her fingers. Karan fell forwards, gasping.

"But I'm having Rulke's tale," Thandiwe added.

"Even if it means we lose the coming war?" said Llian.

"What are you talking about?"

"Rulke spent his entire life trying to protect his people from the Merdrun. His papers must contain a way to beat them."

"Rulke failed and his people are extinct. And I don't believe the Merdrun even exist."

"The magiz is pulling your strings too," Karan croaked.

"After they take Santhenar," said Llian, "there won't be a place for tellers or anything else we care about."

It shook her. Llian could see the self-doubt in her eyes, the fear. But she wanted a Great Tale too desperately.

"I'll take the risk." She turned to Maigraith. "I've done all you asked."

"You betrayed them just as you said you would," said Maigraith, her voice dripping contempt. "Take your prize and go with all speed, and never return to Alcifer."

"The ones in the small pile are written in the common speech," said Llian.

"You've read them already?" said Thandiwe.

"Yes," Llian lied, for the glimmering of a desperate plan was forming.

Could he pull it off? It would take a miracle of telling. "All the others are in the secret Charon syllabary. You'll need Rulke's key to read them."

"Lucky I have it then."

"Teller or thief?" he said pointedly.

Thandiwe rocked back on her heels, then packed all of Rulke's scrolls, codexes and other papers into the titane chest and heaved it onto a three-wheeled trolley. She wheeled it out the door, then ran.

One wheel had a slight squeak. It marked her racing progress down the hall, then she was gone.

As was any hope of stopping the Merdrun.

84

WHERE DID HE HIDE HIM?

After walking back and forth for several minutes, eyeing Llian malevolently, Maigraith stopped and supported herself with both hands on the end of the table. She was shaking. "Give me my ring."

He removed it from his little finger. It had been a tight fit but his hands were so sweaty it came off easily.

She wiped it on her blouse, slid it on her ring finger and studied it for a long time, as if she could not believe she had it back. Then her face hardened.

"So," she said to Karan. "Llian or Sulien? Who's it to be?"

Karan was still on her knees with her hands bound, and her throat was badly bruised. Llian looked into her green eyes, saw she had no answer and knew what he had to do. And what it would cost him.

"Julken is a monster," said Llian.

"He's gone to Garching Nod, the best mancery school in Meldorin," said Maigraith. "The masters will correct his little . . . infelicities."

"Sulien will never be bonded to him. I'd sooner die."

"Then you will," Maigraith said flatly.

"But before I do," he said, improvising desperately, "you must know the complete story of Rulke – the untold story."

"What untold story?" she said suspiciously.

"About his identical twin brother, Kalke, who never left the void."

Maigraith's face normally showed little emotion, but at his words her eyes widened, and he saw a desperate hope there. Then a longing so profound that, even in this situation, it moved him.

Before meeting Rulke, Maigraith had lived a desperately unhappy life, dominated and emotionally crushed by her ruthless liege, Faelamor. Meeting Rulke had transformed Maigraith; she had found the one person who could complete her. But, within months, he was dead, because Llian had pushed Tensor to breaking point.

The dying Rulke had not blamed Llian, but Maigraith did, and as she increasingly rejected the old human and Faellem aspects of her ancestry, her Charon heritage became ever more important, an obsession. Nothing could feed that obsession like Rulke's identical twin – a physically indistinguishable copy of the man she would love until the instant her life's spark was extinguished.

Llian could read her now. Logic told her that Rulke did not have a twin, yet her heart ached for it to be true.

"Why haven't I heard this before?" said Maigraith, her Charon eyes narrowing.

"I only just read it," said Llian. "In the small pile of papers I could read. It was a dangerous secret – dangerous for Kalke, I mean."

"Which of the papers?"

"Fourth from the top."

Maigraith staggered to the opening of the vault, went out and closed it. Without her ring, Llian could not open it again.

"She's gone after Thandiwe," said Karan.

She was studying his face, trying to read what he was up to. He gave an almost imperceptible shake of the head and untied her hands. The cord had cut into her wrists and her fingers were purple. The ropes fell away; she worked her fingers to get the blood flowing.

Thandiwe had run, and she had a lead of ten minutes. Was it

enough? If she had delayed, or Maigraith caught her and read the documents, it was all over and she would kill him out of hand.

"What are we going to do?" said Karan.

"I don't know." He dared not say a word, dared not even hint at his plan by expression or gesture. Maigraith was a formidable mancer and might be able to spy on them in ways he could not imagine.

They sat at the table, their shoulders touching. Karan took hold of his arm with both hands. Llian stared at the faint marks in the dust, all that was left of the papers he had spent the last decade coveting.

"Can Thandiwe make a Great Tale of them?" he said, only because he had to say something and he could not bear to talk about Sulien.

"How good is she?" said Karan.

He considered the question dispassionately. "She was the best student I knew, better than most of the masters."

Karan laid her head on his shoulder and closed her eyes, and he could feel her trembling and sense her dread. He imagined Maigraith staggering after Thandiwe, catching her and reading the papers on the top of the pile.

Half an hour passed. More. Maigraith must have caught Thandiwe. Llian's guts were twisted and Karan looked as though she were about to collapse.

The door opened silently. Maigraith stood there, gasping. Had she caught Thandiwe or not? Llian kept his face impassive; he dared show no emotion except fear for his own life.

"Why was it dangerous for Kalke?" said Maigraith. "Why didn't he leave the void?" Her voice was flat now; Llian could not tell if she believed a word.

"He wasn't strong enough," said Llian. "He still hadn't recovered."

"From what?"

"Thousands of years ago, when Kalke and Rulke were bold young men not yet of age, they set out to prove themselves by making a reckless raid on a Merdrun stronghold. They planned to tweak the nose of the Merdrun leader, Mergriz the Forty-fourth, by stealing the symbol of his authority, the red cube cut from the keystone of the Crimson Gate. They failed of course, and Kalke was captured and tortured in fiendish ways that only the Merdrun would use on another human. He should have died . . . "

Llian left it unsaid, hoping that her yearning to know more would make the story real to her.

"*Should* have died?" said Maigraith.

"I only found the papers this morning. I didn't have time to read the full tale of how Rulke rescued Kalke; I just skimmed it. But what a tale!" he cried. "The rescue was quite impossible, yet Rulke succeeded magnificently. It was the boldest exploit in all the Histories, a story to shade even his tale of the taking of Aachan, *How the Hundred Conquered a World.*" Llian had heard Rulke tell that tale and it had been a barbaric masterpiece.

Maigraith's eyes were shining now, her whole face alight. "In all the Three Worlds there has never been a man the equal of my Rulke."

"He brought Kalke home again but his brother was broken in body and mind. Rulke blamed himself, for he had been the leader on that reckless raid, and Kalke the follower. Rulke spent years trying to heal his twin, at the same time as he was growing into leadership and fighting off the Merdrun. They had the whiff of blood in their nostrils by then and were doing their best to wipe the last of the Charon out. But Rulke hadn't managed to heal Kalke when everything changed . . . "

Llian was thinking back to Rulke's tale and how the Charon had come to escape the void.

"Yes, yes?" cried Maigraith.

"Xesper the Aachim," said Llian.

"What about him?"

"He was a dangerously inquisitive man, and he made a seeing device to look out into the void . . . "

"But?"

"It left a track that identified Aachan, and the desperate Charon, now on the brink of extinction, saw the only chance they would ever get. They followed the track back, found Aachan and took it."

"Though not Kalke?" said Maigraith.

"He wasn't strong enough for that desperate journey; Rulke feared that the trip would kill him. And if by some chance he did manage to survive it, how could they protect him when they were just a handful trying to take a world? They had no choice but to leave him behind."

"To die?" cried Maigraith.

"Rulke loved his brother, and he also owed him. Rulke saw only one hope – to suspend Kalke's life and hide him in a place where he would be safe and no one would think to look for him. And he also hoped, no, believed . . . "

"What, what?"

"That enough time in the suspended state would heal the wounds of body and mind, and restore Kalke to the man of promise he had been before that foolish raid."

"Why would Rulke believe that?"

"The Charon had used life suspension before, on cases that were not amenable to any other form of healing." Llian knew this to be true.

"Where did Rulke hide Kalke?"

"In the frozen core of an asteroid orbiting an insignificant yellow sun."

"But Rulke never went back for him," guessed Maigraith. "Why not?"

"The Charon had taken Aachan, but it did them little good because most of them were infertile there. Their numbers were slowly dwindling, they were afraid of attracting the Merdrun's attention, and they lacked the strength for such a perilous journey across the void. That's why Rulke commissioned the Golden Flute from Shuthdar in the first place – to open a gate directly from Aachan to Kalke's asteroid and bring him safely home. But Shuthdar stole the flute and—"

"That was thousands of years ago," said Maigraith. "Could Kalke still be alive?"

"Rulke believed so." Llian did not plan to say any more. Let Maigraith drag it out of him – it would heighten her identification with the tale.

"The void is limitless," said Maigraith. "How can an insignificant yellow sun be found in a myriad of suns? And how can one asteroid be picked out among millions?"

Llian closed his eyes, as he often did when recalling obscure facts to mind, then opened them and met Maigraith's eyes. He was a teller and he told it to her as truth.

"The galaxy was called Ivellix, the sun was Casulind in the Trabucelus Arm, and it had but three planets, plus an asteroid belt between the first planet and the second. The asteroid, which was three miles by five, was red and covered in sulphur snow. That's all I read."

"You have a remarkably clear memory, considering you read the paper so fleetingly."

"Perfect recall is the first thing a chronicler learns."

Maigraith orbited the table three times. "I'm not sure I believe you."

Llian did not speak.

"And yet," she added, her eyes shining, "it has the ring of truth. It could be true. And since I swore to Rulke, he would want me to do my duty by his brother."

"The void is a dangerous place."

"I've been there, remember? And Rulke gifted me powers no one else on Santhenar has ever held."

If she could have used those powers for the benefit of Santhenar they might have had a chance, but neither Llian nor Karan had ever had any influence on Maigraith. There was no hope of gaining her aid now.

She made another orbit, then stopped in front of Karan. "Your man has earned you and Sulien a reprieve. Use it well, for if he has deceived me you will pay a hundredfold." She left without looking back.

Llian listened to her footsteps until they could no longer be heard. Karan was rubbing her bruised throat. He took her hand and, without saying a word, led her out of the chamber and back to the pool.

"Take your clothes off," said Llian.

She looked at him quizzically, gave an enigmatic smile and said, "All right."

He checked her garments one by one, making sure that Maigraith had not left any tiny spy device on them, then looked her over, back and front, and felt through her red hair.

"You're taking an awfully long time to do a simple job," said Karan.

It was his turn to smile. "Now me."

She checked him just as thoroughly. "Nothing."

"How long have we got?" he said.

"Maigraith will have to make arrangements for Julken's care before she goes to the void, and it'll be a long search. She might not be back for months, even years. Should I get dressed now?"

"The pavilion has a nice soft floor."

She grinned. "I don't see how you can top your performance in Rulke's vault . . . but all right."

Afterwards, when they were lying lazily together, Karan said, "Was there a word of truth in that story about Kalke?"

"Only the bits I cribbed from Rulke's tale, *How the Hundred Conquered a World*."

"You tailored it perfectly to her yearnings."

He did not reply.

She looked down at his untidy yet endearing face. "What is it?"

"I've just broken the most important teller's law of all, and perverted my art. I've created an untrue tale."

"It might be true."

"Any story *might* be true, but that one isn't. If it ever gets out, posterity will only know me as Llian the Liar."

"Would you do it again? To save me and Sulien?"

"Of course. And pay the price. I'm sure there's going to be one."

"How can there be? No one knows save you and me."

"Maigraith will when she returns."

"The void is a deadly place. Let's pray she never comes back."

85

WE'VE GOT TO ACT FAST

"All Rulke's papers are gone," said Llian, "so there's no point staying here."

"And the summon stone is five hundred miles north," said Karan. "We can't get back to it before the invasion. What do you want to do?"

"Go after Sulien." Karan had told him about her trip to Cinnabar, the magiz's attack on Sulien and how she had saved Karan's life.

Tears formed in her eyes. "The magiz will attack again. Sulien is in danger right now and we'll never find her in time." She looked around her, everywhere but at Llian, and her jaw tightened. "I've got to act now. Today!"

"No!" Llian said flatly.

"The magiz is the key to everything: saving Sulien, blocking the summon stone and keeping the Merdrun out. And I'm the only person who can get to her."

"She'll be expecting you."

"I don't have any choice, and if our positions were reversed, you'd do the same."

His shoulders slumped. He knew she would not give in. "How are you going to do it?"

"I haven't got a clue."

Thup-thup, thup-thup.

"What's that?" said Karan.

"Sounds like it's up in the air."

They ran up to the globarium, a tall spiralling tower topped with a half-globe a hundred feet across partly filled with water, with a small pointed island in the middle.

It was breezy here. Karan shook out her hair and it streamed out behind her for two feet. They climbed onto the circular wall. A low range of mountains lay behind them. Ahead, to the east, was the Sea of Thurkad, here twenty-fives leagues across.

"It's a flying balloon . . . " said Llian.

As it came closer Karan saw that it was shaped like a fat lozenge with a smaller lozenge attached to its underside. A pair of rotors whirred at the rear and the vessel had a slight asymmetry that gave its makers away. The Aachim never made two objects exactly the same – for them, that would take away the whole point of designing.

"It's Malien!" Karan cried, taking Llian by the waist and dancing him round in a spiral that took them perilously close to the rim.

She waved furiously, and with her pale face upturned and her streaming red hair she would have been identifiable from a quarter of a mile away. The vessel turned and in a couple of minutes it was hovering over the wall.

"Malien!" Karan yelled.

A door swung open, and framed in it was her kinswoman. Malien tossed down the end of a rope ladder. Karan went up it like a sailor, sprang in and embraced her, then pulled away, watching Llian and biting her lip. He climbed awkwardly, swaying and sweating and missing his footing a couple of times, then froze at the top, not knowing how to get off the ladder.

Malien reached down, wrapped her enormously long fingers around his upper arms and heaved him in.

"Well met, chronicler," she said. "It's good to see, in a world in such flux, that you retain all the flaws you had when we first met."

She was laughing at him, though in a kindly way. They'd had their moments over the years, though Karan knew that Malien, deep down, did like Llian.

Karan pulled the door closed. The cabin was only twenty feet long and eight wide, but the builders had fitted dozens of cupboards into it, all beautifully finished, and every surface was decorated with intricate geometric engravings or carvings of the strange plants and beasts of Aachan.

At the other end, hammocks criss-crossed one another. A dozen Aachim were staring out the oval windows at the city built for their mortal enemy. Karan sighed. She had lived with them for years as she was growing up, and being among them again was like coming home.

But Llian was shifting his weight from foot to foot, and his jaw was knotted. Most of his encounters with the Aachim had been unhappy ones.

"Enough of this terrible city," said Malien.

She gestured to the helmsman, a bony balding fellow with sagging ears. He worked various levers and the sky ship slipped away.

"I wouldn't have thought you'd come within ten leagues of Alcifer," said Karan.

"Nor would I, willingly. I was looking for you."

"How did you know to look here?"

"Three days ago I detected a gate, and Xarah, who has made a science of her art, pinpointed where it originated and where it ended. You remember Xarah?"

A small Aachim, not much taller than Karan, with a pale freckled face and short mustard-yellow hair, and an air of long-felt sadness.

Karan shook hands. "I didn't know gates could be pinpointed."

"They couldn't until now," said Malien. "And only by an adept with the right training."

"How did you know we were in the gate?"

"No one has made one on Santhenar in ten years, then suddenly there are two in three days. Who else could be behind them but the two biggest troublemakers I know."

"*Two* gates?"

"Another went from Carcharon to Vilikshathûr half a day later."

"I suppose that was Shand," said Karan.

"Clearly we have much to talk about," said Malien.

The helmsman took them up the coast to an uninhabited island a few miles offshore. They set down in a sunny glade where the ground was calf-deep in fallen leaves, and the Aachim prepared a hasty meal of smoked meats and pickled vegetables.

"I can't believe that the fate of the world rests on the whim of so shallow and narcissistic an old human as Cumulus Snoat," said Malien after Karan and Llian had brought her up to date. "Truly, your kind is in irretrievable decline."

Karan scowled. The Aachim took every opportunity to point out their own superiority.

"Seven weeks must have passed since the magiz said eight weeks," said Llian. "We haven't got long."

"Ah!" said Karan.

"What?"

"She lied. Syzygy is almost on us."

Llian's breath hissed out through his teeth. "Then we haven't got a hope of stopping the invasion."

"Ship coming!" called their lookout, Nimil, a young Aachim with a metal slit in his throat.

"We'll talk about what to do later," said Malien quietly. "In private."

They scrambled up to the watch post, a flat rock topping a pyramid-shaped hill. Nimil was peering north through a brass and green-enamel telescope. Karan made out a dark speck on the sea.

"Ally or enemy?" said Malien.

"Can't tell." Nimil's voice was a squeaky whistle. "It's racing down the coast, close inshore, keeping out of sight. Could be a smuggler."

Malien looked through the telescope, and so did Karan, but there was nothing more to be discovered. They returned to the fire.

Shortly Nimil reported a second vessel, several miles north of the first and also heading south. "Biggest ship I've ever seen. Flying a purple flag."

"Purple with a yellow book in the middle?" said Llian.

"Yes."

"It's Snoat."

"What does he want?"

"The manuscript of my Great Tale, of course," said Llian. "Can you attack him?" he asked Malien.

"What with?"

"Fire arrows? Or barrels of blasting powder?"

"This sky ship is the first of its kind," she said carefully, "and it was built in great haste. It's not entirely reliable, which is why we've taken so long to arrive. We've had no time to design aerial weapons. And fire is strictly forbidden, or the only blast you'll see will be our disintegration."

"The small ship is heading for Alcifer Cove under full sail," called Nimil.

"It's racing Snoat," guessed Karan. "I'll bet it's some of our allies."

They reboarded and the sky ship slipped away to the south, keeping behind the island until Snoat's flagship was no longer in sight, then the bald helmsman took them low over the racing vessel inshore.

People ran out on deck, staring up at the sky ship. The Aachim design would have been unmistakeable. Someone waved signal flags, spelling *Shand*.

"Tell them we'll set down in the clearing half a mile north of the eastern gate of Alcifer," said Malien to Nimil, who signalled back.

An hour later the party of eight arrived: first Shand, wincing and holding his injured buttock, then Tallia and Nadiril, Lilis and Yggur, Hingis and Ussarine, and finally Esea, who was far behind and looked ghastly. Had Hingis and Ussarine's reunion gone too well?

Shand shook everyone's hands. "We've got a chance now, but we've got to act fast. Let's get to work."

86

WHAT COULD POSSIBLY GO WRONG?

By mid-afternoon, the drumming was pounding in Karan's head. It would not be long now.

"Snoat's coming ashore," a lookout called.

Xarah let out a squawk. Her mustard-yellow hair was standing up. "The flow is rising."

"From the summon stone?" Shand's voice was sandpaper on glass.

"That's what Xarah is monitoring," said Malien. "How can we assassinate a man who's so paranoid and so well guarded?"

Shand whispered in Tallia's ear.

"I don't like it," she said, glancing at Llian.

"I think it's worth a try."

The drumming was rising as well. "What's worth a try?" said Yggur, who was sitting quietly in the background. He looked much better than he had at Chanthed.

"Later," said Shand irritably. He looked around. "Where are Nadiril and Lilis?"

"They went to have a look inside Alcifer."

"Incredible! You'd think we were on a picnic."

He assembled a deputation: himself and the two smallest Aachim men. Karan thought they projected an air of weakness. Perhaps that was his intention.

"Go quickly!" said Malien. "Meet him halfway."

"You have somewhere in mind?" said Shand.

"I'll show you." She led them up a little hillock and focused her field glasses. "The road from the quay passes through a lovely garden, then across an island in an artificial lake – there! It's a beautiful place and Snoat is an aesthete; he'll be drawn to it. Meet him there."

Karan's stomach throbbed; she could only think about Sulien. The magiz could be planning another attack on her right now. She went back and sat next to Llian, who was recording the day in his journal. Malien was ten feet away, her back to a tree and her eyes closed.

"What are they up to?" said Llian.

"I don't know," said Karan. "But I don't like it."

The afternoon crawled towards sunset. "I can't bear this," she said suddenly. "Malien, I've got to stop the magiz opening the gate. I have to go back to Cinnabar."

"You've attacked her twice," said Malien. "You can't use the transpose spell again."

"If my gift for mancery was unblocked—"

"You're too old," said Malien. "The middle-aged brain is too inflexible."

"I'm only thirty-six!" Karan snarled.

"It would probably kill you."

"Every second person I've met lately has wanted to kill me, and if the Merdrun get through, Sulien, Llian and I are at the top of their list. Unblock my damned gift!"

"All right!" Malien snapped. "It'll be worth it to be rid of you." She sucked in a long breath. "Sorry, I take that back. Give me a quarter of an hour." She walked away into the trees.

Llian had gone potato white and was breathing in strangled gasps. Karan took his hand, aching to be able to comfort him.

"Last time you went," he said, "I was sure they'd torture you to death. I can't take any more, Karan."

She gave him a watery smile, the best she could manage. "It's the only way to save Sulien. If . . . if I don't come back . . ." Her voice cracked. "You're my rock, Llian. You've got to be strong, for her sake and mine."

He took her into his arms. "I'll do my best."

"The enemy, they'll . . ." She gulped, swallowed a massive lump.

"I'll find a way."

"You'll explain to her, won't you?" said Karan. "I can't bear to think—"

"I'll tell her why you couldn't answer her calls. She'll understand."

Malien reappeared, carrying a round metal box and looking exceptionally grim.

"What's the matter?" said Karan. "Have you realised that you can't unblock my gift?" She half hoped for that; it would be an honourable way out.

"No," Malien said tersely. "I've realised that I can."

"And?"

"Do you remember the day you gave birth to Sulien?"

What a question. It had changed Karan's life.

"This will be ten times as painful," said Malien.

"You'd better get on with it then."

"Getting your gift back could have . . . consequences."

"I'll take the risk," Karan said recklessly.

Malien took out a strap made of woven wire, with an emerald disc on the front and a black opal disc on the back. She fitted it around Karan's forehead with the emerald disc in the centre of her brow, then pulled the strap so tight that it hurt, and buckled it. She put a similar strap around Karan's chest and a third on her right wrist.

"Ready?" said Malien.

"Yes," Karan said softly. Her eyes slid to Llian, whose fists were knotted in his hair. He was in agony. She swallowed.

Malien touched the emerald disc on Karan's wrist to the one over her heart, then the one on her brow, and whispered a phrase she did not make out.

Pain sheared through her heart, her skull, her belly, then her limbs, as if torturers were pulling her limb from limb. When it finally passed, and she could sit up, she said, "I can't feel the power."

"You don't have any more power than you did before," said Malien.

"*Why not?*"

"Imagine you're an adult with a gift for music, but you've never learned to play. You'd have to practise for years before you could play a complicated piece. It's the same with mancery."

"Then what was the point!" cried Llian.

"Before Karan's gift was blocked she could work simple spells she'd learned as a child. Now she can use them again."

Llian exploded. "So you're sending her against the magiz – the greatest sorcerer the enemy have – armed only with kiddie magic?"

"Malien isn't *sending* me," Karan said quietly. "I'm going because it has to be done, so please stop shouting." She turned to Malien. "I'm worried about returning to Cinnabar via the disembodiment spell. After I used it last time I couldn't stand up."

"As I warned you," said Malien. "But you knew better."

"Is there another way of sending me to Cinnabar?"

Malien hesitated. "Ordinarily, no."

"But?"

"It wouldn't work for anyone else, which is why the enemy haven't sent anyone to Santhenar. But because you've been to Cinnabar three times already, and the path is embedded in you, a *physical* sending could work, though . . . "

"It'll be the most agonising thing I've ever experienced," Karan muttered.

"One of them," Malien said drily.

"Why don't you go too?" said Llian. "You could take the magiz on."

"A sending spell can't be worked on oneself. That's why it's called a sending. I'll get ready then. My preparations will take a few hours. You might want to . . . "

"Write my will?" said Karan.

The levity sank without trace. Llian looked on the verge of collapse.

"It'll be all right," she said feebly.

"That's what you said last time!"

They sat together, not talking. Last time Karan had been sick with dread, but she was quite numb now, barely able to feel at all.

As it grew dark, Shand's party returned. Yggur, who had spent the afternoon at the sky ship, also appeared, though Nadiril and Lilis were not yet back.

"Well?" said Yggur.

"The only envoy Snoat will listen to is Llian," said Shand. "And only if he brings, as a gift, his *Tale of the Mirror.*"

Karan reeled. Now, *now* she could feel. A shriek burst from her. "No, no, no!"

Malien turned to Xarah, who was crouched over a little device with concentric brass rings and sliding pointers mounted on a circular wooden base.

"How is the summon stone now?" said Malien.

Xarah moved one of the pointers a fraction. A tiny red crystal at the centre began to flash, faster and faster. "It's almost ready to bring them through."

"When the invasion comes," said Shand, "we can't be distracted by Snoat. Whatever the cost —" he glanced at Llian, then quickly away "— he's got to die tonight!"

Why was he so cold, so indifferent to Llian's fate? It had to be the drumming, which had driven the allies to fighting and bickering for the past month. "The moment Snoat gets Llian's manuscript," said Karan, "he'll have him killed."

"We've got a plan," said Shand.

"Why can't someone else take it?"

"Only Llian can get through to Snoat."

"Then I'll be his attendant."

"What about Sulien?"

"You bloody old bastard! I'll get you for this."

Llian stood up. He looked as though he wanted punch Shand in the mouth — and Karan half hoped he would. "You're sending me off to die, yet you haven't even bothered to consult me."

"There wasn't time," said Shand, avoiding his eyes.

"Liar! You made this plan hours ago. You don't give a damn any more, do you?"

"It's our only hope, Llian."

"I can see that. That's why I'm going."

"No, you're not!" snapped Karan.

"You didn't ask my permission about Cinnabar," Llian said gently. "I have to go because no one else can get to Snoat. What's the plan, Shand?"

"Your escorts will be Ussarine, Hingis and Esea. Strength and mancery, but the twins won't use any until after you pass the booby-trapped manuscript over."

"What am I supposed to do with it?"

"Kill Snoat if you can, or injure him so Ussarine can finish him off. Then get the Command device."

"Why?"

"Snoat used it to divert my gate from Carcharon, and the device will retain that memory. We can use it to remake the gate, open it right next to the summon stone and smash it to bits."

"You're mad!" said Karan.

"I dare say, but we've got to take the risk," said Shand.

"It's Llian taking all the risks."

"Esea and Hingis will keep Snoat's guards away. The sky ship, which he doesn't know exists, will be hanging in the darkness above, ready to pick everyone up."

"Great plan!" sneered Karan. "Four people versus a hundred guards, and the only means of escape an unreliable sky ship. What could possibly go wrong?"

"I don't like it either," said Yggur quietly.

"Given that your only contribution has been criticism ... " Shand broke off. "Time to go."

Karan watched the small party pass over the hill and out of sight, now understanding how Llian had felt when she had gone to Cinnabar. But then ...

Mummy, my nose is bleeding. My head feels like it's splitting down the middle. Mummeeeee ...

The magiz had found Sulien again. There wasn't a second to waste, nor any point in keeping silent now. Karan threw on her cold-weather gear and made a link.

It's all right, Sulien. I'll fix her – for ever! But before she could trigger Malien's sending spell—

A sour chuckle in her inner ear.

A painful jerk, as though an anchor chain had been wrapped around her middle and thrown overboard attached to a huge weight.

Ten seconds of utter blackness.

Then a frigid blast of wind struck her in the face, and she went skidding past the magiz for a good fifty yards on glassy ice, spinning round and round. The magiz had dragged Karan's physical body back to Cinnabar, to the icy plateau above the ring-fortress, and was bent on revenge.

"I *will* drink her life," the magiz shouted over the shrieking wind. "Then yours. It's all been futile, Karan. In ten thousand years no one has ever beaten us."

87

HER – OR ME?

It was a lovely place for the end of everything.

An octagonal pavilion of cream marble crowned the hill at the centre of the little island in the triangular lake. Three elegant arching bridges connected the island to the shore. A magical setting, Llian thought, for the bloody confrontation that would probably end in his death.

It was eight in the evening and cool, with an easterly breeze drifting mist and occasional showers up from the sea. With Ussarine on his left and Hingis and Esea to his right, he went down to Snoat's guards, who stood under bright lanterns at the foot of the western bridge. He could sense the tension between Ussarine, Hingis and Esea. Another worry he could have done without.

His heart was racing and tingles ran up and down his arms. Given that Snoat was paranoid about his own safety, how could this mission hope to succeed? The thick, spring-fired needle that the Aachim's cleverest artificer had inserted in the spine of Llian's manuscript, and the contact poison on the illuminated frontispiece, had been concealed by Hingis's most profound illusions, though Llian felt sure Snoat's mancers would find them.

As soon as the booby trap went off, Llian, who could not fight to save his life, had to make sure Snoat was dead or delay his escape until Ussarine could get there, then snatch the Command device, evade all the guards and get to Malien's sky ship, which was bound to be under attack by then. If he succeeded in so prodigiously unlikely a task, some future teller would surely make a Great Tale of it, he thought sourly. Assuming the Merdrun left anyone alive.

"Halt!" said the leading guard.

Four more guards came forward. One frisked Llian with intimate thoroughness. The others disarmed Ussarine, Hingis and Esea, sneering at Hingis's deformities and leering at Esea's chest. A stocky, over-muscled fellow likened Ussarine to a side of beef. Only a slight hardening of her jaw revealed her pain.

They were escorted across the bridge and up the hill, checked by a second set of guards then, outside the octagonal pavilion, by a mancer and an illusionist. They found nothing and Llian was allowed past. He could not relax; the sternest checks were yet to come.

The drumming resumed, a whisper in his inner ear. He looked up. Was the sky ship in place, hanging in the darkness a hundred feet above the pavilion? If it was not he would die, and Snoat specialised in unpleasant deaths.

The outside of the pavilion had been blocked off with panels of marbled paper stretched across bamboo frames set between the slender columns. An aide escorted Llian in. The pavilion was brightly lit by an array of yellow paper lanterns suspended from the roof in interlinked circles. Snoat, wearing a silk mask to conceal his scarred nose and chin, and grey silk gloves over his amputated fingers, sat at a deep-blue lacquered desk in the centre. A stand beside him held a magnificent malachite box with gold hinges. The area behind him was screened off with green paper panels.

"You mustn't use the Command device," said Llian. "The Merdrun—"

"The only *story* I want from you is the one in your hand. Put it there." Snoat indicated the edge of the desk.

Llian put the manuscript down. Ifoli came out from behind the green panels, checked the manuscript with gloved fingers, opened it to the title page, then the frontispiece, and frowned. She took a cloth from a bag, wiped the frontispiece down, presumably removing the poison, and sniffed the cloth. She folded it over carefully, slipped it into the bag along with her gloves, and tossed the bag into a glass receptacle in the corner.

She turned the rest of the pages, closed the book and ran her fingers over the top and bottom edges, then down the back of the binding. Llian tensed. She must discover the needle. But Ifoli closed the book. "It is Llian's Great Tale, Cumulus, and there is no mancery on it." She went behind the panels.

Snoat heaved a great sigh, dabbed at his eyes with a triangle of white linen, then glanced lovingly at a display case behind Llian. It contained the first twenty-two Great Tales. The drumming swelled. Llian felt a suicidal urge to leap over the desk and strangle Snoat. He fought the urge and it faded.

Snoat opened the *Tale of the Mirror*, laid his gloved hand on the inside of the cover, and a hidden spring fired the thick needle up into his chest. But instead of penetrating his heart or lung, it embedded itself deep in a rib.

"Ugh!" he cried, trying vainly to pull it out. "You useless fool, Ifoli!"

"Ussarine, now!" roared Llian, and leaped at Snoat.

From outside came a series of thuds. Hopefully they indicated that Ussarine had disarmed the guards, armed herself and was on her way. Marble creaked and cracked and the paper panels shook; Esea was to bring the pavilion down in such a way as to block the guards. Hingis's linked illusions were intended to lead them astray long enough for everyone to get away, though with a hundred guards on the island they could only escape if the sky ship was there.

A marble column toppled outwards, shaking the pavilion and snapping in two when it hit the ground. Dust thickened the mist; the copper roof lifted and tilted, and a heavy rain shower peppered Llian's eyes; for a moment he could not see. He wiped his eyes and saw Snoat backing away, the needle still embedded in his chest. He had the manuscript in his left hand and the malachite box under his right arm.

Llian dived at Snoat, brought him down and went for his throat. Snoat fought back, and for an aesthete he showed remarkable skill at dirty fighting. He kneed Llian in the groin, then drove an elbow at his throat. Llian twisted aside and headbutted Snoat, cracking him on the right cheekbone. The manuscript went flying.

Snoat rolled away, shouting, "Ifoli, get in here!"

"Ussarine!" Llian bellowed. Where the hell was she?

Snoat wrenched up the lid of the malachite box and grabbed the Command device. Its black crystal glowed and the drumming swelled to a series of thunderclaps. Llian felt an almost unbearable temptation to take the device for himself. He fought it, as he had so many times now, and the urge faded.

Snoat thrust the stubby brass tube at Llian's face. He ducked as a black blast roared from the crystal, singeing his right ear and setting the paper panel behind him alight. It toppled onto his head and his hair started to shrivel and smoke. He thrust the panel aside and beat his hair out.

Snoat, who was shaking, groped for the manuscript with his free hand. Llian got it first, swung it round and smashed Snoat in the mouth with the spine. He stumbled back, dropping the device. Three teeth fell from his bloody mouth.

"Esea, what are you doing?" hissed Hingis from outside.

Llian froze, listening, and Snoat did too.

"I'm giving you one last chance to choose." Esea sounded desperate – no, despairing. "Her – or me?"

88

AND ALL WERE DEAD

Karan looked around desperately. The ring-fortress had been breached in at least eight places and the Merdrun were swarming through the gaps, then up onto the flat top of the mountain. Behind her the surviving defenders had formed a hundred-yard-wide ring around the Crimson Gate, preparing to defend it to the death. And she still did not know why.

Karan had no hope that they could succeed; the Merdrun were too many and too tough. She ached all over from the magiz's brutal summoning and from Malien's spells before that. She staggered away towards the ring of defenders, the icy air burning her nose and throat with every breath, trying to work out a plan. The magiz, clearly, had recovered from Sulien's attack, but did not follow.

Karan was here in physical form this time and even in her down-filled garments and fur-lined boots it was unbearably cold, far worse than it had been down below. How could the defenders live up here? How could they fight?

The earnest, black-haired boy she had met last time stood with his father. The lad looked terrified yet determined. All the defenders were resolute, prepared to fight and die as they had sworn to do all those centuries ago.

"Is the gate a sacred place to you?" Karan asked the woman with the ink-stained fingers. There was blood all down her front, her skin was saggy and her eyes showed bleak despair. The defenders knew they were going to die.

Her face twisted. "It's profane! Evil!"

Karan looked up at the great gate. Even with her unblocked gift for mancery she knew there was nothing she could do to harm it.

"Then why defend it at such cost?"

"To prevent it ever being used."

The Merdrun were a quarter of a mile away, forming their lines. It would not be long now, and when they charged they would cross the distance in little over a minute. Minutes after that it would be over for everyone, including the wide-eyed boy who was surely no older than Sulien. The thought was unbearable.

Karan was picking frozen tears out of her eyes when something a defender had mentioned previously struck her. "What's the story of the Fallen Gate?"

"It's said there was another gate," said the boy's father. "The same as this one, only blue, standing beside it. But the blue gate was toppled by the people who gave us this world nine thousand years ago – toppled and buried."

"What did they call themselves?"

"It's not recorded, though they were a big dark people."

"Not the Merdrun?"

"They didn't have the tattoo, but their eyes were similar."

"Charon!" said Karan.

The man shrugged. "They were good people, faithful in their dealings with us and true to their word."

"Then why bury the Azure Gate?" Karan said to herself. "There's something wrong here ... Why are you here anyway? This isn't your fight."

"We swore to defend the gate," he said coldly, "and defend it we will." His voice cracked; he gathered his son to him, hugged him desperately and turned away to face the enemy.

"Is this the end, Daddy?" the boy said.

"I fear it is, Heydy. But we'll face it together as bravely as we can."

Was it better for father and son to die together? If it were her and Sulien ... No, it was unimaginable. Karan made her way through the lines of the defenders towards the red trilithon. No one hindered her. It was as if they were already beyond the material world. Or they thought she was still a spirit.

If the people who had toppled and buried the Azure Gate nine thousand years ago had been Charon, what had they been doing? Why topple the *good* gate?

She reached the great gate. All was still; the defenders were silent and so were the more numerous Merdrun. There was no sound save for the wind whistling through the fringe of icicles hanging from the capstone of the Crimson Gate. Again Karan caught that faint smell of onion soup, the defenders' last meal.

High above, the three moons – little yellow and black Cromo, red Wolfrim and huge green Stibnid – formed a line pointing directly at the gate. Syzygy. The time was now.

She touched the nearest upright but felt nothing. Where was the Azure Gate? Since they had stood side by side, and it had been buried where it fell, it must be close.

Karan scanned the ice-covered ground. It was uneven, though she saw no outlines that would indicate a buried object. But if the Azure Gate, a structure of vast and ancient power, was here she should be able to detect it with her sensitive's gift. She walked around the gate, swinging her right arm back and forth, and sensed something below her. She was standing on the toppled gate; it was just inches below the ground.

Could she do anything with it? No – mancery was an art long in the learning and difficult to master. Though Malien had unblocked her gift, Karan still had to painstakingly learn all but the simplest of spells, ones a gifted child might use instinctively. Could she wake the gate and hope that Stermin's Gates of Good and Evil might interfere with each other?

A skilled mancer might have done so but Karan had no idea how. She pointed her right hand at the place where she sensed the capstone of the gate to be and said, "Wake!"

The ice above the buried gate took on a faint glow, but it faded almost to nothing.

There came a colossal roar from behind her, then the ground quivered as the Merdrun army charged. From the defenders there was silence apart from a single boyish cry soaring above the thunder and the rumbling. It was quickly stifled.

Karan turned, her heart thumping slowly as she counted the seconds down. On sixty-three the attackers struck the defenders in an irresistible mass, armour clanging off armour, sword ringing on sword, roars and shouts, screams and sickening crunching sounds. The wind carried the smell of cold blood to where she stood, revolted by the brutality, the savagery and the waste of a good and decent people who had not asked for any of this.

She would be next.

A squad of Merdrun burst through, led by Gergrig and the big man, one of their generals, with the flattened nose and the metal plate in his head. Gergrig had a long sword in his right hand and a war hammer in the left. Behind them loped the round-faced young woman whose yellow hair was plaited into a loop above her head. What was her name? Uzzey. Her face was radiant as she approached the Crimson Gate.

"At last!" she cried, then stumbled and fell, a spear embedded in her neck. None of the attackers looked at her; to the Merdrun death was failure.

Karan looked away from Uzzey's death throes. She'd had a conscience; she'd been one of the better ones. What had her life been for?

"Take Karan!" roared Gergrig. "Unharmed."

Two soldiers split from the pack and, before she could move, grabbed her and bound her arms behind her back.

"Where's the magiz?" Gergrig bellowed. "Hurry!" He pointed to the line of moons.

The defenders were still fighting furiously, though they were failing; the gap in their lines was getting wider by the second. Four soldiers hurried up escorting the magiz, who was limping on her artificial leg and surrounded by a dozen acolytes in grey fur cloaks. She was lit from within, so charged with power from all the lives she had drunk that an oily green light was radiating out of her.

She cast a shiny-eyed glance at Karan but continued to the Crimson Gate and gave low-voiced orders. The acolytes began to set out small devices on the ground, in three concentric circles centred on the gate. Karan could not tell what they were – charged crystals perhaps.

Again Gergrig pointed to the three moons. Karan hoped to see some change in them, a sign that syzygy would soon be over, but they remained in a straight line.

The magiz was chanting, and so were her acolytes, who, Karan saw, were all female. Their voices soared, high and beautiful. The magiz swung her arm down, the chant cut off, and from every one of the devices on the ground a raw beam of red light sizzled out and lit up the Crimson Gate. The ground shivered and the gate began to glow a deep and penetrating red.

In her inner ear Karan heard a scream that seemed to come from the other side of the gate, then the space between the uprights turned misty. The gate was opening. What was happening in Carcharon? Had it just fed on Wilm or Aviel?

The magiz fell, gasping, and she was not glowing now. Opening the gate had drained her to the dregs. Her acolytes were scattered like grey leaves across the ice-sheathed ground.

Gergrig sank to his knees, his cruel face alight with joy, and all the other soldiers emulated him. But he sprang up again. "Soon, my people, we will have our own beautiful world – all to ourselves!"

My world, thought Karan. Santhenar, reduced to an empty shell for the most brutal human species ever to have existed.

"To the gate!" Gergrig raised his sword and ran between the uprights into the mist, along with twenty of his fellows.

Instantly they began to scream; they were rolling their eyes, clutching their heads with their hands and foaming at the mouth. Then they turned on one another, soldiers who had fought side by side all across the void for years, and hacked at each other in an orgy of bloody ruin.

"Hold!" roared Gergrig, who alone was unaffected. "Put down your blades! What's the matter with you?"

The soldiers inside the gate could not stop; utter madness was on them. Someone struck the general in the head, sending his skull plate flying to clang off one side of the gate. Gergrig, slipping on blood, dived back out onto the ice, gasping. Behind him his soldiers cut each other down until the gate was piled with bodies and all were dead.

He pounded across to the magiz, caught her by her scrawny throat and jerked her to her feet. "What have you done?"

She staggered but did not fall, then raised her right hand. Gergrig released her. Her lips moved; Karan thought that she was interrogating the gate.

"I don't understand," said the magiz.

Gergrig stumbled back to the gate and swung his war hammer at the closest upright, knocking off a shovel-sized piece of rock. He inspected the exposed stone of the upright, which was as red as the outside.

He turned, staring at the ground where the rock had fallen. "What the . . . ?"

He picked up the broken piece of rock. The freshly exposed surface was azure blue.

Karan's heart soared. The gate was a trap, one the Charon must have set up nine thousand years ago when they gave Cinnabar to the defenders. They had toppled the Crimson Gate and buried it, then disguised the Azure Gate with a permanent illusion, making it appear crimson. But the Azure Gate had been the *ennobling* gate, changing the people who chose it, just as the Crimson Gate had corrupted those who passed through it.

That was why the troops in the gate had turned on one another. The conflict between the ennobling gate and their own corruption had been too great; it had driven them insane. And since their entire lives had been devoted to killing, in their madness all they could do was kill.

What would the Merdrun do now? First of all, with their hopes shattered, they would torture her to death. Could she get away? No, she had to finish the magiz or die trying.

Gergrig dropped his war hammer and his sword, raised his scarred right fist and shook it at the false Crimson Gate. He strained, then said in a commanding voice, "Asunder!"

The uprights shook back and forth, the capstone grinding on their tops, then it faded to azure and the entire structure toppled backwards, hitting the ice with three ground-shaking thuds.

"Mancers, to me!" said Gergrig. "We . . . will . . . succeed!"

Dozens of Merdrun mancers ran forward and stood to either side of Gergrig. He pointed to the ground, where the faint shimmer of the true Crimson Gate could be seen.

"Raise the true gate!" said Gergrig.

It took all the power they had, but the two uprights rose slowly to the vertical, shedding chunks of frozen ground, and inch by inch the capstone lifted, hovered and settled on top. The true gate was not a thing of beauty as the false gate had been; it was battered and cracked, and covered in red iron stains and clots of frozen earth and mud. But it stood.

Gergrig cast an anxious glance at the three moons. They were still in line, though it was not as straight as it had been; the littlest moon was creeping to the left and the huge green moon to the right. Syzygy would soon be over and so would their hope of opening the true Crimson Gate.

"Get up!" he said to the magiz, who was lying on the frozen ground again. "Empower the gate!"

The magiz's acolytes lifted her to her feet and held her upright. "Can't . . . do it . . . twice."

"You must!"

The magiz looked around. The surviving defenders had fled. "Their lives wasted!" she said bitterly. "Got . . . no source . . . power."

"You've got her," said Gergrig, gesturing to Karan. "She reeks of power, and so does her daughter. Drink Karan's life and then the brat's, and open the damned gate!"

89

I PITY YOU

"Can't . . . just kill her," said the magiz. "To drink all *her* power . . . must defeat her one on one . . . then tear out . . . living heart."

Karan shuddered; the magiz said it so gleefully. Yet for the first time since she had been dragged here, she felt a surge of hope. If she could delay the magiz long enough for syzygy to be over, the invasion of Santhenar would be delayed by years. Then, before they cut her down, she would do her best to kill the evil bitch.

"Do it!" snapped Gergrig. "You're a foot taller and the most experienced mancer in the void. And she doesn't know how to use the gift she's just had woken."

"Move back!" said the magiz.

Someone untied Karan's wrists. The Merdrun, who numbered many thousands, backed off to form a circle beginning forty yards from her. Gergrig joined them. The only people in the circle now were Karan and the magiz, ten yards away.

Karan weighed her up. The magiz limped on her replacement leg and could not be as fast or as dextrous as before, but if she kept her distance she would not need to be. With all that power she could blast Karan down.

Or could she? If *one on one* meant physical combat, it would give Karan a better chance, though the magiz would undoubtedly fight dirty.

"You old humans are so weak," sneered the magiz. "So fettered by useless emotions. I pulled your strings through your pathetic love for your daughter." She made it out to be a disgusting weakness.

"I pity you," said Karan. "Your lives are empty, meaningless and sterile."

"Victory gives us all the meaning we need. Your man is in Snoat's hands, and he's about to die, as your doomed daughter foresaw."

A steel fist clenched around Karan's heart. Sulien and Llian needed her and she wasn't there for either of them. She had not been there for a long time, and now she never would be. The pain was unbearable.

"Get on with it!" Gergrig glanced anxiously at the moons.

Karan did not look up. Only the magiz mattered now. She had to beat her as quickly as possible, but how?

"Your death will be a beautiful irony," said the magiz. "Even better than my pet traitor."

Yggur! "How did you get to him?" said Karan.

"I embedded a link in him when he unwittingly went near the summon stone a month ago," the magiz gloated.

What?

Yggur hadn't been anywhere near Carcharon; he could not be the traitor. Neither had Nadiril or Hingis or any other male who could be described as a leader. The only one who had was Shand, when he had been searching for Maigraith above the Black Lake.

Shand, Karan's old friend and companion of many journeys, was the unwitting traitor. How was she to tell him? It would shatter him.

Now she thought about it, it was clear that he had been affected by the drumming when she'd met him in Chanthed. It explained his rages against Llian, the false accusations Shand had made against herself, and all the other odd things he had done.

"Your life will give me the power to open the gate," said the magiz. "You will be responsible for the death of everyone on Santhenar, including your daughter."

She drew a foot-long knife with a narrow blade not unlike the boning knife poor Benie had used to kill Cook. Shimmering in the multicoloured moonlight, it looked sharp enough to split a human hair.

Karan got out her own knife from the hidden sheath on the inside of her right thigh. It wasn't very sharp and it wasn't nearly long enough. How could she even the odds?

What was the magiz's biggest weakness? It had to be her addiction to drinking lives. And right now, utterly drained from opening the wrong gate, she was desperate to drink Karan's life. The craving must be consuming her; how could Karan use that?

Theoretically she could use mancery now, though she had not practised a single spell. Besides, no attack of hers could penetrate the magiz's mighty defences.

The magiz leaped forward, slashing with her long blade. She was faster than Karan had expected; there was scarcely a wobble of the artificial leg and she used the knife like an experienced dueller. Karan felt a tickle of fear. What if the magiz was her match in single combat as well?

Karan's strengths had always been her lightning reflexes and remarkable dexterity. She had lost the edge of both with time and injury, but she was still very fast. She leaped left, feinted, tensed as though she was going to go right, then leaped left again and attacked the magiz's unprotected side, swinging high to cut through her coat deep into her shoulder, then low – a slash into her side.

The second blow would have been a crippling one had Karan's knife been longer and sharper, but it caught in the magiz's coat and only gave her a flesh wound. Karan sprang back, then lunged for the magiz's belly.

Somehow she got her knife up in time and the tip skated across Karan's wrist, nicking the artery. Blood spurted. Karan tried to spray it into the magiz's eyes but she wove out of the way and it painted a red line across her throat, then froze there like a gory gash. If only.

Karan leaped back, holding her thumb over the artery. To fight, or stop the bleeding? She could not do both.

The magiz did not attack at once; she was pale and shaky. The shoulder gash was a deep one and perhaps she was in shock.

"The craving to drink my life must be eating you up," said Karan. "It must be almost unbearable."

"The longer the wait, the greater the ecstasy," the magiz said between her crooked teeth.

Her colourless eyes reflected the light of the green moon; they were like pale green crystals bedded in soot. But Karan could see how she was suffering; the addiction was consuming her. Could it be fed?

The magiz slashed again. Karan parried then lunged. The magiz swept her arm aside and brought her metal knee up into Karan's crotch with all her strength behind it, lifting her off her feet. Pain spiked through the pelvic bones she had broken long ago as she landed on her back. Her elbow struck the ground and the knife jarred from her hand.

The magiz approached warily, then kicked Karan in the side of the head, a stunning blow. High above, the line of the three moons still held. There was yet time for the Merdrun to open the gate. If she did not think of something fast, she was going to die and all would be lost.

Karan allowed her eyes to flutter then almost close, as if she were losing consciousness. It might give her a tiny chance. Her wrist had stopped bleeding. The cut had frozen.

The magiz bent and wrenched off Karan's down-filled coat. Instantly the cold struck her, so intense here that she would lose consciousness in minutes, though that hardly mattered now. The magiz tore Karan's shirt open, baring her from throat to belly, and grinned.

"I'm going to gut you before I take your living heart. How does it feel, Karan?"

She went to her knees beside Karan.

"Hurry!" yelled Gergrig.

The magiz was taking her time. "How I'm going to enjoy drinking *your* life."

Karan saw the only chance she would ever get. She forced three fingers into the magiz's open mouth and cast the one spell she was confident of working, a simple freezing charm she had used as a little girl, long before Tensor had blocked her mancery. At any other place the spell might not have worked, but it was easy in this glacial wilderness. And the magiz, brilliant mancer though she was, had no way to block it because it had been cast inside her mouth – inside her defences.

As Karan wrenched her fingers out, cracking and crunching sounds issued from the magiz's throat and middle. Her knife, which had frozen to her hand, plunged down at Karan's unprotected belly. She rolled out of the way and the thin blade snapped on impact with the iron-hard ice.

Karan wrapped her coat around her, gasping from the cold and almost collapsing from pain and aftersickness. The magiz rose to her feet, then seemed to freeze in place apart from her bloody right arm, which slowly creaked towards Karan as if to blast her down.

She ducked. Needles of red ice burst out of the magiz's eyes, nose, mouth and ears; she was freezing inside. Her arm stopped, pointing at the Crimson Gate. She tried to speak but her lips were frozen shut. Had Karan won?

No. As the magiz died, the monumental power released upon the death of a great mancer seared from her fingertips, through the air and into the gate.

It glowed, just as the false gate had, and a crimson mist formed inside it. The gate was open!

A big, handsome woman cried out in ecstasy, "Gergrig, is it time?"

He sprang into the gate and stood there for a moment, his shaven head cocked. "It's good," he said. "You and you," he said to the nearest two soldiers, "cut Karan down. This is the hour!" he roared. "Merdrun, to Santhenar!"

The Merdrun army flooded forward. The two soldiers came at Karan, swords raised. But the spell the magiz had used to drag her to Cinnabar had failed on her death, and Karan felt herself being drawn home. The last thing she saw before Cinnabar vanished was a bluish glow from the fallen Azure Gate. It was still open, but where did it lead to?

She felt an overwhelming sense of relief. With the magiz dead, surely Sulien was safe. But would Karan get back in time to save Llian?

She felt a sickening terror that Sulien's second nightmare had already come true – the one where she had seen Llian, dead.

90

THERE'S NOTHING YOU CAN DO

Karan materialised at the top of the little hill near the clearing. She staggered across to Malien's night-glasses, which she had left on a stump, and focused them just in time to see chaos erupt at the pavilion in the lake – collapsing columns, sudden blazes and jagged black flashes that had to be someone using the Command device.

"Llian, get out of there!" But the sky ship had drifted in the wind; it was hundreds of yards away. "Malien," Karan said uselessly, "what are you doing? *Go back!*"

The sky ship kept drifting away; its twin screws must have failed. Dread enveloped Karan. For a moment she could not move, could not speak. Even if Llian survived, he had no way of escape. There was no sign of Hingis, Esea or Ussarine either. What the hell was going on?

Then Karan remembered Esea stumbling into the clearing that afternoon, and *knew*. Her face had shown utter despair. Why had Shand sent the three of them? How could he have not seen the danger? Because the magiz had been pulling his strings.

She ran down to the clearing. Shand was there, talking to Yggur, Nadiril and Lilis.

"It's failed!" Karan screamed. "Damn you, Shand!"

She turned away. She had to get down there now.

"There's nothing you can do," said Shand.

There was an odd, glazed look in his eye. The drumming was affecting him again, corrupting him just as it had poor Benie. He sprang at her. She leaped away from him, every muscle aching, and fury flared, at all those people, friends and enemies, who had taken it upon themselves to control her life and her family.

"On Cinnabar I discovered who's been betraying us to the Merdrun all this time," she said coldly. "The magiz was boasting about using her *pet traitor.*"

"Who?" Shand croaked. He turned towards Yggur as if to accuse him.

"You!" she cried. "She put a link in you when you went to Carcharon, looking for Maigraith. And you had the nerve to blame *me!*"

He doubled over, gasping, and she felt a second's remorse, but she would pay the price later. She dashed down the road towards the bridge, which was still guarded. Could she get to the island in time? Seconds counted now.

The shoreline was not guarded. Karan stripped off her boots, tied them to her belt and slipped into the water. She was a good swimmer, but at this time of year the water was miserably cold. The drumming was getting louder every second; it was almost deafening now and she saw the moment when it overcame the resistance of the guards and they turned on one another – just as it had turned her allies against each other. Was this how Santhenar was to end?

The pavilion was down but the black flashes kept coming. Why had Llian needed to be there anyway? Was he just a decoy, a sacrifice?

Karan crept out of the water and tripped over the body of a guard, lying where he had been slain. His sword was gone but there was a long brown club on his belt. She took it and, swinging it back and forth, ran barefoot up towards the pavilion.

There were bodies all around it – Snoat's guards. Another guard loomed up. She thumped him over the head. A second man, very tall, appeared behind him. Karan was about to whack him as well when he hissed, "Yggur!"

"Help me look for Llian."

"All right," Yggur said mildly. At least he was unaffected by the drumming.

Karan went back and forth through the ruined pavilion. There was no sign of Llian. The light was fading; whatever had caught fire down near the water was burning away. Then, circling the ruins again, she trod on something soft, and it groaned.

"Ussarine?" said Karan. "Are you injured?"

"Broken legs."

She was half covered by debris – twisted copper sheets and broken screens. Karan heaved them aside. Underneath, two of the slender pavilion columns had fallen on Ussarine, one across her chest and the other over her shins.

Karan could not budge either. Yggur materialised out of the darkness and lifted them away.

Karan sat Ussarine up. "Have you seen Llian?"

"No," said Ussarine.

"What happened?" said Yggur.

"Knocked out, then the pavilion brought down on me," Ussarine said grimly. "Do you know where Hingis . . . ?"

From the tone of her voice, she feared him dead. "No," said Karan.

She caught another dark flash a long way to the east, followed by a bright flare. An image flashed into her mind – Llian's body lying on an expanse of smooth stones. The image Sulien had seen in her second nightmare. Karan stifled a cry; she had to keep going.

"We can't stay here," said Yggur.

Only then did she take in what Ussarine had said. *Knocked out, then the pavilion brought down on me.* "Are you saying Esea attacked you?"

"If she hadn't," said Ussarine, "I would have got Llian out. And the Command device."

A blistering fury swelled in Karan. Esea had been willing to sacrifice Llian, and their hopes of killing Snoat and taking on the Merdrun, solely to rid herself of a good woman who had come between her and her twin.

Karan looked up as the sky ship, its rotors spinning furiously, appeared above the wrecked pavilion.

"Hoy!" she yelled. "Two broken legs. Lower a rope."

A rope was dropped. Karan tied it under Ussarine's arms. Yggur bent and, with an effort, lifted her. The Aachim raised her into the sky ship. Karan dragged herself up the ladder, wet and cold and utterly shattered, and Yggur followed.

"It's a disaster," she said in a deathly voice. "Shand has been corrupted by the drumming; Llian is lost because Esea betrayed us; Snoat got away with the Command device . . . and the Merdrun are coming through the Crimson Gate who knows where."

91

A SCORPION IN MY HOUSE

"Please don't do this," Hingis said hoarsely from outside the pavilion.

Llian could hear each breath rasping as Hingis fought to draw air into his withered lung. What was the matter with Esea? Had the drumming driven her over the edge? Was it affecting both of them?

"Her – or me?" Esea repeated.

"Don't say it, Hingis," Ussarine said softly. "You mustn't choose."

"You forced me, Esea," Hingis choked. "And I choose . . . Ussarine!"

Esea let out a cry of anguish, then shrieked, "Then join her – forever!"

An almighty blast tore the copper roof off the pavilion and sent it whirling down the slope, scattering blazing paper lanterns everywhere. The rest of the columns fell. Outside, Ussarine screamed in agony, then fell silent. Some distance away a man groaned. A woman stumbled off, howling in grief and despair. Esea, surely. Had she killed them?

"Esea?" Llian called. "Hingis? Ussarine?"

No reply. He was on his own.

He realised that he had dropped the manuscript. Snoat rose, holding it in his left hand, the stubby Command device in his right. He was trembling all over, presumably from the effects of the deadly device. He pointed it at Llian, who hurled himself back over the desk. He landed on a burning paper lantern, extinguishing it, and pain seared up his back. The black blast peeled curling layers of bright blue lacquer off the desk and tossed them in all directions like wood shavings in the wind.

"No, Cumulus!" Ifoli cried. "You'll let the Merdrun through."

Snoat was shuddering now and his teeth were chattering. "What's the matter with you?" he snarled. "Let ... me ... go!"

Thump. Llian peered over the desk. Ifoli was staggering backwards, a fist mark on her cheek. The drumming became a thumping crescendo that rattled his ribs. He could feel it calling him again – *take the Command device and cut the bastard down.*

"Get the Great Tales!" said Snoat.

Ifoli swept them into a large bag and slung it over her shoulder. Snoat jammed the manuscript into a leather bag.

Outside, fighting broke out in many places. Had the drumming made Snoat's men turn on one another? It was too much to hope for. Llian scrambled out of the ruined pavilion. Something was burning down near the water. The sky ship should have been lit up by the flames but there was no sign of it.

Snoat was lurching down the slope towards the eastern bridge, waving the Command device wildly, and Ifoli was running after him, bent under the weight of her bag. Llian wanted to bolt back to the clearing and Karan, but the job had not been done. He followed Snoat and Ifoli down, across the bridge and onto a broad expanse of polished paving stones.

"Cumulus, you must not use it again," cried Ifoli. She grabbed Snoat's arm.

"How dare you question me!"

He struck her on the side of the head with the Command device, knocking it from his trembling hand and dropping the manuscript as well. The drumming roared in Llian's ears. Was this his chance? He had to take it. He shouldered Snoat out of the way, snatched up the device and pointed it at his enemy's half-masked face.

"Die, you bastard!"

"You imbecile!" said Ifoli. "*You* can't use it." She dropped the book bag and tried to snatch the device from Llian's hand.

In a moment of drumming-fuelled madness, he turned to blast her down.

"Stop!" said Ifoli.

"How dare you tell me what to do?" Llian raged, and was about to end her when he remembered Sulien saying, "No, Daddy." He lowered the device. Fool, what are you doing?

Ifoli hooked his legs from under him. He fell to the ground and the device skidded away across the stones. "Stay down!" she hissed.

"Guards," Snoat bellowed, "to me!" He turned to Ifoli. "Kill him."

Ifoli looked from Snoat to Llian, then back to Snoat. She shook her head.

"So," he said. "It's as I suspected. All this time there's been a scorpion in my own house."

What was he talking about?

"Who are you spying for?" said Snoat. "It's pointless to deny it."

"Nadiril," Ifoli said softly.

"That doddering old fool!"

"He sent me to you in the first place. He's fooled you all these years."

No guards had answered Snoat's call, but now a one-armed mancer ran up, carrying a snake-shaped staff. Scorbic Vyl, Llian assumed.

"Kill them," said Snoat.

Vyl pointed his staff at Llian and Ifoli. Llian tried to get up.

"Stay *down*!" Ifoli mouthed.

"No, do it with that!" said Snoat, pointing at the Command device.

Vyl picked it up and was about to blast Llian and Ifoli when Esea staggered out of the darkness, her beautiful face twisted in despair. She extended an arm towards Vyl.

Snoat let out a derisive snort. "You don't even have the power to tickle him."

"Reshape it!" said Esea.

White fire roared from her fingertips and struck the Command device, reshaping it into a brass sphere with the dark crystal embedded in it like an evil eye. But the reshaping had perverted the intention of its design and the strain was too much: it shook, shuddered, shrieked and the crystal began to throb.

"Now reshape *them*!" said Esea, swinging her arm in a circle.

Ifoli dropped beside Llian, covering her face with her hands. As he did the same, the Command device exploded in a blast that reshaped Vyl grotesquely, hurled him backwards for fifty feet and set fire to the very stones he had been standing on. It reshaped Snoat too but left him where he stood.

"Can't ... be happening," he gurgled, lurching around in a circle. His face was inside out, his belly outside in. "Not ... to me! Can't ... go like this. Ifoli, my Great Tales ... bring."

She did not move. Esea, whose throat and chest were peppered with shards of brass, let out a little sigh, crumbled to the stones and lay still. Her face relaxed, and all the grief and anguish was gone.

"Damn you!" Llian snarled. He forced himself to his feet, picked up his precious manuscript, hesitated then tore the pages out and tossed them on the burning flagstones. Snoat screamed as though the very point of his life had been denied him, then staggered to the fire and threw himself onto it, as if to extinguish the flames with his own body. The fire roared higher, then, just as suddenly went out.

A shimmering red bubble formed around Llian and Ifoli. In a series of flashes he saw the Merdrun army, an icy plateau with the Crimson Gate at its centre, then Wilm in a luridly glowing cavern with a small silver-haired girl. Aviel.

Then the red bubble shrank to nothing and they were gone.

92

I'VE RUINED EVERYTHING

After Shand and Ussarine were hurled away in the gate, Aviel dared not remain in Carcharon. She and Wilm gathered food, water bottles, weapons and camping gear from the four frozen bodies in the yard. One body had a small coil of rope; he took it as well.

"Where can we hide?" said Aviel.

"Llian mentioned a way station further up the ridge," said Wilm. "It's out of sight of the tower; maybe Unick doesn't know it exists."

He made a ladder with the rope so they could climb down the rear wall. Aviel found it hard going. The way station turned out to be a tiny hut, ten feet by nine, built from slabs of shiny schist. It had a fireplace, a rough stone floor, no furniture and no window. Wood was stacked between the chimney and the wall. The door, though draughty, was sound.

Wilm lit the fire. Aviel put the food and water bottles near the heat to thaw. They ate and sat together, warming their hands on mugs of tea. Wilm kept looking at her sideways as if he did not know what to make of her. She was not the girl she had been when he left Casyme.

She was also mindful that he had made a friend in Chanthed and they had worked together to rescue Llian, then Unick had murdered her in front of him. Wilm must be angry and confused, and perhaps he felt guilty that he had not been able to save her.

Aviel was not confused about anything. She had expected to die a dozen times in the past weeks, and she knew exactly what she wanted: to rid the world of the stone and, if she survived, master the art of making scent potions.

"You look exhausted," she said. "Get some sleep."

"Do you want me to bind your ankle?"

"No!"

"Sorry," he said hastily. "Just trying to help."

"I'm used to doing everything for myself."

He hunched his shoulders and stared at the fire. "What are we going to do about the stone?"

"I haven't thought it through yet."

"I don't suppose you need my help with that either."

Aviel realised that she was being mean-spirited. He had come all this way to save her from a brute, at great cost to himself. She did not like to touch, as a rule, but he was her oldest friend. She took his big hand and even drew some comfort from it.

"I'm really sorry, Wilm. Look, I don't need the sleep, but you do. Why don't we talk about it when you wake up?"

He took off his boots and lay down in his blankets. Aviel got out the grimoire and moved closer to the fire. The small, squashed writing was hard to read by the flickering light. She studied the Electuary of Compulsion. Could she compel Unick to destroy the stone that meant everything to him?

Ultimately, all forms of attacking mancery came down to a contest of wills, and his whole life had been a contest: himself versus the world. As for her, from the day she was born it had been her versus her six sisters, and her father, and everyone she had ever met save Wilm and Shand. Being crippled, overworked, underfed and chronically unlucky, her inner strength had to be all the stronger. She had to beat him.

Wilm was asleep, one fist clenched around his blankets. No one could have had a better friend. She smiled, rubbed salve into her swollen ankle and took up the grimoire.

Immersed in the work as she was, the night and the next day passed swiftly. The instructions for making the potion were complex and difficult, and made doubly so because she did not have all the scents she needed and had no way of making them here. She had to substitute them with ones she did have, but first she had to work out exactly how to use them and in what order, otherwise the completed potion could prove fatal.

"What are you doing?" said Wilm the following mid-afternoon.

Aviel sniffed the phial she was using, added another drop, sniffed again and frowned. "Step nine requires oil of bergamot and I don't have any. I'm trying to make a substitute with lemon and almond oils, plus a hint of lavender and a few other things, but it's not working. I'll have to start afresh."

"You're so clever," he said. "I wouldn't be game."

"Says the man who taught himself how to use a sword then beat Snoat's best assassin."

She might have said *killed* but Aviel did not want to think about that.

"How long is it going to take?" said Wilm.

"Another day or two – if we get that long. The drumming is getting louder."

"It was in my dreams the whole time I was asleep. Is there anything I can do to help?"

"Not really."

"Then I'll go and spy on Carcharon."

Fear shivered through her. "Be careful."

The next day passed, and the day after. The drumming grew ever louder, reminding Aviel that her work was urgent, but whenever she tried to hurry she made mistakes and had to do it all over again.

That evening the scent potion was finally done, and she knew it was as close to the true Electuary of Compulsion as she could make it. But would it work? There was no choice but to try it on Unick, and pray.

When they entered the yard of Carcharon it was clear that something had changed for the worse. The ground was shuddering beneath them, the drumming was loud and frantic, and showers of crimson and orange light kept bursting out of the tower windows and the air vents. She really did not want to go down there.

"Do you think this is the end?" said Wilm.

"Yes. I think it is."

As they crept hand in hand down the yard, the tower shook; loose stones slid out of the wall and tumbled down the ridge, crashing and smashing all the way to the bottom. It had been sunny during the day and the frozen corpses of Rasper and his three assistants stood out above the melting snow like zombies in a white fog. It was a horrible omen.

"What if we're too late?" said Wilm as they went in.

"We've got to keep going."

"But the Merdrun drove the mighty Charon into extinction. What can *we* hope to do?"

Aviel was thinking the same thing but saying it aloud did not help. "Ordinary people have beaten great enemies before."

Wilm's silence was eloquent.

"Wilm?" she said, desperate for some encouragement, even the smallest.

"Malien said don't use mancery near the stone. And scent potions are mancery."

"What choice do we have?"

She took his cold hand in her freezing one. He seemed to take comfort from her courage – if only he knew how despairing she was – and they crept down between the juddering walls and through the cracking and crumbling passages. She was shaking and he was too. She did not want to go in; she never wanted to see Unick again. Most of all, she did not want to go anywhere near the stone. If he caught her he would feed her to it, and she was a bit corrupt now – this time it might take her.

Finally they approached the cavern. It was sweltering and the glow from the summon stone was such a lurid and penetrating crimson that it passed through the solid rock, lighting it up like glass. They turned the corner and Aviel's knees gave.

"I . . . don't think I can do it."

Wilm held her up. "Yes, you can. You will."

The summon stone seemed to have grown, though that might have been the baleful red corona surrounding it. The drumming, however, was oddly thick here, as if muffled.

"The time must be close," croaked Wilm. Then he jumped. "Aviel, I can hear people talking."

She could too, distant, echoing voices. "Lots of people . . . as if they're on the other side of a wall. And one deeper voice. It sounds like he's giving orders but I can't make out the words."

Wilm turned slowly to face her and in the garish light his eyes appeared to be bleeding. "Is he giving orders to an army," he whispered, "or to the stone?"

Then one voice soared above the rest. *Gergrig? Is it ready?*

Almost.

"Quick, use the scent potion," whispered Wilm.

"I can't use it on the stone," said Aviel. "Only on Unick. Where is he?"

"He's here!" said Unick in a clotted voice. He stepped out from behind the stone, the Origin device swinging from what remained of his left hand.

Aviel let out a scream. All his toes were gone save for the big ones, and he had lost two fingers on his left hand, three on the right, and both ears. He was a lurching, scabrous monstrosity who should have been dead. Perhaps only willpower kept him alive, and how could she hope to master a will that strong? Surely only death could.

The floor quivered violently, tossing her off her feet. A crack formed across the middle of the cavern, opened to the width of a foot, then snapped closed, squirting dust up in a series of little grey fountains. The summon stone flared. Aviel's innards knotted.

"Soon," Unick said to the stone. "Very soon now." He took a step towards her.

Wilm drew the black sword and sprang. But Unick ducked, caught Wilm's free arm and jerked him forward so hard that he flew through the air towards the stone.

Aviel screamed.

He struck it side on and the sword was jarred out of his hand. The right side of his head hit the summon stone, there was a red flash and a puff of smoke, and the drumming became a thundering roar. Wilm hurled himself aside, gasping and clutching at his bloody ear. Where his clothing and hair had touched the summon stone he was unharmed, but the top half of his right ear was gone, taken by the stone.

He began to shake uncontrollably. He reached for the sword but his knees gave and he went down on his back. Unick had been disabled for some minutes after the stone fed, and Wilm would be too.

Aviel felt sick, and guilty. He was only here because of her, and now he was going to die. She fumbled the scent potion out of her pouch, her hands trembling so badly she could barely undo the wrappings. Unick, who was bending over Wilm, turned and stared at her, a half-smile playing across his broken mouth.

As she dropped the wrappings and took hold of the stopper, the summon stone projected a red-tinged shadow onto the end wall, though the space between the two uprights was open, not closed. Was it the other side of the gate? Was it Cinnabar?

Through the gate Aviel saw the outline of an armed host. The Crimson Gate must be opening.

Gergrig, there's someone at the summon stone.

Gergrig, a lean man with a shaven skull and a dense black beard, brandished a recurved blade in Aviel's direction.

"That's a good sign!" she said in a croaky voice. "He's afraid we can still block him."

"Use the potion, quick!" yelled Wilm.

Unick lurched towards her, smiling sickeningly. Aviel rehearsed the compulsion she planned to use on him – *Smash the stone!*

She tugged on the stopper – which stuck. Curse her bad luck. As she heaved on it her right foot twisted on a patch of jellied blood, she lost her balance, and the phial flew from her hand. She dived after it, ignoring the agony in her ankle, but the phial struck the wall and smashed. He wouldn't even get a whiff of the potion she had spent so long making.

"I'm sorry, Wilm!" she wept. "I've ruined everything." She knelt, paralysed, as Unick lurched towards her.

Wilm let out a howl of anguish. "You're not touching her!" he cried. "You're NOT!"

He managed to crab backwards and grab the black sword. Still lying on his back, he slashed the blade straight through Unick's left wrist. His hand went in one direction and the Origin device in the other. Aviel reached up with both hands and caught the heavy device, dropped it but caught it again.

But the figures were thickening on the other side of the shadow gate, becoming more solid. Unick, his wrist spurting blood, kicked his severed hand at the summon stone like a sacrificial offering, and it flared.

The shadow gate hardened. The army started to firm and become real. Unick staggered towards Aviel, clearly intending to feed her to the stone.

Wilm forced himself to his feet and, as Unick reached for Aviel, coldly ran him through. "That's for Dajaes too," he said softly.

Unick grunted, dragged himself off the blade, lurched around in a spiral and crashed face first into the summon stone.

And as it took him, he let out a dreadful screech of horror and despair. "You can't do this to me! I opened you. *I'm special—*"

First it took his face, then his head, neck and body, all gushing stinking brown smoke as he was drawn in and annihilated. His legs went, his hideous feet, then with a flash of crimson he was gone, leaving nothing behind but smoke and a lingering stench, and a pair of ragged big toenails pinging off the walls.

The shadow gate became a real gate, the Merdrun real soldiers. They were about to come through. Aviel reacted without thinking, just knowing that the summon stone was like a live thing now, and live things could be poisoned. She twisted the tubes of the Origin device apart, took the heavy glass container of quicksilver from inside and hurled it at the stone. It smashed, and deadly quicksilver drenched the summon stone.

It flashed crimson, black, crimson, then a deeper, impenetrable black. The Merdrun cried out in terror. The uprights of the summon stone ground together, separated, crashed together again and the shadow gate split into two separate gates. The one with the Merdrun in it, which was a brilliant throbbing crimson now, began to spin, faster and faster until it was a red blur, then shot upwards and vanished.

The other gate, which had an azure hue, enveloped Aviel and Wilm, spun like a top, appeared to drill down through the solid rock below the cavern, and took them with it.

93

AND WIPE THEM OUT

At the far western tip of frigid Shazabba, in an abandoned village built on stilts at the centre of a partly frozen lake, Sulien watched the Whelm gather on the grey pine boards.

Every day on the long journey west, then the wild boat trip south down the west coast of Meldorin to Shazabba, and every day since their arrival here, they had formed their sensing and scrying circle.

It was the only time she ever had to herself. The only time she was

free of the endless work, the harsh, cold treatment and her daily punishment. She sat on the edge of the deck, shivering and gazing north
towards home. Would she ever see Gothryme again, and Mummy and
Daddy and dear old Rachis? Sulien did not think so. Karan had not
answered her last, despairing call.

Had she forgotten her? Or were she and Llian dead? Was Sulien condemned to spend the rest of her life with the hideous Whelm, trapped
at the bitter end of Santhenar? She was one of them now. They had
initiated her and she did not think they would ever let her go.

Their chanting grew louder. It was horrible, like everything about
them. They sounded like a flock of evil crows. The Whelm were searching for the one thing that could complete them – a master they could
serve and obey without question. They had sought in vain since the
death of Rulke, their perfect master, ten years back.

But when Sulien had made that desperate link to blind the magiz
and save Karan's life, it had revealed Gergrig to the Whelm, and this
had changed everything. They were desperate to see him again; they
no longer scried in despair, but in a fervid ecstasy.

Only Idlis, who had sworn to protect Sulien with his life, abstained
from the circle, though she could see the yearning in his black eyes too.
How long could he hold out?

Karan had told her to run but Sulien had no money, she did not
know the land, and the long southern winter had already begun. She
had nowhere to go.

Suddenly, in her inner eye, something flashed crimson, black, crimson, then black again – a seeing. Karan's seeing?

"Mummy!" she cried. "Where are you? What's happening?"

No answer, but the Whelm's cawing cries swelled to a roar, and she
saw, projected on the icy lake, the red-tinged shadow of two standing
stones with a third across their tops. The shadow looked like a gate,
and through it she saw the waiting Merdrun army. Their leader raised
his sword.

A handsome woman with glowing eyes said, *Gergrig, is it time?*

This is the hour! he roared. He thrust the sword forward and the army
charged the gate.

The cries of the Whelm cut off, then into the silence soared a single high voice, Yetchah's voice.

"Our perfect master! Yes, yes, *yes!*"

Karan did not know what to do. Join Malien in a desperate attempt to locate the invading Merdrun, though she had no idea where to begin?

Give the war up as lost and try to find Llian, who was probably dead?

Or race all the way to Shazabba – a month's hard riding – and try to hide Sulien from the most vicious warmongers the void had ever spawned?

Mummy, the Whelm have gone crazy.

Karan's skin crawled at the image Sulien had sent her. Yetchah's thin arms were outstretched towards Gergrig and her eyes were alight with longing. *Our perfect master!* she cried. *Yes, yes,* yes.*

She turned to the other Whelm. *Gergrig wants the child. If we give her to him, he will surely agree to be our master. Take her!*

That was all Karan saw. "Sulien, run!" she screamed. "Anywhere! I'm coming, I'm coming!"

But then the adverse consequences Malien had warned her about, the consequences of Karan getting back her gift for the Secret Art, became horribly apparent. She could no longer send to Sulien, nor could she link to her.

Karan could not warn her in any way.

There was only one thing to do and she did it without a second's thought. She bolted down through the forest to the little glade where Malien's sky ship was moored. Karan cast off all but one of the ropes and, as the craft lifted, ran up the ladder. She was about to cut the last rope when Yggur appeared below her.

"You're not stopping me," said Karan.

"You don't have the power to fly it."

She slumped. He was right, of course. How could any novice operate such a craft, which was driven by subtle aspects of the Secret Art?

"Then Sulien will die and the Merdrun will win," she wailed.

"But *I* can fly it." Yggur sprang up the ladder, took the control levers and said, "Which way?"

She had never liked Yggur, and he frightened her. How could she possibly trust him?

Half a dozen Aachim raced into the glade, led by a red-faced, furious Malien. "How dare you! Get out!"

"To Shazabba," said Karan, and slashed the last rope.

The story continues in

BOOK TWO:

THE FATAL GATE

Coming Spring 2017

GLOSSARY OF CHARACTERS, NAMES AND PLACES

Aachan: One of the Three Worlds, the realm of the Aachim and, after its conquest, the Charon.

Aachim: The human species native to Aachan, who were conquered by the Charon. The Aachim are a clever people, great artisans and engineers, but melancholy and prone to both hubris and indecision.

Aftersickness: Illness that people suffer after using the Secret Art or using a native talent or gift. Sensitives are very prone to it.

Alcifer: The greatest of Rulke's cities, designed by Pitlis the Aachim.

Aviel: A crippled girl, fifteen, who lives in Shand's workshop and is training herself to become a perfumer.

Bannador: A narrow, poor, hilly land on the western side of Iagador.

Basunez: A distant, mad ancestor of Karan. He built Carcharon and carried out forbidden sorcery there.

bel Soon, Tallia: Formerly Mendark's chief lieutenant, and now Magister of the High Council, she is a mancer and a master of combat with and without weapons. Tallia comes from Crandor.

Benie: A former cook's boy at Gothryme Manor, now apprenticed to the chef.

Bufo: The captain of Wistan's college guard.

Calendar: Santhenar's year is roughly 395.7 days and contains 12 months, each of 33 days. The months are: spring – Thays, Criffin,

Bunce; summer – Bolland, Guffins, Thisto; autumn – Mard, Pulin, Ballin; winter – Sord, Galend, Talmard.

Carcharon: A tower built on a rugged ridge high above Gothryme Forest by Karan's mad ancestor Basunez at a node where the Secret Art was especially powerful.

Chacalot: A large water-dwelling reptile, somewhat resembling a crocodile.

Chanthed: A town in northern Meldorin, west of the mountains. The College of the Histories is situated there.

Chard: A kind of tea.

Charon: They fled out of the void to take Aachan from the Aachim long ago but were sterile there. Ten years ago the last of them went back to the void to die.

Chronicler: A graduate in the art and science of recording and maintaining the Histories.

Citadel: A fortified palace in Thurkad.

Clysm: A series of wars between the Charon and the Aachim between 1500 and 1000 years ago, resulting in the almost total devastation of Santhenar.

College of the Histories: The oldest of the colleges for the instruction of those who would be chroniclers, tellers and even lowly bards. It was set up at Chanthed soon after the time of the Forbidding.

Construct: A machine at least partly powered by the Secret Art.

Council, also Council of Santhenar, Great Council: An alliance of the most powerful mancers for the protection of Santhenar.

Crandor: A rich tropical land on the north-eastern side of Lauralin. Tallia's homeland.

Duril, Anjo: A sly, corrupt master at the college.

Elienor: A great heroine and subsequently a clan leader of the Aachim from the time when the Charon invaded Aachan.

Esea: A beautiful, clever but troubled reshaper. Twin sister to Hingis.

Faelamor: Leader of the Faellem species, who came to Santhenar soon after Rulke to keep watch on the Charon and maintain the balance between the worlds. She led her followers back to Tallallame, and self-immolation, ten years ago.

Faellem: The human species native to the world of Tallallame. A small dour people who are forbidden to use machines and particularly magical devices but are masters of disguise and illusion. Some still dwell on Santhenar, in Mirrilladell.

Fiz Gorgo: A fortress city in Orist, flooded in ancient times, now restored; the stronghold of Yggur.

Flute; also Golden Flute: A device made in Aachan at the behest of Rulke, by the brilliant smith Shuthdar. He subsequently stole it and took it back to Santhenar. When played by one who is sensitive, it could be used to open the Way Between the Worlds. It was destroyed by Shuthdar, and this created the Forbidding.

Forbidding: See *Tale of the Forbidding*.

Galliad: Karan's father, who was half-Aachim but exiled from them. He was killed at Carcharon when Karan was eight.

Gate: A structure controlled by the Secret Art which permits people to move instantly from one place to another. Also called a portal.

Gellon: A fruit tasting something between a mango and a peach. Shand makes an incomparable gellon liqueur.

Gergrig: Leader of the Merdrun.

Ghâshâd: The ancient mortal enemies of the Aachim. They were corrupted and swore allegiance to Rulke after the Zain rebelled 2000 years ago, but when Rulke was imprisoned in the Nightland 1000 years later they forgot their destiny and took a new name, Whelm. Since Rulke's death they have been a lost people.

Gift of Rulke; also Curse of Rulke: Knowledge given by Rulke to the Zain, enhancing their resistance to the mind-breaking spells of the Aachim. It left a visible stigmata that identified them as Zain.

Gothryme: Karan's impoverished estate near Tolryme in Bannador.

Great Library: Founded at Zile by the Zain in the time of the empire of Zur. The library was sacked when the Zain were exiled, but was subsequently re-established. Its current librarian is Nadiril the Sage.

Great Mountains: The largest and highest belt of mountains on Santhenar, enclosing the south-eastern part of the continent of Lauralin.

Great Tales: The greatest stories from the Histories of Santhenar, traditionally told at the Festival of Chanthed and on important ceremonial occasions throughout Santhenar. A tale can become a Great Tale only by the unanimous acclamation of the master chroniclers. In 4000 years only 23 Great Tales have ever been created, the most recent being Llian's *Tale of the Mirror.*

Grint: A copper coin of small value.

Griveline: A fast-acting herbal extract than induces numbing and partial paralysis. Lethal in large doses.

Gyllias: See *Shand.*

Hingis: A clever but physically grotesque illusionist, maimed by a kick from a mule as a boy. Twin of Esea.

Histories, the: The collection of records which detail more than 4000 years of recorded history on Santhenar. The Histories consist of historical documents written or held by the chroniclers, as well as the tales, songs, legends and lore of the peoples of Santhenar and the invading peoples from the other worlds, told by the tellers. The culture of Santhenar is interwoven with and inseparable from the Histories and everyone longs to be mentioned in them.

Hrux: A dangerous pain-relieving drug produced by the Whelm. Addictive and can have strange side effects, especially to people with Charon blood.

Huling's Tower: The place where Shuthdar destroyed the Golden Flute and Yalkara subsequently murdered the crippled girl.

Human species: There are four distinct human species: the Aachim of Aachan, the Faellem of Tallallame, the old humans of Santhenar, and the Charon, who came out of the void. All but the old humans can be very long-lived – Tensor, Rulke, Yalkara and Faelamor, for instance, all lived for thousands of years.

Hundred, the: The Charon who survived the taking of Aachan. Rulke was the greatest.

Hythe: midwinter's day, the fourth day of Endre, midwinter week. Hythe is a day of particular ill-omen.

Iagador: The fertile and wealthy land that lies between the eastern mountains of Meldorin and the Sea of Thurkad.

Idlis: Formerly the least of the Whelm, also a healer and long-time hunter of Karan and the Mirror. Karan spared his life three times, a debt that he repaid by healing her bones after she was gravely injured in Shazmak, and once a year bringing her a small supply of the pain-relieving compound hrux.

Jepperand: A province on the western side of the mountains of Crandor. Home to the Zain; Llian's birthplace.

Karan: A woman of the house of Fyrn, but with blood of the Aachim from her father, Galliad, and old human and Faellem blood from her mother. This makes her triune. She is also a sensitive. Llian's partner; mother of Sulien.

Lauralin: The continent east of the Sea of Thurkad.

League: About 5000 paces, three miles or five kilometres.

Librarian, the: Nadiril the Sage.

Lightglass: A device made of crystal and metal that emits light after being touched.

Lilis: Once a street urchin in Thurkad, rescued by Tallia at the age of twelve and apprenticed to Nadiril, now his anointed successor as Librarian.

Link, linking; also talent of linking: A joining of minds by which thoughts and feelings can be shared and support given. Sometimes used for domination.

Llian: A Zain from Jepperand, partner to Karan and father of Sulien. He is both a master chronicler and a teller, a rare combination. After his *Tale of the Mirror* was voted a Great Tale he was banned from practising for meddling in the Histories.

Magiz, the: the greatest sorcerer among the Merdrun. She gains power by drinking people's lives.

Magister, the: Mendark, a great mancer, chief of the Council of Santhenar, and Magister for 1000 years, he renewed his body an unprecedented 13 times. He was killed in Shazmak at the end of the Time of the Mirror (see below).

Maigraith: An obsessive, cold, repressed triune. She is a master of the Secret Art. Mother of non-identical twins Julken and Illiel, nine, fathered by Rulke, though Illiel, who takes after the Faellem, lives far away with them, and Maigraith has nothing to do with him.

Malien: An Aachim of House Elienor, now leader of the Aachim.

Mancer: A wizard or sorcerer; someone who is a master of the Secret Art.

Master chronicler: One who has mastered the study of the Histories and graduated with the highest honours from the College of the Histories.

Master of Chanthed: Currently Wistan; the Master of the College of the Histories is also nominal leader of Chanthed.

Meldorin: The large island that lies to the immediate west of the Sea of Thurkad and the continent of Lauralin.

Mendark: See *Magister*, the.

Mirror of Aachan: A device made by the Aachim in Aachan for seeing things at a distance. In Santhenar it changed and twisted reality and became corrupt, but stored many secrets. Yalkara took it to the void with her.

Moon, the (Santhenar's moon): The moon revolves around Santhenar about every thirty days. One side (the dark face) is blotched red and black, and because the moon rotates on its axis much more slowly, the dark face is fully turned towards Santh only every couple of months. This rarely coincides with a full moon, but when it does it is a time of ill-omen.

Murg, Magsie: The evil old owner of a tannery in Casyme.

Nadiril: The head of the Great Library and the most senior current member of the Great Council.

Nightland: A place, distant from the world of reality, wherein Rulke was kept prisoner for 1000 years.

Norp, Basible: A self-effacing master at the college.

Old human: The original human species on Santhenar and by far the most numerous.

Osseion: A former captain of Mendark's guard, a huge dark man, now the innkeeper of Ninefingers. Father of one child, a daughter, Ussarine.

Pitlis: A great Aachim of the distant past, whose folly betrayed the great city of Tar Gaarn to Rulke and broke the power of the Aachim. The architect who designed Tar Gaarn and Alcifer, he was slain by Rulke.

Portal: See *gate*.

Rachis: Karan's steward at Gothryme Manor, now an ancient, frail man.

Ragred: a collectably ugly man, but a fine servant to Snoat.

Rasper, Jundelix: A master assassin.

Recorder: The person who set down the account of the four great battles of Faelamor and Yalkara, among many other tales. His name was Gyllias (see *Shand*).

Reshaper: A mancer who can change the form and structure of matter.

Rula: The Magister before Mendark. She was regarded as the greatest of all.

Rulke: The greatest of the Charon. He enticed Shuthdar to Aachan to make the Golden Flute. After the Clysm he was imprisoned in the Nightland until a way could be found to banish him back to Aachan. When Tensor opened a gate into the Nightland Rulke escaped, later occupying Shazmak and Carcharon. He died in Shazmak at Tensor's hand.

Julken: the obnoxious son, aged nine, of Maigraith and Rulke.

Santhenar, Santh: The least powerful but most populous of the Three Worlds, home of the old human peoples.

Secret Art: The use of magical or sorcerous powers (mancing). An art that very few can use and then only after extensive training. Notable mancers have included Mendark, Yggur, Maigraith, Rulke, Yalkara, Tensor and Faelamor.

Sending: A message, thoughts or feelings sent from one mind to another.

Sensitive: Someone whose human senses and feelings are far more acute than normal. Sensitives, for instance Karan, may have *seeings* of things happening far away. Rarely they can make mind connections such as one-way *sendings* and two-way *links*. Sensitives can be unstable because they feel things far more strongly than other people.

Shand: A friend of Karan's late father, also known as Gyllias and the Recorder. He had a daughter, Aeolior, with Yalkara. Aeolior, who died young and tragically, had a daughter, Maigraith.

Shazmak: The forgotten city of the Aachim in the mountains west of Bannador, now largely abandoned.

Shuthdar: An old human of Santhenar, the maker of the Golden Flute. After he destroyed the flute and himself, the Forbidding came down, closing the Way Between the Worlds.

Sith: A free city and trading nation built on an island in the River Garr in southern Iagador.

Snoat, Cumulus: A wealthy, narcissistic, power-hungry collector.

Span: The distance spanned by the stretched arms of a tall man. About six feet, or slightly less than two metres.

Sulien: Karan and Llian's only child, a girl aged nine. She has unknown gifts.

Tale of the Forbidding: Greatest of the Great Tales, it tells of the final destruction of the flute by Shuthdar more than 3000 years ago, and how this created a Forbidding which sealed Santhenar off from the other two worlds.

Talent: A native skill or gift, usually honed by extensive training.

Tallallame: One of the Three Worlds, the home of the Faellem. A beautiful mountainous world covered in forest, recently invaded by savage creatures from the void.

Tar: A silver coin widely used in Meldorin. Enough to keep a family for several weeks.

Tell: A gold coin to the value of twenty silver tars. Enough to keep a family for a year.

Teller: One who has mastered the ritual telling of the tales that form part of the Histories of Santhenar. Great tellers also write their own tales and a rare few of these may become Great Tales.

Tensor: The former leader of the Aachim. He saw it as his destiny to restore the Aachim to finally take their revenge on Rulke, who betrayed and ruined them. He was proud to the point of folly. He died in Shazmak ten years ago.

Thandiwe: Llian's former lover, now a master chronicler desperate to have her own Great Tale.

Three Worlds: Santhenar, Aachan and Tallallame.

Thurkad: An ancient, wealthy and notably corrupt city on the River Saboth and the Sea of Thurkad. Seat of the council and the Magister.

Thyllan: Once a warlord of Iagador and former member of the council, now known as the Impotent. A troublemaker.

Time of the Mirror: The period of several years, beginning about twelve years ago, during which the events set down in Llian's *Tale of the Mirror* took place.

Tirthrax: A city of the Aachim in the Great Mountains.

Tolryme: A town in northern Bannador, close to Karan's family seat, Gothryme.

Triune: A double blending – one with the blood of all Three Worlds, three different human species. They are extremely rare and almost always infertile. They may have remarkable abilities. Karan is one, Maigraith another.

Turlew, Legless: A malicious former college servant who wants revenge on Llian.

Unick, Gurgito: a genius at inventing magical devices, but a sociopathic, depraved drunk.

Ussarine: Osseion's daughter. A huge, kindly warrior.

Voice: The ability of great tellers to move their audience to any emotion they choose by the sheer power of their words.

Void, the: A place where life is more brutal and fleeting than anywhere. The void teems with the most exotic life imaginable, for nothing survives there without remaking itself constantly.

Vyl, Scorbic: A mancer in the service of Snoat.

Way Between the Worlds: The secret, forever-changing and ethereal paths that permit the difficult passage between the Three Worlds. They were closed off by the Forbidding.

Whelm: Former servants of Yggur – his terror-guard – they are now masterless and dwell in the frigid southland of Shazabba.

Wilm: A good-hearted country lad aged seventeen, who always gets things wrong.

Wistan: The dying seventy-fourth Master of the College of the Histories.

Xarah: A young Aachim woman in Malien's group, twin to Shalah who was killed in Katazza.

Yalkara: The last of the three Charon who came to Santhenar to find the flute and return it to Aachan. She was Shand's partner for a time. Maigraith is her granddaughter.

Yetchah: A Whelm woman, partner to Idlis.

Yggur: A great, powerful but troubled mancer and warlord, and a former member of the Great Council. Last year he had a relapse and withdrew from all his captured lands, creating a power vacuum that Cumulus Snoat has taken advantage of. Yggur is now mentally unstable and withdrawn.

Zain: A scholarly race which once dwelt in Zile and founded the Great Library. They made a pact with Rulke. After he was imprisoned in the Nightland most were slaughtered and the remnant exiled. They are still hated.

Zile: A city in the north-west of the island of Meldorin. Once capital of the empire of Zur, now chiefly famous for the Great Library.

GUIDE TO PRONUNCIATION

There are many languages and dialects used on Santhenar by the four human species. While it is impossible to be definitive in such a brief note, the following generalisations normally apply.

There are no silent letters, and double consonants are generally pronounced as two separate letters; for example, *Yggur* is pronounced *Ig-ger*, and Faellem as *Fael-lem*. The letter *c* is usually pronounced as *k*, except in *mancer* and *Alcifer*, where it is pronounced as *s*, as in *manser*, *Alsifer*. The combination *ch* is generally pronounced as in *church*, except in *Aachim* and *Charon*, where it is pronounced as *k*.

Aachim *Ar'-kim*
Chanthed *Chan-thed*
Charon *Kar'-on*
Faelamor *Fay-el'-amor*
Iagador *Eye-aga'-dor*
Karan *Ka-ran*
Llian *Lee'-an*
Maigraith *May'-gray-ith*
Neid *Nee'-id*
Rael *Ray'-il*
Shuthdar *Shoo'-th-dar*
Ussarine *Oos-sar-een*
Whelm *H'-welm*
Yggur *Ig'-ger*
Xarah *Zha´-rah*

extras

orbit

meet the author

IAN IRVINE, an Australian marine scientist, has also written thirty-one novels. These include his internationally bestselling Three Worlds epic fantasy sequence, comprising The View from the Mirror quartet, The Well of Echoes quartet and The Song of the Tears trilogy, and a related fantasy series, The Tainted Realm trilogy.

His other books include a trilogy of eco-thrillers, Human Rites, set in the near future when the world is undergoing catastrophic climate change, and thirteen novels for younger readers. He is currently writing book two of The Gates of Good and Evil.

introducing

If you enjoyed
THE SUMMON STONE,
look out for

BATTLEMAGE

Age of Darkness: Book 1

by Stephen Aryan

"I can command storms, summon fire and unmake stone,"
Balfruss growled. "It's dangerous to meddle with things
you don't understand."

Balfruss *is a Battlemage, sworn to fight and die for*
a country that fears and despises his kind.

Vargus *is a common soldier—while mages shoot lightning*
from the walls of the city, he's down in the front lines
getting blood on his blade.

Talandra *is a princess and spymaster, but the war may*
force her to risk everything and make
the greatest sacrifice of all.

CHAPTER 1

Another light snow shower fell from the bleak grey sky. Winter should have been over, yet ice crunched underfoot and the mud was hard as stone. Frost clung to almost everything, and a thick, choking fog lay low on the ground. Only those desperate or greedy travelled in such conditions.

Two nights of sleeping outdoors had leached all the warmth from Vargus's bones. The tips of his fingers were numb and he couldn't feel his toes any more. He hoped they were still attached when he took off his boots; he'd seen it happen to others in the cold. Whole toes had come off and turned black without them noticing, rolling around like marbles in the bottom of their boots.

Vargus led his horse by the reins. It would be suicide for them both to ride in this fog.

Up ahead something orange flickered amid the grey and white. The promise of a fire gave Vargus a boost of energy and he stamped his feet harder than necessary. Although the fog muffled the sound, it would carry to the sentry up ahead on his left.

The bowman must have been sitting in the same position for hours as the grey blanket over his head was almost completely white.

As Vargus drew closer his horse snorted, picking up the scent of other animals, men and cooking meat. Vargus pretended he hadn't seen the man and tried very hard not to stare at his longbow. After stringing the bow with one quick flex the sentry readied an arrow, but in order to loose it he would have to stand up.

"That's far enough."

That came from another sentry on Vargus's right who stepped out from between the skeletons of two shattered trees. He was a burly man dressed in dirty furs and mismatched leathers. Although chipped and worn the long sword he carried looked sharp.

"You a King's man?"

Vargus snorted. "No, not me."

"What do you want?"

He shrugged. "A spot by your fire is all I'm after."

Despite the fog the sound of their voices must have carried as two others came towards them from the camp. The newcomers were much like the others, desperate men with scarred faces and mean eyes.

"You got any coin?" asked one of the newcomers, a bald and bearded man in old-fashioned leather armour.

Vargus shook his head. "Not much, but I got this." Moving slowly he pulled two wine skins down from his saddle. "Shael rice wine."

The first sentry approached. Vargus could still feel the other pointing an arrow at his back. With almost military precision the man went through his saddlebags, but his eyes nervously flicked towards Vargus from time to time. A deserter then, afraid someone had been sent after him.

"What we got, Lin?" called Baldy.

"A bit of food. Some silver. Not much else," the sentry answered.

"Let him pass."

Lin didn't step back. "Are you sure, boss?"

The others were still on edge. They were right to be nervous if they were who Vargus suspected. The boss came forward and keenly looked Vargus up and down. He knew what the boss was seeing. A man past fifty summers, battle scarred and grizzled with liver spots on the back of his big hands. A man with plenty of grey mixed in with the black stubble on his face and head.

"You going to give us any trouble with that?" asked Baldy, pointing at the bastard sword jutting up from Vargus's right shoulder.

"I don't want no trouble. Just a spot by the fire and I'll share the wine."

"Good enough for me. I'm Korr. These are my boys."

"Vargus."

He gestured for Vargus to follow him and the others eased hands away from weapons. "Cold enough for you?"

"Reminds me of a winter, must be twenty years ago, up north. Can't remember where."

"Travelled much?"

Vargus grunted. "All over. Too much."

"So, where's home?" asked Korr. The questions were asked casually, but Vargus had no doubt about it being an interrogation.

"Right now, here."

They passed through a line of trees where seven horses were tethered. Vargus tied his horse up with the others and walked into camp. It was a good sheltered spot, surrounded by trees on three sides and a hill with a wide cave mouth on the other. A large roaring fire crackled in the middle of camp and two men were busy cooking beside it. One was cutting up a hare and dropping pieces into a bubbling pot, while the other prodded some blackened potatoes next to the blaze. All of the men were armed and they carried an assortment of weapons that looked well used.

As Vargus approached the fire a massive figure stood up and came around from the other side. It was over six and a half feet tall, dressed in a bear skin and wide as two normal men. The man's face was severely deformed with a protruding forehead, small brown eyes that were almost black, and a jutting bottom jaw with jagged teeth.

"Easy Rak," said Korr. The giant relaxed the grip on his sword and Vargus let out a sigh of relief. "He brought us something to drink."

Rak's mouth widened, revealing a whole row of crooked yellow teeth. It took Vargus a few seconds to realise the big man was smiling. Rak moved back to the far side of the fire and sat down again. Only then did Vargus move his hand away from the dagger on his belt.

He settled close to the fire next to Korr and for a time no one spoke, which suited him fine. He closed his eyes and soaked up some of the warmth, wiggling his toes inside his boots. The heat began to take the chill from his hands and his fingers started to tingle.

"Bit dangerous to be travelling alone," said Korr, trying to sound friendly.

"Suppose so. But I can take care of myself."

"Where you headed?"

Vargus took a moment before answering. "Somewhere I'll get paid and fed. Times are hard and I've only got what I'm carrying."

Since he'd mentioned his belongings he opened the first skin and took a short pull. The rice wine burned the back of his throat, leaving a pleasant aftertaste. After a few seconds the warmth in his stomach began to spread.

Korr took the offered wineskin but passed it to the next man, who snatched it from his hand.

"Rak. It's your turn on lookout," said Lin. The giant ignored him and watched as the wine moved around the fire. When it reached him he took a long gulp and then another before walking into the trees. The archer came back and another took his place as sentry. Two men standing watch for a group of seven in such extreme weather was unusual. They weren't just being careful, they were scared.

"You ever been in the King's army?" asked Lin.

Vargus met his gaze then looked elsewhere. "Maybe."

"I reckon that's why you travelled all over, dragged from place to place. One bloody battlefield after another. Home was just a tent and a fire. Different sky, different enemy."

"Sounds like you know the life. Are you a King's man?"

"Not any more," Lin said with a hint of bitterness.

It didn't take them long to drain the first wineskin so Vargus opened the second and passed it around the fire. Everyone took a drink again except Korr.

"Bad gut," he said when Vargus raised an eyebrow. "Even a drop would give me the shits."

"More for us," said one man with a gap-toothed grin.

When the stew was ready one of the men broke up the potatoes and added them to the pot. The first two portions went to the sentries and Vargus was served last. His bowl was smaller than the others, but he didn't complain. He saw a few chunks of potato and even one bit of meat. Apart from a couple of wild onions and garlic the stew was pretty bland, but it was hot and filling. The food, combined with the wine and the fire, helped warm him all the way through. An itchy tingling starting to creep back into his toes. It felt as if they were all still attached.

When they'd all finished mopping up the stew with some flat bread, and the second wineskin was empty, a comfortable silence settled on the camp. It seemed a shame to spoil it.

"So why're you out here?" asked Vargus.

"Just travelling. Looking for work, like you," said Korr.

"You heard any news from the villages around here?"

One of the men shifted as if getting comfortable, but Vargus saw his hand move to the hilt of his axe. Their fear was palpable.

Korr shook his head. "Not been in any villages. We keep to ourselves." The lie would have been obvious to a blind and deaf man.

"I heard about a group of bandits causing trouble in some of the villages around here. First it was just a bit of thieving and starting a couple of fights. Then it got worse when they saw a bit of gold." Vargus shook his head sadly. "Last week one of them lost control. Killed four men, including the innkeeper."

"I wouldn't know," said Korr. He was sweating now and it had nothing to do with the blaze. On the other side of the fire a snoozing man was elbowed awake and he sat up with a snort. The others were gripping their weapons with sweaty hands, waiting for the signal.

"One of them beat the innkeeper's wife half to death when she wouldn't give him the money."

"What's it matter to you?" someone asked.

Vargus shrugged. "Doesn't matter to me. But the woman has two children and they saw who done it. Told the village Elder all about it."

"We're far from the cities out here. Something like that isn't big enough to bring the King's men. They only come around these parts to collect taxes twice a year," said Lin with confidence.

"Then why do you all look like you're about to shit yourselves?" asked Vargus.

An uncomfortable silence settled around the camp, broken only by the sound of Vargus scratching his stubbly cheek.

"Is the King sending men after us?" asked Korr, forgoing any pretence of their involvement.

"It isn't the King you should worry about. I heard the village Elders banded together, decided to do something themselves. They hired the Gath."

"Oh shit."

"He ain't real! He's just a myth."

"Lord of Light shelter me," one of the men prayed. "Lady of Light protect me."

"Those are just stories," scoffed Lin. "My father told me about him when I was a boy, more than thirty years ago."

"Then you've got nothing to worry about," Vargus grinned.

But it was clear they were still scared, more than before now that he'd stirred things up. Their belief in the Gath was so strong he could almost taste it in the air. For a while he said nothing and each man was lost in his own thoughts. Fear of dying gripped them all, tight as iron shackles.

Silence covered the camp like a fresh layer of snow and he let it sit a while, soaking up the atmosphere, enjoying the calm before it was shattered.

One of the men reached for a wineskin then remembered they were empty.

"What do we do, Korr?" asked one of the men. The others were scanning the trees as if they expected someone to rush into camp.

"Shut up, I'm thinking."

Before Korr came up with a plan Vargus stabbed him in the ribs. It took everyone a few seconds to realise what had happened. It was only when he pulled the dagger free with a shower of gore that they reacted.

Vargus stood up and drew the bastard sword from over his shoulder. The others tried to stand, but none of them could manage it. One man fell backwards, another tripped over his feet, landing on his face. Lin managed to make it upright, but then stumbled around as if drunk.

Vargus kicked Lin out of the way, switched to a two-handed grip and stabbed the first man on the ground through the back of the neck. He didn't have time to scream. The archer was trying to draw his short sword, but couldn't manage it. He looked up as Vargus approached and a dark patch spread across the front of his breeches. The edge of Vargus's sword opened the archer's throat and a quick stab put two feet of steel into Lin's gut. He fell back, squealing like a pig being slaughtered. Vargus knew his cries would bring the others.

The second cook was on his feet, but Vargus sliced off the man's right arm before he could throw his axe. Warm arterial blood jetted across Vargus's face. He grinned and wiped it away as the man fell back, howling in agony. Vargus let him thrash about for a while before putting his sword through the man's face, pinning his head to the ground. The snow around the corpse turned red, then it began to steam and melt.

The greasy-haired sentry stumbled into camp with a dagger held low. He swayed a few steps one way and then the other; the tamweed Vargus had added to the wine was taking effect. Bypassing Vargus he tripped over his own feet and landed face first on the fire. The sentry was screaming and the muscles in his arms and legs lacked the strength to lift him up. His cries turned into a gurgle and then trailed off as the smoke turned greasy and black. Vargus heard fat bubbling in the blaze and the smell reminded him of roast pork.

As he anticipated, Rak wasn't as badly affected as the others. His bulk didn't make him immune to the tamweed in the wine, but the side effects would take longer to show. Vargus was just glad that Rak had drunk quite a lot before going on duty. The giant managed to walk into camp in a straight line, but his eyes were slightly unfocused. Down at one side he carried a six-foot pitted blade.

Instead of waiting for the big man to go on the offensive, Vargus charged. Raising his sword above his head he screamed a challenge, but dropped to his knees at the last second and swept it in a downward arc. The Seveldrom steel cut through the flesh of Rak's left thigh, but the big man stumbled back before Vargus could follow up. With a bellow of rage Rak lashed out, his massive boot catching Vargus on the hip. It spun him around, his sword went flying and he landed on hands and knees in the snow.

Vargus scrambled around on all fours until his fingers found the hilt of his sword. He could hear Rak's blade whistling through the air towards him and barely managed to roll away before it came down where his head had been. Back on his feet he needed both hands to deflect a lethal cut which jarred his arms. Before he could riposte something crunched into his face. Vargus stumbled back, spitting blood and swinging his sword wildly to keep Rak at bay.

The big man came on. With the others already dead and his senses impaired, part of him must have known he was on borrowed time. Vargus ducked and dodged, turned the long blade aside and made use of the space around him. When Rak overreached he lashed out quickly, scoring a deep gash along the giant's ribs, but it didn't slow him down. Vargus inflicted a dozen wounds before Rak finally noticed that the red stuff splashed on the snow belonged to him.

With a grunt of pain he fell back and stumbled to one knee. His laboured breathing was very loud in the still air. It seemed to be the only sound for miles in every direction.

"Korr was right," he said in a voice that was surprisingly soft. "He said you'd come for us."

Vargus nodded. Taking no chances he rushed forward. Rak tried to raise his sword but even his prodigious strength was finally at an end. His arm twitched and that was all. No mercy was asked for and none was given. Using both hands Vargus thrust the point of his sword deep into Rak's throat. He pulled it clear and stepped back as blood spurted from the gaping wound. The giant fell onto his face and was dead.

By the fire Lin was still alive, gasping and coughing up blood.

The wound in his stomach was bad and likely to make him suffer for days before it eventually killed him. Just as Vargus intended.

He ignored Lin's pleas as he retrieved the gold and stolen goods from the cave. Hardly a fortune, but it was a lot of money to the villagers.

He tied the horses' reins together and even collected up all the weapons, bundling them together in an old blanket. The bodies he left to the scavengers.

It seemed a shame to waste the stew. Nevertheless Vargus stuck two fingers down his throat and vomited into the snow until his stomach was empty. Using fresh snow he cleaned off the bezoar and stored it in his saddlebags. It had turned slightly brown from absorbing the poison in the wine Vargus had drunk, but he didn't want to take any chances so made himself sick again. He filled his waterskin with melting snow and sipped it to ease his raw throat.

Vargus's bottom lip had finally stopped bleeding, but when he spat a lump of tooth landed on the snow in a clot of blood. He took a moment to check his teeth and found one of his upper canines was broken in half.

"Shit."

With both hands he scooped more snow onto the fire until it was extinguished. He left the blackened corpse of the man where it had fallen amid wet logs and soggy ash. A partly cooked meal for the carrion eaters.

"Kill me. Just kill me!" screamed Lin. "Why am I still alive?" He gasped and coughed up a wadge of blood onto the snow.

With nothing left to do in camp Vargus finally addressed him. "Because you're not just a killer, Torlin Ke Tarro. You were a King's man. You came home because you were sick of war. Nothing wrong with that, plenty of men turn a corner and go on in a different way. But you became what you used to hunt."

Vargus squatted down beside the dying man, holding him in place with his stare.

Lin's pain was momentarily forgotten. "How do you know me? Not even Korr knew my name is Tarro."

Vargus ignored the question. "You know the land around here, the villages and towns, and you know the law. You knew how to cause just enough trouble without it bringing the King's men. You killed and stole from your own people."

"They ain't my people."

Vargus smacked his hands together and stood. "Time for arguing is over, boy. Beg your ancestors for kindness on the Long Road to Nor."

"My ancestors? What road?"

Vargus spat into the snow with contempt. "Pray to your Lantern God and his fucking whore then, or whatever you say these days. The next person you speak to won't be on this side of the Veil."

Ignoring Lin's pleas he led the horses away from camp and didn't look back. Soon afterwards the chill crept back in his fingers but he wasn't too worried. The aches and pains from sleeping outdoors were already starting to recede. The fight had given him a small boost, although it wouldn't sustain him for very long. The legend of the Gath was dead, which meant time for a change. He'd been delaying the inevitable for too long.

introducing

If you enjoyed
THE SUMMON STONE,
look out for

HOPE & RED

The Empire of Storms: Book 1

by Jon Skovron

In a fracturing empire spread across savage seas, two young people from different cultures find common purpose.

A nameless girl is the lone survivor when her village is massacred by biomancers, mystical servants of the emperor. Named after her lost village, Bleak Hope is secretly trained by a master Vinchen warrior as an instrument of vengeance.

A boy becomes an orphan on the squalid streets of New Laven and is adopted by one of the most notorious women of the criminal underworld, given the name Red, and trained as a thief and con artist.

When a ganglord named Deadface Drem strikes a bargain with the biomancers to consolidate and rule all the slums of New Laven, the worlds of Hope and Red come crashing together, and their unlikely alliance takes them further than either could have dreamed possible.

1

Captain Sin Toa had been a trader on these seas for many years, and he'd seen something like this before. But that didn't make it any easier.

The village of Bleak Hope was a small community in the cold southern islands at the edge of the empire. Captain Toa was one of the few traders who came this far south, and even then, only once a year. The ice that formed on the water made it nearly impossible to reach during the winter months.

Still, the dried fish, whalebone, and the crude lamp oil they pressed from whale blubber were all good cargo that fetched a nice price in Stonepeak or New Laven. The villagers had always been polite and accommodating, in their taciturn Southern way. And it was a community that had survived in these harsh conditions for centuries, a quality that Toa respected a great deal.

So it was with a pang of sadness that he gazed out at what remained of the village. As his ship glided into the narrow harbor, he scanned the dirt paths and stone huts, and saw no sign of life.

"What's the matter, sir?" asked Crayton, his first mate. Good fellow. Loyal in his own way, if a bit dishonest about doing his fair share of work.

"This place is dead," said Toa quietly. "We'll not land here."

"Dead, sir?"

"Not a soul in the place."

"Maybe they're at some sort of local religious gathering," said Crayton. "Folks this far south have their own ways and customs."

"'Fraid that's not it."

Toa pointed one thick, scarred finger toward the dock. A tall sign had been driven into the wood. On the sign was painted a black oval with eight black lines trailing down from it.

"God save them," whispered Crayton, taking off his wool knit cap.

"That's the trouble," said Toa. "He didn't."

The two men stood there staring at the sign. There was no sound except the cold wind that pulled at Toa's long wool coat and beard.

"What do we do, sir?" asked Crayton.

"Not come ashore, that's for certain. Tell the wags to lay anchor. It's getting late. I don't want to navigate these shallow waters in the dark, so we'll stay the night. But make no mistake, we're heading back to sea at first light and never coming near Bleak Hope again."

They set sail the next morning. Toa hoped they'd reach the island of Galemoor in three days and that the monks there would have enough good ale to sell that it would cover his losses.

It was on the second night that they found the stowaway.

Toa was woken in his bunk by a fist pounding on his cabin door.

"Captain!" called Crayton. "The night watch. They found...a little girl."

Toa groaned. He'd had a bit too much grog before he went to sleep, and the spike of pain had already set in behind his eyes.

"A girl?" he asked after a moment.

"Y-y-yes, sir."

"Hells' waters," he muttered, climbing out of his hammock. He pulled on cold, damp trousers, a coat, and boots. A girl on board, even a little one, was bad luck in these southern seas. Everybody knew that. As he pondered how he was going to get rid of this stowaway, he opened the door and was surprised to find Crayton alone, turning his wool cap over and over again in his hands.

"Well? Where's the girl?"

"She's aft, sir," said Crayton.

"Why didn't you bring her to me?"

"We, uh...That is, the men can't get her out from behind the stowed rigging."

"Can't get her..." Toa heaved a sigh, wondering why no one had just reached in and clubbed her unconscious, then dragged her out.

It wasn't like his men to get soft because of a little girl. Maybe it was on account of Bleak Hope. Maybe the terrible fate of that village had made them a bit more conscious than usual of their own prospects for Heaven.

"Fine," he said. "Lead me to her."

"Aye, sir," said Crayton, clearly relieved that he wasn't going to bear the brunt of the captain's frustration.

Toa found his men gathered around the cargo hold where the spare rigging was stored. The hatch was open and they stared down into the darkness, muttering to each other and making signs to ward off curses. Toa took a lantern from one of them and shone the light down into the hole, wondering why a little girl had his men so spooked.

"Look, girlie. You better..."

She was wedged in tight behind the piles of heavy line. She looked filthy and starved, but otherwise a normal enough girl of about eight years. Pretty, even, in the Southern way, with pale skin, freckles, and hair so blond it looked almost white. But there was something about her eyes when she looked at you. They felt empty, or worse than empty. They were pools of ice that crushed any warmth you had in you. They were ancient eyes. Broken eyes. Eyes that had seen too much.

"We tried to pull her out, Captain," said one of the men. "But she's packed in there tight. And well...she's..."

"Aye," said Toa.

He knelt down next to the opening and forced himself to keep looking at her, even though he wanted to turn away.

"What's your name, girl?" he asked, much quieter now.

She stared at him.

"I'm the captain of this ship, girl," he said. "Do you know what that means?"

Slowly, she nodded once.

"It means everyone on this ship has to do what I say. That includes you. Understand?"

Again, she nodded once.

He reached one brown, hairy hand down into the hold.

"Now, girl. I want you to come out from behind there and take my hand. I swear no harm will come to you on this ship."

For a long moment, no one moved. Then, tentatively, the girl reached out her bone-thin hand and let it be engulfed in Toa's.

Toa and the girl were back in his quarters. He suspected the girl might start talking if there weren't a dozen hard-bitten sailors staring at her. He gave her a blanket and a cup of hot grog. He knew grog wasn't the sort of thing you gave to little girls, but it was the only thing he had on board except fresh water, and that was far too precious to waste.

Now he sat at his desk and she sat on his bunk, the blanket wrapped tightly around her shoulders, the steaming cup of grog in her tiny hands. She took a sip, and Toa expected her to flinch at the pungent flavor, but she only swallowed and continued to stare at him with those empty, broken eyes of hers. They were the coldest blue he had ever seen, deeper than the sea itself.

"I'll ask you again, girl," he said, although his tone was still gentle. "What's yer name?"

She only stared at him.

"Where'd you come from?"

Still she stared.

"Are you..." He couldn't believe he was even thinking it, much less asking it. "Are you from Bleak Hope?"

She blinked then, as if coming out of a trance. "Bleak Hope." Her voice was hoarse from lack of use. "Yes. That's me." There was something about the way she spoke that made Toa suppress a shudder. Her voice was as empty as her eyes.

"How did you come to be on my ship?"

"That happened after," she said.

"After what?" he asked.

She looked at him then, and her eyes were no longer empty. They were full. So full that Toa's salty old heart felt like it might twist up like a rag in his chest.

"I will tell you," she said, her voice as wet and full as her eyes. "I will tell *only* you. Then I won't ever say it aloud ever again."

She had been off at the rocks. That was how they'd missed her.

She loved the rocks. Great big jagged black boulders she could climb above the crashing waves. It terrified her mother the way she jumped from one to the next. "You'll hurt yourself!" her mother would say. And she did hurt herself. Often. Her shins and knees were peppered with scabs and scars from the rough-edged rock. But she didn't care. She loved them anyway. And when the tide went out, they always had treasures at their bases, half-buried in the gray sand. Crab shells, fish bones, seashells, and sometimes, if she was very lucky, a bit of sea glass. Those she prized above all else.

"What is it?" she'd asked her mother one night as they sat by the fire after dinner, her belly warm and full of fish stew. She held up a piece of red sea glass to the light so that the color shone on the stone wall of their hut.

"It's glass, my little gull," said her mother, fingers working quickly as she mended a fishing net for Father. "Broken bits of glass polished by the sea."

"But why's it colored?"

"To make it prettier, I suppose."

"Why don't *we* have any glass that's colored?"

"Oh, it's just fancy Northland frippery," said her mother. "We've no use for it down here."

That made her love the sea glass all the more. She collected them until she had enough to string together with a bit of hemp rope to make a necklace. She presented it to her father, a gruff fisherman who rarely spoke, on his birthday. He held the necklace in his leathery hand, eyeing the bright red, blue, and green chunks of sea glass warily. But then he looked into her eyes and saw how proud she was, how much she loved this thing. His weather-lined face folded up into a smile as he carefully tied it around his neck. The other fishermen teased him for weeks about it, but he would only touch his calloused fingertips to the sea glass and smile again.

extras

When *they* came on that day, the tide had just gone out, and she was searching the base of her rocks for new treasures. She'd seen the top of their ship masts off in the distance, but she was far too focused on her hunt for sea glass to investigate. It wasn't until she finally clambered back on top of one of the rocks to sift through her collection of shells and bones that she noticed how strange the ship was. A big boxy thing with a full three sails and cannon ports all along the sides. Very different from the trade ships. She didn't like the look of it at all. And that was before she noticed the thick cloud of smoke rising from her village.

She ran, her skinny little legs churning in the sand and tall grass as she made her way through the scraggly trees toward her village. If there was a fire, her mother wouldn't bother to save the treasures stowed away in the wooden chest under her bed. That was all she could think about. She'd spent too much time and effort collecting her treasures to lose them. They were the most precious thing to her. Or so she thought.

As she neared the village, she saw that the fire had spread across the whole village. There were men she didn't recognize dressed in white-and-gold uniforms with helmets and armored chest plates. She wondered if they were soldiers. But soldiers were supposed to protect the people. These men herded everyone into a big clump in the center of the village, waving swords and guns at them.

She jerked to a stop when she saw the guns. She'd seen only one other gun. It was owned by Shamka, the village elder. Every winter on the eve of the New Year, he fired it up at the moon to wake it from its slumber and bring back the sun. The guns these soldiers had looked different. In addition to the wooden handle, iron tube, and hammer, they had a round cylinder.

She was trying to decide whether to get closer or run and hide, when Shamka emerged from his hut, gave an angry bellow, and fired his gun at the nearest soldier. The soldier's face caved in as the shot struck him, and he fell back into the mud. One of the other soldiers raised his pistol and fired at Shamka, but missed. Shamka laughed triumphantly. But then the intruder fired a second time without reloading. Shamka's face was wide with surprise as he clutched at his chest and toppled over.

The girl nearly cried out then. But she bit her lip as hard as she could to stop herself, and dropped into the tall grass.

She lay hidden there in the cold, muddy field for hours. She had to clench her jaw to keep her teeth from chattering. She heard the soldiers shouting to each other, and there were strange hammering and flapping sounds. Occasionally, she would hear one of the villagers beg to know what they had done to displease the emperor. The only reply was a loud smack.

It was dark, and the fires had all flickered out before she moved her numb limbs up into a crouch and took another look.

In the center of the town, a huge brown canvas tent had been erected, easily five times larger than any hut in the village. The soldiers stood in a circle around it, holding torches. She couldn't see her fellow villagers anywhere. Cautiously, she crept a little closer.

A tall man who wore a long, hooded white cloak instead of a uniform stood at the entrance to the tent. In his hands, he held a large wooden box. One of the soldiers opened the flap of the tent entrance. The cloaked man went into the tent, accompanied by a soldier. Some moments later, they both emerged, but the man no longer had the box. The soldier tied the flap so that the entrance remained open, then covered the opening with a net so fine not even the smallest bird could have slipped through.

The cloaked man took a notebook from his pocket as soldiers brought out a small table and chair and placed them before him. He sat at the table and a soldier handed him a quill and ink. The man immediately began to write, pausing frequently to peer through the netting into the tent.

Screams began to come from inside the tent. She realized then that all the villagers were inside. She didn't know why they screamed, but it terrified her so much that she dropped back into the mud and held her hands over her ears to block out the sound. The screams lasted only a few minutes, but it was a long time before she could bring herself to look again.

extras

It was completely dark now except for one lantern at the tent entrance. The soldiers had gone and only the cloaked man remained, still scribbling away in his notebook. Occasionally, he would glance into the tent, look at his pocket watch, and frown. She wondered where the soldiers were, but then noticed that the strange boxy ship tied at the dock was lit up, and when she strained her hearing, she could make out the sound of rowdy male voices.

The girl snuck through the tall grass toward the side of the tent that was the farthest from the man. Not that he would have seen her. He seemed so intent on his writing that she probably could have walked right past him, and he wouldn't have noticed. Even so, her heart raced as she crept across the small stretch of open ground between the tall grass and the tent wall. When she finally reached the tent, she found that the bottom had been staked down so tightly that she had to pull out several of them before she could slip under.

It was even darker inside, the air thick and hot. The villagers all lay on the ground, eyes closed, chained to each other and to the thick tent poles. In the center sat the wooden box, the lid off. Scattered on the ground were dead wasps as big as birds.

Far over in the corner, she saw her mother and father, motionless like all the rest. She moved quickly to them, a sick fear shooting through her stomach.

But then her father moved weakly, and relief flooded through her. Maybe she could still rescue them. She gently shook her mother, but she didn't respond. She shook her father, but he only groaned, his eyes fluttering a moment but not opening.

She searched around, looking to see if she could unfasten their chains. There was a loud buzzing close to her ear. She turned and saw a giant wasp hovering over her shoulder. Before it could sting her, a hand shot past her face and slapped it aside. The wasp spun wildly around, one wing broken, then dropped to the ground. She turned and saw her father, his face screwed up in pain.

He grabbed her wrist. "Go!" he grunted. "Away." Then he shoved her so hard, she fell backward onto her rear.

She stared at him, terrified, but wanting to do something that would take the awful look of pain away from his face. Around her, others were stirring, their own faces etched in the same agony as her father.

Then she saw her father's sea glass necklace give an odd little jump. She looked closer. It happened again. Her father arched his back. His eyes and mouth opened wide, as if screaming, but only a wet gurgle came out. A white worm as thick as a finger burst from his neck. Blood streamed from him as other worms burrowed out of his chest and gut.

Her mother woke with a gasp, her eyes staring around wildly. Her skin was already shifting. She reached out and called her daughter's name.

All around her, the other villagers thrashed against their chains as the worms ripped free. Before long, the ground was covered in a writhing mass of white.

She wanted to run. Instead, she held her mother's hand and watched her writhe and jerk as the worms ate her from the inside. She did not move, did not look away until her mother grew still. Only then did she stumble to her feet, slip under the tent wall, and run back into the tall grass.

She watched from afar as the soldiers returned at dawn with large burlap sacks. The cloaked man went inside the tent for a while, then came back out and wrote more in his notebook. He did this two more times, then said something to one of the soldiers. The soldier nodded, gave a signal, and the group with sacks filed into the tent. When they came back out, their sacks were filled with writhing bulges that she guessed were the worms. They carried them to the ship while the remaining soldiers struck the tent, exposing the bodies that had been inside.

The cloaked man watched as the soldiers unfastened the chains from the pile of corpses. As he stood there, the little girl fixed his face in her memory. Brown hair, weak chin, pointed ratlike face marked with a burn scar on his left cheek.

At last they sailed off in their big boxy ship, leaving a strange sign driven into the dock. When they were no longer in sight, she crept back down into the village. It took her many days. Perhaps weeks. But she buried them all.

Captain Sin Toa stared down at the girl. During her tale, her expression had remained fixed in a look of wide-eyed horror. But now it settled back into the cold emptiness he'd seen when he first coaxed her out of the hold.

"How long ago was that?" he asked.

"Don't know," she said.

"How did you get aboard?" he asked. "We never docked."

"I swam."

"Quite a distance."

"Yes."

"And what should I do with you now?"

She shrugged.

"A ship is no place for a little girl."

"I have to stay alive," she said. "So I can find that man."

"Do you know who that was? What that sign meant?"

She shook her head.

"That was the crest of the emperor's biomancers. You haven't got a prayer of ever getting close to that man."

"I will," she said quietly. "Someday. If it takes my whole life. I'll find him. And kill him."

Captain Sin Toa knew he couldn't keep her aboard. It was said maidens, even eight-year-old ones, could draw the attention of the sea serpents in these waters as sure as a bucketful of blood. The crew might very well mutiny at the idea of keeping a girl on board. But he wasn't about to throw her overboard or dump her on some empty piece of rock either. When they landed the next day at Galemoor, he approached the head of the Vinchen order, a wizened old monk named Hurlo.

"Girl's seen things nobody should have to see," he said. The two of them stood in the stone courtyard of the monastery, the tall, black stone temple looming over them. "She's a broken thing. Could be a monastic life is the only option left to her."

Hurlo slipped his hands into the sleeves of his black robe. "I sympathize, Captain. Truly, I do. But the Vinchen order is for men only."

"But surely you could use a servant around," said Toa. "She's a peasant, accustomed to hard work."

Hurlo nodded. "We could. But what happens when she comes of age and begins to blossom? She will become too great a distraction for my brothers, particularly the younger ones."

"So keep her till then. At least you'll have sheltered her a few years. Kept her alive long enough for her to make her own way."

Hurlo closed his eyes. "It will not be an easy life for her here."

"Don't think she'd know what to do with an easy life if you gave her one anyway."

Hurlo looked at Toa. And to Toa's surprise, he suddenly smiled, his old eyes sparkling. "We will take in this broken child you have found. A bit of chaos in the order brings change. Perhaps for the better."

Toa shrugged. He'd never fully understood Hurlo or the Vinchen order. "If you say so, Grandteacher."

"What is the child's name?" asked Hurlo.

"She won't say for some reason. I half think she doesn't remember."

"What shall we call her, then, this child born of nightmare? As her unlikely guardians, I suppose it is now up to us to name her."

Captain Sin Toa thought about it a moment, tugging at his beard. "Maybe after the village she survived. Keep something of it in memory, at least. Call her Bleak Hope."